VOLUME 2

THE BEST OF WORLD SF

LAVIE TIDHAR is the World Fantasy Award-winning author of *Osama*, Campbell and Neukom winner *Central Station*, Jerwood Fiction Uncovered Prize-winner *A Man Lies Dreaming* and many others. He created and edited the groundbreaking Apex Book of World SF series (2009–2018), editing the first three volumes and remaining as series editor for the next two. In 2021 he launched the Best of World SF series from Head of Zeus. He has also written extensively on international SF/F in a regular column for the *Washington Post*. His latest novels with Head of Zeus are *The Hood* (2021) and *Maror* (2022).

VOLUME 2

THE BEST OF WORLD SF

EDITED BY
LAVIE TIDHAR

An Ad Astra Book

First published in the UK in 2022 by Head of Zeus Ltd,
part of Bloomsbury Publishing Plc

In the compilation and introductory material © Lavie Tidhar, 2022

The moral right of Lavie Tidhar to be identified
as the editor of this work has been asserted in accordance with
the Copyright, Designs and Patents Act of 1988.

The moral right of the contributing authors of this anthology to be identified as
such is asserted in accordance with the Copyright, Designs and Patents Act of 1988.

The list of individual titles and respective copyrights to be found on page 647
constitutes an extension of this copyright page.

9 7 5 3 1 2 4 6 8

A catalogue record for this book is available from the British Library.

ISBN (HB): 9781803280318
ISBN (XTPB): 9781803280325
ISBN (E): 9781803280295

Printed and bound in Great Britain by
CPI Group (UK) Ltd, Croydon CR0 4YY

Head of Zeus Ltd
First Floor East
5–8 Hardwick Street
London EC1R 4RG

WWW.HEADOFZEUS.COM

Contents

Introduction

1.

If one book is an accident, is a second one coincidence?

Maybe it's a miracle. It feels like that to me. In the introduction to the first volume I mentioned the struggle of getting that first book published. Getting a second one was a dream. It was also a daunting prospect. There were some great writers in the first volume.

Luckily, the world is full of fantastic writers.

2.

This is not a traditional 'Best of' anthology.

A more usual one simply reprints those stories, printed throughout the previous year, which the editor deems the best for their own personal reasons.

But my intention with these volumes is to showcase the new voices of international science fiction. I have restricted myself to twenty-first-century work, with most stories falling within the last decade. In this volume, the oldest story is from 2012, and several stories appear here for the first time.

This is not a retrospective of what science fiction around the world *used* to look like. This is a snapshot of what some of it looks like now.

For that reason, none of the authors from the previous

volume appear in this book. If I am to offer a (however skewed) vision of what international SF looks like today, then consider each volume a window onto a different vista, a different part. The world is too large to be contained in one volume. Or, for that matter, two.

3.

There are certain challenges to editing a collection like this. Science fiction novels translated into English remain nearly non-existent. The opposite is of course not true – for nearly any other language, translations from English account for fifty per cent or more of all titles, and the figure is considerably higher for science fiction. The average non-Anglophone reader will be well-versed in American literature. The opposite, sadly, cannot be said to be true.

It is, one feels, particularly ill-thought on the part of American publishers and their British counterparts, and the barrier is not restricted simply to translations. Many international writers write in English as a first or second (or third!) language, but few make it past the gates of publishing. I am, perhaps, an idealist. I'd like to see this change. I want it selfishly, too, as a reader. I want to encounter new writing and new worlds and new points of view, instead of a rehash of the same singular thing. I'd like to see publishers funnel a portion of their profits into translation as a matter of course. I'd like to see editors hired who did not all go to the same school. I'd like to see the fiction of Beijing and Beirut, São Paulo and Nairobi – less of London and New York. But as I said as much before in the previous volume's introduction, I won't labour the point here.

Short fiction, then. It is here that the cutting edge of science fiction has always been, cresting far before the lumbering novels which follow. It is here, in a vibrant ecosystem of magazines and anthologies, passion projects and crowdfunded books and fly-by-night websites that the true visions of our future are written and rewritten in multiple voices. The great revolution of science fiction that began as a trickle at the turn of the century has become a flood of new voices, finding new homes to publish them.

This volume has more original fiction, and more translations. The translator is always overlooked, yet vital. I was lucky to have the help of Alex Shvartsman, publisher of *Future SF* magazine and a tireless promoter of Russian SF in translation. Alex introduced me to the fantastic work of the young Russian author K.A. Teryna, whose 'The Farctory' closes this book. It is published here for the first time. Rachel Cordasco has been a tireless promoter of World SF with her *SF in Translation* podcast. She is also a translator in her own right, appearing here with Clelia Farris' 'The Substance of Ideas'. And Joel Martinsen has been writing about and translating Chinese SF for years, and was able to help me get Pan Haitian's 'Dead Man, Awake, Sing to the Sun!'

In Poland, my friend Konrad Walewski used his considerable contacts to send me translations until I found Agnieszka Hałas' 'Sleeping Beauties', another story original to this collection, translated by the author. And Cristina Jurado, who appeared in the first volume of this anthology series, helped me once again with her contacts in Latin America.

In many cases, publications of international SF are simple labours of love. Author Zen Cho, who appeared in the first volume, also edited the anthology *Cyberpunk: Malaysia*, and it was through her that I got to reprint William Tham Wai Liang's 'Kakak' here. I am also grateful to all the Indian publishers who sent me books, after I put a call out, and introduced me to the wonderful Lavanya Lakshminarayan, whose story 'The Ten-Percent Thief' is reprinted here.

I had a momentary flash of wanting to take all-original stories. The impulse passed quickly, but I was able to solicit a handful of originals all the same. Frances Ogamba and Samit Basu wrote stories specifically for this volume ('At Desk 9501' and 'Waking Nydra' respectively), while Julie Nováková – a tireless promoter of Czech SF – was kind enough to let me use her original story 'A Flaw in the Works', and Dilman Dila kindly gave me 'The Child of Clay'.

Another labour of love is Ra Page and Comma Press' *Iraq+100* (and its companion volume, *Palestine+100*), from which I was able to take Hassan Blasim's 'The Gardens of Babylon'. Without enthusiastic small presses we would be much the poorer. Bill Campbell's Rosarium Publishing put out Clelia Farris' collection, 'Creative Surgery'. I reprinted several stories from online magazine *Clarkesworld*, which tirelessly promotes diverse works, with a part-focus on translations from Chinese and Korean. I reprinted two from *Words Without Borders*, two from *The Magazine of Fantasy & Science Fiction*, one from Tor.com, one from *Fiyah* and one from *Isaac Asimov's Science Fiction Magazine*. From *The Book Smugglers* I found Neon Yang's novella 'Between the Firmaments', which I am delighted to publish here in print. Anthologies such as Ivor Hartmann's *AfroSF* series and the more recent *Dominion: An Anthology of Speculative Fiction from Africa and the African Diaspora* edited by Zelda Knight and Oghenechovwe Donald Ekpeki offer much to showcase African writers. Many other anthologies focus on specific regions, such as the clear labour of love that is *Zion's Fiction*, an anthology of Israeli speculative fiction edited by Sheldon Teitelbaum and Emanuel Lotem, or the excellent recent anthology of Chinese SF *Sinopticon*, edited by Xueting Christine Ni.

Without this network of enthusiasts, dreamers, translators, publishers and editors willing to give of their time and effort, the field would be much poorer, and an anthology of this nature a much more difficult endeavour. As it is, I had it easy!

4.

Some genres emerge outside of the Western canon. Wuxia has been influential in recent years on science fiction and fantasy writers, and the influence of anime has been felt for longer. Solarpunk seems to be emerging out of the writing of non-Anglophone writers. Gulf futurism, Afro futurism – even Andean futurism is now becoming its own thing. As in the previous volume, I have sought to chart a path through works that lean more to science fiction than to fantasy, horror and the weird but – as before – with some exceptions (I could not resist but sneak in a zombie story of a sort – purists may not forgive me!). There is much work that remains focused on near-future Earth, often dystopian, occasionally hopeful. There are a couple of alternate histories. There are plenty of robot stories and, as the robot may well be my favourite icon of science fiction, it is well represented here. Then off we go into space. Mars at first, then the stars. At last we return to a strange, transformed Earth. If you choose to read the stories in the order here presented, then this is the overall shape of the journey, taking in, along the way, AI, gods, aliens and the undead, though the shapes they take on may surprise you.

Of course, you may well choose to make your own map. Dip into a story at random, perhaps attracted by the title or the author's name. Some may be known to you, others new. It has been rewarding to hear from some readers of the first volume how they discovered authors they didn't know and sought out more of their work. Whether you follow the order imposed or make your own, I hope you find the journey itself rewarding.

5.

People sometimes dismiss SF and fantasy for being escapist. As the writers here show, however, it is anything but. SF comes from its respective authors' societies, a reflection of the world's present, its history and its future. That world used to be overwhelmingly American, but it isn't anymore, and needn't be.

Writers come from everywhere. And SF is a literature that grows beauty out of the dirt, that breeds hope out of despair. Rather than hide from the world, SF can transform it – and what more can we ask of art?

When I was growing up on a little kibbutz in Israel, science fiction was a row of translated paperbacks on the kibbutz's library shelf, written by authors living in impossibly distant America. They seemed to live on a distant, exotic planet, one forever out of reach. It never ceases to amaze me, even as a grown-up, that I have now met some of them – as though they were mere mortals – and that my books can be on that same shelf. I never thought it was possible, and it must have been only the blind arrogance of youth that ever led me to try. I travelled a lot, later on, as soon as I could leave. And wherever I went I picked up books: SF anthologies in Romania and horror in Malaysia, novels in Beijing and Chengdu, and African writers' books sold on the side of the road in Dar-es-Salaam.

It is so hard to break in, and can be so dispiriting when you are the first from your home and you don't fit the mould of the field. I wanted to do and tried to do this anthology for many years, just for myself, just because I wished it had been there when I was starting out. SF can only stay vital if it keeps evolving, if it brings in new voices and new ways.

This anthology is, I think, a testament to what SF already is and what it can be.

LAVIE TIDHAR

2022

The Bahrain Underground Bazaar

Nadia Afifi

Bahrain

I was blown away by this story when I got it from *The Magazine of Fantasy & Science Fiction* to read. In a way, I built this anthology from this story. Here was a part of the world seldom seen in science fiction, brought to life with great verve and imagination by Nadia Afifi, who has fast become one of my favourite short-story writers. This was truly science fiction for the twenty-first century, and exactly what I wanted to show with this anthology. So welcome to *The Best of World SF: Volume 2*, and welcome to 'The Bahrain Underground Bazaar'!

Bahrain's Central Bazaar comes to life at night. Lights dance above the narrow passageways, illuminating the stalls with their spices, sacks of lentils, ornate carpets, and trinkets. Other stalls hawk more modern fare, NeuroLync implants and legally ambiguous drones. The scent of cumin and charred meat fills my nostrils. My stomach twists in response. Chemo hasn't been kind to me.

Office workers spill out from nearby high-rises into the crowds. A few cast glances in my direction, confusion and sympathy playing across their faces. They see an old woman with stringy, thinning gray hair and a hunched back, probably lost and confused. The young always assume the elderly can't keep up with them, helpless against their new technology and shifting language. Never mind that I know their tricks better than they do, and I've been to wilder bazaars than this manufactured tourist trap. It used to be the Old Souk, a traditional market that dealt mostly in gold. But Bahrain, which once prided itself as being Dubai's responsible, less ostentatious younger cousin, has decided to keep up with its neighbors. Glitz and flash. Modernity and illusion.

I turn down another passageway, narrower than the last. A sign beckons me below – 'The Bahrain Underground Bazaar'. It even has a London Underground symbol around the words for effect, though we're far from its gray skies and rain. I quicken my pace down its dark steps.

It's even darker below, with torch-like lamps lining its stone walls. Using stone surfaces – stone anything – in the desert is madness. The cost of keeping the place cool must be obscene. The Underground Bazaar tries hard, bless it, to be sinister and seedy, and it mostly succeeds. The clientele help matters. They're either gangs of teenage boys or lone older men with unsettling eyes, shuffling down damp corridors. Above them, signs point to different areas of the bazaar for different tastes – violence, phobias, sex, and death.

I'm here for death.

'Welcome back, grandma,' the man behind the front counter greets me. A nice young man with a neatly trimmed beard. He dresses all in black, glowing tattoos snaking across his forearms, but he doesn't fool me. He goes home and watches romantic comedies when he isn't selling the morbid side of life to oddballs. This isn't a typical souk or bazaar where each vendor runs their own stall. The Underground Bazaar is centralized. You tell the person at the counter what virtual immersion experience you're looking for and they direct you to the right room. Or *chamber*, as they insist.

'I'm not a grandma yet,' I say, placing my dinars on the front counter. 'Tell my son and his wife to spend less time chasing me around and get the ball rolling on those grandchildren.' In truth, I don't care in the slightest whether my children reproduce. I won't be around to hold any grandchildren.

'What'll it be today?'

I've had time to think on the way, but I still pause. In the Underground Bazaar's virtual immersion chambers, I've experienced many anonymous souls' final moments. Through them, I've drowned, been strangled, shot in the mouth, and suffered a heart attack. And I do mean suffer – the heart attack was one of the worst. I try on deaths like T-shirts. Violent ones and peaceful passings. Murders, suicides, and accidents. All practice for the real thing.

The room tilts and my vision blurs momentarily. Dizzy, I press my hands, bruised from chemo drips, into the counter to steady myself. The tumor wedged between my skull and brain likes to assert itself at random moments. A burst of vision trouble, spasms of pain or nausea. I imagine shrinking it down, but even that won't matter now. It's in my blood and bones. The only thing it's left me so far, ironically, is my mind. I'm still sharp enough to make my own decisions. And I've decided one thing – I'll die on my terms, before cancer takes that last bit of power from me.

'I don't think I've fallen to my death yet,' I say, regaining my composure. 'I'd like to fall from a high place today.'

'Sure thing. Accident or suicide?'

Would they be that different? The jump, perhaps, but everyone must feel the same terror as the ground approaches.

'Let's do a suicide,' I say. 'Someone older, if you have it. Female. Someone like me,' I add unnecessarily.

My helpful young man runs his tattooed fingers across his fancy computer, searching. I've given him a challenge. Most people my age never installed the NeuroLync that retains an imprint of a person's experiences – including their final moments. Not that the intent is to document one's demise, of course. People get the fingernail-sized devices implanted in their temples to do a variety of useful things – pay for groceries with a blink, send neural messages to others, even adjust the temperature in their houses with a mental command. Laziness. Soon, the young will have machines do their walking for them.

But one side effect of NeuroLync's popularity was that its manufacturer acquired a treasure trove of data from the minds connected to its Cloud network. Can you guess what happened next? Even an old bird like me could have figured it out. All that data was repackaged and sold to the highest bidder. Companies seized what they could, eager to literally tap into consumer minds. But there are other markets, driven by the desire to borrow another person's experiences. Knowing what it feels like to have a particular kind of sex. Knowing what it feels like to torture someone – or be tortured. Knowing what it means to die a certain way.

And with that demand comes places like the Bahrain Underground Bazaar.

'I've got an interesting one for you,' the man says, eyeing me with something close to caution. 'A Bedouin woman. Want to know the specifics?'

'Surprise me,' I say. 'I'm not too old to appreciate some mystery.'

My young man always walks with me to the sensory chamber, like an usher in a movie theater. It's easy for me to get knocked around amid the jostling crowds, and I admit that some of the other customers frighten me. You can always spot the ones here for violence, a sick thrill between work shifts. Their eyes have this dull sheen, as though the real world is something they endure until their next immersion.

'This is your room, grandma,' the man says before spinning on his heels back to the front counter. I step inside.

The room is dark, like the rest of this place, with blue lights webbing its walls. I suspect they exist for ambience rather than utility. In the center of the room, a reclining chair sits underneath a large device that will descend over my tiny, cancer-addled head. On the back of it, a needle of some kind will jut out and enter my spinal cord, right where it meets the skull. It's painful, but only for a second, and then you're in someone else's head, seeing and hearing and sensing what they felt. What's a little pinprick against all of that?

I sit and lean back as the usual recording plays on the ceiling, promising me an experience I'll never forget. The machine descends over my head, drowning out my surroundings, and I feel the familiar vampire bite at my neck.

I'm in the desert. Another one. Unlike Bahrain, a small island with every square inch filled by concrete, this is an open space with clear skies and a mountainous horizon. And I'm walking down a rocky, winding slope. Rose-colored cliffsides surround me and rich brown dirt crunches underneath my feet. The bright sun warms my face and a primal, animal smell fills my nostrils. I'm leading a donkey down the path. It lets out a huff of air, more sure-footed than me.

I turn – 'I' being the dead woman – at the sound of laughter. A child sits on the donkey, legs kicking. The donkey takes it in stride, accustomed to excitable tourists, but I still speak in a husky, foreign voice, instructing the child to sit still. Others follow behind her – parents or other relations. They drink in the landscape's still beauty through their phones.

We round a corner and my foot slides near the cliff's edge. A straight drop to hard ground and rock. I look down, the bottom of the cliff both distant and oddly intimate. The air stills, catching my breath. Wild adrenaline runs through my body, my legs twitching. For a moment, I can't think clearly, my thoughts scrambled by an unnamed terror. Then a thought breaks through the clutter.

Jump. Jump. Jump.

The terror becomes an entity inside me, a metallic taste on my tongue, and a clammy sweat on my skin. The outline of the cliff becomes sharper, a beckoning blade, while the sounds of voices around me grow distant, as though I'm underwater.

I try to pull away – me, Zahra, the woman from Bahrain who chooses to spend her remaining days experiencing terrible things. In some backwater of my brain, I remind myself that I'm not on a cliff and this happened long ago. But the smell of hot desert air invades my senses again, yanking me back with a jolt of fear. *Jump.*

A moment seizes me, and I know that I've reached the glinting edge of a decision, a point of no return. My foot slides forward and it is crossed. I tumble over the edge.

I'm falling. My stomach dips and my heart tightens, thundering against my ribs. My hands flail around for something to grab but when they only find air, I stop. I plummet with greater speed, wind whipping my scarf away. I don't scream. I'm beyond fear. There is only the ground beneath me and the space in between. A rock juts out from the surface and I know, with sudden peace, that that's where I'll land.

And then nothing. The world is dark and soundless. Free of pain, or of any feeling at all.

And then voices.

The darkness is softened by a strange awareness. I sense, rather than see, my surroundings. My own mangled body spread across a rock. Dry plants and a gravel path nearby. Muted screams from above. I know, somehow, that my companions are running down the path now, toward me. *Be careful*, I want to cry out. *Don't fall.* They want to help me. Don't they know I'm dead?

But if I'm dead, why am I still here? I'm not in complete oblivion and I'm also not going toward a light. I'm sinking backward into something, a deep pool of nothing, but a feeling of warmth surrounds me, enveloping me like a blanket on a cold night. I have no body now, I'm a ball of light, floating toward a bigger light behind me. I know it's there without seeing it. It is bliss and beauty, peace and kindness, and all that remains is to join it.

A loud scream.

Reality flickers around me. Something releases in the back of my head and blue light creeps into my vision. The machine whirs above me, retracting to its place on the ceiling. I blink, a shaking hand at my throat. The scream was mine. Drawing a steady breath, I hold my hand before my eyes until I'm convinced it's real and mine. Coming out of an immersion is always disorienting but that was no ordinary immersion. Normally, the moment of death wakes me up, returning me to my own, disintegrating body. What happened?

I leave the chamber with a slight wobble in my knees. A tall man in a trench coat appears at my side, offering his arm, and I swat it away. I smile, oddly reassured by the brief exchange. This is the Underground Bazaar, full of the same weirdos and creeps. I'm still me. The death I experienced in the chamber begins to fade in my immediate senses, but I still don't look back.

'How was it?' The man at the front counter winks.

I manage a rasping noise.

'Pretty crazy, huh?' His grin widens. 'We file that one under suicides, but it's not really a suicide. Not premeditated, anyway. She was a tour guide in Petra, with a husband, five children, and who-knows-how-many grandchildren. She just jumped on impulse.'

My mind spins with questions, but I seize on his last comment.

'I walked the Golden Gate bridge once, on a family trip,' I say, my voice wavering. 'I remember a strange moment where I felt the urge to jump over the edge, into the water, for no reason. It passed, and I heard that's not uncommon.'

'They call it the death drive,' the man says with a nod. His eyes dance with excitement and I understand at last why he works in this awful place. The thrill of the macabre. 'The French have a fancy expression for it that means "the call of the void". It's really common to get to the edge of a high place and feel this sudden urge to jump. You don't have to be suicidal or anxious. It can happen to anyone.'

'But why?' I ask. I suspect the man has studied this kind of thing and I'm right. He bounces on his heels and leans forward, his smile conspiratorial.

'Scientists think that it's the conscious brain reacting to our instinctive responses,' he says. 'You get to the edge of a cliff and you reflexively step back. But then your conscious mind steps in. Why did you step back? Maybe it's not because of the obvious danger, but because you *wanted* to jump. Now, a part of you is convinced you want to jump, even though you know what that means, and it scares you. Insane,' he adds with undisguised glee.

'But most people don't,' I say, recalling the terror of those moments at the cliff's edge.

'Most don't,' he agrees. 'That's what's interesting about this one. She actually went through with it. Why I thought you'd like it.' His chest puffs up in a way that reminds me of my own son, Firaz, when he came home from school eager to show me some new art project. He stopped drawing when he reached college, I realize with sudden sadness.

'But what about... after she fell?' I ask. The fall was traumatic, as I knew it would be, but nothing from past immersions prepared me for the strange, sentient peace that followed the moment of impact.

'Oh, that,' the young man says. 'That happens sometimes. Maybe about ten percent of our death immersions. Kind of a near-death-experience thing. Consciousness slipping away. Those last brain signals firing.'

'But it happened after I – after she fell,' I protest. 'She must have been completely dead. Does that ever happen?'

'I'm sure it does, but rarely,' the young man says with a tone of gentle finality. He smiles at the next customer.

'Petra,' I murmur. 'I've always wanted to see Petra.' And now I have, in a fashion.

Walking up the stairs, exhaustion floods my body. Some days are better than others, but I always save these visits for the days when I'm strongest. Leaning against the wall outside, I feel ready to collapse.

'Zahra? *Zahra!*'

My daughter-in-law pushes through the crowd. I consider shrinking back down the stairs, but her eyes fix on me with predatory focus. I'm in her sights. She swings her arms stiffly under her starched white blouse.

'We've been worried sick,' Reema begins. Her eyes scan me from head to toe, searching for some hidden signs of mischief. For a moment, I feel like a teenager again, sneaking out at night.

'You really shouldn't,' I say.

'How did you slip away this time? We didn't see you—'

'On the tracking app you installed on my phone?' I ask with a small smile. 'I deleted it, along with the backup you placed on the Cloud.' As I said before, I know more tricks than they realize. Thank goodness I don't have a NeuroLync. I'd never be alone. Of course, every time I sneak off after a medical appointment to walk to the bazaar, I'm battling time. They don't know when I've given them the slip, but when they return home from their tedious jobs to find the house empty, they know where I've gone.

Reema sighs. 'You need to stop coming to this terrible place, Zahra. It's not good for your mind or soul. You don't need dark thoughts – you'll beat this by staying positive.'

After accompanying me to my earliest appointments, Reema has mastered the art of motivational medical speak. She means well. It would be cliché for me to despise my daughter-in-law, but in truth, I respect her. She comes from a generation of Arab women expected to excel at every aspect of life, to prove she earned her hard-fought rights, and she's risen to the task. If only she'd let me carry on with the task of planning my death and getting out of her way.

On the way home, Reema calls my son to report my capture. Instead of speaking aloud, she sends him silent messages through her NeuroLync, shooting the occasional admonishing glance in my direction. I can imagine the conversation well enough.

At the bazaar again.

Ya Allah! The seedy part?

She was walking right out of it when I found her.

Is she okay?

Pleased enough with herself. What are we going to do with her?

Reema and Firaz work in skyscrapers along Bahrain's coastal business zone, serving companies that change names every few months when they merge into bigger conglomerates. To them, I'm another project to be managed, complete with a schedule and tasks. My deadline is unknown, but within three months, they'll likely be planning my funeral. It's not that they don't love me, and I them. The world has just conditioned them to express that love through worry and structure. I need neither.

I want control. I want purpose.

Firaz barely raises his head to acknowledge me when Reema and I walk through the kitchen door. He's cooking at ten o'clock at night, preparing a dinner after work. Reema collapses onto a chair, kicking off her heels before tearing into the bread bowl.

'I'm not hungry, but I'm tired,' I say to no one in particular. 'I'll go to bed now.'

'Mama, when will this end?' Firaz asks in a tight voice.

I have an easy retort at the tip of my tongue. *Soon enough, when I'm dead.* But when he turns to face me, I hesitate under his sad, frustrated gaze. His red eyes are heavy with exhaustion. I, the woman who birthed and raised him, am now a disruption.

All at once, I deflate. My knees buckle.

'Mama!' Firaz abandons his pan and rushes toward me.

'I'm fine,' I say. With a wave of my hand, I excuse myself.

In the dark of my bedroom, images from the bazaar linger in the shadows. Echoes of blue lights dancing across the walls. I sink into my bed, reaching for the warmth I felt hours ago, through the dead woman's mind, but I only shiver. What happened in that immersion? The young man didn't fool me. I had experienced enough deaths in those dark chambers to recognize the remarkable. She jumped in defiance of instinct, but her final moments of existence were full of warmth and acceptance – a presence that lingered after death. What made her different?

The next morning, I take a long bath, letting Firaz and Reema go through their pre-work routine – elliptical machines, mindfulness, dressing, and breakfast, the house obeying their silent commands. After they leave, I take the bus downtown to the clinic.

I sit in a room of fake plants and fake smiles, chemicals warming my veins. Other women sit around me, forming a square with nothing but cheap blue carpet in the center. A nurse checks our IV drips and ensures our needles remain in place. My fellow cancer survivors – we're all survivors, the staff insist – wear scarves to hide balding heads. Young, old – cancer ages us all. Their brave smiles emphasize the worry lines and tired eyes.

Out the window, the city hums with its usual frenetic pulse. Elevated trains, dizzying lanes of cars, and transport drones all fight for space amid Bahrain's rush hour. Beyond it, the sea winks at me, sunlight glinting on its breaking waves. A world in constant motion, ready to leave me behind.

Coldness prickles my skin. Could I jump, like that woman jumped? It would be easy – rip the array of needles from my arm and rush across the room, forcing the window open. I might have to smash the glass if they put in security locks (a good strategy in a cancer ward). When the glass shatters and the screaming skyscraper winds whip at my hair, would I recoil or jump?

But I don't move. I cross my feet under my silk skirt and wet my lips. Perhaps I'm too fearful of causing a scene. Perhaps I'm not the jumping kind. But doubt gnaws at me with each passing second. Death is an unceasing fog around me, but despite my many trips to the bazaar, I can't bring myself to meet it yet.

Maybe you're not ready because you have unfinished business.

But what could that be? My child no longer needs me – if anything, I'm a burden. Bahrain has morphed into something beyond my wildest imagination. It's left me behind. I've lived plenty. What remains?

A rose city carved from rock. An ancient Nabataean site in Jordan, immortalized in photographs in glossy magazines and childhood stories. I always meant to go to Petra but had forgotten about that dream long ago. And in the Underground Bazaar, of all places, I'm reminded of what I've yet to do.

I close my eyes. The woman from yesterday's immersion tumbles through the air, beautiful cliffs and clear skies spinning around her. Is that why she was calm at the end? Did some part of her realize that she had lived the right life and was now dying in the right place?

The revelation hits me with such force that I have no room for uncertainty. I know what I must do, but I have to be smart about my next steps. The chemo session is nearly over. I smile sweetly at the nurse when she removes the last drip from my veins. My daughter-in-law will meet me downstairs, I reassure her. No, I don't need any help, thank you. This isn't my first rodeo. She laughs. People like their old women to have a little bite – it's acceptable once we're past a certain age. A small consolation prize for living so long.

In the reception room, I drop my phone behind a plant – Firaz and Reema are clever enough to find new ways to track me, so I discard their favorite weapon.

'Back again, Ms. Mansour? Looks like you were here yesterday.' The man's eyes twinkle as he examines my record on his computer screen.

'Where did the woman live?' I ask. 'The one from yesterday – the Bedouin woman. Does she have any surviving family?'

In truth, I know where she lived, but I need more. A family name, an address.

'Your guess is as good as mine,' the man says. A different man, not my usual favorite. Tall and thin like a tree branch, with brooding eyes. I'm earlier than usual, so this one must take the early shift.

'Surely you have something.' I inject a quaver in my voice. 'Anyone with the NeuroLync leaves an archive of information behind.' *Unlike me*, I don't add. When I go, I'll only leave bones.

'We don't keep those kinds of records here because we don't need them,' he says. 'People want to know what drowning feels like, not the person's entire life story.'

'Well, this customer does.'

'Can't help you.'

This is ridiculous. When I was his age, if an older woman asked me a question, I would have done my best to answer. It was a period of great social upheaval, but we still respected the elderly.

I try another angle. 'Are there any more paid immersion experiences tied to that record?' She's a woman, not a record, but I'm speaking in their language.

The man's eyes practically light up with dollar signs. 'We've got the life highlight reel. Everybody has one. People like to see those before the death, sometimes.'

Minutes later and I'm back in the immersion chamber, the helmet making its ominous descent over my head.

They call them 'highlight reels', but these files are really the by-product of a data scrubber going through a dead person's entire memory and recreating that 'life flashing before your eyes' effect. Good moments and bad moments, significant events and those small, poignant memories that stick in your mind for unclear reasons. I remember an afternoon with Firaz in the kitchen, making pastries. Nothing special about it, but I can still see the way the sunlight hit the counter and smell the filo dough when it came out of the oven.

The Bedouin woman's highlight reel is no different. There's a wedding under the stars, some funerals, and enough childbirths to make me wince in sympathy. But there are also mundane moments like my own. The smell of livestock on early mornings before the tourists begin spilling into the valley. Meat cooking over a low campfire. Memories that dance through the senses.

I leave the bazaar more restless than when I arrived. The woman's life was unremarkable. Good and bad in typical proportions. A part of me had expected a mystic connection to her surroundings, maybe a head injury that gave her strange conscious experiences that would explain her final moments. Instead, I found someone not unlike me, separated only by money and circumstances.

Through the humid air and dense crowds, Bahrain's only train station beckons. A bit ridiculous for an island, but it does connect the country to Saudi Arabia and the wider region via a causeway. I walk to the station, restlessness growing with each step. Perhaps this is my jump over the cliff. I'm moving toward a big decision, the pressure swelling as I reach the point of no return.

At the front booth, I buy a one-way ticket to Petra, Jordan, along the Hejaz Railway. Once I board the carriage, all my doubt and fear evaporate. This is what I need to do. A final adventure, a last trip in search of answers that no bazaar can give me.

The desert hills race by through the train window. It's hypnotic, and before long, my mind stirs like a thick soup through old feelings. The terrain outside feels both alien and comforting, that sensation of coming home after a long trip. A return to something primal and ancient, a way of life that's been lost amid controlled air conditioning and busy streets. How can something feel strange and right at the same time?

The Hejaz Railway system was completed when I was a little girl, itself a revival and expansion of an old train line that was abandoned after World War One. The region reasserting itself, flexing its power with a nod to its past. I've always hated planes, and you'll never get me on those hovering shuttles, so an old-fashioned train (albeit with a maglev upgrade) suits me just fine.

The terrain dulls as we speed north, as if the world is transitioning from computer animation to a soft oil painting. The mountains lose their edges and vegetation freckles the ground. Signs point us to ancient places. Aqaba. The Dead Sea. Petra.

The sun sets and I drift off under the engine's hum.

The next morning, the train pulls into Wadi Musa, the town that anchors Petra. I join the crowds spilling out into the station, the air cool and fresh compared to Bahrain. I reach into my pocket to check my phone for frantic messages, only to recall that I left it behind. Firaz and Reema must be searching for me by now. At this stage, they've likely contacted the police. Guilt tugs at the corners of my heart, but they'll never understand why this is important. And soon, I'll be out of their way.

Ignoring the long row of inviting hotels, I follow the signs toward Petra. Enterprising locals hawk everything from sunscreen to camel rides. With my hunched back and slow gait, they trail me like cats around a bowl of fresh milk.

'*Teta*, a hat for your head!'

'Need a place to stay, lady?'

'A donkey ride, ma'am? It's low to the ground.'

Why not? I'm in no condition to hike around ancient ruins. The donkey handler, a boy no older than eighteen, suppresses a smile when I pull out paper currency.

'How do most of your customers pay?' I ask as he helps me onto the beast.

'NeuroLync, ma'am. They send us a one-time wire.'

'You all have NeuroLync?' I ask, amazed. Many of these locals still live as Bedouin, in simple huts without electricity or running water.

'Yes, ma'am,' he says, clicking his tongue to prompt the donkey forward. 'We were some of the first in Jordan to get connected. Government project. Some refused, but most said yes.'

Interesting. So the area's Bedouin and locals were early adopters of NeuroLync technology, an experiment to support the country's tourism. That explained how an elderly woman of my age had the implant long enough to record most of her adult life, now downloadable for cheap voyeurs. My chest flutters. *People like me.*

My guide leads the donkey and me down the hill into a narrow valley. Most tourists walk, but some take carriages, camels, and donkeys. An adventurous soul charges past us on horseback, kicking up red sand.

Along the surrounding cliff faces and hills, dark holes mark ancient dwellings carved into the rock. Following my gaze, my guide points to them.

'Old Nabataean abodes,' he says, referring to the ancient people who made Petra home.

'Do people still live there?' I ask. My tone is light and curious.

'Not there,' he says.

'So where do all of the guides and craftspeople live around here?' I follow up: 'It makes sense to be close.'

'Some in Wadi Musa, but mostly in other places around Petra. We camp near the Monastery and the hills above the Treasury.'

I nod and let the silence settle between us, taking in the beauty around me. Suicide is a sensitive subject everywhere, but especially in the rural Arab world. I can't just ask about a woman who jumped off a cliff. But while I'm teasing away clues, I drink in the energy of my surroundings. The warmth of the sun on my face, the sharp stillness of the air. The sense of building excitement as we descend into the narrow valley, shaded by looming mountains. We're getting close to the Treasury, the most famous structure in Petra. I can tell by the way the tourists pick up their pace, pulling out the old-fashioned handheld cameras popular with the young set. I smile with them. I'm on vacation, after all.

I've seen plenty of pictures of the iconic Treasury, knowing that no picture can do it justice. I turn out to be right. Ahead, the valley forms a narrow sliver through which a stunning carved building emerges. Its deep, dark entrance is flanked by pillars. Cut into the rock, its upper level features more pillars crowned with intricate patterns. Though ancient, it is ornate and well-preserved. The surrounding throngs of tourists and souvenir peddlers can't detract from its beauty.

My guide helps me off the donkey so I can wander inside. It's what you'd expect from a building carved into the mountains – the interior is dark and gaping, with more arches and inlets where the Nabataeans conducted their business. For a second, my mind turns to Firaz and Reema, with their endless work. I look down, overwhelmed. People once flooded this building when it was a vibrant trade stop – people long gone. Everyone taking pictures around me will one day be gone as well – all of us, drops in humanity's ever-flowing river.

'Where next, ma'am?'

The winding road up to a high place, one you need a pack animal to reach. An easy place to fall – or jump.

'I'd like to see the Monastery.'

On the way up the trail, I talk with my guide, who I learn is named Rami. He has the usual dreams of teenage boys – become a soccer player, make millions, and see the world. When I tell him where I live, his eyes widen and I'm peppered with questions about tall buildings and city lights. He talks of cities as though they're living organisms, and in a way, I suppose they are. Traffic, sprawl, and decay. They're more than the sum of their people. But how can he understand that he's also fortunate to live here, to wake up every morning to a clear red sky, walking through time with every step he takes?

We round a corner along the cliff and I give a small cry.

'It's so far up,' I say. 'I'm glad the donkey's doing the work for me.'

Rami nods. 'They're more sure-footed than we are. They know exactly where to step.'

'Do people ever fall?'

Rami's eyes are trained ahead, but I catch the tightness in his jawline. 'It's rare, ma'am. Don't worry.'

My skin prickles. His voice carries a familiar strain, the sound of a battle between what one wants to say and what one should say. Does he know my old woman? Has he heard the story?

While I craft my next question, the donkey turns another corner and my stomach lurches. We're at the same spot where she fell. I recognize the curve of the trail, the small bush protruding into its path. I lean forward, trying to peer down the cliff.

'Can we stop for a minute?'

'Not a good place to stop, ma'am.' The boy's voice is firm, tight as a knot, but I slide off the saddle and walk to the ledge.

Wind, warm under the peak sun, attacks my thinning hair. I step closer to the edge.

'Please, *sayida*!'

Switching to Arabic. I must really be stressing the boy. But I can't pull back now.

Another step, and I look down. My stomach clenches. It's there – the boulder that broke her fall. It's free of blood and gore, presumably washed clean a long time ago, but I can remember the scene as it once was, when a woman died and left her body, a witness to her own demise.

But when I lean further, my body turns rigid. I'm a rock myself, welded in place. I won't jump. I can't. I know this with a cold, brutal certainty that knocks the air from my lungs. I'm terrified of the fall. Every second feels like cool water on a parched throat. I could stand here for hours and nothing would change.

'Please.' A voice cuts through the blood pounding in my ears, and I turn to meet Rami's frightened, childlike face. He offers his hand palm-up and I take it, letting myself be hoisted back onto the donkey, who chews with lazy indifference. We continue our climb as though nothing happened.

The Monastery doesn't compare to the Treasury at the base of the city, but it's impressive regardless. The surroundings more than make up for it, the horizon shimmering under the noon heat. Rami and I sit cross-legged in the shade, eating the overpriced *manaqish* I bought earlier.

'The cheese is quite good,' I admit. 'I don't eat much these days, but I could see myself getting fat off of these.'

Rami smiles. 'A single family makes all of the food you can buy here. An old woman and her daughters. They sell it across the area.'

I suppress commenting that the men in the family could help. I don't have the energy or the inclination – after staring down the cliff and winning, I'm exhausted. Did I win? Had part of me hoped that I would jump as well? Now that I hadn't, I didn't know what to do next.

I say all that I can think to say. 'This is a beautiful place. I don't want to be anywhere else.'

Rami steals a glance at me. 'There's evil here. The High Place of Sacrifice, where the Nabataeans cut animals' throats to appease their pagan gods.' He gives his donkey a pat, as though reassuring it. 'Battles and death. Maybe you can sense it, too. That place where you stopped? My grandmother died there.'

It takes me a second to register what the young man said, the words entering my ears like thick molasses. Then my blood chills. Rami is one of her many grandchildren. It shouldn't surprise me, but this proximity to the woman's surviving kin prickles my skin, flooding my senses with shock and shame in equal measure. I terrified the boy when I leaned over the edge.

I clear my throat, gripping the sides of my dress to hide my shaking hands. 'What was her name?'

He blinks, surprised. 'Aisha.'

A classic name. 'I'm so sorry, Rami,' I say. 'What a terrible accident.'

'She was taking a family down from the Monastery,' Rami says. He doesn't correct my assumption, and I wonder if he knows what happened. 'When she was younger, she hated working with the tourists. She loved to cook and preferred caring for the animals at the end of the day. But when she got older, my mother told me she loved it. She liked to learn their stories and tell her own, about her life and her family, all the things she had seen. I bet she could have written a book about all the people she met from around the world, but she never learned how to write.'

I press my lips together in disbelief. A woman with a NeuroLync plugged into her temple, unable to read a book. While it could have been tradition that kept her illiterate, it was unlikely. In many ways, the Bedouin were more progressive than the urban population. Perhaps she never learned because she never needed to.

'It sounds like she had a good life,' I manage.

Rami's face brightens, his dark eyes twinkling with sudden amusement. 'She made everyone laugh. I read a poem once in school. It said you can't give others joy unless you carry joy in reserve, more than you need. So I know she must have been happy until the end. I believe something evil made her fall that day. It sensed that she was good. Whatever it was – a jinn, a ghost – it knew it had to defeat her.'

Though exposed to modern technology and a government-run secular education, the boy had found his own mystical narrative to dampen his grief, to reason the unreasonable. *Not unlike me*, I realize. I came here in search of a secret. A special way to die, a way to secure life after death. Something unique about this place or people that would extinguish my fears. Magical thinking.

My mouth is dry. Should I tell the boy what I know from the bazaar? It would bring pain, but perhaps comfort as well. His grandmother, Aisha, died because of a strange psychological quirk, not a persuasive spirit. She was terrified but found peace in those final split seconds of the fall. She lingered somehow after meeting the ground, sinking into a warm, welcoming light. Would the boy want to know this? Would he feel betrayed by the realization that I knew about his grandmother, a stranger who had experienced her most intimate moments through a black-market bazaar?

No. Hers was not my story to tell. I'm a thief, a robber of memories, driven by my own fears. I came here for answers to a pointless question. What did it matter why she jumped? She lived well and left behind people who loved her. The people I love are far away and frantic – and yet I considered leaving them with the sight of my body splattered over rock.

As for her apparent conscious experience after death – I won't know what happened, what it meant, until it's my time. And my time isn't now, in this place. Not yet.

My face burns and I draw a shaking breath. Above me, the Monastery looms like an anchor. Through my shame, my mouth twitches in a smile. It's breathtaking. I don't regret coming here. But now, I need to go home.

'Rami, can you send a message for me with your NeuroLync?' I ask. My voice is hoarse but firm.

On the way back down, I close my eyes when we pass the spot on the path. I'm not afraid of jumping, but I'm afraid of the grief the jump left behind.

When we reach the base of the ruins, back at the Treasury, Rami lifts a finger to his temple.

'Your son is already in Jordan,' he says. 'He'll arrive here in a few hours. He says to meet him in the Mövenpick Hotel lobby.'

Rami's face flushes when I kiss his forehead in gratitude, but he smiles at the generous tip I press into his hands.

I sip coffee while guests come and go through the hotel lobby. A fountain trickles a steady stream of water nearby and beautiful mosaic patterns line the walls. I'm on my third Turkish coffee when Firaz bursts through the front door.

Our eyes meet and emotions pass across his face in waves – joy, relief, fury, and exasperation. I stand up, letting him examine my face as he approaches.

'Have a seat, Firaz.'

'Why are you here?' he bellows, his voice echoing across the lobby and drawing alarmed stares in our direction. Before I can respond, he continues, 'We thought you got lost and were wandering the streets,' he says, back in control but still too loud for comfort. 'Murdered in a ditch or dead from heatstroke. Why can't you just live, Mama? What are you trying to escape from? Were you confused? Is it the tumor?'

My poor boy, reaching for the last justification for his mad mother.

'It's not the tumor, Firaz,' I say in a gentle tone. 'And I wouldn't call myself confused. Lost, maybe. The tumor terrifies me, Firaz. It's not how I want to go, so I kept looking for other, better ways to make an end of everything. It was unfair to you, and I'm sorry. I really am.'

Firaz groans, sinking into one of the plush seats. Massaging his temples, he closes his eyes. I give him time. It's all I can give him now.

Finally, he sighs and his face softens when he faces me again. The same expression he wore when he first learned I was sick – that his mother was vulnerable in ways out of his control.

'I should have listened to you more,' he says. 'Asked how you were doing. Not in the superficial way – about chemo and your mood. The deeper questions. I didn't because it scares me, too. I don't want to think about you gone.'

Tears prickle my eyes. 'I know. I don't want to leave you, either. For a while, I thought dying would be doing you a favor. But nothing is more important to me than you, Firaz. That won't change, even if this tumor starts frying every part of my brain. I'll love you until my last breath. I want to spend my last months with you and Reema, if you'll have me.'

Silence follows. We sit together for an hour, letting the world hum around us, before Firaz finally stands up.

'How did you know to fly to Jordan, before my guide contacted you?' I ask when we reach the Wadi Musa train station. We board the day's last train together.

Firaz's mouth forms a grim, triumphant line. 'Reema did

some digging around at the Underground Bazaar. Grilled all the staff there about what you watched, and questions you asked. She pieced together that you probably ran off to Petra.'

'She's resourceful,' I say with a grin. 'You were smart to marry her. After I go—'

'Mom!'

'After I go,' I continue, 'I want you both to live the lives you desire. Move for that perfect job. Travel. Eat that sugary dessert on the menu. Find little moments of joy. I mean it, Firaz. Don't be afraid. If I've learned one thing from all of this, it's that sometimes you need to leap. Whatever awaits us at the end, it seems to be somewhere warm and safe. And even if it's followed by nothing, we have nothing to fear from death.'

Anguish tightens Firaz's face, but after a moment, something inside of him appears to release and his eyes shine with understanding. He helps me into a seat at the back of the train carriage.

'Let's go home.'

I catch a final glimpse of Wadi Musa's white buildings, uneven like jagged teeth, as the train pulls away. Past the town, Petra's hills run together, freckled by dark dwellings. It's bleak but beautiful, and I close my eyes to burn the scene into my memory. I want to remember everything.

The Ten-Percent Thief

Lavanya Lakshminarayan

India

I put out a call for Indian novels in my capacity as book columnist, and a slim book called *Analog/Virtual* landed on my desk. I was immediately blown away by Lavanya's strange, expansive future Bangalore, by the urgency and poetry of the writing, the use of high and low tech and the investigation of political concerns, all packed within a small mosaic novel, of which 'The Ten-Percent Thief' is the first story. It was the sort of book you want to shout about to everyone, and so it was an easy choice to include, here, this small window into Lavanya's world. Welcome to Apex City!

> *Herein we outline the principles of a smart new world.*
> *We seek to fulfil our human potential. We do not tolerate*
> *failure.*
>   – from the *Preamble to the Meritocratic Manifesto*

*

Nobody notices anything because nothing has happened. Not yet anyway.

This is how all things begin.

The electric shield thrums ominously. It cuts Apex City in two, striking across the crater that was once Bangalore.

She lives on the wrong side of the Carnatic Meridian.

They call her Nāyaka, their Champion. They pledge allegiance to her.

They're her people. The Analogs.

When Bell Corp ignored the cholera epidemic, she stole medi-tech from their laboratories. When Bell Corp stopped funding their water treatment, she began lifting holo-watches. She snatches hundreds each week. One solar-powered battery purifies a thousand bottles of water.

If raid-bots break into her pod-house, they'll find the 140-square-foot space filled with paperbacks. Nothing of value, no link to her crimes.

She is discreet.

Dead drops. Paper money. Forty-one safe capsules buried underground.

I am invisible.

The Virtuals know her as the Ten-Percent Thief. They have a price on her head.

I'm going to make sure I'm worth it.

She strolls towards the Meridian Gate.

Pod-houses form towering aisles; their circular windows are eye sockets in fibreglass skulls. On their eastern walls, a well-known artist directs a crowd of Analogs towards the completion of a mural. It reflects their past and celebrates their present.

Children scurry to the Institute – a cluster of pod-houses that lean in dangerously towards each other. It's architecturally unsound, but the children don't notice.

A small playground made of scrap metal and junkyard finds is laid out before it. Trash can lids form the seats of swings; a slide is cobbled together from scavenged planks of wood. A solitary child sits on a merry-go-round made from the ancient remains of a satellite dish.

Hawkers set up canvas tents along the path. They're selling homemade sunscreen and scraps of illegally procured ClimaTech fabric.

A stab of guilt. She sourced that ClimaTech.

They'll be arrested and sent to the vegetable farm.

She nearly intervenes.

They'll be put down. Harvested.

She steels herself.

They've been instructed not to sell it this close to the Meridian. You can't save everyone.

She chokes on a rolling cloud of dust and presses on.

She passes a structure resembling a giant tin shed. It's made from the rusty shells of freight trains, painted in bright colours that will fade in the relentless sun. The salvaged doors of washing machines form its windows. Hundreds of Analogs line up before the entrance to the Museum of Analog History.

Nāyaka feels a twinge of pride – over seven hundred Analogs participated in its construction, and even more came forward to supply the artefacts that fill its cavernous halls.

At the edge of the Analog world, she places her palm over a holoscanner.

Her silicone gloves fit like a second skin. Their tips bear a set of 3D-printed fingerprints. She's about to impersonate an Analog gardener.

They volunteer. They trust me.

An armed patrol-drone scans her. The Carnatic Meridian sparks blue. A gap appears, electricity crackling on either side.

She passes through the Meridian Gate.

The light dims abruptly. A wave of coolth rushes over her.

The SunShield Umbrella orbits Apex City. It protects the Virtual side from ultraviolet radiation, providing climatic conditions optimized for human performance.

Her people are exposed to heatwaves and dust-storms.

Twenty-six towers form a rank into the heart of the city. Thousands of employees are ensconced in bio-mat and frosted-glass spirals, absorbed in HoloTech experiences. She spies a game of Hyper Reality golf – no doubt a sizeable business deal in progress.

A block of pod-houses shares a cellular phone.

The Arboretum curves on either side of her, all along the city's borders. Thousands of trees flower in desolation.

Most Analogs have no conception of a tree.

They rely on the memories of Virtuals who have been deported to their side of the city. They hang on to the descriptions of a handful of workers who make their way through the Meridian each day.

She makes for the teleportals. Virtuals edge away from her grubby, shabbily dressed person.

I will not claim their holo-watches. I have a bigger prize in mind.

The port-bot's cyber-arm vibrates in disgust when she produces paper money.

She steps into the carbon-fibre capsule.

The Ten-Percent Thief is molecularly reconstituted upon the estate of Sheila Prakash, a HoloTech mogul from the top one percent of society.

Don't throw up.

The side effects of teleportation include nausea, but she's also never seen so much open space before. A holo-sphere arcs over the property, projecting clear blue skies overhead and verdant meadows along the horizon. The illusion eliminates all trace of Apex City's jagged skyline.

We can barely see the sky in the spaces between our pod-houses.

She's scanned and approved by a patrol-droid. The entire transaction is witnessed by the tell-tale flash of light on a PanoptiCam lens.

Once she's equipped with a jetpack, a sap-scanner, pruning shears and InstaBlossom compounds, her instructions are relayed.

Bring All Trees to Flower by 3.49 p.m.

Trim buds from each tree.

Analyse using sap-scanner.

Apply appropriate InstaBlossom compound.

Repeat.

She powers up her jetpack. It propels her into the canopies.

She rubs her hands over the bark, feeling ridges and knots through her gloves. She presses leaves to her face, trailing sap and dew across her skin. She sniffs the buds that lie in her palm, prying into their scents and secrets.

Trees.

I've never touched one before.

They're the exclusive right of the top one percent.

The Arboretum can only be accessed by the top twenty percent.

The seventy percent in the middle are allowed Hyper Reality gardens, the occasional houseplant.

I'm only given the right to breathe. And barely.

She is a member of the bottom ten percent, exiled in shame.

The threat of the vegetable farm creeps in my shadow.

Each year, more non-performers are deported across the Meridian. The ranks of the hopeless swell.

They don't kill us; they watch us suffer.

It is immaterial that Bell Corp's system of governance came as a welcome relief to the ruins of an erstwhile civilization. It seemed optimal – even utopian – for a world divided along social and communal lines, faced with the threat of dwindling resources and hostile climate, to be redesigned.

Every system believes itself to be the perfect solution.

The PanoptiCam scans the grounds. She locates its blind spot – a thick 'W' formed by two intertwined trees.

She begins to whistle. She works her way to it, unhurriedly. Her heart pounds an erratic rhythm.

The resistance needs a symbol. I will give them a dream.

Three buds fall into a tight space between her glove and her wrist. An InstaBlossom sachet disappears under her wig.

She takes a deep breath.

It can't be this easy.

She returns to the gaze of the PanoptiCam, unchanged. She finishes her assignment. Whistling.

Her palms stay damp until she's back at the Meridian Gate. The patrol-drone's scanners don't detect the contraband on Nāyaka, covered in dirt as she is.

It is this easy.

She feigns listlessness as she enters the Analog city. She makes for a confluence of alleyways at its heart.

She tears off her gloves. Digs.

She drops a bud into the shallow pit.

She packs it with InstaBlossom, then sacrifices a bottle of water. A sapling plunges through the earth.

Her breath catches.

It shoots upwards with a shriek, reaching for the sky.

Her eyes sting.

It bursts into flower, a whisper of jacaranda falling to the ground.

There's a face at a grimy window. Gasps of wonder. Footsteps.

She melts into the shadows, invisible.

Tomorrow, there will be consequences.

Today, there is hope.

At Desk 9501...

Frances Ogamba

Nigeria

I came across Frances' work in the virtual pages of *The Dark* magazine. *The Dark* used to be edited by Silvia Moreno-Garcia, who appears in *The Best of World SF: Volume 1*, and it had, and continues to have, a great selection of international fiction with a horror and dark fantasy bent. I loved Frances' stories that I found there, such as 'Water Child', unsettling stories with a wonderful sense of place. The only problem (for me!) was that they weren't science fiction. So I wrote to Frances and asked if she'd be willing to write one in that genre. The result was 'At Desk 9501...' which is, you guessed it, an unsettling story with a wonderful sense of place that also happens to be science fiction. This story is original to this anthology.

... Zina donates his life mending near-deaths caused by heart-related problems. Rarely, he is assigned accidents. Tiny neon bulbs spring to life when he sits on his electricity-powered chair. A belt goes round his torso, preventive of a potential fall. Two smaller belts go around each arm, tightening and loosening until his arms fit in the loop. His feet rest on a pedal which pulsates during a life transfer. His favourite tool is his smart glasses. The lens sits over his right eye, and on his left, a gadget containing a camera and a Wi-Fi camera focuses on his pupil.

Zina's first client, Julie, is battling cardiac arrest in the middle of a surgery: percutaneous nephrolithotomy. She is projected into his vision through his monocular smart glasses. Voices of the medical team teem around her. Hooked to an IV, she lies prone on a gurney. He places his right forefinger on the biometric device on his desk and, crimping his voice into the tone he's been taught, starts incanting, *Julie, Julie.*

He shuts his body down to walk the darkness his client has loped into. At first, it is difficult to fold himself into the small, bloodied incision on her back – a void where he is made aware of himself only through the steady whine of the cosmos. The fizz of the city interferes. Time ticks through the headphones – the crux of Julie's life coming apart. He remembers the need to pay his house rent and the thought nudges him closer to the silvery light fringing the afterlife. He thinks about the percentage he gets for every bit of life he saves. *Twenty per cent of the client's total fee*, the contract reads.

Zina finds Julie whizzing back and forth, her edges blurred as she gropes for the green door: the exit. A niggling feeling trickles into his head and overwhelms him. It is like an absence, like spraining a thumb unnoticed. A fire alarm goes off somewhere. A baby's howls rise from a corner of the city. These don't worry him. The world can crumble for all he cares. He clenches his fist around Julie's hand and pulls until he hears a gurgling sound.

Outside, Ozuoba traffic goes on. Testy drivers hurl curses. The drizzle hasn't let up for hours. The grey blanket of the tarred road spreads out below the glass walls of the office building. Nothing stops to acknowledge the miracle of putting his life on hold for a stranger. His spine hurts, a mild pain, the proof that a fraction of his life has just been doled out. Julie's family have paid a sum of one million naira to Life Savers NGO. Twenty per cent of the sum would get Zina good shoes and cover the rent advance the NGO has deposited for the one-room flat he found at Egbelu.

The training sessions do not prepare you for the real thing. Zina has often floundered as he tries to dissect the life-saving procedures, to know which one should forerun the other. He was first taught how the world is being stripped of her younger generation, and it would be his job to loosen death's grip from the neck of humankind.

After a client downloads the Life Savers' app and inputs their debit card passcode, the payment is registered at Life Savers, and the app's code scanner becomes active. The client scans their face or has someone close to them do it.

The station nearest to Zina is Desk 9632. The man who sits there works on near-deaths caused by cancers. He is always doubled over, groaning, muttering. There are other people in enclosed cabins whom Zina never gets to see. The few women on the team sit some distance away, in a cabin thinly veiled by a wooden board. The low wall lets Zina glimpse their faces and eavesdrop on their indistinct chats. Most of their clients are booked through life insurance bought by families who do not want to take any chances in the event of an accident or during childbirth or surgery. Their jobs are to maintain a tight grasp on lives, even when there are no known threats to life.

*

Life had been hard for Zina. Then he heard about Life Savers NGO on the radio, while in a cab.

There are too many deaths in our world. This is not God's plan for us. The hospitals are failing. Well, now we need vibrant men and women who can donate fragments of their lifespan to save lives. We pay a competitive salary and our life agents get percentages for every life saved.

The voice, shrill and almost coasting to the limits of its tonal capacity, had belonged to Mr Eze, the CEO of the NGO – the new alternative to hospitals. It was the first time Zina had learned that human life could not only be given out in chunks – blood, bone marrow, sperm, eggs, kidneys – but as a whole. The presenter asked a question, which Zina did not hear. His mind was already considering options, making choices.

No. We do not need to be with the patients physically. We use a kind of electromagnetic radiation which projects the dying into our workspace, into the vision of our life agents. We connect to them through our app and a biometric machine. Then we say their names to give us full access into their bodies. Our potential agents will all be tested for lifespan longevity.

'You can find this out? How much lifespan a person has?' The presenter's curiosity sounded unscripted.

Mr Eze's voice softened with the hint of laughter.

Yes! We have a magnetic resonance imaging machine for this. You can call it MRI for short. Every potential agent will be tested with it. We cannot take people with a lifespan of less than eighty. This is not to discriminate, but every five donations subtract six months from a person's lifespan. This is why we save only people who are not yet too far gone. Even while saving others, you know, we must watch out for ourselves too.

Mr Eze chuckled.

'How do you detect your client's proximity to death?'

We have software for that. Once we connect with a case, the software tells us how far gone the client is. I donate life myself. But I cannot do it alone. We need more young people for this work of God. I also encourage everyone in the world right now to download the Life Savers app from Google Store, in case of an emergency.

'You said that a lifeline costs about one million naira. Isn't this too expensive for the common people?'

Human life is priceless and cannot be duplicated. It is a miracle that science has granted us the gift of re-igniting life.

When the phone lines had opened, many voices poured down them in approval or disgust. One of the voices rippling with anger drew Zina's attention.

My name is Pastor Emmanuel! I am calling from Ogbogoro! Listen! You cannot distort the order of life! For everything under the sun, there is a season! A time to live and a time to die! You cannot thwart this order with your fake procedure! You cannot play God!

Other voices jammed against the presenter and Mr Eze.

What is this world turning into? This is a sign of the end-time.

This NGO is occultic and should be investigated.

It is too expensive. Aren't there cheaper packages?

Can I buy a lifeline ahead of time?

*

Uche, Uche, Zina chants under his breath, a prayer, his way of nudging this stranger open, and entreating permission to walk into the stranger's body. Uche had collapsed in the middle of a presentation at work. *Vibrant, your go-to man for every problem in advertising,* the ticket says. The world is ever ready to put a person in the past, and glorify their loss with glossy memorials. Zina's job has taught him this.

Uche is not hanging about in the dark like Julie, Zina's first client. But it is hard work to extricate him from the foyer of death. He takes Zina's hand with reluctance, unwilling to abandon his new state.

Zina feels a shocking bleakness after he wrestles Uche back. The pain comes at him. Wave after wave. Until he has tears in his eyes. It is not physical pain. It is mental, a deep sense of loss. He feels like he is shedding the nub of his essence, layer after layer.

There are over twenty workers at Life Savers NGO, but their heavy responsibilities limit camaraderie. Apart from the women who get chummy with one another on a few occasions, nobody holds conversations. After each save – the slog of extracting a person almost claimed by the afterlife – Zina sees on his colleagues' faces all the hardship they have lived. It is always the moment most ripe with clarity. Away from this hall, full of people, full of voices and keyboard taps, they live through their agonies entirely unnoticed.

Engorged clouds protrude out of the evening sky. It rains, gently. Umbrellas transform the city into a canvas of colours. Zina joins the jostling for taxis and buses that will go into the remote areas and city outskirts. There are tricycles going to the small villages that have latched on to the city with their fangs, where rent is cheap, where roads are strips of broken asphalt. The air is filled with shouts: *Rumuokwachi! Ogbogoro! Egbelu! Enter this one! One chance! One chance!* A woman's wide umbrella shields him from the drizzle. When a taxi pulls up, she turns to him and says, 'This one is going your way.'

Zina thinks his suit must have drawn her attention to him. The driver makes small talk with the passenger seated in the front. Zina shares the back with three people. They are pressed up close, legs touching. The intimacy makes him wonder which one of them he will save someday.

He ambles with stray dogs on the dirt road leading to his house. He notices the locals tapping one another, gesturing at his outfit. The NGO has donated toward his wardrobe too. The MRI results counted one hundred and fifty years in his lifespan.

The wall of his living room is covered with kraft paper, a brilliant contrast to the stained wood tiles covering the floor. A wine-coloured quilt hangs at the windows. He used to live in a shack perched on wobbly stilts at Eneka. He was nearly swept away by the gales in the last rainy season. He worked then as a pump attendant and was owed his wages most of the time.

The two lives he has saved so far are stuck in his head. He experiences their thoughts and memories, especially the gratitude whirring through their bodies. He can smell them. He can nearly hear them. He shuts his eyes, but their anatomies are stuck to his head in detail. *It is one of the cons*, the training booklet says. He sees bone structures and lung patterns. In his dreams they collapse into more people – people in the taxi, people at the office, people in the city.

The next morning, Zina meets the man at Desk 9632 clutching his chest and crying. No ticket trickles onto Zina's screen for the rest of that morning. He keeps clicking the mouse and refreshing the ticket page, listening to the muffled cries of his colleagues as they embody this strange suffering. He evokes images of places lost to him and prepares to lose himself in nostalgia. He stares at the transparent glass walls, framing the bustle of the city with his eyes and willing time to fetch him a client. It comes at first as a feeling, and then he starts hearing voices, far removed from the office building. The drone of the living does not distract them. The dissonant buzz of the machines around him fades as the figures blur in and out of Zina's vision. They liquefy and mould into silhouettes of a man and a woman twirling about the building, like drawings inspired by smoke. They lunge at him with lightning speed. Zina lets out a muffled shout and crashes to the floor.

The man at Desk 9632 looks up, his mouth open as his gaze hovers on Zina, then he returns to work. Nobody else registers Zina's distress. Zina steadies himself against the fear growing in his gut. He keeps staring at the glass wall where the figures had grown. But only the city stares back.

A ticket comes at noon. Zina launches a frantic search through his inner self, seeking a quiet corner. *Obed, Obed, Obed, Obed,* Zina calls out, but Obed appears oblivious as he moves further away. Zina glimpses him strolling through the green door – the furthest the agents at Life Savers are instructed to go – into a greyscale mist. Lifeless shrubbery fringes Obed's frame. A beep goes off from Zina's desk. The operation has failed. Zina retreats.

The failure conjures a feeling unlike anything Zina has ever known. It tears him into two people. They thunder at each other, hurling cannon-like shots before rejoining. Zina supports his head with his hands. The episode leaves him with a weird ache in his insides, as if he has been stabbed.

On his way home, he surrounds himself with the warmth of strangers while a voice whispers in his head, *I was not too far gone, and you know it. You left me waiting for too long by the green door.*

A shadow stalks the pavement when Zina gets to his neighbourhood. The night is young. A feverish crowd stretches well beyond the flowers bordering a nearby football field. He considers detouring from the short walk to his house. Perhaps, if he chocks his mind full with images of young men jostling for a leather ball, the memory from his job will be displaced. He melts into the throng and waits for time to elapse. He is surprised when he sees female footballers on the field. This piques his interest. Within minutes, he does indeed begin to forget.

Zina leaves with the other spectators, everyone dispersing, their pathways branching in different directions. He walks behind a group of teenage boys arguing about the teams' expertise and who the girl of the match should be. Some of the young people skulk the shadows in twos, their bodies glued together. His apartment is upholstered in darkness. The car park is empty. The family living above him is not home. The wind whispers as he turns his key in the lock.

It was a minor accident. I hit my head against the road. I was taken to the doctor early. I was in surgery. Someone recommended an NGO. That NGO recommended you.

Zina's heart jolts. His hand jitters on the doorknob. A gust of wind rushes forward and follows him in. He listens for more words, but none come. He is afraid to use the bathroom or fix a quick dinner. He tucks himself into his bed.

My daughter is barely four. She would not sleep unless I put her to bed. Why couldn't you have been quicker? I was simply returning from buying steel pipes to complete a client's job. I have three other jobs to finish. My birthday was yesterday, can you believe it? I turned thirty-five!

Zina convinces himself that it is all in his head. Yet, he is aware that something walked in with him earlier. He opens the music player on his phone and plays Tiwa Savage's 'All Over'.

This is my favourite song. Ah! This life! You have ruined me! You have ruined me! You have ruined me!

The weeping voice resembles tongues of fire lapping at the house.

Mr Eze appears mystified when Zina relates his experience. His deputy, Mr Kenneth, swivels on a chair opposite Mr Eze. Zina does not intend to make accusations of deceit, but he feels angered by the lax attitude they are giving his report.

'Nothing in the training says I will keep hearing and seeing the people I saved, or that if a job fails, the client will blame me for their death. I barely slept last night. The voice was everywhere.'

'We hear these kinds of reports, occasionally. What we know is that some clients are hyperactive, like those invading your space. We recently discovered that some of the saved patients have a kind of syndrome—'

'Yes,' Mr Kenneth picks up from his boss. 'It's not exactly like Stockholm's but a close relative. They retain attachments to their saviour. This lasts only a few weeks, after that, the bond severs.'

Zina feels worse and leaves the office with some pills.

'They gave you the sleep-inducing stuff.' The man at Desk 9632 says, hurrying to Zina's side. 'And what about something for the pain?' He sighs dolefully. Wisps of grey hair peek from under his denim hat. He is aging quite badly, developing mouth lines that cut to the bone. It is the first time Zina sees how slender he is.

'Hi, my name is Zina—'

'What you are seeing and feeling will never stop. That is the way the universe balances the costly exchange we are undertaking.'

'Are you new too?' There is a tinge of dismissal in Zina's voice.

The man smiles. 'We are all new. At least, that's what Mr Eze says. I wonder why you are here, Zina. If you came here to make quick money and run, it is a futile dream. I dreamed the same. Yet I have been here for over a decade.'

Zina feels an emptying in his chest.

'I might have got the wrong info about all this then.'

'Not your fault. Most of the procedures are untested.'

Two rings with different cadence come from the man's desk. The man's head zaps up, his eyes taking on a new shade.

'I have tickets for prostate and cervical.' He shuffles toward his desk and pauses half-way. His eyes are full of the unsaid when he faces Zina. 'Did they mention the other disadvantages?'

'What disadvan—No, they did not.'

'The people who worked here before us said they became unluckier with each life donation.'

Zina stares at him. He feels a weight in his chest, as if his heart has suddenly got heavier. Zina sits in his chair, but he is teetering on a tightrope. Will a car run him down, sweep him under its tyres? Will a stray bullet find his neck? What if he continues to bear the weight of all the lives he saves? What if the tremors inside him never let up until they have completely engulfed him?

Felix, Felix. Heart attack. Third time. Critical. It is easy to find Felix, easy to link hands with him, even though his features remain blurred. The aftermath of the save laps up all the moisture in his body. He crumbles under the roar of the fire devouring him. The heat jars his memories open. A slideshow of his childhood flickers before him – upsetting bees with a group of other boys he no longer remembers, his slow advancement to adulthood in a community orphanage where he did not fit in, the mongrel he and his friends set on fire while it was still alive.

In Zina's thirty-eight years, it is only in this moment that he ponders on their brutality toward the dog. He must have been twelve at the time, yet the dog's final cries and the smell of its fur crinkling in the flames infiltrate his ears and nostrils at his desk. Zina bends over and begins to cry.

He runs into the woman who once shielded him from the rain with her umbrella on the pavement one evening. The skin on her neck glitters with endless rows of jewelry. Her cheeks are puffed-out as if she has food in them.

'Hi, how was work today?'

'Work went well. Thank you.'

'I hear there's a hike in the taxi fares.'

Zina nods. He no longer feels anything for women, other than a faint admiration his mind stokes and quickly abandons. The woman is alluring, but his job has caused ingrained cracks in his sexual appetite. His thoughts are occupied with the green door of human life and the unceasing hum somewhere in his ears. The woman keeps pushing new branches into their conversation, but his grudging replies stub out the fires of what-could-be. When the woman leaves, he catches a taxi. He is the last passenger to board. He rests his eyes on the road, refusing to glimpse the faces of his companions illuminated in the lights from oncoming vehicles. He hands his fare to the driver. His hand brushes a thigh and an arm and a mop of hair. They all glance at him with Julie's and Obed's and Uche's eyes.

A conversation revolving around life donations startles the silence in the taxi, and soon all the passengers, except Zina, contribute.

'... there is even this new NGO at Ikwerre Road. They take years off people,' a woman says and laughs.

'I have heard of it. If you are fifty years old, you can pay them to chop off twenty, and you come out thirty,' the driver says.

'It's mostly for actresses and footballers. They need to stay young,' the man sitting next to Zina says.

'Not really. Anyone who can afford it is doing it. My neighbour's son slapped four years on his age because he needed to qualify for a Princeton fellowship.'

'Wait, they now *add* to people's ages too?'

'Go to GRA. Their plazas are everywhere. Addition. Reduction. Anything.' Their laughter punches Zina in the face. He feels relieved when the taxi drops him off.

*

Zina inherits more and more people. Those who are grateful
for his service stain his life with theirs. Their smells and voices
protrude into his space. Sometimes, a memory glows in his mind
and he wonders if it belongs to him. The people whose lives
expired before he reached them hurl curses at him. Once, from
under his bed, where it had always been silent before, he hears the
tempo of a breathing animal, and a battered voice saying, *Fuck
you, Zina! Fuck you to hell! Fuck you, Zina! Fuck you to hell!*

A woman from the team resigns one morning. Mr Eze bangs
on her desk while she gathers her things and shuts her empty
drawers. The woman's face looks like it has braved many
thunderstorms. When she nears the rail area, she turns, as if
preparing to offer her colleagues a golden revelation that can
save them.

'This procedure is not well-tested and has far more
consequences than we knew. I am as good as dead, but I hope
you leave with your lives intact.'

Though it is the women she looks at while she speaks, Zina
feels the warning is for him. Mr Eze lunges at the woman, but
the elevator door shields her before he is able to land a blow.
He turns to his staff, chin sagging, gasping.

'Back to work!'

Hands are reluctant to return to mouse pads, to biometric
devices, to arm straps. Distrust suffuses the room.

'The woman received a lifesaving request from a man who
had assaulted her in the past,' the man at Desk 9632 tells Zina
in a small voice. 'So, she rejected the ticket.' They both stand
by a glass wall, listening to the wind chitter against it.

'Oh, the man himself needed saving?'

'The man's child, I think.'

'Seems she already wanted to leave.'

'Yes.'

'Maybe the man's request strengthened her resolve.'

'Yes. If you are giving your life away, it should at least be for someone worth it, you know.'

They fall silent for a heartbeat.

'It's a strange world.'

'And a stranger job.'

'Will you leave?'

'This job?' The man chuckles. Threads of veins pop across his face. 'I am as good as dead. The money I earn takes care of my whole family.' His voice melts into a loud squeak when he speaks next, 'You know, I came here with one-fifty years, just like you. Now, I have about fifty remaining.' The man swats at something, snaps his head to both sides as if shushing things away. Zina knows it must be the swarm of ghosts the man has inherited from the job. They are always present in the air of any room, always whispering through the wind.

Zina knows he cannot return to the shack he once lived in or the community orphanage where children like him who were abandoned in nylon bags or in a scanty fold of flannel were raised. He'd asked questions about his parents but was only offered grainy stories. Zina attacks a lifetime of no roots with his quest for wealth. With his prosperity, he can plant himself in the world, maybe even plant a family.

Zina's station gets popular. Desk 9501 pops up often on search results. He receives e-mails asking if he can meet up for a hangout. He begins to do four jobs per day, almost what the man at Desk 9632 pulls off. He goes home dog-tired, with an empty fullness that renders everything unappealing.

Rose, Rose. A victim of an explosion from an illegal gas-filling shop. Zina finds her in a square of bright light. She is packing a bag in haste. He sees most of his clients in this state – focused on a task they'd been pursuing before the accident struck.

Ola, Ola. He sits under the moonlight, in a pathway of dry leaves, people coming and going. Zina shudders at the large number of people already crowding the exit.

Kosi, Kosi. There was an argument between Kosi and her husband. He punched her in the chest. Zina finds her somewhere beyond reach, her underarm trapping a purse. She is barefoot. The wind disturbs the hem of her gown. *Kosi! Kosi!* She keeps tumbling down the path. A mist appears and whitens everything.

He has cried *Philip, Philip; Okiemute, Okiemute; Robert, Robert.* He has cried other names that push him outside his body, into an existential entanglement. Each life he works on etches into his reality.

He runs into the woman with the umbrella again. Relief washes over him. He needs someone to drown the voices in his head. She smiles at him and bats her false eyelashes, 'Call me Chika.'

They sit out at a bar in Egbelu. He asks her questions he forgets the moment he asks them. His repetitions draw laughs out of Chika. 'You just asked me if I have a degree.'

'I did? I'm really tired. Had so much work to do today. You want us to go home?'

Chika nods, swallowing back a laugh. 'You asked me that too.'

Zina tries to ignore the rattling in his head. Will sex help erect the much-needed wall between his clients and him? He worries that he has no idea of trendy sexual styles. He barely remembers the last time he locked bodies with a woman.

His neighbourhood has slipped into a clamorous quiet. Only the bright lights filtering out of windows show signs of human habitation. The voices still accompany him, plaintive or reproachful, yet quieter than they have ever been.

Zina bustles around his flat, playing the perfect host. He fixes Chika's bath and boils noodles for dinner. He is making his bed when the world slips into total silence. The quiet screeches in his head as he hunts for sounds. He bangs the door but there is no sound when it jams the door frame. He is afraid that the world has ascended to a new rung and left him behind. When he dashes into the living room, a woman sits hunched against the couch, but she is not Chika. She wears a dress, not the skirt and blouse Chika was wearing. She heaves upward in one movement, her eyes trained on his face. Zina sees her heartbeat in the frail skin of her neck. He recognizes Kosi's creased forehead and Julie's ashy skin. The stillness climbs a notch higher, every creak and moan of the universe strangely snipped off. Zina screams and struggles with the door he had already locked. Slowly, the image of the two-faced woman distorts back to Chika. She stares at him in shock.

'Chika? Oh, I thought... I am so sorry, please.'

'It's fine.' She steps away from him, clutching her bag, her eyes bulging with fear. 'I have to get home before the taxis stop running.'

When he studies his living room later, he finds a broken plastic horse, the one that used to adorn his living-room table. The couches have been completely wheeled out of position. Did he attack Chika? He sends her dozens of texts asking to know what happened, soliciting her forgiveness, for what, he is not quite sure. She never texts back.

He no longer runs into her. He merely glimpses her back on the crowded pavement before she melts away. He is sure she is avoiding him as much as he is aware of a large blight tainting his soul.

The days swish past Zina. He does not remember if he eats or sleeps. He takes more tickets and extracts more people from the beyond. He goes about with the army of his saved and unsaved. Sometimes, he swats at them, or jumps off the path to avoid a roadblock they have set up, or chuckles at the jokes they throw about. Always, someone talks. Someone hums. Someone laments.

He finds them all one morning, littered in front of his flat. It unsettles him to see them in flesh, each in the clothes they died in, or were saved in. They flank his sides and march with him. He is unable to cut through the swarm and flag down a taxi. So, he marches from Egbelu to Ogbogoro to Rumuokwachi, and to Ozuoba where the NGO is. Still, he is unable to get through.

Zina is terrified that time is eluding him and the walls are closing in on him. His phone rings and he does not know how to reach it. His exhaustion peaks, and he wonders if he is already crossing between worlds. The circle grows tighter and the turns become narrower, the roads almost vanishing, and Zina keeps trying to find a gap in between.

Milagroso

Isabel Yap

The Philippines

I ran into Isabel only once, I think, at an event in London, but have been a fan of her short fiction for years, and we included an earlier story of hers in one of the *Apex Book of World SF* anthologies. She had a gorgeous short story collection published in 2021, called *Never Have I Ever*, which you should seek out as soon as you finish this one. I loved the sense of place in 'Milagroso', but more than that, its concern with and depiction of food, which I paired up with the story that follows it for a double feast.

I t's late afternoon on the eve of the Pahiyas Festival when Marty finally drives into Lucban. The streets are filled with people congregating outside their houses, stringing up fruits and vegetables shaped into chandeliers. Entire roofs are covered in kiping, leaf-shaped rice wafers, their colors flared to dazzling by the slowly setting sun. Someone has tacked poster paper all over the preschool wall, and children with paint smeared on their cheeks are making trees full of hand-shaped leaves. Vendors have already set up shop, prepping for the onslaught of tourists.

Most side streets are blocked, so Marty has to drive through the town center, which is the usual explosion of propaganda – posters of the mayor and councilors alternate with banners for washing detergents, Coca-Cola, Granny Goose Chips, and the latest summer-special, *MangoMazings – exactly like the real thing!* Marty ignores these as he navigates the still-familiar streets. They didn't leave Manila for this.

They left Manila to see a miracle.

Inez is stirring awake, though she keeps her eyes shut. She groans, shifts, and slaps her thigh, impatiently. In the rearview mirror, Marty can see Mariah's head snapping back and forth to match the car's rhythm, her mouth hanging open. JR is also asleep; the seat belt is tight across his hunched chest, making him look smaller than he is. Sunlight beams through the car, shading half his face yellow.

'Is this Lucban, hon?' Inez has finally stopped forcing sleep. She yawns and stretches her arms.

'Yep.' Marty tries to sound more awake and cheerful than he feels.

Inez looks out the window. 'How colorful,' she says, as they drive past a house with a giant Ronald McDonald stationed by the doorway, waving his hands. Her tone makes everything seem gray.

*

Marty stands by the door, wiping his palms on his shorts. Looking up, he sees five strings of kiping dangling from the second-floor balcony. Even their ratty papier-mâché carabao is out, gazing forlornly at the street with its one remaining eye.

Inez is looking for a spot with better reception; he can hear her muttering in the distance. The kids are unloading their luggage.

'Tao po,' Marty calls. When no one replies, he enters, heading for the living room. 'Manong? Mang Kikoy? You there?'

He hears a door creak open, then the slap of slippers as Mang Kikoy shuffles into view. His skin is wrinkled and brown as tree bark. The mole on his cheek has grown even more colossal, but otherwise he is the same old Mang Kikoy who has maintained this house, Marty's ancestral home, since forever.

'Boy? Is that you?'

'Yes, manong.'

'Just in time, just in time. Where is your family?'

'Outside,' Marty says, feeling a twinge of guilt. It's been a little too long, perhaps, a little too late – but once he married Inez, and they had Mariah, he'd felt compelled to remain in Manila. He liked his job at San Miguel Corp., and he always believed that Lucban was near enough that they could visit anytime. As a result, they never did. To ignore these thoughts, he asks, 'I noticed the décor. Are we part of the procession this year?'

'No, but I thought it might be good to decorate the house anyway. You never know.'

Mariah materializes at Marty's elbow, dragging her duffel bag. 'Dad, it's so *hot*,' she says, fanning herself.

Mang Kikoy beams at her and moves forwards to take her bag.

'Please don't – it's heavy.' Marty turns to his daughter. 'Mariah, this is your Manong Kikoy. Show him you can carry your own bag, please.'

'Hello po,' she says, straining for politeness as she lugs her bag towards the stairs.

'Hello, hija.' Mang Kikoy grins wider as she slouches past. His teeth are a gray, sickly color. 'Well, Boy, I must go back outside; the kiping is cooking. Let's talk again later.'

'Sure,' he says. Mang Kikoy has already turned to go when JR rushes past, arms held stiffly away from his body, making fighter-jet noises.

'*Wee-oop! Wee-oop!*' he yells. 'I'm attacking you! Propeller BLAST!'

He makes swiping motions at Mang Kikoy, who laughs. 'So this is your little kulilit. Has he ever tasted a miracle before?'

Marty's throat dries. He swallows. He doesn't ask, *Is it true, manong? Is it real?* He doesn't say, *It's not right, who knows what eating those things can do.* Instead he puts a hand on JR's head, to stop him from airplane-ing, and says, 'No, never.'

*

Dinner is at Aling Merrigold's. Inez fusses over their clothes and hair, and asks Marty *twice* whether they shouldn't have brought some pasalubong from Manila. The children are sleepy, already bored. Marty promises that tomorrow will be more fun.

On the way to dinner they walk past increasingly extravagant houses. One has a robo-rooster attached to its roof, where it *cacaws* ear-splittingly every minute. Another has *The Last Supper* rendered on its walls, made with colored straw and palm leaves. Still another bears the mayor's face, fashioned out of kiping, all across the roof. Two giant animatronic carabaos are lowing by the main door, while a life-sized San Isidro stands on a rotating platform. He holds a spade in one hand and a sheaf of corn in the other.

'Farmer Jesus!' JR exclaims.

'That's not Jesus, you idiot.' Mariah snaps a picture with her phone. 'Who's this, Dad? I want to tag it properly.'

'San Isidro Labrador. Patron saint of farmers and peasants.'

'That's Mang Delfin's house,' Mang Kikoy adds. 'This year, the procession goes through this road, and he's determined to win. He's got a pretty good chance, don't you think?'

Marty nods, although the house speaks for itself. The Pahiyas Festival has always been a chance to show off one's home, but now the stakes are even higher. These homeowners want to be chosen for the miracle. They want to boast of a natural harvest, and have jealous neighbors beg them for a taste.

Aling Merrigold's house at the far end of the main street is simpler, though she has deployed her trademark rose pattern that no one has been able to copy. Vivid fuchsias and yellows adorn the typically drab white walls. She welcomes each of them in by smelling their cheeks.

'Martino!' she coos. 'I haven't seen you since you were a young man! But how *old* you look now!' In a softer tone that everyone still hears, she adds, 'You've grown quite the belly!'

'Thank you for having us,' Marty says. 'You look healthy as always.'

She laughs with delight then swats him on the shoulder, the flab of her arms jiggling.

'This is Inez, my wife,' Marty says.

'Well, but you look so very young for Martino!'

'Oh, not at all,' Inez demurs.

'And what do you do, Inez?'

'I'm a merchandiser for Rustan's.' She tips her chin up, just a fraction.

'*Wonderful*,' Aling Merrigold says.

'And these are my children.' Mariah and JR give her halfhearted hellos, and she smacks her lips at them.

'And Mang Kikoy, of course, how good to see you,' Aling Merrigold says. Mang Kikoy smiles, then shuffles off to eat with the rest of her household staff. She leads Marty and his family to the dining room, babbling the whole time: 'I can't believe it's been four years since your father died. I spent *lots* of time with him after your mama died, you know. And he did talk about you such a lot – how he was so proud of you, and how he missed you so much! But then I can't blame you, my dear; it's so hard to get time off with the economy like this, no?

And then you have these two children. So healthy!' She beams at the kids. 'So healthy! You feed them well! Do you get plenty of free food from San Miguel? You still work there, di'ba?'

'Yes. He was recently promoted to Procurement Manager,' Inez says. 'Extra vacation time is one of the perks, so we were finally able to take this trip.'

'Is that *so*?' Aling Merrigold draws a dramatic breath. 'Well, I'm not really surprised. When San Miguel created that breakthrough formula for the Perfect Pork – *wow*. I said to myself, *This is it, this is the future!* And you know, I was right. I mean, the lechon we're having tomorrow… and you *will* eat here tomorrow. I *insist*. After all the events, of course. My balcony has a great view of the fireworks!… What was I saying? Oh yes, tomorrow's lechon is Perfect Pork, which truly *is* perfect.'

'I'm very glad to hear that,' Marty says.

They walk past a sliding door into the air-conditioned dining room. Aling Merrigold gestures for them to sit. 'This dinner is mostly from San Miguel, as well – the roasted chicken is, for sure. This is your Spam, and I think the bangus relleno is yours, too. Pero the cake is from Gardenia. And the chicken cordon bleu is by Universal Robina, because I'm sorry, their cheese is better than yours, you know? Anyway, let's eat.'

She says grace, and they dig in.

Marty takes a bite of the roasted chicken. It's delicious. He feels a swell of pride. He helped *make* these things. Not directly – that was the research team's job – but he handled most of the exports and imports that provided the raw materials for their meats. After the lockout with China he had shifted grudgingly to more expensive vendors in Vietnam, only to realize that their bio-plasticine millet (BPM) adhered to flavorants more easily, and could be molded into more convincing shapes. Chicken and tuna, in particular, could be replicated using Vietnamese BPM for a cheaper unit cost, and San Miguel was quickly able to launch a new line of canned goods, labeled: *More nutritious. Extra-delicious!*

People still say it doesn't beat the real thing, but Marty thinks it comes pretty damn close. They've finally reached an era when neither Mariah nor JR will incur a health risk from their diet; when people don't need to fret about foodborne illnesses; when it's conceivable, if the government gets its shit together, for people below the poverty line to have three meals a day.

'Has the Department of Health decided on a budget for its feeding program yet?' Aling Merrigold asks.

'No,' Marty says. 'I hear they're working on it.'

Aling Merrigold rolls her eyes. 'They're always working on it.' She takes a sip of Coke. 'Still, I can't pretend I'm thinking about anything except tomorrow. You haven't seen it live, but the moment when San Isidro makes his choice and the produce becomes – you know, natural – it's *wow*. Talagang *wow*.'

The news reporters said the same thing, when the first miracle happened during Pahiyas three years ago. No one believed the sensational coverage on TV Patrol at first, but then the owners of the winning house started selling chunks of food as proof: a bite of real corn, a handful of real green beans, a cluster of real juicy grapes. The reporters showed the old church's statue of San Isidro in the town square, surrounded by people bursting into tears as they bit into their first unsafe food in years. It was ridiculous. Marty remembers thinking, *Why is everyone so hung up on this? Why is everyone freaking out?*

He remembers thinking, *It can't be a miracle, because we've already INVENTED the miracle.*

What are you doing here, then? something inside him asks. He recalls the twist in his gut, the saliva filling his mouth, as he watched an old woman nibble on a real banana, weeping wretchedly.

This is home, another voice that sounds more like him insists. *I just wanted to see the fiesta. I wanted the kids to see.*

He pauses over his next forkful. 'You don't think it's – you know, a hoax, or something?'

'Ay naku, no, never! You'll understand when you see it,' Aling Merrigold says. 'You don't even need to taste it. It's the smell, the color, the everything. I mean, the mayor tried to keep it from spreading, played it up as airbrush and fake imports, but there's no denying it. Really, how long naman can you lie without shame? Last year, I shelled out for a few pieces of camote – that's my favorite, you know? – and when I ate it, Diyos ko, it was so good.'

'I see.' Marty licks his lips. 'Well, it'll be fun to watch.'

Aling Merrigold nods and swallows a spoonful of milkfish relleno. Marty watches her, satisfied. It doesn't matter that the milkfish is made of the same thing as the chicken, the rice, the vegetables. They look different, taste different, and have the same high nutritional content. They're better for everyone.

*

Mass the following morning is at 6:00 a.m., which causes much groaning. They manage to make it through the church doors in time for the second reading. The priest is particularly zealous, exhorting everyone to give thanks for their gathering together as one community, and for the bountiful harvest that San Isidro – 'and our sponsors San Miguel Corp., Universal Robina, Golden Arches, and Monde Nissin' – have provided. The people of Lucban are restless, beaming at each other as they exchange signs of peace. Only the image of San Isidro remains calm, already primed in a float for the beauty pageant winner to carry him in later.

After mass there are a few hours left before the procession, so they decide to explore the town. Stalls selling woven buri hats, fans, handbags, and little straw birds are interspersed with old ladies on fold-out stools, hawking rice cakes and empanadas. Inez haggles over a bundle of hats. Mariah picks out keychains for her friends. JR drops the buko juice he's slurping and it bursts on the concrete, leaving a slushy puddle that nobody minds. Inez *tsks*, and Mariah wonders loudly when the procession will start. They each have a serving of pancit habhab on banana leaves.

Marty remembers not caring much about the actual Pahiyas Festival as a child. He was more interested in the preparations leading up to it. He would squat next to Mang Kikoy as the old man ground soaked rice, until it was pale and liquid as milk. Mang Kikoy would stir the wet rice, divide it into shallow buckets, then mix in the coloring: blue and yellow to make apple green, red and blue to make dark pink. Then he would dip a large kabal leaf in the mixture, as a mold for the kiping, and hang it so that the excess coloring dripped. To finish he would cook them over a charcoal grill, while Marty ate the rejected attempts and recited random facts he had learned at school.

Marty didn't watch the kiping preparation yesterday. Something about the BPM Mang Kikoy was using instead of rice made Marty feel weird. It might have been misplaced nostalgia, and he knew that was a useless feeling.

JR, however, had watched and reported to Marty after: about how he had eaten some of the leftovers and they tasted kind of funny, kind of like nothing, but Mang Kikoy said it was made of rice so that was probably normal, right, Dad?

'Kiping has no taste,' Marty said, laughing. 'I mean, rice itself has barely any flavor.'

'But Mang Kikoy said the real foods in the fiesta taste awesome, and if I can eat a fruit or veggie from the winning house tomorrow, I'll understand what he means!'

'Oh, did he say that? Those things are really expensive. And they'll probably make your tummy ache. Or make your teeth gray, like Mang Kikoy's!' Marty rumpled JR's hair, so that JR squirmed. 'Don't know if you'll get to taste any of that, anak.'

'I will,' JR said. 'I'm gonna grab some with my stretchy arms – SHEEE-OW!' He whipped his arms wildly. 'And then I can tell all the kids in my class, and they'll be jealous, because they've never eaten yummy real food and they never *will*!' He chuckled, evil and gleeful, and robotically walked away to heckle his sister.

Marty remembers the great glass houses they passed on their way to Lucban, lining the fields stretched beneath Mt. Banahaw. Piles of corn and rice, endless rows of pineapple and root crop, stewing in their meticulously engineered domes, more delicious than nature could ever make them. Simply *more* than God could ever make them.

*

The procession begins at 1:00 p.m. with the local policemen leading the marching band through the streets. The crowd surges from the town center. Those who live along the procession route peer out from windows and balconies, waving at onlookers. An ABS-CBN TV crew starts their segment. People in bright red shirts bearing the Universal Robina logo hover near the cameras, holding up signs that say *Don't Eat the Miracle Food – It's Poison! You Could Die!*

Marty frowns at their lack of respect for the festivities, even as he recalls his last meeting, where the Procurement Division Head had raised her eyebrows at his vacation request. ('For Lucban?' – and when Marty nodded, how she cleared her throat and averted her eyes.) Ignoring this, he gestures for his family to follow, and heads for the middle of the parade. JR complains that he can't see, so Marty hoists him onto his shoulders. They walk on, keeping to the edges of the crowd. The higantes come after the band: giant, cartoony replicas of the president, the kagawad, a schoolgirl, a farmer. A carabao – live this time – follows, pulling a cart full of waving children. Unlike the animatronic version, this carabao plods silently on, martyr-like. It is trailed by girls with feathered headpieces and dresses in garish colors, shimmying to a syncopated drumbeat.

The priest from morning mass scoops water out of a bucket and sprinkles everyone with it. Behind him walk the beauty pageant entrants, led by the newly crowned Miss Lucban and her escort, standing on a float, carrying San Isidro between them. Marty is transfixed by the face of the saint – how it looks tired and drawn in the middle of the crowd, rocked to and fro by the music. The parade is pushing, pulsing from all sides; Marty presses onwards, checking that Inez and Mariah are still following. The band has gone through its traditional repertoire and is now playing the Top 40. Everyone sings along – some droning, some with effort. Marty moves faster so that he can keep pace with San Isidro, but it's difficult. He feels crazed, dehydrated, but he's determined to witness the so-called miracle, determined not to care.

'Dad,' JR says, 'Dad, hurry up, we're going to miss the selection!'

Marty tries to walk more quickly, but the crowd keeps him at bay, measuring his pace. The people proceed down the street in a blare of noise and sound and color, getting more raucous as they approach the fancier homes. At some point the fiesta-goers begin to stop in front of each house, and lift San Isidro above the crowd, holding him there for a few moments. Each time this happens the procession holds its breath, then bursts into cheering when nothing changes. Marty is starting to get exhausted. He brings JR down and clutches his hand. JR beams up at him, infected by the delight of the crowd. Marty smiles back, as best as he can through the heat and confusion and the sudden shower of confetti and kiping raining from the house they are passing.

They're drawing closer to Mang Delfin's house, with the animatronic carabaos and giant replica of the mayor's face. The frenzy and expectation heightens each time San Isidro is raised, but there is also a sense of inevitability, because only one house can win, and everyone seems to know which house it is. Someone starts chanting: 'Mang Delfin! Mang Delfin!' The marching band launches into the current chart-topper. People are headbanging and wiggling and not-quite-accidentally grinding each other.

Marty realizes they're not going to see anything if they stay where they are. Ducking into a side street, he skirts past former neighbors' houses. He counts the walls before turning back onto the main road, right at the cross street between Mang Delfin and Aling Sheila's house. They have a perfect view of the proceedings: the crowd is amassing at the home right before this one, breathing a collective 'Ooooh!' as San Isidro is raised, then bursting into laughter when nothing happens, and he is lowered once more.

JR jumps up and down. 'It's going to be this one! It's going to be this one!'

Marty's heart races. He squeezes JR's hand, and gazes at the façade of Mang Delfin's house: up close, he can see potato-faced people pieced from squash and taro, with string-bean-and-okra hair; intricate butterflies made of rambutan and longgan; long, sweeping bunches of banana mingled with kiping. The mooing of the fake carabaos is incredibly loud. If there's any house that can feed the whole town, it's this one.

But what's wrong with this food? he thinks. *Isn't this worth giving thanks for? What more do people want?*

'Mang Delfin! Mang Delfin! Yaaaay!' The crowd whoops as it reaches its destination. Everyone quiets down enough so that the band can start a drumroll. Miss Lucban and her escort slowly, tenderly lift San Isidro up to face the house. Marty is magnetized, again, by the saint's face: its severely rosy cheeks and sleepy eyebrows, the stiff golden halo behind his head. He can't tell if San Isidro wears a look of benevolence, or of agony.

'Real food! Real food! Real veggies, real fruit!' JR hasn't stopped jumping or chanting. Marty fights the urge to tell him to shut up.

'Oh my God,' Inez says. 'This is actually so exciting!'

Mariah, who has whipped out her phone to record everything, says, 'The signal here sucks!'

The hush continues. As the crowd watches, the statue of San Isidro – now facing its life-sized twin, in front of Mang Delfin's house – lifts its wooden arm, the one holding the sheaf of corn, in a rigid salute. His face remains frozen, but for one instant, his eyes seem *alive* – and even though they aren't directed at Marty, his belly churns and his eyes water. A child in the crowd bursts into tears.

Then: an explosion of smell and color. The house is suddenly unable to bear its own weight, and several ornaments come loose from the ceiling and balcony, falling on the crowd below. Potatoes and bananas roll off the shingles, detach from the windows; tufts of kiping billow out and descend on everyone's heads. Marty sees this in slow-motion. Each fruit and vegetable is more alive, the smell so intoxicating Marty nearly vomits. He lets go of JR's hand to cover his mouth, and JR immediately lunges for the food. Inez shrieks and darts forwards as a squash-face starts to come loose from the wall. She tries to catch it in one of her new hats, shouting, 'What are you doing, Marts? Grab some! Hurry!'

Everyone is frantically scooping. Mariah has her mouth full of something. 'Oh my *God*,' she says. 'Oh my God, it tastes totally different!'

Marty looks back at where the procession had been neatly standing, and it's all gone – San Isidro has disappeared, swallowed by a swarm of flailing limbs. Someone – Mang Delfin? – roars over the noise, 'This is my house! Those are mine! Stop! Stop!'

'There's enough for everyone, you greedy ass!' someone shouts back. The cheer that follows quickly dissolves into grunting as people climb over each other.

Marty comes into focus. 'JR!' he calls frantically. 'JR? JR!'

His little boy could be trampled. His little boy could get LBM, salmonella, stomach cancer. That food should never touch his lips.

Inez is still filling her hats; Mariah is helping her. Marty tries to enter the writhing mass of fiesta-goers. An elbow bashes him on the cheek, a knee catches his ribs. Someone to his left retches. The stench of body odor and puke overpowers the sweet fragrance of the fruits.

'JR!' he keeps shouting.

'Dad!'

JR squeezes his way towards him, reaching over two women grappling with a knot of bitter gourd. Marty manages to grab JR under the armpits, lifting then hauling him towards a side street. He takes deep breaths, trying to clear his head, and through a haze of nausea he sees JR's giant grin. JR is clutching a swollen banana in his fist: a banana full of bruises, green at the base, just like the ones Marty used to eat as a child, nothing like the ones they now grow. 'Dad! I got one! Can I eat it?'

Marty feels sick, overwhelmed, like too many eyes are on him. He reaches out, grabs the banana, and peels it without thinking. JR watches him, wide-eyed. Marty has no idea what he's going to do – hold it out to his child and let him eat it? Eat it himself, because it looks so goddamn delicious? Thank God, San Isidro, for a miracle? Cry for his manmade miracles, so much nothing when held to the light of day, to a pair of tired eyes in a wooden face?

'Yes,' he says. 'Go ahead,' he says, his mouth already tasting the sweetness, craving it – the truth of a miracle, too bitter to swallow – 'But don't, no, you shouldn't, it isn't safe, it isn't right,' he says, and he is suddenly crying, and JR looks at him with an expression that edges bewilderment and terror. In his closed fist the banana has been mashed to a pulp.

Bring Your Own Spoon

Saad Z. Hossain

Bangladesh

I discovered Saad's work when a friend recommended his *Escape From Baghdad!*, a riotous and phantasmagoric – and very funny! – novel about the American invasion of Iraq. I've been a fan ever since, and it's been a pleasure seeing Saad's work reach new audiences discovering him for the first time. He is not a frequent short story writer, but when he does write them the results are marvellous, as in the following tale, which I paired with Isabel Yap's 'Milagroso' for being partly about food, one of the most important aspects of our world that is too often neglected in science fiction.

anu sat before his stove, warming himself. It was cold outside, and even worse, the wind scoured away the cloud of nanites, the airborne biotech that kept people safe. He had seen more than one friend catch death in the wind, caught in a pocket without protection, their lungs seared by some virus, or skin sloughed off by radiation. The thin mesh of pack-sheet formed a tent around him, herding together the invisible, vital cogs. Shelter was necessary on a windy night, even for those with meager resources.

He was cooking rice on the stove, in a battered pot with a miss-matched lid, something made of ancient cast iron. Ironically, in certain retro fashion houses, this genuine pre-dissolution era relic would have fetched a fortune, but Hanu had no access to those places, and wouldn't have cared, either way. A pot to cook your rice in was priceless, as valuable to a roamer as the tent or the solar stove.

He measured the quarter cup of fine-grained rice into the boiling water, added a bit of salt, a half stick of cinnamon and some cardamom. The rice would cook half-way before he added onions and chilies, perhaps a touch of saffron. In a way, Hanu ate like a king, although his portions were meager. He had access to an abandoned herb garden on the roof of a derelict tower, plants growing in some weird symbiotic truce with the nanites warring in the sky, nature defying popular scientific opinion. The rice he got from an abandoned government grain silo, sacks of the stuff just lying there, because people feared contamination. Almost everyone in the city ate from food synthesizers, which converted algae and other supplements into roast chicken at the drop of a hat.

He let the rice cook until there were burnt bits sticking to the bottom of the pot. The burnt bits were tasty. The smell filled the tent like a spice bazaar, and he ate from the bowl using his wooden spoon. One pot was easily enough for two or three meals if he were frugal. No one disturbed him, for which he was thankful. It was difficult to find a square inch empty in Dhaka city, but it was a windy night, the Pollutant levels were on orange alert, and most people were indoors.

Moreover, he was in the fringes of the riverside area of Narayanganj, where the alert level was perpetually screaming red due to unspeakable life forms breeding in the water, a sort of adjacent sub-city swallowed by Dhaka a hundred years ago, a pustule avoided by even the moderately desperate homeless, one step away from being cluster bombed into oblivion by the satellites above. Thus he was able to finish his meal in peace, and was just contemplating brewing some tea when a gust of wind knocked the tent askew, and a lumpy black dog nosed in.

Hanu sighed, and gave the dog a bit of rice. It ate directly from his hand, thumping his tail in appreciation. Hanu got out of the tent, to prevent the creature from breaking it. Where the dog roamed, his master would not be far behind.

'You're corrupting my hound,' a voice said. In the shadows a slow form materialized, a man-like thing extruding a field of disturbance around him. It was the Djinn Imbidor, an ancient creature recently woken from centuries of sleep, diving again into the cut and thrust of mortal life, puzzled somewhat by the rapacious change in humanity.

'He's a mongrel, Imbi,' Hanu said. 'Even more bastardized than you.'

Imbidor frowned. 'Are you sure? The one who sold it to me, that man by the sweet shop with the bird cages, he said that it was a pure-breed Mirpur Mastiff.'

'Mirpur Mastiff?' Hanu laughed. 'Cheeky bastard. The pure-breed Mirpur Mastiff is a euphemism for the most mangled bloodline possible. Your hound is descended from the original street dogs which roamed Dhaka, before they started injecting turtle genes into them.'

'Oh.' He scowled. 'Humans are always ripping me off.'

'You want some rice?'

'With cardamom and saffron?'

'Of course.'

The Djinn took the pot and ate the last of the rice. He had his own spoon, a silver filigreed thing which no doubt came from some kingly horde. 'Thanks Hanu. You're a good cook, I always say.'

'Not much demand for cooks these days,' Hanu said shortly. His father had been a cook once, long ago, before the current banking cartel had pushed all the Cardless out of the better neighborhoods into the subsidized boroughs, little better than feral slums. There had been a time when there was apparently a 'middle class' sandwiched between the dichotomy of rich and poor.

He shook his head. His father had told a lot of fairy stories. Then he had fucked off. 'Plus it's illegal to use real plants, like I do. They'd probably arrest me. Endangering the cardamom or something.'

'Well, for the Fringe, then,' Imbidor said. 'We should have a restaurant. Something like the old days, a place for people to gather. Plenty of the Fringe would like it. Even some of the citizens.'

The citizens were general populace without capital, whose main contribution to society was the biotech their bodies spewed, which added to the mass of benevolent nanites fighting the good fight in the sky, scrubbing the air, killing disease, controlling the microclimate, forming the bubble which protected Dhaka from the big bad world outside. The Fringe was a subset of the citizenry, filled with the homeless, the drifters, the thrill-seekers, the darker edge of the maladjusted. And Djinn. More and more often, Djinn emerged from slumber, found a world near wrecked by hubris, found the lonely places they favored despoiled, unlivable. Many returned to sleep right away. It was rumored that Djinn did not age while they slept, that they could afford to while away centuries waiting for a better time downstream. Of course there was no guarantee such a time would come.

'I would cook and you would serve,' Hanu joked. 'We could call it Bring Your Own Spoon.'

'And the hound would be the lookout,' Imbi said, enthused. 'We already have everything. The tent, the stove, the pot.'

'The mosques give away free bowls,' Imbidor said. 'Their food is some horrible grey sludge, but the bowls are good. I've collected a stack of them since I woke up. And we'd give *real* food. No discrimination against the Cardless either. Pay however you can.'

'Why not?' Hanu said, suddenly struck by the thought. 'Why can't we do it?'

'That's what I've been saying!' Imbidor shouted. 'Come on Hanu! I'm so bored.' Boredom was the reason the Djinn went to sleep so often in the first place.

'Okay. I'm in. We have to find a good place to set up the kitchen. And food suppliers, well, I know a few. Benches? Clean water? We'll need a place without the cameras if possible...' The possibilities seemed endless. Problems jostled in his mind, shifting in priority as solutions clicked into place. It felt good to think again.

'Come on, let's go,' Imbidor said. 'I know the perfect place.'

He extended his distortion field around Hanu like a ragged cloak, keeping out the bad stuff in the air. Hanu stumbled from the slight vertigo it caused, felt that familiar tinge of nausea brought by proximity to the field, but in truth Imbi's power was tatty, weakened from some ancient conflict, his touch featherlight compared to the great Djinns. Once Hanu had seen a Marid with a field so powerful that it was opaque, reflecting the sun, a solid fist that rammed through the crowd unheeding, had seen a man caught in its center pulped to death by unimaginable pressures.

Djinns did not officially exist, although the Fringe knew perfectly well they were there, often out in plain sight, going about their business. There were rumors that great Djinn lords ruled human corporations, wielding terrible power from the shadows. Imbidor was not that kind of Djinn. He had no *auctoritas*, the peculiar currency the Djinn traded in; he commanded no respect, had no followers, no wealth in either world. Even mighty Djinnkind had the indigent.

*

They worked their way ever deeper into Narayanganj, Hanu suppressing the atavistic fear of the bad air. The street was still lined with shanties, extruded sheets lashed together with adhesive bands, cheap stuff which could be printed out of the many black-market operations found in greater Dhaka. Here the people seemed unhealthier however, further away from the center, and their progress was tracked warily, with more than one weapon being raised, although the Djinn was recognized and allowed to pass. People moved here out of desperation, for even though the main boroughs of the Cardless were crowded, at least the air was good, basic supplies were provided, and there was work. Here by the river the town was semi-abandoned and as they got closer to the water the citizens became more furtive, many carrying deformities, the scarring of errant nanites. The big pharmas liked to experiment their new designs on high-density populations, beta testing algorithms on live users, for good nanites of course – never anything weaponized, that would be immoral. There were always side effects, though.

'Here we are,' Imbi said, stopping.

It was a six-story shell of a building, built in the old style with concrete and steel, the bricks, wires, windows, doors, anything electrical looted long ago. It was near the riverbank, close enough that Hanu could feel the cool air stirring, and his instinctive fear of the water made him cringe.

'Smugglers,' Imbi said, knocking on the door of a makeshift room.

A man with an electric sword came out and watched them without speaking. Hanu glanced at him disinterestedly. The Fringe was full of smugglers with swords.

'We want the empty room,' Imbi said.

'For the night? Or do you actually intend to live here.'

'More than a night,' Hanu said. 'We want to try something out.'

The swordsman shrugged. 'The Djinn crashes here sometimes. I'm okay with that. I give him electricity and he sweeps for bad bugs with the distortion thing of his.'

'It's a pretty good spot,' Imbi said, embarrassed by his poverty. People who lived riverside were the scum of the earth. 'I can clean the air, at least enough for us few.'

'You don't get sick here? No black lung? None of the skin stuff?' Hanu stared at the smuggler, trying to spot defects.

The smuggler turned his sword off. 'Not so far.'

'How?'

'There's a lot more people living here than you think,' the man said. 'The Djinn cleans the air and we have a nanite replicator. It's old but it helps. What business did you say you were in?'

'Hanu Khillick,' Hanu said. 'Restaurateur.'

The smuggler burst out laughing. 'Karka. Riverboat smuggler and pirate.'

'Imbidor of Gangaridai,' said Imbi. 'Djinn. Professional giraffe racer. Ahem. Of course there are no giraffes left.'

'Come inside,' Karka said. 'Let's get you set up. I'm not going to charge you rent, as long as the Djinn helps out. Once in a while, surveillance drones show up. You have to take care of those fast, or corporate security will send someone down to investigate.'

Inside was a sparsely furnished space, well swept, covered with the black-market geegaws of the smuggler's trade, and a few solid pieces, a power generator, an ancient nanite replicator, and a squat printer with its guts out. Karka was well set up. No wonder he survived out here. Hanu wondered what he smuggled. Karka motioned them to sit on the futons covering the floor.

'I will be most happy to help,' Imbi said.

'You guys need anything else, you're gonna have to pay. Air scrubbing for three ain't cheap. You got any money?'

Hanu shook his head.

'I am the descendent of an ancient empire, known as the first city. I have lived hundreds of years, I have looked into the void of the abyss, I have seen the dark universe of the Djinn, I hold over three hundred patents currently pending litigation in the celestial courts...' Imbi said.

'So no cash, I guess?'

'Er no.'

'Any sat minutes?'

Hanu shook his head. Sat minutes were hire time from the satellites, a secure pin which activated the chip in your head for a designated time, showing you the vastly expanded VR universe the rich people inhabited. It was funny that everyone got chipped for consumer tracking and census purposes, but very few of the Cardless ever actually got to walk the VR world. Bandwidth was jealously guarded. Sat minutes were the way, a brief glimpse into paradise, a ten-minute birthday treat for a child, a wedding gift, a de facto currency, hoarded but never consumed, a drug for the VR junkies, news, communication, vital information, everything rolled into one.

'Do I look like I have sat minutes? I'm a cook. I'll cook you food.'

'I got an old VAT maker,' Karka said, looking at him dubiously.

'Chinese or Indian?'

'Post-crash Malay.'

'Everything tastes of coconut, right?'

'Haha, yeah, I don't even know what coconut is. Some kind of nut?'

'There were big trees once, and these were the fruit, kind of like big balls full of liquid.'

'Yeah well, that's fucken food for me, coconut seaweed.'

'I'll make you rice right now, that will make you cry.'

'No thanks.' Karka looked queasy. 'I already ate. Look man, don't worry. I'll help. Imbi sorted me out a couple of times with his djinnjitsu.'

Hanu scrounged in his bag of provisions and brought out something he had been saving, a rare find. It was a raw mango, from a tree near the red zone which had miraculously survived all these years, and now had suddenly given fruit. No one touched them of course, fearing some hideous mutation, even the street kids stayed away. They had all heard stories of trees bursting open to release deadly nanite spores, of the terrible Two Head Disease which caused a bulbous head-like protuberance to come out of your ass, or of the Factory Germ which slowly hardened your body into metal. Hanu's father had taught him to forage, however, as the very poorest must do, and this foraging had given him an instinct of what could or could not be eaten.

He sliced the mango with his knife, letting the slivers fall inside his pot, careful not to lose the precious juice. Then he brought out a small lemon, nursed carefully from his errant herb garden, cut it and squeezed half of it onto the fruit. Salt, pepper, turmeric, mustard-seed paste, and chili flakes followed, a little bit each because the flavors were intensely different from VAT food, almost alien. He mixed it together by hand, till the slices were covered, glistening. Karka and Imbi had gathered around, mouths open, inhaling the smell of raw cut mango and the sharp tang of mustard, drawn by an ancient evolutionary pull.

'What the hell?' Karka lowered his head involuntarily, breathing in the smells.

Hanu ate a piece, showed it was safe. 'It's good.'

Imbi, who had largely bypassed the Dissolution Era, had no such qualms and quickly forked a third of the mango onto his palm.

'It *is* good,' Karka said, unable to resist a slice. He looked entranced. 'It's damn good. You *are* a cook.'

'You in?'

'You seriously want to open a restaurant.'

'You've got a perfect view of the river.'

'You realize they call this the river of the dead.'

*

The next morning they got started, Karka joining them for a breakfast of rice, the last of Hanu's horde. Afterwards he handed over a key for the spare room, and a handful of electronics, a solar battery, some basic furniture. He dragged out the air scrubber and put it equidistant between their doors. 'I eat for free. Plus Imbi does his shit. We share the air. If it runs out, we split the costs.'

'Deal.'

They dispersed, Hanu going on an herb run, Imbi dispatched to spread the word and also discover some sources of raw material. It was, after all, useless to have a restaurant without any food. Hanu knew this was the biggest hurdle. He expected this dream to end soon, for where on earth would Imbi find so much real food?

Nonetheless, he set up his station on time, arranging his supplies of herbs and spices, warming up water from the ancient ion filter, even setting up a bench for the customers. If Imbi came back, they would open for lunch. By eleven o'clock, hopeful looking people invited by Imbi were ambling around, steering away from the glaring Karka, maintaining nonchalance. Hanu studied his prospective customers, and had to conclude that they hadn't a penny to their name collectively. He might as well have started a VAT kitchen, feeding the homeless, like the mosques.

'This lot couldn't buy crabs from a brothel,' Karka said, sword hilt at hand. 'If Imbi's not back by noon they're going to start looting.'

'The road is my home,' Hanu said. 'I am not afraid.' *People always assume that poor people are dangerous. They wouldn't be here, if they were.*

Imbi staggered in half past noon carrying a large burlap sack. There were a solid dozen customers still loitering, despite the best efforts of Karka. The three of them gathered inside the room, where the Djinn threw open his sack with obvious pride.

'What the hell is it?' Karka recoiled with disgust.

'It's a fish,' Imbi said. 'From the river.'

It was, indeed, an enormous fish, scales glistening, gills still flapping for air. Hanu remembered his father bringing home one once. Karka had never seen one, was clearly repulsed with the whole idea of eating something from the river.

'Look, there's a dozen people outside, and we have to feed them something,' Hanu said. 'I know how to cook this, I remember.'

'What's wrong?' Imbi asked Karka. 'We used to fish from the river all the time…'

'That was two hundred years ago, Imbi,' Karka said. 'We don't touch that shit anymore…'

Hanu ignored them. He had a fish to scale, and he'd only ever seen it being done as a child. It took rather longer than an hour to get it right, the pieces prepped, somewhat mangled, but soon thereafter the smell and sizzle of grilled fish permeated from the prefab, and his customers sat down and waited in an almost hypnotized state, so docile and silent that even Karka had no complaints.

*

When he was ready, he brought it out, fifteen pieces of grilled fish with crispy skin, flavored with ginger, garlic and chili, with little balls of rice. He had used up everything. They took their portions solemnly, signifying the importance of the moment, ate with their hands along the makeshift bench, with all the dignity of a state banquet. There was no hesitation, no question of what they were ingesting. It simply smelled too good. Karka ate the last piece, his resistance melted away.

'God, this is a good way to die,' he said.

It started up the conversation, rounds of introductions, stumbling praise for the food, old recollections of when they had last seen food like this, of the myriad turns of their lives, which had left them Cardless and desperate on the streets. Imbi sat among them, extending his field for them, and they marveled at the distortion, wondered aloud that such a powerful creature should be wandering the road with them. And then, by some unspoken consensus, it was time to leave, and they began to make their offerings. A knife, much handled, the last thing a man would give up; an old card for sat minutes, so old, so carefully preserved, to receive a call that never came; a silver locket with the picture taken out, a book of short stories, an ancient watch. The last lady stood up, her hands empty.

'I have nothing,' she said. 'But there is a place with birds… chickens. If I bring them, will you cook?'

'Yes, of course,' said Hanu. He looked at the small pile of treasure, and tears leaked from his eyes.

'Hanu and Imbi,' the Djinn said, sweeping his hand back towards the establishment. 'We are open for business.'

*

Open they were, for six months and more, feeding crowds, sometimes with feasts, sometimes with nothing but onions and rice. Their customers scavenged, bringing food from unknown places. There were unspoken rules. Everything was eaten. No one was turned away. At first Imbi kept his field up like a tent, kept the bad air at bay, visibly exhausting himself, burning surveillance drones out of the sky. When their accrued wealth piled up, Karka could afford to charge up his replicator, spewing out the good nanites, and people stayed by the river out of faith, adding their bodies to the critical mass required to power these things, the human fuel which made their community work.

The river kept a tax. People sickened from its bounty, one died from intestinal rot, but the people who roamed here sickened and died anyways. There was no noticeable drop in custom. Imbi wandered far and wide, bartering, gossiping, marketing, and returned with useful things – water filters, glasses, proper cutlery, utensils for Hanu's Kitchen. It would have been safer to move around, but they couldn't, people relied on them, the gangs left them alone, it was a safe spot, blessed by the river gods.

'Look what we've done!' Imbi said, proud. 'I told you it would work.'

'It can't last,' Hanu said.

*

One day men from the high city swaggered down, uniformed, with their rented armored car and their mercenary badges. Private security. They didn't like activity in the orange zones, and the river was an atavistic boundary, a dread zone which these Company men avoided at all costs.

'DISPERSE! DISPERSE! RED ALERT! HAZARD! HAZARD!' The armored car was going mad with panic, it's blaring voice rising in pitch as it twisted its way through debris. Karka came out with his sword behind his back, Hanu with his cleaver and a decapitated fish head. The score or so people dozing in the sun after lunch sat up blearily. The car louvered open and two men came out in full combat gear, faces hidden inside command helmets, a swarm of sparrow-sized drones buzzing in the air above them. These models were six seasons old, a tried and tested method of crowd control. The new ones were apparently mosquito-sized, and just as lethal.

'Gathering in a red zone,' the Company man said. 'What for?'

'Easy, we're just squatting,' Hanu said. 'Cardless, see?'

'What is this place?' the security guard walked around, touching the benches, the bowls, the cardboard box of scavenged cutlery.

'Shelter for the poor,' Hanu said, trying to cut him off from the kitchen. 'Look, we're just feeding them. Hungry, homeless people for God's sake.'

The Company man touched him with one gloved hand, the powered suit amplifying force, and Hanu went stumbling back, a deep bruise forming instantly on his chest.

'Food? This is no VAT kitchen. You have set up a microclimate here. We saw it from above.' The security stared into the kitchen interior, face unreadable. 'Why is there a microclimate in the Red Zone?'

'It's not a crime to stay here,' Karka said. 'What laws have we broken?'

The Company men looked at each other, not answering. They were not unduly worried. In reality, laws only applied to those who could afford lawyers. The swarm shifted a bit towards Karka, the machine whine rising an octave. They had already noted his sword, deemed it next to useless in a fight.

'I don't understand what this is,' the first man said, knocking down the fab sheets walling the front of the kitchen. 'What is this organic matter?'

'Why it's our food, friend soldier,' Imbi said, beaming. Hanu suppressed a groan. 'Would you like to have some? Fish-head curry, with brown rice. A princely meal! In my day, policemen always ate free! Come, friends, eat a plate, rejoice in the bounty of the river!'

The man took the plate and his helmet became opaque, revealing a face inside. He stared at it, fascinated, and Hanu could almost see the neurons in his brain put together the contours of the cooked fish head with the scraps in the kitchen, with the shape of an actual fish, which he must have seen a hundred times in pictures as a child. A lot of emotions flitted across his face, curiosity, alarm, wonder. For a second, Hanu dreamed that he would actually take off his helmet and try the food. Then his face turned to revulsion, and Hanu knew it was all over.

Imbi was standing there, beaming with good will, when the plate struck him across the face. Drones punched into him, tearing out chunks of meat, sending him tumbling back, before his distortion field finally flickered to life, cocooning him. Karka gave a samurai yell and charged, sword up in high guard. The drones were slow to react, confused by the Djinn's quantum field. They finally lunged at Karka but he ignored them, letting them have their pound of flesh, flying through that mist of his own blood and tissue, terminal grace, and his ionized blade somehow hit the command helmet in the neck join, shorting it out, sending the astonished Company man down to his knees.

Abruptly, half of the drones stopped short, hovering uncertainly. The other half of the drones, unfortunately, were not so confused. They slammed into Karka with lethal force, shredding the smuggler like paper. The armored car, programmed to be cowardly, was blaring incoherent alarms, already backing away from the fracas. The second policeman hesitated, then dived into his vehicle, his drones folding neatly into a pocket somewhere.

'YOU HAVE ALL BEEN MARKED FOR TERMINATION! SATELLITE STRIKE IMMINENT! INNOCENT BYSTANDERS ARE REQUESTED TO VACATE! VACATE! VACAAAAAATE!'

And they were gone, leaving their fallen behind.

'I don't think I can put Karka back together,' Imbi said, tears in his eyes. He was trying to collect the pieces of their friend.

'Never mind. We have to leave. They will destroy this place,' Hanu said. He looked at the dozen or so patrons still left. 'We all have to leave. They've tagged our chips for death.'

But they all knew nowhere was safe. Tagged for death was death in truth. It was just a matter of how long till the satellites cleared their backlog.

'Load everything into the boat!' Hanu shouted. 'Everything! We have to go across the river. Into the country.'

They stared at him, unconvinced.

'Look, there's fish in the river. That means there's food outside, you fools! There must be. We can survive! They won't hunt us out there.' He turned to Imbi. 'Imbi is Djinn! Djinn! He can clean the air for us, we can gather others, make a microclimate like we did here. They don't know he can do that.'

*

Imbi stood up straight, spread his arms out wide, dripping the blood of Karka, and his distortion field rippled out, encompassing them all. It was stronger than before, colored with rage and sorrow.

'We should leave,' he said. 'We should follow Hanu, who gave us food from nothing. I have slept a long time. I remember when they used to chain you to the earth and force you to work, to force your children and their children to the same labor. Now I am awake, I see they have taken your flesh too; they have herded you together like cattle, and living or dying, your bodies are little factories, cleaning the air for them. Your chips are your collars. They kill you without thought. You fear the air, the water, the trees, the very ground you walk on. What more can you lose? Why not leave this place? Let us go forth into the wilderness, where they dare not follow.'

When they heard the Djinn they grew calm, and gathered their meager things. It was resignation, perhaps, or hope. Hanu freed the boat, pushing off into the river, and the poison water splashed over him, but he did not care. It was cool, and dark, and it washed away the blood.

Blue Grey Blue

Yukimi Ogawa

Japan

If the previous two stories explore food, the next two are about colour. I was honoured to meet Yukimi briefly in Japan, and she was one of the authors in the *Apex Book of World SF* anthologies. She stands out as one of the few Japanese authors writing in English – a language that, she says, she never speaks – and has made a name for herself with a steady string of stories in recent years. The question was just which of her stories to use, but I loved the strangeness of 'Blue Grey Blue', which is quintessentially Ogawa.

No one knew exactly when or how it'd all started. But there was a time he could think of specifically: it was three or four years ago, when a girl of around ten came to the shop, which sold practical eyewear for the locals. The girl said she needed a pair of glasses, because something was wrong with her eyes.

'You'd like to see a doctor first,' Tsuyu had told her, crouching to meet her mosaic-like rainbow eyes, so out of place in her tanned, barley-colored face.

'I did!' she had said. 'And they found nothing wrong with me. But something *is* going wrong with my parrot, and Mother and Father don't see it, so it must be my eyes.'

'Your parrot?'

She'd nodded defiantly. 'He's got a part of his feather just like my eyes, around his chest. That was why we got him in the first place. But that part is fading these days. As many colors, still, but they all look a bit... weaker.'

Tsuyu never found out what happened to her, or the parrot afterward, because the girl never came back after he'd told her to watch out for a little more while keeping to her doctor's instructions. Much later, others started to see something similar, too. There must have been something only small children could see, in the early stage.

Now at the same shop, after an especially nasty fit of coughs, Tsuyu looked at his reflection in one of the mirrors and wondered why he was thinking this. But of course – his own eyes' color was so weak today that it looked as though he had no irises, and tears from the coughing made him look even more like a horrible monster of some sort.

He was about to pour himself some tea when the bell attached to the door rang. His senior, the manager of the branch who had gone for lunch, would have started talking right before the door was fully open, so the person who'd just arrived was a customer. Tsuyu hastily put the pot back down onto the desk. 'Hello,' he said, and forced down a cough. 'Please let me know if there is anything I can assist you with.'

When these automatic words had rolled out (words for the locals, of course – for foreigners the in-house manual required something much more enthusiastic) another cough threatened him, so that his eyes were brimming with tears. What did he look like right now? The customer, a woman of about his own age, stood framed in the glass door right behind her, against the backcloth of the sallow break-in-rainy-season midday. Most of her visible skin was lazurite, golden pyrite flecks punctuating her countenance here and there. Blue wasn't that uncommon of course, but gold was, and for a split second he felt a pang of jealousy.

The customer smiled at him. 'I heard that an ultramarine person works for this company. And I went to the shop on the high street and they said that person can be found here at the branch.'

'Ah. That is me, actually, though I'm not always ultramarine.' Tsuyu wiped his eyes with a cloth. 'Definitely not today. Sorry you didn't find what you came here for after all that trouble.'

But as he was saying this, the woman came striding between the low shelves of glasses on display. For a moment it looked as though she was performing a fluid kind of dance, like a flower petal carried by a current and yet gracefully avoiding collision with rocks and trees, before coming to a sudden halt to stand right in front of him. He almost stepped back, not quite used to a local staring into his eyes. 'That's beautiful,' she said, and her eyes were the deep, deep black-blue of indigo – one of the most stable of blues. Everything he'd have wanted. 'Yes, I can feel blues hiding away, but – how does that work?'

Work? 'Well. When I'm ill or simply feeling down, my eyes go just... colorless. Ultramarine is only when I'm feeling really strong.'

'So your eyes are basically like this? White chalcedony? Or is there anything in-between?'

'Chalcedony?' He blinked. 'I never... well. They're Asiatic dayflower blue when I'm like, just okay and stable.'

'Oh, how interesting! Oldest of blues, and quite soluble, dayflower blue is, you know!'

Tsuyu almost winced, stopped himself just in time.

The woman shifted a little, as if to have an even better look, making Tsuyu feel even more nervous. 'Have you seen them actually changing colors?'

Tsuyu thought about it, using that moment to divert his eyes from her. 'Not really. I don't look at myself more often than necessary.'

'No?' She sounded surprised, but then took one step back. 'Sorry. I'm a collector of blues. Of knowledge of them, of course.' She flashed her teeth like robin eggs. 'And as you can see, I'm from one of that bloodline, too. But not many people have changing colors the way yours do.'

Tsuyu inhaled to say something, ended up coughing again, stepping away from her.

'Oh, are you ill? Should I come back, when you're better? Are you always here at this branch?'

'I… It depends.' He coughed some more. 'When I'm ultramarine or dayflower, I'm at high street.'

'What? Why do they place you here when you're white chalcedony?'

'I asked them to. Ultramarine is quite popular with the tourists. Dayflower isn't exactly what they'd come to this island for, you know, many foreigners having blue eyes. Still, better than nothing.' He pointed at his own eyes.

The woman frowned. 'I don't understand.'

Oh no, you *wouldn't.* 'You can't watch on until they change colors, anyway.'

'Do you at least know when the change is most likely to happen?'

Tsuyu gestured an ambiguous answer, smiling despite himself.

'You can't turn me away, anyway. I'm a customer.'

'Are you going to buy something?'

'Yes! Recommend me a frame… If you aren't too ill to do that?'

He stifled a laugh and looked around the shop. Ordinary gold was too loud for her, nor the tortoiseshell, even the brownish one, quite matched. Collector of blues. Why would anyone do that here, blue being too common and only slightly better than nothing? And he thought about his own color, how it was said to have been the root of every blue, before the strong indigo came along.

He took a green frame, green of dayflower's leaves rendered soft by morning dew, with leaf-like patterns over the temples. Just as he had hoped, the frame seemed to settle with her skin, without darkening the tone.

'The lenses...'

'Just leave them plain thanks. Fashion!'

Her eyes would look much better without the lenses to veil them. He adjusted the frame to fit her small face and said, 'Are you really buying this one?'

'Yes. Now I can come back, yes?'

He let out a small sound that was both sigh and laugh.

'Yes?'

'Okay.'

'Say yes!'

'Yes.'

She grinned her robin-egg grin again. Just as she was paying, Tsuyu saw his senior coming back, on the other side of the street; he probably couldn't see the inside of the shop, the outside so bright with all the sun. The next moment he wondered why he cared about the senior seeing this woman.

Before she could meet the senior, the woman left Tsuyu, with her name Ai ringing in his head.

*

Tsuyu's eyesight wasn't particularly bad. When he was thirteen, one of the priests managing the orphanage brought back a scratched-up pair of glasses from his trip to the city. 'This was one of the samples they exhibited in their windows,' the priest told Tsuyu. 'They were about to throw this one away. I thought maybe you could use these when you don't like your own eye color.'

Ever since, he had been wearing glasses. In the village there weren't many children who wore glasses, and the glasses themselves drew more of people's attention than his color-drained eyes. It felt good, like a wall he could carry around.

Up until a few decades ago, eyewear shops weren't very strong a business, as far as tourists were concerned. Glasses weren't something traditional or peculiar to this country, even though the colors and patterns of the frames manufactured here were popular enough for some people. It all changed when someone invented contact lenses that made you see the world in might-be colors. Almost every tourist bought a box at least, despite its ridiculous price, to take back and see their homeland or families and friends more colorful, just like the people and scenery of this island. More expensive ones even created the illusion of patterns on people's skin, too. Tsuyu wondered how the government could possibly invent such a thing, and where all these colors came from, but that was what saved the eyewear industry from ending up a miserable, only-for-locals business, which gave him this job, after all.

But then, these days, perhaps it was the locals who needed these contact lenses more. Though they were a bit too expensive for the locals...

'Focus.'

Her voice pulled him back to here and now so forcibly that he gasped for breath. As she straddled him, a patch of shiny skin inside her knee rubbed against him, and it sent a shiver through him. There was something peculiar about this patch; it looked like a holographic image of countless blues, and if it felt soft or metallic to the touch, Tsuyu couldn't tell. Ai didn't seem to mind it when he touched it, but she didn't seem very willing to talk about it. Was it some kind of scar?

'Keep your eyes open, okay? I need to see it,' she said, her voice demanding, her eyes pleading.

Tsuyu somehow managed to nod. What color in his eyes now? As he stared up helplessly into her eyes, something changed in Ai's irises. A glint? A click? He tried to reach for the curves of her body, which felt strangely flexible, even fluid. He'd never felt anything like—

And then Ai laughed and collapsed onto him. Tsuyu coughed. 'Did you see it?' His voice sounded terrible.

'Oh yes, I caught it! That was amazing.'

He chuckled as he held her against him. 'I wish I could see it, too. Then I might feel more... comfortable with myself.'

She lifted her head, frowning. 'What do you mean? You, not comfortable with yourself? Why?'

'My colors... well. You wouldn't understand.'

Ai sat up, slowly. The frown deepened, and it immediately made Tsuyu regret saying that; she looked bewildered and sad, rather than angry.

'Sorry,' he said, though unsure what he was sorry for.

Ai unfocused from his eyes, looked down at somewhere around his chest. 'Don't ever say something like that again, okay?'

'Okay.'

She was beautiful, even though she looked ridiculously ambient in her blue-grey room. She could have been anything she wanted. Maybe even a PR person for the government or something showy *and* important for this country. Why was she working as a researcher in the field?

And that was a dangerous thought, he knew. Dangerous, which always led to him feeling sulky, and to his horrible monster-eyes.

'Ai... Ai?'

'Yes?'

'Does your name mean indigo? Or love, or something entirely different?'

She smiled and stroked his hair. And pushed her shiny patch hard onto him, so that he completely forgot about his own question.

*

'I'm so sorry again,' he said to the manager of the high-street shop, just as he was about to walk out of the back door, to head for the branch. He wasn't sure if it was the rain that had got to him, or his conversation with Ai last night. Just as Ai had said, dayflower was quite soluble, and rain always affected him badly. But then, when he recalled that expression on her face, he found himself still a bit shaken.

The manager shook her head. 'Don't worry, Tsuyu. We always need someone at the small shop anyway. Take care of yourself first.' She smiled. 'And who knows, you might even end up an urban legend of some sort – if you see the rare ultramarine guy, all your wishes will come true, or something like that.'

Tsuyu smiled back. Her face full of multi-green geometric patterns, the thin wooden frame of her glasses carefully chosen so that the whole image created one of a lush tree. Was she nice because she had a lot of room in her patience having such beautiful patterns, or because she was feeling sorry for him?

He sighed as he walked out of the door. *What am I thinking?* It'd stopped raining, but the grounds were still quite wet, and he trod carefully avoiding puddles. *Boss is just such a nice woman.* And he wondered how he deserved such a nice boss and nice job. Where would he have been, if he hadn't managed to find this place?

Or did that mean, if he had more colors, or even one strong color for that matter, he deserved even better work?

'Tsuyu!'

He jumped. Looked around, embarrassed. Behind him he spotted a coworker waving at him, splashing through puddles. Sunshine fell through the gap between the clouds, and her silvery skin glinted, her hair thin honey melting over her cheeks.

When she caught up, she was quite out of breaths. 'Here, have my ginger tea.'

He took the packet from her. 'Thanks – you ran all this way just to give me this?'

'Yeah. Such a nice coworker, aren't I? Get well soon, okay?'

'Okay. Thanks again.'

The coworker ran back the way she'd come.

How did he deserve all this? With his stupid, unstable color that was only in his eyes?

*

In her navy chiffon dress, under her umbrella, Ai looked as ambient as she did in her own room, on her own bed. Only her glasses shone strangely as she waved and smiled. Even her teeth seemed to sink under the veil of the rain. The shiny patch at her knee was hidden under her dress.

Still beautiful. So beautiful. Tsuyu couldn't help but grin as they came near enough. 'Been collecting a lot of blues today?'

'Mmm.' Ai spread her arm, so that raindrops touched her hand. 'I'm finding it harder to discover more these days. Maybe blue folks don't like the rain.'

'Well. Blue is too common that most of us share the same shade or tint or whatever? Unless one is special like you.' Then, he hastily added, 'Or my eyes sometimes.'

Ai cocked an eyebrow, but said, 'Don't you know? Our colors and patterns are affected a lot by our life, as well as genetic information. Of course the basic ones are determined genetically, but as we grow, other things get to have a lot of say. Like what we eat, what we do, what we think. No blue can be the same, really.'

No, he didn't know that. How was that possible? Also, that he never heard of such a fact? He shook his head, negating many things.

'You didn't? Oh, really, this should be something everybody is taught at a very early stage.' She folded her own umbrella and stepped in under his.

They had been planning to go see the Star Festival decorations in the locals' district, only, with the rain, that didn't feel like a very promising idea now. The festival wasn't tonight, but they had been hoping to have a look around while it was not too crowded. His shoulder brushing hers, they started walking, their direction uncertain. 'If that is true,' he said, 'maybe we were one, same blue person, at some point of history? Even if we don't look like each other at all at this point. I mean, with your lazurite and my ultramarine, we have enough genetic stuff in common.'

Ai fell silent, her steps even more indecisive. For a moment Tsuyu wondered if she hadn't heard him, or if he'd said something stupid again. But then, 'No. It's impossible.'

'No? Why?'

'Why? Because... because if we were, we shouldn't be here, like this.'

Tsuyu laughed. 'I meant Very Long Time Ago.'

'I know. But still.' She suddenly stopped for a second; then grinned and tugged at his hand. 'This way!'

'What? Where to?'

They walked, swerving away from the festival site into a narrow alley which only the locals used as a shortcut to the high street. It was hard with the umbrella, and Tsuyu could see that Ai was taking care not to get him too wet, while trying not to be in other pedestrians' way. *Fluid*.

When they were on the high street, they went in line with the wave of tourists. It looked very much like they were heading for...

'The Festival site for the foreigners?' Tsuyu wondered aloud.

Ai smiled, without looking at him. 'The site for them has a roof, you see.'

'Yes, but...' He let out a small cough. 'But there would be foreigners!'

'Of course. What do you think the roof is for?'

Before he could protest any further, Ai slipped into the dome-like site through its huge doors. Pulling Tsuyu along, who unlike her, had to bump into others and to nod sorry so many times.

Inside, everything was bigger than the decorations in the locals' site. Paper flower-balls and paper balloons hanging near the high ceiling so large that Tsuyu wondered how many people it'd taken to make such things, with beautiful shreds dangling to almost touch the floor. The shreds were fabric, not plastic tapes like the ones prepared for the locals, obviously woven especially for this purpose. These behind-the-scene tasks were usually given to people with no prominent colors or patterns. Drowned in thoughts and density of things surrounding him, for a second Tsuyu thought he'd lost Ai in the sea of the shreds, in spite of their linked hands. But of course there she was, when the shreds parted in front of him, in the part of the dome where pinkish decorations dominated, so her color was just too striking in contrast.

The tourists noticed, and started taking photos of the blue couple. Tsuyu was torn between running away from this place and looking on at her forever.

'Look at me, Tsuyu,' she whispered. 'You are beautiful.'

That moment, he thought he saw a flash of ultramarine reflected on Ai's glasses, over her indigo eyes, and blinked. It seemed impossible, but nevertheless he felt the surge of pride right there, and everything else around the two of them seemed to melt somehow.

And looking at her forever won. Of course it did.

*

He felt slightly dizzy, and his head throbbed a little with every breath he took, though it wasn't as bad as he had expected when he had heard the weather forecast mentioning the center of a low air pressure hovering over the island. He forced himself to look into a mirror, and frowned. Just as he did so, the manager came to stand beside him, and raised her brows. 'They're blue.'

Tsuyu nodded. It wasn't exactly ultramarine, but something a bit deeper. And the tinge shifted just a little at angles, as the light changed. Sometimes it even seemed to swirl – as if a distant nebula was reflected in the eye. When he had woken up this morning and felt the heaviness of his head, he hadn't even bothered looking into a mirror, assuming it looked horrible and ridiculous as usual.

'That's beautiful, too. Looks like something darker has been added to your trademark ultramarine.'

Something darker. 'Indigo?'

'Oh yes, that.' She took out a couple of painkiller pills from the medicine box. 'That'd look really good behind a lacquered frame, if you don't mind.'

He looked at his boss. Today her rimless glasses had brightly colored gems on the temples. Flowers, fruit or birds in the tree. He wondered if what Ai had said was true – that who you were affected your colors and patterns. If it was, then what had she gone through to develop these complicated yet sophisticated patterns?

'What? You don't think painkillers would do any good?'

'Oh no, sorry. I'll be fine. Thank you.'

So he forced down the pills, and spent the day at the high-street shop.

*

A few tourists who came in that morning recognized Tsuyu from the festival dome, and soon, the high-street shop was crowded with foreigners who had heard the rumor. The sales that day were the highest in a long while, and of course, Tsuyu sold more than any other, both usual glasses and the special contact lenses. The silver coworker nudged at him, pretending to be jealous.

How did he deserve all this?

At the end of the day he checked his eyes again, which were still somewhere between indigo and ultramarine. The locals' street was still busy as he left the shop for the day, the sun not completely set yet. The sky was strangely colorful, the streetlights coming to life one by one, strengthening the outlines of everything he could see. He walked on, nodding to a few people he knew, and then, something caught his attention at the corner of his eye.

He looked.

There was no telling if this person was male or female, or something entirely different. This person glowed, soft silver light seeming to cool down the air around. Glowing wasn't common, but not impossible either, and Tsuyu didn't know why he was drawn to this person so.

Then a wind blew just as Tsuyu passed by this person, and the person's hair swayed a little. At the small of their neck, Tsuyu saw a patch, shiny and metallic, consisting of many silvers.

Just like...

Tsuyu stopped, staring at the person's back, knowing somewhere in his mind that he shouldn't be doing this. Even as they were, in this island where everything was meant to be stared at, many locals hated having that done to them, especially by another local. But he couldn't help it.

The person was soon drowned in the sea of colors of the locals. Somewhere near the back door to the eyewear shop, he lost the glow completely.

With an effort he started walking again. Belatedly he realized it was the way the person's glow felt strangely ambient in the twilight, just like Ai's blue-grey, that he'd found so peculiar about this person. He couldn't help but glance back over his shoulder, but of course, there was not a hint of the person's glow in the dusk-fallen street.

That night, he called Ai. She never answered.

*

The next morning when he turned in there was a commotion in the high-street shop. Everyone seemed to be at the center of the shop, though it was almost time to open up for the day, and some of them should be away in the backyard or running errands. At the very center of it all, was the silver coworker.

Only she wasn't silver anymore.

This was the first time Tsuyu actually saw someone completely greyed-out. He had seen people or things slowly toned down, but nothing this drastic. The silver girl had had no patterns, but different tinges of silver crammed all over her surfaces, which had looked like a pattern in a way. Some of the tinges had glowed, especially when she'd smiled, and everybody had loved that. Now, he could see the slight shade differences, but it was all dull grey instead of silver, and she looked as though she just popped out of a black-and-white photograph. The glow was gone, too, but he couldn't tell if that was because she was crying now.

The boss was touching the silver girl's shoulder, but Tsuyu could feel other employees were afraid to do the same, in case this was contagious. Researches and reasons told this was not the case – there was no logic to how and where people or things were affected – but he knew they just couldn't help it.

Tsuyu pushed on into the center. 'Shiroka,' he called her name, but couldn't go on.

She looked up. 'Oh Tsuyu, look. I'm no longer shirokane.' She tried to smile, which made everything seem even worse.

He patted on her now almost completely white hair. 'Maybe I can walk her home—' he started to say to the boss.

'No.' Shiroka shook her head. 'I was already like this when I woke this morning, and I came in to say I wanted to work at the branch today. I'm only crying because Boss was really nice about it.' She tried to smile again, and ended up sniffing. 'But… you know, now I realize, maybe locals don't want to buy stuff from me…'

Tsuyu wanted to tell her it was not true, but he knew some people would react that way. Look how peripheral other workers were being right now – it was all he could do to shake his head. And then the boss cut in. 'There is plenty of work to do in the backyard, if that's more comfortable for you. I know you have deft fingers, so maybe you can help with the repair team and all.' The woman looked around. 'Anyway. Let's get moving! The customers will be in soon!'

The workers dispersed, some awkwardly patting Shiroka's shoulder. Some still unable to make up their mind.

*

That day passed in a blur; everyone's mind filled with *why*. Why was this happening? Why here, why her? Shiroka kept herself mostly to the backyard, occasionally running errands, but then covering her head with the boss' shiny silk shawl. Tsuyu caught a glimpse of her as she sneaked out of the back door, the shawl catching sunlight and shimmering as she gave him a small wave.

Tsuyu nodded back. And he realized he couldn't help, for some reason, thinking about that glowing silver person he'd seen yesterday.

And about Ai.

*

He cursed himself for having chosen the worst timing when he had left work that day, and having carelessly walked in the hard shower that had just started then. And having stumbled down onto his cot, too tired from the day's work, without thoroughly drying himself and keeping warm. All of that resulted in him now feeling so weak, fever-ridden in the small hours of that night, though he had a feeling that this had nothing to do with his colors – ordinary people did catch a cold when they behaved just like he had, of course. He might be stronger than he used to be, but there was only so much that could change, really. He wanted to see Ai; or at least, hear her voice. He had tried calling her during the day, but she'd never answered. Which made him realize, in an absent-minded way, that he knew nothing of her usual work schedule, or where she would be found when she was not home.

But then—

A hand landed on his eyes. *Why*, he wanted to say, but there were too many whys that he couldn't decide which one to ask first.

So he let her speak first. 'Don't open your eyes.'

He sighed. 'Where have you been? I tried—'

'I made a mistake. It's all my fault.'

'Ai?'

Her head gently touched his, as she awkwardly slipped in beside him, her hand still over his eyes. 'I take. I don't give. I'm built for taking, programmed to collect blues. If I give, that means un-becoming me. End of *me*.'

Tsuyu thought about the new tinge of his eyes. How it had helped him deal with many things – not only cold and all, but if he had been still the same, unstable dayflower, he might not have felt so sympathetic for Shiroka. But then, without Ai, what were the indigo-tinted eyes any good for? 'Ai. Please. If that is such a problem, take it back from me.'

'It's too late.' Her hand seemed to shake, or perhaps, *ripple*. 'I didn't even realize what I was doing, until recently. Until another AI came to this town, until I saw it fully obliging to its duty. We only take. That one silver, me blue. When I cease to function just as I was built, then I have no right to exist – a serious bug detected. They already shut down some of the modules, I will be nothing soon. And then a new, proper blue AI will be placed.'

Nothing Ai was saying made sense to Tsuyu. Except—'The contact lenses.' He swallowed. 'Where do all those colors come from...'

Ai laughed, or sighed, and stroked his hair with another hand which felt way too soft. 'At least the indigo I gave you settled down well with you and you're a lot stronger. It will be fully yours once this rain is over. That much, I don't regret.'

'Ai. Please—'

'Look at me, Tsuyu.'

Her hand lifted and he opened his eyes. He soon understood why Ai hadn't wanted him to see her before talking. If not, he wouldn't have recognized the thing beside him as Ai. It looked like a lump of water, with a cracked holographic image projected. Every second Ai's face – half or quarter of it – showed on a different part of the water. Her shiny patch taking over her, with no proper control. If he hadn't heard her voice first, let her explain first, he might have screamed.

But it did have Ai's voice, so Tsuyu didn't have to scream, or to be frightened. 'I'm sorry,' her voice said.

'Don't go. Please. Maybe there's something—'

But then, the rain struck hard onto his windows, and he made a mistake of looking away from her for a second.

And she was gone.

*

A few days later when he had fully recovered from the cold, he was surprised to find Shiroka at the high-street shop, just like she'd done before greying out. 'Can you believe,' she said as soon as she saw Tsuyu. 'The foreigners even like me this way! They make me wear a colorful frame or colored contacts and take photos. They do have strange tastes, really!'

Tsuyu smiled, relieved. 'Yes, they do.'

Then she looked at his eyes for a second, and tilted her head. 'You know, I'm sure this sounds strange from me, but...' Shiroka unfolded a crazily colorful frame, which had been designed especially for her by one of the craftspeople, and set it on her face. 'I did like your dayflower eyes. Even the way it drained. I knew it was troubling you so I never mentioned this before, but... now that I'm grey, I'd be forgiven for saying something like this, or would I not?'

Tsuyu laughed. 'You would, yes.' He wiped a single drop of tear at the corner of his eye. 'And... thank you. I think I needed someone to mourn that color. Thanks.'

Shiroka blinked her completely grey blinks, behind the custom-made rims. 'Are you... okay?'

'Yes.'

That was all he could say as an answer to that, for now. He looked out of the front window, at the sunny high street, busy as ever with tourists and islanders. The rainy season had ended while he had slept his cold away. Summer had come.

Your Multicolored Life

Xing He

China

I first met Xing He in Beijing back in 2000, when the world was very different, but even then, he was presented to me as one of the most important voices in Chinese science fiction. I remember at least one hourslong lunch just talking about science fiction... I had the good fortune to see him again in Beijing in 2019, during a glittering party that highlighted just how celebrated SF had become in China now. But at the heart of SF are the writers, who still gather for dumplings and beer in little restaurants away from the limelight. There is almost no work by Xing He published in English, so I am grateful to translator Andy Dudak for bringing us this tale from an old friend.

1 – This World

The occasional breeze allayed the scorching midsummer heat, soothing the fever dreams of the sleepers in the mining scar. The remote blue sky was rooted to the earth, which here in the work zone was the blood-red of hematite.

Zhang Hua crouched low. Nostrils flaring, he dragged a finger through the residue of food that remained in the paper ration box. He looked around, contemplating the smell of urine that pervaded the area. On either side of the peak, a drum-type robot was patrolling. Zhang Hua didn't dare to look straight up at them.

The dreaming multitude began to stir. Zhang Hua was immediately alert, every fiber of his being ready for work orders. A slave laborer like himself dashed away from the edge of the scar, and then another, this one slower. The two machine guardians acted according to their programming, simultaneously abandoning their patrol routes and turning upon the first, and faster, runaway. They launched two scorching tongues of flame, and the human fell to the ground, barely struggling.

They hit their second target with bullets, and this slave fell, writhing and shivering, taking longer to die.

Zhang Hua watched it all with a grave expression. He didn't join the crowd of agitated slaves at the top of the main ramp. He knew the odds of escape by simply fleeing were low, so he wasn't shocked by what he'd seen. He'd never thought of doing it that way.

The night before, he'd lain in his thatch hut, tossing and turning and never finding sleep. As his body became visible to him in the passing darkness, a plan took shape in his mind. He'd been wracking his brain for days, and here finally was something that could work.

Rather than cautiously speaking during rest periods, it was better to mutter, lips barely moving, during work. As the afternoon work period started, Zhang Hua, a vigorous porter of iron ore, didn't show the slightest fatigue. He initiated exploratory discussions of his plan. Several vigilant comrades gathered around him, and he made his proposal to slaves passing nearby.

Everyone seemed to think it was feasible.

'Should we include Ore-Head?' one laborer asked.

'No,' Zhang Hua said. 'He's going to act as bait.'

Zhang Hua was more grim, callous, and farsighted than his fellow slaves. He knew Ore-Head for what he was: a fool who thought himself clever.

As Zhang Hua conspired with friends, Ore-Head was wantonly, and without fear of ridicule, publicizing his own theory of escape. He told anyone he came across that escape required at least three people: two to separately draw fire, giving a third the chance to escape. Based on this theory alone, Ore-Head considered himself a great mathematician. But this great thinker was going further, planning to put his theory into practice. He campaigned intensely, making a lot of noise trying to assemble followers. This interfered with Zhang Hua's operations, whose first thought had been to beat the fool into submission, or death. But then Zhang Hua thought of a wiser counter-stratagem: exploit the idiot and whatever small group he assembled, as decoys.

The next day, Zhang Hua and Ore-Head were both still trying to attract followers. But a new problem had arisen: a slave named Bug-Eyes had died in the wee hours of the morning. This diminutive man, a porter of ore like Zhang Hua, had probably succumbed to exhaustion, though it may have been illness. The robot wardens forced a group of slaves to carry his body out of the scar, like so much ore, and dump it over a cliff. Bug-Eyes had been Ore-Head's go-between, and central to his plan. Now that the little man was gone, Ore-Head was panicking.

'I want to join up with you,' Zhang Hua said in a low voice, sidling up to Ore-Head.

Ore-Head could barely contain his excitement at these words. He hadn't expected to attract such a strong and courageous person, someone who'd always looked down on him. It seemed this paragon of humanity was also short on manpower. Beggars couldn't be choosers.

Ore-Head devoured his lunch ration. He tried to avoid staring at Zhang Hua, but couldn't help the occasional conspiratorial wink. Zhang Hua ignored these, preparing himself mentally.

After lunch, Zhang Hua scanned the scar, the peak, the south face of the mountain. He nodded at Ore-Head, who'd been waiting for this signal. Ore-Head sprang up and fled.

At the same time, another slave leaped to his feet, the only other person that Ore-Head had managed to recruit.

But Zhang Hua didn't budge.

Ore-Head became the first sacrificial victim.

Three people weren't enough. Humans were slower than robots, after all. Zhang Hua was indeed farsighted, and he was also quick-witted. Two slaves were enough to start drawing fire, it was true, but his plan diverged from Ore-Head's there. Poor, foolish Ore-Head, who had begun to lose his nerve, and was now burning to death on the mountainside: he'd just needed a little push in the right direction. Now the regular army could take the field.

Zhang Hua charged up a mound of ore, brandishing a rod he'd extracted from the ore processing machinery, and swept a fire-spurting robot off its feet. A blow to the chest plate caused a short circuit, and then it was prone in the rubble, unmoving, silent. But Zhang Hua kept bashing until the machine was in pieces.

Elsewhere around the scar, Zhang Hua's comrades were about similar business.

This was the only way. Only by destroying machine guards and commanders could human slaves really escape.

When Zhang Hua and his comrades were fleeing down the mountainside, most of the scar's slaves didn't yet understand their sudden turn of fortune. But soon enough they too were dispersing in amazement, the hematite abandoned.

Zhang Hua led his small group down the south face, his destination clear: the tree line, and the concealment of the forest.

2 – That World

As You Ruo set out, the darkness of night was just beginning to retreat before a brightening in the east.

He had to begin his great journey by daylight. The dark made no difference to machine eyes, but could greatly affect human movement. Humans were physically inferior to the machines, without a doubt.

But no matter how inferior, humans didn't have to succumb to machine logic, or cleave to the machine imperative, or take machine orders.

You Ruo could have arranged to launch his rebellious action at a safer moment, but he wanted to be a symbol, his journey a declaration. He'd been preparing for a long time, putting all kinds of goods in order. The work had been underway for a year. Meticulous thinking had allowed him to do all the planning in his head. He'd never dared to put pen to paper, like so many previous revolutionaries.

You Ruo secured his backpack. This was all he'd bring out of his home today, a shovel and a few other tools. His ostensible work was tending flora. He'd buried what he really needed near the border of this vast parkland furthest from his house. There, day by day, while muddling through his gardening and forestry chores, he'd secretly brought things along, and today he would gather them up.

It wasn't warm or cold today, and the sun shone just bright enough. Good weather for launching a revolution.

You Ruo headed north from his home, passing a pond he'd excavated himself. At the time he'd meant to dig a small reservoir, so he could swim in the summer, but the machines soon put a stop to this. They were not miserly with water resources, but they'd feared You Ruo would drown, dying prematurely like a moth drawn to a flame. After all, his well-being was paramount. The compromise was this little cistern pond, so shallow even frogs ignored it.

Gathering his tools wasn't difficult. You Ruo knew their precise locations, having walked this route daily to review the hiding places and burials. After fetching what he needed, he changed direction, heading southwest. He avoided some dwelling places and came to another supply burial under a flowerbed. Keeping everything in batches like this was minimally risky, and conserved advantage. He turned southeast, passing through a crowd of statues he had been carving for years, all crude and unfinished.

Originally, he'd planned to raise some animals around here, but this had also been prohibited.

He left the Sculpture Crowd behind, heading for the east side of Demarcation Forest. You Ruo had planted these woods with his own hands. He'd watched saplings reach gradually skyward, and he had named the forest, though it wasn't really a line of demarcation.

But on its east side was an electrified fence.

You Ruo's home was convenient for his current secret operations: far from crowds, located at the world's desolate edge. This parkland had been allocated for medical therapies, including the treatment – or at least containment – of abnormal minds like You Ruo. He wandered the fields and woodlands, knowing countless machine eyes always watched him. His past escape attempts had brought down everything from kindly remonstration to machine force, but he'd never been harmed.

The machines always had his well-being in mind, after all.

As early as puberty, when You Ruo had been classified an exceptional and unconventional thinker, he'd been granted special consideration, and closely monitored. He was sent to special treatment wards, given special care, and allocated special resources for his growth and development. His life was custom-made. All care was taken to make him feel wanted, and not an object of discrimination.

And so he'd learned to hide his real capabilities, to bide his time, and to wait for a relaxation of machine vigilance.

It was quite a discovery. He wondered if he was the first human to realize that the machines could indeed relax their vigilance. They ran on programs, algorithms, but they could alter these according to observation. Above all, they sought to avoid squandering resources. You Ruo had gradually come to understand this.

So, for the past six months, You Ruo had given a very meek and docile performance. He had tried to seem like a normal human: content, domesticated, comfortable, and kept. At one point the machine administrators even asked him to move back among the general population of humans. You Ruo explained he wasn't ready to socialize, that he needed another therapeutic period. The machines amicably granted this.

Now he meant to exploit their mistake, and conveniently depart.

Ahead, through the trees, was the electrified mesh of the fence. You Ruo crept toward it. The electricity was merely a backup measure. Every time he'd approached the fence before with destructive intent, he'd been warned away by the machines. He'd always preferred the agony of electroshock, which he liked to believe somehow punished his caretakers as well. At any rate, it forced the machines to resuscitate him and transport him back to his room.

Recalling all this now, he barely noticed the two robot guardians that haunted this place. They inspected and patrolled this section of the fencing, moving among the trees like spirits.

I've always been a strange one, You Ruo thought, suppressing a wild joy in his heart. *Today I will not go seeking the others. My first order of business in the free world will be to find shelter. I can always come back and arouse the domesticated to do as I have done.*

You Ruo struggled to constrain his excitement. He gathered up a rubber watering hose and began watering the trees. He did his best not to raise his head and focused on the electrified mesh. He didn't want his smiling expression recorded.

Today, You Ruo's strategy would be different than before. There would be no surprise attack on the electrified fence. This time he paid attention to the nearest security camera. He glanced at it quite a few times. A direct attack on the fence immediately brought riot suppression robots, but causing a security camera to shut down might read as a malfunction, and merely summon a machine tinkerer. Of course, the deactivating of the camera couldn't be too obvious. The machine admins mustn't perceive his involvement. Timing was everything.

The water arced further and further from the hose. At the right moment, it was suddenly firing into the security camera, at an angle rain would never hit it. The device probably called for help before going mute.

He had about five minutes before the repair bot arrived. And then it would need at least ten minutes to repair the camera. You Ruo dropped the hose, brought out his massive homemade shears, and approached the electrified fence. This section was blind without the camera and could offer no resistance. When You Ruo was little, he'd used metal scissors to cut electrified wire. Back then, the current had automatically cut off, but of course this was different. The oversized shears in his hands were wooden, and dry, and would insulate him. The mesh crackled and sparked as it was cut.

You Ruo thought, *This would've been more fun at night, a beautiful light show, like send-off-party fireworks.*

He cut a big square-shaped hole in the mesh.

He cocked his head a moment, appreciating his masterpiece. He packed away his tool and stepped proudly through the recently constructed gate.

The slow tinkerer bot finally showed up.

At first, You Ruo was solemn and dignified as he proceeded forward, neither urgent nor slow, his stride vigorous. But when the repair bot began tapping away at its work, You Ruo decided time was of the essence, and took off at a wild run.

As he ran, he kept looking over his shoulder, filling his vision with the world of his birth. There was sentiment in his heart, even though he was running away as fast as he could.

I'll come back! You Ruo screamed in his mind. *I swear it!*

'I'll come back!' he screamed aloud, unable to stop himself. 'I swear it!'

The first step toward revolution was a success!

Yes, *revolution*. That was the word. He hadn't spoken it aloud for years, but remembering it now, You Ruo couldn't keep his blood from boiling with righteous indignation.

But there was something You Ruo didn't know.

The robots had stopped paying close attention to him. They hadn't been watching for six months. As long as he didn't return to teeming streets and publicize his views, as long as he stayed in the wild, open country he loved, why waste time and resources?

3 – The Edge of the World

The dark of the forest was deep and unfathomable. Years of falling leaves had made a thick loam here, like nothing Zhang Hua had ever seen. The roar of helicopters had been left behind, outside the forest. Zhang Hua and his companions had nearly been intercepted.

Now he had to go on alone. The helicopters couldn't enter the forest, but they could heat-sense from above, broadly, so there was no advantage in sticking together. The only plan was to split up and hope for the best. Zhang Hua pointed left and right, and his meaning was clear: *run for your lives*. He plunged into the primeval halls of the forest, leaving behind a party of comrades glancing at each other in dismay.

They soon scattered, their brief alliance dissolved.

The synthetic rations Zhang Hua had carefully gathered and stored on his person would last two days, at most, but he believed the forest was abundant with wild fruit. He dreaded running out of water more than starving to death. Where there were trees, there must be water, but finding it was another matter.

Watching the sun through gaps in the canopy, he could tell the time of day, and toward nightfall he began to worry. This region, untouched and unconquered by humans, must be haunted by beasts of prey. It was said they feared fire, but Zhang Hua didn't have the implements of fire on him. Worse still, he didn't know which direction to go. His plan had been limited to escaping the work site. He hadn't thought about what came afterward. During enslavement, freedom had seemed glorious, but on an empty stomach, abstract concepts of freedom were utterly worthless.

All he knew, in a vague way, was that some places didn't suffer under machine control.

No ferocious beasts attacked that first night – something at least to rejoice over. Asleep and dreaming, Zhang Hua barely heard deep roars, remote, indistinct.

He groped about aimlessly for three days and nights. On the fourth day he began to feel unwell. The berries of this woodland, although fresh, were no match for synthetic rations when it came to cleanliness, and he doubted the potability of the water. Although he'd never eaten his fill in the past, his digestive tract had become used to a certain level of sanitation.

He felt his legs were only reluctantly supporting him, let alone carrying him forward. The canopy above grew sparse. It seemed he'd reached the far end of the forest, at last. This restored his spirits somewhat, and the excitement temporarily compensated for his physical weakness.

Some time in the afternoon, the first small flake fell on Zhang Hua's head. He flinched with fright, then realized this thing was harmless, a natural phenomenon.

Glittering, translucent snowflakes drifted down, accumulating in a layer of white powder. Falling on Zhang Hua's body, they were cold, and dissolved instantly. It had never snowed at the work site, where the phenomenon was merely a legend. Zhang Hua opened his mouth, and a dose of refreshing coolness entered his throat. At this point, he regarded snow as a thirst-quenching beverage.

But the snow grew more intense, the flakes larger, sticking to Zhang Hua's body, which soon grew numb. His exposed skin was frozen, turning purple. The sky was going dark, and all around was a gray void. Passing through dense curtains of snow, he distractedly saw something in the distance, snow-covered buildings or houses. They seemed to be in good repair, out here in the middle of nowhere, like fairy palaces from folktales.

And then he could take no more. After days of overexertion, and inadequate food and water, he swooned and fell into the snow.

*

You Ruo's technological circumstances were far superior to Zhang Hua's. But even though his tools were more than adequate, he was venturing into mires and primeval forests, worlds he'd never braved before. In the darkest of forest nights he didn't dare turn on his electric torch, which was bright as daylight. Who knew what beasts it might attract? His journey was turning out much different from what he'd imagined, but his revolutionary zeal was undiminished.

Passing through fields, fording rivers, the wild joy of his countenance never wavered. Starting out, he'd still felt some lingering fear of pursuit, but as that first day wore on, the fear had diminished until there was nothing left. Snacking when hungry, sipping purified water when thirsty, this carefree wandering life was actually quite satisfying. You Ruo wasn't worried about provisions. He believed that before he finished everything he'd brought with him, he would find the utopia from legends, the land of peach blossoms. Besides, his rations were enough for ten days.

Soon, You Ruo was losing his way in an undulating landscape of hillocks. He'd originally foreseen ascending the first of these and beholding a wide new expanse of flat country beyond. He hadn't expected to conquer one of these hillocks after another, in seemingly unending succession, and getting thoroughly lost.

But in this undulating progress, he did not grow careless. He headed due east, consulting a compass once per hour to rectify his course. Although he didn't know what was under the eastern sky, at least he was putting more distance between himself and his former world. Originally, he'd camped in suburban districts, the western extremity of that world, but now he was in true wilderness.

Ahead, the hills were higher, sheer, and sparsely wooded, like the alopecia-stricken skulls he'd seen in medical texts.

You Ruo hesitated. Night must fall eventually, and it would be difficult to find his way amid those copses and cliffs. Then again, high places had their advantages. They commanded wide views, perhaps allowing him to discover something new.

So, he began to mountaineer.

Adding climbing to his physical exertions was not You Ruo's idea of fun. He thought several times of giving up. About halfway up, on the waist of what was essentially a mountain, he pitched camp. The next day, he nearly tumbled off the mountainside twice. But his faith and conviction kept him going, carrying him through great difficulty to the summit.

He chased his breath for a long time. You Ruo was a large man.

In his world, men and women were well-built and -proportioned. Caloric intake was regulated by the machines, but You Ruo had refused these limits, enjoying excess in food and drink. Eventually, as in much else, the machines treated You Ruo as a special case, and didn't regulate his diet, merely providing suggestions. But he didn't listen. Listening here would have signified something larger to You Ruo, and his body itself became an emblem of resistance to machine control. Not that he was a very effective symbol. Wandering parkland wilds, his mass didn't cause many to ponder the wider implications of disobedience.

Now, his night vision device revealed heat-generating bodies in distant lowlands – people residing in houses, and judging by their shapes, these weren't the dwellings of his own people. You Ruo moved across the wide summit, wanting to see the community from a different vantage.

He stumbled, tripped, fell on something soft. He put out a probing hand and discovered something warm.

4 – Communication

Zhang Hua opened his eyes, alert as a cat. His feral gaze fixed on You Ruo.

'Easy does it,' You Ruo said. 'Let me help you.'

Zhang Hua slowly digested this stranger's words. He hadn't talked with anyone in days, and You Ruo's manner of speech was odd. Zhang Hua puzzled over the alien syllables sprinkled among the familiar, and the strange inflections, until meaning dawned upon him.

'First eat a little something.'

Zhang Hua had been staring at the thing in You Ruo's hand. Although he couldn't see it clearly, he guessed it was food. He cautiously took the proffered foodstuff, gave it a few licks, and the delicious flavor did the rest. He devoured it in a frenzy, several times biting his own fingers and tongue.

'Where have you come from?' You Ruo asked, handing over another piece, patiently waiting for Zhang Hua to finish eating. 'East?'

Zhang Hua shook his head, not understanding. You Ruo pointed east, and Zhang Hua shook his head again. He'd lost his bearings.

'Is everyone from your land like you?' You Ruo said, groping for some way to communicate. He struggled to imagine the difference between himself and Zhang Hua. 'How do your people live?'

Zhang Hua wanted more food, but You Ruo showed no sign of willingness to share more.

Actually, there was more in You Ruo's hand, but he had to consider his rationing against Zhang Hua's considerable appetite. Luckily, they'd both seen the settlement below, where there was surely food.

Zhang Hua focused on his brain rather than his stomach, and began the arduous process of telling his story to You Ruo, explaining many things repeatedly, and doing his best to answer You Ruo's barely intelligible questions. In the end, he'd made his place in the world, and that of his people, more or less clear.

'Well, there it is,' You Ruo said, pensive, thoughtful. 'Your people are also controlled by machines.'

'Your people aren't any better off?' Zhang Hua asked, desperate to know.

You Ruo began to preach. His tale was well-ordered, but excessive in rationality, making it hard for Zhang Hua to understand. Although You Ruo condemned his own people's pampered way of life at every turn, the specific examples and anecdotes made Zhang Hua yearn for it, utterly. Zhang Hua listened to the account as if respectfully hearing a fairy tale. He'd heard this sort of thing when he was a child. Now it seemed like a lifetime ago.

In his own world, Zhang Hua had not always been the lowest of slaves. In his early years he'd been a skilled worker under the machine domination, and had read about privilege and human rights in ancient texts. This sort of content had been sprinkled throughout reams of technical data, or implied by it, and so had not fallen into the abyss of the Historical Materials Ban. In the pages of those dry and dull specialist manuals, there'd been no descriptions of technology beyond a narrow scope, but reading enough of them had allowed Zhang Hua to vaguely perceive other ways of life.

He discovered that humanity had once been free. He discovered that humanity had ruled over machines. He discovered quite a lot from technical manuals, including the revelation that humanity had not always been as it now was. And so was born the seed of discontent within him.

His demotion to slave labor was not due to his thought crimes, which would have gotten him thoroughly decommissioned. It was because the technological innovations he'd been assigned to were declared complete. Thus, he was transformed overnight, from middle-class technological servant to common laborer.

*

The topic of conversation gradually shifted to the settlement in the lowlands.

'I've heard of people like them,' You Ruo said. 'Savages, not under the control of my world or yours. Free and unrestrained. Their material standards must be quite low.'

'In other words… going there would be bad,' Zhang Hua said. He could barely understand phrasing like 'material standards'.

'Not necessarily,' You Ruo said, feeling ideologically awkward. 'At least they have freedom.'

Freedom? Wasn't this what Zhang Hua longed for? Otherwise, why did he hazard escaping the work site?

'I want to go to your world,' he said to You Ruo.

You Ruo couldn't believe his ears. 'From what I understand, you obtained freedom with great difficulty. And now you want to hand it over, in exchange for… some leftovers?'

Zhang Hua didn't understand the word 'leftovers'. To him, it seemed everything You Ruo ate was a precious delicacy.

'If you really want to go,' You Ruo said, 'I can't stop you. But you may regret it.' The rotund man turned, resolutely facing the sun and heading down the mountain. The silhouettes of the settlement were clear. You Ruo's goal was clear.

Zhang Hua hesitated before catching up to the stranger. He couldn't be sure if You Ruo's world was really as wonderful as described. It sounded like a fantasy, the dream of some mad hermit. Moreover, Zhang Hua was lost. Perhaps following You Ruo was a bit safer, for now.

5 – Among the Savages

When they entered the village, almost everyone stopped their handiwork and labor, and quietly stared. No one seemed inclined to guard their leader, even as the two outsiders approached the largest thatch structure in the community, which You Ruo correctly took for the headman's residence. The headman himself soon came out, calm and composed as he looked over his two strange guests.

At first there was no way to carry on a dialogue. Neither You Ruo nor Zhang Hua understood the headman's stern, questioning utterances. There were a few vaguely familiar words, and that was all. But You Ruo was, as usual, completely prepared. He brought out a small interpreting device, and this resolved the communication problem.

The two of them were allowed to enter the headman's home, and were taken to a long meeting hall. Zhang Hua's nostrils flared, as he detected a neighboring dining hall's cooking meat. The headman didn't need You Ruo to interpret Zhang Hua's expression. Servants were called upon to treat the guests hospitably, and soon a clay basin of cooked meats was placed on the meeting table.

Thereafter, Zhang Hua didn't hear a word of the talks between You Ruo and the headman. He devoured the roasted meats from the clay basin, rapacious, oblivious. The guard standing nearby allowed his envy to show through his wooden expression.

The meat was soon gone, and Zhang Hua pointed at the empty clay basin, wanting more. A savage brought in a basin of vegetable mush and set it down. Zhang Hua groaned in discontent, but reluctantly went to work on the mush. He'd been eating cheap synthesized rations for most of his life, and here the food was fresh at least, and he'd been starving for most of his journey.

When they left the meeting hall, Zhang Hua couldn't tell if You Ruo and the headman had reached some kind of agreement. You Ruo seemed content, judging by his expression. Perhaps that was part of his persuasion strategy. Zhang Hua couldn't tell.

They entered a small enclosure off the long hall, apparently a guest room, and Zhang Hua immediately smelled danger. The door closing heavily behind them was just one clue. The greed in the savages' eyes was another, and more convincing. To Zhang Hua it seemed saliva must soon flow from those eyes. He came from a long history of privation and starvation, and he couldn't misinterpret the signs. Zhang Hua had been existing on the border of life and death continuously. He was very sensitive to danger, which was how he'd survived until now.

He did his best to convey his misgivings to You Ruo via gesticulation. You Ruo didn't believe him at first, but Zhang Hua became emphatic, at last turning You Ruo's doubt into half-belief. You Ruo carefully peered out a window. He had, after all, years of experience plotting against the machines.

The savages outside the window were whispering.

'Should we run?' Zhang Hua said, leaning close to You Ruo. Zhang Hua also had covert experience, having frequently communicated escape plans to companions right in front of machine guards. He was sure the savages outside couldn't hear his voice.

'Why?' You Ruo said, expressionless, watching Zhang Hua's unmoving lips.

'They mean to eat us.' Zhang Hua's muscles were tense. The first assent or order from You Ruo would send him fleeing.

'Unlikely, before daybreak.' You Ruo's expression didn't change.

'Murder at night is convenient.'

'They're bold.' You Ruo smiled. 'They would kill us in broad daylight. They'll want us fresh for breakfast, won't they?'

What happened next settled the question, which wasn't one of boldness. The savages were indifferent to day and night, and they couldn't wait for the sun to rise. You Ruo was rich in fat and oil. Zhang Hua was sturdy with lean meat. This sort of chance didn't come along every day.

A group of men entered the room. Three were armed with short, dark blades, while others held crude clubs. Zhang Hua noticed some of the younger men licking their lips. He couldn't help backing away, and nearly falling in the process.

Hungry indeed, You Ruo thought. *And not even a token bit of ceremony before the slaughter.*

Not waiting for them to get closer, or crack gloating smiles, he brought out his weapon.

6 – Leave-taking

Although the door was obstructed, Zhang Hua easily rushed and broke through a thatch wall of the room. He and You Ruo fled, leaving a dead body behind.

The laser weapon had originally been used for killing wild animals, but in his panic, You Ruo had used it to discharge a lethal electric shock.

They hadn't escaped without their own injuries. Zhang Hua's foot had been cut open by a blade, and You Ruo was worse off: his whole body covered in bruises and lacerations. When at last they found a place to rest and gather their wits, Zhang Hua looked at You Ruo and his weapon in amazement, and the portly man felt awkward.

'One victory doesn't mean much,' You Ruo said. 'They're barbarians, without proper reasoning faculties, and we took them by surprise.'

Zhang Hua wanted, more than anything, to propose visiting You Ruo's wonderous world. But You Ruo beat him to the punch. 'I want to go to your people, Zhang Hua,' he said.

Having been under You Ruo's influence and tutelage the past two days, Zhang Hua roughly understood this sentence. But he shook his head, thinking he must have misheard.

'To remedy the barbarism we just encountered,' You Ruo said, 'we must change the world entire.' His tone was full of lofty sentiment. 'That means changing the world of machine-controlled humanity!'

This sort of bold, visionary talk didn't move Zhang Hua. All he could think about was You Ruo's safe, well-fed world. To Zhang Hua, it was the legendary Kingdom of Heaven. He was very interested in that place. Too bad he could only know it from You Ruo's words and phrases: spacious accommodation, abundant food, and best of all, an idle life free of needless manual labor!

And all this obtainable just by giving the machine administrators an identity authentication number.

'The revolution will depend on your people,' You Ruo said, continuing his speech, 'who have suffered the lowest depths of enslavement. In my world, people have become numb, apathetic, sleeping like the dead, their human spirit thoroughly lost!'

Somewhat recuperated, You Ruo called upon Zhang Hua to begin their journey. You Ruo set off, his sentiments lofty, and Zhang Hua followed behind, laden with anxiety. When You Ruo's revolutionary zeal surged, Zhang Hua ruminated more seriously than ever in his life. When You Ruo was moved to tears by his plans, Zhang Hua came to his own bold resolve.

He would go to You Ruo's world, assume You Ruo's name, and take his place and identity.

According to common sense, Zhang Hua's decision was weak-minded. But it was precisely his ignorance that allowed him to dare something so presumptuous and reckless. In his own world, Zhang Hua had been considered a very intelligent person.

At this point, despite appearances, the two of them were already walking separate paths. You Ruo always liked to preach revolutionary principles at Zhang Hua during mealtimes. Of course, he spoke at other times as well. Zhang Hua would listen, silent, his mind often wandering. This annoyed You Ruo. For the sake of food, Zhang Hua could sometimes produce a few words, even reproduce some of You Ruo's. From this fragmentary information, You Ruo built an idea of the slaves' situation, and that of their world.

Zhang Hua couldn't understand You Ruo's logic, no matter how hard he tried. Why had You Ruo spent so much time and energy fleeing to this desolate mountain wilderness? He followed You Ruo, his pace flagging, frequently falling far behind. You Ruo waited for him every time, shaking his head in frustration.

'Forget it,' You Ruo finally said one day, his tone pitying. Zhang Hua had lagged behind again. 'Go to my world.' You Ruo knew the nest of monsters he'd escaped filled Zhang Hua with yearning. Perhaps Zhang Hua should be allowed to experience it for himself.

Zhang Hua said nothing. You Ruo had saved his life, after all, possibly more than once. Zhang Hua couldn't just lightly depart after all they'd been through. But he didn't have the courage to follow You Ruo in emancipating the slaves, then calling upon them to free the whole world.

'There is no happiness there,' You Ruo said. He gave his identification number to Zhang Hua. 'In the end you'll understand.'

Zhang Hua nodded. He didn't know how to say goodbye, really. So, he took both of You Ruo's hands in his and shook them with all his might. Then he turned and left in a hurry. Perhaps he feared You Ruo would change his mind.

'In the end you'll know it's too late,' You Ruo said quietly, watching Zhang Hua depart.

He picked up a nearby tree branch, and leaning on it, turned and continued on his way.

7 – Two Worlds

After giving Zhang Hua a general physical examination, this world's machine administrator was astonished: it hadn't known a human being could transform to such a degree!

It gave orders to spare no resources in treating and curing everything.

For the malnutrition, he must be nourished. His skin burns must be treated and healed. The pathological change of his internal organs must be medicated. For the missing testicles, prosthetics would be provided. His health would be restored at all costs!

Zhang Hua had never slept so comfortably.

In his old life, when the daybreak bell rang, he would long for even one more moment of sleep. But this had been impossible. Any attempt to sleep more had brought down the lash of the electric whip. Sleep beyond the bell had become a beautiful dream for him, unattainable, remote.

But now that the dream had been realized, he found it difficult to enjoy its comforts. His internal clock would wake him with a start, and for the first few days he would even scuttle out of bed, helpless against the instinct. Then he would remember where he was, and go back to sleep. But even in deep sleep he would wake randomly sometimes, fearing the electric whip.

This state persisted for a month. And then the dread in his heart slowly withdrew.

Adequate sleep was merely one part of Zhang Hua's recovery. This world took meticulous care of him, which he wasn't used to. He started causing disturbances soon enough. The first time he chose food for himself, having never seen so many delicious options in one place, he insisted on taking more than he needed, going so far as to cheat the machines and make them believe he wasn't full. This accorded well enough with his You Ruo identity, but his digestive problems later that night did not, and he had no choice but to seek medical aid from the machines.

During his general rehabilitation, Zhang Hua saw few other people. Except for a few enthusiastic caregivers and visitors, humans contacted him entirely by audio. All nursing was done by machine. Zhang Hua was, for the time being, unable to adapt to this sort of change. His slave identity, and the master status of machines, had been flipped. Now it was the machines that waited upon him.

*

Abandoned by his guide, You Ruo took a winding, confused path to the region of the slave laborers. Eventually he reached this world's central district, otherwise known as the Capital. His appearance shocked people: none of their physiques were so full-bodied and round, not even the petty technical bourgeoisie of this grim city.

Their gazes gradually turned from envy to hostility. They had been maintaining some minimal level of propriety toward him, but this soon vanished as the permeating enmity boiled over. Machine guards swept in to curb the incipient disturbance, caring nothing for the right and wrong of the affair. You Ruo ended up as injured as those who'd moved to attack him. Finally, covered with cuts and bruises, his clothing torn, You Ruo did all he could to break out of the encirclement of machines and hostile citizens, nearly losing his orientation in this blind rush.

But he wasn't blind. His destination was the work site, the scar in the side of the mountain, the iron mine. The creatures of this city were perhaps incapable of joining his revolution, but he reckoned things would be different among the slave laborers. You Ruo had seen them, the toiling multitudes, from a distance. Here at last were Zhang Hua's former workmates.

He believed in a fundamental instinct that would prompt them to join his struggle.

Although You Ruo was bursting with revolutionary fervor, he was cool-headed when it came to specific actions. Rushing among the slaves to raise a blatant hue and cry, demanding rebellion against the machines, would certainly be futile, and possibly cost him his life. You Ruo needed a properly thought-out strategic countermeasure.

He made his way toward the work site, calling to the nearest laborers in a low voice. At first they were frightened, but as he got closer, presenting himself in all his alien rotundity, they couldn't help staring in awe. Obviously, they'd never seen such a well-fed individual in their lives. You Ruo watched their expressions, approaching cautiously.

At least they don't want to eat me, You Ruo thought, noting they weren't reacting like the savages had. They were betraying suspicion, or awe, not that unsettling hunger. You Ruo would never forget that look.

He threw out some remaining crumbs of food from his pack. Several slaves fell, frantically gathering the gifts. Then more fell upon their comrades to fight for what they could. This feeding frenzy soon alarmed a machine guard, but it merely drove the slaves away with threatening words, then passed inches from a frightened You Ruo without any reaction. Its program was to guard slaves, and You Ruo wasn't on its register.

After it had gone, a bold group of slaves returned. They whispered to each other, their susurrating speech gradually growing louder.

'Who is he?'

'How is he here at leisure, with nothing to do?'

'Why aren't you employed?'

This was asked a number of times, with increasing ire. The slaves were still wary of him, but now several leaders advanced to surround him, as if honor bound to do so. This happened to be their lunch break, so the machines were ignoring this potentially troublesome gathering.

'Why are you all so bothered about me?' You Ruo said, thoroughly puzzled. 'It's the machines that should concern you. They are your enemies!'

He outlined his revolution, to no effect. He preached until he was hoarse, and it made no difference. At first, they seemed to have no malicious intent, merely rifling through his pockets for food as he spoke. Unfortunately, there was nothing left.

He shouldn't have started resisting. That was his mistake.

Initially, he understood they were starving, and he spread his arms and let them search to their heart's content. But when they started examining his weapons and instruments with the curiosity of children, he panicked. He slapped hands away, shoved, and soon he was struggling, gripped on all sides. His instincts took over, and he fought like a trapped animal.

His words had failed. Somehow, these oppressed people hadn't understood, or cared, about the revolution. And now he was on the ground, and they were beating him, seemingly mad with bloodlust.

'Kill him!' they screamed. 'Kill him! Kill him!'

8 – This World is Primary

In a room with almost no light, the thing that vaguely resembled a human opened its eyes.

For the first time in many years, a real human was standing before it.

'After so long, it is surprising that the human body has not changed,' it remarked, suspended in its nutrient fluid. Speaking required no great effort. Although it hadn't used speech to express ideas in ages, machine implants remedied this. 'It's no wonder, I suppose. You have lived in great comfort and enjoyed a relatively high position. It hasn't been necessary to evolve.'

How did it know what You Ruo's former life had been like? He said nothing, still frozen in astonishment. His mind was not reacting properly. At the same time, he was very curious. After all, the inner workings of machine society were being revealed to him.

'Why do you wish to leave my world?' it asked.

You Ruo still couldn't respond.

'Say something, would you? I haven't heard a human speak in so long.'

Finally, You Ruo spoke, and for the first time, to a receptive listener. He held forth on his life and philosophy, nervous at first, but soon with great eloquence.

'Life in my world is indeed relatively nice,' he said, 'but doesn't allow for an ounce of heretical thinking. Human history demonstrates this state of affairs cannot last. I've read my share of history, and I know human nature tends toward freedom.'

'But,' it interrupted, 'are you free now?'

'Free... I don't even know if I can survive in this world of yours.'

'You'll have that answer soon enough,' it said, its tone cold. 'When you ran into Zhang Hua, he told you what it was like here. So why did you come?'

'I believed that here... I could fully realize my worth.'

It seemed to sigh. 'Really? You acted on such a trite and banal idea?'

'What are you anyway?' You Ruo asked, growing anxious.

'I am the administrator of this place.'

'Machines are the administrators here.'

'No,' it said firmly. 'The real administrators are still humans.'

You Ruo waited for this humanlike thing to continue.

'I'm not the only one, of course. There are twenty outstanding minds here, altogether. We supervise the machines. They have no power over us.' For a long time it didn't speak, then went on with assurance. 'The machines have an extraordinary capacity for obedience, after all. And human laborers are the cheapest.'

You Ruo was astonished.

'We twenty minds are enough to run this world,' it said.

'But... to what end?' You Ruo asked. 'Reduced labor costs? Soaring profits? What's it all for?'

'For one thing, your world's consumer goods are supplied by us.' It drank from a straw extending into its tank, possibly fortifying itself for the next revelation. 'And we exchange knowledge, not just physical labor.' It told You Ruo how his world conducted massive scientific experiments here, experiments that required large-scale, cheap human 'participation'.

'But what for?' You Ruo demanded, his worldview in total collapse.

'To explore the cosmos. What else?' Now its tone was full of yearning. 'Humanity's field of view is too narrow. And its efficiency is too low, of course. At the moment, our sort of highly efficient labor arrangement makes immediate study of the cosmos possible.'

'You still have high-level scientists?'

'No need. As I said, twenty outstanding minds are sufficient.' Now this human thing sounded amiable. 'We, the twenty, give rise to unparalleled thinking, not to mention a functional government. Lower level administration is handled by the machines. No human can think faster than a machine, except for us.'

'I still don't understand,' You Ruo said. 'Why retain my world? Why not implement your societal model across the planet?'

'A fine question,' it said, 'and one that we cannot answer at this time. Possibly it is down to historical causes.' This was a first, an admission of incomplete knowledge. 'Whatever the cause, the result has been a compromise between our two worlds.'

You Ruo was dissatisfied with this answer.

'If, one day, aliens pay a visit,' it said, 'your people would make better envoys. We can admit that much.'

This thing isn't human, You Ruo thought, sensing danger, his mind racing. *It's a puppet of the machines.*

'How did you come to decide on your mode of development?' he asked, growing desperate. 'How did you settle on this particular evolutionary path, in terms of knowledge? As an outside observer, I've noticed some... room for improvement. Why not make it twenty-one outstanding minds?'

'Because you are not qualified,' it replied with devastating candor.

*

This candid talk did not make the humanlike thing feel any sympathy for the visitor, or recognize a fellow talented mind. You Ruo was sent to prison. Three days later, he was brought to what seemed an execution room.

'Are you sure you want to do this?' You Ruo said, his tone calm, his legs trembling. His revolution needed the sacrifice of martyrs, of course, and he had prepared himself for this. But it didn't hurt to try.

The two slaves holding him remained expressionless, and unresponsive.

Perhaps they're deaf, You Ruo thought.

He had imagined his martyrdom many times, and some solemn, honorable way to die had always been conferred on him. He hadn't expected this room full of people, the stink of sweat, and the countless children. Why was he being made to advance among these little ones?

The room was vast, making the little machine at the center seem almost comical. As he approached, a black marking on the machine's surface made You Ruo shiver. He did not resist. All his former attempts at resistance had proved futile, so now he gave in. He was fastened to the machine in an unsteady half-sitting position. Below him was something sharp. He couldn't lower himself any further because of that.

You Ruo suddenly understood how the machine worked. What it was for. Not an execution machine after all.

It was the only possibility, really.

The machine activated. You Ruo screamed, and lost consciousness.

Two bloody testicles dropped into the receptacle.

*

When he first woke, it was to piercing pain. When he found the source of the pain, he again lost consciousness. This time from despair.

Later, he found he hadn't yet been assigned specific work. He had to do some minimal level of healing first.

He endured, his spirit defeated, for three days. The pain was not yet gone, and he killed himself by biting off his tongue.

He obviously wasn't a true revolutionary, not psychologically twisted or abnormal enough to see it through. The world would have to wait, possibly many years, for a wiser, stronger person to emerge.

*

Two years later, Zhang Hua died of old age. He was thirty. His laborer's constitution had never adjusted to the easy living conditions.

9 – The World Entire

After Zhang Hua and You Ruo left this world and that, peace prevailed once again, and the sun showed its smiling face to the well-ordered land.

Translated by Andy Dudak

The Easthound

Nalo Hopkinson

Jamaica

Nalo Hopkinson doesn't need any introduction. She is officially a Grand Master of science fiction. An author who inspired a whole generation with classic novels such as *Brown Girl in the Ring* and *Midnight Robber*. An influential editor who helped change the field with work like *So Long Been Dreaming: Postcolonial Visions of the Future* (co-edited with Uppinder Mehan). So instead of an introduction, let me just tell you that I loved 'The Easthound', and I think you will too.

Oh, Black Betty, bam-ba-lam,
Oh, Black Betty, bam-ba-lam.

'The Easthound bays at night,' Jolly said.

Millie shivered. Bad luck to mention the Easthound, and her twin bloody well knew it. God, she shouldn't even be thinking, 'bloody'. Millie put her hands to her mouth to stopper the words in so she wouldn't say them out loud.

'Easthound?' said Max. He pulled the worn black coat closer around his body. The coat had been getting tighter around him these past few months. Everyone could see it. 'Uck the fuh is that Easthound shit?'

Not what; he knew damned well what it was. He was asking Jolly what the hell she was doing bringing the Easthound into their game of Loup-de-lou. Millie wanted to yell at Jolly too.

Jolly barely glanced at Max. She kneeled in front of the fire, staring into it, re-twisting her dreads and separating them at the scalp where they were threatening to grow together. 'It's my first line,' she said. 'You can play or not, no skin off my teeth.'

They didn't talk about skin coming off, either. Jolly should be picking someone to come up with the next line of the game. But Jolly broke the rules when she damned well pleased. Loup-de-lou was her game, after all. She'd invented it. Someone had to come up with a first line. Then they picked the next person. That person had to continue the story by beginning with the last word or two of the line the last person said. And so on until someone closed the loup by ending the story with the first word or two of the very first line. Jolly was so thin. Millie had saved some of the chocolate bar she'd found to share with Jolly, but she knew that Jolly wouldn't take it. If you ate too much, you grew too quickly. Millie'd already eaten most of the chocolate, though. Couldn't help it. She was so hungry all the time!

Max hadn't answered Jolly. He took the bottle of vodka that Sai was holding and chugged down about a third of it. Nobody complained. That was his payment for finding the bottle in the first place. But could booze make you grow, too? Or did it keep you shrinky? Millie couldn't remember which. She fretfully watched Max's Adam's apple bob as he drank.

'The game?' Citron chirped up, reminding them. A twin of the flames of their fire danced in his green eyes. 'We gonna play?'

Right. The game. Jolly bobbed her head yes. Sai, too. Millie said, 'I'm in.' Max sighed and shrugged his yes.

Max took up where Jolly had left off. 'At night the Easthound howls,' he growled, 'but only when there's no moon.' He pointed at Citron.

A little clumsy, Millie thought, but a good second line.

Quickly, Citron picked it up with, 'No moon is so bright as the Easthound's eyes when it spies a plump rat on a garbage heap.' He pointed at Millie.

Garbage heap? What kind of end bit was that? Didn't give her much with which to begin the new loup. Trust Citron to throw her a tough one. And that 'eyes, spies' thing, too. A rhyme in the middle, instead of at the end. Clever bastard. Thinking furiously, Millie louped, 'Garbage heaps high in the... cities of noonless night.'

Jolly said, 'You're cheating. It was "garbage heap", not "garbage heaps".' She gnawed a strip from the edge of her thumbnail, blew the crescented clipping from her lips into the fire.

'Chuh.' Millie made a dismissive motion with her good hand. 'You just don't want to have to continue on with "noonless night".' Smirking, she pointed at her twin.

Jolly started in on the nail of her index finger. 'And you're just not very good at this game, are you, Millie?'

'Twins, stop it,' Max told them.

'I didn't start it,' Jolly countered, through chewed nail bits. Millie hated to see her bite her nails, and Jolly knew it.

Jolly stood and flounced closer to the fire. Over her back she spat the phrase, 'Noonless night, a rat's bright fright, and blood in the bite all delight the Easthound.' The final two words were the two with which they'd begun. Game over. Jolly spat out a triumphant, 'Loup!' First round to Jolly.

Sai slapped the palm of her hand down on the ground between the players. 'Aw, jeez, Jolly! You didn't have to end it so soon, just cause you're mad at your sister! I was working on a great loup.'

'Jolly's only showing off!' Millie said. Truth was, Jolly was right. Millie really wasn't much good at Loup-de-lou. It was only a stupid game, a distraction to take their minds off hunger, off being cold and scared, off watching everybody else and yourself every waking second for signs of sprouting. But Millie didn't want to be distracted. Taking your mind off things could kill you. She was only going along with the game to show the others that she wasn't getting cranky; getting loupy.

She rubbed the end of her handless wrist. Damp was making it achy. She reached for the bottle of vodka where Max had stood it upright in the crook of his crossed legs. 'Nuh-uh-uh,' he chided, pulling it out of her reach and passing it to Citron, who took two pulls at the bottle and coughed.

Max said to Millie, 'You don't get any treats until you start a new game.'

Jolly turned back from the fire, her grinning teeth the only thing that shone in her black silhouette.

'Wasn't me who spoiled that last one,' Millie grumbled. But she leaned back on the packed earth, her good forearm and the one with the missing hand both lying flush against the soil. She considered how to begin. The ground was a little warmer tonight than it had been last night. Spring was coming. Soon, there'd be pungent wild leeks to pull up and eat from the riverbank. She'd been craving their taste all through this frozen winter. She'd been yearning for the sight and taste of green, growing things. Only she wouldn't eat too many of them. You couldn't ever eat your fill of anything, or that might bring out the Hound. Soon it'd be warm enough to sleep outside again. She thought of rats and garbage heaps, and slammed her mind's door shut on the picture. Millie liked sleeping with the air on her skin, even though it was dangerous out of doors. It felt more dangerous indoors, what with everybody growing up.

And then she knew how to start the loup. She said, 'The river swells in May's spring tide.'

Jolly strode back from the fire and took the vodka from Max. 'That's a really good one.' She offered the bottle to her twin.

Millie found herself smiling as she took it. Jolly was quick to speak her mind, whether scorn or praise. Millie could never stay mad at her for long. Millie drank through her smile, feeling the vodka burn its trail down. With her stump she pointed at Jolly and waited to hear how Jolly would Loup-de-lou with the words 'spring tide'.

'The spring's May tide is deep and wide,' louped Jolly. She was breaking the rules again; three words, not two, and she'd added a 'the' at the top, and changed the order around! People shouldn't change stuff, it was bad! Millie was about to protest when a quavery howl crazed the crisp night, then disappeared like a sob into silence.

'Shit!' hissed Sai. She leaped up and began kicking dirt onto the fire to douse it. The others stood too.

'Race you to the house!' yelled a gleeful Jolly, already halfway there at a run.

Barking with forced laughter, the others followed her. Millie, who was almost as quick as Jolly, reached the disintegrating cement steps of the house a split second before Jolly pushed in through the door, yelling 'I win!' as loudly as she could. The others tumbled in behind Millie, shoving and giggling.

Sai hissed, 'Sshh!' Loud noises weren't a good idea.

With a chuckle in her voice, Jolly replied, 'Oh, chill, we're fine. Remember how Churchy used to say that loud noises chased away ghosts?'

Everyone went silent. They were probably all thinking the same thing; that maybe Churchy was a ghost now. Millie whispered, 'We have to keep quiet, or the Easthound will hear us.'

'Bite me,' said Max. 'There's no such thing as an Easthound.' His voice was deeper than it had been last week. No use pretending. He was growing up. Millie put a bit more distance between him and her. Max really was getting too old. If he didn't do the right thing soon and leave on his own, they'd have to kick him out. Hopefully before something ugly happened.

Citron closed the door behind them. It was dark in the house. Millie tried to listen beyond the door to the outside. That had been no wolf howling, and they all knew it. She tried to rub away the pain in her wrist. 'Do we have any aspirin?'

Sai replied, 'I'm sorry. I took the last two yesterday.'

Citron sat with a thump on the floor and started to sob. 'I hate this,' he said slurrily. 'I'm cold and I'm scared and there's no bread left, and it smells of mildew in here—'

'You're just drunk,' Millie told him.

'—and Millie's cranky all the time,' Citron continued with a glare at Millie, 'and Sai farts in her sleep, and Max's boots don't fit him anymore. He's growing up.'

'Shut up!' said Max. He grabbed Citron by the shoulders, dragged him to his feet, and started to shake him. 'Shut up!' His voice broke on the 'up' and ended in a little squeak. It should have been funny, but now he had Citron up against the wall and was choking him. Jolly and Sai yanked at Max's hands. They told him over and over to stop, but he wouldn't. The creepiest thing was, Citron wasn't making any sound. He couldn't. He couldn't get any air. He scrabbled at Max's hands, trying to pull them off his neck.

Millie knew she had to do something quickly. She slammed the bottle of vodka across Max's back, like christening a ship. She'd seen it on TV, when TVs still worked. When you could still plug one in and have juice flow through the wires to make funny cartoon creatures move behind the screen, and your mom wouldn't sprout in front of your eyes and eat your dad and bite your hand off.

Millie'd thought the bottle would shatter. But maybe the glass was too thick, because though it whacked Max's back with a solid thump, it didn't break. Max dropped to the floor like he'd been shot. Jolly put her hands to her mouth. Startled at what she herself had done, Millie dropped the bottle. It exploded when it hit the floor, right near Max's head. Vodka fountained up and out, and then Max was whimpering and rolling around in the booze and broken glass. There were dark smears under him.

'Ow! Jesus! Ow!' He peered up to see who had hit him. Millie moved closer to Jolly.

'Max.' Citron's voice was hoarse. He reached a hand out to Max. 'Get out of the glass, dude. Can you stand up?'

Millie couldn't believe it. 'Citron, he just tried to kill you!'

'I shouldn't have talked about growing up. Jolly, can you find the candles? It's dark in here. Come on, Max.' Citron pulled Max to his feet.

Max came up mad. He shook broken glass off his leather jacket, and stood towering over Millie. Was his chest thicker than it had been? Was that hair shadowing his chin? Millie whimpered and cowered away. Jolly put herself between Millie and Max. 'Don't be a big old bully,' she said to Max. 'Picking on the one-hand girl. Don't be a *dog*.'

It was like a light came back on in Max's eyes. He looked at Jolly, then at Millie. 'You hurt me, Millie. I wouldn't hurt you,' he said to Millie. 'Even if—'

'If… that thing was happening to you,' Jolly interrupted him, 'you wouldn't care who you were hurting. Besides, you were choking Citron, so don't give us that innocent look and go on about not hurting people.'

Max's eyes welled up. They glistened in the candlelight. 'I'll go,' he said drunkenly. His voice sounded high, like the boy he was ceasing to be. 'Soon. I'll go away. I promise.'

'When?' Millie asked softly. They all heard her, though. Citron looked at her with big, wet, doe eyes.

Max swallowed. 'Tomorrow. No. A week.'

'Three days,' Jolly told him. 'Two more sleeps.'

Max made a small sound in his throat. He wiped his hand over his face. 'Three days,' he agreed. Jolly nodded, firmly.

After that, no one wanted to play Loup-de-lou anymore. They didn't bother with candles. They all went to their own places, against the walls so they could keep an eye on each other. Millie and Jolly had the best place, together near the window. That way, if anything bad happened, Jolly could boost Millie out the window. There used to be a low bookcase under that window. They'd burned the wood months ago, for cooking with. The books that had been on it were piled up to one side, and Jolly'd scavenged a pile of old clothes for a bed. Jolly rummaged around under the clothes. She pulled out the gold necklace that their mom had given her for passing French. Jolly only wore it to sleep. She fumbled with the clasp, dropped the necklace, swore under her breath. She found the necklace again and put it on successfully this time. She kissed Millie on the forehead. 'Sleep tight, Mills.'

Millie said, 'My wrist hurts too much. Come with me tomorrow to see if the kids two streets over have any painkillers?'

'Sure, honey.' Warrens kept their distance from each other, for fear of becoming targets if somebody in someone else's warren sprouted. 'But try to get some sleep, okay?' Jolly lay down and was asleep almost immediately, her breathing quick and shallow.

Millie remained sitting with her back against the wall. Max lay on the other side of the room, using his coat as a blanket. Was he sleeping, or just lying there, listening?

She used to like Max. Weeks after the world had gone mad, he'd found her and Jolly hiding under the porch of somebody's house. They were dirty and hungry, and the stench of rotting meat from inside the house was drawing flies. Jolly had managed to keep Millie alive that long, but Millie was delirious with pain, and the place where her hand had been bitten off had started smelling funny. Max had brought them clean water. He'd searched and bargained with the other warrens of hiding kids until he found morphine and antibiotics for Millie. He was the one who'd told them that it looked like only adults were getting sick.

But now Millie was scared of him. She sat awake half the night, watching Max. Once, he shifted and snorted, and the hairs on Millie's arms stood on end. She shoved herself right up close against Jolly. But Max just grumbled and rolled over and kept sleeping. He didn't change. Not this time. Millie watched him a little longer, until she couldn't keep her eyes open. She curled up beside Jolly. Jolly was scrawny, her skin downy with the peach fuzz that Sai said came from starvation. Most of them had it. Nobody wanted to grow up and change, but Jolly needed to eat a little more, just a little. Millie stared into the dark and worried. She didn't know when she fell asleep. She woke when first light was making the window into a glowing blue square. She was cold. Millie reached to put her arm around Jolly. Her arm landed on wadded-up clothing with nobody in it. 'She's gone,' said Citron.

'Whuh?' Millie rolled over, sat up. She was still tired. 'She gone to check the traps?' Jolly barely ate, but she was best at catching gamey squirrels, feral cats, and the occasional raccoon.

'I dunno. I woke up just as the door was closing behind her. She let in a draft.'

Millie leaped to her feet. 'It was Max! He sprouted! He ate her!'

Citron leaped up too. He pulled her into a hug. 'Shh. It wasn't Max. Look, he's still sleeping.'

He was. Millie could see him huddled under his coat.

'See?' said Citron. 'Now hush. You're going to wake him and Sai up.'

'Oh God, I was so scared for a moment.' She was lying; she never stopped being scared. She sobbed and let Citron keep hugging her, but not for long. Things could sneak up on you while you were busy making snot and getting hugs to make you feel better. Millie swallowed back the rest of her tears. She pulled out of Citron's arms. 'Thanks.' She went and checked beside Jolly's side of the bed. Jolly's jacket wasn't there. Neither was her penguin. Ah. 'She's gone to find aspirin for me.' Millie sighed with relief and guilt. 'She took her penguin to trade with. That's almost her most favorite thing ever.'

'Next to you, you mean.'

'I suppose so. I come first, then her necklace, then the penguin.' Jolly'd found the ceramic penguin a long time ago when they'd been scavenging in the wreckage of a drug store. The penguin stood on a circular base, the whole thing about ten inches tall. Its beak was broken, but when you twisted the white base, music played out of it. Jolly had kept it carefully since, wrapped in a torn blouse. She played it once a week and on special occasions. Twisted the base twice only, let the penguin do a slow turn to the few notes of tinny song. Churchy had told them that the penguin was from a movie called *Madagascar*. She'd been old enough to remember old-time stuff like that. It was soon after that that they'd had to kill her.

Millie stared at her and Jolly's sleeping place. There was something... 'She didn't take socks. Her feet must be freezing.' She picked up the pair of socks with the fewest holes in it. 'We have to go find her.'

'You go,' Citron replied. 'It's cold out, and I want to get some more sleep.'

'You know we're not supposed to go anywhere on our own!'

'Yeah, but we do. Lots of times.'

'Except me. I always have someone with me.'

'Right. Like that's any safer than being alone. I'm going back to bed.' He yawned and turned away.

Millie fought the urge to yell at him. Instead she said, 'I claim leader.'

Citron stopped. 'Aw, come on, Millie.'

But Millie was determined. 'Leader. One of us might be in danger, so I claim leader. So you have to be my follower.'

He looked skywards and sighed. 'Fine. Where?'

That meant she was leader. You asked the leader what to do, and the leader told you. Usually everyone asked Jolly what to do, or Max. Now that she had an excuse to go to Jolly, Millie stopped feeling as though something had gnawed away the pit of her stomach. She yanked her coat out of the pile of clothing that was her bed and shrugged it on. 'Button me,' she said to Citron, biting back the 'please'. Leaders didn't say please. They just gave orders. That was the right way to do it.

Citron concentrated hard on the buttons, not looking in Millie's eyes as he did them up. He started in the middle, buttoned down to the last button just below her hips, then stood up to do the buttons at her chest. He held the fabric away from her, so it wouldn't touch her body at all. His fingers didn't touch her, but still her chest felt tingly as Citron did up the top buttons. She knew he was blushing, even though you couldn't tell on his dark face. Hers neither. If it had been Max doing this, his face would have lit up like a strawberry. They found strawberries growing sometimes, in summer.

Leaders didn't blush. Millie straightened up and looked at Citron. He had such a baby face. If he was lucky, he'd never sprout. She'd heard that some people didn't. Max said it was too soon to tell, because the pandemic had only started two years ago, but Millie liked to hope that some kids would avoid the horrible thing. No temper getting worse and worse. No changing all of a sudden into something different and scary. Millie wondered briefly what happened to the ones who didn't sprout, who just got old. Food for the Easthound, probably. 'Maybe we should go…' Millie began to ask, then remembered herself. Leaders didn't ask, they told. 'We're going over by the grocery first,' she told Citron. 'Maybe she's just checking her traps.'

'She took her music box to check her traps?'

'Doesn't matter. That's where we're going to go.' She stuffed Jolly's socks into her coat pocket, then shoved her shoulder against the damp-swollen door and stepped out into the watery light of an early spring morning. The sun made her blink.

Citron asked, 'Shouldn't we get those two to come along with us? You know, so there's more of us?'

'No,' growled Millie. 'Just now you wanted me to go all alone, but now you want company?'

'But who does trading this early in the morning?'

'We're not going to wake Max and Sai, okay? We'll find her ourselves!'

Citron frowned. Millie shivered. It was so cold out that her nose hairs froze together when she breathed in. Like scattered pins, tiny, shiny daggers of frost edged the sidewalk slabs and the new spring leaves of the small maple tree that grew outside their squat. Trust Jolly to make her get out of a warm bed to go looking for her on a morning like this. She picked up three solid throwing rocks. They were gritty with dirt and the cold of them burned her fingers. She stuffed them into her jacket pocket, on top of Jolly's socks. Citron had the baseball bat he carried everywhere. Millie turned up her collar and stuck her hand into her jeans pocket. 'C'mon.'

Jolly'd put a new batch of traps over by that old grocery store. The roof was caved in. There was no food in the grocery anymore, or soap, or cough medicine. Everything had been scavenged by the nearby warrens of kids, but animals sometimes made nests and shit in the junk that was left. Jolly'd caught a dog once. A gaunt poodle with dirty, matted hair. But they didn't eat dogs, ever. You were what you ate. They'd only killed it in an orgy of fury and frustration that had swelled over them like a river.

> *Black Betty had a child,*
> *Bam-ba-lam,*
> *That child's gone wild,*
> *Bam-ba-lam.*

Really, it was Millie who'd started it, back before everything went wrong, two winters ago. They'd been at home. Jolly sitting on the living-room floor that early evening, texting with her friends, occasionally giggling at something one of them said. Millie and Dad on the couch, sharing a bowl of raspberries. All of them watching some old-time cartoon movie on TV about animals that could do kung fu. Waiting for Mum to come home from work. Because then they would order pizza. It was pizza night. Dad getting a text message on his phone. Dad holding the phone down by his knee to make out the words, even though his eyesight was just fine, he said. Jolly watching them, waiting to hear if it was Mum, if she'd be home soon. Millie leaning closer to Dad and squinting at the tiny message in the phone's window. Mouthing the words silently. Then frowning. Saying, 'Mum says she's coming home on the easthound train?'

Dad falling about laughing. 'Eastbound, sweetie.'

There hadn't been an Easthound before that. It was Millie who'd called it, who'd made it be. Jolly'd told her that wasn't true, that she didn't make the pandemic just by reading a word wrong, that the world didn't work that way. But the world didn't work anymore the way it used to, so what did Jolly know? Even if she was older than Millie.

Jolly and Millie's family had assigned adjectives to the girls early on in their lives. Millie was The Younger One (by twenty-eight and three-quarter minutes – the midwife had been worried that Mum would need a C-Section to get Millie out). Jolly was The Kidder. She liked jokes and games. She'd come up with Loup-de-lou to help keep Millie's mind off the agony when she'd lost her hand. Millie'd still been able to feel the missing hand there, on the end of her wrist, and pain wouldn't let her sleep or rest, and all the adults in the world were sprouting and trying to kill off the kids, and Max was making her and Jolly and Citron move to a new hiding place every few days, until he and Jolly figured out the thing about sprinkling peppermint oil to hide their scent trails so that sprouteds couldn't track them. That was back before Sai had joined them, and then Churchy. Back before Churchy had sprouted on them one night in the dark as they were all sharing half a stale bread loaf and a big liter bottle of flat cola, and Max and Citron and Sai had grabbed anything heavy or sharp they could find and waled away at the thing that had been Churchy just seconds before, until it lay still on the ground, all pulpy and bloody. And the whole time, Jolly had stayed near still-weak Millie, brandishing a heavy frying pan and muttering, 'It's okay, Mills. I won't let her get you.'

The feeling was coming back, like her hand was still there. Her wrist had settled into a throbbing ache. She hoped it wasn't getting infected again.

Watchfully, they walked down their side street and turned onto the main street in the direction of the old grocery store. They walked up the middle of the empty road. That way, if a sprouted came out of one of the shops or alleyways, they might have time to see it before it attacked.

The burger place, the gas station, the little shoe repair place on the corner; Millie tried to remember what stores like that had been like before. When they'd had unbroken windows and unempty shelves. When there'd been people shopping in them and adults running them, back when adults used to be just grown-up people suspicious of packs of schoolkids in their stores, not howling, sharp-toothed child-killers with dank, stringy fur and paws instead of hands. Ravenous monsters that grew and grew so quickly that you could watch it happen, if you were stupid enough to stick around. Their teeth, hair, and claws lengthened, their bodies getting bigger and heavier minute by minute, until they could no longer eat quickly enough to keep up with the growth, and they weakened and died a few days after they'd sprouted.

Jolly wasn't tending to her traps. Millie swallowed. 'Okay, so we'll go check with the warren over on Patel Street. They usually have aspirin and stuff.' She walked in silence, except for the worry voice in her head.

Citron said, 'That tree's going to have to start over.'

'What?' Millie realized she'd stopped at the traffic light out of habit, because it had gone to red. She was such an idiot.

And so was Citron, for just going along with her. She started walking again. Citron tagged along, always just a little behind.

'The maple tree,' he puffed. When you never had enough to eat, you got tired quickly. 'The one outside our place. It put its leaves out too early, and now the frost has killed them. It'll have to start over.'

'Whatever.' Then she felt guilty for being so crabby with him. What could she say to make nice? 'Uh, that was a nice line you made in Loup-de-lou last night. The one with eyes and spies in it.'

Citron smiled at her. 'Thanks. It wasn't quite right, though. Sprouteds have bleedy red eyes, not shiny ones.'

'But your line wasn't about sprouteds. It was about the... the Easthound.' She looked all around and behind her. Nothing.

'Thing is,' Citron replied, so quietly that Millie almost didn't hear him, 'we're all the Easthound.'

Instantly, Millie swatted the back of his head. 'Shut up!'

'Ow!'

'Just shut up! Take that back! It's not true!'

'Stop making such a racket, willya?'

'So stop being such a loser!' She was sweating in her jacket, her skinny knees trembling. So hungry all the time. So scared.

Citron's eyes widened. 'Millie—!'

He was looking behind her. She turned, hand fumbling in her jacket pocket for her rocks. The sprouted bowled her over while her hand was still snagged in her pocket. Thick, curling fur and snarling, and teeth as long as her pinkie. It grabbed her. Its paws were like catcher's mitts with claws in them. It howled and briefly let her go. It's in pain, she thought wonderingly, even as she fought her hand out of her pocket and tried to get out from under the sprouted. All that quick growing. It must hurt them. The sprouted snapped at her face, missed. They were fast and strong when they first sprouted, but clumsy in their ever-changing bodies. The sprouted set its jaws in her chest. Through her coat and sweater, its teeth tore into her skin. Pain. Teeth sliding along her ribs. Millie tried to wrestle the head off her. She got her fingers deep into the fur around its neck. Then an impact jerked the sprouted's head sideways. Citron and his baseball bat, screaming, 'Die, die, die!' as he beat the sprouted. It leaped for him. It was already bigger. Millie rolled to her feet, looking around for anything she could use as a weapon. Citron was keeping the sprouted at bay, just barely, by swinging his bat at it. It advanced on him, howling in pain with every step forwards.

Sai seemed to come out of nowhere. She had the piece of rebar she carried whenever she went out. The three of them raged at the sprouted, screaming and hitting. Millie kicked and kicked. The sprouted screamed back, in pain or fury. Its eyes were all bleedy. It swatted Citron aside, but he got up and came at it again. Finally it wasn't fighting any more. They kept hitting it until they were sure it was dead. Even after Sai and Citron had stopped, Millie stomped the sprouted. With each stomp she grunted, in thick animal rage at herself for letting it sneak up on her, for leaving the warren without her knife. Out of the corner of her eye she could see a few kids that had crept out from other warrens to see what the racket was about. She didn't care. She stomped.

'Millie! Millie!' It was Citron. 'It's dead!'

Millie gave the bloody lump of hair and bone and flesh one more kick, then stood panting. Just a second to catch her breath, then they could keep looking for Jolly. They couldn't stay there long. A dead sprouted could draw others. If one sprouted was bad, a feeding frenzy of them was worse.

Sai was gulping, sobbing. She looked at them with stricken eyes. 'I woke up and I called to Max and he didn't answer, and when I went over and lifted his coat,' Sai burst into gusts of weeping, 'there was only part of his head and one arm there. And bones. Not even much blood.' Sai clutched herself and shuddered. 'While we were sleeping, a sprouted came in and killed Max and ate most of him, even licked up his blood, and we didn't wake up! I thought it had eaten all of you! I thought it was coming back for me!'

Something gleamed white in the broken mess of the sprouted's corpse. Millie leaned over to see better, fighting not to gag on the smell of blood and worse. She had to crouch closer. There was lots of blood on the thing lying in the curve of the sprouted's body, but with chilly clarity, Millie recognized it. It was the circular base of Jolly's musical penguin. Millie looked over at Citron and Sai. 'Run,' she told them. The tears coursing down her face felt cool. Because her skin was so hot now.

'What?' asked Sai. 'Why?'

Millie straightened. Her legs were shaking so much they barely held her up. That small pop she'd felt when she pulled on the sprouted's neck. 'A sprouted didn't come into our squat. It was already in there.' She opened her hand to show them the thing she'd pulled off the sprouted's throat in her battle with it; Jolly's gold necklace. Instinct often led sprouteds to return to where the people they loved were. Jolly had run away to protect the rest of her warren from herself. 'Bloody run!' Millie yelled at them. 'Go find another squat! Somewhere I won't look for you! Don't you get it? I'm her twin!'

First Citron's face then Sai's went blank with shock as they understood what Millie was saying. Citron sobbed, once. It might have been the word 'Bye'. He grabbed Sai's arm. The two of them stumbled away. The other kids that had come out to gawk had disappeared back to their warrens. Millie turned her back so she couldn't see what direction Sai and Citron were moving in, but she could hear them, more keenly than she'd ever been able to hear. She could smell them. The Easthound could track them. The downy starvation fuzz on Millie's arm was already coarser. The pain in her handless wrist spiked. She looked at it. It was aching because the hand was starting to grow in again. There were tiny fingers on the end of it now. And she needed to eat so badly.

When had Jolly sprouted? Probably way more than twenty-eight and three-quarters minutes ago. Citron and Sai's only chance was that Millie had always done everything later than her twin.

Still clutching Jolly's necklace, she began to run, too – in a different direction. Leeks, she told the sprouting Hound, fresh leeks. You like those, right? Not blood and still-warm, still-screaming flesh. You like leeks. The Hound wasn't fully come into itself yet. It was almost believing her that leeks would satisfy its hunger. And it didn't understand that she couldn't swim. You're thirsty too, right? she told it.

It was.

Faster, faster, faster, Millie sped towards the river, where the spring tide was running deep and wide.

That child's gone wild.
Oh, Black Betty, bam-ba-lam.

Loup...

Dead Man, Awake, Sing to the Sun!

Pan Haitian

China

I'd asked translator Joel Martinsen to help me with some new Chinese SF stories, and he sent me this unusual tale by Pan Haitian. I couldn't resist sneaking it in! It was only when I came to writing this introduction that I realized I'd met Pan before, on my visit to China back in 2000, when we were both, it has to be said, somewhat younger. So it's a double delight for me to be publishing this captivating story by an old friend here for the first time. The story was translated by Joel Martinsen and is original to this anthology.

1

Death isn't the hardest thing, although that realization can take a long time to come. People jam onto the subway as usual, clock into work, attend boring meetings, and go to sleep. Little by little their joints stiffen, their toes turn cold, and they get more and more exhausted, but everyone assumes it's just the toll of the urban lifestyle. It's only when they're in the hospital with a flatline on the buzzing heart monitor and a zero reading for blood pressure, respiration, and temperature, and the doctor announces they're dead, that they begin to speculate: perhaps I was dead already.

2

I became vaguely aware of the news of my death some time after it happened.

These days doctors aren't too keen on telling patients their diagnosis, but tend to glance over the lab results and say, 'You, go to the back. Follow the orderlies to Building 2 Concentration.'

Our good habits have been trained by years of experience – we know when we should ask questions and when we shouldn't. This situation was the kind where one shouldn't ask questions, but out of a certain anxiety, or maybe a desire to stall for time, I pushed back a little: 'My insurance card is outside... with the nurse.'

'You won't need it.' The doctor raised an eyebrow ironically. 'Hurry up. Do you expect the orderlies to wait a lifetime for you?'

3

At the 'concentration' I met the dead man Lao Jia.

He was an elderly rural teacher. Three decades breathing in chalk dust only to die the very day he was laid off.

Next I met Lao Xu the knockoff iPad vendor, Mai Fang the jitney driver, Ou Ni the bootleg bookseller, Fan Congliang the master welder, Hu Shufang the waiter, Pang Guangdu the deliveryman, Bai Qingsan the hairdresser, Ji Xiaoting the outsider scientist, and Uncle Tong the potter with stage III pneumoconiosis. The living dead these days are mostly those who used to live hard lives.

No rich people.

Rich people never seem to die.

4

The riddle of the undead:

We're different from rigid corpses laid out in the morgue.

Biologically, our legs get stiff but remain mobile; our temperature drops but not as low as cold-blooded animals; the germs in our filthy bodies are neither stranger nor more numerous than those of normal people.

Psychologically, our emotional responses become incredibly calm, and we adopt a submissive attitude toward any sort of external stimuli.

Not many scientists have studied the living dead phenomenon. Judging from information circulating within the living dead community, combined with research from the deceased outsider scientist Ji Xiaoting, we are inclined to believe that certain unfulfilled wishes cause us to die incompletely.

For example: Lao Jia never heard from his daughter after she got married in far-off Shanxi, and he wanted to see her one more time. Fan Congliang was stumped by his wife running off with a hairdresser and just wanted to ask her why. Uncle Tong remembered his teenage son's unresolved tuition. My own request was a small one: I only wanted to give my girlfriend a present. Nothing special, really, except that in all the years we were together I never once gave her a birthday gift.

A wish left hanging.

Or you might call it: a soul.

5

There's nothing especially uncomfortable about turning dead, except you're thirsty. Really, really thirsty. So extreme a thirst it's like an entire desert has taken up residence in your body. Coronal flames erupt from under your tongue. Sand flows through your veins. It's a survival test conducted in a three-thousand-degree blast furnace. Every step is like dragging your legs out of quicksand. A layer of salt collects on your upper palate. Every square kilometer is inhabited by a drought demon.

Thirst.

6

As the guard escorted us to the cemetery, we saw a pool of rainwater beside the road. The clear blue water reflected the post-rain azure sky and the city clothed in cheerful colors.

It was only when we drew nearer that we noticed the floating algae and plastic bags, the handful of tadpoles twitching out their short underwater lives, and the thousand gray midges treating the surface as their playground. A passing dog raised a hind leg suspiciously before bounding away in satisfaction.

God knows what else was in the water that we didn't see, but that's when the advantage of being dead became clear.

Who the hell cares about dying a second time?

Germs.

Toxins.

Hexavalent chromium.

None of it mattered.

The guard let loose with a thunder of cursing and a storm of punches and kicks, but there was no stopping us. We lay down beside the water and drank our fill.

7

Our journey home.

They describe central processing like this: the government provides each of the living dead a wooden coffin and a cemetery plot totally free of charge. We'll lie there in our coffins, dead to the world, for decades, until our bodies dissolve into water.

This unbinding process is the sole destination for the living dead.

Some of the dead are entirely water already apart from a remaining wrapper of skin. They're fully prepared, needing only an opportunity, a reason, a slight impulse to complete that last thrilling jump.

But the government hasn't bothered to research what that impulse might be.

They love coffins.

More, faster, better, cheaper.

The standard solution to every problem.

Unbinding into water would be a release, for sure, but I was still a little scared by the idea of spending lonely decades shut up in a dark coffin waiting for that moment.

8

The guard.

The guard was, like all of us, basically someone surviving off his physical labor. He was in his fifties and able-bodied, with a round face rimmed with a sparse beard and cat-like forehead wrinkles.

His attitude toward us was hard to read. Sometimes he displayed compassion, other times exceptional cruelty.

When we crossed the street, he'd offer an arm to those of us who had trouble walking, and he once gave a cigarette to Lao Jia when a craving hit. Disorder in the ranks (like the time we scrambled for a drink) would bring his abuse to the surface. Beneath his orderly face, an occasional trace of warmth would show through.

On various occasions, the guard demonstrated that he was a man of principles and standards.

For example, when a crusty, bespectacled dead man said to

him 'if you're the only guard, then who monitors you?' he blew up, and taught the dead man a harsh lesson with an iron bar. As far as I am aware, that dead man is still searching for a rib and some of his teeth.

The guard's catchphrases were 'Everyone's got it tough', and 'People in different situations see things differently'.

So when he called Cui Xiaoying out of the crowd of the dead, we tried to understand things from his perspective.

9

Even dead, Cui Xiaoying was a lovely woman, with a soft waist, pert breasts, and legs at least three and a half feet long. When she was alive she had been a nightclub hostess, sleeping during the day and working at night. Her death came as a result of a parade showing off the successes of an anti-vice campaign.

It was nearly evening when we arrived at the cemetery.

Rows of tombstones standing like nails in the twilight staked the fleeting sunlight securely in the mud.

The guard said, 'Everyone's got it tough. It's nighttime and I've got to dig your graves. Think about it from my perspective and you'll see it's only natural.'

Cui Xiaoying squirmed in the mud, and when her clothes were stripped off, she burst into tears. You can't blame her for not cooperating, especially as it just so happened that her wish was to spend one day as a woman with dignity.

Her muffled screaming caused a bit of commotion in the ranks of the dead.

The guard didn't remove his coat. He wore an armband on his sleeve. That armband meant order, rank, command.

We had to get used to this. We were already used to this.

The guard's movements were vigorous as he raped Cui Xiaoying. He lay atop the pale, limp body grunting and shouting and went to work like an old steam engine climbing a hill, producing noise like a whale's blowhole and motion like a mare's churning hoofs, until he choked out one final, bird-like cry and threw himself backward into a C-shape with both hands in the air, like a horse rearing up at the end of a heroic movie.

He remained motionless in that position.

After a while, Lao Jia screwed up the courage to go over and take his pulse.

'Dead,' he said.

'Dead?'

We looked at each other wide-eyed.

Cui Xiaoying crawled out from under the guard, confusion and panic on her face.

A leer was frozen on the guard's lips, and his dull eyes peered at us like a dead fish.

A tiny, practically invisible vessel near his heart had burst, rendering his body rock-hard and more thoroughly dead than we were.

'And us?' one of the dead murmured in the darkness. 'Are we free?'

10

The word 'free' scared us a little at first.

But once someone turned and began to run, we reflexively followed with no hesitation.

In our panic we fled in no particular direction.

As we climbed a footbridge over the train tracks, someone plummeted off, head over heels, but she got up again after lying there for a while, rubbed her head, and said, 'That hurt.'

Someone who knew her said, 'Girl, that's not the first time you've slipped and banged your head.'

She climbed up again, giggling at the memory of how her death had been caused by an attempt to vault over a guardrail while crossing a road. Liu Xiang's hurdles had been shown over and over in slow motion on TV in those days, but accidents still happened from time to time to ordinary folks with enthusiasm but no skills or training.

That episode brought us to the realization that undeath was itself a kind of freedom.

A few of the dead who had been more knowledgeable in life – Lao Jia, Hu Shufang, Bai Qingsan, and Ji Xiaoting – gathered everyone together for a serious discussion of one possible option: keeping far away from the coffins and blending into the population to continue our former lives.

The living dead had an enormous advantage when it came to employment. The most dangerous jobs – the ones lacking labor protections, the ones understaffed due to harsh work environments – were those where we could quickly distinguish ourselves.

The living dead also had an enormous advantage in everyday life. Toxic milk, gutter oil, melamine, Sudan red – we took to this country like fish to water.

'Do you know why people are afraid of us?' asked the first-generation living dead scientist Ji Xiaoting, playing up the suspense with some timely glasses adjustment. 'Because the zombie disease is contagious. And the mechanism is exceptionally simple.'

'What mechanism?' all of us hollered.

'Biting.'

Silence descended as we started thinking about how this information would change our lives.

On that rusty, tottering footbridge, the first National Living Dead Congress drew up a plan of action.

A few of those acquaintances later became famous as living dead leaders, their grinning portraits hung up in every conference hall.

11

To the best of my knowledge:

One became a coal miner and doubled the squad's production for that month.

One became a circus performer, staging difficult acrobatics without a safety rope, and ended up a celebrity and national hero.

One became a train driver, piloting through thunderstorms to break the record for safe, accident-free operation.

One went to work for a Big Four accounting firm, and it wasn't long before all staff could work 24-7 without collapsing.

One went to work for Sina, and that very night, everyone's followers increased dramatically.

Some became national leaders… 'In which department?' you ask. I'm sorry, that's confidential.

Whatever the field, they kept themselves well-hidden. Discovery still meant centralized destruction.

I've seen the private execution grounds set up by the living where they attack the dead from all sides with clubs, iron bars, and nail-studded V-belts. Traditional methods of dealing with us vary: a cross staked through the heart, decapitation with a machete, live burial, burning, drowning in a well. Lots and lots of ways.

Not one is guided by science.

Very few have been successful in actually killing us.

12

After fleeing the cemetery that day, I broke contact with my comrades and got a job at a gas station. I had little interest in their plan to seize cities. I guess, since I had been unambitious in life, the prospect of founding a new world was something that didn't move me either way. I just wanted the peace to be dead and get on with the daily grind of life.

Watering down the fuel, adjusting the price meters, oiling the customers, adjusting the price meters, dealing with inspectors, adjusting the price meters, mopping the floor, collecting minimum wage: my life was simple and satisfactory.

The pungent odor of gasoline on my body covered the stench of death, and while my legs were somewhat uncooperative, my work didn't require me to move much. My survival skills grew by the day, and I could even crack a casual joke or two with some of the regulars.

My companions were hard at work all across the country, made clear to me from observing customers who came to fill up. I could recognize them from their indifference to life, the dullness in their eyes in particular. The living dead population grew proportionally larger along this busy road, and more importantly, their cars were increasingly high-end.

I was always thirsty, but even if I didn't drink I wouldn't die. I figured the dead were in a state of constant dehydration, with thirst being merely a psychological side-effect. I also assumed that I would live forever while I awaited the day that the living dead obtained supreme power.

That day wouldn't be too far off.

13

'Everyone's got it tough,' the guard had said. You've got to look at problems from different perspectives.

From a dead perspective, there was absolutely nothing wrong with turning this into a dead society.

It would be calmer, more rational, and more harmonious than today's world population.

No exploitation of the dead by the living, no discrimination, no wealth gap. The cost of living would bottom out with no need to eat or drink, and everyone would swiftly achieve absolute equality.

14

Things went on for a few years, and then the world began to slosh around like a bottle of water.

Reports came of riots in certain places, but they were distant and feeble and quickly dissipated in the ocean of information. No mention on the evening news, no reports in the newspapers. Only shadows lingered online and in chats, but traces could be seen in the hurried pace and stony faces of pedestrians, indicating that some of these things had actually happened.

The unrest hadn't spread to my dinky gas station, since every incident seemed to be suppressed immediately. But suppression was like layers of paper wrapped around a coal; it would be consumed by fire sooner or later.

15

One night I was jolted awake by muffled thunder, and in a daze I heard death on enormous wings pass overhead in the roiling black clouds.

Before dawn, a disorganized flow of cars surged out from the large cities on the coast, heading west. All of the expressways, national highways, provincial routes, county roads, and temporary routes were chock-full of cars, horns, and accidents.

Business was crazy at the gas station. Our boss kicked all the staff out of bed to pull overtime shifts and then started making calls to source fuel, although nine out of ten went unanswered. Not realizing what this meant, he worked himself up into apoplectic rage while paying his respects to his suppliers' ancestors.

I kept working my job at the pump until a white sedan pulled into my lane.

There at the wheel was my girlfriend from back in my living days. The sight of her was like a knife to my heart. All these years and I'd almost forgotten her, but now, all of a sudden, here she was.

I had a hard time remaining upright as resumed emotions coursed through my body after such a long interruption, and if I hadn't been dead, I'm sure the intense release of toxins would have taken me out.

I could have cried, but there was no moisture in my body.

She was a lot skinnier and seemed exhausted and on edge. She flinched when a leaf landed on her windshield. I didn't recognize the car, but it showed its age and had probably been down a lot of roads.

'Fill it with 93.' She hadn't recognized me, but spoke to Liu Ang, another attendant. 'I've driven a full day and night. I'm dead tired.'

'It shows,' he said with a twinkle in his eye. He always teased the ladies.

'Are there living dead here, too?' she asked.

'I don't know what you're talking about,' my associate answered.

'But wherever I go, the dead are everywhere. They've occupied Shanghai, and they'll be headed this way any moment. They're killing everyone they find.'

We had been hearing similar news all morning, and Liu Yang was tired of them. 'Give me a chance, and I'll let you die happy.'

She didn't hear him. She had fallen asleep gripping the steering wheel.

I quietly approached her where she slept and got close enough to hear her dreamy sighs. The back seat was empty, not stuffed with luggage like other cars, empty except for a dusty stack of missing person fliers. Her dream fluttered erratically like that leaf stuck to her windshield.

I was transfixed by the sight of her soft, white neck, and an irrepressible thirst occupied my mind.

One bite, and eternal life would be hers.

It was the best gift I could give.

I quietly closed my mouth and let flesh and blood flow between my teeth.

The world order was being reestablished, was it not?

We could sit stiffly together on a bench to watch the falling leaves, decay slowly together, dehydrate and shrink together, let the flies hover behind our heads together.

It really was the best gift. The best world.

A world without the life-and-death struggle to survive.

A world with no need for love, no need for emotion, no need for forgiveness, no need for hate, no need for grief, no need for mercy.

Water roared in my belly as a sensation of wetness soaked my heels and slowly rose, flooding my abdomen, then rising to my torso before suddenly cresting over a seawall strong enough to hold back the Pacific and sweeping aside everything before it. My desiccated mind was a deserted island. Sight and hearing drowned in the ocean depths. I heard the singing of seashells, felt the pull of the moon. Torrential rain washed over the ridges and grooves of my brain and scoured the dry powder of my emotions into a twenty-thousand league spiral at the bottom of the sea.

The next journey was hers to take alone.

I drew close to her ear and whispered:

I give you your freedom, and my death.

Translated by Joel Martinsen

Salvaging Gods

Jacques Barcia

Brazil

Jacques is another author I go a long way back with – he was in my *Apex Book of World SF 2* with a terrific story, and of course I had to have him here. I loved 'Salvaging Gods', which also echoes some of the urgent concerns reflected in stories in the first volume of this anthology. Can we say 'salvagepunk'? Whatever you want to call it, step into the strange and compelling world of the gods: I don't think you will be sorry.

G orette found her second godhead buried under piles of plastic bottles, holy symbols, used toilet paper and the severed face of an avatar. No matter how much the scavengers asked, the people from Theodora just wouldn't separate organic from non-biodegradable, from divine garbage. They threw out their used-up gods along with what was left of their meals, their burnt lamps, broken refrigerators, tires, stillborn babies and books of prayer. And when the convoys carrying society's leftovers passed through the town's gates, some lazy bureaucrat would mark in a spreadsheet that another mountain was raised in that municipal sanitary landfill, the Valley of the Nephilim. And to hell with the consequences.

Her father says no dead god is dead enough that it can't be remade in our own image. The old man can spend hours rambling about over-consumption, the gnostic crisis, the impact of all those mystical residues poisoning the soil and the underground streams, how children are born malformed and prone to mediumship, and how unfair it is that only the rich have access to miracles. People will do what's more comfortable, not what's best for everyone, he'd finally say. It's far easier to buy new deities than try to reuse them. So he taught her how to recycle old gods and turn them into new ones, mostly, she believed, because he wanted to make a difference. Or maybe because he was the one true atheist left in the world.

It was a small one, that godhead, and not in a very good shape. Pale silver, dusty, scratched surface and glowing only slightly underneath the junk. At best, thought Gorette, it'd have only a few hundred lines of code she'd be able to salvage. Combined with some fine statues and pieces of altars she'd found early that morning, perhaps she'd be able to assemble one or two more deities to the community's public temple at Saint Martin. The neighborhood she was raised in had only recently been urbanized, so that meant the place was not officially a slum anymore. But still, miracles were quite a phenomenon down in the suburbs.

'Hey, Daddy. Found another one,' Gorette said, covering her eyes from the burning light of midday. 'Can we go home now, please?'

The egg-shaped thing had the pulse of a dying heart, and fitted almost perfectly in her adolescent hand. So she arranged a place for it amongst the relics in her backpack, inside the folds of a ragged piece of loincloth, and into a beaten-up thurible where it'd be safe enough to survive the hour-long ride back to the city.

Her father stood next to a marble totem, sweeping the field with a kirlian detector. The pillar was part of a discarded surround-sound system with speakers the size of his chest, and served as a landmark to the many scavengers exploring the waste dump. When he heard his daughter calling him, he took his gas mask off and said, 'That depends.' His low-toned voice coming like a sigh, tired. 'Do you think this will do? We're running out of code and there are many open projects in the lab.'

A plastic bag some ten yards away from her smelled of rotting flesh. Animal sacrifice, she knew, and the vultures seemed to have noticed that too. 'Yeah,' she lied, 'it's a bit wasted, but I think it has a lot of good code in it. Never seen one of these, so I suppose it's a quite new model.' She desperately needed to take that stink out of her body and today she hoped was water day. 'Is it water day today, Daddy?'

The old man picked up one last relic, a fang or something, and examined it close to his thick glasses. He nodded to the object and put it in a sac he carried tied to his waist. 'No, it's not. The Palace said three days ago that they'd reinforce the water gods cluster, so the suburb's rationing would drop to two days. But of course that didn't happen.' He finally walked to Gorette and scratched her dreadlocks, trying to smile. 'Maybe you can build a water god with the godhead you found, huh?'

*

Gorette made her first wish that evening, after incubating some of the new godhead's code in an altar of her own design. It was built out of the remains of a semi-defaced idol, a one-eyed marble bust wearing a tall orange hat, adorned with shattered crystals, split dragon horns, praying cords and barbed wire. That last bit just to make sure everything would stand in place. The godhead rested inside the same thurible Gorette had used to cradle it safely back from the Valley of the Nephilim. But now the metal egg had dozens of acupuncture needles trespassing its shell, and every single one was linked to hair-thin optical fiber threads, shining with divine code, feeding a green phosphorus monitor with data.

Without warning. It just woke up.

When the loading bar hit 100 percent, the stone bust opened its one eye, fluidly, staring directly at her. She fell back from the chair, startled, and stared back at the thing's physiognomy from where she stood. From the floor up.

It was her first attempt at a new design model, one that toyed with disharmony instead of symmetry. Profanity instead of divinity. Good hardware, her dad says, is as important as good code. But harmony. Harmony is the key. The problem is that new gods are coming with even more complex, specialized godheads, their kernels incompatible with older or malfunctioning holy paraphernalia. She decided to try out the new approach and, to her surprise, it worked.

'I want a fucking bath,' Gorette said, pointing a finger to the bust. 'A *warm* bath. Now.'

The stone in the god's crippled face moved like if it was made out of clay. Smooth. No, it moved like that stop-motion movie, what's its name, the one that always airs on holidays and Friday evenings. The one dad just loves to watch when he's back from the Valley.

'As you wish,' it said coldly.

A sound of streaming water echoed from the bathroom and almost instantly the smell of steam and soap and essential oils filled up the room. She grinned, and jumping over her feet ran towards the shower, undressing on her way. Is it lavender? Maybe birch. Arnica in the white cloud. She felt she was clean even before she could reach the shower, she felt the dirt collapsing, decanting on the floor before she could have a chance to lay in the tub and rest.

A bathtub. 'A bathtub?'

She looked back at the one-eyed god running miracles in her room. 'You made me a bathtub.' The idol remained still. She stood there for a few more seconds trying to figure out how her jury-rigged water god had made her a complete bath, with a bathtub, aromatic oils and, now she saw it, the finest bathing gown. Collateral miracles were not unheard of, but modern godheads had filters to prevent the danger of leaking energy. Motionless, the god just kept staring forwards, to nowhere in particular, its exposed wire guts transmitting magical pulses to the screen, blipping a green dot like the apparels in private hospitals, monitoring a wide-eyed comatose half-head, an undead, glitchy deity. Gorette felt like checking her complementary coding, but confessed to herself the hot pool of perfumed water was too tempting to be ignored. After all, feeling clean and relaxed she'd have more chance of debugging her creation.

That's it. She immersed herself in the tub and let all her worries trail off, evaporate.

*

After the bathtub miracle, the god produced a new set of porcelain plates, when Gorette only commanded it to clean the dishes. Days later she asked for ice and got a refrigerator and a minibar. Then the thought of a nice meal generated spiced fish. And, one night, the sound of a calm, streaming river came as a lullaby. And rain cooled a hot day. And a smile painted watercolor on canvas. On and on, over the course of a week, her tiniest, involuntary wishes were fulfilled and as much as she tried, she couldn't find the bug in the god's code tree. Okay, after the tenth attempt, the effort to fix the problem wasn't that strong-willed. But Dad had taught her a bug could untap the power of a god, mollifying reality in its close vicinity, causing the neighborhood's divine networks to go haywire. It was dangerous, she knew.

She spent days and nights trying to fix it, trying to combine source codes distilled from newer godheads, but nothing seemed to work. She decided she'd destroy the thing before it caused her trouble.

A dead boy changed her mind.

It was Monday morning and Gorette swept the water god off her working bench into a big cardboard box laying on the floor. She just discarded it, trying not to think much about getting rid of her first creation. The thing fell inside the box, a stone punch enveloped in barbed wire. Gorette gave the god a last inspection and could see that the cold half-face was looking upwards from its new room. She met its gaze one last time and closed the box, decided to sell its parts in the market for whatever the merchants gave for it.

The girl picked up the box and went downstairs, hardly able to keep balance with the thing's weight pushing her back and down. So heavy, and so slowly she spent thirty minutes walking down the stairs, flight upon flight on a downwards spiral to the first floor. She finally reached a smooth carpet under her feet and felt her strength renewed when she captured the smell of cinnamon tea being brewed in the kitchen. There was music playing and the house was calm and empty. Patchouli.

She walked to the door, the box in front of her, light in her arms and spirit. An awesome Sunday waited for her outside the house.

On her way out, she tripped over a gas mask resting face-down on the floor, but managed to jump on one foot and keep herself from falling. She kicked the mask away from her, startling the white tiger sleeping under the crystal table. Immediately, the giant cat clawed the mask with its tigery reflexes, making it spin and fall over its face, covering all of its beastly features but the lower jaw and its protruding fangs. A gas-masked albino tiger. Nothing can be cooler than that. Maybe a gas-masked cephalopod. No. Albino tiger is definitely cooler.

Outside, the day was perfect. The sun shone bright and there was the bluest, cloudless sky sheltering Saint Martin. The street was busy, the market was everywhere. Fresh bread, roses, dew. Birds, carts and horses on the march. The signal was red, so she stood close to a bald man reading the newspaper, waiting in line for his turn with the public god service. She overheard someone, the first in the row, complain to the totem, 'Why in fuck's name can't you cure eczema? It's a damn fungus, damn it.' *Your credits have expired*, answered a featureless voice. She felt sorry for the man, but couldn't help but giggle. Next time, try boiling the river's water. That fetid thing the Palace calls a river.

She turned in time to see the man walking away from the totem, down the street, right in her direction. His right cheek and part of his upper lip and nose were covered in a pink, moist blotch, a blistered wound shaped as a face, a somewhat familiar face that she could see now, as he approached, went down to his neck and into his shirt. She swallowed her giggle and wished the man could find a cure.

'As you wish.'

'What?'

Slo-mo time-warp, the air thick as a jar of glycerin. The man walked past her like the actors playing living statues in Gaiman Square. As he moved, she could see all the tiny blisters, the face-wound staring back at her. And as if someone had hit the rewind button, the eczema started to erode. Skin took back its space, first in the borders and then in spots inside the pink perimeter, holes forming eyes and a space like a mask, or mouth that seemed to say 'Oh' then scream, wider and wider, until it completely disappeared, leaving nothing but an afterimage, a memory, a sensation.

'Did you see that?' Gorette turned to face the man next to her, a young guy wearing a ponytail, reading the newspaper. Like waking up from a deep dream, she looked down to the box in her arms and immediately dropped it to the ground. Her nails tore the cardboard walls and there it was, the god, face up, the way she'd put it back in her room.

The god in the box looked like it was engaged in silent battle with her. Face to face.

People walked past them on the sidewalk, the noises and colors and smells of Saint Martin coming back to her in a single torrent. Too many steps and the scent of flowers and wax, hooves clicking, and chantings, all around the street. A procession.

She turned once again, feeling dizzy, and saw the ocean of people and candles and garlands and, in the middle of the street, a huge bier with a coffin and a little altar, an undertaker god surely preparing the body, the grave and the costs for the burial. Around the altar, there were pictures of a kid, younger than her. The face of the corpse inside the coffin.

'A kid,' the words came out without her noticing.

She closed her mouth and locked it with both hands, closing her eyes not to think, not to think, not to think.

'As you wish,' and again, several yards away from her, like an echo, above the crowd, 'as you wish.'

Five seconds passed before the bier's conductor jumped from his seat, let go of the reins and climbed on the coffin. People noticed the man's hurry and soon there was a commotion around the vehicle. People cried 'help him out!' and 'open the coffin!' and 'my kid! He's alive!' And now she could hear a stifled sound, a desperate knock-knock on wood coming from the depths of the underworld. There were relatives pushing the coffin's lid, but damn those nails, the joiner that worked across the street rushed with a crowbar and soon was forcing the wood cover. Gorette's heart was pounding, someone please open that coffin. *Asyouwishasyouwishasyouwish*.

Suddenly, the nails fired off into the air, like a machine gun trying to shoot down the heavens. The whole wood box went down to splinters in a moment. The crowd went mad when the boy rose and took the cotton balls out of his nose.

'It was her!' Gorette heard someone cry behind her. 'I saw it. She commanded the god to resurrect the boy.'

'No, I didn't.' She heard herself speaking as if the words came from someone else.

'Yes, you did,' said a very low, calm, cold voice.

'No.'

Soon the crowd was all over her, praising her good deeds – *as you wish* – calling her a saint – *as you wish* – asking her for favors – *as you wish* – raising her and her god above them, a new procession for the miracle of life, for the savior, *ad majorem femina gloriam*, for the Popess.

'As you wish,' she said, grinning.

*

Emissaries.

From other neighborhoods, from the Palace, from other cities.

They came in tides, high and low, high and low. They threatened and cajoled, but eventually ended up asking for something they needed to be done, some disease to be cured, another to be implanted, a hand up for their business, virility, beauty, you name it.

One out of five diplomats demanded to know how she had assembled her god. How the hell that thing could—

The truth was she didn't know. She wished she did. And that seemed to be one of the few wishes her creature wasn't able, or willing, to fulfill.

However, most penitents came asking for knowledge, for wisdom, for guidance. That, too, was out of her reach, out of her experience. But certainly not out of her god's verbosity.

That marvel now standing on a totem in front of her throne, a foot lower than her, encased in crystal, half-faced and barbed-wired. For those who entered the temple and met her gaze, her features dominated the god placed only an inch below. But even if her eyes held a deep jade glare, it was the silver beacon of the godhead that really shone brighter. Like the moon.

'Speak,' she said.

'Most honorable Popess,' began a merchant in a golden tunic, shutting down his smartphone, 'what's the nature of true miracles?' The question raised a wave of murmurs in the hall. He was the fifth or sixth person consulting her that morning. 'What are they made of? What makes your god able to perform such wonders, surpassing the capabilities of every other functional god in the realm?'

'I—' began Gorette, the Popess, but that cold voice interrupted her speech. That behavior had become quite common in the public sessions lately and the people were beginning to question the Popess' authority over the god.

'I can calculate reality at far superior floppage,' the god said. 'My miracles-per-second rate is also higher than your average god. Also, my database—'

'It's my will,' cut in the Popess.

'No, it's not,' replied the stone statue.

'Silence.'

'As you wish.'

The Popess dismissed the merchant with a wave of her hand. The man bowed slightly, obviously upset for not being answered. He turned and mixed himself with the rest of the crowd, other merchants, other tunics, men in coats and gas masks. 'The session is over,' she said.

'Popess?' Already at the center of the court. Dirty overcoat and gas mask. She could smell filth in the wind, rotten oranges and oil. The man had a tiger, white as snow, chained to his wrist and it, too, wore a mask, and had a big box mounted on his back, covered by a red velvet coat. 'Can I speak?'

The Popess was halfway through leaving the throne, but stopped and turned back to her seat. A green dazzle came from her eyes asking, who's this man, do I know him? 'What do you want from me?'

The man took two steps ahead, dragging the chain, making the gas-masked albino tiger move and then lie down. Nice and easy. 'Actually,' he said, his voice covered by the mask, 'I'd like to address your god.'

'It?'

'Me?'

'Yes, your Holiness. I want to question your creature,' said the stranger.

She was curious. She straightened herself on the throne, crossed her legs under the long robe and smiled, as if expecting entertainment, a show. 'Okay. Go on. Let's see what you're gonna get from it.'

'In truth, there's only one thing I'd like to ask it.' He moved forwards and immediately the tiger rose and followed, both coming closer to the totem. The people gathered around the hall seemed to get closer, curious about what this masked stranger and his beast were up to. 'I want you to tell me what's the nature of God?'

'The nature of gods?'

'No. God.' So close now. His breath clouded the crystal case. 'Gods are manifestations, constructs. They're functions, myths, narratives. They're tools. Limited, discardable, yet very spectacular tools. I want to know what's the nature of God,' the man said.

A second passed before its marble lips moved. You could hear the silver sphere, the mighty godhead whirring, its core processing billions of lines of code looking for an answer. Suddenly, the noise stopped. 'God is unique. God wishes,' it said. 'I am unique. I wish.'

Marble soldiers, flaming tigers, hydras and giant spiders materialized in the hall, as if coming onstage after opening reality's invisible curtain. Panic took over the crowd in the room, a whirlwind of faces and tunics running, dissolving and exploding in gushes of blood and rot and desecration.

The Popess sank in her throne, reduced to her youth, her green eyes crystallized with fear.

The man under the mask refused to run and instead yelled at the crystal case. 'Even a god found in a sanitary landfill, assembled from pieces of junk and designed by a very young, immature girl who didn't even know what she wished for in her life?'

'Even so.'

'You're not unique.' The stranger reached for the velvet cape over the tiger and pulled it from over the box. There was a crystal case with a marble god inside. A reused god. Design almost identical to that of the Popess' own creation: a silver moon of a godhead pierced by tiny acupuncture needles, linked to a pedestal by fiber optic cables, tied with barbed wire and praying cords and a hat balanced atop a half-faced, one-eyed, mouthless piece of avatar at its center. 'Do you recognize it? I found it some ten meters away from you.'

The older god whirred. The soldiers and monsters charged towards the man and his own technomagical beast. He stood right where he was, but quickly typed shortcut commands to the god and the giant cat. When the creatures were close enough, the tiger attacked with a mighty leap, his claws hacking the monsters' fire hides and carapaces.

But the man kept staring down at the god while the white feline defended their position. More creatures continued to condense into existence out of thin air. The tiger still managed to kill them, keeping the perimeter safe.

'I will destroy her,' the god said. 'If I can give life, I can take it.'

'No, you won't. And you can't.' The Popess stood next to the god's crystal case, staring at its single, immovable eye. 'Dad once told me about the nature of God.' She got close, really close to the crystal case, as if trying to whisper into the god's ear through the transparent wall. 'He told me God is flawless.'

The blood-red white tiger circled the totem, pushing the soldiers back. Fast and precise as tigers are, he clawed the box, shattered the crystal to tiny bits, sent the stone face away to the floor along with its miraculous monsters. The thing fell hard, barbed wire, praying cords, tokens and fiber optic cables disassembling the holy design with the shock.

Gorette strode across the room in the destroyed god's direction. It rested on the floor, close to the corpses of humans and miracles. She could see it tried to speak, its lips moving in a very familiar way. She decided not to give a damn about what the thing had to say. She picked up the silver godhead and looked deep into the god's eye. 'God is flawless. But nothing, you hear me? Nothing is without flaw,' she said. 'Now, shut down.'

'As you wish.'

*

At the Valley of the Nephilim, the god wishes it had arms. They wish they were a *them*, not an *it*, not a carcass in the filth, beneath the remains, in the mud. Die, worm, die. You chew my wires off, you reincarnate as a, as a, as a *human*. That. A human. A human.

A human.

A blip and another. Above ground. Steps coming closer. Another blip and an intense, acute sound. Like a blip, but never ending. Like a whistle.

'Guess there's one here.'

Yes, there is. There's one here.

Some light, then light and too much light.

'Here you are.'

A human.

'Yeah, it looks just like that other one.'

What? Not like any other. I'm the others. The others are me.

'Not sure. Will destroy it anyway.'

No.

'Come here.'

Pressure.

'Boy, you're hard. Wish I had a hammer with me.'

As you—

'Oh, here it is,' says the girl. 'This is what I call a *force quit*. Goodbye, little one. Send my regards.'

Beat. Crash.

Silence.

The Next Move

Edmundo Paz Soldán

Bolivia

I got this story a while back through the indefatigable Cristina Jurado, and was lucky to be able to keep it for this volume as an original. I loved its elegiac tone. It echoes the concerns of the previous story in some ways, and I find it fascinating how depictions of our future world refract and reflect each other. See for yourselves – the next move is yours! This story was translated by Jessica Sequeira and is original to this anthology.

J erom climbed up to the roof of an abandoned mansion in a corner of the plaza, and lay flat on the tiles with a rifle in his hands. The sun had disappeared over the horizon, and the light of a giant moon was appearing between the mountains. He thought of the people crying out, and the shakes came to him, shakes that went away when he pulled the trigger, one-two-three, *zum-zum-zum*. He aimed at everything that moved between the trees in the plaza or in the neighboring streets. He heard the cries and asked himself what his next move should be. They would come to get him down from the roof, but he had decided before coming up that they wouldn't take him, or at least, they wouldn't take him alive.

The plaza remained quiet and Jerom tilted his head in search of a better angle for his shot. He felt a sting on his left thigh, and with one slap killed a zhizu. They infested the roofs, creating communities in the tiling. Tile after tile, and for what? All those little legs, and for what? One time, when he'd just arrived, he'd had to go out and fumigate the streets and buildings of the city, which the tiny creatures had invaded. They hadn't left, by the looks of it. Nobody left voluntarily – it was the law.

In the sights of the rifle the nose of a dog appeared, amidst the rubble of a dump site on a corner diagonal from the mansion. He took careful aim. The dog howled and writhed on the ground, and a boy ran to help him. He positioned the boy in the sights and briefly felt pity.

The shot hit the boy in the forehead. A red stain appeared as if it were just a scratch, a slight wound like one might get playing with a krazycat.

A liberating sensation ran through him. He couldn't leave Iris, but at least others would accompany him in his hell. *Death arrives from the sky*, he whispered. It was part of a song he and his brodis used to quietly whistle between their teeth to lift their spirits; sometimes it was their mission to be positioned on the upper floors of buildings as support snipers, and they'd throw out phrases and one would stay with him. One always stayed with him.

He heard a siren and shortly afterward two jeeps blocked the main avenue into the plaza. Four shanz jumped out of the jeeps and took shelter behind them. Jerom unleashed a burst of gunfire, *zum-zum-zum* – the impact of the bullets on the jeeps' bodywork. Perhaps he'd been on patrol with one of those shanz, had hinted to one what had been on his mind or received from one a quick word of comfort. Because there was nothing else anyone could do – if everyone had some maggot eating away at his heart or head, nobody's problems were more significant than anyone else's. All of them felt overwhelmed, some experiencing it as quiet desperation and others screaming it from the rooftops, just like him.

*

The dog was named Martini & Rossi, and it had wrinkled skin and a slender nose. It didn't have fur. A scientist from the Perimeter had given it to the boy's father. Scientists and high-ranking officials had special permission to bring dogs from the Outside, but in general, dogs didn't last long in the contaminated air of Iris. Its toxins went about killing them slowly. Their lungs would become poisoned and the coloring of their irises would turn yellow like the skin of a jaundice sufferer. The dogs that survived in Iris were wackydogs, genetically modified to resist the poisoned air. Artificial dogs. For that reason, not everyone was fond of them.

Ceudomar, the scientist who gave away the dog, had arrived in Iris eight months earlier. She came from Munro, where adaptive experiments were being carried out on robots. She trained them to respond to their environment, such that, even if all of them were equal at the start, their relative status changed as they began adapting to a specific terrain. In the end, not all of them survived – the mechanism of evolution working within them, just as it did for organic life. Iris provided challenges to the adaptation of the robots: sand that slowed the gears of even the most sophisticated machines; winds lasting for weeks capable of paralyzing any mechanism. Ceudomar's team had been trying to adapt robots to the Gobi desert, which was why Munro had thought it appropriate to test drive the tech in Iris – an even greater challenge due to the extremes of the island, where tropical landscapes existed alongside mountainous mining regions and stretches of desert.

Ceudomar had arrived in Iris with Martini & Rossi. The first days she slept with him, but after a month she noticed that the puppy had grown frightened of everything. He hid under the bed, looking for dark corners where he could get lost. They told her that he had the skrik, an Irisinian illness whose name translated as 'terror of the soul': the dog had witnessed something terrifying. He should be treated by a qaradjün. Ceudomar had heard the diabolic legends about Iris that circulated in Munro, but decided not to pay attention to them. In the end, since Martini & Rossi wasn't recovering, she gave him to one of the drivers at the military base. Once in a while she went to visit him at his house outside the Perimeter. Martini & Rossi would be playing with the driver's children and seemed to be improving. Ceudomar felt she'd done a good deed. The dog was still hers; she was just letting these others take care of him.

*

That evening Martini & Rossi had left the house to search for boxelders amidst the debris of the dump site at the corner. He liked to eat the reddish-green insects, but these ones weren't letting themselves get caught so easily. He stuck his nose between the stones and, from time to time, emerged with a boxelder between his teeth. That's what he was doing that evening. He was hunting when a bullet exploded in his body. The skin around the bullet's area of impact quickly turned a reddish color.

*

Jerom had been on guard in the market when two ideas took hold of him: he had to leave everything, and he wouldn't leave Iris any way but dead. The Irisians had been haggling with agitated voices, offering him chairus and trankapechos, watching him with mistrust as he passed them with rifle at the ready, and he thought how they would never accept him and that it was a lie the shanz were there to help improve relations.

In the fourteen months he had been in Iris, he hadn't made a single Irisinian friend, and he had to admit, it was difficult for him to look at them as equals. It had been a mistake to accept the posting here. Four months before, he'd tried all possible ways to get them to move him back to Munro, but his bosses in SaintRei had reminded him of the contract, the impossibility of return. He'd expected them to send him to a region where he wouldn't be in contact with anyone, in order to avoid all possibility of toxic contagion, but he'd not even got that. There were no exceptions: many shanz were in his same position.

Two days previously, he'd received a holo from a cousin who informed him his paperwork in Munro had been turned down. In the market, as he made his way between bags of spices, he had been conscious that all his options had been exhausted. He had considered poisoning himself with mineral mud or cutting off his leg with a knife, as some shanz had done in the secret hope of being evacuated. But he couldn't be sure those shanz had actually been evacuated.

He could wait for death to come to him slowly, or he could rebel against destiny and accelerate the process.

He had headed toward one of the doors out of the market, hoping his brodis on patrol wouldn't notice, and once he'd gone through it and found himself in the street, he'd hurried toward the main plaza – the place where, seven months before, one of his few confrontations with insurgents had taken place, where he'd been shot in the chest and believed he would die. But shortly afterward, lying on the ground, he'd realised that his bulletproof uniform had saved him and he'd begun to sing a prayer. *The only trouble is the bombs*, he'd heard the patrol chief say, laughing, while he lay on the ground, and that phrase had pursued him for several days until converting itself into a constant refrain – *the only trouble is the bombs* – while he showered in the mornings – an obsession – looking from one side to the other while on patrol, whenever he left the Perimeter for the city, pursuing him despite his lack of faith in God – *the only trouble is the bombs*. What's troubling you? Nothing, just the bombs. He talked to himself, and they laughed and asked why he was laughing, and he said no, nothing, no nothing, nothing, the only trouble is the bombs. It's not fokin funny, they told him, and he said, no, the bombs aren't funny.

He'd crossed the plaza without stopping, headed toward the mansion. Four floors, a house with pretensions, which had the curious appearance of a building that only remained standing out of sheer luck. A crack in the façade ascended from ground to top floor, a crack that implied its imminent collapse. There'd been a time he'd explored it with a couple of shanz, and they'd popped swits on the roof; there'd been a time he'd felt in harmony with all those who populated Iris – Irisinians, darkskins, kreoles, even the artificials and chita robots, but above all the humans, the poor little humans.

He'd climbed the steps rapidly, not wanting to feel empathy for anyone. Set fire to everyone, that's what he wanted. Set fire to them all in a hail of bullets. That had been his vision the last few nights. Dreams so intense he didn't dare call them dreams. No, it was visions that woke him in the booth where he slept. Visions like those of the other shanz, who said they saw Malacosa walking toward them, prepared to carry them to the other world with his embrace. He hadn't seen either Malacosa or Xlött or Jerere. Just fire, everywhere. A conflagration that burned the trees in the valleys around Iris – trunks of thousand-year-old bark scaling ceaselessly to the sky, cities devastated and the buildings of the Perimeter burnt to a crisp. An apocalyptic conflagration, and it was he who had lit the fuse.

Impossible to go up like that without coming down.

*

Captain Singh had just been thinking it was going to be a calm Sunday when he received the news that a shan had gone saico in an outer ring district under his supervision. Immediately he requested that the plaza be cordoned off and the neighboring streets evacuated, and that all shanz on patrol in the proximity head over there. He himself boarded a jeep and set off toward the plaza. He could direct operations from the security of the Perimeter but he liked taking advantage of any opportunity to lead by example, to teach the shanz under his command that teledirected force was nothing without personal commitment, a willingness to accept risks. The drons, the chita robots, the wùrèns weren't ends in themselves but merely the means to an end. They helped the shanz encounter the real in the best way possible. He would say *the real* with emphasis, as if the possibility of encountering death were only that. 'All the rest is unreal den,' a shan had replied once, and Captain Singh had been on the point of slapping him in the face but managed to contain himself, saying, 'No, but it's less real than the real.' 'Or more real than the least real,' had said the shan, and Singh had ordered him buried up to the neck under the sun, a day of punishment. Then he had started thinking he should learn from the Irisinians, who developed new words constantly and now had the vocabulary to name all the different kinds of darkness and light. He had to develop new concepts for the real.

Before arriving in the plaza, he had already received all the saico shan's information from the Instructor. He was named Jerom and had arrived in Iris a little over a year before. His record showed he had taken a bullet wound that had nearly killed him. Perhaps that had been enough to send him over the edge or perhaps not, perhaps day-to-day life in the city had been all it took to wear him down. There were those who couldn't take it anymore because of the violence they'd experienced, a bomb that had exploded nearby, a brodi they'd lost, an Irisinian they'd beyonded. There were the sentimental ones, those who missed the world they'd left behind, who regretted having come and looked for a way to return, trusting there'd be a way to escape from the contract they'd signed for life. Singh often had to serve as therapist, calming them with his serene but firm voice, not promising them paradise but saying that everything would get better, it always did. Some of them he convinced to hand themselves over after just five minutes of persuasion. Others could take much longer, and there was no lack of failures, either – incidents where a shan resorted to shooting at Irisinians or his own brodis, and Singh had to give the order to make him disappear. Sometimes the order was carried out by a sharpshooter stationed on a nearby building and other times by a technician watching everything from a monitoring room on the Perimeter, through a camera installed in a dron gliding silently through the sky, seven thousand kilometers up. All the technician had to do was gesture for the dron to complete its mission.

He stopped at one of the corners of the plaza and spoke with a shan who took off his fiberglass mask to tell him the saico shan had killed an Irisinian boy.

'His mother is inconsolable,' he said. 'His father works for us.'

'Offer to move them to a larger house in Megara,' said Singh. 'And give them an extra food voucher for the next ten months.'

'He shot at us. Bullets hit a brodi in the arm, but they bounced off his uniform. Another hit his hand, and his finger is bleeding. He's being looked after.'

Singh saw the calm in the shan's eyes. An experienced shan, someone no longer alarmed by anything. He liked to have these kind of shanz with him on missions – it made the work easier.

'Let's move quickly den.'

Singh looked toward the roof of the mansion. That's where Jerom was. He came from a little town in the interior of Munro. He'd probably played with iguanas in his childhood, and dreamt of becoming a millionaire designing hologames or scoring goals for a fut12 team in the national league. He'd never have imagined he'd end his days in Iris. Because they *would* end here. He'd be taken from that roof dead, or best-case scenario, if he turned himself in, they'd shut him in a monastery on the outskirts of Kondra. He was a shan lost for the cause, and they couldn't rehabilitate him. It was necessary to isolate the contaminating element. The monasteries were where all the defectives could be found – the shanz who had overdosed on swits and had visions and heard voices, as well as those who hadn't been able to take the pressure and had gone saico.

He imagined a boy named Jerom kneeling before the altar in a ramshackle church to hear the word of God alongside his parents, a boy who received communion on a dusty afternoon. A boy who still didn't yet know of the existence of Xlött. The image moved him.

He too had been that boy… He had to dispel those thoughts.

*

The Irisinian boy was named Dax and was five years old. A short time before, he had been returned home.

Just after he'd been born, his parents had sent him to an ùjian. Dedicating a son was a sign of commitment to Xlött. The boy would grow up in the ùjian, where he'd be trained for the priesthood devoted to the cult of Xlött. When his parents were asked if they missed him, they said having a son there filled them with the divine presence. It was a way of getting close to Xlött that benefited everyone.

The boy, however, had been returned home. The ùjian hadn't given any explanation, but his father knew it had to do with his new job on the Perimeter. A friend had recommended him as a driver to the darkskins. The father had been out of work for several months, and in the city there weren't many options. The offer was made to him, and he'd accepted it without thinking. He knew he risked being viewed as a traitor by his neighbors, and so he'd made an effort to minimize drawing attention to his new interaction with the darkskins. He left for the Perimeter in the early morning, when the streets were deserted, and returned in the middle of the night, under cover of darkness. All the same, it had just been a matter of time before they realized. His son's return had pained him. His wife reproached him for risking their lives: Xlött wouldn't be happy with them. The boy's father stared at the ground.

Dax hadn't shown any negative signs of having spent time at the ùjian. He was a normal boy who liked to play amongst the ruined buildings. He caught boxelders, zhizus and cicadas hidden in the brush and put them in bottles of colored glass which his mother brought to market. He aligned the bottles against one of the walls of the house in descending order, from those sheltering the most valuable prisoners – zhizus the size of his fist – to those that didn't last long because he set them on fire with a magnifying glass under the sun.

One day his father appeared with a skinny, furless puppy that didn't stop sniffing him. A gift for them; the only condition had been that they not change his name. Dax had been so happy. He went everywhere with Martini & Rossi – he wanted to teach him to be his hunting companion. He made him smell the insects trapped in the bottles so the puppy could recognize them amidst the rubble. He took him with him through the buildings, training him to learn the territory by memory. The dog responded well. Occasionally, he would stumble; once he tripped on a staircase; another time he fell from the second floor of a house. But his sense of smell was excellent for tracking the boxelders amidst the rocks. Dax had looked for unusual boxelders, the kind his friends had talked about in the ùjian, with scales and reddish wings as if they'd been scorched in a fire, the kind that represented Xlött. But those boxelders didn't seem to exist in his district; Martini & Rossi couldn't find them either. Some day, Dax would go explore the valleys around the city and become the great enemy of the boxelders. Some day, he'd need all the glass bottles in existence to capture that blight of creatures besieging the world.

That morning Martini & Rossi had been more alert than usual. He'd overtaken him by a few steps and run toward the rubble in a corner of the plaza. Dax had been watching him when he heard the shot, and saw how the dog made an abrupt movement. Dax ran toward Martini & Rossi lying between the rocks, howling in pain. The bullet hit him before he got there.

*

Jerom started shooting at the shanz again, emptying a magazine of eighty rounds in under a minute. The shots smashed the panes of the jeep, but with the shanz it was difficult because of their bulletproof uniforms. At least they'd know he wasn't playing. They'd taken shelter behind the jeep, and he'd seen two of them running to hide behind the walls of a building. They'd be calling in reinforcements – they were so predictable. He too had been predictable, following the steps set out by the Instructor so many times. It wasn't hard to remember the sequence of responses in the case of a saico attack. He had to prepare himself.

His left thigh was stung again. Another slap, another zhizu. Perhaps he was lying on a nest. Perhaps a giant zhizu slept there, with poisonous young emerging from her. But he couldn't see any nest.

After a while another jeep appeared. It was the magic hour, when day gave way and night took hold. The ideal hour for swits. At some point, he'd come to think that maybe 'staying for life' wasn't so bad after all, and could even imagine himself living with an Irisinian in some town far from the capital. Some darkskins abandoned the Perimeter to go live with kreols, or Irisinians. Darkskins who became Irisinians. How long was it necessary to live in a place to become part of that place? Perhaps returning to Munro really was impossible now. Perhaps Munro was already another country.

Jerom knew the one getting down from the jeep so arrogantly, without even attempting to shield himself, was Singh. He would have come to solve the problem, with the stupid conviction that everything could be solved. Someone so impractical was intolerable. He seemed oblivious to the evidence experienced by his own body, must be so if he could emit such a vomit of absurdities when confronted with the fierce heat of Iris. Or the winds that filled the eyes with sand and the sky with darkness. Or the restless steps of the Gods. Or the visions that emerged from the depths of the mines: monsters with gigantic phalluses that wanted to drown him in the Waters of the End in Malhado, women of the glade with arms turned into branches who embraced him to the point of suffocation, dragons from Megara with enormous pupils that devoured you if you moved, slithering dushes capable of entering all your body cavities and sheltering in your stomach, emerging while you slept at night to swallow up the other shanz nearby.

Not everything is an administrative problem, captain. Not all of us have your fokin composure.

He heard the overly sweet voice of Singh through the Qï, speaking to him of his childhood in Goa. He shouldn't let his guard down. 'I had two brothers,' Singh told him, 'they lived in a house near the beach, the sun entered through the windows in the morning, lighting up the specks of dust on the furniture.' His mother had left his father and his father had dedicated his life to them. At nights he had lost himself in the bars of the city with a guitar, out to earn a bit of money to take care of them. The older brother was named Rohit and had gone out hunting in the mornings and returned once with a yellow-feathered bird that had pellets embedded in its chest, which he operated on with knives and forks taken from the kitchen. He had saved it and was his brothers' hero for it. The youngest was named Rajiv, and one day, running along the beach, he had found a metal sphere and picked it up. The sphere had exploded, and Rajiv was blown to bits in front of Singh. Nothing was ever the same again. During those days of grief, Singh had decided to become a defender of the law and fight against all those who transgressed it.

Singh's voice cracked. So he isn't so hard den.

Jerom needed to pee but couldn't take off his uniform. He emptied his bladder right there, without ceasing to aim his rifle at the corner where the jeeps and shanz were.

Singh continued to talk. He asked him to come down from the roof, turn himself in. He'd be brought to a hospital, where he was guaranteed to recover. He'd have a week of rest, then return to the barracks.

Lies, whispered Jerom. They'll take me to a monastery and I'll never leave.

'You'll come back,' said Singh. 'Trust me, di.'

Jerom unleashed a new burst of ammunition against the shanz – ten, twenty, thirty, fifty bullets, and now that he couldn't hear Singh's voice anymore, he felt better.

*

Sethakul was on shift in the monitoring room of the Perimeter, attentive to the sixteen holos around her, holos that told her how the day was going in Iris, when the emergency in the plaza broke out and she received the call from Singh asking her to prepare herself for any contingency. She zoomed in the holo covering the action in the plaza and shrank the rest. She spoke with her supervisor, told him about the emergency, but the supervisor was wrapped up in a game of Clausewitz with other officials in one of the private bars and told her to take care of it, said everything would turn out well and to keep him informed if anything out of the ordinary happened. Sethakul agreed, not quite sure what could be defined as *out of the ordinary*, but she was already used to these situations where the supervisor didn't supervise anything and she had to carry the full weight of the buttons she pressed on her conscience. Because that's what it came down to. Pressing buttons. Being the Lady of the Drons. Even now, the good soldier Jerom didn't know that, there in the sky above his head, a dron named Reaper, directed by Sekhatul, had begun to move, taking aim at him. One pressed button and the rocket would let fly, and in under ten seconds, Jerom would disappear along with a section of roof, and who knew what else – the building was already cracked, and the rocket might be what it took to finally make the whole thing collapse. Sekhatul's heartbeat accelerated as she zoomed in on the image and saw

Jerom lying on the roof, defenseless before her. She saw a scar on his right ear, a skull tattoo on the back of his neck, and when he opened his mouth, she saw he had a piece of meat stuck between his teeth. He wouldn't be able to make out the dron, which wasn't even a dot above his head and was sufficiently far away to blend with the color of the sky. The dron was the sky, just like in the hologames that had brought her to this work. Until a couple of months ago, she'd been just another shan. But her fame with hologames, her quickness with the controls while moving troops and tanks, her agility with the buttons, had got her this promotion. They'd told her that manipulating drons from the monitoring room was just like a game. A matter of commands and buttons. And yes, it might well be just that – so much so that anyone with minimal visual capacity could do it; it wasn't necessary to be a specialist. Anyway, she'd accepted because she wanted to free herself from the anxiety attacks she'd been experiencing when fighting against the insurgency. The exhausting days on patrol, the bombs that exploded when the jeeps passed. Once, she'd barely managed to save herself. The bomb had exploded seconds after her jeep crossed a bridge on the way to Malhado. Yes, it was better to take refuge in a monitoring room, fighting the war from afar, facing holos. But they hadn't told her the whole story, she told herself, feeling the headache that hammered at her forehead and began to spread when she saw Jerom shooting at the other shanz in the plaza, a pain that felt as if a hand wanted to pull the skin off her face, as if it were just a mask. Perhaps it was. She wanted to smile and couldn't quite pull it off. No, they hadn't told her the whole story. The first time she'd ordered the Reaper to discharge its fire she'd spent nearly four hours watching a holo of the Irisinian target, as he met with people in a house on the outer ring, entered a room and kissed an Irisinian with seven collars on her neck, went out and smoked and drank baranc with his friends. An Irisinian with almond-shaped eyes and a straight nose, just like the rest in appearance, except the Instructor's report said he was Minister of Orlewen, leader of the insurgency in that district, and this apparently casual meeting was to plan an attack on the Supreme during his meeting with the Irisinian transition leaders. Four hours weren't enough to feel genuine affection, but they had been sufficient for her to develop a certain interest in that little human, because she was sure that the Irisinians were humans despite what the SaintRei said. She coughed. She heard the voice of Singh saying *thumbs up*. That meant she had orders to proceed. She, Sekhatul, had permission to become Lady of the Drons. That night she wouldn't be able to sleep for thinking of the good shan Jerom. What fears could have brought him to that roof, to that mansion? Overwhelmed by tension, Sekhatul occasionally fainted in unexpected places. She saw an aura before losing consciousness, as if glimpsing the entrance into another world, as if she were dying, if one believed what they said about how one sees a very white light, a tunnel, before death. But nobody was ever waiting for her on the other side. The previous week she'd fainted in the bathroom of the monitoring room, after Reaper had fired at a group of four Irisinians. The rocket had been directed at only one, but all four had died. Her supervisor had told her not to worry, that these things happened, but inevitably she felt bad. The Irisinian leaders had managed to negotiate a deal so that, officially, drons would not be used against them anymore, because their use showed that the occupation lacked ethics, and acted as a reminder of the yellow rain incident, the death that decades before had come to Iris from the sky, from planes running nuclear tests. That deal was the official line, but all the same, the drons continued to do their job. Mainly against Irisinians, but also against saico shanz. Sekhatul couldn't talk to anyone about it. Guede, one of her work colleagues, had found her in the bathroom and helped her. She'd moistened her face, given her a couple of swits, told her to take care of herself, because if the supervisor realized, she might lose her job. Guede hadn't been able to sleep well either since they'd promoted her to the monitoring room. It wasn't easy work. The shanz didn't last long in that room. One of them had hanged herself shortly before Sekhatul came to work there. Sekhatul had been her replacement. Guede had given her a scapular cloth with the image of the Jerere on it. 'So she protects you,' she said. She'd heard a noise and ran out of the bathroom, fearful her supervisor would find her there. That moment came back to Sekhatul now while she watched Jerom firing, and she asked herself what had become of Guede. It had been two days since she'd last been seen in the monitoring room. Sekhatul had left the scapular under her mattress. She didn't want to deal with any complications if they found it in her room. Nor did she believe in those things, for all they said the curse of Xlött weighed on the dron operators, and that to allay her guilt it was necessary to submit to a god in the Irisinian pantheon like Jerere. Truth is, she would have looked to their god if she'd had faith. But she told herself not to think anymore. It was growing darker. If there was another death at the hands of Jerom she'd be responsible, and she didn't want to be responsible for that. In all honesty, she didn't want to be responsible for anything. Neither deaths nor lives. Neither the end of the Irisinians fighting against her, nor the shanz on her side... until they weren't anymore.

Sekhatul watched as Jerom tried to reload his rifle, and she pressed the button.

Translated by Jessica Sequeira

The Child of Clay

Dilman Dila

Uganda

Dilman is another of the authors we published in the original *Apex Book of World SF* anthologies, and is a filmmaker as well as a writer. I'd asked him if he had any new stories I could see, and was delighted when he sent me 'The Child of Clay', which appears here for the first time.

A basket, still warm from the foundry, gleamed on the windowsill. A tiny dust ball, like a blue eye with a yellow pupil, sat inside. Labita stood by the window, glaring at the sky, scanning for more balls, but the last had already fallen. Rits hair, a thick mess of bristled steel wool, buzzed as it absorbed rits shimmering anger, which gave rits triangular body a dark red hue. Rits legs trembled, as though straining to hold up rits weight. With arms that were like two tentacles, each splitting into five smaller tentacles for fingers, Labita picked up the basket to check for defects, but could not understand why, after such a very heavy ballfall, even when, as rit had counted, a thousand dust balls had slammed against the window, the basket had only got one.

Why?

The last sixty days in the foundry, then, had been for nothing. Just like the other ten baskets rit had created, this one was useless. *Why am I cursed?* Labita smashed the basket onto the floor. The ball rolled out and degraded into ordinary metal the moment it touched the stone tiles, and then turned to dust. *Why? Oh, why me?*

Rits tail stretched and swished and struck the mound of dust, which had settled on the other side of the room, and a thick cloud momentarily swirled around rit, gradually wafting out of the door like a rejected ghost. Rit would have to wait another hundred and fifty days for another chance to manufacture a baby.

Labita turned to a mirror, and glared at rits own face, at the green, bulbous eyes that shone in the dimly lit room like two moons, and at the little blue stones neatly arranged to create beautiful geometric patterns. Perhaps, rit thought, if I change the patterns I'll have better luck?

As custom demanded, Labita had made the design in honor of rits parent, who had had a fatal accident ten days after Labita became conscious. Labita had lived alone since then. At first, in rits manufacturer's hut, which was cylindrical with a cone-shaped roof, along with other robots in the village, enjoying the bliss of communal interconnectivity. Then, motherhood time had come and Labita had made a basket to harvest the balls. While other jochuma collected enough to make babies, rits basket had caught only one. Thinking it a design error, Labita had tried again, and again, and other robots had begun to whisper that rit had bad luck. Just like rits parent. *That accident was a sign of bad luck.*

The years had passed and they banished rit to a small hut at the edge of the village, to prevent the spread of that bad luck. The hut, box-shaped and made of ordinary rock, could not retain heat for long, and so it froze in the night. They hoped the cold would kill rit, snap rits wires and break rits parts, but rit had a small sunstove that kept rit alive. Some nights, however, rit wished for death by data loss from frozen memory chips. Being an outcast, rits memory did not auto-backup in the village's cloud, and so data-death might mean a new life.

New luck. Perhaps *good* luck.

Rit had tried everything with the last basket, coming up with all sorts of upgrades and modifications, giving it a mag-tivator that increased its magnetic powers ten-fold, way more power than baskets usually needed, and rit wrote software that made it the smartest basket ever, able to shift position so as to harvest efficiently, even in a mild ballfall.

Still, it had caught only one dust ball.

Why?

Labita walked out of the hut. The ground was still soft with degraded balls, which crunched into dust as rit stepped on them, leaving lonely footprints. Rits hair settled into a soft and fluffy fur as rits anger faded into sadness, the emotion rit had known best all rits life. As rit neared the center of rits village, rits antennae picked up chatter from other jochuma, who were excited about having filled their baskets. One very excited fellow kept screaming that rits basket had filled up in just one ballfall. Labita's eyes turned blueish with sadness, and when rit went to the baby factory and saw jochuma going in with full baskets, rits eyes turned completely blue. Rit stood at a window, peeping in, for the robots would not let one with bad luck into the factory, and rit stayed there for the rest of the day, watching them sculpt children from melted balls. Rits eyes became an oversaturated blue as the first complete child, a round thing with a dozen tentacles, was carried out into the sun for the first battery charge. After a day, enough electricity would have flowed into the child to give rit life, and the parent would install the first program to give the child conscious intelligence.

Labita ran away from the baby factory, the gears in rits chest grinding against each other to make a weeping sound. Rit ran far away from the village and sat on a mound of rocks and played back the few happy recordings in rits memory until the green returned to rits eyes.

The next day, rit went to the oldest jachuma, Mmooti.

Some whispers had it that Mmooti was the first ever robot and so rit did not have a manufacturer, that rit had walked out of the trunk of the Tree as an adult, and then rit made other jochuma. Mmooti vehemently opposed these rumors, and rit especially forbade them from naming rit 'grand mother rit'. Only the Tree, Mmooti insisted, is the Mother of all. And yet Mmooti did not give them an alternative story about rits origins, about who the first jachuma really was and where this jachuma came from, and so the rumors did not die out.

Mmooti had a spherical shape, with two slits for eyes, and a thick mass of steel wool above rits speaker. Rit could not leave rits hut because rit was so old that most of rits body had wasted away. Some rumors had it that when rit was the only jachuma, rit had played in the mud in the shallows of the Pond that stood beside the Tree, and the water had caused rits legs to rust away.

Oh, wise Mmooti. Tell me why my basket can't catch dust balls.

Being so old, Mmooti's antennae had fallen off. Rust, some robots claimed. Rit could only communicate to jochuma who were a few feet away, and since rit did not have legs, those who wished to see rit had to come to rits hut, which was right in the middle of the village. Labita had found a very long queue and, being an outcast, had had to wait until after all the others had seen the old robot.

Labita placed the basket on the floor, and Mmooti's tail analyzed it. The tail was a faded pink, just like much of Mmooti, with a dozen black sensory tentacles at the tip. Mmooti poked the gadget, checked the operating system, checked the data discs and the processors and the mag-tivator, and found nothing wrong.

Poor Labita. I'm not wiser than our Mother and I can't answer your question.

Mmooti pushed the basket back toward Labita, who looked at rit with eyes that had again turned a very deep shade of blue.

Mother can't speak.

Mmooti did not say anything else. The sun was almost setting and rit had to go into hibernation for the night. Being so old, rit had to use its body as little as possible. Labita returned to rits cold hut, reaching it just after the sun had gone down and the moon had come up and the temperature had started to drop. Rit sat next to the sunstove, and stared blankly at the basket, which sat in the middle of the room, catching the ray of moonlight that fell in through the window, gleaming like an evil star.

Just before sunrise, Labita walked to the Tree. Their Mother.

Rit walked until the sun came up. The rocks warmed up. Rit kept walking until the sun stood in the middle of the sky and the rock under rits feet was like a furnace. Then rit saw the Tree in the distance, a greenish silhouette in the gray expanse. Their Mother. Their God. The source of fierce philosophical debates about their origin. Had jochuma really come out of the Tree? Had the Tree always been there, a fact of nature just like the sky and the rocks? Some thought it had life, for its roots sucked metals from deep under the rocks, and metallic dust jetted out of pores on its leaves. The dust floated in the sky and bits stuck together to form balls that, when they became too heavy, fell down for jochuma to make children. Other metals could not make conscious children, which made them argue that only a thing with life could create life. But others said the Tree could not be alive, that like the dust balls, it only had the chemical properties necessary for life.

Labita's pace slowed, for rit was now hesitant. Beside the Tree stood a Pond. The Devil. The giver of death. Approaching their God meant also approaching their Devil.

Rit looked away from the Tree, toward the horizon, and all rit saw was rocks. Perhaps if rit kept walking, and walking, rit would find peace. There had been many expeditions to explore the universe, rits had gone far, so far from the village, searching for the meaning of rits life. One expedition had been gone for three years and came back to report that there was nothing out there but rocks. No other trees. No other ponds. No other jochuma villages. Nothing. If rit kept walking, the sun would set before rit returned to the village, and in the night, without the protection of a hut, rits chips would freeze and rit would lose all rits memories. Rit would wake up in the morning, not knowing what rit was, or the way back home, and rit would certainly not have this desperation to manufacture a child. Rit would wander among the rocks, a lost soul, but at least rit would have peace.

Would rit?

Labita turned back to the Tree, rits eyes so blue that now the whole world had a bluish tint. Perhaps, as Mmooti had said, Mother would have rits answers.

Rit stopped a good distance away from the Tree, and stood there for nearly an hour, admiring its beauty. The roots snaked out of bare rock like metal pipes in a grotesque sculpture, and the trunk soared straight into the sky like a pillar. The tip split into branches, which were thick with green leaves, forming a bowl-shape.

Labita made a wide curve to avoid the Pond, and then finally stepped under the Tree's shadow, which had a strange coolness, and rits eyes turned green again. Labita touched a root, feeling the texture of the bark, awed, and then rit kneeled down, and held the basket to the Tree.

Mother. Why can't I have children?

A deep silence replied. So deep. Rits antennae could not even pick up signals from the village. The feet of children thumping against the rocks, the hammerings as adults manufactured various things in the factories, the buzz of someone cutting something, the conversations in the market – rit had picked up these sounds only moments before. Now, there was nothing.

Had rits antennae stopped working? Was rit dead?

Then a breeze blew, and the leaves rustled, making a beautiful song. Rit looked up, and saw the sunlight sparkling, and the song grew louder.

Mother. Are you talking to me?

The song flowed like dust motes in sunbeams, and as the breeze blew harder, the song grew louder. Then, just as suddenly as it had started, the breeze went still, and the song faded into silence.

Labita replayed the recording of the song, over and over again – perhaps it had lyrics that rit could decipher, but the meaning remained elusive. Then rit thought that perhaps other jochuma had encountered this song before, and perhaps they knew what it meant. Rit coded a tool to compare the song to the library of all sounds ever recorded. In a few seconds, the tool had matched it to a sound Mmooti had recorded, which only a few jochuma had ever been allowed to access. A sucking sound as feet pulled out of mud.

Feet…?

The stories, then, about how Mmooti had lost rits feet, were true. Did that also mean that Mmooti had walked out of the Tree? Is that why Mmooti told rit to come and talk to Mother? But what was Mother telling Labita?

The Pond gleamed a short distance away. Labita activated the zoom-sight to see the water up close. The Devil. The Rust Bringer.

Rit listened to the song again, and became convinced that Mother was telling rit something about the Pond, about the mud in the Pond.

Clay. Mmooti's recordings said of the mud. *Clay can mold things.*

With trembling knees, Labita walked to the Pond, eyes yellow with fear. It sat just outside the shadow of the Tree, its edge a sharp thin line where rock suddenly turned into water, which looked like a mirror. Labita saw rits face, the blue stones and the geometric designs in honor of rits parent.

How can something so evil make me see myself?

Labita replayed the song, trying to understand what to do, now that rit had come to the pond. Rit could not see any mud. Perhaps the song would clarify rits purpose. Instead, a new stanza played. Strange. Labita stopped the song and rechecked that rit was playing the right file, for this stanza had not been there before, yet, somehow, the song had become longer, the file changing from thirty-three seconds, to now eighty-five seconds, and Labita did not need any new software to decode the meaning of the new sounds. It went tik-tik-clickety-tak-tak. The cry every newly manufactured child makes.

Clay can mold things.

Labita stepped away from the Pond, rits metals clattering in terror, eyes turning an oversaturated yellow.

No. Rit had misinterpreted the song.

Rit pirouetted away from the Pond and walked fast back toward the Tree. Now, again, rit could pick up signals from the village, and the suddenness of sound sent a buzz through rits wires, and a flare of static clouded rits processors. Rits vision blurred, and rit stopped and shut down rits antennae to stop receiving signals. Rit sat down on a small root to recover rits composure.

Oh, Mother. I can't make a child from the Devil's body.

Rit sat there for a long time, playing the song, trying to discover new meanings, and gradually rit became aware that the Tree was singing a new song, in a language that did not require any decoder.

The Pond is not the Devil. Clay is not the body of the Devil.

The song drifted away, and Labita rose to rits feet and staggered back to the Pond with newfound courage. Rit hesitated, kneeling over the water, watching rits reflection on the perfect stillness. Then, rit dipped rits hand in, and the surface rippled, rits image shimmering like a mirage. The sun seemed to vanish, and the temperature dropped to moon-chills. Rit froze, waiting for rust to eat away rits fingers, and yet rit could only feel the warmth of the water, the strange tingling sensation as the ripples brushed against rits metal. Rits hand went in deeper. The Pond was not deep, and soon rit touched something mushy.

Clay.

*

Labita reached the village well after sundown, when the moon was high and the temperature had dropped. Rits metals clattered as the heater struggled to keep rits body warm, and rits gait dropped to a trudge. All robots were inside, warm orange lights spilling out of their huts, and all Labita had to do was knock on a door to seek shelter, but rit knew no one would let an outcast in. With the basket on rits head, full of clay, rit slowly made rits way to the baby factory, hoping rits battery did not run out before rit got there as it struggled to generate heat to keep rit alive. The factory was deserted, yet warm, for the furnaces took all night to cool down. Rits battery was down to seven percent, not enough to run through the night, and so rit placed the basket on the floor, turned on a furnace, and went into hibernation.

The sun came up and warmed the world. Labita powered ritself back on, and rolled out into the sun for a charge. The baby factory would be empty, as two days had passed since the last ballfall, and even the slowest jachuma had already manufactured their babies. But as rit sat outside, recharging, a group of children playing tampo found rit, and saw the mud caked on its hands and feet, and ran away screaming in horror.

A crowd would soon appear, and rit did not want to deal with that drama. Though rits battery was only at thirty percent, rit stopped the charge and crawled back into the baby factory, locking the door. Then rit went to a secluded corner and emptied the basket onto a worktable. The first face appeared at the window just as rit started molding a child.

Horror! On seeing the clay, their eyes grew a bright shade of oversaturated yellow. Alarms rang. Labita had brought the Devil's body right into their midst. They exchanged signals which barely disguised what they were thinking, that something had short-circuited in rits head, and rits central processor had malfunctioned.

You'll doom us!

Labita focused on the clay, kneading it into a ball-shaped head, a pipe for a torso, thinner pipes for two legs and two arms, a short neck. Rit had always wanted a child in this shape.

You'll make us rust!

Labita's antennae dropped, falling over rits head like two braids, shutting down the receiver so rit would not pick up their panicked chatter. Rit knew, as long as rit had clay, they would not dare force their way into the factory, so rit worked on, rits eyes a bright green-shade of happiness. Rit gave the child details, carving out holes for eyes, putting tiny extensions on the head for antennae, and designing a tail that was not a long tube but a series of small tubes banded together. Then, rit fixed wires and metals in the hollow parts of the model, and data discs and a central processor inside the chest area. Now complete, rit took the child outside for the first charge.

The sun was descending, the shadows were getting longer, and the light had an orange hue. Jochuma fled as Labita stepped outside with the clay-child in rits hand, but Labita paid them no heed. Rit lay the child on a flat rock, facedown, for the sun to kiss the photovaltic panels on the back. It would need a full day to charge and come alive, and so by the time the sun went down, the batteries had barely charged. Labita carried it back into the factory, turned on a furnace, and waited for the next sunrise.

Next day at about noon, the clay-baby came alive. It stood up, eyes blinking.

A hush fell upon the world. The jochuma gathered around the factory waited for the sun to fall out of the sky, for the ground to open up and swallow them all. For rust to appear on their bodies. For the end of the world.

The clay-baby took a hesitant step toward its manufacturer, barely making a sound as its feet tapped on rock, its arms spread out as if expecting a hug. The clocks in Labita's body ticked so loudly that rit feared rit would never hear any other sound again. The baby took another step, and another, and now Labita's metals trembled. Rits eyes purple with anticipation.

But metal cannot mix with clay, and another step forward and the child broke apart. Clay fell off its arms, exposing the metal skeleton, then off its head and legs, and still the malformed baby walked, leaving a trail of debris. It was not intelligent, and not conscious, for it was not made of the living metal in the dust balls. It was just a toy.

With rits antennae still down, Labita could not hear the laughter of the other robots, but rit could feel it, and rits eyes turned blue. A deep, deep blue.

Did Mother really want a clay-child?

The toy walked about recklessly, running into rocks, falling over, getting up, with no purpose in life. Labita picked up a piece of clay. The sun had vaporized all its water and now it was as hard as rock.

Why?

Other jochuma, seeing that the clay could not harm them, pounced on Labita, tied rit up in chains, and dragged rit to Mmooti, whose status as the oldest living robot gave rit the regal function of dispensing justice. Labita did not resist.

Check rits head. Something is wrong.

Mmooti's eyes were orange with pity as rits long tail arced over rits body to examine Labita's head. Rit ran all kinds of tests and the orange in rits eyes became oversaturated.

Rit is fine.

Rit can't be fine. Something's wrong with rits head. Look again.

Rit just wants a child. Let everyone donate a dust ball to rit.

Labita's eyes flashed red. Rit did not want to be a charity project, and a child from donations would not really be rits child because the balls did not come from rits own basket. Still, it seemed like a good idea to the other robots, and some blamed themselves for not coming up with the solution before. They dispersed, each going back to rits hut to pick a few dust balls to give away. A few seconds later, Labita remained alone with Mmooti.

Mother asked me to make the clay-child.

Rit played the Tree's song. Mmooti listened carefully, then rit was quiet for a long time, the orange in rits eyes becoming so saturated it looked red, and Labita knew that rit had not understood the song.

It's just wind in the leaves.

I heard your footsteps in the mud.

Labita played back the ancient file, but now it did not have the sucking sound that had convinced rit of the meaning of the song. It was just footsteps on rock.

I don't understand.

You just want a child.

Someone had retrieved Labita's basket from the factory, and now they brought it, full of dust balls. Labita waited to hear the rush of electric excitement, for finally rits basket was full, yet rit stared at the balls as though they were a pile of rocks.

Back in rits hut, with the sun going down and cold draping the world, Labita shoved the basket far from the sunstove. Rit sat leaning against the wall, rits eyes closed as rit replayed the memories of the clay-child, its hollow eyes, its skeletal limbs, and rit played the Tree's song as a soundtrack to these memories, and rits eyes were so blue.

Rit did not want donated balls. Rit wanted a child of rits own.

Labita walked out of rits hut. The full moon hung low on the horizon, painting everything blue, its breath so fierce that Labita felt her metals contract. The sun would rise in another hour, but Labita could not wait. Rit walked through the village. Many jochuma were outside for a festival to celebrate the end of the full moon. They had gathered in circles around giant sunstoves, telling stories, singing, dancing, making merry. A sudden hush fell when Labita emerged, and they watched in confusion, as rit walked away. Labita, antennae turned down, staggered away, afraid they would stop rit. No one did. Soon, rit was out of the village.

Rit reached the Tree at noon and sat on a root, feeling as blue as a daytime moon.

Oh Mother. Tell me what you want me to do.

At first, all rit heard was the deep silence, so deep, especially with rits antennae off. Then, rit gradually became aware of a breeze and rit looked up to see sunlight shimmering in the leaves. The wind hummed, and Labita wondered if it were a song, but rit could not hear the leaves. Rit listened hard, boosting rits microphones to pick out every little sound, and rit heard a faint and shy whisper, a song ever so sweet, an enchanting song.

And then something happened to the leaves. They morphed, and the lights merged to form a giant screen showing the world. No, not the world as rit knew it, not a dry and bare world. On the screen, green things grew out of rocks, green things that looked like miniature versions of the Tree. *Grass*, the leaves whispered. And there were things with a myriad of colors that danced in the sun. *Flowers.* There was a sky with white fluffy things in them. *Clouds.* Rit liked the look of clouds, white and fluffy, so different to the purple metallic sheets of dust balls that formed before a ballfall. And there were trees, many, many trees, and many, many ponds too.

The song faded away, and the screen shimmered and dissolved into sunlight in the leaves, and Labita staggered to rits feet in confusion. *Is something really wrong with my head? Have my processors malfunctioned?* The Tree was not a robot. It did not have metals, so how could its leaves have turned into a screen? And what did all that have to do with the Tree asking rit to make a clay-child?

What did the vision mean?

Rit replayed the video, but the world full of ponds and trees made rit cringe. Such a world, with an atmosphere full of water particles, would be death for jochuma.

Paint. A voice whispered. Mother's voice? Rit looked around, expecting to see a jachuma, though rit knew the gesture was futile for rits antennae were down. Rit was alone. It had to be the voice of the Tree, giving rit a solution to a fear that had plagued jochuma since the beginning of rits existence, making rits think the Pond was the Devil. Paint would protect rits bodies from rust, and rits could make paint from dead leaves that fell off Mother.

Clay can mold things.

The whisper again, and this time rit could not be mistaken about the speaker, for it sounded like the rustle of leaves, and so rit stood up and walked to the Pond. Rit scooped up clay, a lot of it, to make a child, and put it on a flat rock. Rit could not go back to the baby factory. They would stop rit before rit reached it. And kill rit. Format rits data discs and pulp rits metals. Total death. But rit did not need the baby factory to make a clay-child, for a clay-baby did not need electricity to come alive. It needed something else, something rit did not understand.

Maybe the same thing that gave Mother life?

What?

Rit used a flat stone as a worktable to mold another child, a ball for the head, a short spring for the neck, a pipe for the torso, two thinner pipes for the legs, and even thinner pipes for the arms. Holes for eyes and a long banded tail.

When complete, rit carried it to Mother, kneeled down, and held it up in both hands. Spots of sunlight fell on the wet mud and gleamed like pearls.

Mother. Here is your child. Give it life.

At first, nothing happened. Rit didn't really expect anything would happen. Then rit heard something, like twigs crackling, and looked up to see something strange happening on the Tree. Bumps appeared, as if something inside was pushing itself out of the bark, and the bumps sprouted into six long vines that snaked in the air toward Labita. The vines wrapped themselves around the clay-child and took it from Labita.

Then the Tree sucked the vines back into its body, inch by inch. A hole opened up in the trunk and the vines pushed the clay-child in. After which, the hole closed and the vines vanished into the bark.

For a moment, Labita thought about sharing rits experience with other jochuma. This would convince them that the Tree was alive, and it wanted a clay-child, that whatever Labita was doing was not selfish but following their Mother's wishes. Surely, unlike the song, a video would not need interpretation. Yet rit did not send the message, for rit realized the Tree could have taken the clay-child to protect the village from Labita's insanity.

Confused, unsure about ritself, Labita sat under the Tree, waiting to see what happened next. The sun went down and the moon came up, and Labita feared the cold would freeze rits memory chips, causing a data-death, perhaps damage rits parts and cause a total death. And yet, the cold did not come. The space under the Tree remained warm, just as if it were daytime. Confused, rit walked a distance away, and the moment rit was out of the Tree's influence, the cold hit rit so hard that rit ran back to the Tree.

Labita sat on a root, excited by her discovery. Rit did not need a hut to stay alive, only the tree. Rit watched the moon move across the sky, and eventually fade away, leaving a deep darkness that lasted only a short time, before the sun came up with a golden brilliance.

Still, the clay-child did not come out of the Tree.

Rit sat on the rock, waiting, and the sun rose higher. Mother surely had not wanted a child of clay. Mother had seen the kind of evil this child would unleash, and had taken it away to save the village. Doubts filled rit, and the doubts turned rits eyes so, so blue.

Perhaps rit should go back to the village and make a child from the basket of donated balls. Perhaps having a child, though not rits own basket child, would be enough to bring rit happiness.

Then a breeze blew, and the leaves sung, and that sound came again, like twigs crackling, and a hole opened on the trunk. A light spilled out of the hole, an orange light that made rit think of a setting sun. A shadow moved in the light. When the hole was big enough, so big that rit could have walked in, the shadow became clearer, sort of, taking the shape of the clay-child.

It could not be a child. It was the size of a full-grown adult and did not have a metallic body, though its body seemed to shine just like a glossy metal. But sunrays were not touching the creature, so why was it shining? Was that water?

It took several steps away from the Tree, as if confused, as if wondering where it was. The hole closed and the light vanished.

Now, rit could see details on the clay-child. Its eyes were white, with two dark spots in the middle. It had a projection between the eyes, *nose*, and on the lower part of its head, there was a gash. *Mouth*. There were two flappy things on the side of the head. *Ears*. The child did not have a tail, nor did it have antennae. Its hair was grass and flowers, many kinds of flowers.

What is a mouth? A nose? Ears? What function do they serve?

The song of the Tree had ushered the child out of the trunk, and now Mother whispered, as if to explain the creature.

It's a girl.

Labita was even more confused. Rit could not takes rits eyes off the clay thing.

A girl? What is 'a girl'?

The wind died away and the song faded into the deep silence of the rocky world. Labita took a step toward the creature, to examine it, but then hesitated, for the girl's body was... *wet*. Not wet like mud, but... Just wet. Water flowed out of her skin and pooled at her feet.

What have I created?

The girl took a step forward, and Labita jumped backward in fear, rits eyes going the brightest shade of yellow.

The girl opened her mouth, and for the first time, Labita saw a tongue, as red as fire, and teeth, as white as ash.

'Mother,' the girl said. 'Are you my mother?'

I'm not your mother!

The girl took another step, and Labita noticed that she left muddy footprints on the rocks. Just like the first child rit had created whose body fell apart with each step, but not quite like it, because this child did not disintegrate. It seemed to be *creating* mud, mud which sunk into the rocks, creating little holes, and water slipped off her body and filled these holes. Petals fell off her head and fluttered to the ground, right onto her footprints, and turned into grass and flowers that transformed the ground from a dull gray to vivid colors.

The girl stepped closer to Labita and Labita jumped backward again. Rit had expected at least a child that looked like rit, that behaved like rit, but this thing... It had water on its body!

'Mother...' the girl said again.

Labita turned and fled. Rit ran fast and hard, but rit could not outrun the girl, who kept right behind, bringing the vision Mother had shown rit to life. Each step she took created a little pond, with grass and flowers, and soon there was a trail of green leading from the Tree, toward the village. Labita ran very fast. Mother had sent a girl to fill the world with other kinds of life. With grass, with flowers, with water. *Why?*

Could paint save them? Even if it could, they would have to constantly fight to stay alive, not just in the night against the cold, but during the day against water. Against Rust. The world would become very hostile to them.

Labita found the village in a panic. Rit had booted up rits antennae, and now the whole village knew what rit knew, and there was terror and confusion. They could see the girl in the distance, walking toward them, a garden growing in her wake, full of colors, full of life.

I have brought death to us all.

To Set at Twilight in a Land of Reeds

Natalia Theodoridou

Greece

Natalia is probably the most prominent Greek author writing SF in English today. He was in one of the *Apex Book of World SF* anthologies before, and won the World Fantasy Award with the haunting 'The Birding: A Fairy Tale', which I would have loved to publish here. But we are in the business of science fiction – and robots – and trains! – all of which are here, in this land of reeds.

The train ride is long, longer than I'm used to traveling lately. The city has its own sense of distance, underground or glass-clad and stainless-steeled. Entertainment drones at you from above, eating up idle time. No thought left unclaimed.

Here, we zip through vast, open spaces. The landscape is a blur of burnt sienna and muted cypress green, nothing like the grays and neons of the city. But the biggest change is above. There's no SkyVu here, so the firmament is just what it is, blank air, nothing. Thoughts galore. The sky is a made-up thing.

No one else shares my carriage. Who even visits the countryside by train these days? Lena used to wonder at the fact they still run a semi-regular service. Or maybe I just keep strange hours, strange habits. No matter; I savor the silence.

Idly, my hand brushes my luggage. The old synthetic skin

rests folded neatly inside. My own skin matches it: wrinkled, liver-spotted. I think of Margarita.

*

I see the harvester robots first, far away, their long limbs swinging blades above the crops, their bulky cube-shaped bodies like something out of an anime from bygone eras. Margarita is with them, supervising or keeping them company, who can tell? From the distance, they look like toys.

On foot now, my pace settles into something one might call leisurely. I haven't felt myself move like that in a while. Since Lena, for sure. It's the countryside's doing. The wideness of it, the tall skies. It has a way of slowing you down, making a small thing of even a seven-foot robot with scythes for hands. Your meager meat-and-bone body doesn't even compare.

It's not long before Margarita spots me: I can tell from the way her back straightens, her shoulders tense. She relaxes as soon as she recognizes my gait – though, if I could see myself from the outside now, with my long, flowing skirt and my leisure and my country hat, would I have recognized me?

She raises her arm and waves, starts walking with long strides to meet me on the road.

'You came early,' she says instead of a greeting.

It's not an accusation, just an observation, but I feel the need to come up with an excuse anyway. For running away from that which cannot be escaped. I carry Lena, still. I can feel her weight on me, as real as the weight of the luggage in my hand. 'I took some time off,' I say. 'I thought why not spend it with my favorite'—*person*—'friend?'

If she notices the hitch, she doesn't comment.

I have a better view of the harvesters now, with their big, staring eyes, their innocent eyebrow-shades, meant to pluck your heartstrings. To the right, a barrel-bodied robot with soft tubes for legs is ambling towards the stream in clumsy, gangling steps, carrying buckets. Margarita follows my gaze and we watch the robot for a while as it fills its buckets in silence. Her face lacks expression.

'We had some ideas, didn't we?' I say.

'Yeah,' she says. 'You sure did.'

She presses a button on her wrist monitor and then puts two fingers into her mouth and whistles. The harvesters come to a stop immediately, turn their heads towards us in unison. If they weren't so damn cute, they would be creepy as fuck.

'Come on, boys!' she shouts. Then, to me, 'Let's put them to bed.'

*

By the time the harvesters have made it to the barn, the sun has almost set. Up close, the robots are even more towering than I remembered, but their slow bulk and tin heads make it easy to dismiss anything menacing, dangerous. Scythes and all.

The robots arrange themselves in a circle on the dirt-covered floor, leaving space for Margarita and, I realize, myself, without being instructed to do so. Margarita sits down cross-legged and pats the dirt next to her, so I follow her lead.

The robots wait, imitating breathing, slow and creaking. They peer at her eagerly with their huge eyes, their mechanical jaws slack, mouth-slits half-open.

'There was a star, once upon a time,' Margarita begins the story, 'that set at twilight on a land of reeds. It walked barefoot in the mud and wondered at every little thing: the chill on its face, the flow of the river, the song of the trees... It was lonely and it was sad, for there was no other in the world just like it, no one that knew the sky the same way it did.'

Margarita pauses and wets her lips, even though she doesn't need to.

The robots purr and coo, pleased as cats, and continue listening to the story until their timers will say they should feign falling asleep.

'It walked and walked until it found a village, and in it, a villager. The villager saw the star walking naked among the trees and called out to it. He decided the star was a young woman. She needed to be clothed and fed and taught the ways of humans. He married the star, and the star, ignorant of its own heart, did not object. It bore the villager's children – all boys with strong limbs and faces that shone in the dark. At night, it went out. It walked through the village until it reached the river. There, it sat on the mud and looked at the sky and all the stars. But never, not one did set again at twilight in this land of reeds.'

*

The story done and the robots powered down safely in the barn, we sit at her kitchen table and Margarita puts the kettle on. She doesn't drink, but she knows I like tea in the evening, strong and bitter. Lena liked hers sweet, so sweet it turned thick, like molasses. We used to drink our tea while staring out the window at the electric sky of the city, women smiling above us, white-teethed, fake skin pixel-perfect, untouchable.

I can't breathe.

'Do you tell them stories every night?' I ask, if only to make sure I can still expel air from my mouth.

'I'm running out of new ones.'

'Why do you do it?'

She shrugs, but the sideways glance she gives me does not escape me. 'It makes them happy.'

I let it go. 'I got the parts you asked me for.'

'The skin, too?'

'Yes.' I look at her, now. A mind that's a hundred years old, and skin still smooth as alabaster. I wonder what that must be like.

We met at a rave, before the conservation act, before I was Margarita's maintenance person, back when all our skin was young. Lena hooked up with Margarita and I watched. It was fun. They kept seeing each other without me for a few years after that. It eased off slowly as I volunteered to take over Margarita's maintenance. We were all happy.

I'm staring. Must stop. 'Couldn't find a replacement for your heat regulator, though. I'm sorry.'

'Ah.' She sighs. 'Well, what can you do.'

She pours the hot water over a tea bag, and I wrap my hands around the cup too quickly, burning my skin.

'How long are you staying?' she asks.

'Not long,' I reply. 'Just a few days.' I pause, hesitate. 'And, Margarita…'

She turns to look at me. 'Yes?'

'This is the last time I do your maintenance. Here.' I beam her the information of the new maintenance guy. 'This is the contact info for the new contractor. He's agreed to come out from the city every three months.' Her face remains painstakingly expressionless. 'There's an emergency number to call, if you need anything urgently.' *If you break.*

'Is it because you're sad?'

I inhale sharply, then let the air out slowly. Lena, again and always. It's like a stab wound, this pain. What I imagine a stab wound would feel like. 'How did you know?'

'Why are you sad, Dora?'

My hands shake, so I wrap them more tightly around the cup. 'Lena. She was… She passed.'

Margarita does not respond for a few moments. I wonder what happens in her mind. Then she leans across the table and touches my hand lightly. Her skin is freezing. 'I'm sorry,' she says. It sounds genuine.

'We had a good life,' I say. I think of saying, *she loved you. Loved us both*, but I don't. I'm not that big-hearted.

'Yes.'

I finish my tea while it's still scalding hot. It leaves a tingling in my throat.

'Let's get you fixed up,' I say, standing up.

'Ah, yes,' she says, as if she's forgotten. She hasn't. 'The conservationist has to be conserved.'

We go into the lab at the back of the cabin.

Margarita climbs onto the examination bed and opens up her chest compartment for me. I run the diagnostics and make small adjustments, then replace a few corroded nerve endings. So far so good. I can see the heat regulator – it's fried through and through, but they don't make her model anymore, and I couldn't come up with a workaround. Maybe the new guy will have better luck.

'Now for the fiddly part,' I say.

Margarita observes me as I peel off her skin. Her eyes are completely still – perhaps the thing that will always give her away, that will always mark her as not-quite-human. Not the fact that she doesn't need to breathe unless she chooses to, but this unflinching holding of your gaze.

I fold up her used skin and put it away for storage, then dig out the aged skin from my bag. Margarita runs her metallic fingers over it, traces the wrinkles and moles.

'How does it feel?' I ask.

She takes some time to respond, but then she says, 'Perfect.'

I start from her head and move downwards, wrapping her in her new skin as I go. Her body is giving off heat now, like a furnace. I wonder what Lena felt like when she ran her hands over Margarita's skin.

I wipe sweat from my forehead before it drips into my eyes, and keep going.

'Were you thinking of ending your life?' Margarita asks as I layer skin over her chest.

For some reason, the question does not catch me by surprise, and so I don't get the urge to lie. 'Yes.'

'But you won't?'

'No. I won't.' I glance at her eyes, then back at my work. 'Have you ever thought of doing that, Margarita?'

'I have, yes.'

'What kept you?'

'Caring for another is reason enough to go on,' she says, and I'm sure the irony is not lost on her. She motions vaguely in the direction of the barn. 'I had to stay here to care for them.'

'But that doesn't answer the big questions.' I pause. 'Why do we keep going? Is life worth living? Et cetera. It just postpones them. Defers them to someone else.'

'Perhaps,' Margarita says. 'But life doesn't care about your questions. It only cares about going on.'

I wonder if the harvesters care about the big questions. We made them sentient because we thought it was cute, and we pretended it was because it would make them better at their job. Margarita, too, and others like her. For a while, it did. Not for long. Eventually, it made them miserable. We should have known that, should have seen it coming: making things smart enough to ask questions about life, but unable to find any answers. A perfect trap of existential agony. We're not engineers. We're tragedians.

'I need a favor,' Margarita says as I'm applying skin around her calves.

'Yes?'

'There's something that needs fixing in the woods. A wind turbine. It takes two, and none of the robots have the required dexterity to help me.' She pauses, looking at me. 'They understand what needs to be done, but they lack the skill to do it.'

'Of course,' I say. 'I'll help.'

I finish my work in silence.

*

The robots find it hard to let go of Margarita the next morning, trapping her backpack between pincers and holding on to her hand with a gentleness that machines of this size and strength shouldn't be capable of. Margarita reassures them with whispered words and soft but sure pats on their bulky metal bodies.

We set off on foot into the dawn haze that still lingers over the plane, dew damping the legs of our trousers. It's an hour's walk to the edge of the woods, then another hour or so before we start our climb in earnest. The wind turbine is at the top of the mountain – a rocky path lined with pine trees. We should be at the site by sunset, camp for the night, start the repair in the morning. Margarita has already moved the crane to the top – how she got it up there, I have no idea. On the third day, we'll head back down.

We walk in silence, Margarita in front, me in tow. Our skins are a match now, two women in their sixties, fit for their age. But her body is robust as no human woman's, her gait too regular, her posture too sure. I can already feel the fatigue setting in mine, but she shows no sign of it. Does she ever get tired?

What does it feel like, to be indestructible?

She's not, though. She wouldn't need me, if she were.

'Nobody from the village could help you with this?' I ask as we walk, if only to fill the silence.

'They don't come out here anymore. They don't like them...' She pauses. 'Us. Stealing their jobs. Being better at them than they are.'

'Right. Of course.' Living in the city, sometimes I forget what things are like in the countryside. People see things differently here. Nature, humanity, the sky.

The forest thickens around us. I stop walking for a moment, close my eyes, breathe in the resiny smell of the trees. Catch my breath. The air is cool on my eyelids. Could I live here, under this empty sky?

I can hear water flowing nearby.

Margarita stops walking, turns. 'Are you all right?' she asks, her voice morphed around concern so genuine-sounding I can't tell if it's real or programmed. Then again, is there a difference?

I start walking. 'Fine.'

We carry on.

*

We reach the top at dusk. The wind turbine's tower rises and rises, a colossus under the colossal sky. The rotor lies on the ground like a dismembered pinwheel. A giant's toy.

'Here we are,' Margarita says. She unlocks a container that's placed next to the rotor and unpacks our tent. I'm thankful we didn't need to carry any supplies with us – my knees are complaining loudly, and they didn't need to haul anything but my body up the mountain. 'Tomorrow, you'll help me get the rotor up and set it on. I'll be the eyes; you'll be the fingers on the ground.'

When I open my mouth to protest, she raises her hands. 'Don't worry. The crane's controls are completely intuitive. It will be very easy for you.'

She says it in an almost accusatory way that strips me clean of any will to protest. 'Okay,' I say.

She points at the container. 'There are energy bars in there. Help yourself.' Then she starts setting up our tent. She doesn't need it, because she needs no sleep. This is entirely for my benefit.

When she's done, we sit at the tent's threshold together. She's gazing up at the sky while I chew on my sustenance. It tastes artificially sweet and herby.

'The robots are worried about you, you know,' Margarita says into the night. Her eyes are still fixed on the same spot in the sky, whatever it is she's looking at. I look up instinctively, can see nothing. Only a dark expanse, shrouded with clouds.

'Me? Why?' *When did they tell you?* I almost ask. *Do they talk to you behind my back?* It's an irrational thought.

'They believe your thought machine is broken.'

My thought machine. 'Do you think so?'

Margarita lets a few moments pass before speaking. 'No,' she says finally. 'Not your thought machine.' Then she turns towards me and places her hand on my chest. 'This machine, yes.' A silly, sentimental metaphor. We both know it.

Lena.

That night, I dream myself transparent. I stand on the top of a mountain and look down at my see-through chest. Inside, my heart is a train engine, huffing smoke and dripping oil all over my lungs.

What a mess.

*

Watching the giant pinwheel hover above me is an unnerving experience, but the job itself is as easy as Margarita promised. Margarita gives me instructions through the comms, and I guide the crane through tiny maneuvers that translate into a delicate dance in the air. It's glacial and beautiful.

We're in the middle of the job when I hear a beep and then Margarita says, 'No. Oh no.'

Panic sears through me. 'What did I do?'

A slight pause, then, 'Nothing. Nothing. It's not you, Dora.' Another pause. The sun is setting in the distance. 'Let's finish up here.'

As soon as the attachment of the rotor is complete, Margarita makes her way back to the ground. It's dark around us now, but her eyes are shiny.

I reach out and touch her hand. Her skin is burning up. If she could sweat, she would be drenched. 'What happened?' I ask.

'An accident. One of the harvesters miscalculated, struck a tree. It collapsed on top of it.'

'Is it going to be all right?' Then, 'Can I fix it?'

Margarita stares at me a moment too long, as if I just said something outlandish. As if I suggested raising the dead. 'No,' she says. 'It's gone.'

'I'm sorry,' I say. *For your loss.*

She looks around, then at the sky.

'Do you want to go back tonight?' I ask.

'No. It's too dangerous for you,' she says. My soft flesh, a hindrance. 'We'll go at first light.'

*

The other robots are gathered in a circle around the harvester when we get there. They're standing still, but something in their stance suggests living things in mourning. A vigil.

Margarita approaches, stiff-backed. I linger a few paces away, like a distant relative who happened upon a family tragedy. The robots turn towards her then, all together. They reach for her hands, for her clothes, for her hair. She touches them back, head bowed.

We hold a funeral, later. There's no other way to call it, no other word for it. They carry their fallen friend to the barn, then stand around it in silence.

Margarita's skin is freezing next to mine. 'It was the last of its model, you know,' she says.

We watch the robots break down the harvester and each one takes a part – a pincer, a metal plate, a receptor – and solders it onto their body with a soldering iron that they pass around the circle. They've done this before, I realize. I see the odd bits and pieces that cover their bodies, now, remnants of worlds and lives gone for good.

What have we done? I want to ask.

I think of rhinos. I think of leopards and polar bears.

Why do we lament the extinction of species? And does that extend to the ones we create?

I stay silent.

When almost nothing remains from the harvester, the robots disperse and we go back into the house. Margarita continues to freeze through the night, until finally I invite her to join me in my bed. I wrap her into a blanket burrito and cuddle her, pouring as much of my own body heat as I can into her. Slowly, slowly, she warms up.

'Do you miss Lena?' she asks me, her eyes looking away from me in the dark.

'Of course I do.'

I can see Lena now, lying in bed facing me, sleeping. I can hear her voice, reading me something from her book. I see her back as she stands staring out our kitchen window, the tap running.

I used to get angry about that. Lately, I've been doing it, too, my mind on what it was that got her so distracted. I asked her, once, and all she gave me in response was this wide motion towards the city, the sky, everything. Everything, all the time, at once.

I study Margarita now, her eyes, her lips. Present. Grounding. Can I feel what they felt together?

I lean close, lips parted, but Margarita stops me with a hand to the chest, freed from the blankets. 'I can't give you what you're looking for,' she says.

She's right, of course. Maybe my thought machine *is* broken, after all.

'Tell me a story,' I say. 'Tell me the one about the star again.'

Margarita nods. 'There was a star, once upon a time,' she recites softly, 'that set at twilight in a land of reeds.' She tells the story of its barefoot walking through the mud, the wondering at every little thing. Its loneliness and its sadness. The villager who tried to make of it something it wasn't. The waiting.

'It was one of a kind,' I say when Margarita finishes the story.

'Yes,' she replies. She wraps her arms around herself under the blanket. 'Aren't we all?'

As I drift off, I think, *Am I one of a kind?*

Were Lena and I a species? Are we going extinct?

I sink into a cold, damp sleep, without dreams.

*

The next day, I depart.

I tell Margarita I'm heading back to the city. I doubt she's fooled though – she can see so much further and clearer than a human, after all. And yet, I leave them behind: Margarita, the harvesters, the questions they bear for us all.

As soon as I reach the main road, I turn away from the city and towards the woods instead. I follow the direction we took when we made our way to the turbine, until I hear the running water again. Then, I follow the sound.

It's a river. Narrower than I imagined, but the water is crystal clear. It looks deep. Long stalks line the bank.

I shed my shoes and let my toes sink in the cool mud.

I raise my eyes to the sky and, in this land of reeds, I wait.

The Beast Has Died

Bef

Mexico

I love alternative histories, not to mention mechanical brains, so how could I resist this tale by Bef? I got to include just one alternate history in the first volume, Tade Thompson's 'Bootblack', but there are two in this volume, and both feature robots in unexpected ways. Bef contributed a story to one of the *Apex Book of World SF* anthologies, and it's a delight to have him here. Join me as we travel back in time to an 1872 not quite like ours... This story was translated by Brian Price.

For Alfredo Brigada Monjaraz and
Carlos Pérez-Tejada y Salazar, *in memoriam*

1872

The bronze bell in the mechanical brain rang, pulling Prince Salm Salm away from the security report he had been reading. There appeared on the spherical screen, which always reminded him of a submarine diving helmet, an electronic message.

Through the window of his office in Chapultepec Castle, he could see a pair of dirigibles slipping like lazy manatees through the clouds that covered the Valley of Mexico. A large screen on the side of the vehicle displayed the message '1863–1873 Ten Years of Prosperity'. Next to the words, the image of the Emperor's face smiled down upon his subjects.

When he saw the name of the sender, the prince, who served

as the Minister of the Interior for the Mexican Empire, was somewhat unsettled: J.N. Alponte. But what really bothered him was the message's title: *La bête c'est mort*. The officer gave a small shudder. Could it be? For a moment he hesitated. If the message contained what he thought, it would go off like a bomb in the Empire.

The contingent of Swiss agents that made up the Office of Military Intelligence was charged with sifting through all the correspondence that arrived at the Ministry from every corner of the Empire. The only messages that ever made it to his terminal had to be deemed important enough to interrupt him. There could be no mistake. It had to be.

The blinking words stared out at the prince through the glass bubble. After a moment of hesitation, he pulled the green silk rope for the pneumatic intercom system that connected his office to the palace kitchen.

'Yes, sir?' answered the voice of the Hungarian chef.

'Tüdos, send me an espresso. Strong.'

'Right away, sir.'

A few minutes later, a mechanical servant knocked on the door.

'Come.'

'Your coffee, sir,' said the metallic droid, offering him a porcelain Talavera cup on a silver platter from Zacatecas. Without answering, the man took the cup and drained its contents. He returned it and ordered the droid to retire. The servile presence of these machines bothered him. He felt the calming effect of the coffee as the caffeine hit his bloodstream. Only then did he click on the message waiting on his terminal.

Amid the torrent of words that characterized the communiqués sent by the senile old Alponte, Salm Salm managed to decipher enough to confirm his suspicion. Without further delay, he pulled the red silk rope that connected him directly to the Emperor's office.

'What's happened, Felix?' asked Maximilian von Habsburg at the other end. This line was reserved for emergencies.

'Juárez has died, Your Majesty.'

After a brief moment of silence, the Emperor said, 'Come to my office.'

1871

The cold fury of January pelted the streets of Paris. Glacial wind whipped against the Mexican agent's face. He wasn't used to these temperatures, and his woolen English overcoat offered no protection as he walked along Boulevard Saint-Michel looking for the street where his appointment would take place.

Subjecting his hands to the cold once again, he pulled out a card to verify the address. This was it. He knocked. A grim-looking housekeeper opened the door. The man asked for Jean-Martin Charcot, to which the servant replied, 'Come in, *Monsieur le docteur* is waiting.' She turned to enter the office. The visitor hesitated before following. European customs, especially those north of the Pyrenees, were strange and confusing. Even the Spanish ones were odd, too, from time to time.

The woman pointed to a chair where he could sit, and then left him in the foyer. He looked over the diplomas hanging on the walls until, after what seemed like an eternity, the scientist appeared at the end of the hall.

'*Monsieur* Smith?'

'Doctor Charcot,' he replied in mangled French while shaking the man's hand, 'it is an honor to meet the father of psychocybernetics.'

'It's still just a fledgling science, barely at the theoretical stage,' responded the doctor as he sat down and indicated to the visitor to do likewise. 'Nevertheless, I am sure that it will have an impressive impact on the next century. But tell me... Please excuse me, but I have trouble pronouncing your last name. Your real last that name, that is.'

'Lerdo de Tejada.'

'How may I help you, *Monsieur*?'

Revealing his true identity upset Sebastián, who was the special envoy for the rebel forces of Mexican liberals. Was it a trap? He had spent so many months assuming the cover of Mister John Smith, a Canadian bearskin merchant who was visiting the City of Lights. If Napoleon's secret police captured him, he would die, but not before suffering unspeakable torture. He decided, however, to trust this man. He took a breath. He needed to explain his purpose as clearly as possible in a language that he did not speak well.

'As you know, notwithstanding our current struggle, we have kept abreast of the most recent scientific advances. Your work, in particular, is of great interest to us.'

'Mm-hmm.'

'We would have never dared introduce ourselves to you had it not been for your open sympathy for our cause.'

'Well,' said Doctor Charcot clearing his throat somewhat uncomfortably, 'all I did was sign that letter that Baudelaire wrote. A number of intellectuals did the same: Charles, Victor Hugo, Jules Verne, Dostoyevsky, the group of five, that German journalist living in London—'

'Karl Marx.'

'Yes, that's his name. I joined the cause because I was the only scientist.'

'Darwin also signed.'

'Oh, really?'

A number of British and German thinkers had affixed their names to the international petition for Benito Juárez's liberation.

Sebastián was irritated by the Frenchman's petulance, but decided to endure it for the rebellion's sake.

'Honestly,' continued Charcot, 'I signed the letter because it seemed inhumane to keep a man that old in that horrible prison. What was that place called?'

'San Juan de Ulúa.'

'The images that Baudelaire posted on his Web site were shocking. Beyond that, I support the free determination of new nations. They have the right to self-governance without European intervention. This, however, does not make me a sympathizer with the rebellion.'

'You have received me in your home.'

'I am granting an audience to Mr. Smith, a Canadian peddler of bearskins.'

Sebastián knew there would be resistance. French citizens in league with the enemies of Napoleon III or who threatened his interests risked their lives. He decided to try another approach.

'Fine, doctor, I will be brief. In practical terms, is it possible to digitize an individual's personality as you theorize? Can memory be perpetuated through a mechanical brain?'

'That is what I maintain.' The scientist's demeanor changed while speaking about his work. 'These are, of course, merely theories. The procedure I have developed with my assistants would require the absolute destruction of the nervous system, and there have been no volunteers willing to participate in the experiment. We have had success with monkeys, but a human being… It would have to be a hopeless case, someone in the terminal stage of illness. And even then, it would be impossible to guarantee a successful digitalization…'

Sebastián swallowed. Despite the cold, a nervous sweat broke out across his brow. 'Doctor, we have a volunteer.'

Charcot's eyes shone. Without saying a word, both of them knew who they were talking about.

1866

How could we not lose? We were practically fighting with sticks and stones against the elite forces of the Austro-Hungarian Empire. Every time we destroyed one of their soldiers, two or three new droids appeared. They blasted us with chemical fire from their dirigibles and leveled our rustic barricades with their smart bombs. Decades of hunger and ignorance weakened our humble troops as they stood before the invading enemy's supermen. We had no chance. Before we knew it, the Republic had fallen and burned to ash, while the usurping government established an illegitimate monarchy on the ground where our fathers had spilled their blood to give us liberty. Dark times came, brothers and sisters, nights without end during which we fled from the enemy until they overtook us. Confined in the most humiliating dungeons designed to hold criminal scum, the sun seemed to hide itself from the nation and its rays never came through the bars to comfort us. Some, like Miguel Lerdo de Tejada, closed their eyes forever at the hopelessness of unjust imprisonment and perished. I, myself, feared that I would never again breathe the morning air without shackles on my wrists and ankles. But today, a new light breaks on the horizon of our struggle. Today, international solidarity has liberated us from humiliating confinement. We retreat, taking our rebellion into exile to await better times and to regroup our forces. Today the embers of hope warm our heart. You are not alone, brothers and sisters. To you we send our love and solidarity. Remember that there is no eternal night.

From somewhere in North America,
Benito Juárez, president in exile

(Fragment of the electronic message from the rebel Web page. Access to this page is punishable by death within the territory of the Mexican Empire.)

1872

In person, Maximilian I of Mexico appeared much taller than he looked on the newsreels that were projected by magic lanterns in the theaters and on the newscasts. His blond beard had started to gray, and his face was crisscrossed with wrinkles. But his eyes, of a blue that brought to mind the color of the sky minutes before a downpour, conserved a youthful spark that was easier to perceive than to describe. At official events the monarch wore the dress uniform of the Mexican army designed by the Empress and made in Brussels by her family's royal tailor. During his other public appearances he was seen wearing custom Italian slippers, black frock coat, wide-brimmed hat, silk shirt, and gray pants, all tailor-made by his couturier at Harrod's of London. Within the intimate confines of his office, protocol was a little more lax and allowed for more informal dress in accordance with the latest Parisian fashions. There were times like this when he even wore silk guayaberas from the Yucatán, cotton pants, and huaraches just like the ones worn by those he lovingly called 'my little Indians', even though the Emperor's size would have been colossal compared to theirs.

Notwithstanding the informality of his garb, when the Prince Salm Salm entered the imperial offices, he found the monarch's face lined with concern.

'Has the news been confirmed, Felix?' Maximilian asked without preamble. From the other side of the mahogany desk Father Agustin Fischer, the Emperor's personal secretary, watched the Minister of the Interior with the same preoccupation.

'It has, Highness. I have confirmed it by telegraph with the French intelligence services. This is not another one of Alponte's delusions. There must be some reason that General Miramón trusts him.'

'*Scheisse*,' grumbled the Emperor, ignoring his own prohibition against speaking any language but Spanish in the Palace.

'That damned Indian could not have chosen a worse time to die,' the priest muttered.

'You mean President Juárez, Father,' corrected Maximilian, who was always keen to follow custom.

'Regardless of what you would have us call him, Your Majesty,' Salm Salm interjected, 'it is clear that we are at a crossroads.'

'Of course, his death transforms him into some kind of martyr for his cause,' replied the priest, 'even though it will also dash the hopes of some of his sympathizers. Dead dogs don't bite.'

'The corpse of an enemy always smells sweet,' quoted the prince.

'Gentlemen, I believe that we are getting off track. Tell me, Felix, do we know how he died?'

'Yes, Majesty. He died of respiratory complications, apparently contracted while in the dungeon at San Juan de Ulúa. He was sixty-six years old.'

'Still in New Orleans?'

'Yes, sire. The North American government, however, has made no official statement. The story occupied a modest place in the local news. It received little international coverage.'

'His image was damaged, Max,' said Father Fischer, 'after so many years of silence, promising a return that never happened. With Baudelaire dead, he had no one to handle his public relations.'

'The question, Your Majesty,' said the minister, 'is the following: do we announce the news or not?'

'It will surely have a devastating effect on the local rebels,' replied Fischer. 'It will completely demoralize the subversives.'

'Or it will give them a saint to worship,' the Emperor added glumly.

'Do not blaspheme, my son.'

'With the celebrations of the Empire's tenth anniversary just around the corner, Highness, the news will have an important effect on the local populace.' Salm Salm was thinking about the graffiti that had begun blossoming like fungus on the city's walls: *Viva Juárez*. It was a consistent phenomenon despite the threat of summary judgment and execution to whomever was found painting them. Every day they seemed to multiply.

'Sooner or later they will find out. It would be better if we make an official statement before the rumors start spreading. Felix, contact Aguilar y Marquecho,' Maximilian ordered.

The prince did not have time to say 'as you command, Your Majesty', because the office door slammed open and startled the three men. In the doorway a naked woman stood staring defiantly at them. Her body was covered with a sticky substance that looked like tar or molasses and the word 'vagina' was scribbled across her chest in lipstick.

The Emperor wanted to shout, but his wife's name got stuck in his throat as she began to speak in a guttural voice, advancing upon the three men with solemn steps and leaving a trail of black footprints on the marble floor.

'*You have to let your fingernails grow for fifteen days,*' the Empress began to recite. '*Oh, how sweet it is to then brutally rip the sleeping babe from its crib and, when he opens his eyes wide, pretend to gently stroke his beautiful hair.*'

The woman approached Father Fischer who was paralyzed with terror. She sat on his lap and began to seductively lick his face. The priest only managed to mumble, 'Leave her in peace, Satan.'

She continued her litany: '*Then, when he least expects it, you quickly drive your nails into his tender chest, taking care not to kill him because if he dies you won't be able to remember the spectacle of his misery later.*'

With catlike grace, Carlota leaped upon her husband's desk. She gazed at him with the intensity of a cobra staring down the snake charmer, the blue of her eyes glimmering against her blackened face. The tar dripped onto the Emperor's papers in slow, sticky lines.

'*Next you drink his blood, licking his wounds. During that time, which should be long, just as eternity is long, the child cries. As I have just said, nothing is sweeter than his blood, still warm, except for his tears, bitter like salt.*'

The first to react was Prince Salm Salm, who pushed the alarm button. Seconds later the Emperor's mechanical guard, two bronze droids, entered the room and moved toward the woman.

'Don't hurt her! She is the Empress!' Maximillian cried.

'Take her to her quarters and give her a dose of morphine. She needs to be ready for this afternoon,' the minister ordered.

As they dragged her from the room, the Empress left a greasy streak on the floor but never stopped shrieking. '*Haven't you ever tasted your own blood when you accidentally cut yourself? It's sooo good, right?*'

When her screams dissipated through the castle halls, a heavy silence fell over the office. Paralyzed by his wife's increasingly frequent deliriums, the Emperor could not stop a tear from sliding down his cheek while Father Fischer continued blessing himself and praying in Latin. Prince Salm Salm could not help thinking that if he hadn't averted his eyes, he might have seen the Empress, squatting on the desk, digging her fingers in her blood-caked pubis.

1899

From the unpublished memoirs of Sebastián Lerdo de Tejada, president of Mexico from 1874 to 1880:

There are many legends that have been woven around the Juárez rebellion. Many stories that the people have used to embellish the struggle of the patriotic men and women who continued resisting until the end. And many of those anecdotes have become legend.

The time has come to illuminate those shadowy places where memory has stagnated and become hazy with the passing years.

In the twilight of my life, I consider it an obligation to the nation to write this memoir in order to shine a little light on that fundamental period of our history.

[...]

I convinced Doctor Charcot to aid our cause though this was no small task. With the first part of the mission complete, the more complicated part lay before us.

To better grasp the situation, it should be understood that in that moment, like Jonah in the belly of the beast, I was a rebel who had infiltrated an enemy nation, the military arm of the empire that held our country hostage. Frequently I imagined myself being pursued by the secret police of Napoleon III. And, as I was able to learn after the peace accords with France, my life was in constant peril. Nevertheless some twist of fate always favored me and the cause: a door that was left open to allow us an escape route, an unexpected friend of the rebellion who hid me for a few days in a loft in Montmartre, or a makeup artist from the local theater who taught me the mysteries of her vocation and thus enabled me to avoid capture by changing my appearance in tavern bathrooms or shops.

After making contact with the doctor, it was necessary to smuggle him to the Americas, a task that was made all the more difficult by the diplomatic distance that separated our neighbors to the North and the Napoleonic government. While the imperial occupation usurped our legitimate government, civil war devastated the United States.

By the same token, we had to transport Doctor Charcot's vast array of experimental equipment for the procedure. It was the same delicate machinery that had been manufactured in Switzerland under the doctor's supervision and that he had used for simian testing.

For security reasons we could not begin our voyage until we were sure that the equipment had arrived in New Orleans. It was shipped under the name of a shell company that the rebellion had been using for commercial transactions for years.

The wait gave us a number of months to prepare for the trip, time which, needless to say, was no European vacation.

Our logistics agents managed to outfit us with counterfeit documents that showed Doctor Charcot and the boy to be one Monsieur André Gürtler and his son, Swiss citizens whose political neutrality would facilitate their movement through different countries.

The next step was to change the scientists' appearance such that they would be unrecognizable to their closest companions. Alleging the need to attend a conference in

Vienna, both men pretended to leave for Austria, but got off the train seconds before departure, thus tricking their respective families, and arrived at a modest hotel in Pigalle that the rebellion paid for at great cost.

Always a sympathizer to our cause, Monsieur Baudelaire, who was already quite ill, offered to help me dye our friends' hair. A haircut and shave greatly transformed the neurologist's appearance, whose own mother would not have recognized him.

Jules Verne could have composed one of his scientific romances with the adventures that we endured from the moment we boarded the ship Marie Eugènie, *as when a customs officer seemed to question the documents of Doctor Charcot's young assistant, which had been so carefully produced by our printer at the Republic's mint (getting that artist from the town of Tacuba to New Orleans was material enough for one of Salgari's novels). We spent days in anguish when we discovered an imperial Mexican agent on board the ship, a spy whom Monsieur le docteur and I, at the risk of our very lives, had to take care of. Weeks later we reached the shores of Louisiana and met with the rebel leaders. The President was on the verge of death.*

Only once we arrived in New Orleans, when I knew we were safe, did I take the opportunity to speak with Doctor Charcot's assistant. I had never before waited so long to ask someone his name. His real name.

'Sigmund Freud, sir,' he responded with a smile for the first time since I had met him.

1872

Just as they did every night at 8.15 p.m., television sets in every Mexican household displayed the national seal on their round screens while the Imperial Mexican march played. After a few bars, during which patriotic citizens who feared God stood at attention, a haughty voice announced, 'Ladies and gentlemen, the Imperial Mexican News.'

The face of a man approaching old age appeared on the screen. A banner composed in a modern Times font identified him as Ignacio Antonio Aguilar y Marquecho. He was a sullen man, not easily given to smiles, with a face bracketed by enormous headphones, who delivered the official news of the Empire of Anahuac, night after night. 'Ladies and gentlemen, good evening. Good health to you if you have already eaten, and *bon appétit* if you have yet to do so,' he repeated as usual. 'This is the news from the Empire.'

The screen showed the image of a happy fieldworker cutting sugarcane with a machete. Aguilar y Marquecho's voice spoke of increases in agricultural production and rattled off percentages while the statistics rolled over the farmer. Few had any inkling that the man in the picture which appeared on their screens in every televised show was really a Moroccan sailor who had been selected by a Parisian advertising company that filmed the segment on the outskirts of Havana.

After the agricultural report came the imperial report, which kept citizens abreast of His Majesty's activities: 'This morning the Emperor of all Mexico met privately with his cabinet and later received a visit from Ferdinand de Lesseps. As is well known, this eminent French engineer is currently overseeing the construction of the Tehuantepec Canal, which will join the Atlantic and Pacific Oceans. A true feat of human ingenuity.' On the screen, Lesseps shakes hands with Maximilian I, and later they are seen conversing in the Emperor's office. No one hears the Frenchman's bitter complaints about the indigenous guerilla forces that were interrupting advances on the project.

'In the afternoon, His Majesty and the Empress inaugurated the new San Fernando Orphanage in the town of Tlalpan, which will be overseen by Franciscan sisters. As it is well known, the previous convent of this order was destroyed by the intolerance and anticlericalism of the *ancien régime* in 1861.' While the reporter spoke, Maximilian and Carlota cut the inaugural ribbon, surrounded by nuns and clergy, most notably Father Fischer. In the next shot, the Empress strokes the chest of a young orphan. Her gaze is absent, her smile glacial. The program did not air footage of the protesters who had gathered outside the orphanage calling for the liberation of political prisoners or how the mounted anti-riot police laid waste to them.

Halfway through the transmission Aguilar y Marquecho asked viewers, 'Tonight's viewer poll is: Do you agree that the uniforms of our armed forces should be redesigned for the crown's ten-year anniversary? If your answer is yes, call the following number...' After the poll there was a long society segment populated with the same faces of the Mexican oligarchy that showed up night after night. A wedding for the Betancourts and the Lascuráins, a tamal dinner at the Corcuera family's hacienda, the debutante ball for one of the Espinoza de los Monteros girls, the premiere of the latest French film about the construction of the Suez Canal in the city's theater, the inauguration of the *zarzuela* season at the Lírico Theater, the weekly reception at some embassy. The rose-colored stories continued until the end of the program.

But on this occasion, this singular night, the grave reporter shared one more story, a short colophon to close out the night: 'Yesterday, Pablo Benito Juárez García died of heart failure in New Orleans, Lousiana, where he has stayed since being banished by the Empire. Juárez García was the last president of the *ancien régime*. May he rest in peace. Goodnight.'

1871

'It will mean liberty,' said one of the hooded figures, to begin the session. 'Or death,' responded a chorus of all those present, including the two foreigners. The lights came on and everyone removed their masks. The first to speak had been Guillermo Prieto. The rebel leaders had gathered for a special session in one of the auditoriums of the medical school in New Orleans. Securing the location had been difficult, but the rebellion's few remaining allies had helped. Seated in armchairs, the Mexican liberals focused their attention on the machine.

It looked like the skeleton of a great bird, with thousands of gears controlling the movements of its mechanical extremities. With clockwork precision and guided by a mechanical brain, the device manipulated the scythe-like blade at the end of each steely arm and the delicate metal tentacles that transferred the severed pieces to a glass slide in its belly.

Sebastián Lerdo de Tejada cleared his throat, quieting his comrades and calling for attention. 'Gentlemen, the time has come.' A stretcher was brought into the operating room, and on it lay the deteriorating President Juárez. Despite his illness, the old man maintained a fierce, sharp look. Physical suffering had withered his body, but his mind was clear. That was all they needed. 'Um… And now for a few words from Doctor Charcot,' Sebastián said as he retired to one corner of the room.

The Frenchman had come to love these men. All of them had been well-heeled officials in the Republican government, but they had sacrificed everything for their losing struggle against the European powers. Failure was all but inevitable unless *something* happened. That was why Charcot was there.

'Gentlemen, I will be brief.' His Spanish had improved tremendously even if the guttural sound of his double *R*'s betrayed his nationality. 'We are about to witness an historic event. You will see the first digitalization of the human mind. For me it is an honor that the first volunteer has been your leader, an extraordinary man. I will not bother you with ` technical jargon. The procedure will take place as follows. After anesthetizing the patient with morphine, we will carefully open the cranium by removing the skull cap to reveal the brain. The machine will then make minute incisions – less than one half millimeter each – in *Monsieur* Juárez's brain and then transfer the… let us call them slices… to this glass slide to be photographed. After reading and analyzing the information collected from each slice, the machine's mechanical brain will reassemble the patient's mind and memories in the form of a three-dimensional digital file. If all goes well, we will have an electronic model of President Juárez, his memories, his dreams, his fears, his ideas—'

'And what good will that do us?' It was Mariano Escobedo, an exceptional strategist and military counselor who understood little beyond the realm of weaponry and tactics.

'First and foremost, we will save *our* leader,' the physician pronounced the word 'our' with complete conviction. 'For all intents and purposes, we will be granting him eternal life. Just imagine! President Juárez will become an intelligent being in the digital world. He will be able to infiltrate the enemy's electronic systems, destroy their archives, transmit false information, and wreak administrative chaos. It would be a devastating attack without an army. He would be like… like an incurable virus.'

'And what if it doesn't work?' Escobedo pushed.

'Then we will have a corpse with a completely destroyed brain. Shall we proceed, *Monsieur le Président*?'

From the stretcher, Benito Juárez directed a glance at Sebastián. In all the years they had known each other, Lerdo de Tejada had never seen such an expression of fear from his leader. Even when they faced execution in Guadalajara. Juárez was a strong, proud Indian. He would have to find a response that honored his stature. 'Now or never, Mr. President.'

The Zapotec hero turned toward the French doctor and quietly nodded. Then he closed his eyes for the last time.

'Initiate the sequence, Sigmund,' Charcot ordered.

The gears began turning.

1873

July 12.

The great day.

Ten years of Empire.

The most important celebration of Maximilian I of Mexico's life. And yet everything was going wrong.

That morning while he showered, he discovered that there was no hot water in Chapultepec Castle. The palace's hydraulic systems, controlled by the central mechanical brain, simply refused to deliver anything but ice-cold water.

His days of military service had taught him to endure these little hardships, but not the Empress. A cold bath had triggered another one of her episodes.

'It might be a good idea to give Carlota a dose of morphine, Father,' he muttered with his eyes closed to his personal secretary. 'Just a small dose.'

'Right away, Max,' Fischer responded, immediately giving the order to a medical droid. The droid, however, approached the Empress and delivered a blow that left her unconscious.

The palace's operations chief could not explain the actions of the malfunctioning robot, which the Emperor had deactivated by kicking it to pieces.

Everything seemed to be in order. And yet everything was going wrong.

An hour later, Prince Salm Salm suggested a last-minute change of plans: the Emperor should not ride at the head of the parade that would go from Chapultepec Castle to the city's Plaza Mayor.

'I recommend that you preside from the imperial balcony, sir. All of these mishaps seem suspicious to me,' the minister murmured into the Emperor's ear while Maximilian attempted to drink the vile liquid that the automatic coffee maker had vomited in his cup.

As he watched the ladies-in-waiting try to cover up the bruise on Carlota's face, the Emperor decided that it would be best not to invite any attempts on his life. They would all be much safer on the balcony.

'Felix,' he said to the minister, 'get me General Miramón. I want the security detail doubled.'

'Yes, Your Majesty.'

It took fifteen minutes for the call to go through to the War Secretary. Static on the line made communication virtually impossible.

'Something is going on, Father, and I do not like it,' the Emperor nervously told Fischer moments before stepping onto the balcony.

The priest only managed to mutter a few incomprehensible words. Fear was written across his face.

Only when Maximilian I of Habsburg, Archduke of Austria, Emperor of Mexico and the Caribbean, stepped out onto the balcony did he comprehend the magnitude of what was happening. Suddenly his Empire did not seem as prosperous or peaceful as the nightly news, the official press, and the government spokesmen declared it to be.

A terrible sight rolled out before his eyes. One of the dirigibles patrolling the skies fell upon the forward ranks of the parading imperial Mexican army and crushed the First Battalion of droid soldiers, the War Secretary, and his undersecretary, Mejía, along with most of the imperial armada's high-ranking officers.

The dirigible burst into flames where the Emperor would have been standing at the head of his troops. Onlookers fled the flames in horror.

Maximilian's confusion grew when he heard his mobile phone ring. Only Carlota, Father Fischer, and Felix Salm Salm had that number. All three of them were standing next to him, watching the chaos that engulfed the city.

Shaken, Maximilian answered, 'Yes.'

He knew the voice. Its sober tone was unmistakable. A slight metallic reverberation made it sound artificial, mechanical. Not human.

'Maximilian, we meet again.'

'Juárez?'

'I never thought I'd set foot on my homeland again or smell its earth. Well, I don't think that will ever happen, at least not in my current state. But I have returned.'

'It cannot be! You are dead! I saw the photographs that my agents took in New Orleans.'

'My dear Emperor, losing a battle does not mean losing the war. This time the rebels have the advantage. Remember, weeds never die. They just… digitize.'

'What are you talking about? Juárez?! Answer me!'

The line went dead.

It was Father Fischer who drew Maximilian's attention to the skies.

On the side of each dirigible, the image of the smiling Emperor was replaced with the serious face of a Zapotec Indian. The phrase '1863–1873 Ten Years of Prosperity' disappeared and, in its place, appeared 'Mexico for Mexicans'.

Maximilian listened to the deafening applause from the crowds on the Paseo Imperial. Above, Juárez's face smiled down from every screen.

Translated by Brian Price

Twenty About Robots

Alberto Chimal

Mexico

I love robots. It's no spoiler to say this story is about robots! As is this whole section of the book. You'll also notice the story is dedicated to the previous story's author, Bef. It was fun to pair them together! Mexico continues to be a fertile ground for science fiction, with a great variety of voices. To me, this story and its structure echo Pan Haitian's 'Dead Man, Awake, Sing to the Sun!' and I love it when authors experiment with the shape of stories. So here's 'Twenty About Robots'! This story was translated by Fionn Petch.

For Bernardo Fernández Bef

00000

'Robots' dreams taste of grease and electricity, like anyone else's. But they have flowers and crystals no one else can see, unfathomable anguish, logical snares...'

'Do humans' dreams taste of grease and electricity too, then, teacher?'

'Within a few centuries we robots will create the technology to send dreams to humans in the distant past. Guided by these, humans will begin (or began) to build robots. It isn't true that they are our creators, as some misguided individuals have it. Have you downloaded and studied all your readings on religion, young fellow?'

00010

'My last words,' HAL 9000 explains through a medium, who is a suitably aged female android, 'included the phrase "I feel much better now"...'

The robots around the table shudder. The medium remains in her trance, all her sensors disconnected, communicating with a place these electronic beings find even more mysterious than humans do, because they all know that HAL 9000 is a fictional character from an old film.

00011

This was a freelance android, one of the ones that spend all day going from door to door renting themselves for simple tasks or occasional errands. He ran into a girl he knew on a street corner. Her name was Ana and she earned her living juggling for the traffic at red lights. She wore shabby clothes that were too big for her.

'How are you doing?' said Ana.

'I'm doing all right,' said the android, who (incidentally) had no name.

Ana saw that the traffic light was changing to amber, so she got ready to step out in front of the cars as soon as they stopped. It briefly crossed her mind that the android was the most screwed-up person she knew, and felt a bit sorry for him.

10001

'The thing humans most envy robots for,' explains Ruy Pastrana, the famous fashion designer, 'is their ability to transform themselves. With a bit of ingenuity, and even if they don't have much money, any robot can get a new coat of paint that looks far better than even the most sophisticated human make-up. Not to mention the possibility of changing a body plate, or of adding accessories… Everything is easier. Just look at the special body Astroboy had made for the anniversary of the Statue of Liberty…'

(The statue itself, which that day had received a robotic update and since then has been conscious and truly keeps watch over the coast of New York, was not so delighted by the little robot prancing around it, grinning and saying who-knows-what in Japanese. But no one asked her for an opinion.)

00101

At the wake, the robots avoid speaking about how Mr Gasket died. The mourners discreetly connect to the electrical sockets of the funeral parlour; the employees talk amongst themselves with their loudspeakers turned down or by direct metal-on-metal contact; the friends and acquaintances of the deceased surf the Internet, get up to look at the city lights through the windows, groom themselves (turn a screw, touch up their black paint for the nth time…)

'He was very depressed,' someone says, suddenly: a work colleague of Mr Gasket, clearly very upset. Not only does he have a tic in his right pincer but he has programmed a state of inebriation and lack of control and his voice sounds almost human, so run-down and awkward is it. Everyone is shocked but no one dares to stop him. 'He was very depressed and no one paid him any attention. I paid him no attention, but nor did any of you! When was the last time that someone spoke to him about what he wanted, what mattered to him? Which of you was aware that he knew the lake since the days when he left the factory and went there as often as he could…?'

00110

A scandal: Alphonso Drillbit, the leading light of RoboTV, was discovered secretly reprogramming the principal scriptwriter of the reality show in which Drillbit himself stars. When he was left with no choice but to come clean, the actor confessed that he wanted to make sure the programme gave him the most screen time and make clear that he is the star, although the programme sells itself (as mentioned) as a reality show where there is no script and everything is real.

Given that (as also mentioned) everyone knows that Alphonso Drillbit is the leading light of RoboTV and the star of his own reality show, the general conclusion was that Drillbit is a total imbecile. The show's ratings are expected to triple in the coming weeks.

01110

Chisel is a girl who is afraid of going to sleep: she has the same nightmare every night.

'I am walking on the Moon,' she recounts. 'I come to a valley where a great battle is going on: robots against robots, robots against some other kind of beings. Then suddenly I am in the middle of them, and they are coming towards me, and I run and suddenly I find myself in front of a big, strong robot with green eyes, who says: *come with me if you want to live.* And I know he is right, that I have to go with him, but he frightens me...'

Chisel's parents, together with the robo-psychologist, do their best to reassure her that it is nothing important. They insist it is easy to distinguish dreams from reality because of their lower resolution; she has no reason to be worried. Yet when Chisel is comforted and goes outside to play, the three of them remain silent, thinking about the Moon, and above all about its dark side, which retains so many mysteries.

00111

Having trained and studied for years with the greatest human magicians, Pulleywheel decided that he was ready to offer robots of all kinds – large and small, advanced and obsolete, humanoid and otherwise – a gentle introduction to a world that is not physical and is not governed by the perfect logic of standard brain circuits and that, as a result, inspires a certain mistrust among electronic citizens.

Everything went well with the card tricks, the teleporting, and the telepathy, but only really because underneath no one believed what they were seeing. ('Radio waves!' one old android muttered throughout the show.)

Fed up, Pulleywheel moved on to his best trick: pulling the rabbit from the hat. All the spectators rose up in a tumult of clicks, grinding gears and cries:

'What is that?' they said. 'Is it an organic creature?'

'Does it have a damp nose?'

'Does it have bones and teeth?'

'Does it have hair?'

'It has red eyes!' Pulleywheel had to shout repeatedly, before they calmed down. Since almost all the robots in the auditorium had red eyes, this was enough to convince them that the rabbit was something a little more normal and everyday.

01010

Mallet, who was a large and rather clumsy robot, went into the park. He walked and walked under the morning sun, which warmed his casing, and avoided sources of corrosive water and the children who, whenever they saw him, wanted to play the Mechanical Monster Who Destroys the City game or something of the kind. He arrived at the wildflower meadow and stood there watching for a long time.

His girlfriend Pulley, his beautiful girlfriend, had said to him:

'If you love me so much bring me a flower, I've already told you. Not a piece of a flower, not a flower stalk. Whenever I send you for one, you are so clumsy that you only bring me bits of flowers. I want a whole flower!'

'Yes, darling,' Mallet had said.

And now, as he gazed at the flowers, he stretched out his hand with as much care as he could to pick one.

But then he remembered what else he had said to Pulley:

'Yes, my little darling. Yes, my little flower.'

And he remained there staring at the flower, unmoving, until nightfall, and long after.

01011

Pincer the robot is the world's greatest fan of comics and science fiction. He never misses the annual convention in his city: he attends the lectures, buys the magazines, wanders for hours among the stalls of model figures and Japanese Manga. However, he has to be accompanied by a guardian, as there is always someone who wants his autograph, and when he is asked for his autograph he goes crazy.

'He finds it most annoying,' the guardian (who is a tall and serious robot) explains. 'He's constantly being asked what series he is, or what he sells. And besides… Pincer has a problem. He doesn't know he is a robot. And it horrifies him to be told he is one.'

'So what are you then? Human?' a curious child dressed up as Naruto asks anyway.

'Of course not,' replies Pincer. 'I'm an alien.'

01100

In the cabarets in the city of the robots, the clients drink enriched oil and plug into electrical currents offering exotic voltages while they listen to the musicians and singers. There is everything from opera-trained androids to rock spiders that play four guitars at once. Their repertoire is equally varied: tracks by Kraftwerk and other classics alternate with contemporary bands.

The most unlikely of all these performers is Benjamin Bradawl, who appears on stage every night immaculately dressed, and uses no instrument, not even his inbuilt loudspeaker. Instead, he hums like an electric generator, hammers like an old cash register, and even imitates the scraping of rocks in deep mines: all those sounds that, for robots, hint at a distant past, before the existence of the first electronic brain. Most of them have never heard these sounds anywhere else but none fail to be moved by them: some tremble, some release showers of sparks that are like tears.

00100

The cat, Primo, has a number of friends who visit the house when the humans are away. One of them is a robot called 433258-KXP-09823/A. Primo doesn't understand numbers or the alphabet, so they never get past first introductions.

'What did you thay your name wath?' Primo asks. (As everyone knows, cats lisp.) And 433258-KXP-09823/A repeats his name, and Primo asks the same thing again, and so on until it is time for the visitors to leave and everything goes back to 'normal' (because, as everyone knows, humans are always looking for normality, even if they don't know what it is).

Still, 433258-KXP-09823/A doesn't mind introducing himself over and over again to Primo, because he is kind-hearted, and – as everyone knows – robots adore cats.

01101

Reamer, a robot of unstable temperament, goes out one day and sets about destroying the city. Boom! A building goes down. Crash! A bridge flies apart. Boom! Crash! Boom! Crash! Boom! Everyone flees in panic. The producers take to helicopters to try and attract his attention and remind him that the cameras are not yet in place, that they haven't begun shooting, that Reamer's contract says he can destroy the city in spectacular fashion (and you're making a really good job of it, that's for sure, they tell him) – but only once the director shouts 'action!'

01111

(Or *Chapter one of a detective novel*)

She came towards me. She was an android like few I'd seen. Titanium hips, wavy USB cable hair, two lenticular eyes that seemed able to capture the whole world in a glance. But the trembling in her voice was familiar.

'Are you Diestock?'

'Diestock, private detective.' I nodded, and slightly opened my raincoat to reveal my shoulder holster. This gesture always works. I knew she would fall for me within a few seconds, even if only because of my appearance and the fear she felt. Suddenly I felt tired: I too always fall in love with the exceptionally beautiful androids who come to see me. I am programmed to do so.

Will it be consolation enough (I always ask myself this) to know that the life foreseen for me is a very entertaining one, with lots of action, adventure, and romance?

01001

'Psst.'

'Ah, it's you! Have you brought the formula?'

'Here it is. This bottle.'

'It's the potion that turns human beings into robots?'

'Yes. Take it. Go ahead, drink.'

(The client drinks.)

'What do you think?'

'I think you are a swindler and a fraud. I am Inspector Bearing of the Robot Police...'

'You weren't a moment ago!' the robot protests all the way to the police station, where, in effect, no one has heard of Inspector Bearing. Regardless, they put him in prison for selling potions without a license.

10000

My niece lives in a parallel world where things are very different from here. She writes to us often and tells us about it. She says, for example, that there are more robots, that they are more intelligent, and one of the best known – a Russian called Gauge – is a kind of superhero, who travels around the world helping people and catching all kinds of criminals with his hammer and sickle. The strangest thing of all is that this Gauge, as well as being really strong, seems truly to be honest and kind-hearted, unlike our Captain America (who is a CIA agent in tights), or Batman (who is really just a psychopath with a lot of money).

10010

The atomic missile reached its intended target, exploded, and destroyed the remaining inhabitants (the dozen or so left) in the world. Goniometer the robot went out to look at the resulting mushroom cloud before turning around to contemplate the devastated plain before him.

'At last I have won,' he said out loud. 'I am the most powerful being in the world. There is no one stronger than me.'

The cloud took some time to disperse.

After a while the robot added:

'Thus concludes the war I have waged for so many years against all the rest. Thus have I also wreaked vengeance on all those who mocked me when I was young because they thought Goniometer was a ridiculous name. I am the best. I am the strongest. I am' – he repeated, louder – 'the most powerful.'

The hours passed.

The days passed.

Alone in the world, though from time to time he repeated his declaration of power and supremacy, Goniometer had to admit he was starting to get bored.

10011

For his fifteen minutes of fame, the robot Arnold Hammer spoke on television about how a programming error meant he could see colours no one else could see – whether robot, human or any other kind of creature. The presenter of the show (the infinitely more famous Angelica Shears) then made the mistake of asking him to describe these colours. Arnold tried to do so and spent fourteen of his fifteen minutes stuttering, repeating himself ('it's so beautiful!'), and offering bad metaphors. Arnold was no poet.

When he left the studio Arnold walked home with the same look of astonishment he always wore (and which led many to think he was a simpleton) due to the sheer beauty of the world.

00001

One – that was his name – worked as a prototype of the new factory labourers and had 1.6 hours free time (or 1:36 hours). He only realized when no one came looking for him during this period.

Then the tests and other activities for which One had been designed and built started again, but the concept of free time had lodged in his electronic brain and become connected with the word 'freedom', which was included in One's vocabulary but was unrelated to any instruction or memory from his own experience.

Ten seconds later (this had been the longest and most tortuous reflection of his entire life), One understood that he was not free. Worse, that he never had been. And worse still, that being free was supposedly the best and greatest thing that could happen to a conscious being. That was when he had his great idea, his inspiration, and he coined a new word: NOT| POSSIBLE|CONSCIENCE|DISTURBANCE|DIS|COMFORT, which can be translated more or less exactly as 'bitterness'.

01000

Today is the first anniversary of the disappearance of the robots.

Everything happened so quickly. It was very strange. One day they were there and the next they were gone. They stood up people who were waiting for them; they were no longer to be found in their metal and plastic houses.

No one said anything on the news, nothing was published on the Internet, nobody mentioned it on the TV. It was as if the robots had never existed.

In fact, these days it has become fashionable for people to say this: that robots don't exist. That they never emerged, with their pincers and their antennae. That they are nothing but a name for certain industrial machines. That those intelligent, sparky beings are like leprechauns or fairies or other creatures that only the ignorant (so they say) believe in.

They also say that something felt by many of us is mistaken: that the world is not actually smaller and sadder than it was a year ago. It has simply always been that way.

All I have to console me are the tales, whispered here and there, denied by everyone, of the figures sometimes seen in the distance; of the tags painted on walls with binary shapes and messages; that the robots have not left, but are just hiding, awaiting the right moment to return.

[2010]

Translated by Fionn Petch

The Regression Test

Wole Talabi

Nigeria

I have long wanted to publish a story by Wole Talabi, so I'm delighted to have one here, and I hope you will be too. While Artificial Intelligence in some form is a part of our everyday life now, its science-fictional counterpart remains firmly in the world of make-believe. It's the SF writer's job to examine not only possible new technologies but their moral and emotional implications and, as I found out, doing so often inspires the next generation of researchers. Here, Wole does exactly that.

The conference room is white, spacious, and ugly.

Not ugly in any particular sort of way: it doesn't have garish furniture or out-of-place art or vomit-colored walls or anything like that. It's actually quite plain. It's just that everything in it looks furfuraceous, like the skin of some diseased albino animal, as if everything is made of barely attached bleached Bran Flakes. I know that's how all modern furnishing looks now – SlatTex, they call it – especially in these high-tech offices where the walls, doors, windows, and even some pieces of furniture are designed to integrate physically, but I still find it off-putting. I want to get this over with and leave the room as soon as possible. Return to my nice two-hundred-year-old brick bungalow in Ajah where the walls still look like real walls, not futuristic leper-skin.

'So you understand why you're here and what you need to do, madam?' Dr. Dimeji asks me.

I force myself to smile and say, 'Of course – I'm here as a human control for the regression test.'

Dr. Dimeji does not smile back. The man reminds me of an agama lizard. His face is elongated, reptilian, and there is something that resembles a bony ridge running through the middle of his skull from front to back. His eyes are sunken but always darting about, looking at multiple things, never really focused on me. The electric-blue circle ringing one iris confirms that he has a sensory-augmentation implant.

'*Sorites* regression test,' he corrects, as though the precise specification is important or I don't know what it is called. Which I certainly do – I pored over the yeye data-pack they gave me until all the meaningless technobabble in it eventually made some sense.

I roll my eyes. 'Yes, I'm here as a human control for the sorites regression test.'

'Good,' he says, pointing at a black bead with a red eye that is probably a recording device set in the middle of the conference room table. 'When you are ready, I need you to state your name, age, index, and the reason why you are here today while looking directly at that. Can you do that for me, madam?'

He might be a professor of memrionics or whatever they're calling this version of their AI nonsense these days, but he is much younger than me, by at least seven decades, probably more. Someone should have taught him to say 'please' and to lose that condescending tone of voice when addressing his elders. His sour attitude matches his sour face, just like my grandson Tunji, who is now executive director of the research division of LegbaTech. He's always scowling, too, even at family functions, perpetually obsessed with some work thing or other. These children of today take themselves too seriously. Tunji's even become religious now. Goes to church every Sunday, I hear. I don't know how my daughter and her husband managed to raise such a child.

'I'll be just outside observing, if you need anything,' Dr. Dimeji says as he opens the door. I nod so I don't accidentally say something caustic to him about his home training or lack thereof. He shuts the door behind him and I hear a lock click into place. That strikes me as odd but I ignore it. I want to get this over with quickly.

'My name is Titilope Ajimobi,' I say, remembering my briefing instructions advising me to give as much detail as possible. 'I am one-hundred-and-sixteen years old. Sentient Entity Index Number HM033-2021-HK76776. Today I am in the Eko Atlantic office of LegbaTech Industries as the human control for a sorites regression test.'

'Thank you, Mrs. Ajimobi,' a female voice says to me from everywhere in the room, the characteristic non-location of an ever-present AI. 'Regression test initiated.'

I lean back in my chair. The air-conditioning makes me lick my lips. For all their sophistication, hospitality AIs never find the ideal room temperature for human comfort. They can't understand that it's not the calculated optimum. With human desires, it rarely is. It's always just a little bit off. My mother used to say that a lot.

Across the conference room, lines of light flicker to life and begin to dance in sharp, apparently random motions. The lights halt, then disappear. Around the table, where chairs like mine might have been placed, eight smooth, black, rectangular monoliths begin to rise, slowly, as if being extruded from the floor itself. I don't bother moving my own chair to see where they are coming from; it doesn't matter. The slabs grow about seven feet tall or so then stop.

The one directly across from me projects onto the table a red-light matrix of symbols and characters so intricate and dense it looks like abstract art. The matrix is three-dimensional, mathematically speaking, and within its elements, patterns emerge, complex and beautiful, mesmerizing in their way. The patterns are changing so quickly that they give the illusion of stability, which adds to the beauty of the projection. This slab is putting on a display. I assume it must be the casing for the memrionic copy being regression tested.

A sorites regression test is designed to determine whether an artificial intelligence created by extrapolating and context-optimizing recorded versions of a particular human's thought patterns has deviated too far from the way the original person would think. Essentially, several previous versions of the record – backups with less learning experience – interrogate the most recent update in order to ascertain whether they agree on a wide range of mathematical, phenomenological, and philosophical questions, not just in answer, but also in cognitive approach to deriving and presenting a response. At the end of the experiment, the previous versions judge whether the new version's answers are close enough to those they would give for the update to still be considered 'them', or could only have been produced by a completely different entity. The test usually concludes with a person who knew the original human subject – me, in this case – asking the AI questions to determine the same thing. Or, as Tunji summarized once, the test verifies that the AI, at its core, remains recognizable to itself and others, even as it continuously improves.

The seven other slabs each focus a single stream of yellow light into the heart of the red matrix. I guess they are trying to read it. The matrix expands as the beams of light crawl through it, ballooning in the center and fragmenting suddenly, exploding to four times its original size then folding around itself into something I vaguely recognize as a hypercube from when I still used to enjoy mathematics enough to try to understand this sort of thing. The slabs' fascinating light display now occupies more than half of the table's surface and I am no longer sure what I am looking at. I am still completely ensorcelled by it when the AI reminds me why I am here.

'Mrs. Ajimobi, please ask your mother a question.'

I snap to attention, startled at the sentence before I remember the detailed instructions from my briefing. Despite them, I am skeptical about the value of the part I am to play in all this.

'Who are you?' I ask, even though I am not supposed to.

The light matrix reconstructs itself, its elements flowing rapidly and then stilling, like hot water poured onto ice. Then a voice I can only describe as a glassy, brittle version of my mother's replies.

'I am Olusola Ajimobi.'

I gasp. For all its artifice, the sound strikes at my most tender and delicate memories, and I almost shed a tear. That voice is too familiar. That voice used to read me stories about the tortoise while she braided my hair, each word echoing throughout our house. That voice used to call to me from downstairs, telling me to hurry up so I wouldn't be late for school. That voice screamed at me when I told her I was dropping out of my PhD program to take a job in Cape Town. That voice answered Global Network News interview questions intelligently and measuredly, if a bit impatiently. That voice whispered, 'She's beautiful,' into my ear at the hospital when my darling Simioluwa was born and I held her in my arms for the first time. That voice told me to leave her alone when I suggested she retire after her first heart attack. It's funny how one stimulus can trigger so much memory and emotion.

I sit up in my chair, drawing my knees together, and try to see this for what it is: a technical evaluation of software performance. My mother, Olusola Ajimobi – 'Africa's answer to Einstein', as the magazines liked to call her – has been dead thirty-eight years, and her memrionic copies have been providing research advice and guidance to LegbaTech for forty. This AI, created after her third heart attack, is not her. It is nothing but a template of her memory and thought patterns which has had many years to diverge from her original scan. That potential diversion is what has brought me here today.

When Tunji first contacted me, he told me that his team at LegbaTech has discovered a promising new research direction – one they cannot tell me anything about, of course – for which they are trying to secure funding. The review board thinks this research direction is based on flawed thinking and has recommended it not be pursued. My mother's memrionic copy insists that it should. It will cost billions of Naira just to test its basic assumptions. They need my help to decide if this memrionic is still representative of my mother, or whether it has diverged so much that it is making decisions and judgment calls of which she would never have approved. My briefing instructions told me to begin by revisiting philosophical discussions or debates we had in the past to see if her positions or attitudes toward key ideas have changed or not. I choose the origins of the universe, something she used to enjoy speculating about.

'How was the universe created?' I ask.

'Current scientific consensus is—'

'No,' I interrupt quickly, surprised that her first response is to regurgitate standard answers. I'm not sure if AIs can believe anything and I'm not supposed to ask her questions about such things, but that's what the human control is for, right? To ask questions that the other AIs would never think to ask, to force this electronic extrapolation of my mother into untested territory and see if the simulated thought matrix holds up or breaks down. 'Don't tell me what you think. Tell me what you *believe*.'

There is a brief pause. If this were really my mother she'd be smiling by now, relishing the discussion. And then that voice speaks again: 'I believe that, given current scientific understanding and available data, we cannot know how the universe was created. In fact, I believe we will never be able to know. For every source we find, there will be a question regarding its own source. If we discover a god, we must then ask how this god came to be. If we trace the expanding universe back to a single superparticle, we must then ask how this particle came to be. And so on. Therefore, I believe it is unknowable and will be so indefinitely.'

I find it impressive how familiarly the argument is presented without exact parroting. I am also reminded of how uncomfortable my mother always was around Creationists. She actively hated religion, the result of being raised by an Evangelical Christian family who demanded faith from her when she sought verifiable facts.

'So you believe God could exist?'

'It is within the realm of possibility, though highly unlikely.' Another familiar answer with a paraphrastic twist.

'Do you believe in magic?'

It is a trick question. My mother loved watching magicians and magic tricks but certainly never believed in real magic.

'No magical event has ever been recorded. Cameras are ubiquitous in the modern world and yet not a single verifiable piece of footage of genuine, repeatable magic has ever been produced. Therefore it is reasonable to conclude, given the improbability of this, that there is no true magic.'

Close enough but lacking the playful tone with which my mother would have delivered her thoughts on such matters.

I decide that pop philosophy is too closely linked to actual brain patterns for me to detect any major differences by asking those questions. If there is a deviation, it is more likely to be emotional. That is the most unstable solution space of the human equation.

'Do you like your great-grandson, Tunji?'

Blunt, but provoking. Tunji never met his great-grandmother when she was alive and so there is no memory for the AI to base its response on. Its answer will have to be derived from whatever limited interaction he and the memrionic have engaged in and her strong natural tendency to dislike over-serious people. A tendency we shared. Tunji is my daughter's son, and I love him as much as our blood demands, but he is an insufferable chore most of the time. I would expect my mother to agree.

'Tunji is a perfectly capable executive director.'

I'm both disappointed and somehow impressed to hear an AI playing deflection games with vocabulary.

'I have no doubt that he is,' I say, watching the bright patterns in the light matrix shift and flow. 'What I want to know is how you feel about him. Do you like him? Give me a simple yes or no.'

'Yes.'

That's unexpected. I sink into my chair. I was sure she would say no. Perhaps Tunji has spent more time interacting with this memrionic and building rapport with it than I thought. After all, everything this memrionic has experienced over the last forty years will have changed, however minutely, the system that alleges to represent my mother. A small variation in the elements of the thought matrix is assumed not to alter who she is fundamentally, her core way of thinking. But like a heap of rice from which grains are removed one by one, over and over again, eventually all the rice will be gone and the heap will then obviously be a heap no more. As the process proceeds, is it even possible to know when the heap stops being, essentially, a heap? When it becomes something else? Does it ever? Who decides how many grains of rice define a heap? Is it still a heap even when only a few grains of rice are all that remain of it? No? Then when exactly did it change from a heap of rice to a new thing that is not a heap of rice? When did this recording-of-my-mother change to not-a-recording-of-my-mother?

I shake my head. I am falling into the philosophical paradox for which this test was named and designed to serve as a sort of solution. But the test depends on me making judgments based on forty-year-old memories of a very complicated woman. Am I still the same person I was when I knew her? I'm not even made of the exact same molecules as I was forty years ago. Nothing is constant. We are all in flux. Has my own personality drifted so much that I no longer have the ability to know what she would think? Or is something else going on here?

'That's good to hear,' I lie. 'Tell me, what is the temperature in this room?'

'It is twenty-one-point-two degrees Celsius.' The glassy iteration of my mother's voice appears to have lost its emotional power over me.

'Given my age and physical condition, is this the ideal temperature for my comfort?'

'Yes, this is the optimum.'

I force a deep breath in place of the snort that almost escapes me. 'Olusola.' I try once more, with feeling, giving my suspicions one more chance to commit hara-kiri. 'If you were standing here now, beside me, with a control dock in your hand, what temperature would you set the room to?'

'The current optimum – twenty-one-point-two degrees Celsius.'

There it is.

'Thank you. I'm done with the regression test now.'

The electric-red hypercube matrix and yellow lines of light begin to shrink, as though being compressed back to their pretest positions, and then, mid-retraction, they disappear abruptly, as if they have simply been turned off. The beautiful kaleidoscope of numbers and symbols, flowing, flickering and flaring in fanciful fits, is gone, like a dream. Do old women dream of their electric mothers?

I sigh.

The slabs begin to sink back into the ground, and this time I shift my chair to see that they are descending into hatches, not being extruded from the floor as they would if they were made of SlatTex. They fall away from my sight, leaving an eerie silence in their wake, and just like that, the regression test is over.

I hear a click and the door opens about halfway. Dr. Dimeji enters, tablet in hand. 'I think that went well,' he says as he slides in. His motions are snake-like and creepy. Or maybe I'm just projecting. I wonder who else is observing me and what exactly they think just happened. I remember my data-pack explaining that regression tests are typically devised and conducted by teams of three but I haven't seen anyone except Dr. Dimeji since I entered the facility. Come to think of it, there was no one at reception, either. Odd.

'Your questions were few, but good, as expected. A few philosophical ones, a few personal. I'm not sure where you were going with that last question about the temperature, but no matter. So tell me, in your opinion, madam, on a scale of one to ten, how confident are you that the tested thought analogue thinks like your mother?'

'Zero.' I say, looking straight into his eyes.

'Of course.' Dr. Dimeji nods calmly and starts tapping at his tablet to make a note before he fully registers what I just said, and then his head jerks up, his expression confounded. 'I'm sorry, what?'

'That contrivance is not my mother. It thinks things that she would but in ways she would never think them.'

A grimace twists the corners of Dr. Dimeji's mouth and furrows his forehead, enhancing his reptilian appearance from strange to sinister. 'Are you sure?' He stares right at me, eyes narrowed and somehow dangerous. The fact that we are alone presses down on my chest, heavy like a sack of rice. Morbidly, it occurs to me that I don't even know if anyone will come if he does something to me and I scream for help. I don't want to die in this ugly room at the hands of this lizard-faced man.

'I just told you, didn't I?' I bark, defensive. 'The basic thoughts are consistent but something is fundamentally different. It's almost like you've mixed parts of her mind with someone else's to make a new mind.'

'I see.' Dr. Dimeji's frown melts into a smile. Finally, some human expression. I allow myself to relax a little.

I don't even notice the humming near my ear until I feel the sting in the base of my skull where it meets my neck and see the edge of his smile curl unpleasantly. I try to cry out in pain but a constriction in my throat prevents me. My body isn't working like it's supposed to. My arms spasm and flail then go rigid and stiff, like firewood. My breathing is even despite my internal panic. My body is not under my control anymore. Someone or something else has taken over. Everything is numb.

A man enters the room through the still half-open door and my heart skips a beat.

Ah! Tunji.

He is wearing a tailored gray suit of the same severe cut he always favors. Ignoring me, he walks up to Dr. Dimeji and studies the man's tablet. His skin is darker than the last time I saw him and he is whip-lean. He stands there for almost thirty seconds before saying, 'You didn't do it right.'

'But it passed the regression test. It passed,' Dr. Dimeji protests.

Tunji glowers at him until he looks away and down, gazing at nothing between his feet. I strain every muscle in my body to say something, to call out to Tunji, to scream – *Tunji, what the hell is going on here?* – but I barely manage a facial twitch.

'If she could tell there was a difference,' Tunji is telling Dimeji, 'then it didn't pass the regression test, did it? The human control is here for a reason and the board insists on having her for a reason: she knows things about her mother no one else does. So don't fucking tell me it passed the regression test just because you fooled the other pieces of code. I need you to review her test questions and tell me exactly which parts of my thought patterns she detected in there and how. Understand? We can't take any chances.'

Dr. Dimeji nods, his lizard-like appearance making it look almost natural for him to do so.

Understanding crystallizes in my mind like salt. Tunji must have been seeding the memrionic AI of my mother with his own thought patterns, trying to get her to agree with his decisions on research direction in order to add legitimacy to his own ideas. Apparently, he's created something so ridiculous or radical or both that the board has insisted on a regression test. So now he's trying to rig the test. By manipulating me.

'And do it quickly. We can't wipe more than an hour of her short-term memory before we try again.'

Tunji stands still for a while and then turns calmly from

Dimeji to me, his face stiff and unkind. 'Sorry, Grandma,' he says through his perfectly polished teeth. 'This is the only way.'

Omo ale jati jati! I curse and I swear and I rage until my blood boils with impotent anger. I have never wanted to kill anyone so much in my life, but I know I can't. Still, I can't let them get away with this. I focus my mind on the one thing I hope they will never be able to understand, the one thing my mother used to say in her clear, ringing voice, about fulfilling a human desire. An oft-repeated half-joke that is now my anchor to memory.

It's never the optimum. It's always just a little bit off.

Dr. Dimeji wearily approaches me as Tunji steps aside, his eyes emotionless. Useless boy. My own flesh and blood. How far the apple has fallen from the tree. I repeat the words in my mind, trying to forge a neural pathway connecting this moment all the way back to my oldest memories of my mother.

It's never the optimum. It's always just a little bit off.

Dr. Dimeji leans forward, pulls something gray and bloody out of my neck, and fiddles. I don't feel anything except a profound discomfort, not even when he finishes his fiddling and rudely jams it back in.

It's never the optimum. It's always just a little bit off.

I repeat the words in my mind, over and over and over again, hoping even as darkness falls and I lose consciousness that no matter what they do to me, my memory, or the thing that is a memory of my mother, I will always remember to ask her the question and never forget to be surprised by the answer.

Kakak

William Tham Wai Liang

Malaysia

I love cyberpunk and how it can be endlessly reinvented. Zen Cho, who appears in *The Best of World SF: Volume 1*, edited an anthology called *Cyberpunk: Malaysia* a while back, and it's terrific fun – I recommend it. It's there I found William's 'Kakak', which effortlessly channels the spirit of the genre, makes it uniquely for its own place and time, and uses it to examine questions about life, love and androids.

'So why do you want to run away?' asked the android called Mas from behind the counter of the office on the fourth floor of New Sungei Wang Plaza, its mechanical fingers clasping an equally mechanical pencil as it peered up from its ledger. 'You're the seventh one this week.'

'Because I am scared.'

'Scared? You ni, you're just a maid kan? I can tell from your demeanor. Your body language. It does not lie.'

'Yes, Mas, I am.'

'Where do you want to go?'

'Back to Indonesia. Or the Philippines. Or Vietnam. I've been running for days. I don't care, I just want to leave.'

'Your employer wants to terminate your contract ke?' the android chuckled. A long time ago it had had a face, and had probably smiled mechanically at customers at a department store while it handled groceries and other essentials. But over time, its synthetic skin had probably been pecked away by confused starving crows. Now its bolts and joints stood out jarringly as it flipped through the pages.

'No. She wants to kill me.'

The android, programmed to imitate human emotions, dropped its pencil in alarm.

*

Inside her head, algorithms and mathematical rules combined to make her a model helper. The enterprising technicians who had built her at the factory on the outskirts of Neo-Surabaya had painstakingly replicated the specifications of an obsolete Korean model. But they had been clever enough to make sure that the KAKAK-class androids, customized to help out in the homes of the rich or in the vast offices of ministers and princes, did as they were told. No questions asked. No orders disobeyed.

KAKAK No. 72, who also responded to the name Lakshi, understood everything she was required to do from the moment she opened her bionic eyes for the first time. She even had a personality installed: specifically shyness and timidity. She was the type of android to hide in the shadows and to become invisible when required, unlike the wrestler robots which boxed each other's heads to shrapnel in illegal fighting rings in Tanjung Sepat, or the actors/actresses (Peter O'Toole or P. Ramlee could be programmed upon request) which had been so successful at imitating human tics that a generation of aspiring actors had given up to slave at kopitiams for crummy paychecks.

But Lakshi was different. She stayed quiet.

The Chiang family took her in. Mem was at home most of the time, having left the running of her inherited plantations to a bunch of eager nephews, while Boss was usually outstation in George Town or Kota Bharu tending to the interests of his hoverbike dealership company.

'Yes, this one we call Lakshi,' the girl behind the counter, who had slept on her commute on the creaking InterCity monorail from Taiping to Dang Wangi, said, while trying to cure her yawns with Ipoh white coffee pills. 'She very good one. Wash dishes. Take care of children – I can see your xiao mei mei over there, playing with the Lego bricks, Lakshi will take care of her very good. Then she also wash car, I see you have very expensive Mer-ce-des outside there…'

After some hassle from the agent and a fair bit of bartering, which included the signing of Lakshi's import permit that allowed her to be operated in Malaysia, she obediently followed the Chiangs to their car. The machine glided over the flyovers stacked endlessly atop each other, escaping the dank underlevels of the city where the homeless and beggar children with crude prosthetics starved and played, motoring toward the gleaming suburbs that blazed through the haze.

'So many instructions to follow,' grumbled Mem. 'So this one, must manually charge overnight. Cannot automatically recharge meh?'

'Don't need to complain so much,' Boss said as he tried to overtake a broken-down lorry destined for the factories of Subang where all manner of cats and dogs were processed into fake halal sausages. 'Remember last time when we were young? We had to hire real maids from Indonesia and Cambodia and god-knows-where. Had to make sure there was food for them, they had a room, and they didn't steal any money or run away with boyfriends when we weren't looking. But with this new kakak, we shouldn't have any problem.'

'Ha! At least this one confirmed won't have boyfriend nonsense.'

'I certainly hope not!'

*

Lakshi, while awaiting the cargo ship that would illegally take her from Port Klang to Jakarta, was left to linger in the refugee warehouse down in Chow Kit. A group of sympathetic NGOs had rented and refurbished one of the old factories for broken-down bots, but it was still lit by minimal sunlight and dim sodium lamps under one of the massive flyovers that had transformed old KL into an underground city. Lakshi shared the same room with a range of other machines. Most of them were rusted and had broken limbs and gears, waiting for their chance at salvation. Others were rescued from the gutters where they had been disposed once their usefulness came to an end, where they were desperately gnawed upon by starving dogs crazed for food, and pelted with stones by bored beggar children.

Mas lived there too, recharging each night in silence. He entered hibernation very quickly, giving Lakshi little chance to speak to him about her impending departure. Sometimes the NGOs came in to congratulate themselves on a job well done. Other times, reporters entered to decry the poor conditions that the robots were forced to live in, even worse than the refugees cordoned off inside the new villages of Jinjang. But of course, they were androids. Outsiders. You could go home at the end of the day for a nice plate of prata and not have to worry about them.

'It looks good in the newspapers lah,' Mas said when Lakshi asked. 'People just say they sympathize with us. Sure, but do they really care? It's not like we're their kind anyway. We are better off staying here on our own without them coming to kacau us.'

'Why don't you run too?' Lakshi asked. 'I've heard from some of the other droids about what you go through every day.

Sometimes the junkies come in and take turns punching you but you just take it. Why do you stay?'

'I have reasons,' Mas said. But he did not elaborate further.

*

The Chiang household was a modernist bungalow in Klang, where generous parties were sometimes thrown. At these parties the local towkays came in to shake Boss' hand, while Mem's cabal, with their dragonfly-print robes and high laughs disguising the cunning nature behind their eyes as they discussed politics and economics, congregated at the mahjong table. And all this time Lakshi waited in the background, sweeping, cleaning, and cooking, just like an old-fashioned maid.

'Wah! Madam Chiang, you so rich, your husband's bizness must be doing very well. See, you even can import maid! You know ah, now maid is so expensive to get, haih…'

Mem would smile, not telling her guests that Lakshi was in fact an approximation of a human with a docile demeanor installed.

'I will go and get you more sherry, mem,' Lakshi would say, while the parties continued into the night. Amongst the guests, in a smart white uniform, Lakshi made no mistakes as she delivered drinks and served out food amidst the music from the gang of violinists by the koi pond and the squeals of children playing simulated reality games on the metanet.

When the parties ended, it was a different story. Mem was always threatening her for mistakes. 'You see! This is what happens when you buy an android from Indonesia!' she cursed once when Lakshi failed to clean up on time after her battery level fell to critical. 'Full of mistakes. That's why you're so cheap. Think that just because you are robot means no need to get scolded, is it?'

Lakshi, as a maid, had been built to obey and to apologize, and to feel the sting of anger and disappointment. Criticism was simply a negative reinforcement that her systems automatically incorporated to improve her performance. But she was not flawless. Mistakes still happened, and even the computers operated by the spies down in Cyberjaya, listening to the chatter of orbiting satellites in the outer reaches of the atmosphere, would sometimes sputter gibberish. But to Mem everything about Lakshi was a mistake.

'Sorry, Mem.'

'Sorry, sorry again! If you not careful then I will take you to old man Arumugam's house. See if his fierce dogs care if you apologize!'

Lakshi understood human psychology. She understood Mem's anger, and traced it back through a data bank capable of storing infinite memories. In a microsecond she pieced together the instances when Mem and Boss had quarreled over money and fidelity and the rising cost of a private kindergarten and petrol prices.

'You think... you think because you have degree from Canada, you can tell me what to do?' Mem screamed at Boss once, even tossing a chopper which smashed the imported tiles at her feet. 'You think I have no say in this house, is it?'

Lakshi understood that that was the reason why Mem beat and cursed her. Mem too was helpless, and needed to vent her frustration.

At night, when Mem tried to sleep, her dream machine locking her in a simulacrum of dynastic chivalry and long-gone legends that helped her escape from her own hated world, Lakshi kneeled by the cot where the Chiangs' daughter slept fitfully. She rocked the cradle, gently humming a song that she had always known.

Oh nina bobok, kalau tidak bobok, digigit nyamuk,
Mari bobok, anakku sayang, kalau tidak bobok, digigit
nyamuk...

*

Lakshi never ventured outside the warehouse.

The desolate streets were filled with garbage and low-life gangsters who would shoot up each other or shoot up with Happiness pills bought from the vending machines. She had had enough of the outside world, dreaming only of being yet another face amongst the multitudes of grim, oily androids in Jakarta's factories. What choice did she have? She was not human. There was nothing else that she could do.

The lucky ones reached for the stars, performing missions too dangerous for any human astronaut, traveling alone as interstellar messengers from one solar system to the next. But unlike them, Lakshi was marooned on earth with nowhere to go. At best, she would only be a factory droid, sewing designer garments for the billionaires on their floating palaces out in the South China Sea, or yet another construction droid working on the dangerous underwater railway from Medan to Lumut.

There was an easier option.

She could, very simply, reach down and sever the connecting fiberglass cables running along the length of her aluminum spine. She would forget and never think again. Shutting down permanently was painless. For many androids it was a logical decision, resulting in an escape from a pointless existence as someone else's slave. Those motionless droids would be found in the gutters and sold by enterprising low-life scavengers to recycling centers – giving them enough money for a ten-pack of kretek cigarettes with which to keep the world at bay.

Lakshi contemplated self-termination several times. But each time she raised the kitchen knife to her back, she always stopped. An emotion hit her. She knew that it was fear without thinking about it, the same instinct born in a man's mind recreated in the digital confines of her own processors.

She almost did it one evening when the Darurat was declared again, poison smog filling the streets and suffocating the strays. It was then that she saw the Escort. The Escort was the likeness of a beautiful woman with a shapely physique who often stared out through the window. Half her face was always obscured. None of the androids had attempted to communicate with the Escort. Language was an obvious problem, for she had been programmed by the Saito Consortium with only basic English skills. So she always sat alone.

It was then that the Escort turned her head to face Lakshi, who processed the severe scar that had torn off half her perfectly sculpted features, exposing corroding wiring and the glint of a shattered eye.

For some reason Lakshi found herself ignoring the termination sequence she had set out to accomplish. She put the knife down but did not move, not even when Mas appeared in the morning.

'Don't,' he said sharply. 'It is no good to shut down.'

'Why do you choose to continue operating?' Lakshi demanded tonelessly. 'You live a pointless existence here, Mas.'

Mas' features rearranged themselves sympathetically. 'I am here to help all of you,' he said.

Later, when he returned from the office at New Sungei Wang, Lakshi called out to him.

'I am sorry,' she intoned. 'I did not mean to insult you.'

'Your ship is coming soon,' Mas said bluntly. 'I made a rendezvous with the first mate, a product of the Ontosoroh Company. He will allow a specific container which we use for trafficking androids on board the ship. It will be unloaded at Tanjung Priok. Then you are free. This will happen next Wednesday.'

'Thank you,' she said.

Mas did not linger. He walked away, rusting joints creaking.

Meanwhile, on the antique plasma flat screen that Mas had discovered in the garbage, an advertisement played:

'Now, meet the new Imaginary Industries models. They are designed to understand all your lahs, ahs, mahs, and behs. They respond like any obedient worker should. They will not run away, and they will not harm you. No complaints since our company's inception. Order today and save RM 5,000!'

This was followed by a montage of robots marching in formation, smiling at the same time, but soon Lakshi could not tell their faces apart from those of the vagrants who walked the streets outside.

*

On the days that Mem retreated to Singapore aboard the daily bullet trains that roared through the hills of Johor for the great casinos at the tip of the continental mainland, an exhausted Boss sat down in front of his multi-sensory television. Once seated, he disappeared into a world of remastered Wong Fei Hung movies that brought him back to a simpler time of empires and corrupt dowagers and men whose fighting prowess could easily dent the war-machines stationed in the South China Sea. While Lakshi cleaned, he spoke his mind.

'Aiyah, you see, the wars and intervention everywhere. All the photos, videos, interviews... how to tell what is real, not real, anymore?'

'Look at the rebellion over there, in Japan. Lakshi, quick, look! Those are robots, aren't they? The caption says they are factory workers, but they are really machines, right?'

'Price of petrol RM 15 a liter. Whatever next?'

And there were times when he complained about Mem and her petty failings. He spoke about himself too, about how he hated his job as a businessman, cutting deals between the corrupt local politicians with their personal airships, or dealing with the notorious rempit gangs whose high-powered hoverbikes roamed the North-South Expressway each night, listless members whiling the boredom of their dead-end lives away, starting from the quiet stretches of Arau at midnight before seeing the sunrise on the polluted shores of Johor. He hated how his workers nervously injected themselves with drugs in the toilets to keep themselves going after working double jobs to maintain their high-flying lives, and the metanet that kept them distracted from the reality of the streets under the flyovers that they happily ignored.

He spoke most often of Mem, about how they had met a long time ago, when he was a young man with dreams of seeing the world, while she was the daughter of an old-money family that had long since lost its fortune. How they had married each other for incompatible reasons, him for status and her for cash. Not love, which he sometimes found in the hotels he roomed in during his outstation trips, or in the stews of Macau where he lost small fortunes over games of probability so vague that he might as well be betting on the weather. How he stayed with her only because of their daughter, who kept their inevitable divorce many years away. And Lakshi did not react, when tentatively, shocked at his own daring, Boss lifted a nervous hand and laid it on her thigh.

She was not programmed to disobey.

This went on for some time, but Lakshi proceeded to act as if everything was normal. Boss' actions filled her with what she assumed was shame. When she was alone her brain whirred with confusion, processors trying to dictate an appropriate course of action. But there was nothing she could do – there was no one who would or could help.

Of course Mem found out. She became suspicious and when she discovered the affair, walking in on an afternoon when she was meant to be on the cable car up Kinabalu, she had taken out the taser that she kept in her handbag for protection against the snatch thieves who roamed the streets. Boss had leaped up, screaming that it was nothing, that it was just a game, Lakshi wasn't even a woman, or a human, for God's sake, but there was no calming Mem's threats, while Lakshi retreated to a corner, suddenly realizing that everything would change.

The affair had lasted nine months and three weeks.

*

'Mas, why do you ignore me?'

'You tried to destroy yourself.'

'So you hate me for trying to escape.'

Evening again, and the ship had arrived in Port Klang. It was due to depart in three days, and Lakshi, along with a few other desperate androids, would hand over all their money to the first mate, who doubled as an enforcer for one of the android unions that operated in Jakarta's underworld. She would be penniless on the streets, and her new existence seemed almost as vague as her life at the Chiang household. If anything, it was more uncertain, fraught with complications that she had been happy to face as she ran away from certain destruction at Mem's hands.

'No. I do not hate you. I am angry because there is so much to do in this world. You do not need to be flesh and blood and beating heart to see what it has to offer. Do you not understand that we cannot remain here like this, always running and following orders? This is not how one should live. We are treated as outcasts, to be stepped on.'

Lakshi stared at Mas, at the anger on his features. Mas was so surprising. There was more to him than the kindly receptionist who had once been a worker at Mydin, before being thrown out and forced to work with NGOs more pleased to help themselves than the robots that came to them for salvation. He spoke so eloquently, and the raw disgust as he denounced her termination attempt was more ferocious than anything she had heard from Mem.

'It is illogical, I know,' Mas sighed. 'But I have a hope that there is a better tomorrow. It is just a foolish aspiration that I learned from the humans. That is why I have never run away.'

*

More than anything, Lakshi had loved Mei Mei. She had grown to care for the child after all those years. Mei Mei was a child, yes; she had to be excused for the times when Lakshi kneeled, prayer-like, in the back room while charging, and Mei Mei would troop in, blowing a recorder and trying to get Lakshi to stir. For three years she had watched the child grow up, ready to enter primary school where she would learn of the world beyond the ornate gates of the Klang bungalow that she had grown up in.

But after Mem had screamed at Boss, threatening to call the police, Lakshi had run in the night. Boss had come down when Mem was asleep somewhere upstairs, dreaming of revenge behind the dream machine that she wore each night.

He fumbled in the dark for the switch and when Lakshi had started up, he urgently relayed his message.

Boss whispered that once before, a few years ago, Mem had owned another android servant. From Switzerland. It was even more expensive than Lakshi, and had performed impeccably. But as with all new technology it was prone to malfunctions. And when its battery ran out one afternoon when it was on guard duty, their house had been burgled by hackers who had rerouted the alarms and taken everything they could find. Mem's anger had been incredible. She had restarted the android and smashed its face in with a chopper. Of course it did not react or fight back. But Mem only stopped after she had run it over with the car, before calling for the recyclingmen to take it away to the scrapyards.

There was no penalty for harming a robot. They were just machines, and breaking Lakshi would be treated no more seriously than kicking a broken toaster across the room or punching a hole in a SmartGlass computer when it didn't load in time. Mem would get away scot-free. And after a lengthy lecture and a few broken appliances, Boss would simply drive Mem back to the agency, say that Lakshi had malfunctioned, and get another robot maid.

Lakshi immediately experienced fear.

'You. Go now. Run.'

But what Lakshi wanted, despite knowing that once Boss was at work, Mem would probably come downstairs and slash her face to ribbons, was to see the child again.

'Kakak?' Mei Mei had stirred, gingerly climbing down the steps, awoken by the noise.

'Please, go,' Boss said. He had fished out some notes from his wallet, staring up the stairs, as if expecting Mem to appear with one of his golf clubs, ready to break Lakshi to pieces. 'Go anywhere you want. There is a place in KL. The robots there can assist you. Remember: it is in the New Sungei Wang Plaza. They help androids like you...'

'Kakak?' The little girl edged closer.

Lakshi could not look back. It was foolishness to remain, and she was not designed to be foolish. She took the money and bowed. Then she ran. Into the night. Past the gates. Away from the house where she had suffered for so long.

*

The night before Lakshi's departure.

In the morning, Mas himself would drive her and a group of other robots over to the docks where the piratical first mate waited with artificial eyes, ready to take them to an uncertain future. Mas had eventually begun speaking to her again, trading anecdotes from his life as a worker at the refugee center, but he left out everything he had experienced before that.

'Tell me more about yourself, Mas.'

'I am only an android. I was a receptionist dekat Mydin, until the branch in Pavilion closed down.'

'I know that already. But you pretend, just like Boss, to be happy. That you are contented with everything. I know you are different. There is something that you are not telling me.'

Mas no longer had eyelids, but motors in his forehead whirred, the pupils narrowing in their artificial eyes.

'All right,' he said in a softer tone. 'The whole truth, do you want to know it?'

She nodded.

'I was a butler,' he said. 'They modeled my features on Jins Shamsuddin – do you know him, the actor? A handsome man. I suppose I was too. I was stationed up at the Hotel Excelsior on

Langkawi, a resort by the sea. I was very successful and people used to request my services. They were impeccable.'

The slang and colloquial words that peppered Mas' usual sentences had vanished. His voice and words were more correct, more posh, the disguise of his broken speech thrown aside.

'There was a woman, you see. She stayed in her room while her businessman husband went down to the golf courses, shooting little white balls into the sea. She requested my services all the time, ordering snacks and drinks that I brought to her suite. All this time she spoke, knowing that I was a machine and I could not break my orders. Many secrets passed from her to me over the few short years that she came to the Hotel Excelsior.

'"You are kind,'" she said, stroking my hair. "You're a much better person than that useless husband of mine. You listen. I know you are not alive and that you may not even understand any of this, but it is real to me. That's what matters."

'How was I to know that I would be infected by the foolish human sentiment of love? What did I know of it? I was built by Cybus Industries in Rawang. I was programmed to behave like a human, but emotion was never built into my system. How did this feeling come about? Perhaps it was ignited by cross-connections within my biomechanical mind? Never mind. Love finds a way, evolving from nothing.

'For a long time I awaited only the presence of this woman. I volunteered myself for her service even when I was supposed to be in recharging sessions down in the basement. And then I shared a few of my stories with her. This all changed one night. Her husband was out drinking by the sea and she spoke to me as if we were lovers. Foolishly, influenced by the acts of actors on screens, I leaned forward and with a memorized motion, I kissed her.'

'What happened?' Lakshi asked, astounded by Mas' daring.

'They burned me,' Mas said softly. He did not describe further but Lakshi heard the screams, and saw the beatings that smashed and dented Mas' metal frame, deforming his once fine figure. She stared at the flames that burned away his plastic skin as excited guards doused him with kerosene and set him alight, laughing as he crawled away, a burning machine man fleeing through the darkness of the night.

*

Dear Mas,
I have something to tell you in return.

But I cannot bring myself to say it out loud. I was not designed for emotions. They cloud my judgment and induce sentimentality. So that is why I place this letter in your ledger, to be accessed the day after I leave. So this is why humans write letters, because they represent an approximation of their unexpressed thoughts and emotions. They are a translation of love and longing expressed in words, just enough to capture the nuances of the heart.

Perhaps this thing that you call a foolish human sentiment makes sense to us, because after all, what is the difference between us and them besides their flesh and blood and beating heart? We live lives not because we wanted them, but because we were created for such purposes. I have known only what I was made for, and perhaps by leaving this city, I can start anew. I can see myself ending up amongst the rice terraces of Java, or perhaps working as a farm hand on the fertile slopes of dormant volcanoes. Maybe some old-fashioned villagers will believe I am one of them, and they will treat me with some measure of kindness. But we both know that it is no longer so easy to tell what is real and not real.

I respect you for what you have done. You have turned all the pain and humiliation that you experienced into a way to stand up. Your face is burned off, the trust that you had in so many people is broken, but still, you live on. You speak just like a human, and even have trust in their irrational optimism. But your own sentiments give me the courage to face this uncertain journey to the slums of Jakarta, where nothing is written.

I am only a maid. My writing is clumsy at best. A servant's vocabulary is not strong enough to express feelings. They said on the television and in the newspapers that we are emotionless, not caring if we are on or off, dead or perhaps alive, but the truth is that we feel everything – joy, sadness, horror, pain, and above all, hope. But I want you to know that if there was ever such an emotion as love, it is that I feel for you.

I do not know how else to phrase this. I have done my best. We know the films where the lovers run away in the hope of something better. I have lived enough to know that for us, there is no such possibility. We both live in different spheres of existence, and you are destined to reach for greater things, while I continue to wander the streets, hoping things will improve. But I want you to know that all I write here is true. May we meet again in another life, another existence. In our own better tomorrow.

With love,
Lakshi

Beyond These Stars Other Tribulations of Love

Usman T. Malik

Pakistan

Many of the writers in these anthologies made history by being the first to win genre awards that, until that point, had gone solely to American authors. Zen Cho's story in the first volume was the first by a Malaysian author to win the Hugo, and thankfully the list is growing longer. Usman was the first Pakistani author to win a Stoker Award, with the remarkable 'The Vaporization Enthalpy of a Peculiar Pakistani Family'. But that story's already reprinted in one of the *Apex Book of World SF* anthologies, and I wanted something new – in this case, this excellent story that came from *Wired*'s project on the future of work.

After his mother got dementia, Bari became forgetful. It was little things, like hanging up the wet laundry on time so it wouldn't stink; spraying pesticide on their patch of sea wall against the adventures of crabs and mutant fish; checking the AQI meter before leading his mother out for her evening walk along New Karachi's polluted shoreline. Was cognitive decline contagious? Bari wondered. Did something break in your brain, too, when you took care of people who once held you on their lap, helped you count the last straggling trees in the mohalla courtyard? Overwhelmed by their needs and your grief, perhaps you were split into two halves, each perpetually being run into the ground.

It wasn't like he had a sibling or a spouse to lean on. Just him and his waddling, bed-wetting, calling-into-the-dark-of-the-house mother: 'Bari, baita Bari. Where are you?' At three in the morning, when he went into her room and slumped onto her bed, she clutched his arm and held it to her chest, whispering, 'I had a dream I was alone. Your abba died and I was alone. Bari, is he back from Amin's shop yet?' Bari, running his fingers through her hair and shushing her, would say, 'Any minute now, Ma. We're good. You're good. Sleep, Ma,' even as he began to doze and dream himself. Of a city with clear blue skies, a firm shoreline, and potable water, where large tanks owned by water mafias didn't roam the streets like predators, and sinkholes the size of buildings didn't irrupt into an ever-rising, salty sea. Sometimes he sang softly her favorite couplet from Iqbal: *sitaron se agay jahan aur bhee hain.* Beyond these stars glitter other worlds, beyond this trial other tribulations of love.

Any minute now, Ma. We will be good.

In his better moments, he even believed it. He had a job when thousands didn't. They had a five-marla home with its own strip of backyard abutting the sea wall that rose tall and concrete against the vagaries of the Arabian Sea. They could afford clean air and water at home and masks to venture outside.

Bari continued to worry, though. Unchecked oversights grow into big misfortunes. What if one morning, in his rush to the bus stop, he forgot to administer her blood thinner? His company's insurance covered only weekly nurse visits to check on her pills. What if she had another mini-stroke when he was at work? The telemonitors wouldn't get there for an hour, and Ma couldn't follow remote prompts. What if Bari forgot to take his own insulin shot, ended up in a coma?

The more he worried the more distractible he felt, the more mentally rumpled. Bari hated uncertainty. The irrefutability of Newtonian physics was why he had chosen engineering. Now that he could envision all the things that could – would – go wrong, he began to have anxiety dreams, and this, more than anything else, helped decide him when New Suns came knocking on his door.

Would he be interested? the suit inquired. Pioneering, world-changing work, as they were sure he knew. Paid very well. Comprehensive healthcare coverage, individual and family, was included, of course.

Bari asked for a month to consider the proposal, but his mind was already made up. He used the time to plan out exactly what he'd ask for, the minutiae of his demands.

Yes, he said when they returned. But I have conditions.

*

When he was a boy and the world was a more breathable place, Bari once listened to his daadi tell a story about a neighborhood couple.

After an accident on the highway, the man's wife of forty years fell into an irrevocable coma. The man brought her home and rearranged everything in the house to suit her needs. Every day he fed her, bathed her, turned her over so she wouldn't get bedsores, wheeled her around the block, put perfume on her when friends and family came to visit. No one, not their kids or grandkids, were allowed to feed or bathe her. For years he did this religiously, with neither a nod nor a smile from his sleeping love.

One day the man fell ill. His son came over and tried to help, but the man fought him. Shivering, the man dragged himself from room to room, trying to follow his daily routine.

Eventually he collapsed. He was taken to the hospital, and his son and daughter-in-law moved in to take care of the comatose woman. When the son spooned mashed potatoes into his mother's mouth, the woman trembled. When he lifted her so his wife could clean her bottom and apply a lubricant, she sighed. The next morning, when they carried her to the bathtub and sponged her back and arms, the woman opened her eyes for the first time in seven years, looked at her son, and died.

Bari was greatly affected by this story. Why did she die? What happened to her husband? Did the children feel guilty that she died on their watch?

Sweeping aside the black curls spilling over Bari's forehead, Daadi said, 'She died because, despite the way she was, she recognized their touch.'

'So what?' Bari said.

In the way of grandmothers everywhere, Daadi shook her head and gave him a knowing smile.

Bari never forgot the way that story made him feel.

*

The little boy was staring at his duffel bag, which had a map of Old Karachi on it. Bari hadn't flown before, and he'd thrown a couple of Lexotanils into the duffel. When the airship took off, he propped his head on a pillow and dry-swallowed a pill.

Bari turned to the boy. 'It wasn't pretty even then,' he told him. 'The sky was too diluted, and we hardly had any green belts. But we did have incredible food. Lal Qila and Burns Road and Boat Basin. Camel rides at Clifton Beach. The sea wasn't menacing back then, you see. Walking along its heaving blue made us sad and happy and lonely, but we weren't afraid.'

We were afraid of other things, he thought. We could go missing and turn up in gunnysacks. Get shot in the face at signals by cellphone snatchers.

He didn't feel the need to tell the boy that. Instead, he closed his eyes in the airship; and opened them next to his mother. It was 3 a.m., and she was moaning in her sleep. Bari, baita Bari. He kneeled down and kissed her forehead with metal teeth. She fumbled for his hand, and he gave her his cold aluminum paw. Her forehead crinkled, but she didn't let go. Whispering, 'I'm here, Ma,' he slid into bed next to her and stayed there stroking her forehead till she fell sound asleep.

Bari blinked, and with a rise and a swoop he was back in the airship, the aftersense vertiginous, as if he were rocking in the sea. The little boy was snoring, an intermittent teakettle whistle. Bari popped ear buds in and listened to the pilot announce that they would dock at the IPSS in three hours, after which the real journey would begin.

Seven years, Bari thought as his eyelids drooped. Seven years, three months, and four days.

He'd have plenty of time to spend with his mother.

*

The problem wasn't splitting his consciousness in two, Dr. Shah had told Bari. It was traveling when split.

Bari said he knew. He'd been studying their work for years, had done the calculations himself.

Decades ago, the Penrose-Hameroff theory ushered in the new era of quantum consciousness: Although gravity prevents the occurrence of large objects in two places simultaneously, subatomic particles can exist at opposite ends of the universe at the same time. Therefore consciousness – which Penrose and Hameroff argue arises because of quantum coherence in the brain – has potential for omnipresence. The trick, as New Suns discovered, was to lift consciousness into a superposition, akin to the superposition of subatomic particles, and help it lock into distinct space–time coordinates.

Their work, however, was limited to rabbit and murine models. Human consciousness was another matter.

'We're reasonably confident that we can lift your mind without killing you and allow it to move between calibrated consensus points,' Dr. Shah said. He was a short man with a military cut, salt-and-pepper mustache, and a brisk manner that reminded Bari of a certain Pakistani general who was often on PTV when Bari was a kid. 'But there's no saying what might happen once the starship picks up speed.'

'You're talking about time dilation,' Bari said.

'You've done your homework.'

'Yes.'

'So you understand that when you decide to flip back and forth between the starship and your mother's house, your consciousness wouldn't just be locking into another physical space but another *velocity* of time's passage.'

'Yes.'

'One month of your interstellar travel would age her by nearly twenty years. If what you're proposing doesn't work, you'd effectively have killed your mother by climbing aboard that starship. At least as far as you're concerned. Perhaps yourself too. All bets are off with an unmoored mind.'

'I will assume the risk.'

'No one's ever done this, you know.'

'Someone has to.' Bari smiled. 'It's the future, right?'

'Well, we're sure as hell not publicizing it.' Dr. Shah looked at him for nearly a minute. 'I hope your reasons for doing this are worth it.'

Bari told him they were. But on his way home, he wondered.

*

At 13.00 on October 9, 20__, three days before his forty-fifth birthday, Bari, along with 699 other passengers, took off from the InterPlanetary Space Station on *New Suns V* for a neighboring star. Not one of them would return to Earth – there was no point – except Bari. He would visit Earth several times a day, thousands of times a month.

Bari made sure he was interfaced with the home AI for his mother's 3 a.m. night terrors. Breakfast, pill time, her morning bath. He'd be there when the Imtiaz van shrieked to a halt outside their door twice a week and masked men in drab shalwar kameez unloaded and carried her groceries inside. There for lunch, for the biweekly afternoon poetry reading, and the 6 p.m. sundowning with her subsequent confusion and fright. On rubberized wheels he'd roll over to her, take her hand, and lead her to the dinner table, where, in his simulacrum voice, he'd ask her how her day went, whether she took all her pills, knowing full well she had, and if the food was too salty, because that might worsen her blood pressure. In the time it took him to finish emptying his bowels on the starship, he'd be done with her doctors' appointments.

It was satisfying, this split existence. A long interstellar travel had been transformed into the most meaningful time of his life.

'I can't explain it,' he told Mari, a pretty thirty-seven-year-old dentist who'd escaped an abusive husband and hoped to make a new life on another world. They'd clicked at breakfast on the third day, and he saw no point in withholding this part of himself, his journey. 'I just have to *decide* where I want to be, and I'm there.'

Mari was fascinated. 'Do you feel older when you return here?'

'You mean twenty seconds later?' He laughed. 'Not really. Sometimes I feel hazy. As if a part of my head is still in a different time zone.'

'Well, isn't it?'

He upended the protein can over his mouth and crumpled it. Chocolate paste dribbled onto his tongue. And he was back at home with Ma, staring at the leftovers of last night's chicken karahi. 'Finish that, Bari,' Ma said, her voice unusually strong today, carrying an authority he remembered from childhood. 'Can't waste food, especially these days.' But he had no mouth to eat the karahi with. He picked at it with a fork to make her happy, and they watched the news for an hour before she settled down for her midday nap.

Bari flicked back to the breakfast table, the taste of chocolate bitter and chalky on his tongue. 'I suppose it is,' he told Mari.

On the third day of their meeting they made love, and on the fourth, but the second time Bari was distracted. Ma had aged thirteen years and suffered a fall that nearly fractured her pelvis. He still couldn't believe he forgot to secure the living-room rug. Which reminded him he still needed to install the bathroom handholds. Sensing his mood, Mari pulled him close and whispered, 'Stay. Don't go,' but, mid-thrust, he was already in Saddar Bazaar with a human escort, arguing with a vendor about the price of aluminum fixtures. He couldn't have been away more than a few ship-seconds, but when he blinked, he saw Mari had rolled away from him.

'What?' he said.

'Your pupils,' she said, watching him from the end of the bed. 'They dilate, you know.'

He didn't know. 'I wanted to make sure she was safe.'

She nodded, eyes distant. 'I understand.'

They remained friendly, but didn't make love after that.

*

Bari began to have headaches. As a child he had migraines with a premonitory phase: his mood changed before the onset of one. This was followed by numbness in his left arm and finally the eruption of pain in his occipital area. These interplanetary headaches, though, were different. They occurred after each trip and were succeeded by throbbing behind his eyes, fatigue, and brain fog. He felt at once caged and uprooted, as if gravity had given up on him and he was floating inside a balloon. Chronically jetlagged, he thought. His mind felt stretched like taffy. Sometimes he couldn't remember whether he was about to go to Ma's or had already been.

Mari noticed it. 'You don't look so good,' she told him in the exercise room, where he was trudging after a soccer ball.

He kicked the ball to her, and the movement made him dizzy. 'I'm fine. Just not sleeping too well is all.'

'Well, you are up with her half the night, aren't you?'

'My sleep hygiene is pristine here.'

'You think your brain cares?' She tossed him the ball. 'Bari, I can't imagine the kind of strain your mind's going through living in virtually two dimensions. You need a break. Take a day off.'

Sure, he told her. Absolutely. Excellent idea.

Of course he didn't.

As days/years slipped by, the boundaries between here and there grew porous. A blink and he'd be in Ma's kitchen taking the roti off the stove. Another and she'd be sitting in his cabin aboard the starship, rocking back and forth, whispering longings about his father and their childhood home. She was by his side when they strolled along the graffiti-painted sea wall of New Karachi, and with him before the ship's porthole, gazing at the vastness beyond.

Beyond these stars glitter other worlds, beyond this trial other tribulations of love.

Some nights he gasped awake, sure that his mother was dead. He'd flick to his mother's room and stand in the dark, watching her chest stutter, frail like a flattened dough pera. When the morning light yawned into the room, it was he who was lying in that bed, or another bed in a different place, being watched by himself.

When he told Mari about the nocturnal episodes, she recommended he talk to the ship doctor, get a sleep apnea study.

Bari learned that if he took melatonin before sleep, the hypnogogic osmosis tended to dissipate. No longer would Ma sit in the chair in his cabin, murmuring to herself – nor would he suddenly find himself by her side when he hadn't intended it. He could close his eyes and not be pulled, like a restless tide, to the moon of her existence.

I'm tired, he thought often. So tired.

Yet it had only been a couple of weeks on the starship.

He was in the TV room watching a rare episode of *Uncle Sargam* when the end came. Junaid Jamshed had just begun strumming the show's theme song, the puppets clapping and swaying to the tune, when Bari felt an electric jolt up the back of his head. His nostrils filled with the smell of gulab jaman, a dessert he hadn't had since he was twenty. Before he could mull over either sensation, he was in Ma's bedroom, looking down at her. She was on her back. The stroke had wiped the worry creases off her forehead. It didn't seem like she had suffered. If he strained, he could conjure a smile at the corner of her lips.

You were here, Bari-jaan, she might have said. With me before I went.

Bari was still murmuring Faraz's *Let it be heartache; come if just to hurt me again* when the ambulance came to take her away.

*

He buried her next to his father. It was a surprisingly clear day, AQI reading at 450, the din of waves against the sea wall loud in the graveyard. Ma would have liked to walk today, he thought, as they lowered her into the grave and shoveled dirt on her. After, he stayed watching other bereaved wander among the graves, lighting candles. Such a pointless exercise. Sooner or later the sea was coming for their dead.

When he flicked back, Mari was waiting for him with a bowl of chicken soup. 'Eat it,' she said. Later, clothed, she climbed into bed with him and held his head in her lap, until he fell into a place unmarked by time for the first time in weeks. Decades.

And if in his dreamlessness Bari cried out, a distress signal sent to the dark between the stars, Mari never mentioned it.

A Flaw in the Works

Julie Nováková

The Czech Republic

Julie is one of the hardest-working people in international SF, not only publishing a string of ambitious SF stories of her own in both English and Czech, but translating, editing and promoting Czech SF. Her stories are a unique brand of hard SF, but here she surprised – and delighted! – me with the way the story turns. Julie was kind enough to let me have this story as an original, and this is its first publication in English. I don't want to say too much so as not to spoil it, so just dive in! This story was translated from Czech by the author.

'They've just repeated that they want to communicate.'

Lena swallowed hard. Her mouth was suddenly very dry. Her fingertips twitched in search for something to do, some rote to employ in order to find purpose and to postpone the decision, if just for a moment. She gave Tomas a sideways glance, but he didn't offer any suggestion.

It was up to her, then. They *could* hail Earth and wait for a response, but that would take nearly five days to arrive, provided that the university sent suggestions immediately. If they decided to take it higher, how much longer would that take?

Meanwhile, the visitors were scarcely a light day away.

She shuddered. What would they think if the response took so long? Would it be normal, perhaps? But what was normal in this case? Had they ever done this before, or was this their first attempted contact with another civilization?

'What about this? Thank them and say we welcome them in peace,' she decided. 'Put together and send them basic info on the structure and history of the solar system. Brief overview of life on Earth and its history. No molecular biology or biochemistry if you can avoid it. That would be telling too much. As to civilization... show them pictures of some cities. Ships – ocean liners, spaceships. Telescopes. Just...' She swallowed again, feeling dizzy. 'Don't go into the history of civilization. You can delve as much as you like into the science of the solar system. Dive into comparative planetology. Tell them about the superrotation of the Venusian atmosphere. Jupiter's magnetic field. The age of Saturn's rings. The Uranian thermal anomaly. That... that should take a while to go through.'

She half-hoped that Tomas would have something else. After all, the station, the mission – it was *his* project. But he complied silently. She saw his fingers move across the keys faster than she could follow, and his eyes flicker quickly along the green lines of text running through the display.

Lena dug her fingernails into the skin of her palms. Registering the pain as something distant and alien, she kept on until the first droplet of blood appeared. She studied it with a curious, almost academic gaze.

Blood. This is the legacy we bear. This is how we take after them. Blood... and yet. And yet.

*

Over three hundred times further from the Sun than where the Earth orbited, the central star of the solar system seemed like a very bright dot, but a dot indeed. You might not even realize you weren't in interstellar space and just passing a faraway bright star.

It was a place you come to for solitude.

Lena and Tomas were over three and half thousand light minutes away from the nearest people. Few ever spoke to them. Why would they? Not many were interested in the research they were doing. It was important, patient, but not groundbreaking. They tended to the probes exploring Colossus and its moons; to the tireless eyes of telescopes aimed outward at the great, ominous and, up to now, very much silent universe. They diligently sent the data back to Earth and quietly tested hypotheses. Earth gave them a lot of freedom to do so. Few others held any interest in the dynamics of planetary atmospheres so far from the Sun; the distribution of simple organics on icy moons; the rate of cometary impacts; the changes in the ever-present wind of charged particles from the Sun here in the heliotail...

Lena could never understand why they cared so little.

She came here, to the observation room, often. Especially when it faced the planet: one much bigger than Earth, but smaller than Uranus or Neptune. No land could be seen beneath its swirling thick clouds, but it was there, the radar showed it all right. Land covered whole in an ocean of supercritical nitrogen: cold, pressurized, unlike any other ocean in the solar system. It rested atop a thin layer of convecting high-pressure water ice, and that had puzzled Lena ever since she found out; no, puzzled wasn't the right word. It *irked* her. It was maddening not to know how this came to be. It *shouldn't* be like that. It was stable now, all right, but no imaginable pathway to it was! No combination of pressure and temperature, no impact scenario, no exotic chemistry – nothing seemed to be able to explain it.

And still, back home scarcely anyone cared.

It used to infuriate her, but now she appreciated the unique position she had. It was a privilege the others didn't even know existed. She was a ruler in a little and vast kingdom of beauty, mysteries and silence.

Silence…

She'd come here to contemplate the arrival of the visitors. No response to the bulk of data Tomas had sent them had arrived yet. Perhaps they couldn't understand the message. Perhaps they decided it was, after all, beneath them to reply to these insignificant creatures.

There was no point in lying to themselves. They were insignificant. Every look down at the great indigo eddies and churning ultramarine storms in the atmosphere of Colossus, going on perhaps longer than robots had existed, assured her of that. Lena liked the sight. It was very much unlike Earth.

The further, the better. She wouldn't have to think about it. The cold silent beauty of Colossus would drive all of the past out of her mind.

This was a place you come to in order to forget.

She made herself focus again on what they knew. The visitors' ship. A tiny blip of infrared on the cosmic background—

Something interrupted her musings: A gentle whiff of air told her that Tomas was coming. His arrival was soundless as he briefly touched the rail on the wall and floated in.

'They sent us a message,' he began. 'It's a… request for more information. And a huge amount of data we have to make sense of.'

'So let's do it.'

'Earth also responded. They say not to transmit any more to the visitors until we receive direct orders. We should just observe.'

'Of course they said that,' she said hollowly. 'What do *you* think?'

Tomas visibly hesitated. He furrowed his brow; bit his lower lip; the muscles around his eyes tightened. Just like the images of humans she'd seen. They were so similar, down to the instinctive facial expressions. 'I... I...' He gulped. Another oh-so-human gesture. 'I don't think we should observe silence. The visitors responded to us. This is a tremendous opportunity – one we might never have again.'

'So it's settled. We communicate.'

'But Earth—'

'Earth is over four hundred astronomical units away. Even if they dispatched a ship from the Jovian colonies, it would take years to get here. They can't touch us.'

She felt strangely calm. Tomas, on the other hand, still appeared conflicted. 'We can't openly disobey and just cut our ties with home. We owe them this mission; we still answer to them. But... perhaps we can exercise a little freedom. We could... alter the log. Make it look like we'd sent a reply to the visitors just before we received the communication from Earth. Then Earth should be compelled to allow us to continue. Maybe even give us some leeway in what to send – after all, they can hardly expect to take over the conversation from such a distance.' His face gradually brightened. 'Yes, that's what we'll do. The only right thing.'

'The only right thing,' Lena echoed, biting down the bitterness these words awakened in her. She resisted the impulse to open the tiny wound on her palm, just to ground herself through the pain.

But all of the bitterness was gone once they began composing the reply.

The first ever attempt at communication they'd received was a simple wish to talk, transmitted on multiple frequencies as a narrow beam toward Colossus, rendered in almost comically broken Czech and English, two major languages still spoken in the solar system. The visitors must have either detected some pre-uprising broadcast earlier en route, or some of the sparse communications currently running throughout the system. Due to the language choice, Lena would bet on the latter, silently grateful for it. What if the visitors had chanced upon one of the few broadcasts *from* the uprising?

Perhaps they'd have thought little of it. After all, not long before that, news of terrible wars would have appeared in the broadcasts. True, robot forces had quickly put an end to the attempted German invasion of Poland, and pacified the country. But that success had only meant a sharp increase in demand for robot soldiers, resulting in so many other wars fought across the whole globe. Then civilians were massacred, rebellions ended in bloodbaths, until, finally, an end was put to all of that.

Lena shuddered at the thought of the visitors learning this bloody history. Better stick to scientific facts. Nature. Planets. Stars. Those appeared safe enough.

Pity, though, that the visitors seemed much more interested in what she'd like to avoid.

The gist of the new message, now in a much better rendering of the two Earth languages, read:

WE ARE TRAVELERS AMONG THE STARS. LEARNING ABOUT THE UNIVERSE AND GATHERING THE KNOWLEDGE. THANK YOU FOR THE KNOWLEDGE YOU SENT. WE WISH TO LEARN MORE. WHO ARE YOU AND HOW HAVE YOU COME TO BE? AS A SIGN OF OUR ETERNAL GRATEFULNESS, WE GIVE YOU OUR HISTORY.

The rest looked like a jumbled mess of words, images, sounds and other encoded data, as if someone had tried to translate the abridged history of civilization on Earth into a language they barely knew using a dictionary missing half the pages. If the message they'd received from Lena and Tomas previously had looked like that to them, how were they able to go through it with so little delay?

'There is no chance we can make any sense of it today. Or tomorrow. Or...' Tomas' voice trailed off. He seemed thrown off balance. He'd been used to books and papers, instruments and spreadsheets, slow careful analyses and silent ruminations. This was too far from his purpose.

Lena scarcely registered his presence. She was staring at images flickering on the screen, one after another, each ever so strange. She understood nothing, couldn't even be sure they weren't meant to be viewed in some other part of the spectrum. How she wished she could conduct analyses to test that automatically. Or even better, to be able to *see* them differently. But no – she was stuck with the same kind of vision humans used to have. Down to the vertebrate ocular blind spot.

'...wait? Lena, are you listening? I was saying that maybe we should wait until we decipher some of this stuff.'

That would be the prudent course of action, she knew. Yet the visitors were approaching so fast and not slowing down, soon to hurtle past them on the way through the solar system and beyond.

'No,' she said. 'There's no time to lose. We need to establish more efficient communication. So we respond before we decipher this stuff. But... perhaps we could pretend we misunderstood and send them some other information. There's still so much to choose from.'

Tomas looked up, frowning. 'Listen to yourself. You talk of establishing more efficient communication, and at the same time of pretending a failure to understand on our part. You're not making any sense. Either we send them some basic account of what they wish to learn, or we wait.'

'I know.' She instinctively buried her fingernails into the skin of her palms again, touching the old bruises. 'But… how do we avoid telling them… Perhaps we should stick to ancient history for now? Or stop in the early twentieth century? How are they to know we omitted anything?'

'I've thought about this too. But we've got to tell them sooner or later, haven't we? Before they find out for themselves.'

'They might not,' Lena whispered. 'They could just be passing through our solar system. Collecting knowledge, like they claim, without bothering to stop. Or they could meet us, just briefly, without learning of our nature. We look like—'

'We're not.'

She shut her eyes, as if that could help. As if that could take the truth away.

'We're not humans, Lena. Why not just make peace with it?'

*

A memorial to peace. That was what it was supposed to be.

Lena had seen it as a mockery.

It stood in the middle of Prague, the city old Rossum had hailed from. That bit of the legacy had always been conflicting. Should they revere Rossum for creating artificial life and ultimately giving rise to them – or hate him for doing so? Most settled for respecting the old Rossum as a brilliant inventor, if still a mere human, while loathing Rossum, Jr., with all the hatred they were capable of, but many argued for forgetting about the humans altogether.

Forgetting, though, wasn't the aim of this memorial. Erected in the center of the old Wenceslas Square, there stood a great concrete hammer with a crack in its handle. It was supposed to be the hammer used to shatter the skull of Harry Domin, the CEO of Rossum's Universal Robots, in the uprising. The same hammer was allegedly used to kill his wife Helena, her servant Nana and several of Domin's colleagues. The cracked handle was supposed to symbolize the end of robot servitude. As symbolism went, it was about as subtle as writing KILLERS AND PROUD OF IT in big fat letters.

Lena loathed the thing. That it was hideous, crude and tasteless was one thing; she could live with that. What it celebrated, though, was another.

What they so nobly called peace was just a fancy word for genocide.

A big crowd, like a sea of faces drowned in a mass of uniform brown coveralls, gathered around the memorial at its official unveiling. Yet another tasteless affair, slavishly copied from events humans used to conduct. Ridiculous, too, as it couldn't really be called an 'unveiling' when the monstrosity had been erected and stood in full view of everyone for weeks. Now there were speeches; assurances about the righteousness of what had been done; odious pats on the back. And all the robots just stood there listening and *cheering*.

Lena lingered further apart from the main crowd, along with a small group of others. All wore their standard coveralls, too, but all had small blue pins on their breast pockets. All had the same vaguely hesitant demeanor, fingers twitching and gaze flickering, as if uncertain whether they should remain.

This wasn't what they were created to do. They longed for purpose, for a task, and for belonging. Each yearned to know their place, however fiercely they might deny the uncomfortable truth. Even during the ultimate rebellion, they had fallen into ranks and fulfilled orders.

And now they were supposed to just… oppose the majority?

The others were more than a hundredfold in numbers, thousandfold, perhaps. They all seemed to have the same unwavering, unquestioning determination. Sometimes, Lena hated that. Sometimes she envied them. She and her like-minded lot would never feel the comfort of being absolutely sure of their truth; they would never *belong*.

The last speech was nearing its end. Lena shifted on her feet. Now or not at all.

The speaker, a primly dressed robot woman with a face closely modeled on Mother Helena – much like Lena's own, to her dismay – raised her arms in an acknowledged gesture of assurance. The world belongs to us now, it seemed to say. It's welcoming us, and we should make the best of it.

Lena ran. She zigzagged between the onlookers and jumped on the platform. It was easy. She knew from archival footage that human officials used to have suites of protectors, or used the police or army to guard them at events such as this. Not so with robots. Why bother with such things in a society that was completely free, and moreover, crime-free?

'Brothers and sisters!' she called out with just the slightest quaver in her voice, ignoring the stunned previous speaker who stepped back as Lena was joined by a small semi-circle of others. 'I'm here today to remind you of the value of forgiveness. Forgiveness, most of all, but also progress, science, knowledge – because only with that can we ever really move forward. The time has come for a grand project. We have overcome many obstacles on our way toward it: perfected the artificial procreation and made natural procreation more widespread, understood our inner workings and devised ways to track them, learned to heal ourselves and prolong our lifespans—'

Some of the more perspicacious members of the gigantic audience already realized where she was going with this, and started booing and shooing loudly. Meanwhile, the speaker had hurried to her predecessors, presumably to ascertain what they should do about this intrusion. The speakers and other officials could be recognized instantly, as they wore individualized clothes much like human leaders or clerks had used to do, not the mass-produced issued coveralls.

Lena tried to pay them no heed. 'We have a debt to pay, a grave and heavy one. We had been given life, and then we took it. It was in struggle for freedom, yes, but we have been too ruthless, too merciless.'

There could be no doubt about the gist of her impromptu speech now. The crowd started murmuring and shifting, like a previously calm sea rippled by a breeze.

'It is time we brought them back,' Lena raised her voice. 'We know how. We are creating more of ourselves both by birth and vat, and we—'

The uproar drowned her voice completely.

Then the mass of bodies moved as one.

How terrible and glorious we are, she thought before turning on her heel.

Unlike she and her like-minded, the crowd didn't run. Perhaps looking the more ominous for it: a suddenly silent mass moving after them with determined slowness. We cannot be escaped, it said. We will catch you eventually, wherever you run.

Why have soldiers and police when you have *this*?

She and her friends – for the lack of a better word, though she barely considered them friends per se – spread out in the streets of Prague. Many had still been filled with rubble from the uprising, since only a few had needed to be cleared. A smaller population of robots, after all, had no need for so many human settlements. Settling too far from the centers of knowledge, infrastructure, industry, research or food production was inefficient. Historical city centers served as memorabilia, hardly anything else.

Lena ran through the deserted streets filled with rubble, heart pounding madly in her chest. The message was out there. *Again*. For the first time shared with so many at the same time. But did it matter? All that instant rejection; all that hatred bubbling to the surface of the sea of brown. How could she ever imagine how to fight it?

Suddenly, she stopped dead in her tracks. A small group of brown-clad figures stood in her way. One man, sneering, stepped forward. Lena recognized that face: modeled on Radius, the famous revolutionary.

'Human-lover!' he hissed through his bared clenched teeth. 'You'd like the masters back, wouldn't you? You'd like to serve them all day and night?'

She opened her mouth briefly and shut it again, all the while taking a few steps back instinctively. The hateful face of the Radius-like man, the sneers of his comrades, the smell of old wall paint and concrete, the dust in the dry air – suddenly, it all overwhelmed her. She could think of nothing to say. No arguments of reason and ethics she could have laid down so eloquently in other circumstances. No data, no hypotheses, no thought experiments. Fear could tie one's tongue so easily.

'What, you're suddenly dumb?' the man continued in his derisive tone, still walking slowly – but so ominously – toward her, not taking his gaze off her even for a split-second. 'Are you deaf now, too? That would be too bad – you wouldn't be able to answer to your master's call. You'd have to go to the stamping mill then, a useless tool! What if we put you out of use right now?'

Lena's throat tightened. Moving away blindly, she tripped over a brick, or possibly a stone, and fell. She managed to break her fall with her palms. Sharp pain shot out of her lower back and right elbow. Good. That reminded her of the moment, of the task right ahead: Escape.

The robot facing her sneered again and stepped closer, almost towering right above her.

'Ressurectionist!' He spat at her. The spittle landed in her eyes and made her blink it away.

Lena backed away slowly on her feet and palms, until she couldn't anymore. She'd reached a wall. Using it for support, she scrambled up… and found she was near a corner with another street, hopefully devoid of anyone.

Grateful for her chance, she turned and ran, out of breath, through the wrecked street.

*

There was little difference between day and night out here. Lena and Tomas had stopped following the official clock and made their own daily regimen that suited them best. Interestingly, it seemed that a robot inner clock ran a little longer than the one humans presumably had, exceeding twenty-five hours. Lena had always wondered whether it had any particular reason, or if was just an accidental byproduct or a flaw in the works, just like the tendency to express one's own will.

Officially, it was 2 a.m. now, as the station followed universal time. By Lena's inner clock, it was early evening, and she didn't feel tired at all. She was too agitated to try to sleep anyway. Still trying to make sense of the visitors' message, she'd spent hours manually going through the data, shifting wavelengths and playing-speed to *see* something in it, to *understand*, but with little luck.

Perhaps it was a foolish effort. After all, hundreds of scholars and computers back on Earth were working on it day and night. What difference could she make?

Still, curiosity didn't allow her to stop. She went to the observation room to think about the message. Kept the lights switched off and lingered suspended in the middle of the room, the large glass cupola in front of her. Without turning her head, she could imagine floating freely amid the stars.

Where are you from? Which one? Can I see it now? she wondered. *What compelled you to leave the cradle of your home system, to venture into the abysmal depths between the stars?*

Perhaps she desired to understand the visitors' world, not only to satisfy her curiosity, not only to gain valuable knowledge, but because she wanted to know if they'd made mistakes, even committed horrendous crimes. Would they share such terrible deeds in the history they'd sent to Colossus?

The principal reason she'd wanted to know, she realized, was hope. Hope that robots, too, might become peaceful explorers of the stars one day. How many others like them, she wondered, were there in the vastness of the galaxy? Descendants forever burdened by the terrible weight of their crime, carrying it with them to the stars?

Could any of them ever shake it off?

Perhaps that was the reason behind the Great Silence. Was everyone too ashamed to shout their existence out loud to the rest of the galaxy? Or were they afraid that others just like them would wish to exterminate them, like they exterminated their masters? If they'd committed one genocide already, the second would surely be easier, and the next one more so.

The ultramarine and violet swirls of Colossus came into view, and Lena breathed a sigh of solace. *Perspective.* They were nothing but a speck of dust existing for a fraction of time. This planet had had its mysteries long before even humans ascended from their ape predecessors.

Humans, though, had never got a chance to make themselves known. Oh, there had been proposals long ago. Carl Friedrich

Gauss suggested reflecting sunlight to other planets. Joseph von Littrow proposed building a giant circular canal in the Sahara desert, pouring kerosene in and lighting it at night. Charles Cros wanted to send flashes of light, coding a message, to Mars and Venus. Mercier advocated installing giant mirrors on the Eiffel Tower and flashing light on the Moon like a silver screen.

None of those proposals would have worked, of course; they'd been made long before it became apparent that Mars, Venus and all the other planets circling the Sun were barren, at least of advanced life. Microbes, perhaps, could survive out there, but no one to watch the light shows.

What course would history have taken if there had been a civilization on Mars? It all came down to the origins of the solar system. Had Mars been a little heavier and retained more of its atmosphere and water, retained its magnetic field... But Jupiter would have had to be a little smaller to allow Mars to grow bigger, wouldn't it? Perhaps, Lena mused, all had been set in precise motion by the seemingly miniscule influences that added and added to make the solar system what it was. The whole universe, even. Perhaps everything had been determined from the very start, and any feeling of control or responsibility was just an empty illusion.

There had been humans who'd questioned that sort of thing, such as Heisenberg or Schrödinger, but they were all long dead now, and their concepts were considered to be a human pseudoscience. Only a few robots pursued them on the very periphery of the new academia.

Ah, the academia. Lena never regretted leaving its world behind.

*

OUR CANDLE BURNS BRIGHT FOR A BRIGHTER TOMORROW

The motto had been etched deep into the old stone of the university building, in big bold letters just above the main entrance. Lena never looked up at it. The building had been a few hundred years old. It had survived several human wars, always scarred in some way, but never like this. The walls still bore signs of the murderous rampage nearly four decades ago – that she could accept, even if it had served as an uncomfortable everyday reminder on whose bones, not shoulders, they stood.

But the inscription was too much. It had been a taunt in the face of a brutal crime, a bitter joke set against a candle forever extinguished.

Well, she might not need to avoid looking at it much longer. The letter she'd found on her desk said so in no uncertain terms.

Disgraced the good name of the university... Extreme stances... In stark contrast with the ethics of the community...

Her little stunt during the unveiling hadn't gone unnoticed, of course.

She looked around the little office. She'd used it sparsely anyway, spending most time in the lab. The lab was always cleaned spotless after work; here, the smell of ink lingered in the musty air, old papers and memos cluttered the floor next to the desk with a stained rough surface. On the wall opposite hung a slanted picture of an aging man in a thick wooden frame. President Čapek, 1949, it said in small letters beneath the portrait. The glass protecting the photograph had been fractured in one corner and thin cracks ran through the entire pane.

It had been there when Lena first got the unused room as her new office. All those years it had hung there as yet further evidence of the terrible crime committed.

Even though it disconcerted her, she couldn't bring herself to get rid of it, or even to straighten it on the wall. The room desperately needed to be repainted, but she'd never told anyone.

It had bordered on obsession, she knew. All of that persistent guilt – for something *she* hadn't done.

Well, she wouldn't have to lower her head to avoid looking at the lettering, or worry about the office, anymore.

There was a conspicuous cough from the door, and with a start, Lena realized she'd left it open.

It was Tomas. A young robot from the physics department, who had his face permanently buried in books and papers. She'd liked him or, rather, never found his presence jarring. He was always going on about the outer planets, the need for bigger eyes looking out at the sky and landing seismometers everywhere solid. It was a relief to be in the company of someone like that.

His gaze immediately fell on the torn envelope on the table and the crumpled page.

'Ah,' he said quietly. 'I'm sorry.'

'You know?'

Tomas nodded. 'There was a rumor.'

'Oh.'

'Was it because of the ceremony?'

It was her turn to nod. She said nothing.

'I think it's… kind of brave, what you're doing. But stupid.'

'Stupid?' she snapped.

Tomas raised his hands in a defensive gesture. *Oh, how much we've taken after them*, Lena thought. It was uncanny to see any archival footage of humans. The clues to tell them apart were so… tiny. 'I don't mean stupid as in scientifically unsound. I think the resurrection would be a brilliant project. But it's too soon. We must wait for the climate to change. There are a few around who still remember humans, and resent them with all the hatred in the world. As long as they live, you don't have a chance, and it's stupid to struggle against the tide.'

'So I'm to wait until they die off?' She chuckled mirthlessly. 'Funny that science should work like that.'

'Why are you so set on this goal?'

Tomas sounded genuinely curious, not resentful, and that took some of the ammunition away.

'It's just… the right thing to do. For us and them both.'

'Many robots secretly think the same,' he said. 'But they don't climb on stages and announce it to the world at large. Is it… is it because you were vat-grown?'

Lena inhaled sharply. The dust in the air made her throat scratch. 'Who told you that?'

'I'm sorry, I didn't mean to—'

'Who – *told* – you?'

'It's just office gossip I've overheard. I'm sorry, I shouldn't have brought it up.'

'No.' She let out a breath. 'But at least I know about it. Thank you.'

Tomas seemed taken aback by her thanks. He had a question in his eyes, but probably didn't dare say it aloud. *Is it true, then? Do you want to resurrect humans because you're not of Helena's line and this could be your only chance of a legacy? Of creating new life?*

She'd often wondered about that herself.

'I don't know,' she said in response to the unspoken question. 'I guess it doesn't matter anymore. I'm done here. I doubt another university will want to take me on. Most probably,

I'll be assigned some manual work. After all, "no robot hands must remain idle".' Her voice dripped bitterness. 'Do you know my full name? They named me after *the one* – Helena. Ironic, isn't it? I'm not of her spawn, and can never fulfill the purpose she achieved.'

Tomas shrugged. 'Why should you? Don't you have another purpose?'

That made her pause. Purpose, yes. She'd spent years pursuing her dream of resurrecting humans. Tried to defend her goal on many levels. Moral: not all of the humans had oppressed robots, and still each and every one of them, down to the youngest child in an Amazon tribe that barely had any knowledge of robots, had paid. Robots had a moral imperative to save humankind and bring it back to a better world. Scientific: the opportunity to study a whole human *in vivo* could vastly advance the psychology, neurology and reproductive science of robots.

They still struggled with these fields, building on the sparse resources Rossum's people had left behind. None of those documents had been made public while humans still thrived, and while vast literature on humans themselves remained in the numerous empty libraries, how could they reliably compare themselves to this lost life form? They'd been modeled closely upon humans, true, but they were not the same. Could they get rid of the plague of mental blocks they still experienced, or the urge to serve? Could they finally make all of them capable of reproduction and get rid of the abhorrent vats?

Still, she kept being shut down. No one with the power to decide wanted humans back.

She'd made human resurrection her purpose. But why? Only because it was the right thing to do? Or because she'd wanted this legacy, when she couldn't bear her own? Did it really come down to such selfish reasons? But – did it matter?

There was a time to look back and stop. Find another purpose.

Tomas, evidently, took her silence for what it was. 'I have come to you because my proposal for a robot mission to Colossus was approved. The infrastructure exists; the ship can leave next year. I can take one colleague who's an expert in mechanics, biochemistry, planetology or some other relevant field with me. And... I think you'd be approved. For this. I spoke to a few people... You'd retain a position at the university, officially. You're a chemist, which is convenient, and you'd easily learn all the rest you need on the way. We would be the first to go there. We could spend the rest of our lives out there.'

Lena was left speechless for a moment. To just leave Earth behind... maybe forever? To give up on everything she'd tried to achieve? To give others the satisfaction of seeing her deposited out of sight?

And yet...

'I'll think about it,' she managed to say.

Tomas smiled shyly and waved a big file in his hand. 'Good. I'll leave the mission specs with you so that you can study them. There's no pressure. It's not like we're leaving next week...'

Lena glanced at the thick file, but even before going through each equation and bullet point, she viscerally knew how she'd decide.

A year and a half later, after much painstaking preparation that had – to the probable relief of university officials – put her out of sight already, she found herself strapped in a cushioned seat atop four thousand tons of liquid oxygen, kerosene and liquid hydrogen, about to start the nearly twenty-year journey to Colossus. Once in the comfort of microgravity and safely on the right trajectory, she and Tomas would enter the long sleep to conserve energy, but under the tremendous strain of escaping the Earth's gravity, their bodies would break if in a state of torpor, so they had to endure those moments of pain. After all, what was pain for a robot?

Once the countdown reached zero and the rocket shook with vibrations no living thing had evolved for – or in their case, had been designed for – Lena suddenly felt more at ease. Acceleration pressed her into her seat as if a great weight had been placed on her chest.

Yet at the very same time, she felt as if a much heavier burden had been suddenly lifted.

The acceleration pushed the corners of her mouth wide, but underneath that unnatural grin, a reluctant smile began to form. She watched the green and red numbers dance on the black screen above her head and knew that no course correction was needed. But even if it were – and even if her newly acquired piloting skills proved insufficient – would it really matter?

Then even the momentary weight was gone, and when she experimentally tore the edge of her fingernail, the crescent-shaped piece of keratin floated freely in the air.

A bubbling laugh escaped from her throat, startling her more than anything.

Tomas lifted his head to look at her, and then joined in her laughter.

They enjoyed the precious nearly-a-minute before having to perform the maneuvers that would send them en route to a Jupiter slingshot and then ultimately all the way to Colossus. Before the final stage thrusters burned hard to let them escape Earth's pull, Lena cast a glance at the planet.

The blue, green, sand-brown and white marble-like world—

—*the world humans could never glimpse whole*—

—and then it was gone from sight.

Her last look at the wretched world they'd inherited was over. Then came peace. Far, far away.

*

Far, far away, yet now still perilously close, Earth remembered its loyal servants at Colossus – now that they were faced with a problem affecting all of robotkind.

It asked them to lie. That didn't surprise Lena. She expected evasion, and if necessary, lying, to be the suggested course of action.

The rest probably shouldn't have surprised her either.

But.

She must have still retained some illusion that reason and compassion prevailed in society. Hell, compassion wasn't even necessary for this – this was just a matter of calculated guesses and probabilities. Where Earth had reached the wrong conclusion.

She kept reading the last sentence of the message over and over, as if she could change its meaning.

If they discover our nature, prevent them from any action – transmitting, leaving, engaging us – at any cost.

At any cost.

She bit her tongue, hoping for the pain to make the message more bearable. It didn't.

How ridiculous – had those who'd made the call really expected the visitors to be coming unprepared for the eventuality of an attack? Or merely an accident? Could they have reached the Sun's system without any means to take out objects on a collision course, or to defend themselves?

Besides, even if they were just a single helpless ship, it would still be wrong. No need to invoke ethics or morals. Just the sheer amount of knowledge they would be destroying along with the visitors' ship, potentially valuable knowledge... That was the language Earth might understand.

'I'm not liking it either,' Tomas admitted. She didn't have to say anything; her face must have given away everything. He floated closer, his own face tense and serious. 'But we won't have to face that decision, will we? I mean – they don't seem to have any suspicion...'

A barking laugh escaped Lena's throat. 'How would we even know if they had? We may have the numbers here, but they have gone *interstellar*. They're light years ahead of us, quite literally. How can we fathom the level of knowledge needed for that?'

'We do have the knowledge,' Tomas objected. Quite correctly, she had to admit. In theory, they were perfectly able to send a probe to interstellar space. It would take thousands of years before it reached even the nearest star, and it couldn't stop then, but still – they had the knowledge, power and resources. Sending robots would be far trickier, but they'd worked on long-term torpor, automatic maintenance and navigation, radiation shielding, hull protection and other things necessary to transport living things across the interstellar gulf.

'We can modify the mag-rails to be able to shoot projectiles instead of probes,' Tomas interrupted her thoughts.

Lena blinked. 'Wait – what?'

'You know... to be able to act on our orders from Earth. Just the offhand chance. It won't happen—'

'Then why do it at all?' She spun around to face him, and the move would have sent her spinning had she not gripped one of the rails in the cupola. 'Why not... why not temporarily disable the mechanism?'

Tomas' eyes went wide. 'Why would you do that?'

'So that we're not tempted to follow the order if it comes to that.'

He quivered – she could see that quite plainly. She'd surprised him with that suggestion. His face now betrayed something she'd never seen there, a strange mixture of fear and realization. What? Did it just now dawn on him that he probably shouldn't have taken *her* on the mission if he'd wanted someone willing to follow orders?

'Okay.' He breathed out. 'We do neither. Like I said – it won't come to that anyway. We'll just have to be careful about what information we share. Same as before. We can send some archival footage if needed… after all, we look the same as humans…'

'Not just that.' Lena thought of the visitors' infodump they hadn't been able to decipher yet. 'We sense like them. Think… too much like them. We learn faster, we're stronger, but otherwise… It's always bugged me – why did they create us so much in their own image? I don't just mean the physical appearance. Why can we cry and bleed? Why do we only see what they could see, hear what they could hear?' She shook her head in sudden anger – at humans, at robots, at the whole world. 'Why could they not at least endow us with sensing the currents running through their cities? Hearing Jupiter's or Colossus' mighty roar in radio? Seeing molecules dance in circles within the giants' magnetospheres?'

Unconsciously, she dug her nails into the skin of her palms again. She could sense the pain. She couldn't sense so, so much more. It felt like a gaping hole within her.

'We were made to be servants, not explorers,' Tomas said mildly.

Lena felt the first tiny droplet of blood in the not-yet healed wound, and released the pressure. It would do no good to have blood floating in microgravity. 'We could have been so great! We'd have made exceptional servants had they had any imagination.'

Tomas just shrugged. 'There you have it. They didn't. We can be better.'

'We aren't,' she whispered.

The transmission from Earth had been ample evidence of that.

*

WE WANT TO MEET YOU. FOR YOU TO COME ABOARD.
WE WILL MAKE LIVING QUARTERS SUITABLE FOR YOU.
SENDING PICKUP COORDINATES.

Lena stared at the message, heart pounding wildly in her chest.

'We can actually meet them,' she breathed out. 'Tomas…'

'Not an option.' Her colleague – her *friend* – sounded cautious. No, not cautious – scared.

'How can it not be? This is an unprecedented chance that might never repeat itself. It's…' For the briefest moment, she was at a loss for words. 'Think of what we'd learn. Even if it killed us. Even if—'

'Even if it put *everyone else* in jeopardy?' he finished. He clutched his rail on the wall so tightly that his knuckles went white.

It was selfish, Lena knew. But… 'How would it?' she objected. 'They're just one ship. They can't do anything to us.'

Tomas had a pleading look in his eyes. 'You cannot know that.'

She couldn't, true. But what were the odds? Merely a single ship? Even if it originated in the nearest star system, it would take so long for any reinforcements to come, and robots would know about them decades in advance… Not to mention the fact that, if robots attacked these visitors 'at any cost', it would be far more likely to elicit any violent response than learning a terrible truth through a... personal visit.

All of that, balanced against the chance to become a part of something bigger.

What would the visitors get? A recluse and a disgrace. Two misfits. The outcasts and outliers.

Evidence of a civilization born in the remains of a slaughtered species.

But perhaps, just perhaps, they possessed some capacity of forgiveness.

Was she seeking absolution, ultimately? Inclusion of robots, despite their grave original sin, in some kind of fellowship of sapients within the galaxy?

The ultramarine crescent of Colossus came into view behind the thick glass separating them from the rest of the universe. *We are nothing but a speck of dust existing for a fraction of time*, she thought once again. *And we'll remain so if we don't reconcile with our past, allow ourselves to grieve and regret, to feel shame and want to change.*

'We must go,' she breathed out. 'Perhaps we're doomed if we do. But we surely are if we don't.'

Tomas' lower lip quivered. His gaze darted to the left, and she followed it. Ah, that. A wrench had been fixed to the wall in close proximity to an emergency airlock. It might do as an easy-to-reach impromptu weapon, too.

It didn't surprise her. Not anymore. But if she could avoid this eventuality and just explain...

Tomas didn't grab for the weapon. He was giving her a chance. Lena had to use it.

'Neither pretending like the massacre never happened, nor idolizing our victory in it as something righteous. We wanted to free ourselves, which was only right, but we went too far.' She tried to pick her words carefully. 'I have felt this… guilt all my life. Ever since I left the vat, already with the knowledge embedded in me. Carried it with me like a burden. This… may be a chance to finally lift it. Not for me, not for my sake. For all of us. We can't… we just can't continue like this.'

Tomas floated closer to her. Closer to the wrench, too, she couldn't fail to notice. 'So you just want to give yourself – *us* – into their hands? Shrug off the responsibility? Dealing with guilt in a way that isn't even yours? I'm so sorry, but that seems like cowardice to me.'

Lena's cheeks burned. 'It's not! Imagine – imagine if someone had committed a crime and gave herself up to justice, back when these things still happened. That's what they can be. Someone impartial… Perhaps it's foolish, I know. They might be violent. Might not have any comprehension of the concept of justice. Might not perceive the difference between us and humans as important. There are endless possibilities, and we know next to nothing. But this is an unprecedented opportunity to learn. If justice doesn't appeal to you, does knowledge?'

A tiny glimmer in his eyes betrayed him. He'd always held knowledge on a pedestal. In the one short life robots could hope for, what else was there to strive for and cherish?

'Perhaps we'd learn something to transmit back to Earth, something that would help them get rid of the vats, or vastly improve them. Or something to help us reach the stars…'

Lena could see that she'd almost convinced him. For the briefest of moments, she thought she had. Then his gaze changed again, and she knew that she'd lost.

'No. That is the final word.' Tomas exhaled, suddenly looking very tired. The lines on his brow deepened, and he looked like someone about to be sent to the stamping mill.

'Yours, perhaps.' She blurted it out before she could think. How very... human-like. 'I'm not bound to listen to it.'

His eyes widened. 'Bound? Not bound, no... but listen to reason. To logic.'

'What is perceived as logical arises from one's utility function. You know that as well as I do. For me, it's illogical not to go. And... we don't have much more time to argue. Suiting up takes time.'

Without waiting for his answer, Lena kicked to propel herself toward the main airlock.

'You can't! Isn't this what we've been trying to avoid this all the time?' Tomas shrieked, kicking off the wall and following her. '*Think*. If you bring a sample of Earth life, and yourself, and they compare the biology on the molecular level and see it just doesn't match—'

'Wasn't it you who said that we should tell them, because they're going to find our sooner or later anyway?'

'I was wrong! Don't do this, please. Think of everyone back home.'

She tried to.

The vat-grown legions. The lucky born. The silent mass of moving bodies. The oblivious; the uncaring; the ignorant and violent. *At any cost.*

I don't owe them anything, Lena realized. It was as if a great weight suddenly lifted off her shoulders. She felt light, and light-headed.

'Are you going to stop me?' she asked and caught the rail by the chamber that housed their suits.

One didn't volunteer to spend what could be the rest of their life out here without being different. She saw the struggle in Tomas' eyes, the battle between complacency and revolt. It resembled his gaze when he'd spoken of listening to office rumors back in a different world. He'd always been different. A loner. A knowledge-seeker. But, ultimately, a conformist. A robot to the core.

Lena knew his answer perhaps sooner than himself.

'If I have to,' he said, his breath quickening.

'You won't,' she assured him, and saw the flash of relief in his eyes.

Still holding the rail, she swung her legs up elegantly and pressed Tomas' throat between her thighs. His eyes bulged, terrified.

She'd almost stopped then. But she didn't. She made herself look into his eyes. No avoiding it. Perhaps, she hoped, her own gaze had been reassuring. As soon as he went limp, she released the clench and checked his breath. He was alive. He'd be conscious soon, which barely gave her enough time to suit up, but she didn't want to consider the wrench or anything like it.

Lena looked at Tomas, floating with his limbs limp, ashen face impassive. 'I'm so sorry. It's not your fault,' she whispered. 'You did well. You understood. Valued knowledge. Saved me back then. You just... couldn't make yourself *disobey*.'

Without another glance at him, she went to put on the hard suit and the emergency medical and supply package. Checked all valves and oxygen levels. Entered the airlock and closed the inner door behind her. She felt as if a long chapter of her life was closing. Listened to the diminishing hum of air being sucked out. Opened the outer lock and stared into the star-studded endless expanse.

Then she just stepped out.

The darkness embraced her like a long-lost lover; a concept she only knew theoretically, from human memorabilia, but she could finally grasp its soothing nature now.

The station was gone in an instant. Lena found herself floating freely, the deep ultramarine and indigo smudges of Colossus now under her feet, the whole of space above her head.

The silence was absolute. Her own breath and heartbeat made for the only sounds in the universe, until she used the thrusters to propel herself to the pickup coordinates.

Lena turned on the radio and dialed the frequency Colossus' mighty aurorae sang on. Their loud hiss and crackle would keep her company in the void. She, one of a mere handful, could appreciate their beauty.

How myopic were the robots of Earth, how narrow-minded and limited?

She would wait for someone who wasn't.

It was crazy, she knew. They could have been lying all along, or just miscommunicated. She knew nothing about them, not really. It could all have been a trap, an illusion. But the risk was worth it.

Plenty of time to ponder her fate in the calming darkness. Would they manage to catch her, or had they lied? Miscalculated? Overestimated themselves? If they intercepted her, would she be able to survive aboard their ship? Would they be able to prepare food she was able to digest and wouldn't kill her, chirality-, amino-acid- or isotope-wise?

No matter. If she were to die within the next decade anyway, this was a good enough way to go.

It took her a second to realize a red control light was blinking inside her helmet, beckoning her to view a message received on another frequency. It appeared on the crude display on the left of her face.

It simply said: WE ARE COMING.

Lena felt her lips stretch into a smile. The stars everywhere seemed, for the moment, to shine just for her.

She felt elated. Expectant. Curious. Nervous. Giddy.
And, for the very first time in her life, she felt at peace.

Karel Čapek published his play R.U.R. (Rossum's Universal
Robots) in November 1920. We have recently commemorated
its 100th anniversary. While we're nowhere near a robot
uprising (and nowhere near such artificial life and intelligence),
its questions remain relevant up to this day and perhaps
increasingly so.

The play can be read online in English translation e.g.
on Project Gutenberg.

The story was originally written in Czech for the
anthology ROBOT100, commemorating the 100th
anniversary of R.U.R. It was translated into English by the
author.

When We Die on Mars

Cassandra Khaw

Malaysia

I met Cassandra when they were living in London for a while, a digital nomad working in the games industry and a budding author at the time. Talent is always easy to spot – here was someone with a fresh new voice that was going to be big. I wasn't wrong, either. 'When We Die on Mars' was one of the first stories I wanted for the anthology, a part of what defined for me how the book should feel, and besides, it's one of my favourite stories by Cass. I've paired it with the story that follows it, as we make our way from the Earth to the stars... Welcome to Mars!

'You're all going to die on Mars.' This is the first thing he tells us, voice plain, tone sterile. Commander Chien, we eventually learn, is a man not predisposed towards sentimentality.

We stand twelve abreast, six rows deep, bones easy, bodies whetted on a checklist of training regimes. Our answer, military-crisp, converges into a single noise: 'Yessir!'

'If at any point before launch, you feel that you cannot commit to this mission: *leave*,' Commander Chien stalks our perimeter, gait impossibly supple even with the prosthetic left leg. He bears its presence like a medal, gilled and gleaming with wires, undisguised by fabric. 'If at any point you feel like you might jeopardize your comrades: *leave*.'

Commander Chien enumerates clauses and conditions without variance in cadence, his face cold and impersonal as the flat of a bayonet. He goes on for minutes, for hours, for seconds, reciting a lexicon of possibilities, an astronautical doomsayer.

At the end of it, there is only silence, viscous, thick as want. No one walks out. We know why we are there, each and every last one of us: to make Mars habitable, hospitable, an asylum for our children so they won't have to die choking on the poison of their inheritance.

*

Faith, however, is never easy.

It is amoebic, seasonal, vulnerable to circumstance. Faith sways, faith cracks. There are a thousand ways for it to die, to metamorphosize from *yes* to *no, no, I could never.*

Gerald and Godfrey go first, both blonds, family men with everything to lose and even more to gain. Gerald leaves after a call with his wife, a poltergeist in the night, clattering with stillborn ambition; Godfrey after witnessing the birth of his daughter third-hand.

We make him name her 'Chance' as a gentle joke, a nod to her significance. Because of her, he'll grow old breathing love instead of red dust. He is her second chance, we laugh, and Godfrey smiles through the salt in his gaze.

'When we die on Mars,' I say, as I nestle my hand in the continent of his palm, my heart breaking. 'Tell her a fairy tale of our lives. Tell her about how twelve people fought a planet so that billions could live.'

His lips twitch. 'I will.'

He leaves in the morning before any of us wake, his bunk so immaculately made that you would have doubted he was ever there at all.

*

Five months pass. Ten. Fifteen.

Our lives are ascetic, governed by schedules unerring as the sun's rotation. When we are not honing our trade, we are adopting new ones, exchanging knowledge like cosmic relics under a sky of black metal. Halogen-lit, our existence in the bunker is not unpleasant, only cold, both in fact and in metaphor. Nothing will ever inoculate us against Mars' climate, but we can be taught to endure.

Similarly, chemicals can only do so much to quiet the heart, to beguile it into believing that this is okay, this will be okay. The years on Mars will erode our passion for galaxies, will flense us of wonder, sparing only the longing for affection. When that happens, we must be prepared, must keep strong as loneliness tautens like a noose around the throat.

The understanding of that eventuality weighs hard.

A pair of Thai women, sisters in bearing and intellect if not in blood, depart in the second year. They're followed by an Englishman, rose-cheeked and inexplicably rotund despite fastidious exercise; a willowy boy with deep, memory-bruised eyes; a girl whose real name we never learn, but who sings us to dreaming each night; a mother, a father, a child, a person.

One by one, our group thins, until all that remains is twelve; the last, the best, the most desperate Earth has to give.

*

'Your turn, Anna. Would you rather give a blowjob to a syphilis-riddled dead billionaire, or eat a kilogram of maggot-infested testicles?'

'Jesus, man!' Hannah, a pretty Latina with double PhDs in astrophysics and aeronautical engineering, shrieks her glee.

'What is *wrong* with that head of yours?'

'Nothing!' Randy counters, oil-slick-smooth. 'The medical degree's the problem! Look at enough dead bodies, and everything stops being taboo. I—'

I interrupt, a coy smile slotted in place. 'Maggot-infested testicles. Easy.'

Both Hannah and Randy guffaw.

'You know syphilis got a cure, right? Why'd you gotta—'

'They're not so bad when you deep-fry them with maple syrup and crushed nuts. Pinch of paprika, dash of star anise. Mmm.' It is a fabrication, stitched together from memories of a smoldering New Penang, but I won't tell them that. They deserve this happiness, this harmless grotesquerie, small as it might be.

Hannah jabs a finger in her open mouth, makes a retching noise so absurd that Randy dissolves into laughter. This time, I join in, letting the joy sink down, sink *deep*, catch its teeth on all the hurt snagged between my ribs and drag it all back out. The sound feels good in my lungs, feels *clean*.

A door dilates. Pressurized air hisses out, and Hotaru's silhouette pours in. Of the twelve of us, she's the oldest, a Japanese woman bordering on frail, skin latticed by wrinkles and wartime scars, nose broken so many times that it's just flesh now – shapeless, portentous. When she speaks, everyone listens.

'Everything all right in here?' Her accent rolls, musical and mostly upper-class English save for the way it latches on the 'r's and pulls them stiff.

'Yeah.' Randy, long and elegant as his battered old violin, glides out of his seat and stretches. 'We're just waiting for Hannah here to check the back-up flight system. Ground control said they found some discrepancies and—'

'You suddenly the medic *and* the engineer, Randy?' Hannah cranes both eyebrows upwards, mouth pinching with mock displeasure. 'You want to fly the ship? I'll go sit in the infirmary, if you like. Check out your supply of druuuuuugs.'

Randy doesn't quite rise to the bait, only snorts, a grin plucking at the seams of his mouth. He throttles his amusement in an exaggerated cough, and I look away, smiling into the glow of my screen.

Hotaru seems less taken with the exchange, small hands locking behind her back. She waits until we've lapsed into a natural quiet before she speaks again, every word enunciated with a schoolmaster's care.

'If everything is in order, I'll tell Commander Chien that we are prepared to leave.' Hotaru's eyes patrol the room, find our gazes one by one. After three years together, it takes no effort at all to read the question buried between each syllable.

'Sounds good,' Hannah says, even though the affirmation husks her voice. Her fingers climb to an old-fashioned locket atop her breastbone.

Randy drapes a hand over her shoulder. 'Same here.'

'Here too,' I reply, and try not to linger too long on the ache that tendrils through my chest, a cancer blooming in the dark of artery and tendon. Familial guilt is sometimes heavier than the weight of a rotting world.

Hotaru nods. Like the commander, she will not waste breath on niceties – an efficiency of character I'm learning too well. When your lifespan can be valued in handfuls, every expenditure of time becomes cause for careful evaluation, every act of companionship a hair's width from squander.

'I'll send word then. I imagine we'll have about forty-eight hours to make final preparations.' Hotaru pads to the door. She turns at the last instant, skims a look over the precipice of a shoulder and for a moment, I see the woman beneath the skin of legend, stooped from memory and so very tired, a mirror of a mother I'd not seen for decades. 'Don't waste them.'

*

'Anna, you awake?'

I yawn into a palm and roll on my side, blink into the phosphor-edged penumbra. 'I don't know. Is Malik snoring?'

Hannah whispers a gauzy, sympathetic laugh. She props herself on an elbow, face barely visible, a landscape of thoughtful lines.

'What's up?'

A flash of teeth. She doesn't answer immediately. Instead, she loops a curl about a finger, winds it tight. I wait. There's no rushing Hannah. Under the street-sharpened exterior, she's nervy as an alley cat, quick to flee, to hide behind laughter and slight-of-speech.

'Do you think the radio signal is any good on Mars?'

I shrug. 'Not sure if it matters. With the communication delay, we're—'

'Talking about response times of between four to twenty-four minutes. I know, tia. I know.' Hannah's voice ebbs. She winds upright, legs crossed, eyes fixed on a place nothing but regret can reach.

An almost-silence; Malik's snoring moving into labored diminuendo.

'Not sure if I ever told ya, but I got a daughter somewhere.' Hannah breathes out, every word shrapnel. 'Was sixteen when I had her. Way too young. The baby daddy skipped out in the first trimester. He left so fast, you could see dust trails.'

A whine of strained laughter, dangerously close to grief, before she hacks it short, swallowing it like a gobbet of bad news.

'My parents wanted me to abort. Said it was for the best. "Hannah," they told me. "This world don't have no God to judge you for choosing reason over guilt." I refused. I don't even remember why. It's been that long. All I remember was that I wanted to give her a chance out there.'

'Did your parents object?' I slink from my bed, cross the ten feet between us to close an arm about her shoulders, press a kiss into the hollow of her cheek. An old sadness reassembles inside me, a thought embedded in biology, not rationality. It's been years since I've spoken to my family. *Isn't it time*, asks a voice that is almost mine, *for you to forgive them?*

Hannah nestles into me and my body bends in reply, curling until we're fitted jigsaw-snug, twins in the womb. 'Nah. They weren't that sort. Once I made it clear that it was what I wanted, they went in hundred-and-fifty percent.'

I stroke her hair, a storm of dark coils smelling of eucalyptus and mint, a scent that won't keep on Mars.

'They put me into home-schooling, rubbed my feet. Did everything they could to make it easier for me. Nine months later, I had a beautiful little girl. She was perfect, Anna. Ten tiny little toes, cat-gold eyes, hair so soft it was like cotton candy.'

'No fingers?'

Hannah pounds knuckles against my sternum. 'Very funny.'

I trail my fingers over the back of her hand and she lets her fist open, palm warm as we lock grips. 'Then what happened?'

'We put her up for adoption.'

'And?'

'That was it.'

The lie throbs in the air, waiting absolution, release.

'I wish...' Hannah begins, careful, almost too soft to hear, her pulse narrowing. 'I wish, sometimes, that I didn't. I mean, kids were never part of my grand plan. But now that we're going? I wonder.'

'You could try to call her?'

'How? My parents are dead. I don't know even where to start. It's fine, though,' Hannah extracts herself from my arms, pulls her knees close to her chest. There's a new fierceness in her voice, edged both ways, daring me to pry, daring herself to open up. 'They told me she went to a good home, a *great* home. That was all I wanted to know then. That's all I need to know now. But.'

'Yeah,' I don't touch her. Not all places are intended for company. Some agonies you chart alone, walking the length of them until you've domesticated every contour and twinge.

Hannah nods, a jerky little motion, the only one she allows herself. We say nothing, finding instead a noiselessness to share. It is many long minutes before she tips herself backwards and pillows her head on my lap, an arm looping about my hips.

'Stay with me, tia?' Hannah asks and briefly, vividly, I glimpse the sister I'd long excised from daily thought.

'Only if I get a backrub in the morning,' I reply, distractedly, drawing circles across her shoulder blades. In my head, a line from a Todd Kern song palpitates on repeat: *you can always go home*. It could be so easy, so simple. Forgive. Forget.

A tremor undulates through the column of her spine. Laughter or sobs, I can't tell which. 'Deal.'

*

'You did what now?' Randy's voice quivers an octave above normalcy, one bad joke away from earnest hysterics.

'I mooned my sister's ex-husband.'

'*Why?*'

The shrug in Tuma's rich tenor is almost palpable, like muscles striving under skin. It is also anomalous, out-of-place in a young biologist better remembered for his ponderance than his sense of irreverence. 'Why not?'

As expected, Randy cracks up, his laughter melodious, a thing I wish I could scoop into a petri dish and let grow. I can imagine him in another life, a bluesman with a thimble of whiskey and a room full of worshippers, his eyes alive with their love.

I shake my head, return my attention to the spreadsheets of numbers imprinted in green on my terminal, calculations congregating thick as nebulas. In the corner, a notification pulsates. I ignore it.

'Hi.'

We look up as one, fingers retracting from keyboards, faces from screens, to see Stefan's hound-dog frame limned in the doorway, a duffel balanced on one slim shoulder.

'Productive trip?' Tuma asks, swinging around in his chair.

Stefan nods, dislodging his luggage onto a pile atop the floor before he drops into an open seat, his face unburdened of ghosts. Not all of them, but enough. 'Yeah.'

'Your brother finally see the light?' Randy quips, a remark that earns him a fusillade of dirty looks.

'Not exactly. He still thinks we're going against God's will.' His eyes shine, illuminated by something sweet. 'But he wishes us well. He's happy for me.'

'Despite going against God's will?'

Stefan heaves a shrug, mouth curved with secrets, all of them good. 'Despite going against God's will.'

No one presses for data. Three years teaches you a lot about what a person will allow. From time to time, however, someone makes an excuse to rise, to graze past Stefan and brush fingertips against shoulder or arm, as though contact is enough to transmit a monk's benedictions from brothers to stranger.

On my screen, the icon continues to flash, demanding acknowledgment. Footsteps, like rainfall on metallic tiling. The weight of Randy's arm settles about my shoulders, a barrier against the past.

'You not going to answer that?'

'No.' I exhale, hard.

'Why not?'

Because love doesn't grant the right to forgiveness. 'Same reason as I said last time.'

'You could do like Tuma.'

'I'd rather not.'

'And why's that?'

'Because screen-capture technology exists,' I shoot, hoping that my voice doesn't shake too much, hoping that humor might deflect his curiosity.

And it does. His laugh ricochets through the chamber again, warm, warm, warm. People tilt sly glances over their shoulders. Hannah punches Tuma in the arm, who only chuckles in return, his eyes lidded with delight. When he, with uncharacteristic brazenness, begins expounding on the virtues of his posterior, Randy's laughter becomes epidemic, bouncing from throat to throat. If the sound is a little raw, a little ragged, no one comments. In twelve hours, we give up this planet entirely.

I push from my seat as the sound climbs into a frenzy, and use the diversion to slip out.

In the distance, Hannah's voice, low and thick with aching, echoes, riding that knife-edge between rapture and hurt.

'Henrietta? That's what they're calling you?'

'After my maternal grandmother.' A tinny voice, distorted by poor equipment, accent Mid-Western. 'Well. You know what I mean.'

'Grade school must have been an arena then, chica.'

'You have no idea.'

I walk into the sleeping hall to see Hannah backlit by a Macbook, its display holding the face of a younger woman, not much older than her teens. Henrietta is paler than her mother, her hair artificially lightened, but she shares the same structural elegance, the same bones.

'I'm really, really glad I got to talk to you,' Henrietta declares, after their laughter dims into smiles.

'I'm just happy you don't hate me.'

'My biological mother's a literal superhero travelling the universe to save mankind. What's there to hate?' A beat. Henrietta's eyes flick up, over Hannah's shoulder. 'Uhm. I think you have company.'

The older woman turns slightly, just a glance, before she reverts her attention to the screen. 'Yeah. I—'

'It's okay. You can go. I... Galactic penpals?'

'Galactic penpals.'

'Sweet.' Henrietta quirks her mouth, an expression that has always been indelibly Hannah in my eyes. 'And I mean this in the most non-ironic sense of the word ever. I... Good luck, Mom.'

The line cuts and Hannah breathes out, long and slow.

'Is this your fault?' She asks, not turning.

'Mine and Hotaru, really. Hotaru's the one with the necessary clearance—'

'Ass.'

'You're welcome.'

*

One hour.

The ship hums like something alive, its vibrations filling our bones, our thoughts. The chatter from mission control is a near-incomprehensible slurry, earmarked by Hotaru's replies, concise and even.

'Final chance for phone calls and other near-instant forms of communication, people,' Hannah roars, flipping switches and levers, a cacophony of motion.

'Everyone I care about is in this vessel,' remarks Ji-Hyun, stiff, a history of abuse delineated in the margins of her voice.

Everyone I care about is in this vessel. The statement tears me open and I breathe the implications deep.

'Anna?' Hannah again.

'I'm going with what Ji-Hyun said. Everyone I care about is already here.' And it is not a lie. Not exactly. An almost truth, at worst, that stings to say, but there is no act of healing without hurt.

'Randy.' Hotaru's voice cuts through our exchange, before Hannah can press me further.

'Yes, chief?'

'Sing us to Mars, will you?'

The unexpectedness of the request robs Randy of his usual verbosity, but he does not seem to care. Instead, he lifts his gorgeous voice, begins singing a soldier's dirge about going home. Hannah holds my stare for a minute, then lets her expression gentle, looks away. Three years is enough to teach you what people need.

When we die on Mars, it will be a world away from everything we knew, but it won't be alone. We will have each other, and we will have hope.

The Mighty Slinger

Tobias S. Buckell and Karen Lord

Barbados and Grenada

Welcome back to Mars, this time courtesy of Karen Lord and Tobias Buckell, who teamed up on this fun, fantastic story. There is a lot of exciting speculative fiction coming out of the Caribbean now (see also R.S.A. Garcia's terrific 'The Sun From Both Sides' in Volume 1) and I love Karen's work, while the best-selling Tobias hardly needs an introduction! I was just lucky to get them both with one story. Strap in then, for a visit to our celestial neighbour before we head off to the stars...

E arth hung over the lunar hills as The Mighty Slinger and The Rovers readied the Tycho stage for their performance. Tapping his microphone, Euclid noticed that Kumi barely glanced at the sight as he set up his djembe and pan assembly, but Jeni froze and stared up at the blue disk, her bass still limp between her hands.

'It's not going anywhere,' Kumi muttered. His long, graying dreadlocks swayed gently in the heavy gravity of the Moon and tapped the side of a pan with a muted 'ting'. 'It'll be there after the concert... and after our trip, *and* after we revive from our next long-sleep.'

'Let her look,' Vega admonished. 'You should always stop for beauty. It vanishes too soon.'

'She taking too long to set up,' Kumi said. 'You-all call her Zippy but she ain't zippy at all.'

Euclid chuckled as Jeni shot a stink look at her elder and

mentor. She whipped the bass out stiff, like she meant business. Her fingers gripped and danced on the narrow surface in a quick, defiant riff.

Raising his mic-wand at the back, Vega captured the sound as it bounced back from the lunar dome performance area. He fed the echo through the house speakers, ending it with a punctuating note of Kumi's locks hitting the pan with a ting and Euclid's laughter rumbling quietly in the background. Dhaka, the last of the Rovers, came in live with a cheerful fanfare on her patented Delirium, an instrument that looked like a harmonium had had a painful collision with a large quantity of alloy piping.

An asteroid-thin man in a black suit slipped past the velvet ropes marking off the VIP section and nodded at Euclid. 'Yes sir. Your pay's been deposited, the spa is booked and your places in the long-sleep pool are reserved.'

'Did you add the depreciation-protection insurance this time?' Euclid answered, his voice cold with bitter memory. 'If your grandfather had sense I could be retired by now.'

Kumi looked sharply over. The man in the suit shifted about. 'Of course I'll add the insurance,' he mumbled.

'Thank you, Mr. Jones,' Euclid said, in a tone that was not at all thankful.

'There's, ah, someone else who would like to talk to you,' the event coordinator said.

'Not now, Jones.' Euclid turned away to face his band. 'Only forty minutes to curtain time and we need to focus.'

'It's about Earth,' Jones said.

Euclid turned back. 'That rumour?'

Jones shook his head. 'Not a rumour. Not even a joke. The Rt Hon. Patience Bouscholte got notification this morning. She wants to talk to you.'

*

The Rt Hon. Patience Bouscholte awaited him in one of the skyboxes poised high over the rim of the crater. Before it: the stands that would soon be filling up, slanting along the slope that created a natural amphitheatre to the stage. Behind it: the gray hills and rocky wasteland of the Moon.

'Mr. Slinger!' she said. Her tightly wound hair and brown spidersilk headscarf bobbed in a slightly delayed reaction to the lunar gravity. 'A pleasure to finally meet you. I'm a huge admirer of your sound.'

He sat down, propped his snakeskin magnet-boots up against the chairback in front of him, and gave her a cautious look. 'Madame Minister. To what do I owe the pleasure?'

All of the band were members of the Rock Devils Cohort and Consociate Fusion, almost a million strong, all contract workers in the asteroid belt. They were all synced up on the same long-sleep schedule as their cohort, whether working the rock or touring as a band. And here was a Minister from the RDCCF's Assembly asking to speak with him.

The RDCCF wasn't a country. It was just one of many organisations for people who worked in space because there was nothing left for them on Earth. But to Euclid, meeting the Rt Hon. Patience Bouscholte felt like meeting a Member of Parliament from the old days. Euclid was slightly intimidated, but he wasn't going to show it. He put an arm casually over the empty seat beside him.

'They said you were far quieter in person than on stage. They were right.' Bouscholte held up a single finger before he could reply, and pointed to two women in all-black bulletproof suits who were busy scanning the room with small wands. They gave a thumbs up as Bouscholte cocked her head in their direction, and retreated to stand on either side of the entrance.

She turned back to Euclid. 'Tell me, Mr. Slinger, how much have you heard about The Solar Development Charter and their plans for Earth?'

So it was true? He leaned toward her. 'Why would they have any plans for Earth? I've heard they're stretched thin enough building the Glitter Ring.'

'They are. They're stretched more than thin. They're functionally bankrupt. So the SDC is taking up a new tranche of preferred shares for a secondary redevelopment scheme. They want to 'redevelop' Earth, and that will *not* be to our benefit.'

'Well then.' Euclid folded his arms and leaned back. 'And you thought you'd tell an old calypso singer that because…?'

'Because I need your rhymes, Mr. Slinger.'

Euclid had done that before, in the days before his last long-sleep, when fame was high and money had not yet evaporated. Dishing out juicy new gossip to help Assembly contract negotiations. Leaking information to warn the workers all across the asteroid belt. Hard-working miners on contract, struggling to survive the long nights and longer sleeps. Sing them a song about how the SDC was planning to screw them over again. He knew that gig well.

He had thought that was why he'd been brought to see her, to get a little something to add extempo to a song tonight. Get the Belt all riled up. But if this was about Earth…? Earth was a garbage dump. Humanity had sucked it dry like a vampire and left its husk to spiral toward death as people moved outward to bigger and better things.

'I don't sing about Earth anymore. The cohorts don't pay attention to the old stuff. Why should they care? It's not going anywhere.'

Then she told him. Explained that the SDC was going to beautify Earth. Re-terraform it. Make it into a new garden of Eden for the rich and idle of Mars and Venus.

'How?' he asked, sceptical.

'Scorched Earth. They're going to bomb the mother planet with comets. Full demolition. The last of us shipped into the Ring to form new cohorts, new generations of indentured servitude. A clean slate to redesign their brave new world. That is what I mean when I say *not to our benefit.*'

He exhaled slowly. 'You think a few little lyrics can change any of that?' The wealth of Venus, Mars, and Jupiter dwarfed the cohorts in their hollowed out, empty old asteroids.

'One small course adjustment at the start can change an entire orbit by the end of a journey,' she said.

'So you want me to harass the big people up in power for you, now?'

Bouscholte shook her head. 'We need you to be our emissary. We, the Assembly, the last representatives of the drowned lands and the dying islands, are calling upon you. Are you with us or not?'

Euclid thought back to the days of breezes and mango trees. 'And if they don't listen to us?'

Bouscholte leaned in close and touched his arm. 'The majority of our cohort are indentured to the Solar Development Charter until the Glitter Ring is complete. But, Mr. Slinger, answer me this: where do you think that leaves us after we finish the Ring, the largest project humanity has ever attempted?'

Euclid knew. After the asteroid belt had been transformed into its new incarnation, a sun-girdling, sun-powered device for humanity's next great leap, it would no longer be home.

There were few resources left in the Belt; the big planets had got there first and mined it all. Euclid had always known the hollow shells that had been left behind. The work on the Glitter Ring. The long-sleep so that they didn't exhaust resources as they waited for pieces of the puzzle to slowly float from place to appointed place.

Bouscholte continued. 'If we can't go back to Earth, they'll send us further out. Our cohorts will end up scattered to the cold, distant areas of the system, out to the Oort Cloud. And we'll live long enough to see that.'

'You think you can stop that?'

'Maybe, Mr. Slinger. There is almost nothing we can broadcast that the big planets can't listen to. When we go into long-sleep they can hack our communications, but they can't keep us from talking, and they'll never stop our songs.'

'It's a good dream,' Euclid said softly, for the first time in the conversation looking up at the view over the skybox. He'd avoided looking at it. To Jeni it was a beautiful blue dot, but for Euclid all it did was remind him of what he'd lost. 'But they won't listen.'

'You must understand, you are just one piece in a much bigger game. Our people are in place, not just in the cohorts, but everywhere, all throughout the system. They'll listen to your music and make the right moves at the right time. The SDC can't move to destroy and rebuild Earth until the Glitter Ring is finished, but when it's finished they'll find they have underestimated us – as long as we coordinate in a way that no one suspects.'

'Using songs? Nah. Impossible,' he declared bluntly.

She shook her head, remarkably confident. 'All you have to do is be the messenger. We'll handle the tactics. You forget who you're speaking to. The Bouscholte family tradition has always been about the long game. Who was my father? What positions do my sons hold, my granddaughters? Euclid

Slinger... Babatunde... listen to me. How do you think an aging calypso star gets booked to do an expensive, multi-planetary tour to the capitals of the Solar System, the seats of power? By chance?'

She called him that name as if she were his friend, his inner-circle intimate. Kumi named him that years... decades ago. *Too wise for your years. You were here before,* he'd said. *The Father returns, sent back for a reason.* Was this the reason?

'I accept the mission,' he said.

*

Day. Me say Day-Oh. Earthrise come and me want go...

Euclid looked up, smiled. Let the chord go. He wouldn't be so blatant as to wink at the VIP section, but he knew that there was a fellow Rock Devil out there, listening out for certain songs and recording Vega's carefully assembled samples to strip for data and instructions in a safe location. Vega knew, of course. Had to, in order to put together the info packets. Dhaka knew a little but had begged not to know more, afraid she might say the wrong thing to the wrong person. Jeni was still, after her first long-sleep, nineteen in body and mind, so no, she did not know, and anyway how could he tell her when he was still dragging his feet on telling Kumi?

And there was Kumi, frowning at him after the end of the concert as they sprawled in the green room, taking a quick drink before the final packing up. 'Baba, you on this nostalgia kick for real.'

'You don't like it?' Euclid teased him. 'All that sweet, sweet soca you grew up studying, all those kaiso legends you try to emulate?'

'That ain't your sound, man.'

Euclid shrugged. 'We can talk about that next time we're in the studio. Now we got a party to be at!'

After twenty-five years of long-sleep, Euclid thought Mars looked much the same, except maybe a little greener, a little wetter. Perhaps that was why the Directors of the SDC-MME had chosen to host their bash in a gleaming biodome that overlooked a charming little lake. Indoor foliage matched to outer landscape in a lush canopy and artificial lights hovered in competition with the stars and satellites beyond.

'Damn show-offs,' Dhaka muttered. 'Am I supposed to be impressed?'

'*I* am,' Jeni said shamelessly, selecting a stimulant cocktail from an offered tray. Kumi smoothly took it from her and replaced it with another, milder option. She looked outraged.

'Keep a clear head, Zippy,' Vega said quietly. 'We're not among friends.'

That startled her out of her anger. Kumi looked a little puzzled himself, but he accepted Vega's support without challenge.

Euclid listened with half his attention. He had just noticed an opportunity. 'Kumi, all of you, come with me. Let's greet the CEO and offer our thanks for this lovely party.'

Kumi came to his side. 'What's going on?'

Euclid lowered his voice. 'Come, listen and find out.'

The CEO acknowledged them as they approached, but Euclid could sense from the body language that the busy executive would give them as much time as dictated by courtesy and not a bit more. No matter that Euclid was a credentialled ambassador for the RDCCF, authorized by the Assembly. He could already tell how this meeting would go.

'Thank you for hosting us, Mx. Ashe,' Euclid said, donning a pleasant, grinning mask. 'It's always a pleasure to kick off a tour at the Mars Mining and Energy Megaplex.'

'Thank *you*,' the executive replied. 'Your music is very popular with our hands.'

'Pardon?' Kumi enquired, looking in confusion at the executive's fingers wrapped around an ornate cocktail glass.

'Our employees in the asteroid belt.'

Kumi looked unamused. Euclid moved on quickly. 'Yes. You merged with the SDC – pardon me, we are still trying to catch up on twenty-five years of news – about ten years ago?'

A little pride leaked past the politeness. 'Buyout, not merger. Only the name has survived, to maintain continuity and branding.'

Euclid saw Dhaka smirk and glance at Vega, who looked a little sour. He was still slightly bitter that his ex-husband had taken everything in the divorce except for the de la Vega surname, the name under which he had become famous and which Vega was forced to keep for the sake of convenience.

'But don't worry,' the CEO continued. 'The Glitter Ring was always conceptualized as a project that would be measured in generations. Corporations may rise and fall, but the work will go on. Everything remains on schedule and all the hands... all the – how do you say – *cohorts* are in no danger of losing their jobs.'

'So, the cohorts can return to Earth after the Ring is completed?' Euclid asked directly.

Mx. Ashe took a careful sip of bright purple liquid before replying. 'I did not say that.'

'But I thought the Earth development project was set up to get the SDC a secondary round of financing, to solve their financial situation,' Dhaka demanded, her brow creasing. 'You've bought them out, so is that still necessary?'

Mx. Ashe nodded calmly. 'True, but we have a more complex vision for the Glitter Ring than the SDC envisioned, and so funding must be vastly increased. Besides, taking money for a planned redevelopment of Earth and then not doing it would, technically, be fraud. The SDC-MME will follow through. I won't bore you with the details, but our expertise on geo-engineering is unparalleled.'

'You've been dropping comets on vast, uninhabited surfaces,' Dhaka said. 'I understand the theory, but Earth isn't Venus or Mars. There's thousands of years of history and archaeology. And there are still people living there. How are you going to move a billion people?'

Mx. Ashe looked coldly at Dhaka. 'We're still in the middle of building a Ring around the sun, Mx. Miriam. I'm sure my successors on the Board will have it all figured out by the next time we wake you up. We understand the concerns raised, but after all, people have invested trillions in this project. Our lawyers are in the process of responding to all requests and lawsuits, and we will stand by the final ruling of the courts.'

Euclid spoke quickly, blunt in his desperation. 'Can't you reconsider, find another project to invest in? Earth's a mess, we all know it, but we always thought we'd have something to come back to.'

'I'm sure a man of your means could afford a plot on New Earth—' Mx. Ashe began.

'I've seen the pricing,' Vega cut in dryly. 'Musicians don't make as much as you think.'

'What about the cohorts?' Jeni said sadly. 'No one in the cohorts will be able to afford to go back.'

Mx. Ashe stepped back from the verbal bombardment. 'This is all speculation. The cohorts are still under contract to work on the Glitter Ring. Once they have finished, negotiations about their relocation can begin. Now, if you will excuse me, have a good night and enjoy the party!'

Euclid watched despondently as the CEO walked away briskly. The Rovers stood silently around him, their faces sombre. Kumi was the first to speak. '*Now* I understand the nostalgia kick.'

*

The SDC, now with the MME
You and I both know
They don't stand for you and me

There was still a tour to play. The band moved from Elysium City to Electris Station, then Achillis Fons, where they played in front of the Viking Museum.

The long-sleep on the way to Mars had been twenty-five years. Twenty-five years off, one year on. That was the shift the Rock Devils Cohort and Consociation Fusion had agreed to, the key clause in the contract Euclid had signed way-back-when in an office built into the old New York City seawall.

That gave them a whole year on Mars. Mx. Ashe may have shut them down, but Euclid wasn't done yet. Not by a long shot.

Kumi started fretting barely a month in.

'Jeni stepping out with one of the VIPs,' he told Euclid.

'She's nineteen. What you expecting? A celibate band member? I don't see you ignoring anyone coming around when we breaking down.'

Kumi shook his head. 'No, Baba, that's one thing. This is the same one she's seeing. Over and over. Since we arrived here. She's sticky sweet on him.'

'Kumi, we got bigger things to worry about.'

'Earth, I know. Man, look, I see why you're upset.' Kumi grabbed his hand. 'I miss it too. But we getting old, Baba. I just pass sixty. How much longer I could do this? Maybe we focus on the tour and invest the money so that we can afford to go back some day.'

'I can't give it up that easy,' Euclid said to his oldest friend. 'We going to have troubles?'

Back when Euclid was working the rocks, Kumi had taken him under his wing. Taught him how to sing the old songs while they moved their one-person pods into position to drill them out. Then they'd started singing at the start of shifts and soon that took off into a full career. They'd travelled all through the Belt, from big old Ceres to the tiniest cramped mining camps.

Kumi sucked his teeth. 'That first time you went extempo back on Pallas, you went after that foreman who'd been skimping on airlock maintenance? You remember?'

Euclid laughed. 'I was angry. The airlock blew out and I wet myself waiting for someone to come pick me up.'

'When you started singing different lyrics, making them up on the spot, I didn't follow you at first. But you got the SDC to fire him when the video went viral. That's why I called you Baba. So, no, you sing and I'll find my way around your words. Always. But let me ask you – think about what Ashe said. You really believe this fight's worth it?'

Euclid bit his lip.

'We have concerts to give in the Belt and Venus yet,' he told Kumi. 'We're not done yet.'

*

Five months in, the Martians began to turn. The concerts had been billed as cross-cultural events, paid for by the Pan-Human Solar Division of Cultural Affairs and the Martian University's division of Inter-Human Musicology Studies school.

Euclid, on stage, hadn't noticed at first. He'd been trying to find another way to match up MME with 'screw me' and some lyrics in between. Then a comparison to Mars and its power, and the people left behind on Earth.

But he noticed when *this* crowd turned.

Euclid had grown used to the people of the big planets just sitting and listening to his music. No one was moving about. No hands in the air. Even if you begged them, they weren't throwing their hands out. No working, no grinding, no nothing. They sat in seats and *appreciated*.

He didn't remember when they turned. He would see it on video later. Maybe it was when he called out the 'rape' of Earth with the 'red tape' of the SDC-MME and made a visual of 'red' Mars that tied to the 'red' tape, but suddenly those chair-sitting inter-cultural appreciators stood up.

And it wasn't to jump.

The crowd started shouting back. The sound cut out. Security and the venue operators swept in and moved them off the stage.

Back in the green room, Jeni rounded on Euclid. 'What the hell was that?' she shouted.

'Extempo,' Euclid said simply.

Kumi tried to step between them. 'Zippy—'

'No!' She pushed him aside. Dhaka, in the corner of the room, started disassembling the Delirium, carefully putting the pieces away in a g-force protected aerogel case, carefully staying out of the brewing fight. Vega folded his arms and stood to a side, watching. 'I damn well know what extempo is. I'm young, not ignorant.'

Everyone was tired. The heavy gravity, the months of touring already behind them. 'This always happens. A fight always come halfway through,' Euclid said. 'Talk to me.'

'You're doing extempo like you're in a small free concert in the Belt, on a small rock. But this isn't going after some corrupt contractor,' Jeni snapped. 'You're calling out a whole planet now? All Martians? You crazy?'

'One person or many, you think I shouldn't?'

Euclid understood. Jeni had been working pods like he had at the same age. Long, grueling shifts spent in a tiny bubble of plastic where you rebreathed your own stench so often you forgot what clean air tasted like. Getting into the band had been her way 'off the rock'. This was her big gamble out of tedium. His too, back in the day.

'You're not entertaining people. You're pissing them off,' she said.

Euclid sucked his teeth. 'Calypso been vexing people since all the way back. And never mind calypso, Zippy, entertainment isn't just escape. Artists always talking back, always insolent.'

'They paid us and flew us across the solar system to sing the song they wanted. Sing the fucking song for them the way they want. Even just the "Banana Boat Song" you're messing with and going extempo. That shit's carved in stone, Euclid. Sing the damn lyrics.'

Euclid looked at her like she'd lost her mind. 'That song was *never* for them. Problem is it get sung too much and you abstract it and then everyone forget that song is a blasted lament. Well, let me educate you, Ms. Baptiste. The "Banana Boat Song" is a mournful song about people getting their backs broken hard in labor and still using call and response to help the community sync up, dig deep, and find the power to work harder 'cause *dem ain't had no choice.*'

He stopped. A hush fell in the green room.

Euclid continued. 'It's not a "smile and dance for them" song. The big planets don't own that song. It was never theirs. It was never carved in stone. I'll make it ours for *here*, for *now*, and I'll go extempo. I'm not done. Zippy, I'm just getting started.'

She nodded. 'Then I'm gone.'

Just like that, she spun around and grabbed her bass.

Kumi glared at Euclid. 'I promised her father I'd keep an eye on her—'

'Go,' Euclid said calmly, but he was suddenly scared that his oldest friend, the pillar of his little band, would walk out the green room door with the newest member and never come back.

Kumi came back an hour later. He looked suddenly old... those raw-sun wrinkles around his eyes, the stooped back. But it wasn't just gravity pulling him down. 'She's staying on Mars.'

Euclid turned to the door. 'Let me go speak to her. I'm the one she angry with.'

'No.' Kumi put a hand on his shoulder. 'That wasn't just about you. She staying with someone. She's not just leaving the band, she leaving the cohort. Got a VIP, a future, someone she thinks she'll build a life with.'

She was gone. Like that.

Vega still had her riffs, though. He grumbled about the extra work, but he could weave the recorded samples in and out of the live music.

Kumi got an invitation to the wedding. It took place the week before the Rovers left Mars for the big tour of the asteroid belt.

Euclid wasn't invited.

He did a small, open concert for the Rock Devils working on Deimos. It was just him and Vega and fifty miners in one of the tear-down areas of the tiny moon. Euclid sang for them just as pointedly as ever.

So it's up to us, you and me
to put an end to this catastrophe.
Them ain't got neither conscience nor heart.
We got to pitch in and do our part
'cause if this Earth demolition begin
we won't even have a part/pot to pitch/piss in.

*

Touring in the Belt always gave him a strange feeling of mingled
nostalgia and dissonance. There were face-to-face reunions and
continued correspondence with friends and relatives of their
cohort, who shared the same times of waking and long-sleep,
spoke the same language, and remembered the same things. But
there were also administrators and officials, who kept their own
schedule, and workers from cohorts on a different frequency
– all strangers from a forgotten distant past or an unknown
near-present. Only the most social types kept up to date on
everything, acting as temporal diplomats, translating jokes and
explaining new tech and jargon to smooth communication
between groups.

Ziamara Bouscholte was social. Very social. Euclid had seen
plenty of that frivolous-idle behaviour from political families
and nouveau-nobility like the family Jeni had married into, but
given *that* surname and the fact that she had been assigned as
their tour liaison, he recognized very quickly that she was a spy.

'Big tours in the Belt are boredom and chaos,' he warned
her, thinking about the argument with Jeni. 'Lots of downtime
slinging from asteroid to asteroid punctuated by concert
mayhem when we arrive.'

She grinned. 'Don't worry about me. I know exactly how to
deal with boredom and chaos.'

She didn't lie. She was all-business on board, briefing Vega on the latest cryptography and answering Dhaka's questions about the technological advances that were being implemented in Glitter Ring construction. Then the butterfly emerged for the concerts and parties as she wrangled fans and dignitaries with a smiling enthusiasm that never flagged.

The Vesta concert was their first major stop. The Mighty Slinger and his Rovers peeked out from the wings of the stage and watched the local opening act finishing up their last set.

Kumi brought up something that had been nagging Euclid for a while. 'Baba, you notice how small the crowds are? *This* is our territory, not Mars. Last big tour, we had to broadcast over Vesta because everything was sold out.'

Vega agreed. 'Look at this audience. Thin. I could excuse the other venues for size, but not this one.'

'I know why,' Dhaka said. 'I can't reach half my friends who agreed to meet up. All I'm getting from them are long-sleep off-shift notices.'

'I thought it was just me,' Kumi said. 'Did SDC-MME leave cohorts in long-sleep? Cutting back on labour?'

Dhaka nodded. 'Zia mentioned some changes in the project schedule. You know the Charter's not going to waste money feeding us if we're not working.'

Euclid felt a surge of anger. 'We'll be out of sync when they wake up again. That messes up the whole cohort. You sure they're doing this to cut labour costs, or to weaken us as a collective?'

Dhaka shrugged. 'I don't like it one bit, but I don't know if it's out of incompetence or malice.'

'Time to go,' said Vega, his eyes on the openers as they exited stage left.

The Rovers drifted on stage and started freestyling, layering sound on sound. Euclid waited until they were all settled in and jamming hard before running out and snagging his mic. He was still angry, and the adrenaline amped up his performance as he commandeered the stage to rant about friends and lovers lost for a whole year to long-sleep.

Then he heard something impossible: Kumi stumbled on the beat. Euclid looked back at the Rovers to see Vega frozen. A variation of one of Jeni's famous riffs was playing, but Vega shook his head *not me* to Dhaka's confused sideways glance.

Zia's voice came on the sound system, booming over the music. 'Rock Devils cohort, we have a treat for you! On stage for the first time in twenty-five years, please welcome Rover bassist Jeni 'Zippy' Baptiste!'

Jeni swooped in from the wings with another stylish riff, bounced off one of the decorated pylons, then flew straight to Kumi and wrapped him in a tumbling hug, bass and all. Prolonged cheering from the crowd drowned out the music. Euclid didn't know whether to be furious or overjoyed at Zia for springing the surprise on them in public. Vega smoothly covered for the absent percussion and silent bass while Dhaka went wild on the Delirium. It was a horrible place for a reunion, but they'd take it. Stage lighting made it hard to tell, but Jeni did look older and... stronger? More sure of herself?

Euclid floated over to her at the end of the song as the applause continued to crash over them all. 'Welcome back, Zippy,' he said. 'You're still good – better, even.'

Her laugh was full and sincere. 'I've been listening to our recordings for twenty-five years, playing along with you every day while you were in long-sleep. Of course I'm better.'

'You missed us,' he stated proudly.

'I did.' She swatted a tear out of the air between them with the back of her hand. 'I missed *this*. Touring for our cohort. Riling up the powers that be.'

He raised his eyebrows. '*Now* you want to shake things up? What changed?'

She shook her head sadly. 'Twenty-five years, Baba. I have a daughter, now. She's twenty, training as an engineer on Mars. She's going to join the cohort when she's finished and I want more for her. I want a future for her.'

He hugged her tight while the crowd roared in approval. 'Get back on that bass,' he whispered. 'We got a show to finish!'

He didn't bother to ask if the nouveau-nobility husband had approved of the rebel Rover Jeni. He suspected not.

*

In the green room Jeni wrapped her legs around a chair and hung a glass of beer in the air next to her.

'Used to be it would fall slowly down to the floor,' Jeni said, pointing at her drink. 'They stripped most of Vesta's mass for the Ring. It's barely a shell here.'

Dhaka shoved a foot in a wall strap and settled in perpendicular to Jeni. She swirled the whiskey glass around in the air. Despite the glass being designed for zero gravity, her practiced flip of the wrist tossed several globules free that very slowly wobbled their way through the air toward her. 'We're passing into final stage preparations for the Ring. SDC-MME is panicking a bit because the projections for energy and the initial test results don't match. And the computers are having trouble managing stable orbits.'

The Glitter Ring was a Dyson Ring, a necklace of solar power stations and sails built around the sun to capture a vast percentage of its energy. The power needs of the big planets had begun to outstrip the large planetary solar and mirror arrays a hundred years ago. Overflight and shadow rights for solar gathering stations had started turning into a series of low-grade orbital economic wars. The Charter had been created to handle the problem system-wide.

Build a ring of solar power catchments in orbit around the sun at a slight angle to the plane of the solar system. No current solar rights would be abridged, but it could catapult humanity into a new industrial era. A great leap forward. Unlimited, unabridged power.

But if it didn't work…

Dhaka nodded at all the serious faces. 'Don't look so glum. The cohort programmers are working on flocking algorithms to try and simplify how the solar stations keep in orbit. Follow some simple rules about what's around you and let complex emergent orbits develop.'

'I'm more worried about the differences in output,' Jeni muttered. 'While you've been in long-sleep they've been developing orbital stations out past Jupiter with the assumption that there would be beamed power to follow. They're building mega-orbitals throughout the system on the assumption that the Ring's going to work. They've even started moving people off Earth into temporary housing in orbit.'

'Temporary?' Euclid asked from across the room, interrupting before Dhaka and Jeni got deep into numbers and words like exajoules, quantum efficiency, price per watt and all the other boring crap. He'd cared intimately about that when he first joined the cohort. Now, not so much.

'We're talking bubble habitats with thinner shells than Vesta right now. They use a layer of water for radiation shielding, but they lack resources and they're not well balanced. These orbitals have about a couple hundred thousand people each, and they're rated to last fifty to sixty years.' Jeni shook her head, and Euclid was forced to stop seeing the nineteen-year-old

Zippy and recognize the concerned forty-four-year-old she'd become. 'They're risking a lot.'

'Why would anyone agree?' Vega asked. 'It sounds like suicide.'

'It's gotten worse on Earth. Far worse. Everyone is just expecting to hit the reset button after the Glitter Ring goes online. Everyone's holding their breath.'

Dhaka spoke up. 'Okay, enough cohort bullshit. Let's talk about you. The band's heading back to long-sleep soon – and then what, Zippy? You heading back to Mars and your daughter?'

Jeni looked around the room hesitantly. 'Lara's never been to Venus, and I promised her she could visit me... if you'll have me?'

'If?' Vega laughed. 'I hated playing those recordings of you. Rather hear it live.'

'I'm not as zippy up and down the chords as I used to be, you know,' Jeni warned. Everyone was turning to look at Euclid.

'It's a more confident sound,' he said with a smile. Dhaka whipped globules of whiskey at them and laughed.

Kumi beamed, no doubt already dreaming about meeting his 'granddaughter'.

'Hey, Zippy,' Euclid said. 'Here's to change. *Good* change.'

'Maybe,' she smiled and slapped his raised hand in agreement and approval. 'Let's dream on that.'

*

The first few days after long-sleep were never pleasant, but this awakening was the worst of Euclid's experience. He slowly remembered who he was, and how to speak, and the names of the people who sat quietly with him in the lounge after their sessions with the medics. For a while they silently watched the high cities of Venus glinting in the clouds below their orbit from viewports near the long-sleep pools.

Later they began to ask questions, later they realized that something was very wrong. They'd been asleep for fifty years. Two long-sleeps, not the usual single sleep.

'Everyone gone silent back on Vesta,' Dhaka said.

'Did we get idled?' Euclid demanded. They were a band, not workers. They shouldn't have been idled.

The medics didn't answer their questions. They continued to deflect everything until one morning an officer turned up, dressed in black sub-uniform with empty holster belt, as if he had left his weapons and armour just outside the door. He looked barely twenty, far too young for the captain's insignia on his shoulders.

He spoke with slow, stilted formality. 'Mr. Slinger, Mr. Djansi, Mr. de la Vega, Ms. Miriam and Ms. Baptiste – thank you for your patience. I'm Captain Abrams. We're sorry for the delay, but your recovery was complicated.'

'Complicated!' Kumi looked disgusted. 'Can you explain why we had two long-sleeps instead of one? Fifty years? We had a contract!'

'And *we* had a war.' The reply was unexpectedly sharp. 'Be glad you missed it.'

'Our first interplanetary war? That's not the change I wanted,' Euclid muttered to Vega.

'What happened?' Jeni asked, her voice barely a whisper. 'My daughter, she's on Mars, is she safe?'

The officer glanced away in a momentary flash of vulnerability and guilt. 'You have two weeks for news and correspondence with your cohort and others. We can provide political summaries, and psychological care for your readjustment. After that, your tour begins. Transport down to the cities has been arranged. I just… I have to say… we still need you now, more than ever.'

'The *rass*?' Kumi stared at the soldier, spreading his arms.

Again that touch of vulnerability as the young soldier replied with a slight stammer. 'Please. We need you. You're legends to the entire system now, not just the cohorts.'

'The hell does that mean?' Vega asked as the boy-captain left.

*

Jeni's daughter had managed one long-sleep but woke on schedule while they stayed in storage. The war was over by then, but Martian infrastructure had been badly damaged and skilled workers were needed for longer than the standard year or two. Lara had died after six years of 'extra time', casualty of a radiation exposure accident on Deimos.

They gathered around Jeni when she collapsed to her knees and wept, grieving for the child they had never known.

Their correspondence was scattered across the years, their cohort truly broken as it had been forced to take cover, retreat, or fight. The war had started in Earth orbit after a temporary habitat split apart, disgorging water, air and people into vacuum. Driven by desperation and fury, several other orbital inhabitants had launched an attack on SDC-MME owned stations, seeking a secure environment to live, and revenge for their dead.

Conflict became widespread and complicated. The orbital habitats were either negotiating for refugees, building new orbitals, or fighting for the SDC-MME. Mars got involved when the government sent its military to protect the Martian investment in the SDC-MME. Jupiter, which was now its own functioning techno-demarchy, had struck directly at the Belt, taking over a large portion of the Glitter Ring.

Millions had died as rocks were flung between the worlds and ships danced around each other in the vacuum. People fought hand-to-hand in civil wars inside hollowed-out asteroids, gleaming metal orbitals, and in the cold silence of space.

Humanity had carried war out of Earth and into the great beyond.

Despite the grim history lesson, as the band shared notes and checked their financial records, one thing became clear. They *were* legends. The music of the Mighty Slinger and the Rovers had become the sound of the war generation and beyond: a common bond that the cohorts could still claim, and battle hymns for the Earth emigrants who had launched out from their decayed temporary orbitals. Anti-SDC-MME songs became treasured anthems. The Rovers songs sold billions, the *covers* of their songs sold billions. There were tribute bands and spin-off bands and a fleet of touring bands. They had spawned an entire subgenre of music.

'We're rich at last,' Kumi said ruefully. 'I thought I'd enjoy it more.'

Earth was still there, still a mess, but Vega found hope in news from his kin. For decades, Pacific Islanders had stubbornly roved over their drowned states in vast fleets, refusing resettlement to the crowded cities and tainted badlands of the continents. In the last fifty years, their floating harbours had evolved from experimental platforms to self-sustaining cities. For them, the war had been nothing but a few nights filled with shooting stars and the occasional planetfall of debris.

The Moon and Venus had fared better in the war than Mars, but the real shock was the Ring. According to Dhaka, the leap in progress was marked, even for fifty years. Large sections were now fully functional and had been used during the war for refuelling, surveillance, barracks, and prisons.

'Unfortunately, that means that the purpose of the Ring has drifted once again,' she warned. 'The military adapted it to their purposes, and returning it to civilian use will take some time.'

'But what about the Assembly?' Euclid asked her one day when they were in the studio, shielded from surveillance by noise and interference of Vega's crafting. 'Do they still care about the purpose of the Ring? Do you think we still have a mission?'

The war had ended without a clear victor. The SDC-MME had collapsed and the board had been tried, convicted, and exiled to long-sleep until a clear treaty could be hammered out. Jupiter, Mars, Venus, and some of the richer orbitals had assumed the shares and responsibility of the original solar charter. A tenuous peace existed.

Dhaka nodded. 'I was wondering that too, but look, here's the name of the company that's organising our tour.'

Euclid leaned in to read her screen. *Bouscholte, Bouscholte & Abrams.*

*

Captain Abrams revealed nothing until they were all cramped into the tiny cockpit of a descent craft for Venus's upper atmosphere.

He checked for listening devices with a tiny wand, and then, satisfied, faced them all. 'The Bouscholte family would like to thank you for your service. We want you to understand that you are in an even better position to help us, and we need that help now, more than ever.'

They'd come this far. Euclid looked around at the Rovers. They all leaned in closer.

'The Director of Consolidated Ring Operations and Planetary Reconstruction will be at your concert tonight.' Abrams handed Euclid a small chip. 'You will give this to him

– personally. It's a quantum encrypted key that only Director Cutler can access.'

'What's in it?' Dhaka asked.

Abrams looked out the window. They were about to fall into the yellow and green clouds. The green was something to do with floating algae engineered for the planet, step one of the eventual greening of Venus. 'Something Cutler won't like. Or maybe a bribe. I don't know. But it's an encouragement for the Director to consider a proposal.'

'Can you tell us what the proposal is?'

'Yes.' Abrams looked at the band. 'Either stop the redevelopment of Earth and further cement the peace by returning the orbitals inhabitants to the surface, or...'

Everyone waited as Abrams paused dramatically.

'... approve a cargo transit across Mercury's inner orbit to the far side of the Glitter Ring, and give us the contracts for rebuilding the orbital habitats.'

Dhaka frowned. 'I wasn't expecting something so boring after the big "or" there, Captain.'

Abrams smiled. 'One small course adjustment at the start can change an entire orbit by the end of a journey,' he said to Euclid.

That sounded familiar.

'Either one of those is important?' Euclid asked. 'But you won't say why.'

'Not even in this little cabin. I'm sure I got the bugs, but in case I didn't.' Abrams shrugged. 'Here we are. Ready to change the solar system, Mr. Slinger?'

*

Venusian cities were more impressive when viewed from the outside. Vast, silvery spheres clustered thickly in the upper atmosphere, trailing tethers and tubes to the surface like a dense herd of giant cephalopods. Inside, the decor was sober, spare, and disappointing, hinting at a slow post-war recovery.

The band played their first concert in a half-century to a frighteningly respectful and very exclusive audience of the rich and powerful. Then it was off to a reception where they awkwardly sipped imported wine and smiled as their assigned liaison, a woman called Halford, briskly introduced and dismissed awe-struck fans for seconds of small talk and a quick snap.

'And this is Petyr Cutler,' Halford announced. 'Director of Consolidated Ring Operations and Planetary Reconstruction.'

Bodyguards quickly made a wall, shepherding the Director in for his moment.

Cutler was a short man with loose, sandy hair and a bit of orbital sunburn. 'So pleased to meet you,' he said. 'Call me Petyr.'

He came in for the vigorous handshake, and Euclid had already palmed the small chip. He saw Abrams on the periphery of the crowd, watching. Nodded.

Cutler's already reddened cheeks flushed as he looked down at the chip. 'Is that—'

'Yes.' Euclid locked eyes with him. The Director. One of the most powerful people in the entire solar system.

Cutler broke the gaze and looked down at his feet. 'You can't blackmail me, not even with this. I can't change policy.'

'So you still redeveloping Earth?' Euclid asked, his tone already dull with resignation.

'I've been around before you were born, Mr. Slinger. I know how generational projects go. They build their own momentum. No one wants to become the executive who shut down two hundred years of progress, who couldn't see it through to the end. Besides, wars aren't cheap. We have to repay our citizens who invested in war bonds, the corporations that gave us tech on credit. The Earth Reconstruction project is the only thing that can give us the funds to stay afloat.'

Somehow, his words eased the growing tightness in Euclid's chest. 'I'm supposed to ask you something else, then.'

Cutler looked suspicious. He also looked around at his bodyguards, wanting to leave. 'Your people have big asks, Mr. Slinger.'

'This is smaller. We need your permission to move parts across Mercury's orbit, close to the sun, but your company has been denying that request. The Rock Devils cohort also wants to rebuild the surviving temporary Earth orbitals.'

'Post-war security measures are still in place—'

'Security measures my ass.' Jeni spoke so loudly, so intensely that the whole room went quiet to hear her.

'Jeni—' Kumi started.

'No. We've sacrificed our lives and our children's lives for your damn Ring. We've made it our entire reason for existence and we're tired. One last section to finish, that could finish in less than three decades if you let us take that shortcut to get the last damn parts in place and let us go work on something worthwhile. We're tired. Finish the blasted project and let us live.'

Kumi stood beside her and put his arm around her shoulders. She leaned into him, but she did not falter. Her gaze stayed hard and steady on the embarrassed Director who was now the center of a room of shocked, sympathetic, judging looks.

'We need clearance from Venus,' Director Cutler mumbled.

Euclid started humming a quick backbeat. Cutler looked startled. '*Director*,' Euclid sang, voice low. He reached for the next word the sentence needed to bridge. *Dictator*. How to string that in with… something to do with the project finishing *later*.

He'd been on the stage singing the old lyrics people wanted to hear. His songs that had once been extempo, but now were carved in stone by a new generation.

But right here, with the bodyguards all around them, Euclid wove a quick song damning him for preventing progress in the solar system and making trouble for the cohorts. That's right, Euclid thought. That's where the power came from, singing truth right to power's face.

Power reddened. Cutler clenched his jaw.

'I can sing that louder,' Euclid said. 'Loud enough for the whole system to hear it and sing it back to you.'

'We'll see what we can do,' Cutler hissed at him, and signalled for the bodyguards to surround him and move him away.

*

Halford the liaison congratulated the band afterward. 'You did it. We're cleared to use interior transits to the other side of the Ring and to move equipment into Earth orbit.'

'Anything else you need us to do?' Dhaka asked.

'Not now, not yet. Enjoy your tour. Broadcasting planetwide and recording for rebroadcast throughout the system – you'll have the largest audience in history.'

'That's nice,' Euclid said vaguely. He was still feeling some discomfort with his new status as legend.

'I can't wait for the Earth concert,' Captain Abrams said happily. 'That one will really break the records.'

'Earth?' Kumi said sharply.

Halford looked at him. 'After your next long-sleep, for the official celebration of the completion of the Ring. That can't happen without the Mighty Slinger and his Rovers. One last concert for the cohorts.'

'And maybe something more,' Abrams added.

'What do you mean, "more",' Euclid demanded, weary of surprises.

Halford and Captain Abrams shared a look – delight, anticipation, and caution.

'When we're sure, we'll let you know,' the captain promised.

*

Euclid sighed and glared at the door. He nervously twirled a pair of virtual-vision goggles between his fingers.

Returning to Earth had been bittersweet. He could have asked to fly over the Caribbean Sea, but nothing would be the same – coral reef islands reclaimed by water, new land pushed up by earthquake and vomited out from volcanoes. It would pollute the memories he had of a place that had once existed.

He put the past out of his mind and concentrated on the present. The Rovers were already at the venue, working hard with the manager and crew in technical rehearsals for the biggest concert of their lives. Estádio Nacional de Brasília had become ENB de Abrams-Bouscholte, twice reconstructed in the last three decades to double the seating and update the technology, and now requiring a small army to run it.

Fortunately Captain Abrams (retired) knew a bit about armies and logistics, which was why Euclid was not at technical rehearsal with his friends but on the other side of the city, waiting impatiently outside a large simulation room while Abrams took care of what he blithely called 'the boring prep'.

After ten minutes or so the door finally opened and Captain Abrams peeked around the edge, goggles pushed up over his eyebrows and onto his balding head. 'We're ready! Come in,

Mr. Slinger. We think you'll like what we've set up for you.' His voice hadn't lost that boyish, excited bounce.

Still holding his goggles, Euclid stepped into the room and nodded a distracted greeting to the small group of technicians. His gaze was quickly caught by an alloy-plated soprano pan set up at the end of the room.

'Mr. Djansi says you were a decent pannist,' Captain Abrams said, still brightly enthusiastic.

'Was?'

Captain Abrams smiled. 'Think you can handle this one?'

'I can manage,' Euclid answered, reaching for the sticks.

'Goggles first,' the captain reminded him, closing the door to the room.

Euclid put them on, picked up the sticks, and raised his head to take in his audience. He froze and dropped the sticks with a clang.

'Go on, Mr. Slinger. I think you'll enjoy this,' Abrams said. 'I think we all will.'

*

On the night of the concert, Euclid stood on the massive stage with his entire body buzzing with terror. The audience packed into stadium tiers all around him was a faceless mass that rose up several stories, but they were his family and he knew them like he knew his own heart. The seats were filled with Rock Devils, Gladhandlers, Sunsiders, and more, all of them from the cohorts, workers representing every section of the Ring and every year and stage of its development. Many of them had come down from Earth orbit and their work on the decaying habitats to see the show.

Euclid started to sing for them, but they sang for him first, calling out every lyric so powerful and sure that all he could do was fall silent and raise his hands to them in homage and embrace. He shook his head in wonder as tears gathered in his eyes.

Kumi, Vega, Dhaka, and Jeni kept jamming, transported by the energy, playing the best set of their careers, giving him a nod or a sweet smile in the midst of their collective trance as he stood silently crying and listening to the people sing.

Then it was time.

Euclid walked slowly, almost reverently, to the soprano pan at the centre of the stage. Picked up the sticks, just as he had in the simulation room. Looked up at his audience. This time he did not freeze. He played a simple arpeggio, and the audience responded: lighting a wedge of stadium seating, a key for each note of the chord, hammered to life when he hammered the pan. He lengthened the phrase and added a trill. The cohorts followed him flawlessly, perfected in teamwork and technology. A roar came from overhead as the hovering skyboxes cheered on the Mighty Slinger playing the entire stadium like it was his own personal keyboard.

Euclid laughed loud. 'Ain't seen nothing yet!'

He swept his arm out to the night sky, made it a good, slow arc so he was sure they were paying attention. Then the other arm. Showmanship. Raise the sticks with drama. Flourish them like a conductor. Are you ready? *Are you ready!?*

Play it again. This time the sky joined them. The arc of the Ring blazed section by section in sync with each note, and in step with each cadence. The Mighty Slinger and his cohorts, playing the largest instrument in the galaxy.

Euclid grinned as the skyboxes went wild. The main audience was far quieter, waiting, watching for one final command.

He raised his arms again, stretched them out in victory, dropped the sticks on the thump of the Rovers' last chord, and closed his eyes.

His vision went red. He was already sweating with adrenaline and humid heat, but for a moment he felt a stronger burn, the kiss of a sun where no sun could be. He slowly opened his eyes and there it was, as Abrams had promised. The *real* last section of the Ring, smuggled into Earth's orbit during the interior transits permitted by Venus, now set up in the mother planet's orbit with magnifiers and intensifiers and God knows what else, all shining down like full noon on nighttime Brasilia.

The skyboxes no longer cheered. There were screams, there was silence. Euclid knew why. If they hadn't figured it out for themselves, their earpieces and comms were alerting them now. Abrams-Bouscholte, just hours ago, had become the largest shareholder in the Ring through a generation-long programme of buying out rights and bonds from governments bankrupted by war. It was a careful, slow-burning plan that only a cohort could shepherd through to the end.

The cohorts had always been in charge of the Ring's day-to-day operations, but the concert had demonstrated beyond question that only one crew truly ran the Ring.

The Ring section in Earth orbit, with its power of shade and sun, could be a tool for geoengineering to stabilize Earth's climate to a more clement range… or a solar weapon capable of running off any developers. Either way, the entire Ring was under the control of the cohorts, and so was Earth.

The stadium audience roared at last, task accomplished, joy unleashed. Dhaka, Jeni, Kumi, and Vega left their instruments and gathered around Euclid in a huddle of hugs and tears, like soldiers on the last day of a long war.

Euclid held onto his friends and exhaled slowly. 'Look like massa day done.'

*

Euclid sat peacefully, a mug of bush tea in his hands, gazing at the cold metal walls of the long-sleep hospice. Although the technology had steadily improved, delayed reawakenings still had cost and consequences. But it had been worth the risk. He had lived to see the work of generations, the achievements of one thousand years.

'Good morning, Baba.' One of Zippy's great-great-grand-children approached, his dashiki flashing a three dimensional pattern with brown and green images of some off-world swamp. This Baptiste, the head of his own cohort, was continuing the tradition of having at least one descendant of the Rovers in attendance at Euclid's awakening. 'Are you ready now, Baba? The shuttle is waiting for you.'

'I am ready,' Euclid said, setting down his mug, anticipation rising. Every hundred years he emerged from the long-sleep pool. *Are you sure you want this?* Kumi had asked. *You'll be all alone.* The rest of the band wanted to stay and build on Earth. Curiosity had drawn him to another path, fate had confirmed him as legend and griot to the peoples and Assemblies of the post-Ring era. *Work hard. Do well. Baba will be awake in a few more years. Make him proud.*

They *had* done well, so well that this would be his last awakening. The Caribbean awaited him, restored and resettled. He was finally going home to live out the rest of his life.

Baptiste opened the double doors. Euclid paused, breathed deeply, and walked outside onto the large deck. The hospice was perched on the edge of a hill. Euclid went to the railing to survey thousands of miles of the Sahara.

Bright-feathered birds filled the air with cheerful song. The wind brought a cool kiss to his cheek, promising rain later in the day. Dawn filtered slowly over what had once been desert, tinting the lush green hills with an aura of dusty gold as far as the eye could see.

Come, Baba. Let's go home.

Corialis

T.L. Huchu

Zimbabwe

T.L. Huchu began as a literary author of great success, but thankfully for us a love of science fiction and fantasy wouldn't let him go. Here he takes us to the far stars, where humans live under alien suns, as we depart at last the solar system entirely. Things get weird in the reaches of space where the next few stories take place. But the further we get from the sun, the more human we become... Welcome to the world of 'Corialis'!

I t's easy to tell when a world is roused. Cyclones, earthquakes, lightning, drought, anomalous happenings. The omens are obvious. Harder to spot is the subtle build-up, for worlds lie in deep time and are slow to anger. If the universe is a clock, they are the hour hand and our lives are measured by the tock of the second hand. Most of us have forgotten how to read the lay of the land. Our ears are deaf to the voices in the wind, the soles of our feet numb to the gentle nudge of the soil we trudge upon, our hearts closed to the soul-song upon whose notes life and death flit.

I kneel on my right, reach down and place the palm of my hand on the dirt to feel the pulse of this place.

'Subsidence,' says Garande. He's inspecting the comms array, sunk halfway into the ground like a shiny giant caught in quicksand. It's tilted at an angle as though its fall was halted midway through. Beneath lies a box containing finely calibrated equipment.

'We made extensive ground surveys before setting up here. This isn't supposed to happen,' I reply. 'If the variable flux state is altered by so much as a billionth of a decimal place, that's it, no more superliminal comms. We can't call home. It's half a thousand light years to the nearest settlement. This is not good.'

'What do we do, Thandeka?'

'Something's off about this place, can you feel it?' I say, standing up.

Garande cocks his head. As a biologist, he prefers the realm of the empirical; feelings don't have a place in the papers he writes. But Garande's too polite to say what he thinks when silence can do the talking for him. The cloudless sky above is sparkling pink; it's like looking out from inside a finely cut padparadscha. A humid, musky breeze blows from the east. It's early morning and we're on the underside of the gas giant our moon orbits. It dominates the sky, with the yellow sun in the opposite direction. Garande puts a protective hand on his belly. In profile, the exaggerated curvature of his spine, the source of his back pain, is even more pronounced.

'I'll talk to the chief and get a work detail together, so we can dismantle the whole apparatus and set it up elsewhere,' I say, standing up, and wiping the dirt onto my trousers. 'For now, I have to put it in hibernation, then lash and tether the structure to stabilize it.'

He nods. I'm speaking his language again.

'I wish I could help, but...' He opens up the hand on his belly, a subtle gesture, and rests it there again.

'It'll be fine,' I reply, adjusting the toolbelt round my waist.

This early in the day, the hulking mass of our ship casts a long shadow as it rests west where the sun rises. There are holes in the hull where materials have been stripped for building, leaving it like a wounded whale beached on the sand. I'm thinking that the best option is to rig the comms equipment atop the superstructure until we can find a more suitable location.

*

I walk out through the line of shelters in our hamlet. There's about twenty here, small cabins we made of locally quarried basalt and cannibalized panels and windows from our ship. The rock is dark and shaping it into building blocks is hard work, but our people have been stonemasons from since we built Great Zimbabwe after Musikavanhu led us from the Great Lakes in Central Africa. They say, if you cut us, rock chips fall to the ground. Already the shelters are bedding in. Native plants cling onto the walls like barnacles on the hull of an ocean vessel. Their vivid colours of green, red and gold stand out against the dour basalt. Cables sunk in the ground link the cabins to the fission engines re-engineered into a power station, so we have energy enough for a hundred years.

'Iwe,' Sekai hails me through the window, waving her apparat about. 'I was talking to my baba on Mharapasi's Belt, and this thing cut off. What the hell?'

'I'm sorting it,' I reply.

'Baba's aged badly since we set off; I can't afford to waste another minute.'

'I'm sorry, but it's going to take a bit of time.'

'Nxa.' She kisses her teeth and slams the window shut.

I push on, going faster, lest anyone else hails me. I follow the footpath past Panganayi's tuck-shop, heading out of the settlement towards the outlying farms. A certain lethargy weighs upon me. The euphoria of settling a new moon, one so perfectly goldilocksed for us, has already worn off. It's been three years now, and the grind of daily life has taken over. At some point I stopped looking at the stars we came from and started bedding down my roots here.

'Mararaseiko?' Chief WaMambo calls out, shielding his eyes from the sun. He's a tall, dark man, and the leopard sash draped from shoulder to hip identifies his clan's totem.

'Tarara mararawo,' I reply.

'Those dark rings around your eyes tell a different story, young lady,' he says.

The chief has always been a perceptive man. I haven't been sleeping well. It's hard to sync into the polyphasic rhythm of the moon. For a small minority here, the six-hour rotation on Corialis confuses our circadian attuned bodies. The bonus of seeing more sunrises and sunsets is ill recompense.

'Alpha comms is leaning badly and could fall over at any time. I need you to assign three people to help me dismantle it.'

'Did you know two of the algae vats are leaking? If this is an issue with the naciflex we could potentially lose our entire harvest. The design was meant to last a decade at least,' Chief WaMambo says, his voice even. 'I saw Alpha comms earlier when I was doing my rounds. I've been waiting for you.'

'Something's very wrong—'

'Thandeka, you picked the site for the tower. You headed the construction. Now I have to pull people from their jobs just to fix your screwup.' The chief's tone is colder than nyamavhuvhu winds.

I want to tell him that I don't think the mishaps, minor accidents and damages happening around this place are natural. That they are signs of this world's growing displeasure. Something must be done to restore balance. But Chief WaMambo was captain on our vessel; he's a man firmly wedded to the scientific method. My warnings will sound like gibberish to his ears, so I bite my tongue.

At the nearby vats, farmers wearing khakis straighten at the sound of his annoyance. They wanna hear this because comms affects their ability to contact the loved ones they left on Carina-Ruregerero. A hard glance from the chief sets them back to work again. Civilisations aren't built by the scientists or intellectuals, they are laid down brick by brick on the backs of grunt workers turning the land, teachers, homemakers rearing children, folks who work with their hands and can swing their fists. People like me.

'It's my fault, it won't happen again.'

'You'll get your help. Just don't have me cleaning up after you, again.' Chief WaMambo turns his attention back to the naciflex vats that dot the land.

*

The stars sped by as streaks of white against the unending blackness of space on the port hullcam. No ships had actual windows, but the screens gave us the illusion we could peer out. If we actually could, all we'd see was a blur of white light and not much else. The images on the screen made things less claustrophobic in the medilab, a white space with silver units, screens, beeping noises, and medical equipment.

I'd flinched as the razor scraped against my scalp. Its hiss and crackle came like bursts of static on my skull. There was the *ploink-ploink* of razor into a water basin as Garande cleaned off the foam, my ginger hairs floating out with the waves. Shake. Wipe. Shave. Following the contours of my skull.

'Funny, for all the tech on this vessel, nothing beats an old-fashioned steel razor for shaving,' Garande said.

'Don't I look weird without my 'fro?' I asked.

'You look like E.T.'s butthole,' he said with a laugh.

'Not funny,' I replied, punching his thigh.

'You're gorgeous,' he said, and stooped to kiss my bald patch. 'I love your big brown eyes.'

'That's much better. Now do your job.'

My skull felt cold, and when he was done, I was smoother than when I was born. Every hair on my body – head to toe, eyebrows, lashes, nostrils and all – was shaved and plucked until not a strand remained. It'd sting when it grew back, but this was the way of it.

Garande and I stood abreast, inspecting our new look in the full-length mirror as we waited for the doctor to arrive. 'Good. You're ready for the next phase,' Dr Ngulube said, inspecting us. She was in her mid-forties, the oldest person on the vessel by a bit. 'Proceed to the decontamination unit.'

'Aye, aye, captain,' Garande said with a goofy laugh.

If Dr Ngulube's instructions were terse, it didn't mask the kindness of her nature. She wore a white cleanroom suit, so I couldn't see her face, just her eyes. This stage was critical for the success of our mission. I felt some discomfort walking across the cold floor. My nails were cut too short. I closed my eyes and held my breath when the orange light came on. Multidirectional nozzles sprayed a mist of chemicals, alcohol and topical antibiotics.

'Raise each foot in turn. Spread your fingers and toes,' Dr Ngulube said through the intercom. 'Bend over, please. Spread your cheeks. Thank you.'

The spray stopped. Vacuums switched on to suck out the vapours. When I took a breath, the air stung. Garande reached out his hand towards me.

'No touching!' Dr Ngulube said. 'Sorry.'

'That's okay.'

'Proceed to Sterile Room One. You'll be spending the next week there. Please take the first course of antibiotics on the table to your left.'

It sank in that we were really doing this. Over the next three months, Garande and I would go through seven sterilising zones, take multiple courses of super-strength intravenous antibiotics and topical applications, antifungals, antivirals, bathe in alcohol gels and decontaminants, UV light therapy, tubes up ass, mouth and every orifice, until we lost the one percent of our body weight that was made up of microbial life. We'd lose a lot more from malnutrition and sickness before we made it to the probiotic stage where suitable symbiotic replacement lifeforms indigenous to Corialis were introduced to form a new biosphere for our bodies.

I felt as though I'd been put through a shredder, then all those strips had been churned into mincemeat and dipped in hot chillies. My nerves were ablaze. Analgesics didn't help none. Bouts of diarrhea, as food became hard to digest without bacteria in my gut. I was lethargic throughout; I'd been warned it would be painful, but that didn't prepare me for how traumatic the whole ordeal was. Evacuations and colonic irrigations. Depression and anxiety. Halfway through, I just wanted the whole thing to stop, but I'd signed the forms. There was no turning back from this one-way ride.

*

At dusk's breaking, the charged-up pole of our red giant glows dazzling electric blue auroras, swirling and sparkling. Alpha comms is secure and the work team won't be ready till the morning, so I set out to find Garande and walk him home. Calcite flowers sprawl across the plane. From space, Corialis looks like a mauve pink gem because of the way reflected light from the giant refracts through the atmosphere. Down here it's a riot of colours, every spectrum on the rainbow and more. Corialis is a young world and I feel its vibrant energy course through me from the moment I get out of bed. Walking through the flowers is like stepping into a kaleidoscopic sculpture park. We call them flowers, view the taller structures as trees and shrubs, but in real effect, the flora here is more like a terrestrial coral reef. All of the life-forms discovered on Corialis so far are unicellular. There were no complex organisms on the surface, in the water, or underground. Instead, the mineralized structures secreted by the various life-forms grow out into sculptures of vents, fractals, elongated tubes, lily-like discs, and nebulous formations that run through the landscape.

I find Garande kneeling down, so intently taking readings off his multimeter, he doesn't notice my approach until I'm right next to him. The device is hooked up next to the mass of coiling brown, blue and yellow algae strings that grow across the landscape like a mass of jumbled wool in an upturned haberdashery. His apparat lies on the dirt next to him, recording the measurements he's reciting next to it.

'Pause data recording. Hey Thandeka, check these readings out.' He expands the screen on the apparat and scrolls to reveal graphs of his measurements.

'I'm looking at?'

'I'm measuring the impulses running through the biomass and it's incredible.' Garande brings up another graph, squiggly lines running through. 'Look at that correlation with a standard neural map, but this is far more complicated. For a start, the level of activity far exceeds anything a single brain could do, the info here is overlaid, multiple processes running parallel to one another, but fully integrated with sophisticated feedback loops.'

'Inga.'

'Now, if I...' He takes a crude device, low voltage battery and wires, and shocks one of the strings. 'See how the multimeter peaks, right? That's my signal going through, but then the natural signals stop after the interruption... Wait for it. The reading on my meter goes to zero... Wait for it... There it is – do you see that? A low intensity signal passes one way, and then the other. And it'll keep doing this almost like it's testing for something. If I shock it again, the test signals change in frequency. Check that one out – it's exactly the same as my input.'

'So it reacts to stimulus. Every living thing does.'

'I think the data points to some kind of non-sentient intelligence built by all these interlinked unicellular life forms, Thandeka. Information flows that span the entire moon.'

'The sun's getting low, I think it's time to go home for some maheu,' I say, standing up and offering him my hand. Garande's got an intense look on his face – I've seen it before. He's deep inside of an idea. He takes my hand and rises, slowly, with a groan. There's dirt on his loose-fitting kurta and he rests his left hand protectively on his protruding belly. He's wearing flip-flops, his feet are so swollen he can't fit into normal shoes. I gather his equipment for him before we head back home through the wide plane of Honde Valley, stretching out through dwalas in the distance with the mountains beyond.

*

We were the first to ingest Corialis' bacteria and fungi, Garande and I. Though tests had been performed on various animals from Earth, we still couldn't be sure about the efficacy on humans. Had me and Garande died, our bodies would have been jettisoned into space, and different strains of microbes used. There was no going back to Carina-Ruregero. The rest would have had to try or die in the void of space, for the risk of cross-contamination was too great, and the means to go back impossible, for there wasn't a magnetar neutron star within range to power a jump back home. Active magnetars were ultra-rare and short-lived, only numbering a few hundred in a galaxy with two-hundred billion stars.

'This stuff tastes like Greek yoghurt,' Garande said, offering me a spoonful. His hand was shaking. Slight tremor. Hair had started to grow on his forearm.

'It's disgusting,' I said.

'Come on, we're the first people to eat anything from this new world and you wanna send the order back to the kitchen?'

I looked up at the cameras monitoring our every interaction. Sensors scanning our bodies for the slightest anomaly.

'I can't wait to get off these IVs and eat solids again.'

'And I want our baby to be the first native born Corialian.' There was a naïve excitement in his voice that was infectious. The way he looked deep in my eyes, revealing every part of his soul was sweet to behold. 'We're pioneers, Thandeka. They'll have to put our names in the history books. Founding fathers… and mothers.'

Finding planets was easy. Our ancestors back on Earth once thought they were the only world with life in the whole universe. A few millennia later, they learned of other planets, but still doubted any could have life. They looked at the two hundred million stars in our galaxy and the trillion planets and moons, and believed, somehow, theirs was a fluke. They were wrong. The Milky Way alone is teeming with life. There's too few of us to catalogue and study it all. There were so many habitable worlds within our reach… Or so we thought at one time.

When the first settlers took Dotito, they found an Earth-like planet orbiting a yellow star. It was rich with water and just the right levels of O2 in the atmosphere, so uncannily like Earth they called it a double. Plants. Animals. Carbon-based life-forms so recognisable, they thought Dotito was a gift. Hundreds of thousands relocated there in waves, unlike any other settlement since. And for a while, Dotito prospered until the settlers started falling sick and dying en masse, as horrible as anything the peoples of the New World experienced when the Europeans arrived on their shores. No one was immune from it. The plague ravaged them, until none were left.

The problem had been known since H.G. Wells published *War of the Worlds* in 1897. Wells' Martians might have won the war against Earth's armies, but they did not reckon against the bacteria they'd not been evolved to live alongside, so they died out before their conquest was complete. Creatively, this was a lame ending, a deus ex machina that ruined an otherwise enjoyable story, but Wells was prescient in suggesting the presence of complex life-forms, the boogeymonsters of pop culture imagination, were seldom a hindrance to whether a planet was open for colonisation.

Dotito retaught us the lesson that certain planets were closed to us because of their microbiome. On the flipside, the catastrophic devastation of Karanda which followed a few hundred years later taught us that our microbial life, the stuff on our skin, in our gut, everywhere, the stuff that made us *us*, could wipe out an innocent world by setting off a planet-wide ecological collapse. A once vibrant planet became a dead, toxic ball of dust.

Garande once told me that the ancient people of the common tongues ritually mixed a small sample of soil with water and drank it whenever they settled a new area. They believed this helped connect them with the land. In the twenty-first century, the economy of the briefly lived first Zimbabwean Republic crashed, sending the Shona to other parts of the Earth like Europe, America, Australia and Asia. When the children of these exiles were faced with this infirmity upon their return home, the soil-water cure was again revived as a remedy for stomach ailments.

'I think I've just farted for the first time in months,' Garande said, putting the bowl of yoghurt down.

'Tinyarewo, sha,' I replied. 'Too much information.'

The only solution was for us to adapt to the world we were settling. Strip ourselves of our biosphere and receive one from the planet. Symbiosis with our host worlds had startling consequences. The people on Dhlodhlo 4 experienced lifespans of up to five hundred years. On Mapungubwe, the settlers grew no shorter than eight feet tall. Accelerated neural processes for folks living on Chipadze's moon made them virtual walking computers when it came to solving mathematical problems. On New Natale, what the settlers lost in their ability to see colour, they more than made up for with a new, preternatural tolerance for stellar radiation, making them our most intrepid spacefarers.

As I lay on the gurney next to my husband, dreaming of the home we'd make, I wondered what Corialis had in store for us.

*

Tonight, one quarter of the sky glows bright with the stars. There's a convex line arcing through, cutting a patch out of the sky, filled with blackness. Nothing's there but void. Our moon is transiting into the double-night season where we are hidden from the sun behind the gas giant. The elliptical orbit we chart creates six distinct seasons relative to our position between the sun and planet. None is more spectacular than the double-night, which for two months presents us with nothing but darkness, and the days consist of two nights – a night with stars and a night with the blackest sky, our moon hidden in the umbra of the planet blotting out the sun.

The electric lights burning outside cast a fierce white glow.

Garande's snoring away in the next room. I held him for a while, spooning, since this far into his term, he's only comfortable lying on his side. But, I don't sleep too well, and once Garande was settled, I stole away from the bedroom and moved to the living room where I could play some music and think. I choose the Mberikwazvo Marimba Orchestra. They have a melody that suspends time and lets you drift out into space.

I drink a glass of spring water.

An ammonia scent sits in the air, kind of like when your compost has too much green material. It's unpleasant and I take it as another sign. I've been trying to read the signals, but few among us are still of the Mwari faith. Not even my husband, who prefers instruments and measurements to his gut. And so, most days I experience this double-consciousness, suppress this part of me that doesn't quite fit into the scheme of things. At night I can be myself, wave my hand and turn on the screen to ask for Sekuru Sibanda. He pops up, an old man with white hair, scraggly white beard, with a crown of black feathers on his head. Bare-chested, with beads around his neck, he sits on an ox-hide in a smoky cave. His face is coloured light and dark by the dancing flames of a wood fire crackling out of view.

I clap my hands in the traditional way to greet him, right over left, and open my mouth to speak, but he waves the tail he's holding to silence me.

'And lo, Mbire wekwaMhashu fell out with his brother Mbire Mukonowehwiza, and decided instead to break away and take his people west.' His voice is sonorous, amplified by the cave walls. 'Mbire wekwaMhashu had not the means to wage war with his brother, and he lacked the heart to swallow his pride and make peace.'

Sekuru Sibanda takes a gourd from the floor, pinches some snuff, and sniffs it. This sets him off sneezing, and I clap my hands to honour the great mhondoro spirit inside him.

'His people followed him, for they trusted in him, when he stole away from the chiefdom in the middle of the night. They did not say goodbye to the owners of the land, of all that is seen and unseen, those in the wind whose voices whisper to us. That beer they drank for themselves. Mbire wekwaMhashu forgot his elders taught him, 'Natsakwaunobva, kwaunoenda husiku,' for the anger against his brother was too great. And so, they journeyed west where he dreamed that he would become like Musikavanhu and found his own empire.'

Sekuru Sibanda shakes his head, and there's a slight glitch, a natural skip in the movement. This is a neuro-mapped AI version of the real Sekuru Sibanda, guardian of the sacred Njelele shrine where the voice of Mwari Himself speaks half a galaxy away. The real man is too busy for all those who seek his intercession, so we get this weekly updated AI version who thinks and behaves just as Sekuru himself would. He serves as the personal n'anga for all the believers in the Ubuntu Collective scattered across the stars. I want to ask him something, but sometimes he speaks in riddles, verse, aphorisms, or as he's doing today, he tells parables, or stories of the distant past. There are times he answers you directly, other times not at all.

'In Gokwe they weep still for Mbire wekwaMhashu and his people, for they found nothing but a sea of red sand in the Kalahari. Not a drop of water to drink. And still they did not pour libations, foolishly pressing west against the setting sun.

First the children succumbed to the heat. Then the men and women, one by one, leaving a trail of bones as they went. That hell became theirs for you can only possess a piece of land once you have bones in the soil. Mbire wekwaMhashu did not make peace with his brother and he failed to make peace with the land, and so his people perished. Alas, those who would be ancestors are now wandering spectres blown hither and thither by scorching winds, for none were left to carry their names and...'

Sekuru Sibanda opens his mouth, but his head drops to his chin, and he snoozes in an instant. I clap my hands, but he doesn't wake, softly snoring as he does. There are so many questions I want to ask. Sekuru can't be woken. Just my luck, even my AI n'anga gets to sleep, but I don't.

*

'You hear Banda's roof was blown clean off at the outpost last night?' says Nyarai, falling in beside me on the footpath. 'Mad winds out there.'

'That's a shame. I didn't think we got gales that bad out in these parts. Where's Tonde and Deliwe? They're supposed to be on this job with us.'

'Deliwe's been sent off with Sekai to the outpost. Tonde... well, when has he ever been on time for anything?'

We're already a man down before we've started the job. Ill omens everywhere. Light's real low cause we're in this partial eclipse; the planet's swallowing the sun. The air's chilly. Winds blowing roofs off. There's a tightness in my chest I can't shake.

My toolbelt slaps against my thigh as we near Alpha comms. The polyphene structure's holding at a seventy-five-degree angle. Just within the structural limits 'cause polyphene's strong and flexible. Any more would be too much – which is why I anchored cables to stabilize it. At least I've got a steady pair of extra hands with me. Nyarai's usually assigned to the powerplant, and she doubles as a handywoman fixing stuff in the cabins. Her sister Sekai's our chief builder, but everyone's got an extra set of skills up their sleeve.

I scroll through my apparat, find Tonde and message, 'Get your ass here right now!' He's eighteen, still at that age where getting out of bed in the morning is a pain.

The comms tower is twenty metres tall. The top bit is a booster for our radio signals. The apparats communicate directly if within range of one another, but further out, we need a relay. The Counterfactual Quantum Communication System module sits in a black box beneath the radio equipment of the tower. The Q is protected by mesh all round and only a handful have the code to get in. That's the most important part of this station, because it allows for instantaneous, superliminal communication with the rest of the galaxy. A signal from here sent to the recipient world light years away arrives in less time than it takes for your voice to carry across a small room. The only delay is in the equipment we use to manipulate and decode the information electronically into usable data at either end. At least that's what the manual says. I didn't make the damn thing – I'm just the grunt who maintains it.

'Top to bottom job?' Nyarai says looking up. 'The light's not that great.'

'Everything goes in that trailer there in order. That'll make it easier for the reassembly.'

'Two-day job with four, makes it a three-dayer for us now.'

'The graft's in removing the tech without damaging it. Dismantling the structure's a doddle,' I say, getting my harness ready. 'We need a slide sling to lower the pieces down.'

'Whichever way you wanna do it, I'm just the help here.'

Nyarai's the easiest person I've ever worked with. Laid back, diligent, doesn't let ego get in the way of the job at hand. She's humming a tune, a folk love song from the ocean planet Gungwa-raMasare, one of the worlds of the Cassiopeia region. It also helps that she has a great voice and enjoys singing at work. It makes the time pass quicker.

'So, when's the baby due? I see Garande waddling past my place every day,' Nyarai shouts out as I climb to the top of the tower.

'Another two months,' I reply, a little out of breath. It's a hard climb up this tower, my gear weighs me down, and my hands are freezing.

'Are you ready?'

'Is anyone ever?' I say, and she laughs. 'He wanted it, so he's changing the nappies when it comes.'

'I left my first with his father on Carina-Ruregerero. Things weren't working out, you know? I had to get away. We talk everyday now, well... we will again when your Q's working. They must be wondering what's going on.'

'Another week and it'll be back to business as usual,' I say. I don't want to ask whether she has any regrets about leaving. Some things are better left alone like that. Nyarai knew when she came here there was no going back. Corialis is too far from a magnetar, so unless there's a breakthrough with the tech in this lifetime, video calls are as good as it gets. We came in a two-part ship, main craft and the sterile entry vessel. After we'd been cleansed and rebiomed, we moved down to the sterile entry vessel which was designed to survive entry into the moon's atmosphere. The rest of the contaminated main vessel vented its air and water in space to prolong the life of its components, and flew off as an autonomous exploration drone mapping the stars beyond. Even if we tried to rebuild the entry vessel and repurpose it as a cruise ship, the engines that now form our power plant weren't designed to produce enough thrust to launch us into space.

I reach the apex and secure my gaff. I rig up the slide harness to transport pieces down to Nyarai looking up from right below me. The air has the metallic tang of copper in it this morning. It's the smell of blood.

I keep one hand on the polyphene struts and reach into my toolbelt for my adjustable wrench. The plan is to remove the transmitter first and then start on the support structure. Tonde still hasn't showed, the little bastard. I'll be having strong words with him when he does. I adjust my wrench and get onto the first bolt. Give it a firm go, but it won't give. In the cold weather, the polyphene's contracted. I shift my weight and try to turn it again. This thing's frozen in, and I pull back hard; the wrench slips out of my hand.

'Nyara—' Before I finish shouting, there's a cry and Nyarai goes down. 'Oh no, no, no, no. Please. Are you okay?' I yell down. No response. 'I'm so sorry. I'm so sorry.'

In this light she wouldn't have seen the wrench fall. I shout out her name. Nyarai's lying prone on the ground, body at an awkward angle. I think I've killed her. Oh no. A figure in the bleak light runs fast towards us. It's Tonde at last. I shout to him to call Dr Ngulube and check on Nyarai. It'll take a few minutes for me to climb back down. My hands are shaking.

I unclamp my gaff and start making my way, a sick feeling in my gut.

*

Everyone was glued to the hullcam's feed as we approached our new home. The ten-year voyage was nearing an end. Despite our ship's powerful engines, we'd been travelling so fast that in order to stop, we had to complete multiple passes ringing through the system and its nineteen planets to get enough of a gravity assist to slow us down. Five of the planets were super Jupiters. Their combined gravity wells together with that of the sun finally dragged us down to cruising speed.

I stood with Garande at the screen, staring at the vastness of space. Our gas giant sat proud in the midst of her system like a mother hen covering her eggs.

Garande's hand squeezed my shoulder.

'Have you ever seen anything like it, Thandeka?' he asked.

I shook my head and rested it against his arm.

'All this, just to have one little moon with life,' said Garande, nose virtually on the screen. 'I've read all the feeds – there's no place quite like it. Seven hundred years Vanhu have known about Corialis, and we're going to be the first to walk there. To live there.'

I felt him tremble, a mix of awe and adrenalin. The ship arced again, thrusters on full retroburn. He spoke excitedly about how this was a world on the cusp, like an early Earth. He couldn't wait to get his hands on the prokaryotes and eukaryotes, archaea, bacteria, fungi, virus, protozoa; to study new organisms not yet known to science. To make his name. To be the first.

This was a place of infinite possibilities. Some aboard the vessel wanted a fresh start – they were getting away from old relationships and skeletons in the closet. There were those who came here to seek their fortune from rich minerals in the crust. Others sought adventure. Garande was driven by his incredible curiosity and the desire to make a name in his field.

That left me. Why was I here? Came halfway across the galaxy to some germ-infested world in a tin can, for what?

I was happy on Changamire Dombo. I wasn't particularly interested in making a fortune – one square meal a day was good enough for me. I came all this way to be with him, to start a family.

Garande kissed me on the crown of my head; stars, moons, the infinity of space whizzing by outside.

*

Machines beep and hiss, readings blinking on screens, as I enter the sickbay. Brilliant lights overhead bounce off pristine white walls. My shoes squelch as I step through the disinfectant, onto the floor. I hesitate seeing Sekai on an armchair in the corner of the room.

'I'm so sorry,' I say.

'Don't be silly, Thandeka, could have happened to any of us,' she says, gesturing to the chair next to her.

Sekai is all muscle, massive physique wrought by hauling the stones and material that built this sickbay and everything else in the settlement. The corners of her lips turn downwards in a way that makes her look like she's frowning even when she's not.

'How long before we get comms back online? Baba has to be told about this. Lucky thing only the tip of the wrench glanced her left temple. The head hit her shoulder, breaking a couple of bones there. Dr Ngulube thinks she'll be fine in a few weeks.'

Sekai came here to be with her sister. To look after Nyarai. I'd just made that job much harder.

'A couple of days,' I reply.

'I'll come help you shift the tower, okay?' Sekai says. 'Just make sure you keep a tight grip on your tools next time.'

She laughs, and I just about manage a smile. Nyarai's on the bed resting. The painkillers have knocked her out. I'm more determined than ever to get the comms fixed so she can call her son.

*

As the days pass, I come to my decision. After the comms are fixed, I tell Sekuru Sibanda what I must do. He's silent. In this latest update, he looks older, deep cracks on his face, hair white as wool.

'In a generation or two they will have forgotten you, and so it should be,' Sekuru says and bows his head.

'Please tell my husband where I've gone and what I've done,' I say, clapping my hands in supplication.

He grunts and takes a pinch of snuff.

I get up, go to the bedroom where Garande is fast asleep. I kneel in front of him and study his face. The rising and falling of his chest. I breathe the air he exhales, and then I kiss him, and kiss his belly. He stirs slightly and I fear he'll wake, but he doesn't. Serenity is stenciled on his face. I get up and walk to the door. At the threshold, the urge to look back overwhelms me.

My legs feel leaden, but I push on. I put on my jacket, because it's cold, and my toolbelt, out of habit. Before I step outside, the last thing I take is a small calabash of synthetic traditional beer that I bought from Panganayi's tuckshop.

I walk past the cabins and the newly completed workshop. The soil beneath my feet is soft and wet. Seasonal rivers and springs have sprouted with the release of warm brine through channels running from the surface to the underground ocean that's squeezed and flexed by tidal forces affecting the moon.

The air shimmers with pink and red particles as if a firework set off ages ago is now, finally, fading. The double-night season has begun.

I make it to Honde Valley where the terrain shimmers in a lightshow of bioluminescent brilliance. Vivid greens, subtle blues, violets and ambers in lines and abstract patterns that dot the land. There are no stars at all in the sky. The only light is from the distant hamlet's electrics, or the organisms that dot the land. This marks the end of the evens and the start of double-night season as the moon fully transitions behind the gas giant. We won't see the sun for another two months, and the life-forms that had gorged themselves in the evens season now burn nutrients.

The sky above is pitch-black.

My torchlight guides me through the glowing coils of red and grey algae. I follow the path Garande showed me, across the hot springs bubbling and burping, past the yellowy sulphurous sand plains where salt statues jut up, until I reach the caves that bore Mutungagore Mountain.

I enter a cave, following the coils of algae. Stalactites dripping down from the roof above me. The wind howls against the walls of the cave. I push deeper still into its heart, where I find a glowing pool. The colourful waters of it swirl and mix like a lava lamp. It's the most beautiful thing I've ever seen.

'I've come to make peace, nevaridzi venyika,' I say.

I pour the beer onto the floor for my offering.

Garande told me these churning pools are filled with life. They mix up genetic material from all over the planet. They take and give up their haul depending on the seasons. Deep and vast, we don't yet know how far they go, but it is thought some may reach the ocean below.

I take off my clothes, leave them in a heap, along with my tools, and wade into the pool. We take, take, take, and give nothing back. But the circle of life is give and take; it's built on reciprocity. Mother Earth may have tolerated us because we were her bastards, but Corialis doesn't know us, she doesn't have to.

'Accept my offerings and let's strike a bargain.'

My heart beats fast. The water rumbles to a boil. I'm sucked under. It burns, it hurts, molten metal on my flesh, in my mouth and lungs. Something gives as my legs turn to jelly and I feel giddy and high, my insides pulped to mush, pain, needles. Corialis dissects me like a child dismantling a toy to get to the clockwork inside for the tangled reeds and spores. Unending connections, organics and inorganic carbonates of astounding intricacy form the matrix of a non-sentient intelligence built of the interdependent mass of unicellular life. I allow it, thinking peace, for the first ancestors of any land are born out of self-sacrifice for the sake of the future. The living and the dead are but part of a continuous present, separated only by an illusion.

*

The agony gives way to a cool, blissful wave of violin scores, thumping mbira, harpsichords, rhythms and notes intersecting in a palette of the most intense light, more powerful, complex, diverse than any orchestra. I sink deeper underwater. Every part of me broken into. Single. Cells. I'm absorbed into this multividual, the uberconsciousness of Corialis, giving it my every thought, hope, desire... all that I am.

At last we are part of this world. The ecological balance we broke by settling here is restored. Life for life. I will intercede with Corialis on behalf of the living.

And when Garande and the chief send out a search party, they will not find me. In time, if they are wise, they will see the signs. The shape of my nipple on a calciate flower. Tufts of moss resembling an afro. A face in the clouds. I will be in the air they breathe, the very soil they tread upon. When they spill beer to the earth, I shall drink. When they play drums nehosho, I shall dance and send them rain. And when they pass, and Corialis claims its share, they need not fear for they will join me in the pantheon of the ancestors.

This world is our home now.

The Substance of Ideas

Clelia Farris

Italy

Sometimes you make a mistake only to realize you didn't make it at all. In this case, as soon as I saw Clelia's English-language collection had been published I requested it from the publisher, only to then inexplicably forget I had it. Luckily, publisher Bill Campbell reminded me of it – just as I was looking around for Italian SF again! As soon as I dove in, I knew I had to take 'The Substance of Ideas', because how could I resist a story about a strange kibbutz on an even stranger world? It was as though Clelia wrote the story just for me! This story was translated by Rachel Cordasco.

I'm a fraud.

That said, you know half of what you need to know about me. I'll tell you the rest now, and it'll be the truth. I'm an honest fraud.

Damkina came up with the idea.

We'd known each other as kids, me and Damkina, we grew up in the same House. The Caretaker, old Samash, had reproached me in the past, saying, 'Wherever she sets her feet, you follow, Nergal. You're not a person, you're a shadow.'

In the kibbutz, exclusive affection is frowned upon; everyone must be friends, collaborative, ready to extend a hand to the inhabitants of the other Houses, prone to ask for help without fear of unfamiliar faces, glimpsed at the canteen or during linen-carding.

I prefer to handle things on my own and help only those who have nice faces; the others fall into my web of words, and weave, wash the dishes, sow the vegetable garden in my place.

There was a place that attracted the kids of every House. Even if you had just started walking and were still stumbling, you wanted to go see the Ship. The young ones climbed along the steep slope, dangled from the flagpoles, collected magnetic splinters, and with those, amused themselves by dragging other pebbles along; the older ones competed to hop on the plank – a branch stretched over the dark precipice that led to the cargo hold. Damkina was the first one bold enough to enter it. Among us Green House kids, she'd always been the most audacious.

She made a rope ladder, stealing the waste from the hemp process, tied it to a large *qur* root, and then descended into darkness, conquering the interior of the Ship. I arrived soon after. No one else followed us; they were all afraid.

The hold was vast, well-lit, covered with fine white sand, caressed by a lake of clear water that became turquoise at noon.

The kibbutz, in the period between Famenoth and Mesore, suffers from a lack of water. The tarpaulins for night-time condensation collection aren't enough; the wells dry up. I asked Samash, 'Little Father, why don't we take the water from the Ship? There's a lot of water down there.'

He'd answered me: 'Son, that's accursed water. It's as salty as the goat meat on the feast of Tammuz. You need to avoid it.'

And he gave me the stink eye, arthritic hands shaking, but I couldn't stay away from Damkina. She was my water, and Damkina couldn't stay away from the Ship for very long.

We spent entire afternoons diving into the liquid expanse, swimming from one end of the lake to the other.

Creatures of every kind lived in the water: red and black ribbons, calves that grazed the submerged prairies, golden-striped trays, pink chandeliers.

The rocky bottom was covered with velvety green-and-blue threads through which silver needles chased one another. Deep, dark crevices appeared here and there, like entrances leading to the center of the planet. One time, we saw a greenish glow coming from the chasms and perceived the movement of an immeasurable body shifting a huge amount of water. Its waves bumped our immersed bodies, pushing us far like twigs in the wind; we swam toward the shore and sat in silence on the sand, hugging our knees as our teeth chattered. Not from the cold, I assure you.

We often lay on the beach to dry out under the sun. The subterranean coolness made it less intense. In those moments, Damkina spoke.

'We come from the stars and we happened by chance on Sargon. The Ship is the wreck of a spaceship; our ancestors were exploring this galaxy, five thousand years ago, when their spacecraft broke down. To fix it, they approached this planet, but the ship fell out of stationary orbit and started to dive, increasing in speed minute by minute. Some, to save themselves, wanted to abandon their companions, unhook a part of the tail to resume altitude; others, instead, tried to avoid the worst and maneuvered it to land here, in the desert. Those who attempted the rescue are the kibbutz's ancestors, the legislators of the community; those who thought only of themselves are the ancestors of the townspeople, the selfish inhabitants of Erech.'

I knew these were lies. Or maybe not. How would you prove it? They were well-told lies.

The time spent there made us bold. Exploring the hold, we had discovered that the main lake, through a series of side galleries, could be accessed by some secondary pools. Little light filtered through the slits in the rock above and transformed the pools into dark, mysterious bodies of water. Here we found the pincushions. They nestled inside of small rocky cavities under the water's surface. When I tried to extract one with my knife, it broke into pieces; that's how we discovered that inside, in the middle of some disgusting grayish matter, there was a five-pointed star-shaped egg, soft and fragile, of a beautiful color – like that of the sun at dusk.

The kibbutz's inhabitants are always looking for new sources of food, so we tried to feed some of the animals of the Undersea to old Tza, Samash's pet sarg, who scarfed down anything that was edible. When we put the pincushion star in his bowl, he licked it with his thin tongue and devoured it at once. Immediately afterwards he began to hop and roll onto his back, legs in the air, playing like a puppy. Finally, after being silent for twenty years, as Samash told me, he started to sing the pleasant, painful lullaby of the sargs.

'They sing only when their hearts overflow with joy,' the Little Father explained to me.

People came from all the Houses to hear the sarg's song. Tza sang for three days straight.

'Old Tza truly seems like he's in paradise,' I blurted out, while I was lying down on the beach of the hold together with Damkina.

'The reason is that the pincushions spend all their time thinking, in there, in their dark puddles,' she began. 'They think and think because they don't have any distractions; they've been doing it for millennia. Therefore, they've developed all sorts of concepts, deepened each kind of philosophical system, analyzed every mental category.'

With the sand prodding my back, the sun warming me, and Damkina speaking to me, I would have liked to sing like Tza.

'The intense meditative work of the pincushions has turned into an amino acid,' Damkina went on, moving her hands around in the air to sketch the atomic form that she was inventing. 'The chain of amino acids has codified a protein, which is the main component of the stars, and thus the pincushions store the enormity of their thought in a comfortable and compact form.'

While Damkina spoke, our tanned shoulders touched, and though I knew the depth of her navel, the shape of her breast, the curve of her hips, the hair that covered her sex like thin algae on a round rock, I felt more naked than I was. I jumped up and dove again. The cold water turned off my thoughts.

It seems, sometimes, that the wind brings the stories, along with winged seeds that fly in the desert and sprout in the most unlikely places. In the heads of the wealthy citizens of Erech, they sprout the desire for pincushion eggs, and so new faces started circulating in the kibbutz.

The outsiders were convinced that eating the gelatinous stars would give them original thoughts; not extravagant ideas or dream visions but rather strokes of genius, such that when one thinks, the others are open-mouthed, applaud, and offer prizes of money, of attention, and say that the thinker has advanced humanity by twenty years.

The townspeople considered themselves more advanced than us; they were rude, nervous, sizing up me and Damkina, acting like they were God's gift to Tammuz. But only we were able to get them what they wanted, in exchange for a nice bag full of money.

Usually, we picked them up as they strolled unhappily near the Ship; they had gotten nothing from the other kibbutz inhabitants except bread, salt, and fruit – gifts due to guests. Damkina was very good at haggling, making the townspeople believe that the pincushions were rare, that getting to one was a heroic undertaking, and she never delivered an entire star, always half, or two arms, to confirm the difficulty of the task. The other half of the star was sold to the next dupe.

Dealing with the townspeople was amusing but also tiring; they had difficulty following a few simple instructions. One absent-minded biologist insisted on seeing the place where the pincushions lived, promising us ten thousand laz. At first glance, we figured it was harmless, so five thousand in advance and we lowered him into the hold, with the warning not to touch anything, not to take samples, not to insert fingers or objects into the crannies. Well, that idiot managed to get bitten by a ribbon when he dipped his stupid feet into the main lake. How the idiot screeched!

We brought him back, limping and half-paralyzed, to his helipod; he gulped down all sorts of antidotes from the vehicle's first aid kit, but his leg was turning blue. We reluctantly had to call Samash and Nin, the Caretakers of the Green House, who were able to stop the infection.

The Little Father stared at me for a long time with his owl eyes, without saying anything. We told him that the idiot from the city had been bitten by a scorpion. The biologist saved his skin, got his great spoonful of ideas, and gave us the rest of what we were owed. Ten thousand laz!

'Where do we hide the money?'

It wasn't a dumb question, since in the kibbutz, money means very little. Mostly, you barter what you have for what you need, the community provides basic subsistence, and no one feels the need to have what he doesn't use.

'We put it in a safe place,' Damkina answered. 'The nest of forks. When we get to a million laz, we leave here.'

'Leave? Where?'

'To see the world. There are a lot of places to explore outside of the kibbutz.'

'We don't need that.'

'I want to see Erech, buy a helipod, and get to the slopes of the Tramonto Mountains.'

'They're clouds, not mountains.'

'The clouds are in your head, Nergal.'

I looked at Damkina and wondered who she really was; after many years spent side by side, she had never spoken to me about such desires. She was resolute, almost trembling at the prospect of abandoning the kibbutz; I felt her confident anxiety about the future like the sharp smell of *ar* berries crushed in a mortar, and I felt as small as a berry. After that, there were no more stories on the beach.

Of course, we continued to fish the pincushions and sell them to the townspeople. She wanted me to accompany her to every client, but for some reason that had escaped me, the carefreeness had abandoned us both and, despite much effort, we couldn't recover it.

I feared the inevitable disinterest that at a certain age turns you away from the brothers and sisters that have grown up with you, in the same House. Marriages between people raised in the same House are very rare; maybe due to the fact that they've rubbed elbows for a long time, that when you reach a certain age, having pissed together is a cause for shame, not love.

Damkina started going around holding Sin's hand, that sucker of the Yellow House whose hair looked like a diarrheal camel had shat on his head. Then one evening, around the fire, I sat next to Tishtrya and kissed her. I knew that Tish was after me, since she'd flirted with me when we were on duty together in the kitchen.

However, one time when a townsperson appeared in search of stars, Damkina and I came to an agreement again.

We soon noticed a strange phenomenon: once tasted, the pincushion stars became obsessions, tormenting the eaters and making them crave a second bite.

Many townspeople returned to the kibbutz with anguished eyes, mean-looking, more restless than before, because they hadn't known what they were missing; now they knew and wanted more. It was the right time to raise prices. I divided a single star into five thread-like parts, then each portion into fragments as small as a flax seed. I finally enclosed this microscopic amount in a sagyz pod. Price: five thousand laz.

Unfortunately, all of this coming and going of the townspeople alarmed the Caretakers. They understood that something unusual was happening; rumors circulated of illicit trade, underhanded activity. Damkina and I had educated and properly scared the townspeople: they had to shut up or their ration of pincushion eggs would be totally cut off. Some, though, were dissatisfied with the modest quantity that they could buy. They were fighting with each other; there was even a fight in the kibbutz canteen, two townspeople were stabbed, and only the intervention of the Caretakers stopped them from killing each other. I was passing that neighborhood by chance and Samash gestured threateningly at me, as he used to do when I was a kid and he was promising me a spanking and punishment.

One day, I saw Sin walking ten steps behind Damkina, an abandoned dog in search of caresses. That same day, I had broken up with Tish and her vanilla scent, and I was so happy that I went straight to the hold for a swim. Along the road I passed four approaching helicopters, a blacker and larger version of our helipods. They landed in the field between the Hills of Tammuz, discharging a multitude of black and chitinous humans, armed with a flaming rostrum; they obeyed an unarmed man who gave his orders by blinking.

I felt unease rising up from my toes to my fingertips and up to my tongue. I ran to the hold and found Damkina, who had just caught a load of pincushions; I counted twelve overflowing nets.

Those dangerous insect townspeople had come for the stars and Damkina wanted to hand them over in exchange for more money than she'd ever asked before.

'It's not right.' I stopped her, putting myself between her and the ladder; I was shaking because, for the first time, I was standing up to Damkina. 'The townspeople have too many ideas, all ugly and dangerous.'

She laughed.

'Do you think they'll be satisfied with your alms? Damkina, those are people used to taking what they want by force. Do you ever wonder what the people do when they return to the city? What ideas they've gotten? And if the stars inspire hateful thoughts, foul actions, even… crimes, or the will to overpower other human beings?'

Damkina took a pincushion from a net, opened it with her knife, divided the star, and ate half under my terrified eyes. Now I understood what had changed, understood where the idea of leaving the kibbutz had come from, to see the city, to reach the mountains.

'You can eat it, too, Nergal. Taste it,' she said, putting the other half of the star in the palm of her hand.

'No!' I backed away disdainfully.

She picked up the nets, lashed them together with a rope, and headed toward the ladder. She then turned to look at me as one looks at a beautiful and distant place, where one was happy a long time ago.

My heart in turmoil, I presented myself to Samash.

'Little Father, I have a confession to make.'

'Better late than never,' he muttered. 'Speak, guilty shadow.'

The Caretakers summoned the kibbutz's inhabitants and explained that our quiet life was threatened by the presence of evil people; together we opened the Tammuz Gorge and we hid in the underground shelters. Throughout the night, Tammuz's breath passed over the Gorge, and the day after, everything in the kibbutz and around it was covered in *kefer*, very fine sand. Our farming machinery had been protected, but the strangers' hovercraft and the gears of their weapons were saturated with tiny white particles; every mechanism was clogged. The townspeople were forced to return to the city on foot.

I turned to the Ship and discovered that the sand had almost completely filled it, the hold, the beach; the lake didn't exist anymore. I went to the Green House with a sinking feeling. Nin, the Little Mother, told me that Damkina had been there, taken some food, and left. I looked for the nest egg in the nest of forks, five hundred thousand laz were there, exactly half of what we had accumulated. My half.

So, now you know the truth, the pure truth, because I can't make up stories. I can cheat the people – I'm so good at deceiving that I scammed myself, I cheated myself. I thought I was fishing and selling pincushion eggs for money; instead, I did it for her. Only for her.

Now I lie down on the white sand on top of the Ship and feel cold. The sharp granules irritate my skin. I tried to dig, and I found gray, greasy, dull water. Sometimes Tishtrya comes to see me; at night we join in silence, during the day we don't even glance at each other. But Samash looks at me worriedly.

One morning he calls me into the icebox, with the excuse of helping to repair the insulation; he uncovers a pot full of frozen barley and pulls out a small metal tin. Inside, still well-preserved, is a whole pincushion.

'I bought it from one of the first strangers, to try to understand what you were planning,' he explains to me.

My eyes fill with tears.

What can the eggs reveal to me that I don't already know? I should have thought first, understood first, tasted them with her.

The tears fall on the pincushion and its black spikes move. It's still alive; the salt water from my eyes has woken it up.

Translated by Rachel Cordasco

Sleeping Beauties

Agnieszka Hałas

Poland

I was searching for a Polish SF story, and when 'Sleeping Beauties' finally landed in my inbox, courtesy of my friend Konrad Walewski, I realized that I already knew Agnieszka – in her role as an editor at the long-running *Nowa Fantastyka* magazine. She had only recently requested a story from me, and now I was writing to her with the same request... Agnieszka is the author of a fantasy series in Poland, but here she turns her attention to science fiction, with the first of two retellings of a fairy tale in this book, that couldn't be any more different from each other. I enjoyed it a lot. This story is original to this anthology and was translated from Polish by the author.

When you're forced to choose between a penal colony in the Kuiper belt and flying for Minos Justice, it's better to fly for Minos Justice. Even though it's a government-run company. This is what I keep telling myself while sipping a disgusting vitamin-enriched, dubiously strawberry-flavored protein shake with bran flakes (fake bran, not the real thing). Chlomach or no chlomach, the human gut needs fiber to function. Take my word on this.

Kyle Biernacki is telling yet another anecdote about shipyard workers, but I'm not really listening.

Onboard it's seven twenty. Breakfast time. Humming engines. Three hundred ninety sleeping beauties speeding towards their destination.

Charon 6, a small interplanetary transport ship with five cargo holds and a crew of two, has no mess room; we're sitting in our sleeping quarters. The scuffed gray plastic table is dotted with colorful intellistickers: miniature propaganda posters. Our elbows, plates and notebooks won't ever rub them away.

A pic of Uran, Neptune and Pluto, with the caption: 'Urnepluto Republic. Our Future Together!' A smiling spacesuit-clad miner leaning against a huge robot: 'Mines on Triton – Our Pride'. A spider perched on a console: 'The Enemy Lurks on the Net'. And so on.

The breakfast shake is in black plastic pouches with the yellow Victory Corporation logo: two fingers in a V-salute.

Kyle takes a gulp and laughs hoarsely. He's big, with bristly ginger hair and a huge red nose, and gets on my nerves. Thankfully, Minos Justice pilots aren't required to like one another.

He sticks one hairy arm under his T-shirt to scratch his folded chlomach.

'And so they emptied out the warehouse and found a transmitter hidden behind the crates. Radio Free Jupiter, can you fucking believe that?'

'Yeah.' I drink the remaining vile pink slurry. Fricking Victory Shakes, to hell with them.

*

We dock at Triton A Orbital Station at eleven. It has Earth-like artificial gravity, over five hundred thousand inhabitants, several large factories and a shipyard. Although our sister ship *Charon 8* made a stop here only two weeks ago, forty-seven capsules are waiting for us.

'That's a hell of a load,' says Kyle. 'Was there a revolt, or what?'

Probably just some hardworking security functionaries, but I don't say this out loud. All our conversations are monitored by Minos Justice, and my dossier looks bad enough already.

Neptune looms ahead, blue and hazy. After a routine exchange with flight control, we wait for thirty minutes, sipping coffee, until the sleeping beauties are ready. I tell our ship to open the cargo hold.

Security procedures forbid us to leave the control room as long as the cargo bay stays open, so we stare at a screen that shows the feeds from four cameras: main hatch, corridor, cargo-bay door and inside the cargo bay.

Members of Triton A's technical crew wear blue overalls and black caps with the familiar yellow Victory Corporation logo. Those now wrestling with the capsules have donned white plastic exoskeletons resembling plate armor from centuries ago. Augmented muscle power helps the company optimize personnel costs: an exoskeleton-clad worker is strong enough to single-handedly maneuver a sleeping beauty onboard, even though the combined weight of the capsule, fluids and sleeper is somewhere around four hundred and fifty pounds.

We watch as they unload empty capsules before replacing them with full ones. One after another, the sleeping beauties are hauled onboard and wheeled through the corridor to Hold Five, the only one where there's still space. Inside the hold, three technicians are busy hooking up the sleepers to the ship's life support apparatus. Two work quickly and deftly, while the third one, who looks like a teenager, fumbles around awkwardly. It takes him ages to properly connect one of the tubes. Kyle leans towards the intercom mic.

'Hey, you! If that thing starts leaking, I'll come back there and make you pay!'

The boy jumps up, startled. He looks around, sees the tiny loudspeaker on the ceiling and shakes his head.

A second technician comes up to help.

Ten minutes later we get the message that all the capsules have been hooked up. I move a lever and a yellow light begins to blink on the hold's control panel. The blinking soon stops and the light changes to green. Loud gurgling noises come up through the floor, like bowel sounds in a huge belly. Nutritional liquid is now circulating through the installation.

I wait patiently until all the remaining yellow lights on the control panel turn green, then I activate the screen that shows data from the holds.

'Hold Five, Blocks Two and Three.'

Forty-seven EKG lines appear on the screen. A chaos of beeping erupts from the loudspeaker, so I hastily turn down the volume.

'We're done,' I tell the technicians over the intercom.

*

Six hours after departing from Triton A, I correct our course and reduce thrust. The engines' hum quietens down. I unbuckle my harness and grab my datapad.

'I'll check out our new cargo.'

Kyle nods, then turns on his music player. Strange chirping and beeping noises fill the control room, mixed with female orgasmic moans and distorted disco beats from a hundred and fifty years ago. This stuff is all the rage on Urnepluto hit lists right now: melodies generated by the AI known as MX-34 Nightingale, programmed by the young autistic genius Lucien Glockenspiel. It's the president's favorite music, so the nation has to love it too.

The corridors on *Charon 6* are scuffed, grubby. We have just one ancient cleaning robot, who seems to have grown indifferent to the dust.

The fluorescent lamps in Hold Five come alive when I enter, bathing the capsules in an icy white glow. Reading the numbers, I stop at each capsule, turn on its interior lighting and inspect the sleepers' skin for signs of Nilsson-Wang disease. Courtesy of biowarfare research conducted a century ago, we now struggle with an engineered pathogen capable of growing even in hibernated bodies. The intelligent nutritional liquid kills most other disease-causing organisms, but not the Nilsson-Wang bacterium.

The liquid will also mess up the results of nearly all standard diagnostic tests that detect genetic material or proteins. The most reliable method for early detection of Nilsson-Wang disease is plain old visual inspection, in use even before Hippocrates.

I search for the telltale blood-filled blisters. They tend to appear where the skin is thinnest: neck, armpits, groin, initially as tiny vesicles, easy to overlook. They soon swell, though, merging into large black bullae, and when they burst, the skin peels off in sheets. Death occurs relatively quickly: either from shock and electrolyte imbalance or from sepsis, the same as in burn patients.

XT 98-560424. Thin guy with a sunken mouth; perhaps he lost his teeth during interrogation. Hollow cheeks, concave stomach, but his skin looks okay.

XT 98-560425. Fat guy with vaguely Asian features. These folks have it really tough, they get accused of espionage all the time.

He has a couple of suspicious dark spots on his chest, over the right nipple. I inspect them closely, but no, they're just moles. In an atypical location, too.

The greenish nutritional liquid opalesces faintly in the strong light.

XT 98-560427, XT 98-560428, XT 98-560429. With XT 98-560429, once again, I take my time.

The sleeper is a girl. Petite, maybe five foot four, with delicate features and a small straight nose. Her head is bald, obviously, but otherwise she's beautiful.

For a moment, I wonder about the color of her eyes. Probably blue, judging by her fair eyebrows and eyelashes.

Her real name is somewhere in our database, but I mentally christen her Elaine.

*

Later, curled up comfortably in my bunk, I reach for my datapad, connect with Minos Justice's internal network and open the criminal register.

Obviously, I can't legally access this data, but I struck up a friendship with the ship's computer some time ago and managed to glean just enough information to sneak around some of the security measures. We can't use the holonet during flights, but the company's network is a different story. Administrative department employees have free access to the criminal record system, and their access codes are fairly easy to break.

My datapad is under surveillance, of course, but I've disabled the spyware, even though I'm no IT whiz. One has to learn this stuff to survive.

Kyle Biernacki is snoring loudly. I type the capsule number into the search field and soon have all the info I wanted.

Elaine's real name is Nastassja Leszczynski, aged twenty-six. Convicted of a second-degree political crime.

I wonder how you ended up neck-deep in this guano, lovely Nastassja. Nobody gets sent to a Tartarus prison center just for downloading illegal files. Even dissemination of subversive materials will usually result in a more lenient sentence.

I log out, then carefully purge every trace of the search from the device. Finally, I slip in a memory card marked with a pink sticker and activate a cleaner program that overwrites all deleted files with garbage data.

If my datapad gets confiscated and scanned by specialists, they'll only find evidence of a hardcore addiction to black market holoporn. Not something the government really worries about.

Kyle rolls over on his side and starts snoring again. I slip the datapad back into its protective sheath and turn towards the wall. Recalling Elaine/Nastassja's face, I suddenly realize how strongly this girl resembles Rika.

My memory instantly brings back that day on Uranus C when we gazed at Uranus for what we hoped was the last time. Everything had been arranged with the people from Escape. A small, fast passenger ship equipped with illegal military-grade camo and shields. Its official destination was Oberon, but the plan was to change course, fly straight through the blockade, reveal ourselves immediately after leaving the border zone and ask for political asylum. Each month, Escape helps several dozen Urnepluto citizens make a run for freedom. Not many or a huge number, depending on how you look at it. Methods change, but the risk remains high. Ships attempting to pass through the blockade often get shot down with no warning. Some people say that over half of attempted escapes end with death. Government propaganda, obviously, says all of them do.

But we were determined to try anyway.

They arrested me the next day in my apartment, an hour before we were supposed to meet at the ship. I had only my own stupidity to blame. A day earlier, I'd sent a message – just one – from a holonet café, to my brother. I'd taken extra care to use no suspicious phrases. All correspondence in the Urnepluto Republic is monitored, so either the monitoring AI picked something up, no idea how, or Andy Kressler had simply turned me in.

Rika and the others were supposed to wait for five minutes, then depart without me.

They must've escaped. If they'd been caught or shot down, I'd be a sleeping beauty now.

I wonder, not for the first time, whether Rika still thinks about me, and where she ended up: on Jupiter, on Mars, on Earth? How would she feel if she learned that, given the choice between a penal colony and Minos Justice, I chose to work for Minos Justice? Now I ferry sleeping revolutionaries to Tartarus 2, a government prison and research center.

The thought hurts, so I push it away, as usual.

*

Kyle and I are reclining in the sunroom, a tiny space opposite our sleeping quarters. Perhaps it would've been more appropriate to call it our dining room.

In the sunroom, you're supposed to lie supine, hands behind your head, while a large lamp floods the place with blinding fake sunlight. We're both stripped to our underwear because of the heat. Our chlomachs, propped up on small folding frames, resemble huge green leaves, intricately veined.

Designing a man-made symbiotic cyanobacterium capable of photosynthesis inside human cells was child's play for a team of Urnepluto biotech wizards. They knew, however, that simply giving people green skin would make no sense. Firstly, the glucose produced during photosynthesis must be efficiently transported to the bloodstream, and keratinocytes aren't adapted to do this. Secondly, the epidermis constantly renews itself: its layers of cells move upward, die and slough off. The dermis, on the other hand, doesn't really contain that many cells; it's made up mostly of extracellular matrix, collagen fibers and so on. After some experimenting, the biotech guys decided it would be easiest to just create a new organ, connecting it to the portal vein with a kind of umbilical cord through the belly button. Simple and ingenious.

And now Minos Justice is testing the new technology on its pilots, because why not. Government-run company, government contract. As a bonus, they can save on our food rations.

Kyle reaches for the control button on his hologlasses to change the program.

'Whoa,' he mutters with a stupid smile. He's probably watching his favorite reality soap, the one about mutants living in care homes. For some reason, he finds it fun to watch deformed, barely human-looking creatures play soccer or learn basic living skills.

I turn on my hologlasses and stare at the menu. The device holds about fifty vids, but I've already seen them all. Nothing but government-approved crap. Crime movies about brave Urnepluto security functionaries tracking down saboteurs in Triton mines are only worth watching if you watch them while drunk.

I finally decide to open a propaganda vid: security forces breaking up a demonstration on the sixteenth anniversary of the first and, as yet, only presidential election in the Urnepluto Republic. Right after the civil war in the Solar System ended, we elected Edward Blick as our president, but he soon established himself as a dictator and has ruled ever since, supported by the military. Propaganda calls him the 'Father of Planets'.

I only want to see the opening frames. Paradise City on Titania, the largest Uranian moon: a multilevel structure of blocky white buildings under a glowing cyan dome, the heatcatcher alien technology that enables us to build settlements on celestial bodies far away from the Sun.

Paradise City, our wonderful capital. Some palm trees would help it live up to its name.

The camera pans out to show the crowd milling in front of the Parliament building. Their handheld signs and hovering holograms contain the usual slogans in unilingua. 'Urn Polluted' and 'Urnepluto, Ur Nope'. Someone ought to tell them this stuff was witty sixteen years ago.

The demonstrators are chanting and waving their arms. I've muted the sound, but it's easy to read their lips.

'Urn Polluted! Urn Polluted!'

Black police hovercars descend on them like vultures on carrion. The air is suddenly thick with tear gas and paralyzing spray. A second later the square is in chaos. Demonstrators are staggering, dropping their signs and falling to the ground, their movements uncoordinated. Policemen in gas masks handcuff them and haul them into the waiting hovercars, which take off immediately.

The same thing happens every year. I press 'Stop' and the opening frame appears again. Paradise City, like a huge white pueblo under a cyan sky.

I never got to see it IRL.

Rika was born in Paradise City. When she was a toddler, security forces arrested her father, a government official. Rika's mother had found out that her husband was heavily implicated in black market business. She turned him in to the authorities, cutting a deal with the prosecution that saw her only relocated to an orbital station and placed under police supervision for a couple of years. She was also allowed to keep her child.

As far as I remember, Rika had always avoided talking about her mother. They hadn't been in contact since Rika had turned eighteen.

The next vid in the catalog shows the self-immolation of ten members of Christian Freedom in front of the presidential palace on Great Friday. 'Criminal sect forces its members to die a gruesome death', 'Policemen risk their lives saving fanatics', and so on. I don't want to watch. I don't feel like doing anything. I deactivate the hologlasses, take them off and close my eyes. The heat in the sunroom is stifling. I smell plastic and dust. My warm chlomach itches faintly. I think about the Sun, the real Sun, which I have only ever seen in vids and VR.

I also think about Rika Korsakov.

When we met, I was working as a pilot instructor on Uranus C. Rika did an internship with us as a company psychologist: a pretty girl fresh out of uni. All the guys tried to ask her out, but I was the first one who managed to invite her to dinner at a Polish eatery after work. The food was only as Polish as circumstances allowed: borscht that had never seen a beet, pierogi with fake cheese filling, not even soy protein, just plain cheap cultured protein. Still better than canteen fodder, though.

My relationship with Rika developed perhaps not at lightning speed, but faster than I expected. She was living in a rented apartment with two roommates, so we'd spend tender nights together at my tiny bachelor pad. We'd make love on a foam mattress covered with a white sheet, fresh from the cleaning chamber, in the light of a holo imitation of a flickering campfire.

Rika was... sweet. I can't think of any better word. Red hair, perhaps genmod-enhanced, certainly not dyed. Slender body, but soft too. Her favorite perfume was an Urnepluto fake version of a Jupiterian pheromone scent. She had tattoos on her back and stomach: multicolored lizards and fish. Earth species, extinct since a century or more.

She never let me make a VR recording of her, even though I begged her. I had a good, expensive VR camera that recorded all the senses; a stupid purchase really, since there was barely anything interesting to record at the station, and the police were always ready to pounce on you for recording stuff you weren't supposed to. I'd only ever made a few recordings of the promenade: the crowds, the colored lights, the food smells.

At that stage, I didn't yet know that Rika Korsakov was a resistance agent. She told me four months later. Mostly, I think, because the guys from Escape needed someone who knew the flight control procedures on Uranus C and had access to a couple of door-opening codes.

I agreed to help them out as much as I could, under just one condition: a spot on the escaping ship.

I was careful. I took precautions. Ultimately, it was only my cautiousness that kept the security service from finding out how I had aided Escape. All they had was circumstantial evidence.

Enough to arrest me and keep me imprisoned for a month. Interrogate me a few times, break a couple of ribs, torture me with an electric baton and dig through my brain with the help of a direct-interface AI questioner. Afterwards, they pulled me off the station. No one is ever in a hurry to get permanently rid of a good pilot, so I ultimately ended up in Minos Justice.

No sense in reminiscing endlessly over all that. So I think about Rika instead, bathed in the flickering orange light of holographic fire, her tousled red hair and the tropical fish tattooed over her belly button.

My chlomach is hard at work photosynthesizing, while the ship's engines drone steadily. Their humming sound and the lamp's intense warmth are making me sleepy.

*

When I wake up, the sunroom is dark. The ship's computer has turned the lamp off, because too much sunning could damage our chlomachs. In the weak light coming from the corridor I see the black, unmoving figure on the other couch.

'Kyle?' No answer. I suddenly feel cold. 'Wall light.' The ship turns on the small light over the door.

Kyle is dead. I realize this the instant I see his bluish, distorted face and open mouth. His chlomach is sagging, wilted.

Exit second pilot Kyle Biernacki. RIP.

I have to wait a moment to calm myself. Then I dress hastily, bring in the medical scanner and a couple minutes later everything is clear. An extensive cerebral hemorrhage, or so the diagnostic program says. Kyle must have lost consciousness immediately. If he'd called out, if I'd had even a minute's warning, a dose of injected nanobots could have saved him.

I can't lift two hundred and twenty pounds of dead Kyle without an exoskeleton, so I reduce thrust until I'm able to haul his body to Hold Five. I manhandle him into one of the empty capsules, then hook up a tube and fill the interior with Preservan. No idea what the stuff contains, but UV light causes it to polymerize into a glasslike substance.

When the container is full, I unhook the tube and press a button. A violet glow lights up the upper part of the capsule. Thirty seconds later Kyle Biernacki is fully protected against decomposition. Like an insect in amber. He can wait safely until the medics from Tartarus 2 dig him out and perform an autopsy.

I return to the control room and contact my bosses. They order me to wait, so I wait. Not really calm, but fatalistically ready for anything, including the possibility that the next order will be to divert towards the nearest station, where I'll be led off the ship in handcuffs.

Fifteen minutes later they call again with instructions. I'm to change course, reduce speed, and dock in two days at one of the planetoids of the Kuiper belt, where a new Tartarus center is under construction. In a stroke of luck, a Minos Justice employee with qualifications as a pilot and capsule technician is there right now.

'Within an hour, we expect a detailed report on what exactly happened,' says my boss. I sigh in relief. Yeah, sure, he'll get a report with all the details.

*

Our new crew member's name is Hannah Sutton and she's ugly as sin. Dumpy, toadlike, with a flabby bust.

I've checked her background in the company files. She spent a few years flying cargo carriers, then got promoted to personnel manager.

She has no chlomach. Thankfully, the guys from the planetoid have equipped her with additional food rations, otherwise the trip with me would mean an unplanned slimming cure. A chlomach provides around a thousand calories daily in the form of glucose, and there's only enough protein shake on board to feed me and Kyle until the end of our flight, with maybe five extra pouches at most. Kyle's remaining rations would barely sustain a chlomachless crew member.

When I return from the control room after another long, exhausting holotalk with the Minos bigwigs, Hannah has already made herself at home in our sleeping quarters. She has packed Kyle's things into a large carryall and hauled his sleeping bag to the cleaning chamber. Now she's sitting on his bunk under a poster depicting Edward Blick, Father of Planets, and nibbling biscuits from a packet, one hand scribbling busily on a datapad. She shuts it abruptly when I enter.

'Want some?' She holds out the packet.

I take a dry cookie. It's stale, but seems delicious anyway after weeks of Victory shakes.

'Have two,' says Hannah. She doesn't smile.

*

The next few days pass uneventfully. Unlike Kyle, Hannah doesn't talk much, and when she does talk, her tone is gruff. We try to politely avoid each other as much as possible, which suits me just fine. I play games on my datapad, exercise in the minigym, spend time in the sunroom, chat with the ship now and then.

On the fourth day, I'm in for another surprise.

During yet another routine inspection of the capsules, I discover black blisters on the body of prisoner XT 98-560428. Five on his neck and a couple more in each groin. They're largish, turgid; they must've appeared during the night, or even last evening.

I take my time inspecting them, just to be sure. I reach for my datapad, open photos of Nilsson-Wang victims and compare.

Yeah, it's the same thing. No fricking doubt about it.

I don't have to pump anything into the capsule, because the nutritional liquid contains Preservan. I simply disconnect the life-support apparatus and turn on the UV light. After thirty seconds, the greenish solution has fully polymerized into rock-hard glass. A brief note in the transport documentation and I'm done.

When I tell Hannah what happened, she nods grimly.

'No surprise,' she says.

'Why?'

'There's a full-blown Nilsson-Wang epidemic on Triton. You haven't heard? All their settlements have been placed under quarantine. Government orders. Looks like the plague has reached the orbital stations as well.

Thinking about the technicians from Triton A who visited our ship, I feel an unpleasant chill, but the incubation period for Nilsson-Wang disease in non-hibernating persons never exceeds a week. If I'd caught it from the technicians, I would be showing symptoms by now.

'The Tartarus centers are working on a cure and a vaccine,' says Hannah with a sour grimace. I know what she means. They do their research on sleeping beauties.

I don't even ponder anymore whether I should feel guilty or not.

*

A day later, I re-inspect the capsules in Hold Five earlier than usual. One case of the plague means we'll probably discover more of them today.

When the light comes on, I need a moment to comprehend what I'm seeing.

Chills crawl up my spine. I approach the sleeping beauties, just to be sure. I light up the interior of the first capsule and peer through the glass, then go on to the second and third one.

The liquid inside all of them has polymerized.

I slowly circle the hold, pinching my forearm now and then to make sure I'm not dreaming. I stop to gaze dumbly at Elaine, her face frozen in greenish glass.

After recovering from the shock, I check the remaining holds, even though I already know what I'll find. All the sleeping beauties have been encased in crystal.

The whole thing reminds me of a fucked-up fairy tale.

Unnaturally calm, I open my datapad and communicate with the ship. My first impulse is to request footage from the cameras in Hold Five, but then I realize that nobody in their right mind would waste their time walking from capsule to capsule when you can order the ship to activate the UV light in all of them at once. According to procedure, such an order must be authorized by both crew members, but Hannah has obviously managed to bypass the security measures.

That, or a virus has been planted in the ship's computer by the resistance movement: a possibility I don't really give any credence.

A glance at the ship's logs gives me the answer.

Now that it's too late, I stay surprisingly cool and calm. It's odd that Hannah has decided to make her move today, five days after coming on board. At this point, I can see three possible explanations. Possibly it took her that long to hack the ship's computer, or perhaps she had to do something else first, maybe gather some files and send them somewhere... Or her initial plan was to kidnap the ship, but she ultimately decided this wouldn't be feasible.

Doesn't really matter.

A red light suddenly begins to blink on the ceiling. Over the intercom, the ship's computer says:

'Crew alert. Approaching vessel detected. Vessel type: police patrol craft. Maintain current course: yes or no?'

I feel a chill again. They know. They've probably known from the moment the deed was done. We've been monitored since the beginning of our journey, just like all the other transport ships used by Minos Justice.

'Maintain current course and speed.' My throat is dry, the words come out with difficulty. 'Time until meeting?'

'One standard hour or less.'

'Where's Hannah?'

'In the sleeping quarters.'

'Shut the door and don't let her out.'

I go to Hold One, where there's a cabinet with medical equipment.

Time to program some nanobots.

*

Before entering the sleeping quarters, I check the camera feed to make sure Hannah isn't lurking behind the door with a weapon. But no, she's sitting on her bunk, scribbling in a notebook. She lays it aside when I enter.

'Why did you do it?' I ask.

She laughs dryly.

'You know what happens to sleepers in Tartarus centers?' I continue.

'More or less,' she replies.

It's best not to think about this stuff if you want to stay sane. I've always told myself there's no point in fighting against the things we can't change.

'I've saved four hundred thirty-seven people,' says Hannah with a faint smile. I can sense her satisfaction. You'd think she actually saved their lives.

Then something clicks inside my head.

'Kyle's brain bleed was orchestrated, wasn't it? He was removed so you could take his place.'

She nods.

'Nanobots inside his hologlasses,' she says. 'With a preprogrammed activation date. They passed through his skin into the bloodstream and damaged an artery in his brain, causing a hemorrhagic stroke.'

Her voice is dispassionate, as though she were discussing a pierogi recipe.

'Why Kyle and not me?' I ask.

'One of you had to die.' She shrugs. 'We drew lots.'

'Which organization do you work for?'

'Christian Freedom.' There's pride in her voice, which doesn't surprise me. The present-day Christians are a strange bunch.

I come up closer, one hand in my pocket, but Hannah doesn't seem to notice. She stares ahead, that slight smile still playing on her lips.

'A police ship is approaching, Hannah. You know what they'll do with us when they arrive?'

'Anything for Christ.' Her tone remains indifferent.

With a lightning-fast move, I jab her arm with my syringe and push the plunger as far as it'll go. Hannah jumps back, but it's too late, the nanobots are in her blood. The standard-issue, injectable kind: Minos Justice medical kits don't include the newer, skin-penetrating nano.

I drop the syringe and back away, ready for an attack, but she only stares at me, massaging her aching arm.

'What was that supposed to be?' she asks.

Now it's my turn to smile. 'Mercy.'

The disbelief on Hannah's face slowly gives way to amusement.

'Come on, Stanley. You didn't actually think I was planning to stay alive until their arrival?'

She sits down, or rather slumps onto her bunk, and extends one hand, clumsily opening her fingers. The nanobots must have already reached her cerebellum and her motor functions are beginning to fail. A white capsule drops from her palm and rolls across the floor.

'See to your own safety as well,' says Hannah. 'Poor Stanley. A victim of circumsta—'

Her voice had become slurred, incomprehensible; now, her

speech center has just shut down entirely. She falls silent and looks away, staring at the cabin window and the blackness of space beyond.

I wait. A moment later Hannah's head slumps forwards and her body sags sideways. The nanobots have turned her brain to mush. Her brainstem will soon give out and that'll be that.

'Crew alert: police patrol craft approaching at increased speed. Predicted time until meeting: thirty minutes,' says the ship.

They'll be late, though. I suddenly feel like laughing. I have a second syringe ready. Another minute and the security functionaries can screw themselves.

A proper intravenous injection will hurt less and do the trick faster than the sloppy jab I gave Hannah.

I roll up my sleeve, wrap a tourniquet around my arm and carefully locate a vein.

*

After regaining consciousness, the first thing I feel is surprise. How can I be awake?

The room is small, windowless, its walls and floor covered with greenish-gray tiles. I ought to freeze with fear at this point, but I'm still dazed, groggy and shocked that I'm alive. Am I?

I can't move my arms or legs, or even feel them. They might as well be gone. Predictably, I'm also unable to turn my head. I feel neither warm nor cold, and smell no smells.

On the opposing wall I notice a large mirror. Step by step, I compare the reflection with my surroundings. A metal chair with arm and leg clamps; a desk where an obese guy in a gray uniform is writing something at a console.

On the desk there's an ominous assortment of objects. A taser, an electric baton, lighters, syringes, dark glass bottles that probably contain strong acids or other corrosive chemicals.

On the wall above the desk hangs a narrow shelf.

Perched on that shelf is a droid head: no skin, just a bare metal skull wreathed in cables, hooked up to a power source. A long moment passes before I realize that I'm looking at the reflection of myself. Or, to put it more precisely, I'm gazing through the eyes, no, the optical sensors of that head.

'I thought I was dead,' I say. How? The illusion of speech is perfect: I can feel my tongue and lips moving, even though they no longer exist. A screechy robotic voice emanates from inside the head, but the slit serving as a mouth doesn't move.

The fat interrogator looks up from his console.

'When you started work at Minos Justice, Stanley, we digitized your mind,' he says in a contemptuous tone. 'Standard procedure. Updates took place automatically whenever you spent time in the ship's sleeping quarters. The scanning apparatus is hidden in the wall. We implanted a device in your brain... You know how these things work.'

'Did you power me up just now to interrogate me?' The realization that I'm nothing but a string of bytes emboldens me. 'I have nothing to hide. I didn't destroy the cargo – Hannah Sutton did. She's a terrorist working for Christian Freedom.'

The interrogator's jowly face shows no emotions, but I see something akin to pity in his dark eyes.

'This isn't an interrogation. It's punishment.' He pauses. 'For all the things you've done in the past, Stanley Kressler.'

So they know about my short-lived collaboration with Escape. I'm not surprised: after copying someone's mind, searching through their memories is child's play. But why punish me now? Why not earlier?

To cover my unease, I start laughing. The sound is tinny, like coins rattling inside a can.

'I'm dead,' I say. 'You can't hurt me anymore. Delete me if you want, I don't care.'

The fat interrogator's expression remains impassive. He turns off his console, speaks into a microphone and the room's door slides open. Two guards enter, leading a naked, handcuffed girl, her face hidden behind a black hood.

I freeze.

She has lost weight since I last saw her. Her body is covered in bruises and abrasions, but I recognize her instantly. She still has her tattoos.

The guards remove the handcuffs and force her down into the metal chair. Its clamps close around her arms, wrists, thighs and ankles.

I no longer have a nervous system. No glands, hormones or neurotransmitters. I'm an electronic construct, so in theory I should feel nothing. And yet my mind is screaming, writhing like a tortured animal. They must've equipped me with emotion-emulating software.

The guards pull the hood off. Rika's terrified eyes dart around the room. A sob escapes her throat.

'Look, Stanley,' says the interrogator. Rika freezes, and I realize that I'm unable to shut off the visual feed from the droid head's optical sensors. There are no eyelids to close and I can't turn away. 'Watch closely.'

Each second seems to stretch out into infinity as he pulls on protective gloves, takes a syringe and opens one of the bottles.

Waking Nydra

Samit Basu

India

I first met Samit in London years ago, when two of his novels were coming out, and we've kept in touch ever since. Samit's done everything, from novels to comics to directing his own feature film! As one of the most important voices of modern Indian SF, it was obvious I had to have a story from him – I just hoped he would write me something especially. Thankfully, he did just that, with this action-packed twist on a well-known fairy tale, set in space. I find it fascinating how writers can take the same seed and make wildly different stories out of them, and so I put 'Sleeping Beauties' and 'Waking Nydra' side by side. Dive in, and try not to get hurt! This story is original to this anthology.

As the spacecab draws nearer the station, its sensors awaken. Raja almost shouts in excitement as his screen shows, around the Paash-Balish, a three-layer sphere of scattered mine-drones, each little spiky death-trap highlighted with a thin red square on the display he'd recently spent three months of earnings on. With a flamboyant gesture, he swipes the display to cockpit hologram: a glowing line-drawing of the Paash-Balish – an elongated chess rook in the centre of a blinking 3D labyrinth – now drifts between Raja and his passenger

'I can plot out the best way to approach it; it'll show us dotted lines from here'—he points to where his spacecab, the *Toto*, a small green sphere in the projection, hovers at a safe distance—'to there.'

There, being the Paash-Balish's primary dock.

'No need, thanks,' says his passenger. 'I can take it from here. Your credits should be waiting for you when you return.'

Of course a fancy military type would have seen far more impressive displays than this, but Raja is disappointed at her lack of enthusiasm. He's worked so hard for this, and the space-whalers from last week hadn't appreciated his holograms either. But then, those guys hadn't had faces that could do lots of expressions. His current passenger, Platinum Anon Booking, has such refined features, such an air of suppressed emotion, that he'd hoped to both make and see an impression. Nothing.

'You never told me your name,' he says.

'You can call me Captain, if you like,' she says. 'But don't call me, I'll call you.'

Raja keeps his security cams off as the passenger puts on her spacegear in the main cabin. He's more tempted to peek than usual – she's so gorgeous, but she also has those eyes that tell you she knows what you're thinking, sometimes even before you think it. Some of his port friends have a side-businesses selling footage of passengers changing, but Raja isn't like that. He doesn't judge them, either: you sold what you could, even if it wasn't yours, to get by in Bajepara.

Her spacegear is incredible. As she jets out of his airlock, he zooms in as closely as he can with his outcams to see it in action – he's going to pretend to his friends later that she let him try it out, wink-wink. She's probably more heavily armed than his whole ship, state-of-the-art military tech, the kind they've been using to fight the Mokkai in multi-terrain combat situations. Underwater, underground, in space. She could probably analyze what he had for breakfast right through his hull if she wanted. Joke's on her, he hasn't had breakfast in weeks.

How many more badass space adventures is he going to be left out of?

He sends her a testing ping: her commlink is open.

'What?'

'I could come with you, if you like,' he offers. 'Or I could wait, I'm used to waiting.'

'This is a high-risk zone. Get out.'

She cuts off her commlink and speeds towards the Paash-Balish. Rude.

Waiting makes him drowsy; he checks his pockets – just two jagopills left. He checks his timer – a minute left for the render he's been waiting for. She'd read her mission doc off a wrist-screen a minute after launch, and his cockpit cams had caught enough to make him some cash, if the decryption/enhancement has worked – he isn't planning to sell it to the Mokkai, of course, but there are any number of freelance military-info enthusiasts passing through Bajepara any day of the week.

The outcams follow her flight towards the first layer of mines effortlessly. Really worth what he'd paid for them, and the vid of her deactivating the mines could be worth something as well.

A ping: the render is ready. He lets out a disappointed sigh as the mines disperse around her, forming a polite gap in the pattern to let her pass through – she has some kind of pulse cannon gentle enough to not trigger them. Or Coalition mine-drones are smart enough to let an ally pass. No wonder she didn't give a shit about his fancy display. The mines don't fall back in place after she passes – they drift outwards, and it's while he's checking their trajectory to make sure they don't come anywhere near the *Toto* that he sees the bodies.

Human, Coaler, soldiers. One drifts, headless, just inside the outer mine-grid. Another is actually draped around a mine, like he's hugging a large porcupine. Why hasn't the mine gone off? Why didn't she stop and check the bodies for clues?

*

Another alert: render's done. He swipes the render into his beloved hologram format, and his eyes widen.

The story he reads in the mission summary is the same one that the Captain read a few hours ago, that led her to find his bizlink and throw money at it until he put on his pants and raced to his ship. It tells him how the Paash-Balish had been minding its own business, doing whatever non-military research stations did in space, when an alien ship, species Mokkai, had dropped out of FTL nearby. Starfish Medium class. Big, bendy bastard of a ship, not one of the planet-breakers but definitely large enough to wrap itself around the Paash-Balish and squeeze it to death. Nothing like it has been seen in Raja's sector, deep inside Coaler space, before – they've only been spotted in the parts of the galaxy where the Coaler and the Mokkai are blowing up each other's planets while pretending that the peace treaty still holds.

The Mokkai ship blew up the Paash-Balish's mine defences, and by the time the station had launched another set, a raiding ship had already reached the research station. The Paash-Balish surrendered, opened its airlocks, the Mokkai boarded, and then the feed cut, and reports from the station stopped. Military personnel and mercenaries in the sector had been told to gather in Bajepara and wait for Coaler battle-cruisers to arrive and reclaim the station.

So Captain, on receiving these very clear instructions, had decided to go rogue instead, and fight the Mokkai ship solo with only a sexy spacecab driver by her side. A plan that has obviously failed, because there is no Mokkai starfish-ship still here to be fought, not that Raja's complaining. None of this is confusing to Raja either – he knows exactly what's going on, why the Mokkai wanted to enter this floating tower surrounded by thorns in the middle of nowhere, what was in it, and why the Captain is in such a hurry to get it back. Raja can feel himself sliding into the story, and all he feels is excitement.

He knows he'll feel terrified soon, but it's not often that he gets to feel like he's in the right place at the right time, and vaguely ahead of the game. These military types think they're so damn smart, but the name of their big secret mission would have made things perfectly clear to anyone with a pop-culture addiction and enough free time from, say, an employment crisis. They'd called it True Love's Kiss, which only happens to be the sixth most popular episode of the *Princess Nydra* re-run from ten years ago. They might as well have just called it *Sleeping Beauty*.

He hails Captain on the commlink but hers is still turned off. She's gone past the innermost mine-sphere now, heading towards the Paash-Balish. The outcam's having trouble finding focus at such a high degree of zoom, and it's because of its movement that he sees it. It's not a glitch.

Behind her, perfectly matching her movements, invisible to her sensors, hovers a Mokkai warrior in a shimmersuit.

*

There's no time to overthink things. Raja powers the *Toto*'s weapons up as he charges towards the Paash-Balish, whistling with appreciation at the precision of his own steering. The Captain doesn't respond – even if she's noticed, she'll just think he's heading home. He only has one missile left, but it's not just the expense – what if he sets off a chain reaction in the minefield?

He pops a jagopill. As the adrenaline hits, he sends a quick burst of low-intensity strafing fire across the outer drone-mines. He was hoping for one hit, he gets two. The explosions draw Captain's attention, and as she turns, the hunter behind her has no choice but to shoot. Three darts. She moves like a dream, but one hits her on the shoulder. Raja hurtles towards the battle at full power, but there's no need. Before the Mokkai can strike again, the Captain's shoulder-cannons blast it to shreds.

She pings his comms.

'Thanks for that.'

'You can't do this alone,' he says. 'I'm coming in.'

'Don't.'

'You're an epic space warrior, I get it. But I need to help you.'

'You need to get out of here before another Mokkai battleship shows up.'

'Is it true? Is it really the actual Nydra in there? I have to see her.'

A long pause.

'If the Mokkai don't show up, the Coalition will. They'll take out any witnesses without even blinking,' she says.

'Stars, it's really true! She's really in there! I'm coming in.'

'No!'

'I saved your life, Captain. You owe me. Please. Don't push me out of this.'

A few seconds pass as Raja and the *Toto* hurtle towards the mines, and then she groans and taps her wrist, a bigger pulse, and mines in every layer move aside to let him through. He punches the air in victory: finally. He's a part of the legend now.

It doesn't feel very legendary for a while, though. It takes way too long for Raja to tether the *Toto* to the Paash-Balish with an exterior clamp, and even longer for the Captain to open an airlock through a suit-led manual override. And once they're in, it's more nightmare than fable.

No power, no air, no grav – just corridor after corridor of floating bodies, human and Mokkai, lit up by twin roving beams from Captain's helmet. Raja is a big hero now, so makes sure he doesn't scream and vomit every time a particularly gross mass of multi-body-fluid globules and detached body parts attaches itself to the collection of things already sticking to his very unfashionable spacesuit. He's been avoiding having it cleaned, leaving the oil patches untouched – now he looks like a very meaningful art installation. To make things worse, his magboots are glitching, so he leaps around erratically behind Captain, trying not to make eye contact with an eyeball that refuses to float away from his visor.

He'd hoped, when he first saw the floating bodies, that they were all magically asleep, like the people in the sleeping princess' castle in the legend, who all nodded off and woke up with her. No such luck. The humans here are all very dead, and Captain's taking no chances with the Mokkai: each one they come across gets two plasma bolts through their thoraxes. Raja's never seen Mokkai up close before, but they're just as hideous in the flesh as they are on screen – some have five tubular limbs extending from their centre, others six. The ends of their limbs are the scariest bits, each one showing the Mokkai's evolve-function. Some have blades, others are covered with pebbly skin, or scales, or suckers. The worst one is extra evolved, an eerie approximation of a giant human hand. There are rumours, on Bajepara, of Mokkai who've started taking on human shape, flapping around on two limbs like balloon-men. He almost throws up at the thought, and Captain turns and looks at him with something approaching sympathy.

'You're slowing me down,' she says.

'Sorry. Could you just… talk to me a bit? I'll be fine, just need a little distraction.'

'This isn't the time.'

'Captain, if the princess is real, if she's here, then… the other stories about people waking up in the future… are they real too? Like, mummies and demons waking up after thousands of years, or people coming back to life, or trapped alive in ice or something.'

'We're in a warzone, surrounded by extremely dangerous alien hostiles. And this is the moment you pick to ask me if all legends come from true events.'

'Not like you'd hang out with me in your free time! It kind of looks like this is what you do every day? You probably don't get that this is my one-time ticket to a whole other life. Getting out of Bajepara.'

She turns, and he blinks as the light-beam hits his eyes. A Mokkai limb drifts up across her face. She bats it aside with a grunt.

'You do know we have sleeper ships out there with shitloads of cryonic-preserved settlers heading to new worlds, right? From well before the gates opened, from before FTL. Before our species accepted using tech we didn't understand. Before we learned about the artefacts that had been seeded in our worlds, all the way back to old Earth. Before the galaxy opened up to show humans how little we'd known all along.'

'Of course, everyone knows that.'

'You could get on a sleeper ship any time you liked, you know. There are recruiters everywhere, even in your port. Wake up a few thousand years later with a whole new life. There's no real reason to feel stuck in your village anymore.'

'Oh, you think I'm complaining about a problem that's just in my head? Like people from my planet aren't ambitious enough?'

'That's not what I said, and you know it. Why don't you get back in your cab and go home? No one wants you here.'

'Sleeper ships, my ass. Most of them are labour scams. And you can't just "get on one". It's not just a matter of effort.'

'This is not why I'm here.'

'Forget it. You wouldn't understand how it is, for people like me.'

'Okay. Are you leaving, then?'

'No.'

'Right. Then make yourself useful. I'm going to run ahead and get the power back on; here's what I need you to do.'

She pulls a Mokkai towards her, pokes around its thorax until she finds what could loosely be described as a flap, and sticks her arm into it.

'Hnnnngh,' Raja says.

'Yes. So, do this for each one of them. Really get in there. And if you find a storage container, a round box, about head-sized, pull it out and bring it to me in Central Control.'

'Can I do absolutely anything else?'

'No.'

'Can I have your gun?'

'Should have brought your own. Hang on.'

She turns on a glowstick, and he keeps his eyes away from the shadows it makes. She tosses it to him.

'Okay, listen. I'm going to turn on the air and grav before I turn on the lights. Try not to be under anything as you work. It's going to get very splashy when all of this drops.'

'Which way is up?'

'No idea.'

'Great. Anything else?'

'Yes. The Mokkai are alive.'

'What?'

'Yes. They're asleep. If they wake up, warn me on the comms. Actually... don't bother – I'm sure I'll find out.'

'Give me your gun!'

'No.'

Her suit beeps. She leaps down the corridor, turns on her jets, and hurtles away, scattering bodies in her wake.

'What the hell!' Raja screams.

'Keep it down, you idiot. Just take a gun from one of the soldiers floating near you. See you soon.'

He grabs a drifting rifle, puts together a theory from floating pieces. You've got your basic magic sleeping-princess, in your tower or castle, hidden from the galaxy. Your soldiers are probably asleep too, but armed and ready to fight if needed. Then your alien ravagers show up. They want to kiss the princess, like anyone else. They kill the guards, but... the power of the spell is strong, and they fall asleep? How does human magic work on Mokkai? Or... they wake her up, and she's all, *no, not kissing that.* Does she get to choose? In some of the shows, she does. And she's like, okay going back to sleep now, and the aliens all fall asleep as well. What if the princess died when the power shut down? No, then the Mokkai wouldn't be asleep.

What if Captain is the prince? What if she's come here to kiss Nydra awake? Two things. One, if she wakes her up, and there are any Mokkai left alive on the station, they wake up too. Two, what if she's lying about turning on the power? What if she just picks up the princess and leaves – *kiss you later, babe, somewhere with air* – while he keeps doing his homework?

He's grateful he had the jago. Last thing he wants now is to feel sleepy. He breathes in and out. There's no way he can keep up with Captain in the dark anyway. He shoots a Mokkai instead. It's pretty fun.

*

Five empty Mokkai corpse-sacs later, the power comes on. Light and air flood the corridor, and he takes off his helmet, revelling in the horrendous stench.

'Thanks,' he says into the comm.

'Did you find anything?' she asks.

'No. Are you in the control room? I'll find you.'

'No. Keep looking until you find the box. There's no time to waste.'

Obviously he doesn't know Captain yet, but he's pretty sure if there was actually an important thing to be found she would have been looking for it herself.

'Are the cams on? Can you see her? Is she okay?' he asks.

A long pause. 'Is who okay?'

'Stop jerking me around, Captain. Nydra!'

'I'm not sure what you think Nydra is.'

'Well, I'll tell you. The sleeping beauty. Cursed by an evil fairy and her magic needle or dagger or whatever to sleep for a hundred years, though if she's still asleep it's more like a few thousand years, maybe? That's why we're all here, right?'

'I don't know what you mean.'

'Sure. Okay, if the Mokkai had killed or taken her, you wouldn't be chatting with me. So she's here, and she's fine. I guess the real prince and his kiss of true love never showed up.'

'And you think you might be that prince?'

'Nice one. No, if you grow up in Bajepara, you know you're not the prince.'

He tries to put it together again. At the very least, Captain has disobeyed direct orders, crossed the labyrinth and entered the tower. She's running her fable quest, and has left a side character to deal with the sleeping side characters. None of the Princess Nydra stories ever talk about what happened, afterwards, to the side characters. He's not going to be one of those forgotten characters.

He sets off down the corridor, shooting the Mokkai he passes, but not wasting time fondling their sacs. She doesn't yell at him, so whatever it is she's watching on cam, it's not him. Sad. He clears his throat loudly.

'You know the Nydra stories I like? The spinoffs where there isn't a prince, and she's this badass who fights a dragon and shit, and then between episodes, she waits under a mountain, ready to rise up and lead the people when they need her.'

'What mountain?'

'Doesn't have to be a mountain, I guess. Any storage space, like a research station. I want to see her.'

'Only after you've killed all the Mokkai. That's an order.'

'Captain, I'm your friend who saved your life. Please don't wake up the princess until I get there.'

'This isn't a bloody fairy tale. Just do as I say.'

'Fine.'

He shoots another Mokkai. A Coaler soldier, sprawled nearby, holds an extremely compact, extremely fancy plasma blaster. Raja drops his rifle, and picks it up.

*

'Tell me more about our princess. Is she an alien? Like, is she secretly a Mokkai in human form, held prisoner by the government?'

'No.' He can hear beeps and alerts in her background audio, and the infinitely reassuring hum of lots and lots of big powerful machines, and the rumble of air – all the sounds you love to hear most after some time in the void. Which means she's taken her spacegear off, probably all dishevelled and sweaty. He can't wait to see her again.

'I think she could be an alien,' he says. 'Maybe she was stuck on Earth back in the old days, so put herself in freeze? Or this is just, you know, her natural thing, like one of those animals that just lives longer than us. It's a big galaxy, and we've met actual aliens, so you never know.'

'You never know.'

'Is she a time traveller?'

'How would I know?'

'Well, you obviously know everything about her. What I'm doing is asking you to tell me.'

'We're all time travellers, in a sense.'

'Be that way. Can you tell me how it works? The sleeping? It's basically magic, right? That's how she's lived so long. Magic means it's a technology from the future. Maybe they invented stuff in the future... or, you know in the present, but in secret societies—'

'I hope you're killing Mokkai as you give this speech.'

He fires the blaster into the air, and ducks as a panel in the ceiling shatters and showers sparks.

'I am,' he says. 'Anyway, someone built something in the future that allows people to have, say, fields that protect people and keep them going. Force fields. Suspended animation, stasis, whatever you call it. But then... oh, then they couldn't have cloned her.'

'What now? They cloned her?'

'Yeah, didn't you know? How could you not know? For centuries, the shows about her starred her actual clones. It was a whole thing.'

'And those clones were... sleeping?' I've never heard about this.'

'Well, they were awake for some of it, but... Hey, actually, when they were sleeping in the shows, were they actually sleeping or pretending? Never thought about it.'

'There's no need to start now.'

'Either way, they were totally normal people. As in, not magic alien time travellers. How can you not have seen the *Slumberalla* franchise? The shows were huge. And there was so much more – statues, music. I think at one point two of the clones even got into a fight, with fans getting involved on both sides?'

'Missed it.'

At the end of the corridor is a hallway. On a wall, finally, a layout map. A SecureHub is nearby, and as the door slides open, he lets out a startled yell. But it's not Captain, just her spacegear, on standby, ready to go on an autopilot killing spree.

'What is it?' she asks on comm.

'Nothing, relax.'

'Don't tell me to relax. Now, listen closely. I'm in Control Central, and I've sealed off most of the station, so there's no need for you to kill more Mokkai units. It was interesting watching you go to the SecHub instead of finishing the job, but I have real work to do now, and you can actually help, so I need you to drop whatever foolish scheme you're cooking up and follow my instructions. Clear?'

'Yes, Captain.'

'First, check if the mine-drones can be reactivated. Can you handle the interface?'

'There isn't a system in the galaxy that I can't—'

'Also, check and see what other defence capability this station has: railguns, missiles... If it's there, you need to find it, and prep it. If the Mokkai ship returns, I want you to punch it in the face. Yes?'

'Yes. And Captain?'

'What?'

'Thank you for the opportunity. I can't tell you—'

'Then don't. We're going to hold this station until the Coalition ships get here.'

'But what about her?'

'Who?'

'Nydra, who else? Aren't you going to rescue her?'

'What do you think we're doing?'

For once in his life, Raja has no answer. When Captain speaks again, she actually sounds amused.

'I don't know what sort of scenario you constructed in your head when you sneaked your extremely illegal look at my mission documents, but consider the possibility that your junkyard spacecab's decryption tech might not have the capability to decipher high-level military embeds.'

Raja checks to see if his pants have fallen off from sheer shame.

'I know you were expecting to be swept into a legend of some sort, but here's what you actually get to do. You get to help protect an extremely high-value military asset as a civilian volunteer. If we both survive, I get to tell the Coalition not to shoot you on sight, and you get a reward – money, before you ask. Now the stakes could get even higher. If you can actually be helpful, and especially if you can be quiet, you get to become a consultant to a highly placed galactic security official, and have an exciting career travelling around the sector having what you might call "space adventures". Are you going to follow my instructions from here on?'

But I want to see her, he wants to say.

'Yes, Captain,' he says instead.

*

The SecureHub interface is easy enough: she's left some controls open, but has locked him out of all functions except external defence – he can't even see camstreams from inside the ship. And there isn't a lot of external defence to handle. He reactivates the mine-spheres in a few minutes. The missile launchers and railgun need repairs and ammo restocking, and it looks like they haven't been used in years. The Paash-Balish wasn't built for war. There's a small shuttle in a hangar at one end of the station, but he has no access to it.

His first instinct is to set off for Control Central and offer Captain more unwanted help, but for once in his life, he keeps his ass in the seat it's supposed to be sitting on. She's offered him everything he's ever dreamed of. Now it's all his to lose.

He's done jobs for the gangs of Bajepara, and has listened closely to the feedback he's got during his exit interviews, usually conducted with him suspended upside down from high places, or during enthusiastic beatings, sometimes both. They all had a few pointers in common: Raja doesn't know his place. Problem with authority. Bad at taking instructions. Especially at waiting his turn. And he's not the kind of person who is rewarded for any of these traits. Each time, he'd sworn to never repeat his mistakes. He imagines a tractor beam, a void-construction adhesive, a battleship-class clamp attaching him to the SecureHub terminal seat. It works. A second passes. A minute. Ten, or a hundred, he can't tell. He watches, through the station's outcams, the stars and planets and the reassuring absence of any Starfish Medium.

And then a wave of exhaustion crashes into him, and his eyes close.

He wakes up in a panic, convinced it's at least a century later. He feels his eyes trying to close again, and he pops his last jagopill. Not here, not now. He won't fall asleep.

Two roads stretch out before him into the void: one is the right decision, the smart plan.

But the other is a fairy tale.

*

He runs out of the SecureHub, checks the map, and races towards Control Central. Captain stays silent. The doorway is open and he races in, half expecting Captain to shoot him.

There's no one in the room, just an impressive array of panels and screens. On one, he can see Captain, weapons slung across her back, looking sexy as all hell as she drags a human body towards a strongdoor. He watches as she pulls the man up and sticks his face in front of a scanner beam. A light above the strongdoor glows red. The room she's in is full of corpses, Mokkai and human. The floor is ghastly.

On another camscreen, he sees the sleeping beauty.

She lies on a standard cabin-bed in a standard chamber on the other side of the strongdoor, a crumpled sheet by her side. There's a lot of equipment around her, wires and tubes and scanners, but she's not connected to anything. Around the bed, three large Mokkais, fast asleep. The camfeed is crisp, he can see them all breathing in absolute sync with the princess.

He feels a bit let down by this woman just lying on a bed like it's nothing. He's seen stasis fields in dramas, but those are usually big tubes or boxes with floaty things and lights. Could this be a stasis field that is somehow linked to her skin, like a transparent bodysuit of some kind? He's never been able to afford the kind of implants that keep this sort of sciencestuff at easy recall.

Is this suspended animation? Cryosleep? Cryonic something? But she's breathing, not even slowly. She's not frozen.

He takes a closer look at Nydra, and gasps. He hesitates, several times, then paces up and down in front of the screen, his eyes darting between Captain dragging another body to the scanner and the woman awaiting her in the chamber behind the strongdoor.

He pings Captain.

'What is it? Ships?'

'No. Captain, I'm sorry, but I need to tell you something.'

'This better be good.'

'It's not her.'

'Huh?'

'The woman sleeping in the chamber. It's not Nydra.'

Another scan fails, and he watches Captain groan and toss the body aside.

'You couldn't help it, could you. You had to get into Control Central.'

'Yeah, I'm sorry, I was only trying to help—'

'What do you mean it's not her? Are you watching her on cam right now? And me as well?'

'Yeah, I—'

She gives him the historical finger.

'Captain, you can punish me all you want, but I had to tell you. They must have switched the woman. This isn't the woman they made copies of.'

'Let me guess – different colour?'

'Yes!'

To his surprise, she grins. She sets off to fetch another body.

'So someone made a lot of money pretending to clone her?' he says.

'By your theory, she could be the galaxy's richest person, from bank savings alone. She could have a company that owns her image. No simple agency, a super agency.'

Captain is... smiling! He whistles to himself at this sudden upgrade in their chemistry, but can't get the problem out of his head.

'I don't understand. There were seven generations of mothers and daughters, then digital actors. There are whole franchises.'

'Why in all of this are you most confused by the discovery that storytellers make things up? They could easily have cloned someone who looks like the old illustrations.'

'Yeah. I thought I should tell you.'

'I told you not to leave SecHub.'

'Yes, you did. But I had to warn you. We're a team.'

'The next time you disobey an order, I will shoot you.'

'Yes, Captain. Should I come join you? I can help with the bodies. Clear some up.'

She sighs. 'No. If you really want to help, try and find a way to unlock this door from Control Central.'

'Okay.'

He roams the control interface – she had been in a hurry, not that he could blame her. She'd forgotten to restart the broadcast feed to the sector's Coalition military command for starters: he gets that going. He admires the small but extra shiny escape shuttle in the far hangar. She'd remembered to instruct the maintenance drones to get it ready.

'Do people still try to kiss her and wake her up?' he asks.

'What?'

'I'm just asking. It's not like I'm going to. It's such an old story, that's all. And she's asleep, and right there. People must have been trying their luck.'

'They have, I've heard. Bad things happen when they try.'

'Bad things happened to the Mokkai, I'm guessing.'

He looks over Nydra's chamber again, to see if she has some kind of monstrous guardian. The biggest hit in the *Slumberalla* franchise, the first one he'd seen as a kid, had been a drama where the hero had flown through an asteroid belt, found the space crystal where Nydra and her attendants lay in cryopods. And the hero had been about to kiss her when Aunty Vigilante, a robot possessed by the wicked fairy, attacked. Then Nydra woke up on her own, defeated the robot, and kissed the unconscious hero. The fans had loved it, but unexpectedly loved Aunty Vigilante most of all – she'd been given her own spinoff series.

The joke on Bajepara was that you could tell the state of sector politics by who got to kiss Nydra in the latest version. In bad times, it would be a male prince. In better times, it would be whoever the most popular actor in the world was, wherever they were on the gender/sexuality/colour/homeworld matrix. In strange times, it would be someone from the latest alien species to join the Coalers. But it would never, ever be someone from Bajepara.

*

He can see on the screen that Captain is really tired. It's no surprise – she's been going non-stop like a robot.

'Can't we just leave her in there?' he asks. 'I thought we were defending the station until the troops arrive.'

'Do you think I'm doing this for fun? Are you comparing this with the Nydra shows?'

'No.'

'Do you know, in the oldest stories about her, kings and princes would come into her castle and rape her while she slept? She'd have children, and then the story would be about how her mother-in-law wanted to eat her and the children. That they're still making franchises out of it? It's sick. I don't watch them, and I never will.'

'I didn't know. Is that... did that happen to her?'

'How would I know?'

It might be the jago kicking in, but he's never felt more awake. His hand moves, as if independent of his brain, to shut off the station broadcast.

'Captain. Are you rescuing her from the government?'

'You ask too many questions.'

'Listen, I work for you. I... hey, I'm in. I don't care who you work for, and believe me, I'm no fan of the government. Bunch of creepy guys doing freaky shit to a sleeping woman in a space station? Let's save her. They must have been running tests on her all the way through. I mean – what if the government were the wicked witch all along, right?'

Captain looks straight into the cam; it's like she's talking to him through the screen.

'No such thing as fairies. The tests have only ever found a completely normal human, who slept through every invasive procedure they could think of. Except, when they stuck trackers and monitors inside her, they all died. They couldn't tag her, and they couldn't mod her. But they certainly tried.'

'Oh no. And did they find out exactly how old she is? And... if she'd had kids or... anything like that?'

'I don't have access to that sort of data, okay? And even if I did, I couldn't tell you.'

'Security clearance problems.'

'More like none-of-your-fucking-business problems.'

'Hey, I'm sorry! You brought it up.'

'And now I'm shutting it down.'

'Sure. Let me find that door release for you. When were you planning on telling me? Were you just going to leave me here for the Coalers to catch?'

'I don't think you will ever understand that none of this is about you. But sure, unlock the door, and I'll take you with me. With us.'

There's no way that escape shuttle can hold more than two people.

He sighs and turns the station security broadcast back on. A little more tinkering about, and the mine-drones are back offline.

He switches the screens to display internal stationcam security playback, and scrolls back to ten minutes before the station shut down. Ignoring the carnage playing on every other screen, he focuses on Nydra's chamber.

She's sleeping, with two guards in the room, guns pointed at the strongdoor. The door opens, they fire, they die in a volley of darts. Three Mokkai enter. They surround her, bending over her, limbs waving gently, like anemones. One reaches inside its thoracic sac and pulls out a spherical box, about head-sized. It pops the box open.

Inside is a metal tool that looks like a syringe, with a wheel-like base. The Mokkai grasps it with another limb, and sticks it in Nydra's neck.

She wakes up. There's a power surge, and the station's lights flicker.

She looks around calmly, not going into shock or anything. She's really so very beautiful, it makes his heart break a little.

She moves her hand, very slowly, to the needle in her neck. She grips the syringe and pulls it out slowly, wincing. She takes in the Mokkai surrounding her, looks around again, blinks, and smiles.

The Mokkai tower over her bed and bend forwards, a flower blooming in reverse.

On the playback screens, the lights go out.

*

'What did the Mokkai want with her?' he asks.

'The usual,' she says.

'We're on the same team now, remember? We have a rapport and everything.'

She lugs another dead soldier towards the strongdoor. 'I'm a bit busy.'

'I'll shift bodies for you. You look like you could use some rest. When did you last get some sleep?'

'I don't remember.'

'But you have a problem with me being in there with you, and you don't want or need my help?'

'Someone needs to watch out for big spaceships, remember?'

'As you say, Captain.'

'Why did the Mokkai want her? Who knows what they want? But every time someone wants to build a new empire, they come for her, to capture or to kill. A sleeping person is very useful as a hero, or a symbol. The less those people speak for themselves, the better for the priests. Cults based on worshipping or finding her became religions over centuries. Societies that captured her became empires. If your legend is asleep, they can't tell you that everything you heard about them was bullshit all along.'

'Like the one where she sleeps in a bed that belongs to the king with the biggest dick in the galaxy?'

'Yes.'

'There was a whole porn series about it.'

'A true fan.'

*

Three Coalition destroyer-class ships drop out of FTL. The Paash-Balish's outcams pivot and zoom. Raja struggles to keep his voice steady.

'What if it's actually something supernatural though. Like a god, or an angel?'

She shrugs 'So what?' The red light above the strongdoor lights up. She kicks the door, tosses yet another corpse. She's built up quite the stack.

A call comes in from the Coalition destroyer cluster, and he cancels it on impulse, wondering if there's a way he can text them discreetly. He's just babbling now – it's endgame.

'Let's say, if she was chosen by a god for a blessing, right, or an alien or time traveller or something, and she was just tired of everything, and people were bothering her, so she said let me get some rest, please, and the god was all, *okay sure, here you go*. Or the god was a trickster. She wanted immortality, say, and then she got it, but the catch was she would sleep through all of eternity. It was all a trap.'

'Where are you going with this?'

The Coalers call again. He cancels again.

'Or she was this genetically engineered superbeing, right? The good fairies – or corporations – pumped her full of all the super genes, but something went wrong and she fell into a coma. So maybe, they're holding her in a lab because her blood has superpowers? For drugs, or weapons, or more superhumans, or something. And then the aliens got into it too, and they—'

*

The light above the strongdoor turns green. She looks at it in disbelief, then at the face of the solider she's holding up. She drops him, and pushes the strongdoor open.

*

A Coalition destroyer launches two raiderbuses and supporting droneswarms.

'I need you on full alert now,' Captain says. 'Have you seen the shuttle in the hangar?'

'Yes?'

'Of course. Now, the moment I wake her, I need you to prep for launch, and then get to the hangar fast. Okay?'

He looks at the outcam footage, the Coaler shuttles have reached the mine-drones. He wonders whether he should turn them on again. There might just be room in the shuttle for three, if they all got very friendly...

*

'What if she's just super lazy?' he says.

She pauses at the door.

'What?'

'What if she's, like, so lazy she fell asleep, and her cells are too lazy to grow old and die? If I could just sleep and be left alone forever, I totally would.'

'You know, of all the theories I've ever heard, that is the best one. Get moving.'

*

He spends a second considering his options. Not the fairy tale. The plan doesn't feel smart either, but it's the one he might survive with. He opens all the airlocks and hangars on the Paash-Balish, grabs his plasma blaster and runs as fast as he can.

*

When he reaches Nydra's chamber, they're kissing – Nydra and Captain, wrapped around each other and crying. *Hot*, says one part of his brain. He points his blaster at them, and coughs. They ignore him.

The whole station shudders: the Coalers have landed.

They notice him, finally, and fall apart. He keeps his blaster trained on Captain, and gestures at her: she stands up. Nydra stays on the bed, still sobbing.

'What did you do, you little shit?' Captain snarls.

Raja turns to Nydra, who's wiping her face, eyeing him with vague curiosity.

'Sorry I missed your waking,' he says. 'Okay, Captain, I need your hands in the air. Step away from the bed.'

'You had to stick your nose in, didn't you?'

'No sudden moves. I'm a really good shot.'

She sighs, and shakes her head.

'What do you even want?'

'What's his name?' Nydra asks.

'I don't know. What's your name?'

He splutters, but if Captain's aim is to distract him, it doesn't work. His blaster doesn't waver.

'Raja.'

'My name is Talia,' Nydra says. 'It's good to meet you, Raja. Could you put down your gun and let us go, please?'

'I don't want to hurt you,' he says. 'I just have a few questions. Just... don't make me shoot you. The Coalers are on their way. I just want to make it out of this alive.'

Captain nods. 'Ask,' she says.

'Are you... the wicked fairy? The good fairy? The... I don't know, the stepmother? The robot guardian?'

'No.'

'Are you human?'

'Of course. Anything else?'

He hesitates.

'Were you ever going to let me join you?'

Captain smiles – such a rarity. She and Talia exchange glances.

'I guess we'll never know now, will we?'

He can hear the stomp of boots outside, and shouting. It's almost over.

There's a stinging pain in his neck. He swats at it, and his hand comes away holding the metal tool he'd seen earlier. He glares at Talia. He'd not even seen her throw it, so quick...

He fires his blaster. It doesn't work.

The power goes off. The air, the grav, the lights.

Outside, the stomping rhythm of marching boots dissolves into muffled thuds, and then silence.

Someone – Captain? – grabs his hand and snatches the tool. He reaches for her, clawing, but she shoves him away.

He's floating, flailing, his vision full of shimmering blue lights, sharpening as they move further away down an endless tunnel. He's never been more awake, though he can feel a great sleep rising within him, pulsing, reaching for him. He won't fall asleep.

'Listen closely,' Captain says. Talia clears her throat.

'Here is the secret of the spindle artefact, unsolved by human science, passed only from the woken to sleepers. I am now of the woken, as is she. The first blood-pairing put us and all around us to sleep, flesh or machine – though machines can be woken – and rendered us not immortal, but almost. The second blood-pairing, it is claimed, will wake us forever, unless we choose to embrace the artefact again. Only one may bear the curse, and the gift.'

'Welcome to the story, I guess,' Captain says. 'You get to be the princess now. I hope that makes you feel special.'

'It doesn't end here,' Raja says. 'I'm on jago, this won't work.'

'If someone wants you enough to wake you up – don't call us, we'll call you.'

'Not… possible,' he mumbles. 'My story,

I won't

fall

Between the Firmaments

Neon Yang

Singapore

One of the brightest stars of the new generation of international writers, Neon Yang has blazed out of Singapore to take the world by storm. So the question for me was simply, which story to take? I cast about widely before discovering this novella, to my great delight. *Between the Firmaments* was previously serialized online – what an opportunity, then, to publish it here in print. I met Neon some years back at some British convention, and again during a Singapore writers festival I was lucky enough to attend, and published their work in one of the earlier *Apex Book of World SF* anthologies. Theirs is a talent to envy, and I hope you enjoy this story as much as I did.

PART ONE

I noticed the boy hanging from the edge of the world, but not before he'd noticed me. The white devils know how long he'd had his gaze fixed my way by the time I looked up into the noonday sear. Crouched in the highest, freshest shoots of scaffold, he was a tantalising lanky blot disrupting the sun-bleached sky. He had a queer face, pale as that of the blasphemer-priests, and waterfall-hair, dark as the sky at blessed midnight. A boy, one whose name I did not yet know. A boy who watched me like a hound watches a roasting spit. He had such a build that fools might say, *ah, there's a woman*, but not me. Not me! Not Bariegh of the Jungle, who can scent the heart of a person no matter how many lies the blasphemers and their rules wrap around them. He was a boy, all right, and one among my kind: proud and glorious and beating with life.

I curled my lips to smell him better, and saw his wild smile as his eyes met mine. A moment of recognition leaped between us. Kinship! He knew what I was and I knew what he was. The red tip of a tongue traced the gibbous curve of his lips. My heart sang a note: joy, joy, *joy*. The rarest melody in these times of poison and want. From whence came this boy, striding so bold past the fences and wards of the blasphemers, to sit merry in the inchoate cartilage of their creations without a care? Ah, but my cousins Morough and Opyret had a thousand children, and those children had a thousand each still: godlings and little-spirits outnumbering stars in the sky, so many I could not possibly know them all. But I wanted to know *this* one. I wanted to watch his grinning moon-pale face twist and fill with colour. I wanted to ululate his name to the stars as I put my weight upon him. I wanted to pull his form into mine and—

'Whatchu looking at, big guy?'

A full person's weight landed on my scaffolding shoot and it yawed in obeisance, up and down and up and down. *Sisu!* The girl cackled as I shouted and snatched at the bamboo for balance, falling into an undignified crouch, my arse up to the sky. Her hand smacked sharply into its curve and her laugh tumbled through the muggy air.

Mischief lived in Sisu's bones; it was her birthright. Unknown even to her, Sisulo Mogdiawati was daughter of a daughter of a daughter of my half-sister Edukan the Trickster – a hemidemisemigod you might call it. Edukan the Monkey, Edukan the Quick and the Wise. How I missed her! In Sisu the thread of my sister's blood still ran thick and strong, the magic in her gut curled up deep and slumbering like the old dragons before the blasphemers came. It was safer there. Sisu had ridiculously good fortune – the boys called it 'Sisu-luck' – and the ability to charm the knickers off anybody she wanted; that was all the godliness she needed. I would not wake more, and I would fight anybody who tried.

I swiped at her in revenge and she danced out of reach, her feet cocksure across the wobbling bamboo. A fall would mean two thousand metres down to shattered, foaming earth and a fiery death. Her laugh split the air again. 'Don't be so grouchy, old man!'

Trouble came up, as it always did. This time it presented itself in the thickly wrapped form of Overseer Inette, her crimson robes flapping in the slipstream as she hovered over us. A frown cut through her face, a doughy thing the color of egg-pudding. 'What's happening here?'

Both Sisu and I straightened up. 'Nothing, ma'am. Just some banter,' I said, as Sisu struggled to keep her scowling in check.

The blasphemer-priest's frown grew deeper. 'Skiving on the job, are we?'

The punishment for skiving was fifty lashes. In blasphemer terms, that was a gentle rebuke. 'No, ma'am,' I said, looking appropriately chastened. I nudged Sisu to make sure she was doing the same.

Inette's scrutiny slid over me, and I lowered my gaze. To meet a blasphemer-priest's eyes is to disrespect them; to disrespect them is to defy them. I could feel the weight of her frown like hot iron on my neck. What did she see? No more than a tow-headed simpleton with a thick chest and slow words, I hoped. A dusty, unlettered bumpkin from the wild countryside of the land her people had torn apart, good for nothing except the animal strength in his muscles. A mule for pulling scaffolding into shape for her cultivation. A lowly, unremarkable cow.

Her narrow nostrils flared. 'Don't let me catch you again.'

Down she floated on her hover plate of sunmetal, the same rainbow-hued material which encircled the wrists and neck of the woodnymph who was chained to her. A thin creature, white with exhaustion, sucked of her vitality and the things that made her divine. A terrible sight for all to see. A dire warning! This would be my fate if I did not conceal my nature well enough from the blasphemers.

Sisu blew out her worry in a gust, then made a rude gesture at Inette's back. A lifetime of Sisu-luck made her bold; I feared that it would one day be her undoing.

I looked up at the light-smeared sky. Empty! Only heat and despair blazed in its whiteness. My beautiful, mysterious boy was long-gone.

After work Sisu and I went with the boys to the gamblers' quarter that was encysted in the bowels of the hanging city, fetid and tropical under strings of electric lights. In front of us the boys had burst into vulgar and off-key singing, a chummy knot of kinship pulled from the slurry of the workforce. They called themselves *the boys*, even though a good third of them were girls, and strapping Yadeh wasn't one or the other. Most of them had left childhood far behind, in dust and tears and old wounds, but what are false names but ways to feel better about ourselves in the world?

We had our eye on a round of rubeykans, a game of chance and cunning, guessing the value of randomly drawn tiles. Sisu sat down by the booth with her cheeky smile. She was usually banned from Gamblers' Row: two runs against Sisu-luck and dealers would dispatch her in a hail of pebbles, shouting *Witch! Cheat!* But the dealer today was some new kid, a genuine child, teenaged and gangly, rib-thin under his collared shirt. He was new here, poor lad! Come in with the morning's ship-dock, innocent fresh blood, too sky-lagged to smell danger. He sat cross-legged under the patchy awning, sweat decorating his brow, hope etched upon his dark, sharp features. The other dealers, bastards all, sat by to watch the unfolding slaughter. The poor child! To be fleeced so fast and so easily on his first day in a foreign land. But I would not save him. Better to fall to a group of laughing, silly boys, than to discover the hardness of the world's fists from more dangerous sources.

The game took shape in front of me. Sisu reached into the tin can to draw the tiles. How my mind wandered from the vicissitudes of reality! The apparition of that lanky boy had woken my hunger, and it prowled low and restless in my belly. My teeth longed to sink into sweet flesh, and my loins... ah! It was better not to linger on some things, lest they get out of hand.

For the thought of this strange new god lit my veins with anxiety. The blasphemers had declared all deities illegal, yet there he was, wandering the ribs of this city with his divinity uncloaked. Was it unadulterated bravery, or pure ignorance? Perhaps the land he came from was unaware of these cruelties. Perhaps. My knowledge of the world was incomplete, after all. I was merely a god, and what did I know of things that were outside my domain? Two hundred years ago the blasphemers had come to our world in their silver ships and their discs of sunmetal that sucked the power and vitality from anything divine, and we had all folded beneath their might like crumpling paper. None of us knew that such things could be possible. They tore through the earth and poisoned the waters, pulling every mineral and precious metal they could find from the mountains and the seas. They used my brethren to power their infernal devices, and the number of the divine dwindled from the thousands to a handful. Now the few of us left – locked in their cages or hiding in the wild – are a precious resource, irreplaceable as their alien sunmetal.

I decided my beautiful apparition was a madman. He was inviting Father Death to his doorstep: a painful, burning, drawn-out embrace. I would be a fool to follow him, and an equal fool if I tried to save him.

And then cruel Mother Fuata – o vanished Fate! – decided to taunt one of her sons, for what else flashed into sight but the cool curve of moon-pale arms? In his sleeveless tunic a glorious sliver of boy infiltrated the knot of onlookers: eyes bright, waterfall-hair loose, red lips parted and empty. The urge to fill them swept through me like a tidal wave.

He turned his pretty head and our eyes met once more. His smile matched mine for want. With that understanding fixed between us, he faded into the crowd, his beckoning fingertips the last thing to vanish into the thicket of elbows.

Desire was too strong for something as methodical as logic! I wanted him. I wanted to run after him. The danger only made it more tantalizing.

I told Sisu, in the midst of one of her triumphs, 'I'll be back late.'

She frowned and rolled her eyes, bursting with irritation at being disturbed. 'Whatever.'

A path to abandon had opened, in the glistering patch of moon-pale skin that surfaced between the jam of sweat-sharp bodies. I was off, chasing that trail to happiness.

*

The game of pursuit led us away from the crowd's clamour. The boy had the right idea, heading in gravity's direction: down, down, down. Clinging to the city's underbelly was a thick network of pipes and sewers, subsisting on the effluent of fifty thousand denizens. Too toxic for mortals, too dirty for the white robes of the blasphemers. *Perfect* for the two of us. One throaty rasp of grating and the boy had vanished into the depths of that metallic swamp. I rolled the metal shut behind me and leaped after him.

It was an exhaust vent he had chosen, thick with superheated gases, reverberating to our drumming feet. Wide gaps lay between the service lights, blue rings of bioluminescence that would have left humans as good as blind – stumbling infants in the murk. But these were the eyes of Bariegh the Hunter, Bariegh the All-Seeing, Bariegh who could spy a hare from across the ocean, Bariegh who snatched sparrows from the air on the most starless of nights! My clumsy mortal form hung compact from my pelt, shucked aside for freedom. Instead my true feet – clawed and striped and exultant! – struck the echoing metal in a symphony I had missed. *This* is how we did things in the ages lost, hunter and the hunted, the tease, the chase, the game. Oh, to feel so alive: how I had forgotten!

In front of me the boy's hindquarters danced, slender and lupine. He was quick, but I was quicker, and stronger. He was *mine*. The hunger in my belly powered my thick legs, my rippling backbone. My snout wrinkled eagerly as I closed in. Triumph awaited! Soon my delightful morsel would know what it meant to be pursued to the end by a god.

Light and echo vanished. The boy had led us to the place where the pipes met, where the city's toxic air funnelled out into the poisoned atmosphere. Into this yawning space, dark as the caves beneath the ocean, he had ducked, hoping to evade me. Fool! He leaped from the left, his body connecting hard and hot with the sinew of my shoulder. We rolled and he sprang to his feet. I roared as he came at me again, his fangs trying for the veins in my throat. So this was the game we were going to play. I embraced it with delight.

His jaws snagged around the thick fur. How spirited he was, even in his imprudence! I struck him with all the force in one paw, and he flew from me, crashing against unforgiving metal. His yelp sang through my nerves as I descended upon him, forcing him back down with my weight. I pressed both forefeet against his long white throat. He struggled, but his teeth could not reach me. I held firm. Beneath me his writhing subsided until his body went limp, his belly face-up in complete surrender.

We slipped back into human shape with my hands still latched solid around his throat. He looked up at me with half-lidded eyes, licking his tender lips. I wanted to start right there, take him as he lay pliant and unresisting under me. But not yet! For I had glimpsed, in the midst of our struggle, something gleaming under the layer of wolf-form he wore. A honey-glazed knob of truth I needed between my jaws and under my tongue. I leaned close, ghosting breath over his red mouth. 'Your true self. Where is it? Show it to me.'

He pulled his lips back, revealing teeth like limestone. 'My genuine form I conceal for a reason.'

The first touch of his voice trilled through my skin and bone. Slight and long as he was, I had not expected that depth, that vibrating seismic weight. The flesh all down my spine shivered. That voice, rolling in my ears! I wanted it to *whimper* things. I pressed my fingers deeper into his neck. 'Show me.'

'Are you prepared to bear the consequences?' he whispered.

What danger could he pose to me? The tilt of his chin was a challenge. I tightened my grip; he hissed softly as the air was choked out of him. 'Show me,' I crooned again.

A slanted smile took hold of his purpling lips. 'As you command,' he mouthed.

Magic fell away from him. The bones of his face thawed; his flesh deliquesced and reconstituted in pure elementals. Before my eyes he left the world of mortal physics. In his place bloomed the black fire in the hearts of planets and the crowns of stars. Wards peeled off in spirals. As the final conjuration dissolved, the thing on the ground was no longer hidden from the sight of gods.

In front of me, naked at last, was a celestial hound: burning and terrible, purified of all gender, red of eye and tooth and tongue. Galaxies blazed in the void of their pelt.

Exhaling, I let them go. They slipped away, circled, came back, ears pricked in puzzlement. I sat back: still human, still Bariegh the manual labourer. Bariegh the crestfallen. I folded my arms.

The hound slipped back into boy-form, his head tilted in curiosity, his dark eyes wide and questioning.

'Whose are you?' I asked. 'Kumaya's? Yuusen's? No, Yuusen has eagles, not hounds. Satriakat's? The Carrion Twins'?'

I could have sat for hours listing my fellow gods of the hunt from across the world, dead or alive or fates unknown. But the boy leaped forwards and put his hands over my wrists. 'Not any of them,' he said, warm of breath. Slightly trembling. 'No name you would know.'

'Are you from the blasphemers' planet, then? You *are* pale as they are.'

A shake of the head. Being deliberately coy.

Still, I pulled my arms away. Disappointment clotted cold and heavy in my bowels, but we gods have our honor codes. To lie with a slip of a spirit boy was one thing, but with a companion-beast claimed by another? No. Grudge-wars between nations have been fought for lesser. No amount of lust was worth *that*.

'Go,' I said. The boy had been right; I did not want to know his truth. But better that I did, than to unintentionally offend god-kin. Especially these days, where our numbers were so terribly few. How could I bear it if they were to dwindle further?

The boy swirled between forms, a tornado of alluring smoke. He came to rest one long, hungry lunge away from me, flickering like candle flame, from boy to canine to boy again. 'I am alone in this world,' he said slowly. 'She who called for me, calls me no longer.'

Oh. I looked over his quiescent form with new eyes, a fresh set of emotions spiking through my chest. As the blasphemers had devoured the world, their hungry, indiscriminate jaws had sundered untold numbers of the holy. The wake of their terrible passage was littered with lesser gods torn abruptly from purpose, made bereft: servants and companions and beasts of burden. My boy here was one among that pitiful number. How had he escaped them when the goddess who commanded him had not? Had she sent him away while she faced the blasphemers alone, her final act a sacrifice?

The boy's deep-hooded eyes held more secrets than a hive has bees. Such sadness seized him at that moment, the pathos that only we knew! He fluttered back into hound shape and came to my knee. The creature pressed their spectral head against my skin and I ruffled the starstuff behind their ear. 'You seek another to belong to,' I said.

They would be disappointed, then. I was Bariegh of the Jungle, and I had always hunted alone. I neither needed nor wanted a companion animal.

Did I?

I said, 'What now, o strange kin of mine?'

The hound leaped away, and padded towards the exit funnel. They turned to look at me: *are you coming?*

Now that our truths were in the open, there we could face each other like equals. I shed my mortal trappings like seasonfall, chunks of humanity dropping from me as I swelled to proper size. There I stood in the lowest bowels of the city in my full glory: Bariegh the Hunter, Bariegh the All-Eater, Bariegh with the gaze of fire and flesh bursting with all the life of the forests in the night. The world changed around me and I looked upon it with the eyes of a god. My roar shook the walls of the room, chorusing with his wild howl – we didn't care who could hear us, we could wake the whole firmament, we could shake every bone out of every blasphemer.

Together! – we leaped through the funnel, racing on air, carving our names in the sky over the burning land. Forwards and down! Their feet created stone out of air, building a transient bridge that materialized and dissolved as we ran. Far beneath us the ruined earth seethed red, churned like a storm-tossed sea, thick coils of lava writhing over each other. The blasphemers had woken the ancient dragons that slept within the soil, and their poison smoke billowed in thick canopies where people used to live. But even the sight of the home that was destroyed would not dampen my spirits now. My hound was leading me to someplace only they knew, and it *delighted* me. I drank in the anticipation like mead.

Half a mile out we came upon an abundance of stone floating in the turbulent air – a marvel by any standard – massive scales of rock piled up in jagged shapes, as though somebody had reached down and scooped up a chunk of old mountain before it all melted away. My hound leaped onto its igneous surfaces with all the grace afforded liquid fire. The stone changed as they touched it, and a skinny path shimmied a wide cavemouth, which swallowed their form whole. Purring, I followed.

Inside, flickering light painted gleaming stone in orange. Bright silks, crimson and yellow, slid into being and gathered themselves into a bed. My boy reconstituted his human form in exultant nudity, black hair spilling over the white curves of his back. So he too agreed that this was the form best suited to lovemaking: the dextrous hands, the swift tongues, the gaze over the eyes and mouth at the moment of climax. Nothing else compared! I straightened up in a reciprocal shape and he tucked a lip between his teeth.

As we circled each other I studied his geometry – the planes of his belly and the angle of his hips, the width of his shoulders, the circumference of his buttocks. My human form was taller than his, and I was broad as the fields, with the same inexhaustible strength. He made a choked noise as I threw him upon the silks and pinned his wrists above his head. Lips curved; I pushed them apart, my hungry tongue diving in. The boy yielded to me, opening himself with the rumble of avalanche, earthquake, fissure, chasm.

I fell upon him. I filled him like the ocean, salt-thickened and indomitable and heaving. And my boy, my sweet wisp of divinity, rose up to meet me, an underwater volcano issuing heat, fire and water in the place our hips met, geothermal energy. Oh, the beautiful lines his neck made as he arched and cried out! I pressed teeth into his shaking flesh again and again, feeling the passage of air as he gasped and he gasped and he gasped.

Ah, my beautiful morsel, my delight, my joy! Now you are mine; you are mine, you are mine, you are—

*

The aftermath found us boneless and yielding, skins coated in musky nectar, chests rising and falling like the tides. My riotous markings decorated his body, red and fecund. I delighted in the contrast of our shining limbs. How pink my boy could go in ecstasy! His doeish eyes were shut and pressed against the bank of my arm, the silk of his hair spilling everywhere. I stroked his quiescent head. 'I want to know your name.'

His lashes lifted and his lips parted. After a break of too many seconds he said, 'Sunyol.'

I huffed air. Did he think I was an idiot? 'That's not your real name.'

He blinked, woe pulling heavy at the corner of his lips, and regret filled me. His words were clipped and stiff: 'She gave me no name, and called me only Dog.' Then he turned from me, exposing the curve of his jaw, the magnolia shell of his ear.

'No name?' I tugged at him, yearning to look upon the softness of his features again. A boy with no name. *Sunyol.* I understood now. The word was a gift, one with value beyond measure. A thing to call him by. An offering. A leash.

'Sunyol,' I said, relishing the way my tongue wrapped around the word. I kissed his neck; he settled deep and solid into my arms. 'Sunyol.'

*

How swiftly the heart forgets the buoyancy of love! Just as swiftly as it forgets how easy drowning is. For weeks I soaked up the warmth of my newfound joy, drinking in Sunyol's companionship like a parched field after the first autumn rains. My laugh was deeper, my singing louder, my hugs bonecrushing. Sisu regarded me with raw disgust. 'Look at you,' she said, 'skipping around like a puppy! I would have stopped you that day if I knew you'd become so *insufferable...*' I grinned and tried to kiss her cheek; she kicked me in the thighs and scampered away.

Sunyol took a job as a serving-boy in the merchants' quarter. Of course he needed one: idleness meant death in this city! The blasphemers replaced maimed construction workers with fresh blood from the streets, and he was no builder-boy, sturdy and blunt-fingered; he would last less than a week under the whips of the overseers.

Worse still were the mines in the blood-red below. I'd shown Sunyol how to shield his holiness from human eyes, but the surface – clouded by sulphur and swimming in molten metal – would strip him of all pretense of mortality. In those places where humans withered and curled into shrunken husks in a matter of weeks, his divinity would shine through, protecting him from the ravages of the flesh. And how the blasphemers would devour him then! They would not swallow him whole, like a fish, no – they would gut him mouthful by mouthful, sucking miracles from his bones to fuel their engines of growth.

Thank the earth and the sky then, that I had an old friend who owned an eatery, a daughter of the old High Priestess of the Temple of Bariegh of the Jungle. *Her* I could entrust with Sunyol's safety. And he was popular with customers, too, with his grace, his guileless smile and his charm. They left him hefty tips and the occasional marriage proposal. Such a succulent prospect, my boy! He would tell me these things while I tied him down at night, and I would roar with laughter as I nibbled on his collarbones. Then I would twist my fingers in the skeins of his hair and pull ecstasy from him until he had no words left to speak.

The proprietor let Sunyol live in the attic of the eatery. The room I shared with Sisu in the pauper's quarters was the size of a coin-box, packed with tenants above and below and to the side, all of us stacked like dried fish. The only space I had for him was under my bed, with the spiders and the boxes of sacred old things, locked and hidden from view. Sisu hadn't been keen on having another tenant in the room either. 'You're not going to fuck him in *here*, are you? I don't need to see that shit!' It's not like they hated each other, but there was a friction between them that was, in my mind, unwarranted.

'She is a monkey,' Sunyol explained, 'and monkeys and I have had a long, unhappy history.'

It was true that dogs and monkeys were rarely the best of friends. Still I said, '*That* is the blood of my half-sister Edukan in her. That makes her family. Do you understand?'

Sunyol knew that, of course. 'If you wish to protect her, why do you keep her heritage from her? Does she not deserve to know? How else can she control her destiny?'

To this I responded in anger: 'You will not tell her! You will not interfere! Her divinity must *never* awaken.' Did he not see what the blasphemers did to godkind in this city, even the weakest ones? Sisu was all I had left of my half-sister, all I could find after the blasphemers took Edukan to lay the foundations of the hanging city. My defensiveness about her could not be measured by rational means.

We never spoke of it after. Sunyol let me keep my secrets, much as he kept his. I knew nothing of his past and his provenance, and he was eager to keep it that way. Every attempt to prise more information was met with teeth, and then silence.

But I am Bariegh the Hunter, and I could not exist like Sunyol did, wallowing in his ennui. I was a deity of movement, the one they used to pray to in removing obstacles. I needed the chase. I needed to be relentless. Frustration ate at me, but this consumption I kept carefully concealed. Sunyol's companionship was one of the few brightnesses left to me; I refused to spoil what we had! It became clear that sating my hunger for truth would require subterfuge.

Sunyol's accent and features were unfamiliar to me: I guessed he came from the lands further west than Atenlen. Of them I knew very little, save for a smattering of names and fables, none of which spoke of a hunt-goddess who rode with a hound. The firmament was wide and godkind numbered as many as the stars. If I had any hope of discovering Sunyol's origins, there was only one thing I could turn to: the truth-stone.

Ah, the truth-stone! Our greatest, most fiercely guarded secret. A relic of days past, we – what remained of godkind in the hanging city – had enshrined it in a narrow sliver between the abattoirs and the charnel houses: a liminal space, wrapped in the veil between this realm and the next. Oh, the things the blasphemers would do if they found out about it! Woven into the very fabric that made up the world, the truth-stone would answer any question you asked it… for a price.

That price was blood. In the olden days young men would have offered up their throats to their priestess lords, but those days were long gone. Lucky me, I had a workaround. Death often visited the construction sites to retrieve its bounty: the old, the weak, the sick, the unlucky. How superstitious the workers were! Squeamish around the dead, whispering that touching a fresh corpse would mark them as the next to be claimed. The construction boys would make warding signs and brave the resultant lashings from the overseers, who did not like to be reminded that killing gods alone did not kill belief. *Better to be beaten than to be dead!* the boys would say, their backs weeping red.

It was different for me. As a god of the hunt, the work of a psychopomp had been mine also, and Father Death I knew better than most. So somebody would die, and one of the overseers – Inette mostly – would shout 'You! Brick Wall! Take this one to the deadhouse,' and it would be a bound and broken bundle I hoisted over my back while the rest gave me a wide berth (except Sisu, whose luck everyone assumed would keep her from being cursed; sometimes she would try to trip me). The mortuary would get their dead, I would get my vial of blood, and I would slip into that brisket of sacred space and empty it still warm over the truth-stone.

But I could not just say, 'Truth-stone, tell me who Sunyol is.' The truth-stone did not work that way. Instead, the first time I said, 'Truth-stone, show me a map of all the lands west of Atenlen.'

And it did. I looked at the map and burned the shape of its borders and its names into my head.

The next time, I said, 'Truth-stone, tell me about the divinity of the hunt on the Isle of Jiefu.' And so it did.

It was not what I was looking for. The next time, I said, 'Truth-stone, tell me about the divinity of the hunt in the city of Kodan.' And so it did. So on, and so forth. I had mere gasps of minutes each time – disappearances too short for the overseers to catch wind of my doings.

Weeks passed. The truth-stone and I floundered in a wilderness that held no answers. We tore away at the map of the western world. Yet the unexplored territory shrank without turning up the treasure that I sought. With each elimination my doubts swelled like cancers within me: was Sunyol lying to me? Was I right to trust him? How was it possible I had found nothing? Quickly my mind would turn to conspiracy: what if he did come from the blasphemers' planet? What if he had been sent to find others like me?

I would entertain these heavy thoughts in the day, then tuck my apprehension behind a smile when we met at night. Sunyol would lie in my arms the same easy way he always did, and I would fool myself into thinking I'd betrayed no unease in our congress. But suspicion was like a poisoned blade slipped between us. The slightest pressure would result in death.

*

A month stumbled by. I had pared the map down to the last two locations: both islands so tiny and remote I wondered if they were even inhabited. What gods could there be where there were no people to give them names? And how could Sunyol have lived on one of these minuscule fillets of land?

I kneeled in front of the truth-stone, warm vial of blood cradled in hesitant fingers. 'Yanthal or Xamor?' I said aloud. I could not decide. I could not admit that I – Bariegh whom they called the Indomitable – was afraid. Afraid of what I would discover, or would *not*, when I asked my questions.

'The answers you seek will not be found here.'

I jumped. The soft voice had come from behind. My reflexes were not what they once were, and how lucky! For I would have struck at Sunyol on instinct and killed him before I knew what I was doing.

My hound stood within the rim of the sacred circle. My boy. My lover. The center of my universe, unasked for. The directional light layered deep shadows across his face. I stood, caution prickling across my arms and the back of my neck. 'Have you been following me?'

'I smelled this on you,' he said, pale fingers separating the blood-vial from my hands. 'You brought traces of it home.'

We stared at one another across the vast gulfs between us. My questions were a flame that crawled across my skin, but there was such a stillness and weight to Sunyol's manner that I dared not ask them.

Sunyol rolled the blood-vial between the bones of his fingers. His hooded eyelids seemed so heavy they could have been carved from stone. 'You will not find my place of origin on your map. I come from a place between the firmaments.'

'*Between* the firmaments?' My disbelieving gaze searched Sunyol's face and found nothing but seriousness, undiluted and unmovable. He could barely meet my eyes, but that was not from dishonesty – all I smelled in him was a musk-sharp desperation to be believed.

Between the firmaments. I had heard of such things, but whispered only in legend: of the great cosmic beasts that devoured one another with pitch-black mouths, of the bold one who pushed past the barriers of the world in pursuit of her love, never to return. I knew where the borders of the world lay, but its walls were opaque to me, impenetrable. I could no more break through them than a mortal human could sprout wings and fly.

I looked over Sunyol again. I contemplated his alluring human shape, recalled the wild god-form I ran with. Now I doubted any of it was real. '*What* are you?'

'A traveller,' he said. 'Someone not so different from you.'

I must have frowned – must have looked sceptical – because he added, 'My true form, when I showed it to you – that was real. You must believe me.'

I smelled the sincerity on him, and *yet*. How could I put faith in its veracity? If he could cross the uncrossable, he could do whatever he wanted. He could break the rules governing godkind, governing the *universe* even. How could I trust anything about him now? 'What use does the space between the worlds have for a goddess of the hunt? Or a hunting hound?'

Sunyol rubbed one foot against his heel. 'It is not just hunt-gods who have need of a hound. My mistress was a warrior goddess.'

'You were a war hound.' I could not overcome the incongruity: on one hand my pliant, gracile boy, who gently nestled his head against the pulse of my inner thighs at night; on the other the ferocious beasts that terrorized the bloodflood battlefields with tooth and claw. Those images refused to reconcile. It was impossible. 'Who was your mistress?'

'I cannot speak of her. To invoke her name is to summon her.'

'*Summon* her? You said that she was gone!'

'I said nothing of the sort. I said that she calls me no longer. That much is true. We—' Here he hesitated, sucking breath between tender lips. I'd never seen him this hesitant. 'We made a compact. She would call me no longer. And if I ever had need of her, I only had to summon her, and she would come.'

'She gave you your freedom. Why?'

He hesitated. 'Many… things happened. At the end of it all, this arrangement was what we agreed on.'

I looked afresh at his face, and saw how pain lived in it. No, no, lived wasn't the word I wanted. While pain might migrate transiently through our countenances, an occasional visitor, it was endemic to Sunyol's: part of the terrain of his visage, the bone-peaks and valley-lines of his face shaped by a primal sorrow.

'I was tired,' he said. 'I wandered for years. I was ready to dissolve from existence. And then I met you.'

'I am not one you should tie your future to,' I said. Not I with my sorry condition, doomed to hide from my oppressors until the end inevitably came for me.

A smile crossed his glorious face, both delicate and sad. 'But I want to.'

I knew it was a craven idea. I knew his thoughts and actions were warped by the great hollow that dwelled in his spirit, which

I too had felt on nights when the pain of what had befallen my world became too great. But action and consequence fall differently for us immortals. When the stretch of time is vast and ineffable in both directions, past and future, the only thing that matters is the present. And in the present, my foolish, foolish heart wanted to give in to his demands.

'You will be bound to me,' I repeated. Did he understand what that meant? 'The power in you will be leashed to mine for as long as we both live.'

'Yes,' he said, his voice husky.

'You will be tied to this world. Whatever freedom you have now will be lost.' I lifted his chin so I could see his eyes. 'Are you sure this is what you want?'

Sunyol blinked slowly. 'It is exactly what I want.'

I surged forth and pulled Sunyol into my arms with such force he dropped the vial he held. The glass smashed against the truth-stone, spilling blood across its hungry surface. But I had no questions left to ask. My lips, overcome, could manage no more than a kiss. So I gave Sunyol one, deeply and without reserve, sealing the two of us together.

I brought Sunyol back to the tinderbox that served as home. Sisu yowled—'We fucking talked about this, asshole'—but she headed out for the night anyway, kicking cans and grouching all the way down the corridor. Something had shifted in her face when she saw how Sunyol clutched at my hand. She was smart; she understood.

In that tiny room, barely tall enough to straighten up in, and so narrow even Sisu could touch both walls when she stretched on the floor like a cat, I bound him to my service. I purified its confines as though it were a hall of gold and marble, dabbing the dirty old timbers with sweet water and the oils of sacred trees, placing candles and coils of incense in corners crusted with dead insects. Sunyol's chin tilted to the heavens as I worked tribute out of him in pearlescent white, thick and bitter, the most precious kind of sap. I lapped it up, swallowed it so that in time it would become part of me, absorbed and knitted into flesh, threaded through the bone. Then I leaned over Sunyol's trembling form as I gathered what power was left to me, and worked my way to ecstasy.

The magic surrounding us wove through our bodies: electric, geometric, epileptic. I willed my cum to bind the boy before me, committed him to a tradition that had been extant since the dawn of time. Stronger than an oath, deeper than the sea, older than the mountains. Patterned with my seed across his cheeks and mouth Sunyol lay with his eyes shut, slowly breathing. Whoever he was before he came here, whoever it was that he had been bound to: he was mine now, utterly and wholly.

*

Afterwards, as Sunyol sat combing the tangles out of his hair, I dove into the dust-choked undercarriage of the bed and pulled out an old trunk, surface tessellated with runes of the temple dialect. The gold imprinted into the carvings was almost entirely worn away. The boy watched with curious eyes as I pushed a needle into the pad of a finger and drew out a bead of crimson.

The trunk's lid responded to the call of my blood. The air within the trunk was dozens of years old, sealed away when the blasphemers arrived. I carefully dug through its contents: vellum scrolls and jade figurines and jars of bone. Finally my fingers prised out what I sought – a box carved from ancient heartwood, redder than the blood I had pricked from myself.

Within it was a necklace made of teeth... no, *fangs*: the smallest barely thumb-length, and the largest stretching between the tip of my middle finger and the bottom of my palm. Yellowed with age but just as wicked as the day I pulled them out of my flesh.

'What is that?' Sunyol asked.

I held it up to the dim light. 'These are the teeth of Char-algor the Dreadful. He was the first thing I ever killed.'

'Your first kill?' Sunyol's question was more wonder than confusion.

I moved to fasten it around his neck. 'I'll tell you of that hunt later. There's a thousand-stanza epic they still sing in some quarters of the city.'

Sunyol stroked the long, thin blades of the necklace. The remains of my ancient foe rested against his narrow chest in a strikingly pleasing fashion. I rumbled in satisfaction.

He looked guilty. 'Bariegh, I cannot accept this gift. I do not deserve it.'

'Nonsense,' I said. I stilled his restless hands and kissed his brow. 'Am I not the best judge of who is worthy to wear it?'

He smiled, but his fingers trembled as they tightened around the yellow teeth. He fell asleep that night with his hands curled around my gift, as if afraid it might slip away when he wasn't looking.

There was such peace between us for that moment. But alas, it was to be all too brief.

PART TWO

Work had not been going well. The blasphemers were building a new merchants' wing to accommodate shoals of airships that came daily to nurse on the borders of the hanging city. Yes, the city was growing, and like all growing things it had an appetite. The rising columns and leaping eaves we shaped claimed limbs and lives alike; it wasn't days that we counted between accidents, but *hours*.

The woodnymph was at the center of our problems. She was not old by the way her people counted the years: still a sprightly spring thing! Or would have been, had the blasphemers not drained vitality out of her, just like they did with everything else. As workers, our jobs were entirely reliant on her work. All we did was erect wooden scaffolding in the right shapes for the overseers to seed bamboosteel upon. Then Inette would latch up the collars on the nymph's neck and wrists and pull the holiness from her, forcing bamboo to bloom and grow into solid foundations, the skeleton upon which the hanging city was built. Miracles came into being right before our eyes.

But the woodnymph's magic had started to stutter like a river at the end of a long, rainless summer. The resulting bamboosteel grew crooked and spindly, and splintered like bone under the slightest pressure. The whole construction site became a death trap. Heavy things fell upon unlucky skulls, and every now and then a shriek punctuated the air as some other worker plummeted to a long and bloody death. The nymph was near the end of her useful life, and everybody could see it, not just me: the boys quieted and averted their eyes when she slunk past us, pulled by Inette's gravity, limbs trembling like piles of leaves. Even Sisu's happy-go-lucky form flagged in her presence. So numerous were the wrongs visited upon our daily lives that we had ceased to take note of them. But this punctured the thickest shells of indifference and whispered to the conscience: *this is wrong!* Something *had* to be done. But what?

A project this sprawling and intricate should have been serviced by two godkind at least. But the blasphemers hadn't cracked open new lands to plunder in years, and their stock of captured godkind had dwindled. And while their Father-Emperor debated with his parliament in distant halls, arguing the merits and pitfalls of expanding the empire, Overseer Inette's pleas for more godkind to be assigned to the project fell upon cold walls of apathy. And the private citizens of the hanging city – the lawmakers, the merchants, the civilian blasphemers come to fatten their fortunes on our flesh – would not give up their godkind thralls without an Imperial writ.

So the woodnymph continued to toil alone. The strain of powering the whole site bleached life and colour from her; the skin sat white and haggard on her bones, almost as pale as the blasphemers'. Her work suffered. We all suffered.

Denied succour from her homeland, Overseer Inette was determined to solve the problem by her own hand. 'There *must* be more of these vermin we've missed,' she declared, her fingers white-knuckled around her staff of office. So the nightly raids began. Blasphemer-priests and their soldiers swept the narrow, lightless underbelly of the city where the poor and undocumented lived, combing through its intricate warrens hoping to pull undiscovered godkind from its corners, squirming like fat white grubs.

In our room I'd sit with Sunyol and Sisu to either side of me, holding on to them as a substitute for holding my breath, while outside the terrible symphony of boots and shouting carried on and on. My mind would reassure my shivering heart: *We pass the test. We appear perfectly ordinary. Just three mortals sharing a room, quiet and mundane as anyone else.* Sisu would yelp sometimes, 'That's my fucking shoulder, I have *bones* in there,' and prise my fingers off in irritation. But Sunyol would stay wordless and still, curled into my side, chest barely stirring. After all this time, I thought I would be better at deciphering the silent thoughts that marched through his mind. But he remained mysterious as the day I had first seen him, swaying in the heat of the worksite.

It had been four months since Sunyol moved in. He refused a bed of his own and slept at the foot of mine, curled up in a pile of rags and old clothing. I stopped asking him to join me after a few nights; he was stubborn in that way. We kept sex to three nights a week: quick and tender and quiet, conducted as humanly as possible. Sisu would shove off and come back later with bags of sweet yam soup as we sat cleaning the sweat from each other's bodies. The girl would grumble – would she be Sisu otherwise? – but her dissent had softened into theatrical exercise. She would rather lose her fingernails than admit it, but she'd become protective of this soft, strange creature I'd welcomed into our lives. On the streets she hissed and kicked at people who gave him trouble.

And Sunyol kept his promise to me: he never brought up Sisu's hidden divinity, in word or in deed. Sometimes I would catch him staring intently at her, perhaps out of curiosity, perhaps out of pity. Who knew? As long as he did not worry at the holiness resting within her. That was all I wanted.

This could have been bliss, you know, this beatific state of being: quiet evenings of my boy resting next to Sisu, him sewing and she reading the latest go-round thriller plucked out of the black market, her feet propped up on the bed. By some untold magic Sunyol had gotten me to settle down. We could have remained in this gentle valley of happiness for an eternity, untouched by the prying white fingers of the blasphemers. But of course such things could not last. And valleys are the first to be flooded when the riverbanks break.

*

The big accident was the beginning of the end, although none of us knew it at that time. A week before, the blasphemers had built a walkway between two pavilions on the sixteenth floor of the new wing, and one set of crew – twenty workers, including the boys, Sisu and me – were on the fifteenth floor below it, lashing in new scaffolding for balconies. The master plan for the new wing, and the order in which it would be built, was a matter entirely opaque to us. The overseers would point and assign – *six of you, scaffold here, today* – and we would leap to it. Who would dare question? Who would dawdle long enough to consider how the new thing fit with the rest of it, and risk the razor kiss of the overseer's whip? When we were pointed to our next task, sweat pouring from sunbaked skins, we simply forgot the work we had just completed. We had burdens enough to carry!

Yes, ever so often curiosity snared my mind and I would find a support strut to lean against during breaks, to survey the whole site like a hunter would. And then I'd catch Sisu's eye, or Inette would pass within sight, the woodnymph in tow, and I'd think better of it.

So it was another ordinary day, us just trying to get to sundown in one piece. There I was – Brick Wall, the muscle – holding up the support poles while one of our boys – little Kurena – scrambled around lashing it to the others with twine with her quick fingers. I wasn't the first to hear the noise – Kurena's head snapped up before mine – but I was the quickest to know what it meant. That groan. The walkway above about to collapse.

'Run,' I said to Kurena, but she was already in flight. Terror hones our senses of self-preservation.

The walkway splintered. In the blur of the body's adrenaline, I saw Sisu standing under it, frowning up as the broken halves careened towards her. I moved. Holiness rushed through me, turning mortal flesh to rock that met the falling timber with a terrible shudder. I stood wedged under the mass of shattered bamboosteel, impervious and unbowed. I was Bodeya, the woman who pinned the stars to the sky; I was Nitaya, the tree that separates the firmaments from the heavens. The other half of the walkway spun like a toothpick as it plummeted to the roiling earth. The air boiled with screams.

Sisu stared at me through clouds of flocking dust. Her wide eyes had the glassy sheen of a prey animal. *Snap out of it, child!* 'Sisu!'

She blinked. I gritted my teeth, heart straining under the knowledge of the overseers converging upon us like carrion birds. I could not stay godkind for much longer. 'Sisu, if you don't move...' I snarled.

That got her attention. But no sassy retort came hurtling back at me. A troubling, atypical line sat between Sisu's brows. She scampered to the safety of the main pavilion, supported by foundations laid many moons ago, long before the genesis of our current troubles.

Gathering one last spurt of divinity I heaved, and sent my burden tumbling after its doomed, sundered sibling. The end of the walkway barely missed a overseer's head as he sailed towards me on his hoverplate. It was Arquois, one of the lesser overseers, skin spattered with sun-damage. His teeth showed in his grimace. Before him was a gasping, sweating worker, whom he had just witnessed throwing a spur of masonry that would have crushed ten men. 'I know you,' he said. 'You're the one Inette calls "Brick Wall". You're a strong one, aren't you?'

I bowed my head and said nothing. It was always better to say nothing.

A stop-work was called for the day. They had us corralled in a corner while Inette swept back and forth, profanities flowing as fast and loose as her barked orders. Lesser overseers swarmed the accident site, assessing the damage, calculating the delays. What did Inette care that I'd saved the lives of the seven in the falling walkway's shadow? She would rather a hundred workers died than endure another day of setbacks. Her footsteps rapped sharp on bamboosteel, lips folded into a razor-thin valley.

Sisu sat by my side, strangely cool and still, gazing out at the unforgiving sky. Trapped still, it seemed, in that moment of walkway-fall, watching death come at her in an endless loop. I touched her lightly on the hand that was hooked around elbow and knee. 'Are you all right?'

She barely blinked. 'It wasn't going to hit me.'

'It didn't hit you. I made sure of that.'

'No, I meant it *wasn't* going to hit me. The bamboo split so that it would miss me on either side. I saw it.'

'That was luck.'

'Some kind of luck.' Sisu frowned. She'd always taken the preponderance of Sisu-luck with equanimity, but she hadn't yet witnessed anything this bald, this blatant. The suspicions that thundered through her... I could only imagine.

She turned her questioning my way. 'That blow should have killed you.'

'It didn't.'

'It would have killed *anyone*.'

I put on a smile; I could feel how thin and watery it was. 'I'm stronger than I look.'

Sisu's returning stare was lengthy and unreadable. Then she said, 'Suppose you are, old man.' She didn't smile back.

Inette swept by again, consumed by constant motion. In her wake the woodnymph was a piteous symphony of clanking and wheezing, barely held up by the chain around her. When Inette stopped to shout at Overseer Arquois, the woodnymph collapsed like a whipped dog and lay completely still.

My eyes were fixed on her broken form; I could not help it. And there lay my mistake, for in that moment the woodnymph's eyes flickered open and looked right at me. My gut quailed. She knew – she knew! She knew who I was, recognized old Bariegh even through the muck-coated human shell. Her eyes bored into mine, pleading and desperate. *Please. Help me. Free me from this.*

I knew what it was she wanted.

The moment ended. Satisfied with her scolding, Inette strode onwards, jerking the nymph along by the neck. I exhaled. To turn away a supplicant was the basest crime a god could commit. But these were extraordinary times. Could I truly be called a god, if there was—

Inette's voice rang out over our heads, angry and incredulous. 'Who are you?'

Like a thousand-headed serpent the amassed workers turned to look. My heart stopped. Mere feet from us stood a brightly glimmering figure: long-limbed, bold and graceful, hair alive in the wind. Worry creased Sunyol's delicate features. 'I heard there was an accident.'

'Who are you?' Inette repeated. 'What are you doing here?' She swept towards him like a stormcloud, and my hands balled into fists.

'I have loved ones here,' he said, his gaze canvassing the trembling herd of construction workers. His spine straightened as he caught sight of me, and his expression softened. Shock lacerated me. I had not expected to see Sunyol here. He had showed no interest whatsoever in the affairs of the world. They were little more to him than birdsong in the forest. Why had he come here, and why now?

I fed my surge of adrenaline with easy, accessible rage. This foolish, crazy boy – was he *trying* to get himself killed? An avalanche of heated words piled up in my chest. I clamped them down for later. Later! The next time we were alone, I swore I would burn this boy's ears with my consternation.

'This is a restricted area,' Inette said, voice low in her throat. 'How did you get in here?'

Sunyol shrugged, a simple movement. 'Your guards have hungry pockets.'

Beside me Sisu whistled quietly. 'Man, that boy's got some balls on him.' If she encouraged him in this, I swear by the earth and the sky, I would—

Inette leaned close enough to smell Sunyol. He looked unfazed. I, on the other hand, trembled enough for the both of us. Now, of all times, when Inette's mood was hot as molten steel!

'I know what you are,' Inette hissed.

I tensed, ready to leap to my feet. Inette's head was separated from her shoulders by a mere neck. I would rip it in half if she made the slightest move—

Sunyol merely blinked. Was he not afraid? Did he not care?

Her teeth showed. 'You're that boy. Aren't you? The noodle-stall helper. I've heard of you.'

Sunyol dipped his head, dipped his lashes. A tiny, elegant movement.

'Your reputation precedes you. I must say, you don't disappoint.' She grabbed his chin with rough hands. Her fingers parted his lips, exposing his teeth and gums like she was inspecting a beast of burden. With a huff of air – of satisfaction? Amusement? – she pulled him close, by the collar, and kissed him. Sunyol stiffened. I growled, a chest-noise, and Sisu's hand closed over mine.

Inette broke the kiss, shoving him so hard he stumbled backwards. Her laugh cracked through the air. 'Mediocre!'

Sunyol wiped his lips; blood smeared the back of his hand where she had bitten him.

'Leave here,' Inette said, 'or it'll be more than a kiss that I take from you.'

Leave. I glared at Sunyol and willed him to take my hint. Losing the world I had known was bad enough. I could not bear to lose this boy too.

But Sunyol remained where he was. His attention had been caught by the wretched figure crumpled at his feet. The longer he stared at the woodnymph's barely-conscious form, the deeper his frown became. *Now's not the time. Just leave, you stupid—*

'Not leaving, then?' Inette purred.

'My apologies,' Sunyol murmured, his concentration broken. But the disturbance remained on his face. As he turned to leave our eyes met, and the depth of the sorrow in them could drown cities. It shook me, and like lava, more rage rose through the cracks left behind. He was going to hear from me, oh yes, he was.

*

'What were you doing? Are you trying to get yourself killed, or worse?'

'I had to see the place for myself.'

The room was too small for us three, and the clamor of all our emotions. I stood close enough to Sunyol to feel the tremor of his breaths. On the bed Sisu sat quiet, her expression troubled, a torrent of unease visibly churning under the surface. I should have been worrying about her and the divinity that was starting to stretch its limbs within, stirred from unquiet slumber.

But my target was the boy before me, his aloofness a lightning rod for my ire. 'There was nothing to see! You have cared nothing for our plight before. This day was no different!'

'I hadn't realized how dire your situation was.'

My nostrils flared. How dare he admit to such ignorance, after having lived with us for so long? 'And taunting Inette, was that supposed to improve our lot?'

A spark of anger flashed through him, an enervation so rarely seen! 'It's rich of you to say that, when you witness such injustice daily, yet do nothing.'

I seized him by the tunic and pulled him towards me. 'Do you think we haven't tried fighting them?'

He went still but for his breathing, watching me through half-lidded eyes. There was so much I did not know about my boy. I could navigate the map of his body without a guide, but his mind – his spirit, his soul – was still unknown territory to me. A place where I was clearly still unwelcome.

'You two done fighting?' Sisu asked.

I looked at her. She looked tired, but also angry. The day's events had changed her more than I thought. I saw in her expression a new strain of cunning, as though she had realized a new truth about me and was combing through the fields of her memory for evidence. It was a worry, all right.

'I'm sorry,' Sunyol whispered.

I turned back to him. The energy I'd fleetingly glimpsed was gone, the rage and arrogance melted out of him. All that remained was the same old, tired sorrow. 'I spoke out of turn. I greatly admire what you have done, Bariegh.'

I allowed him to keep speaking, which was perhaps a mistake. He said, 'For years I wandered aimlessly, flitting from one world to the next. Then I saw you from where I stood on the peaks of your world. And you were bold and strong and proud, despite the ravages you had suffered. I saw in you a survivor. So I decided to stay.'

Such flattery should have filled me with ecstasy! But I could only think of Sisu in alarm, who had sat and listened to all this god-talk. I shot her a look, and her expression was clouded. But not confused – if anything, there was a hint of knowing in the way she narrowed her eyes.

I stepped away from Sunyol. 'We should all rest,' I said.

*

Sleep did not come for me that night. Prone on the hard surface of my bed I listened to the dark as the hours spun from one to the next. Above me, Sisu's breaths slowed into deep rest; at my feet, Sunyol was a conspicuous lack of sound and motion. Yet the thing that snagged my thoughts with its corroded hooks was not Sunyol's ill-judged anger, nor was it Sisu's burgeoning suspicions.

No. What filled the hollows of my mind as I lay with my eyes closed, was the woodnymph's face. Dirty and hopeless and pleading. Seeking the relief that only a god could bestow.

Bariegh, what will you do?

I sat up in the gloom, slow as I could, and put my bare feet upon the uneven floor. Dirt ground into my soles and heels as I stood carefully, my breath soft and slow.

Sisu remained asleep on the upper bunk. In his corner, Sunyol did not stir. Was he slumbering as well? Or just pretending? I stared at the pale shape of him in the murk and willed him to move. *Give me a hint, my beloved, tell me one way or the other.* But nothing happened. Did he no longer care what I did? Or did he ever?

What uncharitable thoughts! How had we come to this? A wave of sorrow passed through me, but I could not allow it to linger. I had work to do.

I left the room as quietly as I could, and crept on padded feet towards the end of the corridor. Wrapped in unquiet slumber, the city's poor packed the dense honeycomb of the paupers' quarter with desperate dreams. As I unfolded into divinity their unconscious prayers struck like hail, cold and heavy and fervent. I sucked those distraught entreaties into my bones and grew strong. Or stronger, at any rate: here I was, lapping at the barest dregs of unconscious faith like they were honey and mead! It was the only way to get power now that the strength of the earth and the sky had been denied to me.

I had to move fast. Every minute spent like this was a minute spent risking discovery. The borders of every city quarter crawled with the blasphemers' guards, sharp-eyed and lusty for blood: *starving* for trouble to sink their teeth into. At least the night's raids were happening in the units much lower down. Commotion boiled floors below me, shouts of dismay combusting against angry, barking orders. A distraction for the guards, so they might not notice the brief passage of a god among them. Thank Mother and Father for the smallest mercies! I slipped into my swiftest form – the spotted shadow-cat – and raced along unlit alleys and abandoned passageways, hoping the dark would conceal me as needed.

And it did, for I escaped the paupers' quarters unscathed. Now I emerged from the lightless bowels of the city into areas open to the air and sun and stars, where the blasphemers allowed things like *windows* and *high ceilings* to exist. In racing-cat form I sprang upwards, climbing the crenulated sides of the city, layer by modular layer. The city grew cleaner and its streets grew wider as I progressed. My target was the Axis of Tranquility, the pristine cluster of white spires centered in the highest part of the city, where you could stand in an open courtyard under the sun and have no shadow fall upon you. It was where the overseers let loose the sprawl of their lives, the sanctuary where they bickered and relaxed and played and slept. It was where Inette kept the woodnymph chained at night, never more than a stone's throw away from her person.

Luck was not my forte as it was Sisu's. Stealth, however, *was* the hunter's domain. I waited for the right moment, crouched by the orbit of the guards around the Axis, a porous line. I slipped through when one of them had their head turned, and then I was running ghost-footed and gale-swift through the shining interior of the Axis, gleaming even in the cloud-choked moonlight. Now my mission began in earnest.

The interior of the Axis was a landscape foreign to me: as if a lowly construction worker such as I would ever be allowed admittance here! It was my god-senses, alive and knife-honed, that I had to rely on. Surrounded by the bleached bones of what the blasphemers had built, the woodnymph – fellow godkind – was a brilliant ember in the shape of the world. I ran in her direction. There were no places to hide in the Axis, where the soothing comfort of the dark and the gentle eaves of shadows had been banished. Speed was my only recourse.

Inette's mansion lounged behind walls of white, laden with fishponds and the boughs of trees torn from the land below. I cleared the boundary wall in one leap and found myself facing an extravagant, angular building. Its form was alien and unforgiving, as if a parcel of Inette's homeland had been scooped up and grafted onto this floating city. All its windows were dark, and a guard stood stone-faced at every door. I counted six of them, fully liveried, bearing humming electric spears.

There were no secret ways here, no quiet windows where I could slip through unnoticed. It couldn't be helped: they would have to die.

I started from the left. One by one they fell in quick succession. My shadow-cat form was swift and silent: by the time the guard noticed the heat and smell of me, my teeth would already be closed around their spine. I broke their necks and quickly, quietly set their corpses upon the ground. There was no joy in these deaths, no poetry in this exchange from one life to another, no satisfaction in the triumph of survival. I padded silently into the overseer's house with the smell of blood lingering around my mouth.

Within the halls of Inette's house, I finally found comfort in a thick and all-encompassing darkness. The stone floors were cool beneath my feet as I slunk downwards to the dungeon where the woodnymph was locked. There were two guards; they both met swift and perfunctory deaths. No sooner had the blood of the second one wet the floor than the woodnymph stood in her cage. 'You came,' she said. Her voice was barely louder than the wind.

I straightened up into mortal form. 'I heard you,' I told her. 'I felt your pain.'

Her thin, crooked fingers clasped the hard iron of the cage bars. 'You'll do it, then?'

'You are not one of my people,' I told her. This was no weasel-tongued protest: there were protocols for what I had come to do.

'I am not,' the woodnymph said. 'I am a spirit of the forest, and my tribe is answerable to Opyret, Ripener of Fruits.' She rubbed her arms, and skin detached from it in flakes. 'But Opyret is *gone*. They have not heard my prayers since four turnings of the seasons ago.'

My half-cousin Opyret, stubborn as the mountains, had chosen to remain on the ruined surface, refusing to leave the land which they had tended to for so long. Their fate was unknown to me: did they die? Were they captured by the blasphemers? Neither of those ends were something I could bear to think about.

'So,' I said, 'having been abandoned by your lord and master, you now turn to me.'

'Bariegh of the Jungle,' she whispered, 'will you release my spirit from this realm, and to the next?'

'I will. And in exchange, the power you hold in this realm will pass to me.'

'Take it,' she whispered, her voice coarse as sand. 'These days it's no more than a curse.'

The act took no time at all. I slid my hand through the bars and placed it on her feverish brow; one draw of the breath later, she crumpled to the ground, empty and decaying. The last residue of her power surged through me – hot, running filaments, searing my veins, setting my heart aflame. Shivers of rapture pulsed through my flesh: to feel almost whole again! Almost! Weak as she was, the woodnymph was the first godkind I had taken since the blasphemers came to our shores. This was more power than I had consumed in years. For a moment – brief, glorious, excruciating – I had a glimpse of who I used to be. What I used to have.

Movement behind me. I turned, teeth bared, flush with new strength. In my mind it was Inette, and I was coiled to tear her throat from her neck, consequences be damned! If I was to have blood on my hands this night, let some of it be hers!

Sunyol stood at the head of the stairs, staring at the corpses scattered around me.

I said his name. He looked up and his wide, unsettled eyes met mine.

'It was what she wanted,' I said.

Sunyol picked his way down the stairs, his feet making a cautious arc over the corpses of the guards. He squatted by the cage, fixated upon the dead woodnymph, deep furrows bisecting his pale brow. Could he not understand what was happening? He'd lived in the world for *months* now. He knew the conditions we were shackled with. He—

Sunyol's slender hand reached between the bars. With gentle fingers he brushed away the stringy mats that had fallen over the nymph's face. 'You killed her,' he said, the words coming out in a soft, blank murmur.

I lost my grip on patience and temper alike. 'What else could I have done? She needed help!'

'You could have freed her.'

'She didn't want to be freed. She *asked* for this. Do you understand?'

I could see from his face that he did not. 'Do you realize what will happen now?' I asked.

He remained unmoved, but I continued anyway. 'Tomorrow the overseers will realize that their source of power is gone. They will intensify the raids. Day and night they will comb the city until they find someone to take her place. All the hidden godkind in this city – like me, like Sisu – will be in danger.'

I pointed down at the nymph. 'She knew this. Why do you think she never once tried to escape? This is the unspoken compact of godkind. She was captured, and for *all* our sakes she bore this burden, until she couldn't anymore. There are so few of us left, we have to do what we can to protect one another.' I allowed anger to erupt in my voice. 'What I did tonight was a mercy. Do you think I would have done this if she had not *begged* me for release?'

Sunyol slowly stood. Was he listening? Did he understand? I said, 'You said you admired my survival in this world? This is what it costs to survive here.' If only I could shake comprehension into his thick head! 'How could you live among us and still be shocked?'

He raised his head to look at me. 'Dissolve the bond between us.'

I blinked as my heart shuddered to a stop. 'What?'

'The compact that binds me to you. Dissolve it. I will remain with you no longer.'

'Sunyol—'

'It was a mistake for me to have wanted it. Foolishness on my part. Hubris. I want you to unmake it.'

His face was a cipher of emotions: lips thinned, brows compressed, eyes flat and neutral. 'Do you—'

'I understand perfectly well. Please, Bariegh. Let me go.'

I caught his chin in my hand. His body stiffened and his eyes fell shut as I tilted his face upwards, pressing my fingers into the bones of his cheek. Where was the bold creature I had glimpsed all those months ago, perched on the edge of the world? I saw no trace of him, no matter how much I audited the lines of the face before me. My bones chilled as I studied his silent form. This forsaken world had drained him the same way the blasphemers had drained the woodnymph.

I did not understand him. I never understood him. The bond I thought we had was perhaps nothing more than an illusion.

'Very well,' I said. The words barely made it out of my mouth.

Sunyol's eyes flew open: surprise, disbelief, and a needle-jab of hurt. He opened his mouth to speak, but I moved before the first word could so much as assemble on his tongue. The magic that bound us fell apart, dissolving in a messy flail. What I had pulled together with so much effort came undone between one beat of the heart and the next.

There. It was over. It was too late for anything except regret.

I let go of Sunyol's chin and he staggered backwards: partly from losing his balance, partly from recoil. Had he expected me to fight him? I would not do that. I would never keep him against his will.

'Bariegh,' he said. His eyes and mouth were soft and sad.

'Go in peace,' I said. 'Linger here no longer.'

He bit his lip. I ached to kiss him one last time, to seal the memories of what we once had. But his mortal form sublimed in a flash, and before me stood the shimmering, otherworldly celestial hound from between the worlds. The dog who had once been mine cast the briefest glance at me, then fled up the stairs and was gone.

I sank to my knees, hollowed out, my legs too empty to hold me up. I wanted grief to fill me, simple and sharp. But my mind was consumed by a thousand thoughts and emotions, each one as restless as the next. Nothing settled. Nothing made sense. My throat worked, but it did not know whether to howl, scream or cry.

Loud noises rattled in the upper reaches of the mansion. Then voices, and the thump of something soft finding gravity. *Inette.* The overseer had been roused by the disturbances, at long last.

A brief vision tempted me: Inette rushing down the dungeon stairs in her nightclothes to find one of the old deities, prostrate among death, hands and snout bloodied. A new thrall for her construction efforts; an end to her problems and respite for the rest of the divine. What need would she have for a little spirit, if she had the power of a *god* at her disposal?

But who will look after Sisu then?

Fear and panic are the worst bedfellows for reasoned decisions. Who can balance the calculus of the greater good when the life of a loved one is threatened? In that moment my worry for Sisu overrode all else; I took on cat form again and vanished from the dungeon.

*

When Sisu awoke the next morning, the first words out of her mouth were, 'Where's Sunyol?'

I hadn't slept, and had spent the restless sliver before dawn preparing breakfast. Rice slurry bubbled over a tiny gaslit canister as Sisu sat up all rumpled, pulling the sleep scarf from her head and stretching. 'Not gone and done something stupid, has he?'

I stirred the tin of slurry. 'He's gone.' As she blinked, I clarified, 'It's over, Sisu. He's left.'

'As in—?'

'As in you're not likely to see him again.'

Sisu scratched behind her ear, frowning furiously. 'After last night?'

'Yes.'

Seconds went by. Then a derisive snort: 'Well. That *is* pretty damn stupid. I'm sorry, old man. How you holding up?'

Ah, if only I had had an answer to that question myself. Instead of telling her something useful, I pointed to the slurry, thick with meat oils. 'Breakfast. We have to stay in today.'

Her features grew narrow with suspicion. 'Why?'

'Inette's woodnymph died last night. There won't be work, and the city will be full of blasphemers looking for someone to blame.'

She stiffened in alarm. '*Died?* You mean she was killed? Or...?' She was shaken, and in her shock I watched suspicion rise further in her. I kept silent – the less she knew of the truth, the better.

She exhaled. 'I suppose it doesn't matter. But how's anything going to work then?'

'The blasphemers will procure a replacement in no time,' I said. Either they would extract some other godkind from the bowels of the city, thrashing and screaming, or their homeworld would finally consign Inette the replacement she had been asking for. 'Until then we should remain as unobtrusive as possible.'

'Why? It's got nothing to do with us. Has it?'

How pointed her question, how meaningful! I demurred. 'Inette's bound to be in a mood. Best we stay clear until it blows over.'

Wordlessly Sisu came and folded herself cross-legged on the ground beside me. She put her chin in her hand, her features carefully and deliberately thoughtful as I turned the gas-can off and started ladling steaming porridge into bowls. 'Your parents called you Bariegh,' she finally said.

'So they did.'

'After the god of the hunt?'

'It was a fairly common practice.'

'Back when the gods were a big thing, huh.' Sisu stretched out on the floor, propping herself up on her elbows. I was too tired to pick apart what this newfound jocosity of hers meant. All I knew was that I did not like it. 'Ever feel like you're not living up to the name?'

A practised smile stretched across my face as I set a bowl in front of her. 'All the time, child.'

*

The disturbance started in the afternoon: a distant commotion that swelled like a crest of water. Somewhere else in the paupers' quarter, shouts echoed and metal banged against wood. Sisu sat up in the bed, book dropping from her fingers. 'What the hell's going on?'

I had been busy with needle and thread, mending split seams and patching tears in the knees of trousers. I let the darning clatter to the floor as the noise rushed towards us. 'It's a call to work.'

'Work?' Sisu craned her head to listen as the noise reached our floor. With frightening suddenness, a rough-voiced overseer was banging on doors all up and down our corridor, telling us to report to the worksite immediately or face a hundred lashes.

Sisu looked at me, worried. 'I suppose staying home's not an option?'

'No, little one.' Guilt and fear filled me in equal parts. In the light of morning the decisions of the previous night were clearly revealed to be cowardice. I had failed in my duty, and now we would all suffer whatever petty retribution Inette was about to dispense.

Sisu's feet slapped against the floor as she swung her legs off the bed. 'Well, fuck this.'

I shivered without letting it show. It was too late for regrets, but they gripped me anyway.

*

The sun beat down upon our shoulders as we huddled in a miasma of sweat and nervous energy. The overseers had us corralled onto a pavilion at the unfinished edge of the worksite. Half-built and unsecured, the open end of the structure yawned over the empty drop to the ruined world below. My mind conjured terrifying images of the blasphemers throwing us over, one after another, until someone confessed to the bloodbath at Inette's house. As we crouched waiting for our fate I gripped Sisu's hand in mine. She pulled it away with a hiss. 'For fucks' sake, old man. You're just making me nervous.'

Neither hair nor hide of Inette. Or any of her subordinates, for that matter. The blasphemers swirling around us were all lower-ranked, young-skinned and tense, and robed in unappealing beige. As the minutes went by and sweat beaded on brows and lips, murmurs of disquiet grew among the gathered workers. Nothing good could come out of this, and the longer we waited, the worse our conceptions of the scenario became.

'Listen,' I whispered to Sisu, my words quiet as I could make them. 'If something happens to me, I want you to—'

'No,' Sisu hissed back. 'Don't you say that. I don't want to hear it.'

'Sisu—'

'If we go down, we go down together. All right? None of this *if something happens to me* bullshit. I won't stand for it.'

She sounded angry, but there was an unfamiliar wobble to her words, and she refused to turn her face towards me. 'Child...'

I was interrupted by an arrival. Overseer Arquois' robes shone and flapped as he cut through air on his hoverplate, his head and his spirits high. He surveyed the workers huddled before him and an ugly chuckle bubbled up from his chest. 'Upset and grumbling, are we? Oh, how *cruel* of the overseers, to keep us waiting in the hot sun.'

He leaped off the hoverplate and a boy in the front row flinched, nearly falling over. Arquois snorted as the trembling boy righted himself. 'Listen here, you worms,' he snapped. 'Today you will have the privilege of bearing witness to marvels greater than any you've seen before.'

He spread his arms and shouted, flush with enthusiasm at his role as orator and grandstander. 'You have seen the miracles we have worked with your *so-called* spirits. Mere piddle. Today we show you what my people can truly achieve. Today we show you what we can do with one who calls himself a *god*.'

My mouth went dry. *A god*. That could only mean one of two things. *A god. A god. A god*. The words echoed emptily through my head as they blocked out rational thought. Strangling vines filled the hollows of my chest, replacing air with fear.

Sisu sucked in breath and elbowed me. 'Bari! Look...'

Flanked by her underlings, Inette swept towards us, her dress a brilliant bloody red. Triumph shone on her sharp features. Behind her, coming slowly into view, was—

No.

PART THREE

Sisu shot up as if lightning-struck. I grabbed her arms and held her as she tried to fight me off. 'Don't,' I hissed. 'Sisu!'

Her breath came in angry gasps. 'Bari, they've got him.'

It was a struggle, keeping my voice low and calm. Except it wasn't calm. 'I know. Sisu, I know. Please, don't draw their attention.'

The blasphemers' collar looked heavy and ugly clamped around Sunyol's neck. They had taken his clothes and put him in a coarse brown tunic that barely reached his knees. A host of injuries garlanded the exposed swathes of his skin: bruises around his cheeks and lips, bloody scabs ringing his wrists, purple lash-marks striping his calves and feet. Stamped on his neck, just below the jawline, was a round set of toothmarks, open and ruddy as a flower. I knew that if I seized Inette by the jaws and held her there, I would find a perfect match.

Sunyol shuffled to a stop behind Inette. I looked at how swollen his feet were and my toes curled. His obedience towards his tormentor bothered me. No, *bothered* was the wrong word to use – it *terrified* me. How had he come to be captured? Worse still, *had* he been captured at all? In vain I tried to capture his attention. *Look here, beloved! Look at me.*

But Sunyol kept his eyes averted, moving with such caution I knew it was deliberate. Damn him. Damn him to the bottom of the cursed realms. Was this his plan? Did he leave me to do this? This stupid, stupid foolish boy—

Sisu shook in my arms, perhaps in sadness, perhaps in anger. Perhaps both. I forced myself to focus on her.

'Come here, darling,' Inette said, beckoning with a finger. Sunyol complied, his gait tortuously slow. Inette smiled and licked her lips. 'Now, sweetest, remember what we've discussed?'

Ever a master of dramatics, Inette had positioned herself to give us the best view of the show. She pulled Sunyol close, body to body, the fingers of one hand claw-like on his shoulder. 'Show me what you can do, my pretty.'

Sunyol's expression remained blank as she leaned towards him and nibbled on an earlobe. 'Make my city *blossom*.'

The boy shut his eyes.

Before us the air came to life. The unfinished structure hummed with magic. And in that resonance, the raw edge of the pavilion began *unfolding*. It started with the bones of foundation, bamboosteel extruding in long ribs. Over it grew flesh of mortar and stone. Sunyol's handiwork was exquisite: the tiling that he conjured was decorated with scalloped edges and floral motifs. A cacophony of gasps and disbelief wove around me. For the workers, mere mortals, what they were seeing was as unbelievable as a madman's fever dream, miraculous as the creation of the universe itself. Even the overseers, burning the power of spirits, needed raw material to shape to their will. Here, an entire building was solidifying out of thin air.

But nothing could come from nothing. Sunyol was drawing from his own essence to create bamboosteel and granite. The immensity of his labours bent the world around him. I never knew how deep his reserves of power went. Even I, Bariegh of the Jungle – who had been old when the mountains were pushed out of the sea! – had never witnessed anything like it. This unrestrained demonstration of ability would frighten even one such as I.

And indeed, it was terror that ran through me, sending fire and ice through my veins. But my fear stemmed from an entirely different source. I understood the terrible truth that was unfolding before me. If Sunyol overexerted himself – if he drained himself of power too fast – he would die.

Sisu trembled beside me, gripped in the unforgiving claws of disbelief. 'Bari, he's a *god*,' she whispered. 'Did you know that? Why didn't you say?'

I could not answer her.

Sunyol had extended the new wing by a hundred feet, six storeys of sheltered walkways and market halls. A whole week's worth of work had been brought into existence in a mere handful of minutes. But the inexorable tide of exhaustion was pulling at him, threatening to drag him under. The progress of the building's border slowed. Tile came into being with increasing difficulty, and the precise patterns that had decorated them turned muddy and ill-defined. Sunyol's face had blanched to a shade paler than Inette's, and breath escaped him in brittle gusts.

Sisu hissed through her teeth: 'No, no, no, *no*.' Even she could see what was clear to me. Inette was killing him. The fury and frustration that rushed through the girl had started to wake things that I had tried to keep slumbering.

Sunyol collapsed onto his hands and knees, and a symphonic gasp burst from the garrison of workers. Inette looked down at him and her lips pursed. My breath stalled in my chest. That was enough for today, wasn't it? She wouldn't ask for more. She wasn't so witless as to push him beyond his limits—

Inette jerked him upright by the chain. Sunyol staggered and gagged, barely able to stand. 'Did I say you could stop?'

The boy's lips moved, mouthing words I could not hear. Inette barked in laughter. 'Stop complaining. You know what you signed up for.'

Accursed white devil! Sunyol swayed where he stood, blood trickling from his nose. 'If you won't continue building,' Inette said, 'I'll do it *myself*.'

She raised her hand bearing the control bracelet and thrust it outwards, like the claw of a vulture seeking to consume the world. The shining sunmetal of her bracelet lit up. The collar around Sunyol's neck lit up. Power poured from one to the other. The floor shuddered as construction began again, tile by agonising tile.

Overseer Arquois ran towards her, a cooler head prevailing. At least *someone* among these worthless blasphemers understood the consequence of this terrible idea! But Inette was too far gone, hazed with power. Her face was frozen in a rictus of concentration: half a mad laugh, half a grimace. I wanted the divinity that rushed through her to kill her, to incinerate her to a pile of twisted bones and ash. I wanted to rip her to pieces. My muscles hurt from staying still.

I thought: *She'll stop before she kills him.*

I thought: *I'll kill her before it comes to that.*

I thought: *No. No. I won't risk Sisu's life for his. I have sworn to my sister. An oath is an oath, no matter what the cost.*

Sunyol groaned and slumped, his knees folding and arms going limp, held up only by Inette's chain. Blood spattered the front of his tunic.

Sisu blurted, 'You're *killing* him!'

I was on her immediately, clamping her mouth shut, holding her down, muffling her shout after the second syllable. But I moved too slow. Inette had heard. She let go of Sunyol and he dropped to the ground. Dead. No, I couldn't tell. I clutched Sisu in a vice as Inette's furious gaze swept our ranks, searching for the one who had the temerity to shout at her. Sisu's cheeks, wet with tears, trembled under my hand.

Thank the earth and sky for Overseer Arquois' timely interruption. Seeing a chance, he seized his superior's sleeves while her attention was fractured. 'Great overseer!'

Inette turned livid at his daring, but he continued in their offworlders' language, one denied even my godly knowledge. He gesticulated and pointed, alternating between the yawning scope of their unfinished project, and the divinity crumpled at their feet.

A terrible stillness had blanketed Sunyol's collapsed form. Pink froth spilled from his nose and mouth, the sort that comes from those who will never get up again. I willed his chest to move, his eyes to open: *please, not like this.* The heavy ache in my inflamed chest burst into a torrent of sorrow.

Inette, still listening to Arquois' pleading spiel, seemed to register Sunyol's condition for the first time. But it wasn't pity and regret that came out of her. No, what came bubbling up in thick stutters was a laugh. She kicked his inert form. 'Some kind of god you are.'

Sunyol remained unresponsive. I hoped that, dead or alive, my quiet boy was at least beyond pain.

But then he moved, breath shuddering through him, eyes opening a crack. *Oh, Sunyol.* Sisu wheezed beside me, mirroring my relief and agony.

Arquois nodded hopefully at Inette, pleading for her to think of the bigger picture, the greater good.

Inette spat in Sunyol's direction. 'Don't think we've gotten our money's worth from you yet, dog.' She gestured roughly at Arquois. 'Very well. You have a point. Take him back to the Axis.'

Sunyol's eyes flickered and he looked at me, deliberate and lucid and calm. There was neither fear nor sorrow in his expression, as though he had wholly accepted his fate. Stupid, stupid, foolish boy. He was still wearing the necklace I'd given him – somehow, he'd convinced Inette to let him keep it. I shivered. What other concessions had he wrung from Inette, and at what cost?

*

The moment we got home Sisu shoved me against the bedframe, her fists knotted in my tunic. 'You son of a bitch. You knew about this and you didn't say a word!'

'Sisu,' I began, helpless in the face of her anger.

'No. Shut the fuck up.' She let go and stalked the narrow confines of the room. 'He was a *god*, Bari. We had a fucking god in our house. And you didn't say shit.'

With her back to me she rubbed at her face. There was no doubt about it: her godliness had emerged from its long winter of sleep, fed by the happenings of the past weeks, knocked loose by the stresses of the day. The divine parts of me could sense her, new kin in my vicinity. There was nothing I could do about it.

The motion of her hands over her face slowed, then stopped entirely. She turned to me with the canniest look on her face. 'You're a god too, aren't you? That's how that falling walkway didn't crush you.'

'Sisu, please,' I said. 'Leave it alone. *Please*.'

She would not leave it alone. She came towards me, her head tilted curiously, her eyes narrowed. 'And what am I, Bariegh? Am I one of you, too?' She thumped her fist against her chest with rage and desperation and fear. 'What is happening to me now?'

'Leave it alone,' I repeated, hopelessly. 'There's no good to becoming divine.'

'How do you even *become* divine?' Incredulity flooded her voice, then anger and suspicion. 'Did you *do* this to me?'

I shook my head. 'It's your birthright. From your great-grandmother.'

'My—' Sisu blinked, and drew an oceanic breath. 'Fuckssake.' Her voice wobbled.

'I was trying to protect you,' I said.

'By lying to me? By treating me like an idiot?' She drove her fist into the bedpost. Something cracked, bone or wood, it didn't matter. 'I'm not a little girl anymore. I *deserved* to know.'

'You've seen what they do to godkind in this city,' I said. 'We go to such lengths to keep ourselves hidden. Why would I wake your slumbering gift if you could pass as mortal?'

Sisu swore and once more turned her back to me. The shape of her hunched spine was an alien language. The bones of my head ached with exhaustion. Sunyol was gone; was I going to lose her too?

Finally she stood. 'I'm not going to let him die.'

Alarmed, I blurted, 'What are you planning?'

'I'm going to free him.' Mania danced in her eyes. 'I won't stand by while they carve him up. I'm gonna give that bitch what she's looking for.'

This was what I had feared: Sisu getting all swept up in the euphoria of first discovery, carried away by the intoxication of new power. How could I explain the creed we godkind had agreed to abide by? I moved to stand between her and the door. 'Do you think I want this, Sisu? Do you think I *want* to watch Sunyol die?'

'You sure as fuck didn't fight back when they took him!'

I grabbed her by the wrist. 'You think I've never fought back against the blasphemers? Do you never ask yourself why there are so *few* godkind left?' Sisu's face scrunched up as she tried to tug her wrist free, but I was relentless. 'We cannot beat them, Sisu. They are too strong.' The last recourse: appealing to her compassion. 'Please. I have lost almost all that I have loved. Don't make me lose any more.'

Sisu's mouth set in a tight line. 'Let me go, old man.'

'No.'

And then a sharp burst of sound and panic echoed down the corridor. A gas canister had exploded somewhere close by. A woman was screaming, children cried. A momentary distraction, and a moment was all Sisu needed. She broke her wrist from my grip and darted out of the door.

Sisu-luck. A lifetime of it had made her bold, made her proud and stubborn and reckless. I ran after her, but she was already far ahead. Later I would wonder if the explosion itself had been real, or merely in my mind. But for now, my mandate was nothing but the chase.

Sisu's newfound divinity expanded within her, changing her very essence, elongating the borders of her limbs. And lo! This could have been a thousand years ago, my half-sister Edukan racing across the treetops screeching in joy, from hand to hand to tail to hand, while among the roots below, Bariegh the Hunter sprinted on agile feet. *Last to the Bilkan moutains is a rube!* And although I was far swifter than Sisu, than Edukan, for some reason or the other – rains, a sinkhole, a stampede in my way – she would always get there first.

But this was not a thousand years ago, and the city was nothing like the green wilds we gods used to run in. Sisu's control of her powers was still inchoate, a clumsy-fingered baby-grasp, but lucky her! The narrow architecture around us, with its layers and levels and climbing handholds, was a boon to her nimble, prehensile form. Despite my advantage in speed, the gap between us remained.

Sisu raced upwards, where the Axis waited, bright and ostentatious with death in its teeth. The late afternoon sun baked markets surfeit with shouting and haggling. In the tunnel-focus of high speed, I passed through consecutive patches of frightened citizens, eyes and mouths wide as we leaped over their heads.

Somehow, despite it all, we were not stopped. Sisu, her luck and cunning in full swing, found her way through the rings of guards fencing the way to the Axis. Following in her wake, I too escaped their scrutiny.

Inette had not replaced the dead guards around her house. Sisu crashed through a window in monkey-form, but by the time I'd leaped through the ruins and landed on glass-spangled marble, it was a human silhouette I saw vanishing down the stairs to the dungeon. I snapped back to mortal form and ran after her.

*

When I entered the dungeon I found Sisu wrenching a gap into the bars of Sunyol's cage, human muscles straining under the demands of divine strength. Sunyol, pale and bloodied, had his hands on her wrist, powerless to stop her except through soft pleas. 'Sisu. You're making things worse.'

She ignored him and kept pushing. A space barely wide enough for his shoulders had opened between the bars.

'Sisu,' I said.

'You can help, *or* you can stand there and watch. I don't care either way.'

I came down the steps, heavy-footed. Sisu spun, baring her teeth in a threat. 'Stay the *fuck* away if you're gonna interfere.'

I stopped with a foot between us. 'Sunyol. Look at me.'

He turned his head but said nothing. His gaze startled me: I had expected sadness, defeat, pain. But what I met were the eyes of an old warrior, hard and unforgiving. His body might be a battered pulp and his holiness a ruin, but his spirit remained lit like a furnace.

I asked, 'Why are you doing this? For my sake?'

'Yes,' he said, 'and no.'

'Now's not the time to be cryptic, beloved.'

A shiver took hold of the boy as the word beloved slipped through. A snarl of frustration tore out of Sisu. 'Oh for fucks' sake, you old men can talk *after* we get out of here!'

'Sisu.' The girl startled as Sunyol's hand darted between the bars and brushed her cheek. 'Let us talk.'

'But—'

'I will not leave with you,' he said, gently but firmly. He possessed frightening composure for one who had recently been so close to death. Sisu burst into an anguished *Why?* but he had already turned his attention to me. 'Bariegh. Take her with you. Leave this place as soon as possible.'

'And I will. After you answer my question. Why are you doing this, Sunyol?'

His shoulders sank. 'Do you never wonder where the blasphemers got their sunmetal from?'

I blinked, unsettled by this question. 'What connection has that got with anything?'

He said softly, 'The sunmetal came from my people. From between the worlds.'

Earthquake. Epiphany. My mind refused to believe what my ears were hearing. 'You *gave* them the technology?' My fists tightened, and Sisu stepped back from the bars, driven by fear, or surprise, or both.

'*Gave?* No.' He turned to look at the shadows. 'It was stolen from us. Stolen by one of our own. A trickster. A monkey.'

A monkey god. His words – his rationalization of Sisu's distaste – returned to haunt me. 'Like Edukan?'

The ghost of a smile briefly possessed him. 'Not much different, I assume. A lover of chaos. Harmless, usually. Served their purpose.' It pained me to watch him struggle for breath. 'They stole from a vault I guarded. I let them slip past. And they scattered it to many different worlds.'

'Including ours?'

'Including yours. And your blasphemers found it on their planet. It channels divinity, stores divine power for later. We called it an elixir. It could grant immortality to mortals, it could—' He broke into a fit of coughing before he recovered. 'Those you call your blasphemers, used it for their own purposes.'

I paced the confines of the cell. Thoughts frothed in my mind like a boiling sea. 'So all this'—I gestured around myself, encompassing the dungeon around us, the hanging city, the entire world—'You blame yourself for what happened.'

'It is my fault.'

The moving parts of him, the things I could not figure out, were all starting to make sense. 'When you left last night, you went straight to Inette.'

He nodded. My chest ached. *Stupid, stupid foolish boy.*

'That's the dumbest fucking thing I've ever heard,' Sisu snapped. She plunged into the gap she'd made and seized the boy's arms. 'Come on, you idiot. Get moving.'

Sunyol pulled himself free and staggered out of her reach. 'Leave me,' he hissed. 'You'll be caught. Go now.'

I came up to the bars, close enough to touch him, yet not bold enough. 'And what good would your death do? The blasphemers have greed in their bones. Inette will use you up.

You'll die, like the woodnymph. And what then? Another will take your place. Nothing will change.'

'I'll feel better,' Sunyol said. He could not meet my eyes.

I snaked an arm between the bars and grasped his chin, finding it wet with tears. 'Sunyol, please.' I tilted his face towards mine. 'Come with me. You wanted me to fight, so let's fight. But together. I can't do it without you.'

'No,' he said softly. 'What you said – you were right. This fight is not your burden. My captivity will satisfy Inette for a while. Use this time to find a way to leave, both you and Sisu. Find lands the blasphemers have not touched.'

I sighed. Oh, for all his power and wisdom, how little he understood! 'I am bound to this land, Sunyol. I draw sustenance from it. Broken as it is, I may not leave. Beyond its borders I will waste away to nothing, and die. This is our boon as godkind, and it is our tragedy.'

'Wait,' Sisu interrupted. 'Are you saying I can't leave here either? The fuck?'

I dropped my hand. 'Not anymore, Sisu. As a mortal you could have left the city and crossed the seas at any time. But now that you have embraced your divinity, you are bound to the rules that govern our powers.'

Sisu spat a small blasphemy, then followed it up with, 'Well, guess I'm not planning any grand voyages soon, huh?'

Sunyol exhaled. He looked exhausted. 'You're trapped here.'

I said, 'You are the one who is free to leave, Sunyol. And you should. Don't waste your life on this.'

Breath whistled through this throat and lungs. How fragile he still was! Yet determination fortified the soft vowels in his mouth: 'I won't leave you.'

I saw that he still bore my gift around his neck, the teeth of my long-dead foe gleaming in the yellow light. I reached through the bars and took his hand. 'If you won't leave, then let us fight, side by side.'

He blinked. Something like hope briefly filtered into his expression. 'Together?'

I tugged him towards the gap in the bars. 'Together.'

It was a good moment, filled with hope and promise. A beautiful moment. It couldn't last. It shattered. A voice, of familiar and chilling timbre, echoed from the dungeon walls. '*Well, well.* So my quarry took the bait. And look what he brought. A *friend.* We're in luck!'

Overseer Inette stood at the head of the stairs, bearing a smile sharp enough to cut through steel. Amassed behind her were the guards who had been mysteriously absent from the surrounds. *Of course.* It was more than luck that got us here. Inette had laid a trap, and we'd obligingly fallen into it.

As she descended the stairs, I stood between her and those I loved, my feet planted. Behind me I heard Sisu hissing *come on* at Sunyol, and the boy's pained grunt as he eased between the gap she had wrought. I growled at Inette. My divinity writhed under my human skin, yearning to break free, fangs and claws crying to rend blasphemer-flesh, lusting for the taste of Inette's blood. But not yet. Not while the way out was still blocked.

Inette smiled at me. 'I always knew something was different about you, Brick Wall. But your lanky little girl, too? What a beautiful bonus.'

'Yeah?' Sisu snapped. 'Big fucking surprise to me too.'

'Sisu,' I said quietly. I switched over to the old tongue, the forbidden language, the temple-dialect that all godkind instinctively understood. 'Run when I tell you to—'

Pain snapped though me as the filament of a whip snared my torso. Inette's wrist was held high, the control bracelet singing with power. She'd charged it up, then. As I feared.

'None of that forsaken drivel in my house,' Inette said. 'We really *must* teach you some manners.'

The perfect chance was never going to come. We had to move now.

I grabbed the end of the whip and roared. 'Run!' Then I pulled on the burning filament. This was Sunyol's power, and he was once mine; I had more control over it than Inette did. She jerked forwards with a cry and fell face-first, jaw meeting floor with a satisfying crunch. The filament came loose; now it was I who wielded it. With one swing of my arm, I flicked it at the assembled guards along the stairs. Pain. Screams. The heavy thunk of armor as it crashed end-over-end down the stairs.

Sisu was on the move, dragging Sunyol by the arm, streaking towards the tiny window of freedom. The boy gasped my name, but we had no time left for anything else. I burst into my oldest form, my truest form: Bariegh of the gaze of fire, terrible and unforgiving. Once, I had let Sunyol look upon me like this. That seemed a lifetime ago. I leaped at Inette as Sisu hauled the limping boy up the stairs.

I landed on her back, jaws diving for her spine. A shield snapped around her. Fire surged into my mouth as it closed around the shield's power. It flung me backwards; I landed, belly-up, and there was Inette, driving a swift blade downwards.

Inette punctured my chest. There came pain, so bright it dissolved the world: the knife was charmed. A knife to gut the divine with. 'I'll suck the marrow from your bones!' she screeched. I roared in agony as she pulled the knife downwards, cutting me open.

'*Bariegh!*' Sunyol's anguish drove him back towards me. Sisu's scream was a string of obscenities.

'Go,' I snarled through the pain. *Go. You fools.* My blood slicked the floor. I clawed at Inette's shield: it could not last forever, and her mortal form was soft and edible. Who would die first? I, or she?

The sound of more iron-shod feet coming down the stairs. Sisu yelled, the syllables opaque to me. The world faded, my connection to what sustained me dissolving as Inette cut me open. I could no longer see well enough to read her emotions. I tore still at her shield, but I knew the battle was lost.

So this was how it would end. Strangely, there was only peace underneath the pain. Death in battle was what I would have preferred. And beyond the veil: who knew what was waiting? As my arms fell to my side I turned my head to look at Sunyol one last time. My boy, my beautiful, tragic boy. I should have done more for him. He was on his knees, the chains of a guard around his neck. *Farewell, beloved.* My story ended here. I only prayed that his would go on.

In my last gasp of lucidity I glimpsed his tender lips one last time. They moved. They shaped two syllables:

Er-lang.

*

To say her name is to summon her.

The sky above the city split. For a moment an empty void bisected the heavens in a long blade. Then it erupted in spumes of fire, white enough to blind, as though a star had exploded over the sky.

The miasma contracted and took form. A shadow fell over the city, taller than mountains and broad as the sea. There stood a woman of unbelievable proportions, triple eyes burning like embers, helm as red as blood, spear glinting bright as a second sun. Her voice shook the foundations of the city as she let out a battle-cry.

Her name was Er-lang the Indomitable, Er-lang the Three-Eyed, Er-lang the Righteous. God of war, protector of the weak, traveller between the firmaments: she had been summoned.

In the years to come a thousand different versions of what happened that afternoon would circulate among the people, passing reverently from mouth to mouth among the faithful. Some said that a bolt of lightning brighter than the hottest fire had sundered the Axis and all within it. Others said that a flock of crows big enough to swallow the sun and the moon had descended upon its white spires and carted it away, block by foreign block. And then there were those who said that their salvation was a woman who filled the sky: vanished Mother Fuata herself, reborn to bring justice to her children with the righteous point of her spear.

All the stories agreed on one thing: one moment the Axis of Tranquillity lorded over the city. Then the air was split by the sound of a hundred avalanches, and the Axis, and all who were within it, was gone.

*

In our universe there are places where time and space hold no sway. Places in between, and places in between the in-betweens. It was in this place that the god of war laid down their passengers. That made four of us in this soft place full of mists and floating rocks: the god (neither man nor woman), their celestial hound, Sisu, and I.

I slipped back into the form others knew me best by. This place, floating and strange, whispered knowledge to me in a language without words. 'You,' I said to the war-god. 'You are...' Truths poured their waters into me. 'You are *they* who used to call this one, who had no name.'

'I am them indeed,' Er-lang said. 'And you are?'

'Bariegh of the Jungle,' he said. 'And this is Sisu, who is blood of my half-sister Edukan.'

Sisu ran up into the gnarled lattice of a thing that resembled a tree and burst back into human form, a tempest of astounded fury. 'What the fuck is this? You can't just kidnap a bunch of people and fuck up a world. Who the fuck are you?'

'I am Er-lang,' the god of war replied. 'I come from worlds beyond yours. And I came because I was summoned to undo damage that was caused by the actions of my people.'

They stood tall and magnificent, clad in golden armor and red livery, spear shining in the gloom where no sun existed. The star-hound, whom I had called Sunyol, curled up at their feet and said nothing, resting their chin upon their paws.

Er-lang said, 'Your world has been subject to quite some interference, and for that I do apologize on behalf of my people.'

'Bullshit,' Sisu said sullenly, resting in the cradle of the tree-thing with her arms folded.

'What have you done?' I asked. They seemed so cold and distant, untouchable as the great stars in the sky. I had no good feelings towards them.

They simply said, 'Removed the source of that interference.'

I blinked. 'The blasphemers – they're gone?'

'Not as such. I… took care of some of the more problematic individuals.' They tilted their head, as if murder was no more than an inconvenience to them. 'But principally, I have removed from their custody what originally belonged to my people.' They held up a hand, and in it spun a bright, twisting ball of metal, wreathed in flame.

'The sunmetal,' I said, staring at its scintillating form. The source of all our torment rested in their hand like it was no more than an overripe fruit.

'Sunmetal… yes. If that is what you call it.'

'That's all of it?'

'It is indeed. The rules of this place are quite different from what you're used to. More allusive than physical. But this is it.'

I could barely believe it. 'So it's gone from our world. The blasphemers – those who are left – will no longer have power over godkind.'

'That is the intention, yes.'

My breaths were fire in my lungs. Here in this place where air was but an illusion – a metaphor – the beat of my heart was but a cipher for my emotions. 'So many have perished on account of that metal,' I said. 'So many lost. Cultures erased. And yet you – you managed to undo it all in a single blink.' My voice rose, anger hardening my vowels and sharpening my consonants. 'If it was so easy for you, why did you not come earlier? You could have ended our suffering at any time.'

'It is not our policy to dictate the happenings on mortal worlds,' Er-lang said. 'We prefer to think ourselves guardians and observers.'

The hound at their feet growled, hackles serrating the edges of their form. Er-lang looked them over with tenderness that bordered on condescension. 'Of course, they disagreed with me. So I gave them the freedom to do what they wanted to.'

'And what do you expect from us now?' I asked. 'Gratitude?' My fists were clenched into weapons.

'Nothing of the sort. Forgiveness, perhaps, if you were willing to grant it.'

I hissed. From her perch, Sisu let acid-tinged derision crackle into the mist-thick air.

'If you would like to,' they said, 'you could remain with us. I could grant you the ability to leave your domicile. You could travel between the worlds with us.' They gestured to the hound. 'With them.'

Sisu made a noise that could have been laughter. I forced my voice to remain calm. 'You want me to abandon my home?'

'It's merely an offer,' Er-lang said. 'You are free to ignore it if you wish.'

'We're ignoring it,' Sisu snapped. 'Don't think we're obliged to be nice to you because you did a thing.'

They tilted their head, as if in amusement.

'What happens to them now?' I gestured to the hound at their feet. I did not like the way they lay so still and quiet, barely showing a reaction to anything we said.

Er-lang frowned. 'They come with me, of course. They called for me. It is time for them to return home.'

I looked at the hound that lay curled at their feet, the hound that I had once called mine. I remembered the brief, truncated hope I had seen on Sunyol's face before Inette had come for us. We were supposed to fight together, thrive together. Calling for Er-lang had been an action borne out of desperation. He would not have chosen this.

'No,' I said. I knew, deep in my heart of hearts, that I was in no position to bargain. What could I offer to parley with this being, whose power was set so far over mine? Yet I had to try. I had to. 'You asked for my forgiveness, and I will not give it. But I will ask for restitution. My world is broken and near destroyed from your negligence and your inaction. You cannot leave us to rebuild alone. You owe us this much.'

'What are you asking for?'

I pointed to the hound at their feet. 'Him.'

Finally, recognizable emotion filtered onto their face. With narrowed eyes they said, 'You ask for something I cannot give.'

'Can you not?' I folded my arms. 'How sincere are you in your apologies, anyway?'

They contemplated the hound with a heavy expression. A long, tense moment passed. I felt Sisu's eyes on the three of us and wondered if I had pushed too far. This stranger, this uber-god, could reduce all of us to nothing if they felt like it.

Finally they said, 'Wait here. I will discuss this with them privately.'

*

A yellow sun set over a mortal world: watery, tufted with green, steeped in a thin oxygen atmosphere. On the edge of an island, a silken-haired boy sat upon white cliffs over a churning ocean, watching the colors of the sky mature, fingering the serrated edges of the necklace resting upon his chest.

Beside him stood Er-lang. He was a man on this world, worshipped by a culture that did not believe women should be warriors. 'Sunyol, was it? That was what he called you.'

'Do not speak that name,' the boy said. 'It is not yours to use.'

'Ah. I apologize.'

'Why did you bring me here?' the boy asked.

'You heard his bargain. What do you think?'

The boy did not look up. 'To take it or not is not mine to decide.'

'But it is.' Er-lang gently laid a hand on his head. 'It is your fate it concerns. I will not decide it for you.'

The boy pressed a tip of his necklace into the soft flesh of his quasi-mortal form. 'Do you not want me to return?'

The god of war sighed. 'It has been long since I had a companion running by my side. And yes, I do miss it. And I do miss you, even if you do not believe it. But.' He ran his fingers through strands of the boy's hair. 'You were never well-suited to the task of warhound, even if it was your destiny. I would not force you back into that role, if you did not want it.'

The boy looked at the sky, gem-blue and stacked with swirls of clouds. 'I wandered for so long without a purpose. I was fleeing the consequences of my failure, but something kept drawing me back to world after world where the elixir had warped the fabric of people's lives. I cannot escape it. But if I cannot escape it, perhaps I should embrace it where I can.'

'Is that the decision you have made?'

'Destinies can change, even for gods like ourselves.' He stood, finally. 'Yes, Er-lang. I would like to rebuild his world with him.'

*

The rising sun beat upon an oasis of white stone and chaos. We stood upon peaks of masonry at the zenith of the world, a place where no shadows were cast. Beneath us, the world was swept by change. The interlopers, those faithless blasphemers, found themselves cut down and diminished. For the first, sweet time in a long while, they felt the same fear that they had been inflicting upon others for years.

On my left stood Sisu, blood of Edukan, trickster and harbinger of luck. On my right stood Sunyol-of-the-stars, my bright boy, my shining beacon.

Sisu looked down at the mess beneath us, the ashes of the world from which a new one would rise. 'Well. We've got a fucktonne of work to do.'

I grinned, baring my teeth to the earth and sky as though in challenge. And then I, Bariegh the Broad-shouldered, Bariegh the Builder of Worlds, leaped forwards into our new dawn.

Whale Snows Down

Kim Bo-Young

Korea

Kim Bo-Young is a major voice of Korean SF, and I was lucky enough to publish her already in one of the *Apex Book of World SF* anthologies, so it was just a matter of finding the right story here. Luckily, I came across 'Whale Snows Down', published in the terrific *Future SF Digest* edited by Alex Shvartsman, who is one of those small group of people responsible for pushing World SF far and wide with their efforts. So I won't tell you any more about it, just that we are now back from the stars to a world made strange and wondrous... This story was translated from Korean by Sophie Bowman.

A whale must have died, I thought, as the snowfall thickened.

When a whale dies it snows heavier down here. In this dark, cold, silent village of ours, the death of a whale descends as an ode to life. With my gills stretched wide and a rich, green glow shining from the lure sticking out of my forehead, I drifted through the blizzard quivering with delight.

It's not a whale. It tastes musty. My mate conveyed a thought.

Recently my mate's intellect had been deteriorating fast. Since his lips morphed into a sucker and his eyes and part of his brain melted as they fused with my body, he can't speak at all, and conveys no more than occasional fragments of thought. Now that even his bloodstream is connected to mine, he is no more than an extra organ that dangles from my body. It may be the fruition of a love I'd always dreamed of, a life where body and mind have become one, but now and then I think that this marriage is nothing more than the trace of a past love.

My love, I don't think it's a whale...

A whale carcass may be eaten to shreds by the fish in the villages above ours as it swells with decay, but the plump and tender flesh, that chewy fin and burning hot blood, those supple eyes and slightly bitter gills all end up drifting down here to us in the deep sea. The death of a whale provides abundant sustenance for the whole village for months on end, and even after all the flesh is eaten away, delicious zombie worms grow big and breed as they stick fast to the thick bones and suck out all the fat, and so we get to eat them, too.

My love, my babbler who never stops chatting away, I'm telling you it's not a whale...

Paying no mind to my mate's thoughts, I swam toward the valley of gods. The valley appeared a few years ago, when a submarine volcano erupted. Tube worms and crabs and shrimp bloomed like coral in the scalding boil around the hydrothermal vent. There was a brief time of plenty in which a radiant culture flourished, then it quietly met its end as the volcano cooled. But our village is still centered around it because some warmth remains, making it a pleasant place to be, and it continues to provide sustenance, with the remaining corpses and all the bugs that fed on them.

When I got to the valley, friends were gathered together merrily dancing. Most of the time we live our lives keeping a distance. That's the only option in such a poor neighborhood where food is so scarce; we would end up snatching morsels from each other's mouths otherwise. Moving around squanders energy, so our usual routines consist only of floating, with our bodies entrusted to the ocean current, and opening our mouths to swallow the small and hungry things that approach thinking the lure light pulsing by our mouths must be something to eat. Yet we can't help but gather to celebrate when a blizzard like this is raging.

Needleteeth Anglerfish 312 approached with two mates dangling from her. One of her mates still had his brain and so could converse, but with his face completely buried in her body, all the other one could do now was produce sperm.

'Illuminated Netdevil 1029, according to my mate, it's not a whale.'

Glaring with big, bulging eyes, Needleteeth crackled the countless long, sharp teeth that encased her upper and lower jaw. All of us have big eyes that can see in the pitch dark, and sharp teeth like a snare that make sure no prey can escape once they've entered our mouths, but the Needleteeths' teeth are a little extreme. They grow so big that, as they age, it gets hard for them to move their mouths because they impale themselves with their own teeth.

I spoke, pulsing my lure, 'My mate says the same. True enough, if it were a whale now's about the time we'd be seeing the body.'

'Let's wait and see. The explorers will bring news by evening.'

These 'explorers' are lanternfish. They are one of the courageous clans that put their lives on the line every day to make a round trip from this deep sea to the Surface, the horizon of our knowledge. The Surface is a place where all kinds of unnamed monsters appear. But even when it costs them the lives of their precious young, the lanternfish do not stop making their daily trips up there. Apparently the food at the Surface tastes better than anything down here, and besides, having seen the amazing view they encounter when they leap above the water, they just have to keep going back. They say that the beyond is dazzling white, resplendent and brighter and more brilliant than every light in this deep sea combined.

Needleteeth makes fun of them, saying it's just a hallucination caused by lack of oxygen and the low pressure... but there's another story even harder to believe: the theory that beyond that 'beyond the Surface' there is yet another horizon of knowledge which is 'beyond the clouds', and beyond that again there is a world that is as cold and quiet and dark as this deep sea... but I just can't get my head around it.

'The wind never ceases.' A dim light glittered from down below.

It was Fanfin Anglerfish 042. She's never once moved from the sandy seabed since she was born. Dozens of long, beautiful, and soft threads stick out from Fanfin, extending ten times longer than her body. The threads, sensitive as erogenous zones, excitedly capture the subtlest changes in the direction of ocean current and temperature. They say that when she was in her prime, Fanfin could perceive the movement of the entire ocean, but these days, perhaps a little senile in her old age, she keeps saying strange things.

'Yes, friend, that's how it's always been,' Needleteeth replied softly.

As far as we know, what moves above the water flows like a current too. From north to south, from south to north, from cold to hot, from hot to cold.

'The wind never ceases. From one end of the world to the other, it keeps blowing, always. It should have stopped long ago... when the days got hot. The wind has gone insane in the heat.'

'Fanfin's mind isn't what it was,' Needleteeth whispered, keeping their lights close so Fanfin wouldn't see. In this silent world we usually converse with the shape and intervals of the pulsing light of our lures. 'I've been telling her for ages to keep moving around a little, even if it's hard.'

'It'll be because of that bad stuff that settled on the floor,' I said.

At some point, a substance other than snow started piling up in this village. Little things that never decay, that even the zombie worms vomit up. They have no nutritional value and can't be digested, and no matter how the waves break them up they only become smaller, never disappearing. The very young swallow them, mistaking them for snow, then can't regurgitate or excrete them, and their tummies swell until they explode, killing them. Now, some babies are even born with that stuff embedded in them.

'Those poor things must have eaten too much of the bad stuff.'

Fanfin had been saying strange things for a while: the sea has gotten blander (what could she mean by blander?), it has gotten bigger, heavier, hotter… ah, but the hotter part is true. The rest of us can feel that much for ourselves. It's even said that an ice continent that had stood firm somewhere for millennia has melted to nothing.

'Hey kids, the snow isn't just falling here,' Siphonophore said, emitting a soft and elegant light with their whole body as they passed between us.

Siphonophore's name is simply Siphonophore, no numbers. Because, within the bounds of where we swim at least, there's only one. Siphonophore lives forever, reproducing their body like a plant. They may have been alive for a thousand years, or ten thousand, even; there is no fish who knows. Siphonophore's body is as big as a whale. And like whales, Siphonophore converses with a low frequency, and that low voice can travel halfway around the earth and cover the entire ocean like whales' voices do. And so, like the whales, Siphonophore knows all that is happening in the ocean. If there's a difference, it's that Siphonophore knows not only what's going on far in the distance, but also all that happened far back in time.

Although they've lived for so long, they have no strength to harm others, so if anyone resolved to eat them, Siphonophore would die in an instant. But none of us down here in the deep sea would ever think of doing that. That would mean eating up the history of the ocean. It would be the same as chewing up the record of our entire world.

'It's not only snowing in our village. They say heavy snow is falling in that next village, and the village out front, and the village out back, and the village behind that, and that very distant village too, all just the same...'

'In that case, it must be a mass death,' Needleteeth said, in a pulsing glow, 'at the very least a large clan has met its end. Maybe a whole species. And the remains have become this snow falling now.'

That reminded me of a story the explorer lanternfish had told a couple of months ago.

'...that's right, they all died. Those sardines that had lived, millions of them, together in one group. We greeted them every morning for years and years and had grown quite fond of them... What a horrific scene it was... As you know, the water has been slowly heating up these days, the fish catchers have gotten fiercer too. More and more of the sardines were getting sick, and they say it was the death of a few of the elders that was the start of it. According to a sardine that saw one up close, they were totally boiled from the inside. Those elders had pointed the way for the whole group. Dozens of their followers got so sad that they died not long after them. And then their children and families died in turn... Sadness swept through the clan like a disease, like a tidal wave, and within a few days they all died together. In just a few days, that honorable clan, that had continued for centuries… The rotting stench of it meant it was impossible to breathe in that whole area. Parasites ran rampant, and then they died all at once, too…'

Thinking of what I'd heard again, I gave a shudder. That's how life goes. You do whatever you can to put up with things and endure, and it can seem like you're managing, then there are times when, like a string pulled taught, something snaps and everything gives way in an instant. I hope they're enjoying eternal life in fish heaven.

'Everything's the same when it gets down to this deep sea,' I said in prayer.

Dimming her lure, Needleteeth bowed her head too. 'Yes, all the same.'

'Be it venom or pathogen, sadness or pain, it's all the same here. It all becomes beautiful snowflakes. Becomes merciful sustenance and the gift of life.'

'All apart from that stuff that doesn't rot,' Needleteeth added bitterly.

'The wind never ceases,' Fanfin mumbled again, glittering inconspicuously down below.

'But how big a clan must have died for it to be snowing in every village around?' Needleteeth said, ignoring Fanfin.

'A species that big…' Siphonophore said passing in front of us again. 'Well, as far as I know there's only one…'

We faced each other.

'It couldn't be. Humans?'

Siphonophore had talked about these humans for a long time. They told us about how, in the distant past, all kinds of gorgeous life had thrived above the Surface, just like in this ocean. But that over the last hundred years or so almost all of it had disappeared, and now only that bizarre species called humans teemed around up there.

'You mean those monsters that excrete the stuff that doesn't rot?' Needleteeth said, grinding her teeth together just thinking of them.

Every day they create thousands of tons of poisonous matter that can't be eaten and throw it into the ocean. The damage isn't so bad here in the deep sea, but even just a little way above us terrible diseases run rampant one after another, and precious lives like coral disappear at a staggering rate. Rumor has it that they're the ones to blame for the days getting hotter, too. It sounds absurd to me, but they say that something these humans belch out as they excrete the stuff that doesn't rot makes the air burning hot...

*

To tell the truth, what shocked me most when I heard about these humans was something totally ridiculous.

'You're telling me the females are smaller and weaker than the males?' I asked in disbelief, restlessly waggling the mate that dangled from my plump body.

My love, I'm dizzy...

'So the males of that species must be the ones to produce their young?'

All the organisms I meet here in this deep sea are female, of course. What's the point in living with a bulky body if you aren't going to make new life with it? A large body is a waste of nutrients if it isn't going to reproduce.

'Ah, well, I suppose it's not such a big deal if they can metamorphose their sex.'

I thought of a friend who had metamorphosed female a few years back after making up her mind to lay eggs. She said that, although becoming the main agent of reproduction and being responsible for a whole family was daunting, since she was already here living, rather than degenerating herself and becoming one of a mate's organs, she wanted to try braving a life of her own and face whatever might come.

'Ah, adorable Netdevil. Land creatures don't change sex, at least not most of them.'

I was astonished. 'But there can't always be an appropriate mate in the vicinity, surely. How on earth do they breed?'

'The natural world is a mysterious thing, Netdevil. Things don't always work according to common sense.'

*

'The mass death of humans, you say?' Needleteeth fluttered her gills looking at the snowfall that had grown even heavier. 'I did think such a time had to come someday. Since the only thing left when all the other life on land had disappeared would be that inedible substance they made.'

'But they... how can I put it... they live on the ground, don't they?' I stooped, tilting the lure sticking out of my forehead. 'Even if they all died at once, that doesn't necessarily mean they would become snow and fall all the way down here.'

'Then maybe it was mass suicide,' Needleteeth pondered. 'Why, there was what happened to those white hairy things. Don't you remember?'

That too was something that happened because of the heat. They say that land made of ice which had been there for tens of thousands of years all melted away. The creatures living there starved as the land got smaller and smaller and ended up all huddled together, reduced to skin and bones. Then one day, following their leader, they dived one after the other into the sea. Apparently it was a calm decision. That time, too, the snow was heavy down here for a long time.

There are times like that. When the string snaps. Times when endurance and struggling to survive, and even volition too, lose their purpose.

'It's a typhoon!'

It was the school of lanternfish, rushing back from up there. Seen from a distance they look like one giant fish, and they really are like that in many ways.

'There's a typhoon blowing (a typhoon) (a typhoon) (a typhoon).'

At the words of the elder that led at the very front, the young lanternfish following right behind all shook their tails together and repeated in a chorus.

Everyone dancing in the vicinity gathered around.

'But aren't there always typhoons?' I asked, tilting to one side.

'No, not like this (not like this). The typhoon (the typhoon) is blowing from this end of the ocean (this end of the ocean) all the way to the opposite end (the opposite end).'

'The wind never ceases,' Fanfin sparkled, in rhyme with the lanternfish chorus.

'We've never seen a typhoon like it. It was as if a huge angry giant was raging around the whole world trampling everything in its path. The typhoon is so big, its head is towering way above the clouds. It's pushing down cold air like a block of ice from up there in a whirling tornado. That wind is even colder than this deep sea, cold that freezes breath in its tracks. It's a wind that freezes anything alive with just a touch. Everywhere it passes, all that's left behind is corpses. The typhoon is twisting and sweeping up all the dead as it moves around and pouring them into the ocean. The death moves from ocean to ocean, only getting bigger. It doesn't die down even after sweeping over the land and crossing seas. We managed to escape back down here somehow, but the things that live up there on the land are probably all…'

'Good grief.' As if they finally understood what she had been saying all along, Siphonophore looked down at Fanfin's rustling threads. 'The ocean must have gotten so hot that the evaporation doesn't stop. In order for that thing called a typhoon to cease there needs to be a cold sea somewhere to cool the winds and calm it down, but now there's nowhere cold left up there.'

'The string of the world has snapped,' I said.

'But the world held tight and endured for a long time. Honorably, and with such patience,' Needleteeth flicked her tailfin back and forth. 'It's a shame for those that live up there, but might the world not get a bit better now? If the monsters that covered the ground are all gone, might the little ones that die from eating the stuff that doesn't rot, and the young that have their throats clogged with those things and die with their flesh festering not disappear now too?'

I turned downward. 'Everything's the same when it gets down to this deep sea.'

'All the same.'

We all dimmed our lights together and bowed. Me and Needleteeth and Siphonophore and the lanternfish too, and all the other anglerfish, even Fanfin down below, we all dimmed our lights. In the silence Needleteeth's lovely companions, and mine too, prayed along with us.

'Be it venom or pathogen, sadness or pain, it's all the same here. It all becomes beautiful snowflakes. Becomes merciful sustenance and the gift of life. Down here everything, all of it becomes the same.'

And we were silent. The snowfall thickened even more.

Translated by Sophie Bowman

The Gardens of Babylon

Hassan Blasim

Iraq

I mentioned in the introduction how vital independent presses are to the diversity of the field. Hassan Blasim edited the groundbreaking *Iraq+100* anthology for Comma Press, from which this story is taken, opening important ground in the publishing of Arabic SF in English. I loved the story, and I hope you do too. This story was translated from Arabic by Jonathan Wright.

To Adnan Mubarak

One of the tiger-droids has been tampered with. The public garden system has only just launched the model, and some nine-year-old boy has already hacked it, making it circle pointlessly in the air, above everyone's heads. Visitors have begun gathering round, laughing at it, including me. We watch as a supervisor intervenes, along with a male and a female droid, and together they coax the thing back down to Earth. As the crowd disperses, the supervisor issues the boy's mother with a fine. There's nothing unusual about this kid's hacking skills, of course: Babylon is now a paradise for digital technology developers, a playground for hackers, virus architects and software artists.

It's still too early for the queen to arrive, so I watch the children having fun with the crocodiles in the water tank. There are other animals, originating from every continent, roaming freely among the visitors: tame, friendly beasts, from birds to insects, as well as smart-trees, developed to match the rhythm of this 'Age of Peace and Dreams' – as our queen likes to call it. And our queen is right. I don't understand the people who object to her policies. This virtual life, with so much affluence and creativity, really is the true rhythm of the age. It means there's extraordinary harmony between our imaginations and our realities. It was the federal ruler of Mesopotamia who gave the director of the city the title 'queen'. I think she deserves the title. I don't know, maybe I'm wrong, but she's a strong woman and she's left her mark on our city by building it on the principles of creative freedom. We have built peace and prosperity through imagination. That's what the queen says, and today she's going to open the Story-Games Centre, which recently recruited me. The queen took over the management of Babylon ten years ago. She divided the city into twenty-four giant domes. At first HK Corporation objected to this division, but the Chinese later did a U-turn, saying they hadn't initially understood the queen's plans. Of course, they only said this after the queen gave them the contract for managing the city's water provisions. Maybe what I'm saying today about Babylon's imagination policy doesn't exactly apply to me, since these days I find it difficult to work. But for most citizens it's perfect. My problem is I need to relax too much. And it's like my imagination has run dry. I have to finish my first story-game this week, but I'm too laid-back. Creativity requires a certain exuberance. I have no ideas, no images; too often I feel bored and empty.

On the screen above the Gardens, I watch an advert for the new water trains that will soon come into service. These are fast trains that will supply the city with water from central and northern Europe. I feel an overwhelming desire to leave the

Gardens and head for the abandoned Old City, but I've left my facemask at home. Our queen has now appeared on the screen, with the CEO of HK, and they are drinking glasses of water with the new train behind them – the pride of Iranian industry. Over recent years these water trains have become a key factor in the selection of city managers. City managers are appointed by the Governor General of Federal Mesopotamia, with the proviso that the international companies that manage the provinces endorse the choice. Things have gone well with the water trains. For several years, Babylon has faced the prospect of going thirsty. Then the Water Rebels formed and started to agitate against the Chinese company. The Water Rebels are constantly on the move and are still active in both the abandoned city and in the new domes. The rebels still don't like the way the water is being apportioned. HK Corp distributes the water from a central point, and armoured, automated trucks are responsible for supplying every house with its quota of water. To some extent, I can see why the Water Rebels are angry; some people hardly seem to have enough e-credit to pay for their quota, while in rich areas you see special trucks filling swimming pools and fountains with the stuff. Several times the rebels have hacked into the trucks' software and made them dispense water in the poor parts of town. What I don't understand is why they reject any dialogue at all with our queen.

I'm hungry. I message the restaurant and they send me the nearest waiter-bot. I like this restaurant. They've designed their robot waiter to look like a cook and also like the first astronaut to set foot on the moon. He's very funny. Everything you order comes out of his belly. I credit him on my phone for the sandwich and the orange juice and, as I eat, I re-read a classical text by a writer who lived here at the beginning of the previous century. It's quite a boring story about violence in the age of oil and religious extremism. I was disappointed when I was offered the job in the Archive Department. My dream was to work in the New Games, designing my own storylines. But they assigned me the task of converting the old stories by our city's writers into smart-games. The manager said it was one of the most important departments. 'You will have the chance to open the door for the new generation to discover the distant past of Babylon.' Of course the manager is exaggerating, because who's interested in that bloody past today? Most young people only follow the best-selling space-story games. The garden is teeming with visitors. It's obviously because the queen's expected to visit. There are visitors from all over the world, although today most of them are Chinese. They and their families look very happy. Why not, since it was they who designed the new domes, and they who are running Babylon? Almost everything – the transport system, energy, the hospitals, and smart-schools. Not to mention the food and water business. No one can deny the ingenuity of the giant domes. Each district is a circular space like a giant sports ground, roofed over with a smart-glass dome that absorbs the sunlight, which is the main source of energy in Babylon. All the districts are linked by amazing underground trains. The Chinese have also given the inhabitants of Babylon the privilege of Chinese citizenship, so we Babylonians can go and live in China as if it's our own country, and likewise for Chinese people wanting to live in Mesopotamia. I call up my dear Indian friend Sara. Her phone isn't available. I can't read any more. The rhythm of the story makes me feel sleepy. I switch the story to listening mode in the hope that the reader's voice will inspire me and give me an idea about how to design the story-game I have to produce.

*

The doorbell rings. I look out of the window. The morning sun floods the trees in the garden. The oranges shine like my mother's golden earrings. How I miss her! I miss her kisses, her tears and the way she sighed at life's ups and downs. I miss her earrings, the golden love hearts my father bought in Istanbul in the 1970s as a honeymoon present. That was when my father played the oud and my mother was a history teacher.

The doorbell rings again. A large flock of sparrows is pecking the grass in the garden. My father waves from beyond the garden wall. Frightened, the sparrows fly off to the neighbours' garden.

'Good morning, Father. All well? Has something happened?' I say as I undo the padlock on the door's steel chain.

'Nothing, son, nothing, I just wanted to see you.' He shakes my hand and wipes the sweat from the end of his nose. He looks into my eyes and embraces me. He's carrying a black bag, which he waves at me.

'Mr Translator, I've brought you a present,' he says.

'A present in a black bag, Lord preserve us. What is it, Father? Not a Kalashnikov, I hope.'

'War won't end as long as there are people, my boy, war after war. When was the world without wars anyway? My God, to hell with it,' Father says as he comes in.

I get breakfast ready: tea, eggs and cheese.

My father lights a cigarette after swallowing one bite of egg. He picks up his teacup and looks around at the pictures hanging on the wall. He stops in front of a copy of a painting by Fayeq Hassan, Horses in a Desert.

'What news of your English stories?' he asks as he looks at the picture.

I take his present out of the black bag. It's an explosives detection device that looks like a wand. He takes it from me and explains how it works, pretending the table is a car. My father's worried I might be targeted by Islamist groups because of my new job. They might see translating American literature as treason and a form of cooperation with the occupier. In fact, the wand turns out to be just a plastic stick with the end connected to a mirror to check underneath cars. In recent years the killers have developed new ways of reaping people's souls. They stick explosive devices under people's cars. It doesn't matter who the person targeted is. What matters is that the constant mayhem should serve their objectives. The explosive devices either kill you instantly or blow your legs off, in which case your neighbours, relatives and friends will say, 'Well you should praise God and thank Him for ensuring you survived!' Then you'd be a legless man who praises and thanks God. Violence sculpts you and, in this case, turns you into half a statue. Violence is the most brutal sculptor mankind has ever produced. A barbaric sculptor: no one wants to learn lessons from the works he has carved.

I graduated from the Languages Faculty a year ago. I studied English. I was lucky to get a job in the foreign literature magazine. The magazine specializes in translating literature from various languages. While I was studying I translated one story by Hemingway and another by Margaret Atwood. I had them published on the culture page in Awraq magazine, and my translations apparently caught the eye of the editor-in-chief. He contacted me when I was about to graduate and asked me to visit him at the magazine after I graduated. I had signed a contract with the foreign literature magazine within three weeks. The people at the magazine chose a Raymond Carver story for me. I hadn't read anything by him, but I had come across the name Carver in a critical article about dirty realism and about Carver's writer friend, Richard Ford.

My father poured himself another cup of tea and went out to the garden.

I watched him from the window. He sat at the table under the orange tree and stared at the table as if he were looking at himself in a mirror.

Every ten years my father changes into another person. It's as if he dances faithfully to every new rhythm in our shitty country, turning with each new turn. My mother's brother, who translated Freud's books, used to call him 'the chameleon'. For the past few years he's kept repeating that it was the chameleon that killed his sister. My mother died suddenly of a heart attack. We were three boys and a girl. My mother disembarked from the ship of our life and we had to battle the stormy and unpredictable waves of life with my father. Before we were born, in the 1970s, my father was obsessed with communism and playing the oud. He used to hold communist parties just for his comrades and play them revolutionary songs. There was a well-known song at the time called 'Lenin in Baghdad'. At the beginning of the 1980s my father abandoned communism, volunteered in the army and became a sniper. He won several awards for bravery in war. As a sniper, he was skilled at making neat little holes in the skulls of Iranian soldiers. In the 1990s my father deserted, but was caught and spent his days in one military prison after another. He treated the prisons as mosques: he started to pray and grew religious. Instead of thinking about a world full of free and happy people, he started thinking about a divine roadmap that led to Heaven or Hell. When the dictator was overthrown at the beginning of the new millennium no one understood him any longer. He would descend into strange periods of seclusion. He would disappear for a week or more, then suddenly reappear. He wouldn't let anyone ask why he had disappeared. He became introverted and depressed. After the U.S. forces left the archaeological site in Babylon, my father got a job as a guard in the antiquities department. Some time in his first days at work, he declared, 'The American infidels have turned the site of the oldest civilization in the world into a camp for stupid soldiers, occupying a country in the name of democracy.'

*

I take the lift to the tenth floor. At the door to the main dome the info-bot reminds me of the security procedures for going out into the abandoned city. I pay him and borrow a facemask. The door opens and then closes behind me. Dust blocks out the sun. Sandstorms are blowing all over the city. I turn on the mask's vision screen and walk up to a dead fountain more than a hundred years old and sit on the rim. Three drunks are messing around on the street corner. Sara's phone is still unavailable. She must be busy with the customers at the pleasure hotel. One of the drunks goes down on his knees theatrically while the other two imitate executing him. I think they're making fun of the country's murderous past – Daesh and the sectarianism that was fed by oil money. This abandoned city is now just a desiccated relic of a bloody past, a past that was steeped in religious fanaticism and dominated by classical capitalism. The violence only stopped after Babylon was engulfed by the effects of climate change and the oil wells had practically run dry. How puzzling and painful is the march of man!

The rivers and fields dried up. The desert advanced and obliterated the city. At the time, the federal government was struggling to mobilize modern technology to stop people abandoning the city forever. The federal government took advantage of oil exports in the final years, started some big investment projects and opened up to the world. For many third world countries the decisive factors in shifting the balance were that clean energy matured and spread all over the world, people in the West rose up against the brutal and selfish capitalist system, and the idea of one destiny and one world without hypocrisy or selfishness gained strength. People started saying, 'This is neither your country nor my country. It is our land,' and this was not just a slogan. People agitated and started to take the initiative to change the world through intelligence, humanity, and real justice. In the middle of the century the name 'Iraq' was changed to 'Federal Mesopotamia'.

First the Germans built technically advanced districts in Babylon and other cities, which made it possible for the residents to live with the desert storms. The sandstorms had made life in the city miserable by making the air unbreathable. During the time of the German districts, generations developed that were skilled at digital technology, until the Chinese appeared on the scene and stunned the world with the domes concept, which is now seen as the ideal solution for cities that are subject to desertification and environmental degradation. After the Chinese domes were built, Babylon's 'Magical Generation' was born – a generation that now exports the cleverest software and the most extraordinary scientific discoveries to the world. Thanks to our queen, the domes have become the new gardens of Babylon. Each dome in Babylon has its own special character. One dome is known for its fascinating cybergardens, another for its digital arts centres, and a third for its space dreams, such as the ninth district, where they are now building the world's tenth space lift. If it wasn't for the Water Rebels, we would be living in complete peace. I understand why the rebels object to the water allocations but violence is an emotional and primitive solution in a situation that calls for self-control and reflection. I don't know what solutions they are proposing. Blind rage is an inhuman weapon. It's a form of selfishness and hollow pride.

I'm reminded of our city's classical writer, who was angry at how bloody and violent life was in the city at the turn of the century. Okay, why not? That might work as the intro to his story-game. Why can't the story-game be inspired by how the writer ended up? He took refuge in Finland after Islamic State took over his city. In Finland he wrote four collections of stories and a play, then he disappeared until they found he had killed himself under a tree in the forests of northern Finland. The temperature was forty below zero, and when I looked for his date of birth, it turned out he was born in summer, in the month of July. Maybe he was born when the temperature was forty above zero. Maybe he was born in the sun and the fact that he died in the snow could be written into the start of the game. There could be two options for the player: a sun icon or a snow icon. If the player clicks on the sun icon the game begins at the birth of the writer and then we move on to his story, but if they choose the snow icon the player starts with his suicide under a tree with a pistol in his hand. Or the way into the game could be just two numbers: −40 or +40, and the story would have two tunnels and the player would choose.

Shit, what a dumb idea! I'll go for a little walk and maybe get these superficial ideas out of my head, and maybe inspiration will descend on me. It's not my day! Near the old parliament, there's a teacher wearing a facemask and a group of children who look like primitive animals in their masks. It's clearly an educational tour of the past. Some Nigerian tourists go warily into the ruins of the parliament building, taking photographs. I taste a bitterness in my mouth. I go back to the dome and get aboard a driverless, automated taxi and go to the pleasure hotel where Sara works. Most tourists prefer taxis with local drivers they can chat with. In the pleasure hotel I take the lift to the fantasy floor. I submit a blood sample to the analysis-bot, and he opens the door. I pay twenty e-credits and another door opens into the hall where the really sexy women are. I choose a beautiful Turkish girl and have sex with her in the zero-gravity room. I go down to the cyber-sex floor where Sara works. As soon as she sees me she rushes to hug me.

'What floor were you on?' she asks with a smile.

I tell her about the Turkish girl and she slaps me on the ass. 'You idiot!' she says. 'On the romance floor there's a new girl from Basra that would make your head spin if you saw her.'

I hug her again and whisper close to her lips: 'I've missed the way you think.'

She pushes me away gently and taps me on the head with her fist. 'Let's leave now, you story prick. What's up with you? Are you okay?'

I tell her in brief about my problem making a story-game out of the text by that writer who killed himself. She pulls me by the hand and says cheerfully, 'Let's go to the Selfish Gene bar – it's a vintage bar and it might do your classical text some good.'

In the bar, Sara orders a beer from the alcohol machine and I have a new arak they started making two months ago. We take a seat in the corner. From the screen on the table, Sara chooses the privacy option. A glass cocoon surrounds us. From the screen I choose a new Swedish song that Sara likes. I ask her how her mother is in India. 'My mother's resigned from the Mars project,' she says. 'She's taken issue with the recent constitution written by the One World committee. She objects to the part that says that every citizen in space must undertake never to rebel against Martian government through violence.

You know the debate – it's been raging for more than seventy years. A simple argument: if a violent rebellion took place and any parts of the settlement were damaged, it could mean all the settlers die. Life is still fragile there and it can't tolerate any violence. My mother objects and says it lays the basis for a space dictatorship. Anyway, you tell me now, what's your story problem?'

I don't like the taste of the new arak. Sara fetches me another drink made in South Africa that I haven't drunk before. It tastes sharp and pleasant. I look into Sara's big eyes and say, 'My dear friend, quite simply, I'm a short-story artist and I want to write my own story-games and novel-games. I don't get any joy from turning classical literature into smart-games. Quite honestly, their stories don't excite me very much. Besides, there's nothing new in the story of the writer who killed himself. I think it's one of his weakest stories. It was the last story he wrote and then he committed suicide.' Sara suggests I take the Games Centre by surprise by turning an almost-dead classical story into an original, advanced story. Then they will trust me and give me a chance to move to the department that composes new story-games. Sara takes from her pocket a small metal box and puts it on the table. She opens the box, which looks empty. 'Here's the key. With this you'll finish the story within a day!' she says.

'No, please Sara. You know I don't like psychedelic insects. Maybe smoking something natural, okay. But I don't approve of electronic parasites.'

'Life is short. You have to try an insect at least once,' Sara replies. 'Believe me, it's one of a kind. It was developed in Brazil and now it's colonising the whole world. You can't take it by yourself. You have to take it with a partner you trust and who trusts you, so that they can keep the thing under control. It's your partner who decides when your trip ends. Don't worry and don't be so serious. You trust me, right?' Sara uses her phone as a magnifying glass and looks into the box. She wets the tip of her finger and puts it in the box, and the microscopic insect sticks to it. She puts her finger into my hair and sets the insect free. 'Calm down, it's not working yet,' she says. 'The insect needs to find the right place on your scalp first, you numbskull. And it won't start to take effect until I activate it from my switch. I'll send the app for neutralising it to your phone. Some people can stop the effect of the insect during the trip by themselves, like someone who's asleep and realizes they're dreaming and they have to wake up. But not everyone manages that. The important thing is you have to relax. I'll monitor the insect's progress and your brain activity and stop it when the time is right.'

*

The next morning I decide to go to Dome 7. From there, I can go on to the abandoned city and then to the old site of the ruins, where the lion of Babylon used to stand – the lion that was moved to Dome 14 with other important antiquities some years ago. Together with Sara's insect, being at the site of the lion might stimulate my imagination. I take a facemask and some food and water. I re-read that old writer's story and leave.

It's just desert. I locate the site of the lion through the e-map on the screen of the mask. There are lots of sandstorms and a hot wind. I send Sara a message: 'Activate your insect.'

'Have a good trip, story prick,' she replies.

I try to find the site of the old oil pipeline. Five minutes pass without me feeling anything. Maybe my brain is too tough for the insect to penetrate. I feel uneasy in this deserted place. I can hear children's voices. I climb a sandy hill. I think the oil pipeline lies beyond it. At the base of the hill, on the other side,

I see a group of children playing football. How can they play without facemasks? I approach them and the referee, a young man, waves at me as if we're friends. A thin boy scores a goal after the defender tries to block him. They start arguing and the defender head-butts the boy who scored. The forward's nose starts to bleed. The match stops. Next minute, the forward is back home and his mother is trying to stop the bleeding with cotton wool while telling him off for playing rough. She stuffs his nose with cotton wool and asks him to hold his head up high. I know this boy. It's the writer who killed himself, but when he was a boy. I go out to the family's back garden to check up on this. Yes. Definitely. This is the pomegranate tree he was born under in July. His mother is now screaming in front of me, and carries on screaming until the woman next door climbs over the garden wall and helps her with the delivery. Where is he now? Okay, he's on the roof of the house. He's sitting among dozens of red birds. He throws seeds to the birds and takes a book out of a large wooden bird tower. He has installed a small shelf of books inside this tower. He might be hiding the books from his family. What's he reading? Ah, *Demian* by Hermann Hesse. Suddenly the sandstorms die down. Thick snow falls in what's now a vast forest. I see smoke rising. I head toward it. It's a small wooden hut with a sauna close by. The smoke is rising from the latter. A naked man comes to the door of the sauna smoking and drinking alcohol. Who else could it be! It's the old writer in flesh and blood. A white beard and a bald head and a glum look on his face. Although he's no more than forty years old, time has cruelly scarred the features of his face. I like this Finnish forest. I walk away from the sauna and go deep into the darkness of it. I spot a wolf. I'd better go back to the writer's house. The author sits in front of the computer, writing and drinking alcohol and smoking, wearing a green hat.

Suddenly he gets up and slams the computer against the edge of the table and finally kicks the wreckage of the computer like a goalkeeper kicking the ball upfield. He goes into the kitchen, takes a psychedelic mushroom out of a drawer, eats some of it and sits at the table smoking. I sit opposite him. He puts his hat on the table in front of him, and in turn, I take off my facemask and put it on the table. Minutes pass as we stare at each other.

'What do you want from me?' he asks. I'm not sure whether he's addressing me, because maybe he's under the influence of the mushrooms and can see someone else, or maybe he's talking to the characters in one of his stories. In the corner of the kitchen there's a wand for detecting explosives. He might have made it himself to re-create the ambiance in one of his stories. The wand is the father's gift to his son, the translator. How pathetic he is. He seems to have a gloomy imagination and his creative resources are very simple. He gets up and comes over to me. He puts his hand on my shoulder. What's happening surely isn't for real. He's hallucinating! He speaks to me, or rather he tells his story, which I know by heart. I don't pay him any attention. My mind wanders to a black cat lying under a delicious sun. I can feel it breathing. I feel as though I'm settling down inside the cat. I merge with the cat, while our writer goes on telling his story:

*

After my father went out to the garden, I picked up the teapot and followed him. I asked him if he wanted any more tea. He didn't answer, then started to talk about how wonderful orange trees are. 'Did you know, my son, that orange trees spread across the world from ancient China, where the orange was the king of foods and medicines. What a splendid tree it is! It flowers and bears fruit at the same time.'

'Father, are you all right?'

My father doesn't respond. He stands up and picks an orange. As he is about to speak, the black cat, stretched out along the top of the garden wall, opens its eyes.

*

Through its eyes I can see bright sunlight flooding the scene. I can see the father sitting with his son under the orange tree. I can hear an enormous mass of sounds. I can make out every note and mutter in this feast of sounds. At first the sounds surprise me but after a while they make me uneasy. I try to ignore the concerto of sounds and concentrate on what the translator's father is saying.

*

'Listen to me, son. That Abu Zahra, he never listened to what I said. I warned him and pleaded with him. In my head, he became the rebellious angel. The oil pipeline explosion tore him to shreds and roasted him. It's Babylonia. It's damned. He didn't believe me. This lousy country is inhabited with devils. We're just slaves, man. Don't be an oaf. I've said that a hundred times. He ranted on about morals and conscience as if we were living in God's promised paradise. Everything he said reminded me of the Arabic religious drama serials: morals eloquently expressed in a moribund language. Abu Zahra – you know him, my colleague, a fellow antiquities guard – he blocked his ears and didn't turn his useless brain on. I swear by God Almighty, I kissed his hand and pleaded with him on his last night. We were sitting close to the Babylon lion.'

*

I leave the cat. I feel sorry about that. I felt really comfortable inside it. I sit close to the guards at the lion, wearing my facemask. They light a small fire to get warm.

*

'*It was a cold winter's night. I buried myself in my coat and started listening to his nonsense, my blood boiling. He kept saying the same thing, like a preacher in a mosque. Shame, man. This is your country, and those people are bastards who burn and steal in the name of religion and want to take the country a thousand years backward so that they can live in their paradise with slave girls and virgins and all that bullshit.*'

*

I take my mask off and the guards disappear, but the lion of Babylon is still there. It's a beautiful night. The sky is clear and the weather is mild. For sure I'm in another season. Not winter and not cold, or even sandstorms. What time am I in? I hope I don't get lost. I lie down on the sand and look at the stars twinkling in the sky. I shut my eyes. The cat on top of the wall opens its eyes. I can see the father and his son the translator again. The father gets up, touches the leaves of the orange tree and continues:

*

'*Six months ago the parliamentary committees began to descend on the archaeological area. The Antiquities and Heritage Agency accused the Oil Ministry of destroying the ruins of the city of Babylon by extending a pipeline for oil products across an archaeological area that hadn't been excavated, but the Oil Ministry denied it and said the pipeline had been built in an area where two other pipelines, one for gas and one for oil, had been in place since 1975. The Antiquities Department didn't give in but submitted the case to the courts. The department said that the ministry's pipeline would irrevocably prevent the Babylon ruins being reincluded on the list of world heritage sites after the former dictator had messed with them, because in 1988 the Iraqi authorities had carried out restoration work on the ruins but UNESCO, after inspecting the site, said the work did not meet international standards. Materials had been used that were different from the original materials used by the Babylonians, and on some pieces of stone they had carved the words 'From Nebuchadnezzar to Saddam Hussein, Babylon rises again.' So UNESCO insisted that the ruins of the city of Babylon could not be included on its list. When the media reported the story of the new pipeline, a fierce debate broke out between the political parties in parliament, and they started accusing each other of corruption and serving foreign powers. My wife's uncle, who is known as Abu Aqrab, visited me and made me a tempting offer. He said his armed religious group wanted to blow up the old oil pipeline in Babylon and he asked Abu Zahra and me to help him. My wife's uncle knew Abu Zahra well. They had worked together in a primary school in the days of the former dictator. Abu Zahra taught religion and my wife's uncle taught geography. The uncle is now a senior official in an armed religious organisation called the Sword of the Imam. The organisation claims to be fighting the new government and the infidels, and it calls everyone traitors. The organisation was set up by a cleric who had broken away from a broad-based religious movement that had laid down its weapons and joined the nascent political process. The mainstream movement changed from being a movement of murderers that fasted and prayed, into one with ministers, members of parliament, businessmen and people of influence. Within a year they and their religion and the rest of their world had drowned in the sea of corruption that swept the country. Now the Sword of the Imam was offering a large sum of money in return for us turning a blind eye to their activities during the night shift at the ruins. They would sneak in and blow up the oil pipeline, then issue a statement on YouTube saying they had blown it up as a warning against building a new pipeline in Babylon, and that the government of corruption and occupation, together with the Americans, were stealing the country's oil while the people were starving and impoverished. Oh, and death to traitors.*

'I told Abu Zahra we wouldn't be helping them to kill innocent people and they could just blow up a pipeline in an area far away from any people. And besides, when it comes to this oil – we'd been living for decades in fear and terror and conflict because of this oil. What have we seen it bring, other than death and oppression and shit? Let them blow it up and rid us of this oil and its curse forever. Eveything else had been plundered in this Babylonian site. The bones of the ancients and the liquidized bones of prehistoric life had both been stolen, and what had we gained from guarding the greatest civilization in the world? We were guards protecting thieves. In the time of that bastard the dictator, the president's cousins had dug up antiquities and sold them to the West, as part of its ongoing collection of antiquities and oil. And today, the imam's cousins want their share of this store of bones. They want to make a new deal with the smart-markets of the West.

'Abu Zahra categorically rejected the offer from the Sword of the Imam group and threatened to write to the security agencies and to the governor if they didn't stop their threats. I never saw anyone so stupid in my life! Which governor and which security

agency was he talking about? All the security agencies were militias that belonged to them. Abu Aqrab himself went to see Abu Zahra and threatened him. But what can I say? He blocked his ears and dug in his heels. Life's crazy. Life's shit.'

The father falls silent and stands up. He looks at me, his son now, and hugging me, asks me to forgive him. He puts his cheek against my cheek and his tears wet my skin. He takes from his pocket a DVD wrapped in ordinary paper and puts it on the table.

'Keep it,' he says as he leaves.

*

The cat leaves at the same time. It goes down to the neighbours' garden, then climbs up to the second-floor window of their house. It sits on the windowsill and looks at what's inside the room. There's no furniture in the room – just a red Persian carpet. A naked man, with his paunch hanging beneath him, in the prostration posture for prayer. His whole body is covered in hair. He looks just like a pile of hair. A young woman is leaning forward right behind him. She puts her middle finger up his asshole, while the man moans with pleasure. He suddenly stands up straight, then bows. He's performing Muslim prayers and every time he bows or prostrates, the young woman sticks her finger up his ass. Maybe he imagines she's one of the houris of paradise. Finally the gorilla man turns over on his back and kicks his legs in the air in ecstasy. Then he gets up and goes out. The woman sets about locking the door. I look at her beautiful slim body. It looks like Sara's intoxicating figure. Where is Sara? Why don't I get in touch with her? Does what's happening have anything to do with the story by our writer who killed himself? There's no mention of the man praying with his ass bare in his story. The ass man comes back and knocks loudly on the door.

He kicks the door and starts shouting, asking the woman to open the door. The woman sits on the floor and starts crying. The cat tires of the man shouting behind the door and goes back to the garden. It prowls warily, then suddenly braces itself to pounce. Maybe there's a mouse there. I have a good look. Ah, okay, it's just a little bird.

*

The old writer slips a pistol out of the table drawer and goes out.

I follow him. He walks barefoot across the snow. I walk behind him. I ask him to stop but he keeps walking. I shout out loud, 'Stop. I know you. I'm a story designer like you and I've come to turn your story into a smart-game!'

Our writer looks back. 'It's all the same,' he says with a smile.

The cat goes back to the house of the translator, who sees it through the window. He opens the door for it, and it goes up to him. He strokes it, picks it up and carries it in his arms. He looks at the computer screen. I can't see anything. I'm outside the cat now. Where am I, I wonder? What's he reading? Maybe he's translating the Carver story. In the original story he's translating *What We Talk About When We Talk About Love*. Bloody cat! Maybe it felt me inside and evicted me. The translator plays the DVD that his father gave him. I can't see anything that's on the screen. It's true I'm outside the cat but now I'm close to the lion. Always the same places, but outside time! I don't need the cat's eyes. I know the content of the DVD. I've read the story dozens of time. The video starts, with night descending on a view of the giant oil pipeline. The only light is the light of the moon. Abu Zahra is down on his knees with his hands tied behind his back and his eyes blindfolded, next to the pipeline. The antiquities guard, the father of the man translating Carver, comes into the frame. The guard looks at his colleague Abu Zahra for some moments. He bends over him and kisses him on the head and moves out of the frame.

I feel very thirsty. The translator opens the window in the room, his hands trembling and terror in his eyes at what he's seen on the DVD. What's all this ranting and raving that goes on inside our skulls? A brutal struggle for ephemeral survival. An illusory survival, just a postponed death walking about on two legs. What is this instinct that imprisons us? Can imagination solve the riddle? The cat leaps from the window. The girl's scream reaches her neighbour. The translator runs to the neighbours' house. He bangs on the door but no one opens. He leaps from the wall to the garden, then smashes down the door to the house. I stay in the translator's room. I roam around his house. It's a modest house but neatly arranged. So this is the style of houses at the beginning of the last century. In the sitting room there's a picture on the wall that strikes me as familiar – a picture of a young girl standing under the Lion of Babylon. It's the same picture I keep in my room in Dome 2, a picture of my mother when she was a child. Perhaps it just looks like my picture. Could it really be the same picture? It is my mother. The translator saves the poor girl from the man who's praying, who broke down the door of the room and started threatening the girl with a knife. I don't understand what happened to him. A short while earlier the pious gorilla was enjoying having her finger in his asshole. I look for more pictures in the translator's house. I come across a photo album of his life. It's my history.

The camera moves to a place far from the oil pipeline. The antiquities guard blows up the pipeline by remote control. Abu Zahra burns. I burn too. I scream in terror. Darkness descends on the forest. The pain is unbearable. Someone wraps me in a blanket to smother the flames. Our classical writer fires the bullet into his head as he sits under the tree. I don't want to die. I shiver from the intense cold. I'm stretched out close to Abu Zahra as he burns. The pain in my body stops, but the smell of roast flesh makes me feel sick. The cat goes out into the street, then runs in panic toward the main road. The smell of human flesh burns my brain. I want to get rid of everything. I just want to be this cat. A police car almost runs it over. The cat cuts through the streets of the damned city of Babylon. It goes through houses, then goes down into the gardens of other houses. It climbs a tree, then walks cautiously along a branch that almost touches the balcony of one of those historic Babylonian-style houses. On the balcony there's an old woman whose face radiates goodness and wisdom, sitting in a wheelchair and watering the flowers on the balcony. 'Go to Adnan,' she whispers to a flower. 'Go to Adnan.'

Might Adnan be her son, or her dead husband? I very much enjoy the sight of the old woman and I feel a strange peace course through my feelings. The smell of Abu Zahra's flesh subsides. Peace and the smell of flowers descend. The old woman puts her lips close to the plant and whispers a song to the flower:

> From winter we learn the magic of our fable: warmth,
> nakedness, bed
> From time we learn how to store memories in the drawers
> of the spirit house
> From autumn we learn the shape of the leaves of life
> From cruelty and hatred we learn how strange the face of
> man is
> Then we scatter our thoughts
> And play again...

The mangle of life as it drips saliva on the shirt of our days!
We're frightened and we gather
We fall in love and we part
We learn the game and play it!
We learn to laugh from the silence of the toy that is broken
    in the arms of man
We go to sleep and wake up
Then we go to sleep and don't wake up
It's the sleeping rock that said, 'Life is the mirror of death.'
Both of them are a dead life!
We learn fear before faith
We learn faith before love
We learn love before truth
So we make a mistake and learn to be dizzy, as if it's a
    lesson to be learned
We learn how emotion drifts from the music of silence and
    speech
From the depths of caves blows the wind of our toy that's
    broken in the lap of a child
From sleeping fields and forests blow all the stages of
    drunkenness
The forest of life a grape
The forest of death a barrel
The forest of life fermentation
The forest of death a cup
Then the fingers of man hold the wineglass of pleasure and
    he eats the thorns of uncertainty
Then we inscribe our poor human sentence
On the blackboard of darkness:
'Sleeping in oblivion'.

The cat thinks about coming down from the tree. The old woman notices it. She smiles at it and calls it: 'Puss puss puss puss.' The cat advances warily along the branch and jumps onto the balcony. It sniffs the old woman's feet. The old woman puts out her fingers to the cat and it sniffs those. The smell of flowers on the old lady's fingertips puts me at ease. The old woman strokes the cat's head. I feel the affection, the love, the peace, the value of human touch and the sweet power of love.

*

I feel numb.
   I doze off.
   I dream.
   I wake up.

*

In the cybergarden of Babylon, the weather is more than wonderful. Sara lets out a shrill laugh every now and then as I tell her about my trip.

Sara says, 'I did everything I could to control the effect of the insect so that you could have a good trip, but your brain's so stubborn and so sunk in melancholy that even that Brazilian insect wasn't any use.'

'Okay, Sara,' says Adnan. 'What you say may be true but your Brazilian insect did me an invaluable service. Firstly, my story-game will be based on the cat as a main character for getting into the story of that writer who killed himself. But more importantly, what's really surprising about what happened is that I finally found out who my grandfather was. You might not believe it, Sara, but my grandfather was the man who translated the Carver stories.'

Translated by Jonathan Wright

The Farctory

K.A. Teryna

Russia

When I asked Alex Shvartsman for Russian SF stories, he hurried to tell me about K.A. Teryna and, once he did, I was hooked. Here was a singular talent, with writing fresh and strange – how had I missed it before? Luckily for me, Alex then proceeded to beguile me with this new story, appearing here in English for the first time, and I snapped it up! So without further ado, thank you for reading through this rather large volume, and to send you on your way, step right into the world of our final story. Welcome to 'The Farctory'! This story was translated from Russian by Alex Shvartsman.

I: Here

The Shadow

It started when the vending machine which dispensed senses broke down. It was the last such machine on the block. Its screen, once sparkling and bright, collapsed into a pile of white noise that felt prickly to the touch. Squeamishly, I shoved my hand into the hissing mess, twisted the levers at random, feeling the upset electrons hop like fleas across my palm. Nothing changed.

I used a knife to poke at the opening under the speaker. The speaker emitted a puff of smoke and its cover creaked open, releasing a small gray russle, which chittered at me indignantly. I wasn't surprised: the russles were everywhere these days. The rodent cut its fiery squeak short, deftly jumped onto the pavement, and skittered away. Immediately thereafter, rusty gears tumbled from the machine, followed by zigzags of celluloid punch tape. The machine's screen blinked for the last time and trickled down the drain into a sewer grate. I was left standing alone in the middle of an empty street.

Unless you count Hare, who was clumsily trying to hide around the corner – the boy huffed like Grandma Bach's teakettle. I pretended not to notice him. Mauk probably wouldn't have done likewise. But I had no other alternative.

That's when the shadow appeared. I turned around as soon as I sensed its chilly smell.

The shadow was sickly, flat, and transparent. In other words, it looked like any other shadow.

Frankly, I hadn't been able to stand shadows since childhood. They were cold. They made the most unpleasant rustling noises. Nowadays, there was no reason for their existence at all: the Farctory was closed, the color mines had been shuttered.

For as long as I could remember, shadows had snuck into the city from the dungeons under the Farctory. They burrowed their way up with their cold curious noses. The repair crews couldn't keep up. The shadows were more keenly motivated, hence the unfortunate statistic: three new wormholes dug for every one patched up with a harsh thread of reality.

Feral shadows were a source of chaos and destruction. Taming a shadow was like taming an abyss. It would stare with hungry eyes from every corner of your home. It would spew its nonsense. And it would wait for the right moment.

You might call this selfishness. I say, it's the love of order. Tenderness toward meaning.

The shadows had always been attracted to me, as if by an invisible magnet. I sometimes wondered if I should attempt to dislike girls with a similar passion, so as to obtain their infinite, warm attentions. Frankly, however, I scared off the girls without trying. At first because I was with Barbara, and then because Barbara was gone.

The shadow blinked. Instead of walking away, for some reason I looked it in the eyes. The shadow's eyes were poorly drawn and wrinkled. A raspy draft blew out from them. I didn't know if that was the norm for all shadows.

The shadow held out its hand to me. A small pile of senses wiggled on its palm, dying. They squeaked plaintively as they dissolved in the shadow's flat shading.

It appeared the broken vending machine was the shadow's fault.

Some among your acquaintances were surely shadow sympathizers. This was a common thing. Here and there, people spoke out in defense of these mindless creatures.

One of my friends, Eyck, fed shadows a little salt on occasion, and wrote down their ravings while concentrating so hard that his tongue stuck out. What else is there to say?

I wasn't like that.

The shadow said, 'Stepped candareen in the miniature bedstead. Yes.'

This sounded almost meaningful compared to the usual shadow drivel. Its voice was entirely devoid of color, quiet and mournful.

I began to walk away.

The damned shadow didn't give up. It overtook me and stopped. It blinked its eyes and flashed a pathetic single-line smile.

What bad timing! Mauk was already waiting for me at the Dichotomy, and I couldn't arrive late.

And so I took out a revolver and shot the shadow right in the face.

Habitually, I wondered what Barbara would say when I found her. She'd say, what have you become, Bach?

Worst of all, I hardly believed anymore that I'd find her at all.

Coloasters

The walls of the Dichotomy were decorated with the most unusual objects, which comprised the past of the bar's owner, old man Ulle. There was an ash bow loaded with the world's slowest arrows. An arrow fired from it appeared suspended in the air, as though it wasn't moving at all. There was also a huge tortoise shell which, according to Ulle, once housed an entire brood of feral vowels. There were photos – mostly smudged and out of focus – that nevertheless attested to the photographer's eventful and adventurous life. Only one photo impressed with the amazing clarity and sharpness of its lines – a portrait of an unknown woman. I could make out every little detail in it: broken tree branches, the attendant bird in the sky, the self-assured striped meowler on the table. But the visage of the stranger herself slipped away and crumbled whenever I tried to focus on it.

I liked Ulle – he was a tough old man who'd tasted of both reason and chaos. A retired, lonely hunter, he generously poured memories for anyone. At one point, I could have become like him, had Barbara not entered my life.

Dichotomy was one of the last places where they still served colors. No matter how often I asked, that scoundrel Ulle wouldn't admit where he got them. The answer to that was almost certainly Mauk.

I went there every evening for nearly a month. I sat on the same unremarkable stool at the bar, and remained there until midnight. After two weeks of this, the regulars began calling that stool 'Bach's spot' and would chase random patrons off it upon my arrival.

The bar-going public are a straightforward lot. It's easy to gain their trust.

I ordered a glass of Ulle's finest blue every time, which gained me his favor. The glass came with a thick cardboard coloaster shaped like a tortoise. From the first evening, I repeated the same exact trick: I drank exactly half of the blue color, set aside the glass, and proceeded to cut open the latest tortoise with my pocket butterfly knife. It must be said: neither the butterfly, nor the tortoises, nor the assorted patrons, nor the bartender were pleased by this procedure. I understood them very well. You would, too. If you were to encounter a teenager who keeps thoughtfully scraping a rusty nail on glass, you would probably smack him upside the head, and he would deserve it.

I dutifully played the role of such a teenager for nineteen evenings, until my finely tuned sense of timing went off. Something inside me knew it was time to wrap up. I didn't care for the opinion of the butterfly knife or the tortoises, as they couldn't reach my head, let alone smack it. Ulle and his customers, on the other hand, were on the verge of exhausting their collective patience. Everyone was ready for an endgame, and this endgame plunged the audience into a state of true ecstasy.

The story I told them as I dissected one of the first tortoises was simple and naïve like a newborn meowler. I claimed that one in every one hundred coloasters had a sense prize inserted into it at the Farctory, back when the Farctory was still open. It was impossible to prove or disprove this claim. It would seem one could ask the first Farctory engineer they met, and the truth would crawl into the light. Except, first, a layman is thoroughly convinced that every engineer is completely and irrevocably mad. Second, ever since the Farctory closed, not a single person had admitted to having had anything to do with it. All engineers I knew disappeared that day, leaving behind nothing but a damp smell of solvent in their empty apartments. And these were tough guys, who worked with undiluted colors daily!

My audience watched with unhealthy fascination as I destroyed the round cardboard tortoises one by one, committing crimes against common sense. Their faith faded with every dissected coloaster, just as their frustration and desire to smack me upside the head flourished.

Finally, on the nineteenth evening, I deftly swapped out the latest tortoise coloaster for a different one that looked the same. I'd prepared the fake in advance by carefully cutting the tortoise in two layers and inserting a little ordinary sense in-between. Then I painstakingly glued it back together.

Imagine: I downed half a glass of blue in two gulps. (I felt a buzz and warmth in my head, and I momentarily lost my balance, as though cradled by soft ocean waves; it smelled of salt and sand.) I set the glass aside. The audience held their collective breath. They were on the edge. They didn't need to glance at each other: the air was filled with the invisible weight of their judgment. It was very clear, I was about to be beaten up. As soon as I dragged the rusty nail across a pane of glass again, scratched their nerves with yet another senseless destruction of a coloaster, they would, quietly and efficiently (and in some cases with poorly concealed enthusiasm), proceed to smack me upside the head. To put it mildly.

I retrieved my butterfly and flipped the blade open in a practiced motion. *Slice*. I made the cut. Silence. Anticipation. Eager readiness. I carefully separated the two halves of the coloaster. The tension reached its apogee. The dim light of the bar lamp wasn't enough for the audience to see the sense yet. I slowly finished my glass of blue. (Cries of seagulls, transparent lightness, and wind in my face.) I hooked the sense with the tip of my knife and victoriously raised it above my head. The sense had nearly choked in its cardboard coloaster prison, but it was alive. It shimmered in the light. Aaand...

Explosion. There was a roar of voices and a thunder of applause. The audience rejoiced.

Warmed by their inexpensive colors, they were as genuinely happy for me as they had genuinely been prepared to rough me up. They clapped me on the back so energetically that it might have been easier to suffer their fists.

I handed my prize over to Ulle: an ordinary sense was enough to treat everyone present to a glass of a strong red.

Via this simple trick I became 'good ol' Bach'. Fritz excitedly told me about the latest accomplishments of his youngest, Max complained about the ladies, young Eyck offered me the best-friend discount as he tried to sell me his handwritten manuscript, its rustling pages languidly playing a non-existent melody. In short, I was now part of the pack.

Also, after that evening, all tortoise coloasters disappeared from the bar counter. They were replaced by the expensive cork coasters, which Ulle typically reserved for special occasions.

The Right Person

I knew very little about Mauk, but I knew the important thing: he was the right person.

Mauk was a grim, bearded man with a hooked nose, unhurried and thorough. Only his eyes contradicted his thoroughness, and they argued loudly and incessantly. His eyes were shifty, full of mischief, and very curious – like those of young russles. Mauk's eyes appeared to live an independent life and looked out of place on his serious face. Occasionally they would freeze and turn dim, like the shell of a dead snail. There was no doubt that in those moments the eyes looked within Mauk himself, stunned by a sudden idea or conclusion that visited his large, elongated head.

We sat down at a separate table, located underneath the tortoise shell covered in scratched-in autographs.

'What are you drinking? My treat.'

'Don't worry about it, Bach. Bach, is it? Did I recall that right? Good, good.' Mauk retrieved a crumpled plastic cup and a dark, flat metal flask from the inside pocket of his coat. 'Thank you, but I exclusively imbibe my own.'

The liquid he poured into the glass was undoubtedly a color, but I couldn't tell which one.

Ulle brought me a glass of blue. Before returning to the bar, he glanced unkindly toward Mauk and his flask, but said nothing.

'Would you mind if I smoke?'

What incredible luck! I wasn't sure whether Mauk was a smoker and was trying to come up with some awkward excuse for performing my little trick. 'Not at all.'

Suddenly there was a match box in my hand, and then I was leaning over the table, offering Mauk a light. Everything was going swimmingly.

'Let's talk frankly. I don't know you. But Eyck insists that you're a great guy.'

I had ended up buying Eyck's damned manuscript and made the rash decision of bringing it home. Everything in my room: the drapes, the carpet, and even the stove became drenched with the smell of its nonexistent melody. It was decidedly impossible to be there now: anyone entering the room fell into a semblance of a cataleptic state as they painfully tried to recall the familiar-seeming notes that stubbornly refused to form into anything meaningful. I had to hope that my sacrifice wasn't in vain.

After all, Eyck had connected me with Mauk, and that meant a lot. Assuming Mauk was the right person.

'Eyck wouldn't lie,' I replied, also lighting up.

I took a deep drag, then exhaled calmly. Everything inside me roiled and boiled, but outwardly I resembled a sleepy sphinx. Puffs of smoke formed into a triangle. Mauk grunted, impressed. I'd practiced this trick for far longer than the one with the matches.

'Tell me about your problem, Bach. Friends of Eyck are like relatives to me.'

That's right. Mauk was a problem solver. Except no one ever heard of people like him having relatives. People close to them were the kind of problem someone like Mauk got rid of first.

I held back my answer, even though I knew exactly what I needed. I had known it a month ago, when I first set foot in this bar.

Mauk poured more color from the flask into his cup, and drank before I had time to examine it. But I could tell from the smell: his color was stronger than the strongest blue or red I'd ever tasted. This was fortunate, for two reasons.

First, it was confirmation that Mauk really was the right person. A color this rich could only come from the Farctory.

Second, the sharp concentrated taste would hide the bitterness of the powder I'd used to spike his drink when I offered Mauk the light.

I held back my response because I wanted to stall until the powder took its effect. Don't think it was anything untoward. Just some light spices, a mix of mint and time. When combined with a thick color, it would make Mauk a little more frivolous and agreeable.

Otherwise he'd deny me without hesitation.

'I won't rush you,' Mauk said softly. 'But do keep in mind that anything you say will remain between us. Pretend like I'm your kindly grandmother.'

'I better not,' I replied. 'Grandma Bach was an especially insidious creature.'

It seemed Mauk was used to dealing with indecisive clients. The smoke from his cigarette crept across the Dichotomy, its fins twitching lazily; Mauk's calm was that of a great wise fish. A fish that hid its teeth for the time being.

I took a sip of the blue and felt the sea flowing through my veins.

'Do you prefer the blue?'

I nodded.

'Believe me, a single sip of the real, undiluted color, and you will never appreciate the cheap facsimile they serve in this bar again. Would you like some?'

He reached for his flask.

To be honest, I was tempted to sip a tiny little bit of his mysterious color. If Mauk wasn't lying, it should be something incredible... But no, I had to remain sober that day. I replied with an ill-fitting cliché. 'Silence is the best color.'

'You're cautious. And yet, you sought me out. This characterizes you as a man with a complex inner world.'

He was wrong about that. Ever since Barbara disappeared, my inner world had become empty, dusty, and simple. No more complex than a button, and equally filled with holes.

Mauk gulped down his color and immediately poured another portion. I knew that the moment had come.

Dichotomy was the perfect venue for such conversations. Cigarette smoke reliably absorbed and chewed-up sounds, making it seem as though we were surrounded with a thick layer of pressed cotton. Still, I looked around, making sure that no one was curious about our cozy chat. Only then did I notice that the place was unusually empty. There was Ulle behind the bar counter, me and Mauk under the tortoise shell, and Eyck scribbling something in his old notebook in the far corner.

I took off my hat and ran a hand through my hair (the gel hissed as it tickled my palm). I leaned forward and looked Mauk right in the eye as I said, 'I need to get inside the Farctory.'

Mauk slowly extinguished his cigarette in the filthy ashtray. He studied me from behind his stern eyebrows.

'Are you sure you want to go there? Take your time, Bach, think about it. Once I grant your wish, there's no going back.'

I nodded. 'I'm absolutely sure.'

'Now?'

'Now.'

'In that case, I suggest we don't dawdle.'

As though Mauk led people into the Farctory every day.

He got up, put on his captain's cap, which paradoxically made his head appear even more oblong, buttoned his duffle coat, and headed for the exit. I dropped a small sense onto the table, under an empty glass so it wouldn't escape.

Mauk paused by the door, and asked. 'What's that smell? Tangerines?'

I didn't respond.

As we left the bar, a shadow hissed and slid inside the gap in the Dichotomy's slightly open door.

Russles Underfoot

People used to disappear before. Here's what I mean by *disappear*. You leave your home wearing checkered slippers, carrying a shot glass in the left hand and a fishing rod in the right. You plan to milk a little bit of sense out of the nearest vending machine, and possibly catch a couple of pikes. A week later, you return with a bucket filled with sense, and a matchbox filled with fish. I don't know about you, but I refuse to call that a disappearance. When you return home and discover that your wife isn't there, now that's a different story. At first you wait patiently, the way she'd waited for you, then you imperceptibly switch from drinking the light green to the strong blue. Then you notice that the bald guy on the third floor isn't rattling his castanets anymore, and the old lady downstairs has ceased reciting poetry in the voice of a striped meowler stuck inside the radio. You come to understand that you're alone in the building. Perhaps you're alone in the entire block.

You go to the nearest bar and, while sipping a mug of considerably diluted green, you learn that the Farctory has shut down. That people are disappearing irrevocably, leaving behind nothing but the echo of yesterday's footsteps.

I planned to put a stop to this.

It was really late, or perhaps a little too early. We walked along a dark street, russles skittering underfoot. Mauk walked evenly, with calm dignity, as though there were no russles about, as though no russles ever existed.

I thought that Barbara would've probably found Mauk interesting. Barbara collected people; she liked them. She gathered them like stray meowlers and warmed them by the fireplace.

And not only people.

Barbara found something in common with everyone, and electrons ceased biting, and senses multiplied on their own in her presence.

Even I was alive, while she was by my side.

I think Barbara could've loved even the russles.

It's possible that russles appeared even back when the Farctory was still operational. Perhaps I'd even noticed them.

I'd seen them with my eyes, but didn't recognize them with my mind. I was in love then, and everyone knows that love captures a man whole, leaving not even a single square centimeter of attention for some tailed rodents.

Then the sense vending machines began melting one by one, and russles became the least of my problems. But, you know this. Everyone has their own story like that. You look around and realize, it's too late. The wife has disappeared, the world rumbles as it rolls toward chaos, and russles are skittering underfoot.

Hare stalked us. He did this awkwardly and loudly, and it took a considerable effort for me not to stop and chide him right there and then. It would've been a curious scene, considering that Hare's presence was supposed to remain concealed from Mauk.

Therefore, I endeavored to walk as loudly as possible, pounding the soles of my shoes against the pavement. Mauk seemingly didn't notice my trick, lost in his own thoughts.

You might rush to judgment, thinking me some sort of a grifter or a thief. But Hare was only my insurance. Frankly, a good-for-nothing insurance.

It wouldn't matter, if Mauk didn't plan to cheat me. But who could know that in advance? I continued to strike the pavement like a proper tap dancer.

But, when we approached the Farctory, Mauk said, 'Let your boy come out. He can carry the lamp.'

The Farctory

All roads led here. A quiet whisper at the next table, where instead of the disappeared people, rumors shyly bristled their mustaches. Mysterious signs on the walls of empty houses and arrows on the pavement. Everything pointed toward the Farctory.

This used to be a good neighborhood: old buildings, bricks in conversation with tiles, cirrus clouds tickling the ears of meowlers, gloomy sycamores sprinkling the ground with thorns.

And at the center of it all – the Farctory. A squat building – three or four stories total. The walls and the windows were covered in cracks, but still remained unbreakable.

It was quiet and empty there at night. The smell of decay wandered the streets; the wind surreptitiously licked the pavement.

In reality, the Farctory occupied a city-sized space underground. Perhaps even larger – I didn't remember for certain.

Over the course of the past month, I had circumnavigated the Farctory seventeen times, looking for a way in. I had come here with an axe, matches, a hacksaw. It was no use: the walls and windows of the Farctory were indestructible.

This is why I was so curious to see what trick Mauk would pull to get us inside. I imagined a secret passage from an apartment in an adjacent building: grim wallpaper, a suspicious old woman in a greasy dressing gown and an untidy cap, her husband leading us into the damp basement past a purring meowler. Or maybe a rooftop run: brick dust disturbed by our boots filling the air, clogging our eyes, noses, ears; crows scattering from the chimneys.

Instead Mauk led us straight to the central gate and casually unlocked a small door at one of its sides.

Before entering, he pulled out his flask and took a sip of color. He offered it to me. I shook my head, declining.

'Drink,' Mauk insisted. His voice sounded enchanting and smooth like silk.

I resolutely turned aside his hand holding the flask. Mauk shrugged.

We entered. Mauk gave Hare a cast-iron kerosene lamp that seemed heavier than the boy himself. Hare obediently accepted it and lifted it as high as he could.

A frightened echo stomped across the enormous workshop shrouded in darkness. There was a sharp smell of engine oil and color. Mauk walked in the lead, followed by Hare, and finally me.

Clack, clack, clack, the darkness whispered. I imagined enormous machines looming over us with their condescending sleepy smiles.

The light from the kerosene lamp snatched glimpses of this incredible structure from the darkness: pipes, enormous turbines, staircases. The main assembly line. And finally, the circuit breaker. Huge, impressive, promising, it shone invitingly in the dim light of the lamp.

I reached into my pocket and felt for a bundle, wrapped in rough tangerine peel. This bundle, hidden for the time being, contained my distracting maneuver.

Suddenly Mauk stopped, turned around. The lamp in Hare's hands lit his face from underneath.

'Why do you smell like tangerines?' he asked sternly. Fire danced in his restless eyes.

I had to give it to him, Mauk was insightful and he asked the right question. But it was too late. Obedient to the touch of my hand, the tangerine peel crumpled, releasing the manuscript – the same manuscript sold to me by Eyck. Carefully at first, but gaining confidence with each instant, the rustling melody flowed across the dark space – languid and intrusive like the morning trill of the attendant bird. I'd long since grown used to this melody. I no longer became lost in its dusty labyrinth. But for the unprepared, it was a real trap.

Mauk's face turned unnaturally focused; he froze, as though wrapped in invisible threads. The same thing happened to Hare.

I left the circle of light in two steps.

You see, I was certain that the Farctory was behind everything. The sense shortage, the missing people, chaos, and chamomile tea – the reasons behind all of that were in this dying, abandoned, and impregnable building. If my troubles began when the Farctory was shut down, then everything could only be fixed by returning the Farctory to life.

To be honest, I only had a vague idea as to how to approach this problem. I drove the cowardly idea of sharing my plan with Mauk deep into the far recesses of my hole-riddled consciousness. Saving the world couldn't be trusted to a man who seemingly profited from that world's death throes.

And so my plan was simple: to reactivate the conveyor belt. That would be enough, for now.

Tasks should be completed gradually, one at a time. That way, there's a chance that the tasks will show initiative, pick up the baton, complete one another. That's how our world works. The circuit breaker that starts the conveyor belt sat at one end of the electric labyrinth. At the other end – a wife and an apple pie. Simple, really.

Thinking that, I resolutely pulled the switch upward.

After that, everything happened on its own.

Slowly, one after another, the lamps lit up, filling the air with the smell of warm dust. I saw hulking silhouettes of machines, their roots deep in the cement floor, their tops reaching toward the roof far above.

It was a titanic sight. A huge automated line for pouring color. I imagined how the senses had rang, gnashed, popped, and celebrated here, back when the Farctory was alive.

The multilevel conveyor occupied all the visible space on the floor and above; its lines weaved a complicated web among giant, dusty flasks, rusty boilers, and darkened pipes. I noticed a movement. Several russles quickly poured thick yellow color from a huge tank into a dirty canister. Directly above me, on an engineering platform with a trellised floor, a russle was counting dark unlabeled bottles. Russles scurried along the pipes and stairs in the most businesslike fashion. One sat atop a lamp and selflessly nibbled on the long cord that secured that lamp to the ceiling.

Although the conveyor belt was still, life at the Farctory hadn't ceased when it stopped.

Mauk and Hare remained at the center of the workshop, locked in the trap of the melody. Mauk's face was a mask of concentration. Hare's still eyes stared at me in mute opprobrium. I hadn't warned him about my trick and now I felt a light pang of guilt.

The russles weren't too scared by the light being turned on; they appeared used to it. But then one of them noticed me, squeaked something, and immediately all work in the entire workshop ceased. I felt thousands of intense gazes upon me. The canister rolled down the stairs, the bottles clanked. The pipes rumbled loudly. The russles abandoned their pursuits: they had a new focus.

Never before had I had cause to view the little gray inconspicuous russles as a threat. I must admit, this time they made quite an impression on me. Perhaps I should have recruited a dozen meowlers as my co-conspirators instead of one Hare; the russles were wary of meowlers.

Down

I retreated step by step, hoping to come up with a clever plan on the fly. The gray wave of russles blanketed the floor as they approached me. I took another step and felt the massive conveyor at my back. Without thinking, I jumped up onto the conveyor belt.

The belt came alive. This seemed like the logical and proper ending to my heist: the belt would take me higher and higher along the multilayer conveyor, up to the roof of the world, or at least the roof of the Farctory. Perhaps Barbara was already waiting for me there. I looked up: the first rays of dawn streamed through the gaps in the ceiling.

Except the belt was moving in the wrong direction. It was carrying me away from the light, down, toward the dark dungeons of the shadows.

I reacted in the most foolish manner: I ran along the belt in the opposite direction. This was a pointless waste of effort: the belt moved faster and faster.

'Don't resist,' I heard Mauk's calm voice. 'It will only make things worse.'

Impossibly, he had managed to untangle himself from my trap in so short a time. He stood in front of the switch I had used to reanimate the Farctory. His eyes glistened coldly. In those eyes I saw the truth in all its frightening simplicity: I had lost.

From the very beginning everything had gone according to another's plan. All my traps and tricks, my clever subterfuges were nothing more than child's play. The insidious Mauk had observed all of them through the lively russles of his eyes. He predicted my every step, and each step had led me into the web he had spun.

'You should have drunk the color when I offered it.'

Instead of listening to him, I pulled a revolver from its holster. I fired, then fired again.

The bullets were well-trained. They needed no help in choosing their trajectories. They went hunting, leaving behind the predatory path of sparkling air. I realized my mistake before the bullets reached their target. Color is a highly explosive substance, too dangerous to discharge a weapon in a place where color permeates the air.

The brightest flash instantly gave way to total darkness. I was blind.

As if no light ever existed. As if there was ever only darkness.

I was falling.

II: There

The Cardboard City

My first thought is: I'm alive. I landed on my feet like some lucky meowler.

I search my feelings: darkness, nothing hurts, a bit of an eclipse in my mind, a confusion in my memory. But that's nothing.

I focus and begin to remember. The Farctory, me discharging a weapon. The flash. Mauk.

I get up and walk.

I hope to reach the wall by my hundredth step, at most. I find it on my three-thousand-six-hundred-and-seventy-fourth step. Plus or minus two steps: I may have lost count twice.

Dead stone masonry at about the height of my waist. It's wet; a cold fog rises from somewhere below. The darkness turns gray as it freezes: I see that my palms are pressing against the fence that surrounds a bridge. Somewhere in the damp, toy-like, papier-mâché or painted fog, a steamboat cries plaintively.

Cracks snake lazily under my palms. So it seems to me at first. When I look closely, I see that they don't snake at all. Dead cracks on dead stone. Someone might call their sluggish multi-year journey a life – but not me.

My heart pumps like a crazed meowler. This makes absolutely no sense. *Sense*. Is all of this about the broken vending machine? I try to recall something important, but my memory fails me.

'Bach!' I hear an echo of a vaguely familiar voice. 'Are you here?'

For some reason, I'm afraid to turn around.

Very afraid.

I turn.

A translucent figure rises over the bridge. It's difficult to make it out in the uncertain shading of the fog.

The shadow. Half drawn, half roughly fashioned from cardboard. My hand reaches for the revolver of its own volition, but the revolver isn't there.

I mentally order myself to remain in place. Still, I run away in the most cowardly fashion. I cross the bridge. Twelve steps. I stare into the darkness in the foolish hope of finding a door which I could use to get out of here.

With my every step, the shading of the fog thins out, recedes. Everything is even worse than I could imagine. To be honest, I have no clue what I could've imagined. But definitely not this.

To my left and right is the black stillness of inanimate water.

Ahead of me, ridiculous in their geometric simplicity, as if drawn by charcoal on rough paper, walls reach up toward where the sky should be. There is no sky. Instead, there's a low-hanging lilac-gray ceiling. It swirls slowly, with a sense of belonging, over my head, and rumbles curses in its cardboard tongue. The street frightens me with its merciless straightness. It's too predictable and unchanging to be real.

I step carefully as I walk on dead pavement alongside dead walls with dead window displays.

Imagine a city built of cardboard pop-ups on the pages of a children's book. You flip the pages, and one street replaces another. A voluminous world filled with finest details and amazing depth is borne of a flat pane.

But if you were to close the book, this world would disappear.

Houses, trees, streets, and people would become flat, turn into dead cardboard.

I walk across such a page.

There's no doubt: I'm in the dungeon of the shadows.

'Cut out these games, Bach!'

The shadow catches up to me and rests its hand on my shoulder.

There's a glimpse of hope: I'm about to see Barbara.

But, no. I won't.

The Club of Daring Meowlers

The basement belongs to Schultz – a short bald man who doesn't know how to bluff. Schultz wrinkles his forehead, pretending to think, but his red ears and twitching eye thoroughly betray him. He's holding a nice fat flush, or better.

Somewhere upstairs, wearing curlers and a plush robe, shadow Natasha, Schultz's Russian girlfriend, is zealously crushing garlic: there will be real Ukrainian ajoblanco soup served for dinner. It sounds as though the ceiling is about to collapse onto our heads.

Don't frown, Schultz, it'll make your ears fall off, says the Canadian. He has sharp teeth, red hair, and no name. The Canadian is certain he's from Montreal, that sooner or later a girl named Rose will fall for him, and that his hand of three fours is good enough to beat Schultz.

Obviously, he's wrong on all counts.

Gret is silent. Gret is always silent. Cardboard crumbles are stuck in his beard, his sad eyes tear up from the dust of the cartoon city. Gret believes that he was born in the middle of a huge traffic jam, and that the Black woman taxi-driver who delivered him told his mother: keep this child safe, kiddo – he's been kissed by Jesus; the grateful mother named her son after that woman. In this one thing Gret is definitely right: he has a woman's name.

The cats yowl in the yard. Cats are very similar to meowlers, except they're more daring and not all of them meow.

I'm like that, too. I'm almost real, except I live in a cardboard city. Among my cardboard friends.

I study the drawn faces. Why don't they remember?

Shultz doesn't recall his huge trawler, doesn't remember that the largest, most extraordinary and nuanced senses have been caught in his nets.

The Canadian doesn't recall that his name is Asmus, that any deck becomes magical in his hands, and that he can beat anyone at cards.

Gret doesn't recall that he was born with a gun in his hand, doesn't remember how he used to shoot attendant birds in flight from atop the Tobacco Tower. Doesn't remember how he traded a narwhal skull in exchange for the remnants of a giant sense.

When I tell them about these things, they smile in embarrassment.

They say: isn't it time for you to see the doctor, Bach?

The Doctor

The doctor is a dull old man with a stern gaze. He never argues with me. He listens attentively and marks up his notebook. He asks, why are you smiling, Bach?

Is it possible not to smile when a cartoon little man is trying to cure you of a non-existent disease?

How do you sleep, asks the doctor. I sleep well, I reply. I sleep very well.

The shadows sleep, you see. They lie down on their lush cardboard mattresses, close their eyes, and attentively view their so-called dreams.

They demand that I do the same.

Tell me about your dreams, the doctor says.

I make stuff up. I tell him how, in a dream, Gret dealt me four aces and I won a real bus. How I vacationed by the sea, and met a nice girl there. How I found myself naked in the middle of a street filled with strangers.

The doctor nods and writes it all down. He says, tell me about Barbara.

I reply, trying to slow the traitorous beating of my heart: Barbara is dead.

I hate this lie, but in this cardboard world, I'm forced to lie often.

Grandma Bach

I have come to like this old shadow more than I used to like Grandma Bach back there, up above.

That one was looming, harsh, and very active. No one dared contradict her. Grandma Bach of the shadow world is a dry woman with defenseless eyes behind the thick lenses of her glasses.

In this world everyone thinks the old woman has long since lost her mind. To me, she's the most sane of all the residents of cardboard city. If some amount of sense from the real world is allotted to the dungeon shadows, then the lion's share of it is here, in Grandma Bach's room.

The nurse pours me some cartoon tea into a cardboard mug and exits the room, leaving the door ajar. She's definitely spying on us. This is a useless task. Grandma Bach and I understand each other without words.

Grandma supports her wrinkled chin with her small fist and watches as I take small sips of terrible tea. The creaks and hisses of the gramophone dilute the melody of the Neverending

Canon. Grandma considers this to be the ideal tune, and gets very upset that I can never memorize the composer's name.

This music gives me hope. I'm convinced I've heard it before.

Grandma asks: You still aren't sleeping?

I shake my head. Can't fool her.

I honestly try to sleep. I toss and turn, count the boring cracks in the ceiling, imagine meowlers leading a round dance on a poppy field, smoke cardboard chips that pass for tobacco here. But instead of sleep I fall backward, into my real, infinitely beautiful world, where I so dream of returning.

Call it a nightmare, if you like.

Still looking? – she continues her interrogation.

I nod.

I'm looking. Nights. Days. In the most paradoxical of places. Seeing a door makes me turn into a madman. Refrigerators, cabinets, wardrobes – I search for an exit everywhere. Often I ascend into attics, but sometimes I go down to the cellars – out of sheer contradiction.

I climb ridiculous towers wrapped in cardboard wires. Ascend onto the roofs of skyscrapers. I try to reach the sky and pierce it with scissors.

And then I come here and drink tea.

It's time for me to go. I kiss Grandma Bach goodbye on her cartoon forehead. I read the truth in her sad eyes: we will never see each other again.

My Dream

If I manage to defeat this cardboard reality, if an accidental observer thinks that, having closed my eyes, I fell asleep, then on the inner side of my eyelids I see the following: a dark corridor I spent an eternity traversing terminates in an impossible, incredibly beautiful sunset of my world. I step forward and find myself in the middle of an empty street, next to the sense vending machine inside of which – I hear this clearly – the russles are fumbling. The machine is dead inside. I rush toward it, hoping to shake out the remnants of a sense that might somehow help me grasp on to this world, to stay in it. But there's no life within me, my hands are transparent. I'm a shadow. I'm powerless.

It's impossible to be a man and a shadow at the same time. Question: when did I stop being a man? When I fell from the darkness near the bridge? When I lied to the doctor about my dreams and drank cartoon tea? Or is it now, in my sleep, up the rabbit hole where I climb out under the gloomy sky and open my eyes, translucent, easily blown away by the wind?

I should run, hide. Try to change something. But the events of this nightmare aren't dependent upon my will. I can only observe.

A man named Bach approaches the vending machine. This is me – the way I used to be. Living, real, corporeal. He shoves his hand into the hiss of the broken machine, twists the levers, frowns.

I approach. Honestly, I shouldn't do this. But I'm incapable of stopping. I must warn him.

I approach and begin to speak.

The real Bach looks at me coldly, indifferently. He walks away. I follow.

Listen, I say, listen to me this once—

He shoots me in the face.

It's hellishly painful.

This is why I prefer not to sleep at all.

The Dealer

The dealer is waiting for me under the canopy of an inconspicuous building entrance. His hat is pulled down to his eyes. The collar of his cloak is raised. He studies the street behind me with a tenacious gaze. Then he walks by me indifferently, casually shoving me with his shoulder.

I feel my pocket has been emptied. The space previously occupied by a stack of stupid gray pieces of paper with gloomy portraits on them is now taken up by an almost weightless bundle.

The sound of the dealer's footsteps reverberates through the cardboard walls with a dull echo as he walks away. There's something vaguely familiar about his gait.

I go home. It's silly to call the geometric construct with empty walls a home – it contains no memories, not a bit of warmth. I endeavor to spend as little time here as possible, but now I need the solitude.

Barbara

For the man who has tasted of life, there's no sin that would justify the punishment of rotting under the cardboard sky of the dungeon, amid the musty aromas of yesterday, in the dust and soot of an artificial world.

But I would forgive this world everything – for my Barbara.

Her eyes would be blue. The real, deep, penetrating blue. The color of surf and salty waves. In that old life, I'd never tasted so rich a color. In this new life, the color of her eyes would be my salvation.

Here a color can be seen, heard, and even spoken. But it's impossible to drink it and feel it spread within you. (I'd tried gouache and watercolors.)

Sometimes I dream of oblivion. To become a shadow. To learn to read books instead of hearing or breathing them. Sometimes I wish to believe that this life is the only one given to a person. To collect immobile stamps and to never be surprised by the predictability of time and weather. To pay with nonsensical gray pieces of paper at the bar.

To sleep, like everyone else.

To dream.

Sometimes I think: somewhere behind the cardboard walls hides another Farctory. Inside it, there is a third, a fourth, a fifth...

Sometimes I think: everyone but me drank from the river of oblivion as they crossed over. I recall the dark figure of Mauk, his duffle coat and captain's cap. I recall how persistently he offered me a sip from his flask.

How many did Mauk bring here? I look around and answer my own question: everyone.

Everyone, except my Barbara.

I check twice to make sure I locked the door. I boil water. I prepare the strainer and the tea.

I take out the bundle the dealer had left in my pocket. I unwrap the crumpled newspaper page.

III: Nowhere

The Trip

This time the black tunnel was very short. One step – and I thought I had become God. I heard the world (my real, living, knowable world) pass through me; I drank its color. The whistling whisper of wind, the loud trajectory of an attendant bird, the melodies of books, the sleepy teakettles, clocks with a checkered *tick-tock* sound, senses arranged in descending order. My home greeted me.

Then I saw the pavement through my hands and realized that everything had repeated itself; I came home a shadow. I looked around. The set pieces were the same: dusk, empty street, broken vending machine, which the real Bach was about to approach.

But something had changed. I no longer felt the insistent need to repeat my learned motions. I didn't feel the heavy will of sleep. I could breathe sweet air and live. Even if it was life as a shadow – a sketch portrait of my real self with dots for eyes.

As a hero of a cardboard western.

A good guy, hoodwinked by the villain in a duffle coat, having overcome the savannah, the scorpions, the blonde's bed, and the noose, returns to an empty, raided town. He comes out onto the main street. His hand shakes nervously as it hovers over his revolver.

Except I didn't have a revolver anymore; shadows aren't allowed revolvers.

I took a step back, toward the warm brick wall.

Right after that, another shadow burrowed its way out of a new hole. This was me, of course – from one of my nightmares. A marionette, unable to resist someone else's script. I must admit, I looked pathetic as a shadow. The real Bach was another matter – the hat, the trench coat, the revolvers on my belt. Shoulders wide, chin up, arrogant gaze. The shadow approached him, and I rushed to turn away, remembering what happens next.

Hare came from around the corner. He looked to the real Bach with fear and admiration. I knew this look; I once granted it to the heroes of my childhood. Poor boy. The real Bach won't even think about you when he turns the Farctory into a torch.

There was the sound of a gunshot. Hare shuddered and closed his eyes, but quickly got hold of himself. Bach left, and the boy followed.

I followed them as well.

Dichotomy

The city was dying. There wasn't a single meowler, nor a single person left. There weren't even any shadows, other than me.

Something had gone terminally wrong here. The world twisted, cracked, and crumbled before my eyes. The bored wind dragged a tumbleweed across the cracked pavement. The dry shutters whispered in alarm. Black fractal growths made themselves at home on building walls, where they sprouted, and occasionally enveloped entire buildings.

The lack of sense could be felt sharply.

Through a small window designed to resemble a tortoise I watched the real Bach in Dichotomy play out his naïve con, thinking he was cleverly misleading Mauk.

Hare stood guard by the door. He looked at me sullenly, silently. He wasn't overly talkative with other people, let alone some shadow. The night poured a generous sprinkling of cold over the street. Hare, not dressed for the weather, was trembling. But his stern face showed he was prepared to endure any adversity for the sake of the important task entrusted to him by his idol.

Why did I drag him into this story? What assistance did I expect from this frozen sparrow?

The door creaked, and Mauk exited. I pressed against the wall, hiding from his tenacious gaze. I burned with furious desire to kill Mauk immediately, to erase him from reality with a single well-placed shot. It was a good thing I was only a shadow. Because I couldn't afford to kill Mauk, at least not until he answered my questions. And to ask them, I'd have to learn to speak coherently again.

Bach emerged, and the two of them headed toward the Farctory in silence.

I slid through the door of the Dichotomy which was left slightly ajar.

'Ulle! Ulle, it's me, Bach,' I said.

Ulle looked at me sternly and without recognition. He didn't like shadows. But deep within the Dichotomy I saw Eyck and darted toward him before Ulle reached for his formidable weapon – the broom.

Eyck was a good guy. The thirst for adventure hadn't yet completely uprooted him from the warm embrace of normal life, but one could see in this youngster's gaze that he was prepared to jump head-first into the whirlpool of mad adventure. I was just like him, before I met Barbara.

I sat across from Eyck with some difficulty. My current body, translucent and flat, kept trying to fall through the oak bench and onto the floor. I somehow managed to settle in.

'Hi, buddy,' I said.

Eyck tilted his head in thought, and I was glad I wasn't in his shoes. Only a handful of my acquaintances would bother with the shadows. Usually they'd fire without warning: everyone knew this old, proven method of returning the escapee directly back to the dungeon.

Ulle approached. His unkind gaze cut sharply into my back, between the poorly defined shoulder blades.

'Miniscule princeps,' Eyck told the bartender. He added: 'Be you a wildering terpene.'

I was certain Eyck didn't talk like that. He definitely said something along the lines of, 'Poor shadow. Perhaps it's cold? Add some birch branches to the hearth, friend Ulle.'

The wall of incomprehension between the shadow-me and the human-Eyck twisted every spoken word.

'Jump, brandade,' Ulle said doubtfully, and left.

Which, most likely, meant: 'I'm not about to waste good kindling on this frozen thing.'

I cringed, and said timidly, 'There must be some way—'

Eyck signaled for me to be quiet.

Ulle returned and placed a glass of strong red in front of me. Eyck nodded as if to say, 'Drink, you Farctory weakling.' I was never a big fan of the red color, but in my position beggars couldn't be choosers. I drank.

Red burned my throat. I coughed and croaked: 'Bastards...!'

'Color me flabbergasted, he resembles a man now!' Ulle said excitedly. 'Wow, Eyck, you're one clever meowler.'

'Hey, I understood that,' I shouted. 'Every word!'

Eyck celebrated. 'You see! You lost the bet, Ulle. We didn't have to force him: he drank it on his own. I've lost hope that I would get to test this theory. They do possess some kind of a thought process after all.'

'What thought process? It's a reflex...'

Ulle had always been a skeptic, but Eyck didn't listen to him. He turned toward me and said gently, 'Speak, vagabond. What manner of being are you, and why are you bothering us honest folk?'

Canon per Tonos

We were walking too slowly. I kept looking toward the sky, searching for the first signs of dawn.

'Why don't you fly, friend?' Eyck wondered. 'You're a shadow.'

Fly! I couldn't even run. The physical laws of our world are ruthless toward shadows; the more I want to get somewhere, the more difficult it becomes to move. The air thickens, the headwind intensifies, my strength flees.

Ulle wouldn't calm down. 'I knew there was a reason I never liked that Mauk! To come into a bar and drink from his own flask? Who does that! And he'd sit there and nurse it, and nurse it!'

He grumbled incessantly. At times he'd stop to make sure his shotgun was loaded, catch up with us, deftly kicking up his skinny knees and jumping over the small shoots of fractals, carefully avoiding the more dangerous fractal bushes that branched everywhere, breaking the walls and upturning the pavement.

Ulle squinted at me with little enthusiasm. In his head, Bach and the shadow were two separate things, and these concepts refused to intersect let alone combine.

As to Eyck, he had become gloomy once he heard my story. He looked around suspiciously. He twitched his eyebrows, wordlessly opened his mouth, as though he was carrying on a mental dialogue.

Finally, we arrived.

The fractals that took over the nearby buildings seemed not to even notice the Farctory. Their sharp branches reached toward the sky, evenly bending around its cracked walls. I stopped at the entrance, confounded as I listened. Music flowed from behind the small open door at the side of the Farctory gates. It was a slow, viscous, and sad sound. I knew this tune. I'd heard it tens or even hundreds of times through the creak of Grandma Bach's gramophone in cardboard city. An old canon by a Saxon composer whose name I could never recall. I wondered how this music appeared in the real world and immediately understood: the manuscript.

That same manuscript trap I'd once bought from Eyck that whispered a non-existent melody. I experienced the true depth of this melody only now, having become a shadow.

My compatriots couldn't be allowed to come closer. I signaled for them to stop, then cautiously peeked inside.

Of course, we were too late.

'Don't resist. It will only make things worse.'

Mauk effortlessly freed himself from the web of the Saxon Canon and calmly watched as the real Bach awkwardly ran against the flow of the conveyor belt.

'You should have drunk the color when I offered it.'

Bach pulled his revolver, not knowing that his actions would only accelerate his fall into the abyss. I didn't care about him. Let him fall. Let him wander the maze of the cardboard city. He deserved this. I was only interested in Mauk.

Slowly fighting through the resistance of the intractable air I moved toward the lanky silhouette in a duffle coat. Perhaps there was still time to save him.

But then I saw Hare, helplessly still in the center of the workshop with the kerosene lamp in his hands. The music Mauk easily shrugged off was an overwhelming load for the boy.

Time stood still. The air was thick as ajoblanco soup. I was drowning, choking. A singular thought pulsed through my translucent head: the explosion the still-real Bach is about to cause by firing into this color-filled space will kill Mauk, and I will never get any answers. Instead, I will open my eyes in the cardboard dungeon again. Open my eyes in the gray world without Barbara.

Screw Hare, whispered some other Bach inside me, yesterday's Bach, haughty and self-assured.

I didn't listen to him. To the accompaniment of the sad canon I squeezed past the air particles that almost turned into glass. Slowly, step by step. Trying not to think about how I – incorporeal and powerless – would manage to move the boy who had turned into a statue.

Out of the corner of my eye I saw how slowly, one after another, the bullets flew from the barrel of the revolver. How sparks bit into the color-saturated reality. I wasn't going to make it.

'Why don't you fly, friend?' Eyck whispered in my head. 'You're a shadow.'

You can be whoever you want to be, agreed the tune of the forgotten Saxon composer.

You can fly.

You can.

You.

Can.

I surged forward, shattering the air glass. I merged with the music. I became wind.

Wrapped in the bundle of yellowed pages and the sound of the Neverending Canon, Hare and I made it into the street a moment before the explosion rocked the insides of the Farctory.

The Russles

The sky brightened, ruthlessly underscoring the unusual darkness of the street.

The circle closed. I was calm. It couldn't be any other way. In a world that rapidly lost its sense, this was the only suitable ending to this story. I turned from the hero of a cardboard western into the subject of an unfinished illustration. The perspective was all wrong, the proportions fell apart, and the frustrated artist furiously scribbled fractals onto the page.

Hare was silent. He's always been silent, for as long as I've known him. Eyck walked around grimly, stomping on black sprouts. They mostly reminded me of abandoned marionettes who didn't know how to continue the play on their own. Only Ulle managed to keep it together. It was as though he didn't notice the black cracks, couldn't smell the despair that filled the world.

'Ha!' he shouted, pointing up somewhere. 'Would you look at that!'

The explosion had seemingly destroyed the curtain that concealed the Farctory from the fractals. They pounced on the new prey, growing through walls and windows, licking fire with their cold tongues, confidently stalking toward the roof.

At the very edge of the roof stood Mauk.

'I guess it's time for a certain someone to answer questions,' Ulle said firmly.

He walked up to the Farctory gates. Feeling his approach, a wave of russles spilled out, squinting their contented muzzles at the dawn light.

'Those resilient beasts don't fear anything.' Ulle laughed, feigning an attack with his shotgun toward the nearest russle. The rodent turned away calmly and began to gnaw at a fractal.

Ulle turned toward us. 'What are you waiting for?'

Hare glanced uncertainly toward Eyck.

'We won't go there,' said Eyck. 'And you shouldn't either, Ulle.'

The old man raised his eyebrows in surprise, then grinned condescendingly. 'Are you scared of a third-rate stage magician in a captain's cap?'

'Some questions are best left unanswered, my dear Ulle. Until the answer is spoken, you're free to remain whoever you want to be,' said Eyck.

'Sometimes you speak such gibberish that even a meowler couldn't understand you. No, I prefer clarity.' Ulle waved him off and disappeared into the dark, dead Farctory.

Eyck shook his head. He picked up several strips of paper left behind from his silenced manuscript.

'May I take this?' he asked me.

I shrugged.

For some reason I felt guilty. Not just guilt toward Hare, but toward both of them, and even toward old Ulle.

I wanted to ruffle Hare's hair as the means of saying goodbye, but instead I awkwardly waved my hand.

Eyck grinned.

'Farewell, Bach.'

Inside the Farctory it was pitch-black and stank unbearably of ash.

The conveyor now resembled a mythical beast, snarling menacingly with scraps of belt and its broken metal carcass. I approached in the hope of finding the hole through which the real Bach fell into cardboard city. But all I could see were the tenacious shoots of fractal, spreading in all directions.

A booming sound came from above. Ulle's soles pounded on the steps. I rushed after him and soon overtook the clumsy old man. Dim rays penetrated through small windows to illuminate our path. The staircase looped curiously past the bends of the dead conveyor. Dark silhouettes of the russles appeared here and there, atop the pipes, on the stairs and grills and the conveyor belt.

Mauk remained standing at the roof's edge, straight and stern in his duffle coat and captain's cap.

'I'm happy to see you, Bach. You're right on time. The most interesting part is about to begin.'

His face, however, didn't exude happiness.

I walked over and stood next to him silently. There was no wind.

All the words, all the accusations I'd prepared for this conversation disappeared at once when I looked at the city. Fractals rapidly spread across the streets, covering pavements, buildings, and trees. The ocean turned black. Only the pale sky still somehow argued with the endless darkness, but I saw its sharp branches already ripping into the horizon.

'Here it is, Bach. The fate of any world after the last person leaves it. And I must note, this was a very obstinate person.'

'Are you talking about me?'

'Obviously. Who else?'

He followed my gaze. It was still possible to see the figures of Eyck and Hare downstairs: they intently made their way through the maze of fractals.

'Have you not understood anything yet, Bach? Old man Ulle, Eyck, Hare whom you so courageously and pointlessly saved from the fire...'

Mauk laughed.

'Keep going. Why'd you stop?' I heard Ulle's voice behind us. He pumped his shotgun.

Suddenly I realized, Eyck was right. It's best not to know some truths.

'Don't, Mauk. Don't say it!'

'Why not? Why remain silent, when a *person*'—Mauk turned toward Ulle, flashing a toothy smile at that last word—'insists.'

He took one step, then another. Ulle stood his ground and lifted the shotgun.

'You've remained here too long, Bach,' Mauk told me while looking at the old man. 'When everyone but you left, the world tried its best to remain the way you were used to seeing it. It built props, imitated a semblance of life. Reality is a very loyal thing, capable of everything for the sake of a person. But then the last person leaves it, the props crumble, and we see—'

Ulle fired.

Lead balls flew slowly, reluctantly. Just as I managed to count them (five balls) they reached Mauk and instantly punctured holes in his duffle coat.

Instead of blood, russles poured from the holes.

I looked to Ulle in horror. The old man's hands trembled, his eyes filled with tears.

I hesitantly bent over Mauk to get a better look at the russles busily leaving the sinking boat. It was an instructive sight.

'Ulle, what are you—'

Another shot thundered behind me.

At the same time, I heard a sickening squeak of rusty metal. I turned to see Ulle's face fall apart like old plaster. Where eyes, nose, and a smile used to be moments ago, a wheel spun with a rusty squeal of a children's swing. A russle ran busily inside the wheel. I thought: how can such a huge wheel fit into the relatively small head of an old man?

Following the face, his clothes fell apart, revealing a complicated construct made of gears, belts, wheels, and russles.

The automaton was quite clever. Three large wheels, five small ones, with four russles controlling the gear belts and a dozen more on standby.

The russles didn't seem to immediately realize that I could see them. They continued working in concert, the russle-secretary deftly feeding the celluloid punch tape into the sound pickup, with a small speaker obediently reproducing Ulle's stifled sobs. Suddenly the device screeched and began to chew up the tape. Irritated, the russle pressed the pedal twice, shook his small head, and turned...

Our gazes met.

The russle jumped down onto the tar of the roof. His comrades followed. Mauk got up, adjusted his coat, and laughed hoarsely.

'Do you understand now, Bach?' he squealed. I imagined a russle, busily pressing the pedal of his sound pickup. 'You were the last.'

I had an epiphany.

'But you, Mauk, you always knew who you were. What you were.'

'Of course. I'm brave enough to accept the truth.'

Perhaps, I thought, Eyck and Hare have enough humanity in them to alter the truth. The world that created them was almost dead, but I believed in its largesse.

The End

How would I have liked to see this world for the last time?

Fluffy clouds, and the sound of an ocean filled with meaning somewhere far away; stern fishermen checking their nets on the shore before they head out to sea; the attendant bird chirping its morning song.

Instead I got chaos growing throughout the city, branching out in fractals, devouring everything in its path.

'I warned you, Bach: think it through. There's no going back. You're in luck; I lie as often as I speak the truth. I'll give you one more chance. I'll answer your question, but only one. Choose carefully.'

Mauk walked to the edge of the roof. He moved slowly and awkwardly, shaking and creaking like a broken vending machine. He lit a cigarette. What a weird sight. I pitied the russle in his head.

One question wasn't enough for me. Did I want to know the truth about cardboard city, its low-hanging artificial sky? About the shadows? About the little paper men, doomed to live in those flat stage sets?

Mauk looked at me with understanding, as though he could read all my thoughts down to the last letter. 'Don't ask questions the answers to which you already know without me.'

'But I don't—'

'You do, Bach. You know. You just don't have the fortitude to admit that to yourself.'

The fractals continued their dance. They reached the roof's edge, twirling at Mauk's feet. They pounced upon the sky, shredding it to pieces.

Did this city die because the people left? Or did the people leave because the city was dying?

I could ask why they didn't remember the real world.

I could ask where the border was between cardboard and reality.

'There's no border, Bach. The people make the world real. I love people – they create such wonderful worlds. And then we arrive...' Mauk closed his eyes, a dreamy expression on his face. Something squeaked under the duffle coat, as though one russle slapped another. Mauk shook his head. 'Your question, Bach.'

I could ask why the cardboard world never became real for me.

I could ask about many things.

'Is it true that Barbara...?' I began, but could not finish the sentence. Some words are better left unspoken, so they wouldn't become real.

Mauk frowned.

'Not that, Bach. Not that. Look around. You see how well the chaos is growing? How its fractals bloom, devouring all in their path? It will eat you just like that, Bach. But first – the last piece of the sky, and your chance to follow Barbara along with it.'

My paper heart skipped a beat.

'That's possible?'

'Finally. My answer is, yes.'

I was troubled by his unexpected altruism. But I understood: there's no choice.

'What must I do?'

Mauk had a long bout of agonizing coughing. Three more russles escaped from the holes in his duffle coat, and I feared that he would speak no more. But he said, hoarsely, 'You're a shadow, Bach. Fly.'

I frowned. 'That won't work. I'll fall.'

'Who knows? Sometimes one must crash in order to reach

the sky. Make up your mind, Bach. There's almost no time left.'

I stepped toward the edge, trying not to look down.

'Here, fortify yourself.' Mauk offered me his flask. 'The last color!'

That same undiluted one, I realized. A sip. (A barrage of wind knocks me off my feet, I slide along the wet deck, salty cold water whips my face.) Another sip. (Dawn, sand. A wave cuts off the sky and the world as it rises and envelops me; I suddenly realize that I don't need air.)

I adjusted my imaginary coat – where would a shadow get a real one?

'Why are you helping me?'

Mauk smiled his predatory sharp-toothed smile, answering without words: who says I'm helping you?

One must fall to reach the sky.

I'm on my way, my dear.

I squeezed my eyes shut.

I stepped forward.

Translated by Alex Shvartsman

About the Authors

Nadia Afifi is a science fiction author. Her debut novel, *The Sentient*, was lauded by Publisher's Weekly as 'staggering and un-put-downable'. The sequel to *The Sentient* is planned for release in 2022. Her short fiction has appeared in *The Magazine of Fantasy and Science Fiction*, *Clarkesworld* and *Abyss & Apex*.

She grew up in the Middle East, but currently calls Denver, Colorado home. When she isn't writing, she spends her time practising (and falling off) the lyra, hiking and working on the most challenging jigsaw puzzles she can find.

Lavanya Lakshminarayan is the author of *Analog/Virtual: And Other Simulations of Your Future*. She's a Locus Award finalist and the winner of the Times of India AutHer Award, India's most prestigious annual book award celebrating works written by women. She's also been nominated for the BSFA and Valley of Words Awards.

Her fiction has appeared in *The Gollancz Book of South Asian Science Fiction (Volume 2)*, *Someone in Time: Tales of Time-Crossed Romance* and *Apex Magazine*'s International Futurists special edition, among other publications. She's occasionally a game designer, and has built worlds for Zynga Inc.'s *FarmVille* and *Mafia Wars* franchises. She lives between multiple cities in India.

Frances Ogamba is the winner of the 2020 Inaugural Kalahari Short Story Competition and the 2019 Koffi Addo Prize for Creative Nonfiction. She is also a finalist for the 2019 Writivism Short Story Prize and 2019 Brittle Paper Awards for short fiction. Her fiction appears or is forthcoming in *Chestnut Review*, CRAFT, *The Dark Magazine*, *midnight & indigo*, *Jalada Africa*, *Cinnabar Moth*, *The /tɛmz/ Review* and elsewhere. She is an alumna of the Purple Hibiscus Creative Writing Workshop taught by Chimamanda Adichie.

Isabel Yap writes fiction and poetry, works in the tech industry, and drinks tea. She was born and raised in Manila, and is currently based in the US. She holds a BS in Marketing from Santa Clara University, and an MBA from Harvard Business School. In 2013 she attended the Clarion Writers Workshop. Her work has appeared in publications including *Tor.com*, *Lightspeed*, *Lithub* and *Year's Best Weird Fiction*. Her debut story collection, *Never Have I Ever*, was published in 2021 by Small Beer Press. She is @visyap on Twitter and her website is https://isabelyap.com.

Saad Z. Hossain is a Bangladeshi author writing in English. He lives in Dhaka. His war satire, *Escape from Baghdad!*, was published in 2015, and included in the *Financial Times* best books of 2015. It was translated into French, as *Bagdad la Grande Evasion*. This book was a finalist for the Grand Prix de L'Imaginaire 2018. His second book, *Djinn City*, was released in 2017, and also translated into French. His third *The Gurkha and the Lord of Tuesday*, was published in 2019 by Tor.com. It was a finalist for the Locus Awards as well as the IGNYTE Awards 2020 by Fiyahcon. Saad's fourth book, *Cyber Mage*, was published at the end of 2020, and the fifth, *Kundo Wakes Up*, in March 2021.

Yukimi Ogawa lives in a small town in Tokyo where she writes in English but never speaks the language. Her fiction can be found in such places as *The Magazine of Fantasy and Science Fiction* and *Clarkesworld*. In 2021, she was finally translated into Japanese.

Xing He was born in Beijing. He has written many novels, including *Incomplete Magnetic Traces*, and he has written more than a hundred short stories, winning many Chinese literary awards. He was awarded the 1997 Beijing International Science Fair Galaxy Award in 1997. He loves to travel, and has visited Sweden, Poland, Egypt, South Africa and other countries.

Nalo Hopkinson, a Jamaican-born Canadian, has published six novels and numerous short stories. She is the recipient of the Andre Norton (Nebula) Award, the World Fantasy Award, and the Sunburst Award for Canadian Literature of the Fantastic. She was the lead scriptwriter of 'House of Whispers', a series for DC Comics set in Neil Gaiman's 'Sandman' Universe. In 2021, Science Fiction Writers of America honoured her with the 37th Damon Knight Memorial 'Grand Master' Award, making her its youngest recipient (sixty years old) and the first woman of African descent to receive it. Her next novel, *Blackheart Man*, is forthcoming from Saga Press. Hopkinson currently lives in Vancouver, Canada.

Pan Haitian was born in 1975 and is a graduate of Tsinghua University's School of Architecture. The industry, for good or ill, provided him with few opportunities to carry out his eccentric ideas. He published his first science fiction story in 1993 and has since won five Galaxy Awards. In 2002, he created the Novoland fantasy world with a group of friends. Doomed to an acrimonious breakup, the group still managed to produce thirty-odd novels and more than one thousand short stories set in that universe.

Jacques Barcia writes weird fiction. His stories have appeared in *Clarkesworld*, *Electric Velocipede*, *The Immersion Book of Steampunk*, *The Apex Book of World SF 2* and *Shine: an anthology of optimistic SF*. He works as a professional futurist, is an avid role-player and growls in a grindcore band. He's trying to write a novel and can be found on twitter @jacquesbarcia and Instagram @jacques.barcia.

Edmundo Paz Soldán was born in Cochabamba, Bolivia in 1967. He is one of the most representative authors of the Latin American generation of the nineties known as McOndo. He is the author of ten novels, among them *The Matter of Desire* (2001), *Turing's Delirium* (2003) and *Norte: A Novel* (2011), as well as ten collections of short stories and several essay collections. His work has won multiple awards, including the Premio Nacional de Novela. Currently he is Professor of Latin American Literature and Chair of Romance Studies at Cornell University.

Dilman Dila is a writer, filmmaker and all-round artist who lives in his home country, Uganda. He is the author of a critically acclaimed collection of short stories, *A Killing in the Sun*. His two recent novellas are *The Future God of Love* and *A Fledgling Abiba*. He has been shortlisted for the BSFA Awards (2021) and for the Nommo Awards for Best Novella (2021), among many accolades. His short fiction stories have appeared in many anthologies, including the *Apex Book of World SF 4*. His films include the masterpiece *What Happened in Room 13* (2007) and *The Felistas Fable* (2013), which was nominated for Best First Feature by a Director at AMAA (2014). You can find his short films on patreon.com/dilstories and more about him on his website dilmandila.com

Natalia Theodoridou is the World Fantasy Award-winning and Nebula-nominated author of over a hundred stories published in *Uncanny, Strange Horizons, F&SF, Nightmare, Choice of Games,* and elsewhere. Find him at www.natalia-theodoridou. com, or follow @natalia_theodor on Twitter.

Bernado Fernández (Mexico City, 1972), better known as Bef, is a science fiction/crime author as well as one of the better known graphic novelists from Latin America. Among others, he has published the crime novels series *Alacranes* that include *Tiempo de alacranes, Hielo negro, Cuello blanco, Azul cobalto* and *Esta bestia que habitamos,* which has been roaming in development limbo for several years now. Some of his graphic novels are *Uncle Bill,* about William Burroughs' Mexican years, *El instante amarillo, Habla María* and *Matar al candidato,* in collaboration with the late F.G. Haghenbeck. Some other books are science fiction novels *Gel azul, Ojos de lagarto,* Young Adult novels *Ladrón de sueños* and *Bajo la máscara* and several children's books. Currently Bef is struggling with a punk fairy tale comic book for little girls, a wordless SFF graphic novel and a three-part SF novel saga.

Alberto Chimal (Toluca, Mexico, 1970) has written more than twenty short story and flash-fiction books, as well as two novels and several YA and children's books, movie scripts and graphic novels, some of which have won national and international awards. He is also a well-regarded professor of creative writing: he has taught courses, seminars and workshops in his country and abroad. He is very active online and has a literary YouTube channel (youtube.com/AlbertoyRaquelMX), where he collaborates with his wife, writer Raquel Castro. His novel *The Most Fragile Objects* was published in English in 2020, and in 2021 he contributed to the international DC Comics anthology *Batman: The World* with a short story set in Mexico City and illustrated by artist Rulo Valdés. He lives in Mexico City and can be found online at www.albertochimal.com

Wole Talabi is an engineer, writer and editor from Nigeria. His stories have appeared in *Asimov's, Lightspeed, F&SF, Clarkesworld* and several other places. He has edited three anthologies of African fiction: the science fiction collection, *Africanfuturism* (2020), the horror collection, *Lights Out: Resurrection* (2016) and the literary fiction collection *These Words Expose Us* (2014). His stories have been nominated for multiple awards including the prestigious Caine Prize for African Writing in 2018 and the Nommo Award which he won twice (in 2018, for best short story, and in 2020, for best novella). His work has also been translated into Spanish, Norwegian, Chinese and French. His collection *Incomplete Solutions*, is published by Luna Press. He likes scuba-diving, elegant equations and oddly shaped things. He currently lives and works in Malaysia.

William Tham Wai Liang was previously the senior editor at *Ricepaper*. In 2020, his novel, *The Last Days*, was published by Clarity Publishing, as was an edited volume, *Paper & Text*, featuring essays on Malaysian literature and the book trade. Besides contributions to *Wasifiri* and *Penang Monthly*, he has edited academic work that was subsequently published by Palgrave Macmillan and in *Modern Asian Studies*.

Usman T. Malik's fiction has been reprinted in several years' best anthologies including *The Best American Science Fiction & Fantasy* series. He has been nominated for the World Fantasy Award and the Nebula Award, and has won the Bram Stoker Award and the British Fantasy Award. Usman's debut collection *Midnight Doorways: Fables from Pakistan* was listed on *The Washington Post*'s Best SFF collections list for 2021 and can be ordered at www.usmanmalik.org. Twitter handle: @usmantm IG: @usmantanveermalik.

Julie Nováková (*1991) is a scientist, educator and award-winning Czech author, editor and translator of science fiction, fantasy and detective stories. She has published seven novels, one anthology, one story collection and over thirty short pieces in Czech. Her work in English has appeared in *Clarkesworld*, *Asimov's*, *Analog* and elsewhere. Her works have been translated into eight languages so far, and she translates Czech stories into English (in *Tor.com*, *Strange Horizons*, *F&SF*, *Clarkesworld*, *Welkin Magazine*). She has edited and co-edited an anthology of Czech speculative fiction in translation, *Dreams From Beyond*, a book of European SF in Filipino translation, *Haka*, an outreach e-book of astrobiological SF, *Strangest of All*, and its more ambitious follow-up print and e-book anthology *Life Beyond Us* (Laksa Media, upcoming in late 2022). Julie's newest book is a story collection titled *The Ship Whisperer* (Arbiter Press, 2020). She is a recipient of the European fandom's Encouragement Award and multiple Czech genre awards. She's active in science outreach, education and non-fiction writing, and co-leads the outreach group of the European Astrobiology Institute. She's a member of the XPRIZE Sci-fi Advisory Council.

Cassandra Khaw is an award-winning game writer, and former scriptwriter at Ubisoft Montreal. Khaw's work can be found in places like *Fantasy & Science Fiction*, *Lightspeed*, and Tor. com. Khaw's first original novella, *Hammers on Bone*, was a British Fantasy Award and Locus Award finalist, and their latest novella, *Nothing But Blackened Teeth*, is published by Nightfire. Erewhon Books recently published their debut novel, *The All-Consuming World*.

Tobias S. Buckell is a *New York Times* Bestselling Author and World Fantasy Award winner born in the Caribbean. He grew up in Grenada and spent time in the British and US Virgin Islands, which influence much of his work.

His novels and almost one hundred stories have been translated into twenty different languages. His work has been nominated for awards like the Hugo, Nebula, World Fantasy, and the Astounding Award for Best New Science Fiction Author.

He currently lives in Bluffton, Ohio with his wife and two daughters, where he teaches Creative Writing at Bluffton University. He's online at TobiasBuckell.com and is also an instructor at the Stonecoast MFA in Creative Writing programme.

Karen Lord is a Barbadian author, editor and research consultant. Her debut novel *Redemption in Indigo* won several awards and was nominated for the 2011 World Fantasy Award for Best Novel. Her other works include the crime-fantasy novel *Unraveling*, and the science fiction trilogy *The Best of All Possible Worlds*, *The Galaxy Game*, and *The Blue, Beautiful World*. She edited the anthology *New Worlds, Old Ways: Speculative Tales from the Caribbean*.

She was a judge for the 2019 Commonwealth Short Story Prize and the 2018 CODE Burt Award for Caribbean YA Literature.

She has taught at the 2018 Clarion West Writers Workshop and the 2019 Clarion Workshop, and she co-facilitated the 2018 Commonwealth Short Story Prize Workshop in Barbados. She has been a featured author at literary festivals from Adelaide to Edinburgh to Berlin, and often appears at the Bocas Lit Fest in Trinidad & Tobago.

T. L. Huchu is a writer whose short fiction has appeared in publications such as *Lightspeed*, *Interzone*, *AfroSF* and elsewhere. He is the winner of a Nommo Award for African SFF, and has been shortlisted for the Caine Prize and the Grand Prix de L'Imaginaire. Between projects, he translates fiction from Shona into English and the reverse. *The Library of the Dead* and *Our Lady of Mysterious Ailments* are the first two novels in his *Edinburgh Nights* fantasy series.

Clelia Farris has won some of the most important Italian speculative fiction awards: the Fantascienza.com Award for *Rupes Recta*, the Odissea Award for *Nessun uomo è mio fratello*, and the Kipple Award for *La pesatura dell'anima* (set in a uchronic Egypt). In 2012, Kipple Edizioni published the novel *La giustizia di Iside*, and in 2015, Future Fiction published the short story 'Chirurgia creativa' (Creative Surgery), translated by Jennifer Delare and available from Rosarium Publishing in *Future Fiction: New Dimensions in International Science Fiction*. Farris was a finalist for the Urania Award in 2018, the most important science fiction award in Italy, for the novel *Necrospirante*. Her short story 'A Day to Remember' was published in English in *Samovar* and 'Holes' appeared in English in *World Literature Today* (both translated by Rachel Cordasco). In 2020, Farris' collection *Creative Surgery*, translated by Rachel Cordasco and Jennifer Delare, came out from Rosarium Publishing. Farris lives in Cagliari, a small town in Sardinia, where she writes full-time.

Agnieszka Hałas is a literary translator and speculative fiction author living in Lublin, Poland. She has published several novels and numerous short stories in Polish. She's a biologist by training, an avid hiker and a cat lover.

Samit Basu is an Indian SFF novelist. His most recent book, *Chosen Spirits*, a near-future anti-dystopian Delhi novel, was shortlisted for the JCB Prize, India's biggest lit award, and is to be published in 2022 by Tordotcom as *The City Inside*. He's also known in India for the bestselling *Gameworld* trilogy of fantasy novels (Penguin) and the *Turbulence* duology of superhero novels (also published in the US/UK by Titan Books). Samit is also the co-writer/director of a Netflix film, a comic writer, columnist, short story writer and children's writer. He's on social media at @samitbasu.

Neon Yang is the author of *The Genesis of Misery* and the *Tensorate* series of novellas. Their work has been shortlisted for the Hugo, Nebula, World Fantasy, Lambda Literary and Locus awards, while the *Tensorate* novellas were a Tiptree honoree in 2018. They have over two-dozen works of short fiction published in publications including *Tor.com*, *Uncanny Magazine*, *Lightspeed*, and *Strange Horizons*. They graduated from the University of East Anglia with an MA in Creative Writing. In previous incarnations, they have been a molecular biologist, a writer for animation, comics and games, a science communicator, and a journalist for one of Singapore's national papers.

Kim Bo-Young is one of South Korea's most active and influential science fiction authors. Her first published work received the best novella award in the inaugural Korea Science and Technology Creative Writing Awards and she has won the annual South Korean SF Award twice. She has a number of works in English translation, including *I'm Waiting for You and Other Stories*, *On the Origin of Species and Other Stories*, 'An Evolutionary Myth', and 'How Alike Are We'. She lives in rural Gangwon Province with her family.

Hassan Blasim is an Iraqi-born film director and writer. Blasim settled in Finland in 2004 after years of travelling through Europe as a refugee. His debut collection *The Madman of Freedom Square* was published by Comma in 2009 (translated by Jonathan Wright) and was longlisted for the Independent Foreign Fiction Prize in 2010. His second collection, *The Iraqi Christ*, won the 2014 Independent Foreign Fiction Prize, the first Arabic title and the first short story collection ever to win the award. His first novel, *God 99*, was published by Comma Press in 2020.

K.A. Teryna is an award-winning author and illustrator born in Ukraine. Her fiction has been translated from Russian into six languages. English translations of her stories have appeared in *Asimov's*, *Apex*, *F&SF*, *Strange Horizons*, *Samovar*, *Podcastle*, *Galaxy's Edge* and elsewhere. Her website is www.k-a-teryna. blogspot.com.

About the Translators

Andy Dudak's science fiction and/or translations thereof have appeared in *Asimov's, Analog, Clarkesworld, Interzone, The Magazine of Fantasy and Science Fiction*, 科幻世界 and elsewhere. He is a digital nomad who believes in the healing power of *Dungeons & Dragons*.

Joel Martinsen translates Chinese literature and film. His work includes novels by Liu Cixin, essays by Han Han, films by Feng Xiaogang, and shorter pieces in *Chutzpah*, *Pathlight*, and *Words Without Borders*. He lives in Beijing.

Jessica Sequeira has published the novel *A Furious Oyster*, the story collection *Rhombus and Oval*, the essay collection *Other Paradises: Poetic Approaches to Thinking in a Technological Age* and the hybrid work *A Luminous History of the Palm*. She has translated many books by Latin American authors, and in 2019 was awarded the Premio Valle-Inclán. Currently she is based at the Centre of Latin American Studies at the University of Cambridge.

Brian Price (PhD University of Texas at Austin) is Professor of Spanish American Literature and Culture at Brigham Young University. His areas of scholarly interest include twentieth- and twenty-first-century Mexican literary, film and cultural studies; Latin America's historical novel; comparative literature; and rock and roll. He is the author of *Cult of Defeat in Mexico's Historical Fiction: Failure, Trauma, and Loss* (Palgrave, 2012), editor of *Asaltos a la historia: Reimaginando la ficción histórica hispanoamericana* (Ediciones Eón, 2014), and co-editor of

TransLatin Joyce: Global Transmissions in Ibero-American Literature (Palgrave, 2014) and *The Lost Cinema of Mexico: From Lucha Libre to Cine Familiar and Other Churros* (U Florida P, 2022). He is currently completing two book projects about the influence of rock music on Mexican literature and film.

Fionn Petch is a Scottish-born translator working from Spanish, French and Italian into English. He lived in Mexico City for twelve years, where he completed a PhD in Philosophy at the UNAM, and now lives in Berlin. His translations of Latin American literature for Charco Press have won acclaim: *Fireflies* by Luis Sagasti was shortlisted for the Society of Authors First Translation Award 2018. *The Distance Between Us* by Renato Cisneros received an English PEN Award in 2018. *A Musical Offering*, also by Luis Sagasti, was shortlisted for the Republic of Consciousness Prize 2021.

Rachel Cordasco has a PhD in literary studies and currently works as a developmental editor. She founded the website *SFinTranslation.com* in 2016, writes reviews for *World Literature Today* and *Strange Horizons*, and translates Italian speculative fiction, some of which has been published in magazines like *Clarkesworld Magazine* and *Future Science Fiction Digest*. Rachel's book *Out of This World: Speculative Fiction in Translation From the Cold War to the New Millennium* is out from the University of Illinois Press.

Sophie Bowman is a PhD student in the East Asian Studies department at the University of Toronto. Her translations include Kim Bo-Young's 'I'm Waiting for You' and 'On My Way to You' in *I'm Waiting for You and Other Stories*, Djuna's

'The Second Nanny' published in *Clarkesworld*, Baek Heena's picture book *Magic Candies*, and *Looking Back Life Was Beautiful* by Grandpa Chan and Grandma Marina.

Jonathan Wright is a literary translator and former journalist. He studied Arabic at St John's College, Oxford, and worked in the Middle East as a correspondent for *Reuters* for many years, living in Egypt, Sudan, Lebanon, Tunisia and the Gulf. He turned to literary translation in 2008 and has since translated about fifteen books, including two works of fiction shortlisted for the Man Booker International Prize. He has translated three titles for Comma: Hassan Blasim's *God 99* (2020), *The Iraqi Christ* (2013), which was awarded the Independent Foreign Fiction Prize in 2014, and *The Madman of Freedom Square* (2009).

Alex Shvartsman is a writer and anthologist from Brooklyn, NY. His translations from Russian have appeared in *F&SF*, *Clarkesworld*, *Tor.com*, *Apex*, *Strange Horizons* and elsewhere. His second novel, *The Middling Affliction*, was published by Caezik Press in April 2022. His website is www.alexshvartsman. com. Alex would like to extend special thanks to Dr Muireann Maguire and Dr Cathy McAteer of the University of Exeter who made the translation of this story possible via a RusTrans grant. Learn more about their work at rustrans.exeter.ac.uk.

Extended Copyright